COMMENCEMENT

COMMENCEMENT
A NOVEL BY LAWRENCE CHERRY

THAT PAGE WITH THE LEGAL STUFF ON IT

Dedicated to our Lord and Savior Jesus Christ.

for without Him this book never would have been possible

COMMENCEMENT

ONE

After the long train ride all the way from Massachusetts, Allen Sharpe looked forward to reuniting with his family and sharing stories over an old-fashioned, home cooked meal. Yet when he got home, all he found was a note on the refrigerator door telling him to come to the New Towers, room B. The New Towers was a luxury condo on Harlem's newly gentrified West Side where his friend, Tim, lived. "Why would my parents want me to come to Tim's building? And what was room B?" Allen puzzled to himself. As many times as he had visited Tim, Allen had never seen a room B. All of the apartments were numbered. He continued to ponder the situation as he took the subway over to the Upper West Side.

When Allen finally arrived at the New Towers, he decided to ask Bradley, the doorman, for more information.

"Good evening, Bradley", Allen greeted the doorman cheerfully.

"Good evening, Mr. Sharpe. Would you like me to ring Mr. Russell for you?"

"Actually, I got this note that says I'm supposed to go to a 'Room B'" said Allen handing Bradley the note. "I'm not sure where that is. Would you know?"

"Ahh, yes. Just take the elevator all the way up to the top floor, to the restaurant and speak with the young woman at the front desk. She'll show you", replied Bradley in his usual courteous manner.

"Thanks", smiled Allen as he made his way toward the elevator. The doorman nodded respectfully.

"So we're having dinner at Menagerie", Allen mused on the elevator ride. "This must be my parents' idea of a present. Tim probably suggested it. But could they have been more cryptic with the note?" Then Allen began to wonder how they could afford to have dinner at such an expensive place. His parents, Lena and Vernon Sharpe, had been religious, hardworking, blue collar people all of their lives. Lena had been teaching at P.S. 118 in Harlem for over 25 years and she was still going. Vernon worked as a maintenance technician for the New York City Parks Department. Despite their combined 50 years of service to the city, their wages only created a modest income relative to the standard of living in the "Big Apple". At the same time, Allen also knew of his parents' ability to stretch a dime. It was this ability that allowed Lena and Vernon to give to their church, Greater Apostolic Church of Christ, charities, and still have money for some of Allen's college expenses, as well as their retirement. "They probably started saving their money in anticipation of this special dinner years ago", thought Allen.

When the elevator opened, Allen walked down the short hallway to the entrance of the restaurant with its heavy glass doors that read "Menagerie" in big frosted script letters. As he entered, he was awash in the elegant ambiance of the place. The terrace windows that wrapped around the back of the establishment afforded a magnificent view of the Upper West Side skyline. There were strings of little orange incandescent bulbs wound around ivory columns and the fixtures along the walls, giving a warm glow to the place. Every table was draped with beautiful silk and linen rose-colored tablecloths, and surrounded by high backed French mahogany chairs, with silk damask cushions. The evening moonlight was reflected in the high quality silverware and crystal on the tables. No matter how many times he had passed by this place, Allen was always astounded by its lavishness. He knew that one day soon he would be a regular customer, but right now he was looking for room B. Allen walked over to the fair-skinned young woman who was impeccably dressed in a black skirt suit with a blue and gray tie, sitting in the maitre'd's booth in the corner near the entrance. Her hair was piled high on top of her head in a French roll. She had her head cocked to the side cradling the receiver of a phone, while busily flipping through the pages of the reservation book she had in front of her. Finally, she hung up the phone and began to scribble something hastily onto one of the pages before typing something into the computer next to her book. She was completely oblivious to Allen's presence, even though he had politely cleared his throat at least several times.

"Excuse, me. I'm looking for a room B", said Allen to gain her attention at last.

"Oh, yes, that's one of the private halls. Are you Allen Sharpe?" asked the young woman, looking up from her work and checking her watch.

"Yes..."

"Good. I'll just make a quick call, and then I'll take you over."

"A private hall?" Allen pondered to himself, as the young woman stepped away to another area to make her call, even though there was a phone right in front of her. He was beginning to think that this was no ordinary dinner with his family.

"Right this way sir", the young woman said reappearing suddenly, interrupting his thoughts.

She led him down a narrow passage way behind the booth that went all the way around behind the restaurant. By now, Allen was too preoccupied with the mystery of this dinner to be tempted to check the woman out from behind, as he usually would in such a situation. The passage opened into a large open area with its own reception and waiting space. From the front, he could see what looked like a business conference room that was labeled "Room A", but nothing else. Allen was about to suggest that the woman had made a mistake, when she sensed his uneasiness.

"Room B is around the corner at the end of the hall."

"Thank You", Allen replied before making his way down to room B.

****

"So this is room B", Allen said to himself. Looking through the little latticed rectangular opening in the door, he noticed it was dark inside. He didn't hear any noise. "Am I early?" he wondered. "Maybe there's some mistake. Maybe this was the wrong room B." Then he heard what he thought were hushed giggles, coming from inside. Finally, he began to realize what was going on. Allen turned the handle on the door and peeked in .....

"S U R P R I S E!!!!!"

A flood of light revealed an amazing spectacle before him. At first, all he could see were tangles of streamers and balloons through a shower of confetti that was being pelted toward him. Then he could see a stage with a podium and a video screen behind it. On the screen he could see the word "Congratulations!" scrolling across with graphics of fire works followed by pictures from his graduation ceremony. Down below the stage there was an adjacent dining area with tables that had burgundy and yellow tablecloths and balloons that were tied to chairs. On the far side of the dance space was a D.J with his turntable, speakers and other equipment. In the corner near the entrance where he was standing was a large table piled high with beautifully wrapped presents. Interspersed within the scenery there had to be about 50 guests. They were all cheering, clapping, shouting, and throwing handfuls of confetti at him. It almost seemed like he was at a presidential convention and he was the party nominee. Allen was completely overwhelmed by the moment. Allen was trying to match names to all of the faces, and trying to think of something to say, when a quick flash of light suddenly stunned him.

"Lena, what are you doin'? You tryin' to blind 'im?" asked Vernon Sharpe trying to shield his son from his mother's outdated digital camera.

"I just wanted to get a picture of the look on his face, that's all", Lena explained hastily. "Baby, I'm so proud of you!" she gushed to Allen. Lena, Allen's mother, was a petite, brown skinned woman whose skin had a glow to it that defied her age. To Allen and his dad, she looked a lot like the woman in those old wedding pictures in the album in the attic. She may have been, at the most, 10 pounds heavier but she wore it well. The only thing that could give any hint to her 48 years was the frumpy looking light blue beaded gown that she wore for the occasion. Overcome by her emotions, she tackled her six-foot-three inch son for a hug.

"Mmph", groaned Allen, a little winded by the embrace.

"Lena, let the boy get some air for goodness sake!" chided Vernon playfully.

Lena had been waiting for this moment since Allen was born. Her only child had just graduated from one of the top Ivy League schools in the country. She could not restrain the excitement, pride, gratitude, and joy that she felt and she didn't want to. As Lena released Allen, he took some time to gather his composure.

"Praise God, he did it! Graduated from Harvard, Thank You Jesus! We got the Victory!" shouted Lena as she "danced like David".[1]

Lena was a devout Christian and she always thanked the Lord for everything. Allen also believed in God, but he could never get as emotional as his mother. His mother's outbursts always seemed to smack of a bit of superstition and naiveté for him. In this public setting, he couldn't help feeling a little embarrassed by Lena's jubilant effusion.

"Well, we all knew he would, and we're proud of him Lena, but we don't have to go crazy", said Vernon sensing his son's uneasiness. Vernon always seemed to be criticizing his wife's "wild holy roller ways" as he called them, but it was more teasing than criticism. Deep down Vernon understood the source of his wife's joy and appreciated her all the more for it.

"Congratulations, Al", Vernon said to Allen, as he reached out and gave his son a normal hug. Vernon could only be compared to a big tall oak tree, so overpowering was his presence, and the dark suit that he wore made him look even statelier. He was the only other person in the room who was taller than Allen. He was six-feet-five inches tall, with a powerful build. Vernon always wore an annoyed expression on his face even when he was happy. However, tonight he was able to crack a faint smile for his son's success.

"Mom, Dad... I don't know what to say. This is too much", was all that Allen could muster.

"You don't have to say anything", replied Lena. "This is your day, baby. You just go ahead and have yourself a good time. Wakeem! Hit the music!"

At Lena's cue the D.J. started to play "Never Could Have Made It Without You" by the Williams Brothers. Then Lena withdrew to direct the celebration, and one by one, Allen's closest friends and family closed in to offer their congratulations and best wishes. The first to grab Allen was his best friend James Reid. No one ever called him James though: just Jim. Allen and Jim had been friends since grade school when Jim had taken Allen under his wing as a little brother after saving him from the school bully. Jim had always wanted a little brother, but his parents never got the chance to have any other children. Allen had always wanted an older brother, so the two seemed to be perfect for each other. Jim was older by two years and though Allen tended to look up to him, there were times when the situation was reversed, as it was at this moment.

"Congratulations, dog!" beamed Jim slapping his best friend on the back and pulling him in for a man hug.

"Thanks, man. Couldn't have done it without you putting up with those late night rants on the phone."

"That's what brothers are for, man. You know I'm always gonna have your back. But this is your night. Forget that modesty stuff. You gotta turn this place out."

"Did you know about all this?"

"Maybe"

As the two men got reacquainted, a young cocoa complexioned woman in a simple black short sleeved dress snuck up behind Allen and threw her arms around him. She was so tiny that she practically had to jump on his back to plant a kiss on his cheek.

"Congratulations, Al!" she chimed sweetly, attempting to cover his eyes with her hands.

"Miko, ?!" guessed Allen, recognizing her voice.

"Who else?" said Jim petulantly, as if their pesky little sister had just interrupted them. Then Allen pulled her around for a real hug. 'Miko' was short for Tamiko. Tamiko Bynum was another childhood friend of Allen's. They met in kindergarten, and their relationship started off rather rocky at first. Tamiko was the only other kid in the class who could even come close to being as smart as Allen, and they were always in constant competition. To make matters worse, Tamiko's father was the pastor at the church his family attended. She was the teacher's pet in school and in the church's Sunday school, and with all the time they spent together, Allen felt like he could never get away from her. Tamiko was always moralizing about one thing or another, expounding various rules of conduct and trying to tell everyone what to do. All the kids used to call her "Miss Priss" back then. But one day at school, someone had broken the class's art project and the teacher was going to cancel the pizza party she planned for the class if she didn't find out who did it. Miko confessed, even though she hadn't done a thing. This Allen knew because he was the one who broke the project, only he didn't say anything because he was afraid of getting into trouble. Tamiko knew this, too, but she took the blame because she knew everyone had worked so hard to earn the party. It was then that Allen realized that Tamiko wasn't just some stuck up do-gooder, who was one way around adults and another way around the kids. She really believed in all of the things she talked about. Allen admired her courage and selflessness and they had been friends ever since. But there was one thing about Miko that Allen didn't think he could ever get used to, and that was her prissy style of dress. Her black dress had princess sleeves, a rounded collar, and came down two inches below the knee. Her shoulder length hair was parted to one side with a hint of curl at the ends, and held in place with a wide tortoise shell headband. To Allen, she looked like she belonged on a Disney Channel sitcom.

"I should be congratulating you, too. Didn't you just get out of Spelman?" remarked Allen.

"Oh no, you don't. This is your night and you don't have to share the spotlight", answered Miko. "Anyway, what are we doing standing here? Come on over to our table. The rest of the guys are waiting for you." Tamiko and Jim steered Allen through a hub of guests, and balloons toward one of the larger tables near the head of the room. As they approached, Allen could see the rest of his friends smiling and signaling him to come over and sit down. There was Tim, who stood out conspicuously from the bunch because of his fair complexion, and sandy brown hair. From a distance and in the dim lights of the catering hall, he could have passed for white. Timothy Russell was Allen's best friend from Harvard who had graduated two years earlier. During his first week at Harvard, Allen suffered some serious culture shock. Allen knew that some of the students at the school were from some of the richest families in America, but this knowledge did not prepare him for his encounters with many of his classmates. A small few went out of their way to be jerks, but most of the kids just ignored him. Then one day, someone walked up to him out of nowhere and asked him if he could make copies of his notes for the open statistics course they were taking. This turned out to be Tim. Tim noticed that Allen was brilliant and Tim always liked to surround himself with intelligent people. So Tim helped Allen navigate the complicated social scene of Harvard. Then there was Callie (which was short for Callilope) Harris. Callie was a girl that Allen met in high school. She was very popular, but because she liked to go to clubs and parties, she had never really noticed Allen who tended to congregate with the geeks. That was until her calculus teacher told her that she was going to flunk the subject. So Callie signed up for a tutor, who turned out to be Allen. Callie ended up with a B+ on the final, which raised her grade to a satisfactory C-. Callie was so happy that she agreed to be Allen's date for the prom, to the dismay of the "cool guys" in school. Allen and Callie got along well, but they decided that it would be best if they remained friends rather than pursue a romantic relationship. Even though Allen was headed to Harvard, and Callie was headed to nursing school, they stayed in touch regularly and became very close.

Tonight, both Callie and Tim were eager to share in their friend's accomplishment. Callie's tall, dark, slender figure looked absolutely resplendent in the silver silk dress with black flowers embroidered on the bodice. She had her shoulder length hair pinned up to the top of her head in a chignon. Tim looked very handsome as well. He had his sandy colored hair gelled back into waves, and his wire framed glassed made him look like the dapper Wall Street type he so desperately wanted to be. His olive colored linen suit made him look a little less washed out than usual, and more like a real brother. When Miko, Jim, and Allen reached the table, Tim and Callie stood up to greet them.

COMMENCEMENT

"Finally, the man of the hour has arrived", said Tim putting one arm around Allen.

"Congratulations, Al", Callie cut in as she moved over to the other side of Allen to place another lipstick mark, under the one made by Miko. "Were you surprised?"

"Kind of…"

"You should have seen the look on his face", laughed Jim.

"You guys - I know this is gonna sound kind of cliché, but I really don't know what to say", said Allen.

"How about 'let's order', because I am absolutely starving right about now", joked Jim taking his seat at the table.

"That sounds like a good idea to me", said Tim who helped Allen to seat the ladies before sitting down himself.

"Oh Snap, look at all this! Fancy silverware, china, menus, that big table of presents over there - this seems more like a wedding reception than a graduation party! Dag!" Allen mused out loud. He was wholly dumbfounded by the expense his parents were driven to in order celebrate this occasion.

"Don't tell me you were expecting your mama to put on some little trifling backyard barbecue with a Carvel ice-cream cake, and some Pepsi", said Callie as she opened her menu.

"No, but I didn't think they would go for broke. Tim, I know you had to have a hand in this. Be straight with me brother, did my parents have to re-finance the house for this or what?"

"Calm down, Allen. Let's just say that a lot of people chipped in to make this all possible, so your parents are not going broke. Enjoy your night. You've earned it, man", said Tim stretching back in his chair.

"Yo! Where my Harvard dogs at!" a voice bellowed from across the room. Everyone at the table looked up to see a tall dark skinned man with a goatee, lots of bling, and a navy and white pinstriped Sean Jean suit with matching Stacy Adams shoes walking toward the table. He let loose a wide grin revealing several shiny, gold-capped teeth.

9

"Up over here that's where they at!" Allen responded, a rhythmic cadence marking his voice. He stood to greet him with the familiar man hug and the pound.

"Congratulations, man! They finally gave you them get out of jail free papers, huh. Now you gon' set if off out there, 'ight!" cheered Richard as he playfully jabbed Allen in the arm and then took his seat at the table. Richard was another friend that Jim had introduced Allen to. They had originally met at a street fair while Allen was on Thanksgiving break from Harvard. Richard was selling books in a booth and was able to provide Allen with a copy of a desperately needed textbook that had been sold out everywhere. Later on Allen found out that Richard sold lots of different things in lots of different places. Due to the peripatetic and transient nature of his business enterprises, many tended to call Richard a hustler, however, Allen was always amazed by how a man with only a high school diploma, and a little bit of street cred could manage his life so well. Richard always lived in the nicest places, had the coolest clothes, and never had a lack of women.

"Look like you settin' it off right now. This party ain't no joke man. Ain't no Chinette and chittlins up in here!" smiled Richard.

"It's about time you got here", sneered Tim. "We were just getting ready to order."

"Order! Dag, it's like that!" said Richard ignoring Tim and opening his menu. Richard always thought that Tim was nothing but an uptight Uncle Tom, and most of the time paid him no attention. "Cold Snap! They even got stuff on here that you can't pronounce! Like what's this, this uh...Cock aw vin stuff? What's that son?"

"It's coq au vin", said Tim with the proper pronunciation, correcting him. And Tim always jumped on any opportunity to correct Richard. "It's chicken braised in a red wine sauce."

"I was down wit' it until you started talkin' bout a wine sauce. The only sauce I like on my chicken is hot sauce, youknowwhatI'msayin. I ain't tryin' to get high off no chicken."

"I feel you", chuckled Allen.

COMMENCEMENT

Jim and the girls laughed as well, while Tim rolled his eyes in disgust. Jim flagged down a waiter to take their orders and within minutes the food was brought to the table. Soon everyone at the table was caught up in the convivial atmosphere of celebration. They sat and talked about old times, caught up with the present, and discussed their future. It was the future that was their foremost preoccupation, especially for Allen, and everyone was full of anticipation to hear what was next on his agenda.

"So, Allen now that you've got your degree, what's next?" asked Tim.

"I definitely want to go into financial consulting and I have a couple of interviews lined up with some really good firms, so we'll see what happens", answered Allen with a sort of practiced humility, trying not to make a big deal of his good fortune.

"Interviews already! You must really be in demand, huh!" cheered Callie.

"But I don't want to get ahead of myself. It's just interviews, nothing's settled yet."

"C'mon Allen, as smart as you are, those companies will be fighting over you before it's all over with", Tamiko gloated while picking at her collard greens.

"As it should be", said Tim in a matter of fact way.

"I don't know if it's going to be that easy", Jim said rather gravely.

"What do you mean?" asked Allen a bit surprised.

"I hear what he's saying", reasoned Tim. "There's been a big downturn in the financial sector since the whole subprime mess started to unravel. There aren't as many jobs as there used to be and it's starting to get pretty competitive out there. Even so, I don't see why…"

"And you know what that means, especially for us", said Jim cutting Tim off, bitterness seeping into his voice.

There was a moment of silence at the table, as everyone looked around at each other, but not at Jim. Finally, Allen decided to break the silence.

"What does it mean? What are you trying to say?"

"Look, Al, you know I'm your boy and I would never say or do anything to bring you down, especially not tonight. It's just....I don't know. Maybe we should talk about this at another time."

"C'mon man, say it. You're my boy. You can be straight with me."

"It's just that everyone is making it seem like good jobs are for the taking. That's just not how the game works in this country. When I got out of St. John's I thought everything was going to fall into place. I had my degree in political science so all I had to do was get a job as a law clerk or a paralegal until I finished law school. Then I'd be a big time lawyer with lots of money. But did it happen?"

"Obviously, no. So what's your point?" asked Tim.

"My point is, even if you have a good education and lots of skills, there are other things that you have to be prepared for. Especially during these hard times", Jim continued.

"Oh? Like what?" asked Tim with just a hint of sarcasm. Tim knew what was coming. They all knew.

"Like racism", Jim blurted out after a few awkward moments. He hated the way his friends always played dumb when he brought up the subject.

"Here we go again", said Tamiko under her breath, shaking her head. Tim shot a knowing smirk at Allen, and chuckled lightly to himself before returning his attention to his meal. Callie fidgeted uneasily with her napkin, while Richard looked around at each of them expectantly, wondering where the conversation would lead. All of them expected nothing less than another bitter diatribe from Jim about the perils of the black man in a white Eurocentric society. Jim believed that racism played a big part in his inability to get a legal position when he graduated college, and he spent a lot of time trying to convince the rest of his friends. Everyone had hoped that if they kept silent and didn't make any eye contact, they could weather the storm of Jim's whining and go back to having a nice dinner celebration. But by the cross expression on Jim's face, it didn't seem likely.

"Most of the legal jobs I was turned down for, I was more than qualified to do! How else would you explain it?!" He continued, the tense emotions spilling over.

"C'mon, Jim. This is Allen's graduation dinner. You should be trying to encourage him, not bring him down with all that racism baggage you're carrying around", said Callie sounding a little disappointed in Jim.

"I'm just tryin' to keep it real. I'm speaking as a black man with experience and I'm lettin' Allen know what the deal is. In times like these, we're the first ones fired and the last ones hired."

"Dude, you're not the only brother in the world and your experience is not the only experience. Despite the fact that you weren't able to get a job in the clerk's office, I happen to know a few brothers that have. There are even black lawyers, judges and even Supreme Court justices now, you know. We even have a black presidential candidate, who looks as if he might make it, for goodness sake. It just so happens to be 2008 and not 1908", argued Tim.

"I don't need you of all people to tell me what year it is, Tim. There's just as much racism today as it was back then. Just look at what's been happening in the last ten years or so. Abner Louima, Amadou Diallo, Sean Bell, The Jena Six... and I don't care if they put this brother in White House. The struggle's not over."

"Look, Jim" said Allen finally speaking for himself. "We're not saying that racism is dead, but this is the new millennium. Racism can't stop you unless you let it. Our ancestors taught us that. If Frederick Douglass could publish a black newspaper when blacks weren't even supposed to be able to read and write, there's no reason why I can't have a job as a financial consultant."

"Amen to that!" added Miko.

"Racism may not stop you, but it can still affect you, knowwhatimean. That racism is still out there, yo. As a matter of fact, look at what they're doing to the black presidential candidate. He can't even fart without some of these folks turning it into a scandal. White folks ain't no joke", warned Richard.

"But there are a lot of white people who are supporting him, too. Not all white people are evil racists, you know", Tim shot back.

"I dare anybody here to name one white person they know that's not", Jim challenged.

"Are you kidding me! If all white people were racists I wouldn't have even been born!" exclaimed Tim.

"I know you're not referrin' to the dude that's been keepin' you and your little sis' a secret from his whole other family-" Richard began.

"Don't even go there, Richard", Tamiko interrupted with a warning. "Let's not make this personal."

"If he didn't want it to get personal about his dead-beat, racist pops, he should have kept him out of the conversation."

"You don't know anything about my father!" shouted Tim angrily.

"And neither do you!" Richard retorted.

"Oooh, that was cold!" remarked Jim.

"Don't let this color fool you. Bright boys can kick-"

"Tim, chill! You know how Richard is. Just let it go. Richard, you know you were wrong for going there. We weren't talking about Tim's family, we were talking about white people in general", said Allen trying to mollify the situation.

"Besides, Tim's right. There are a lot of really nice white people out there who are not racist. If most whites were, none of us would be able to survive", said Tamiko steering the conversation away from the danger zone.

"See you guys are still stuck in the mentality that racists run around with white sheets and fiery crosses. It's far subtler than that. White people don't have to be particularly evil to be racists, just self-interested", Jim insisted, vehemently to the point to where he was pounding his fist on the table. He was always surprised by his friends' blind naiveté about the way the world worked.

COMMENCEMENT

"But that's just my point. You say that most of them are about preserving white hegemony. But if that's true, why are so many African-Americans in very high positions of power. I mean Condoleeza Rice is our secretary of state for crying out loud", continued Tamiko trying to be as sensitive to Jim's feelings as she could.

"Because they know that certain African-Americans are not willing to rock the boat if they can have a few crumbs. Those are the only blacks the white power structure is willing to enter into a dialogue with", retorted Jim.

"Word, True that! Most black folks that get them big gigs is sell-outs, straight up. They climb the ladder to success and then turn around and burn it down, so no other blacks can get up there. Like that dude, in the Supreme Court. This Tom uses affirmative action to get his education on, then he want to take it out so these up and coming young brothers can't get nowhere", added Richard.

"Why is it that if an African-American is successful, and makes a lot of money, some people get the idea that he or she has to be an Uncle Tom? There are many successful African-Americans who help other African-Americans. Look at Magic Johnson, Chris Rock, and Tyler Perry for example. I mean, that's where I want to go with mine. If I got a really prestigious job at one of these consulting firms, I would try to use my influence to create some opportunities for these young brothers out there with nothing to do", said Allen.

"First of all, they'd drop you like a bad habit before you could even think about something like that. Secondly, even if they did let you make such a program, they would oversee it and make sure the only thing to come out of it is a bunch of pre-programmed brothers who won't do nothin' to shake things up in this society", said Jim bursting Allen's bubble.

"Man, you're negative! You're just as bad as these gangsta rappers out here. If all you say is true, what are we supposed to do? I guess Allen shouldn't bother with looking for a job. He should just smoke some crack and die before the white people get him, right?!" exclaimed Callie who by now was fed up with Jim and the whole conversation.

15

"See, you guys are too plugged into the system to understand what I'm puttin' down. I shouldn't have said anything, like I started to."

"Finally, something we can agree on", snarled Tim.

Jim gave Tim a "don't mess with me" look.

"Well, I know there's something else that we can all agree on", said Callie smiling at Allen and raising her glass. "I'd like to take this time to make a toast. To Allen: for whom the best is yet to come. We all believe in you and we all support you; right, Jim?" Everyone at the table gave a hearty "here, here", with the exception of Jim, who was still sulking over the fact that his friends would not validate his ideas.

"You know what? I'm ready to get my dance on, but all you got goin' at this party is church music. When we gonna hear somethin' with some beats?!" said Richard who was ready for a change of scene.

Allen blushed a bit at the fact that his mother's spiritual side was showing again.

"You know my mom. If she organized this celebration, it's gonna be gospel all night."

"You know what, Allen? Your mom's so religious, maybe you should get her to put in a good word with The Man Upstairs for you before those interviews", joked Richard. "It wouldn't hurt." With the exception of Tamiko, everyone laughed.

"I think she's been doing that all of her life."

TWO

"This is Broadway-Nassau Fulton Street, transfer here for the downtown A, C, 2, 3 and 5 trains as well as the J, M, and Z trains. Next stop, Cortlandt Street. Stand clear of the closing doors, please." the smooth voice charmed from the PA. Allen was riding the 4 train, which he knew was Jim's regular line. He also knew for a fact that his friend was driving this particular train. Since Allen was standing at the head of the platform when he was waiting to board the train, he was able to see Jim leaning out of the motorman's car to punch in his stop at the station. Knowing that his boy was driving made him feel a little more at ease, which was helpful right about now. Allen and Jim had managed to reconcile things since last week's graduation celebration. Deep down, Allen knew Jim's remarks stemmed from his over-protectiveness. Jim had been through a lot of hurt and humiliation and he only wanted to shield Allen from a similar experience. But Allen believed he was a different person from his friend, and this was a different situation. Allen was going to make his destiny. Soon. Within the next two stops to be exact.

Allen was on his way to an interview with Hartland Financial Consulting, one of the top-consulting firms in the city. He had spent a whole week doing research on the company, and was excited to find that they had been encouraging newer, mid-sized businesses with a lot of growth potential to go public with stock offerings as a way to build capital. This was the type of thing that Allen liked. The giants in the industry had been there for so long they began to take their public for granted. Allen felt it was time to make some more giants. The only way this could be done would be to encourage the growth of smaller businesses and help them to find their niche in the market. He had seen this done with companies like Google and Yahoo. Allen felt that it was time for some African-Americans to step up and hit the scene with their businesses too, and he would be in the position to help make it happen.

Allen sat back in his seat and crossed his legs, trying not to wrinkle the pants of his charcoal gray suit. Then he took out his burgundy leather portfolio briefcase and opened it on his lap to review some of the notes and data he had gathered one last time. Allen tried to concentrate on what he was reading, but the anxiety he felt created a whirlwind of thoughts that he couldn't keep out of his consciousness. Allen began to consider the tenuous nature of the interview process. "What if there's something they don't like about me?" he pondered. He closed his portfolio, leaned over and put his head in his hands and tried to relax to the rhythmic rocking of the subway car as it barreled down the tunnel, but it was no use. "I should get an offer", he thought. After all, he was articulate, he had experience interning at some pretty well known firms, he had a sound knowledge of the company, good references, and not to mention he had just graduated from one of the top schools in the country. Everyone told him he had a lot to offer, so why should he doubt his capabilities now? Then he could hear Jim's words echoing in the back of his mind. But like everyone else said: this was a different era. Allen felt that America was on the verge of becoming a post-racial society. So Allen brushed away the negative thoughts.

The train slowed down and pulled into the station with a screeching halt.

"This is Wall Street. Transfer here for the uptown trains across the platform. Remember to take all your belongings with you and watch your step on the way out. This is the downtown 4. Next stop Brooklyn Bridge, stand clear of the closing doors, please", said the automated announcer.

This was Allen's stop. He gathered his belongings and his confidence and exited the train and stepped out into the throng of people on the platform. As he scanned the crowd, he noticed most of them were clearly business people with their shiny leather brief cases, and copies of the Wall Street Journal tucked up under their arms. All of them striding confidently down the platform, up the stairs, and off to their respective jobs. These were the movers and shakers: the change makers. As Allen moved along with them, he was confident that he would soon be one of them.

When he had reached the street, he paused for a moment to glance at his watch. It was 9:45. His interview was at 10:00. The building was only a few blocks over, so Allen decided to take his time and look in some of the windows of the shops on the way. The tourists were out, which made it difficult to navigate the narrow sidewalks, however, Allen wasn't bothered by it. He knew why the tourists were attracted to this area. No matter how many times Allen had been down this way, he was always amazed by the opulence of the surroundings. He was not just impressed by all of the big names he saw on the store windows, but by the design of the buildings, the cleanliness of the streets, and the order that seemed to coordinate everything. It was a far cry from his neighborhood back on St. Nicholas Ave. Not that his neighborhood was that bad. Allen would never dream of leaving his beloved Harlem. He wanted to be able to help transform his neighborhood into the busy thriving oasis that he was traversing at this moment. He knew it was possible. If only he possessed the money and the influence. If only someone would just give him a chance to get started. He hoped that this company would be magnanimous enough to take a chance on a 22 year-old dreamer from the inner city.

In the midst of his reverie, Allen almost missed the building. It was a huge glass structure that seemed like an obelisk, especially if you were looking at it from the Brooklyn Bridge. Allen walked in and showed his I.D to the security guard who stood in the lobby. Then he rushed over to one of the elevator banks and grabbed an elevator to the 35th floor. When the elevator doors opened, he could see two big mahogany doors with the words Hartland Financial Consulting inscribed on a conspicuous gold-colored plaque, with the company logo next to it. Beneath it was another one that indicated this was the human resources department. The consultant and analysts' offices had to be on one of the other floors. As he opened the door, he could see the receptionist, a thin, young, white woman sitting behind a large circular oak paneled desk with a headset on. To the left of her there was a short leather couch, and a table with several business magazines spread over it. As Allen walked in, the receptionist looked up, her eyes locking onto his.

"Delivery or pick-up?" she inquired.

"Uh, neither", answered Allen a little puzzled by her question. "I have an appointment for a 10:00 interview with Mr. Ravitch. I'm Allen Sharpe."

"Oh…", she replied, still a little doubtful. "I'll let Mr. Ravitch know you're here. Allen Sharpe, right?"

"Yes."

She leaned forward and pressed one of the buttons on the console in front of her.

"Mr. Ravitch?"

"Ye-es", a friendly voice chimed back.

"Allen Sharpe, your 10:00 is here."

"Give me five before you send him in."

"You got it."

"He'll see you in a few. Have a seat", she said to Allen as she pointed to one of the chairs in the reception area.

"Thank you."

"No problem", she winked.

Allen simply smiled back and adjusted the collar of his shirt and loosened his tie just a bit. He hoped the five minutes would pass quickly before the flirty receptionist made him an offer he had to refuse.

*****

Martin Ravitch, a tall, well-built, middle aged white man with brown thinning hair, leaped out of the chair in his office and headed past a maze of cubicles toward another office in the corner. He stuck his head in and motioned to his associate, Greald Harris, who was neck deep behind a stack of papers. Harris was on the phone trying to wrap up a conference call. Mr. Harris was an older man who was much rounder. He had more hair on his face than he had on his head, most of which was gray and shaggy looking. He nodded at Ravitch's signal, and began to wrap up his call.

"Look, come in on Thursday, and we'll get the paperwork done", said Mr. Harris to the person on the other end of the line as he tried to end the call. "Yes, 9:00 would be great. I'll see you then." Harris wiped his face with his hands before turning his attention to Ravitch who was anxiously waiting in the doorway.

"That Sharpe kid is here. Did you go over his resume?" asked Ravitch.

"Oh, yes. I got it yesterday in your e-mail. Just let me print it out."

"So what do you think?"

"Well, he looks good on paper, but I don't know. Let's see what happens."

"I think this guy is just what we need. I almost proposed to Gertrude for setting up the interview."

"Did you check out his address?"

"He lives up on 127th and St. Nicholas. So?"

"So, what type of people do you think live there?"

"C'mon. I know a lot of people from around that way. It's where all these trendy hipsters live. The neighborhood is changing", said Ravitch nonchalantly. He then checked his watch. "Hey, let's head down, Sofia's gonna send him back soon."

Harris grabbed the printout from the printer and headed down with Ravitch towards the conference room. As they walked in, an admin was busy making last minute arrangements to the room for the interview. She moved some of the chairs behind the conference table, and one chair in front. Harris promptly took a seat and continued to look over the resume, while the admin finished up and left. Ravitch took the seat next to him.

"He's a Harvard guy, but I wish he had a little more experience. He's only had a few internships. He seems a little raw, but I think we could work with him."

"I know you think all interns do is make coffee, but according to his creds, he's been doing a lot more than that. I think he'd be great."

"We'll see. That address still worries me though."

A knock at the door interrupted their conversation. Ravitch rushed behind the desk and took a seat next to Harris.

"Come in", Ravitch sang, his voice full of expectation.

Allen opened the door slowly, and stepped in. The men at the conference table looked up, and an uneasiness washed over them, which Allen could read all over their faces. It made him a little tense. For a moment, Allen thought he had the wrong room.

"Good Morning."

"Yes?" asked Ravitch with a little trepidation.

"I'm Allen Sharpe", announced Allen walking in further and extending his hand for a shake. This made the younger of the men break out of his daze.

"Oh, yes. How do you do?" said Ravitch as he stood up, trying to cover his shock, and forcing a smile as he shook Allen's hand. "Martin Ravitch. I'm the human resources specialist, and this is Mr. Greald Harris. He's the one of the senior consultants, here at the company."

"How do you do?" grunted Harris perfunctorily, who remained seated. He then gave Ravtich a wary look.

"Have a seat", breathed Ravitch, pointing Allen towards a chair. All three men were sitting down and there was a tense moment of dead air between them. Allen noticed that Ravitch's smile seemed pasted on. He sat on the edge of his chair, leaning forward as if he wanted to bolt from the room. He tried staring at the resume as a way to avoid looking at Allen. Meanwhile his associate, Mr. Harris, sat leaning back with his arms folded across his chest. His stare was as cold as his ice blue eyes. The moment lasted only five seconds, but for Allen it seemed like five hours. Finally, Ravitch broke the silence with the first question.

"So, Allen, why do you want to work for Hartland Financial Consulting?"

COMMENCEMENT

"I understand that your company works with small and mid-sized businesses to develop long-term fiscal planning solutions. Correct?"

"Yes."

"I have always had an interest in working with smaller businesses in consulting. In fact, I have had some experience conducting data analysis and evaluating financial plans for such firms as a part of my internship experience. At McFarland Tracy, I assisted consultants in creating a financial restructuring plan for a client that saved the company over 20% in infrastructure costs. This money was then put into investments that increased overall revenues by 30%."

"Do you have any documentation or proof of this?" sneered Harris.

"Yes, of course", said Allen handing him the case study from his portfolio. Ravitch took the portfolio first and looked it over.

"Impressive", he remarked.

"Do you think you could handle a case study on the spot?" asked Harris.

"It would be a challenge, but I'd welcome the opportunity. How much time would I have to make an analysis?"

"I'll give you 45 minutes. There's paper inside the folder for you to jot down your ideas. When we come back you can let us know what your take on it is", said Harris coldly.

Harris took out a folder and handed it to Allen. The folder contained several reports on a mock client's earnings and outlook. It also contained the company's plan and targets for growth and accumulation of capital. Allen carefully perused the sheets, taking notes along the way. Then he made a quick summary of the strengths and weaknesses of the plan, and provided his own preliminary analysis of how the company could reach its growth targets. He had just finished when Harris and Ravitch re-entered the room.

"Are we all done?" asked Ravitch.

"He is done. Time's up", blared Harris snatching the papers from Allen. Harris looked them over. Ravitch had to look over Harris' shoulder to get a glance. Both men studied the papers thoughtfully for some time.

"Hmph, this is impressive", remarked Ravitch out loud in spite of himself, rubbing his chin as he examined the papers. Harris merely rolled his eyes, before chucking them toward Allen.

"There's more to financial consulting than just analysis, research, and planning. There's also a lot of legal work involved. You don't seem to have a lot of experience on that end."

"I may not have a lot of experience, but I do have some experience in the areas you've referred to. At Briers and Lang, I assisted consultants in conducting legal research involving transferring of holdings, liquidations and escrow accounts. McFarland Tracy, I assisted consultants in researching bankruptcy laws as well as mergers and acquisitions."

Another five second silence. Ravitch had taken up the papers Harris had so scornfully cast aside and was now back into the case study analysis, nodding his head up and down like a bobble doll. Harris rubbed his chin thinking of some cunning question to volley at Allen. His next line of attack would be to investigate the validity of Allen's experience. Asking for concrete examples of the people, projects, and customers that he worked with in minute detail. Then Harris interrogated Allen about his plans for the future. Was he working on his MBA? Why or Why not? When did he expect to pursue it? Where did he see himself going on the job? Allen had to think fast on his feet, but he was somewhat used to this as he encountered it before, but not with such ferocity. It was as if Harris was trying purposefully to trip him up. The next 15 minutes was like a verbal tennis match. Harris would serve out an ace of a question that Allen would have to think fast on his feet to return. Ravitch served as the commentator, and made remarks about the cleverness of the question or the shrewdness of the answer. By the end of the interview more than an hour had passed. Allen had managed to maintain a pleasant demeanor through it all, despite the caustic effrontery of Harris' questioning, and the nonchalant disregard of Ravitch.

"Thank you for coming in Mr. Sharpe" managed Ravtich, who still seemed a little uneasy. "We are still in the process of conducting interviews, so we will call you when we make a final decision", he added, extending his hand for a farewell handshake. Harris stood with his arms folded across his chest.

"Thank you", replied Allen. "It was a pleasure meeting both of you. I look forward to hearing from you." Allen extended his hand to Harris despite the fact that the older man's face shot him a look that said, "Don't count on it". However, Harris managed to give him one of the weakest shakes he had ever had.

Allen left the conference room and headed back down the hall toward the reception area, trying to sort out everything that happened in the last hour or so. He sensed that something went wrong, but he couldn't put his finger on what. He was polite. He was articulate. He answered their (or rather Harris's) questions directly, and didn't engage in unnecessary circumlocutions. Ravitch seemed to be impressed with his ideas at times, despite his overall indifference. Could there have been something that he missed?

"Have a nice day", a voice sang behind him. As Allen turned around, he noticed that he had passed the reception desk. He had been so lost in his thoughts that he was almost sleepwalking.

"I'm sorry. You have a nice day, too." He replied absentmindedly. Allen struggled to regain his composure before leaving the office. He would have to think about it again, later. After all, he had another interview in a few days, and he had to go over what went wrong today to keep it from happening again. Allen tried to push the thoughts back as he waited for the elevator to take him to the lobby, but they would not be kept at bay. "Maybe it was something that had to do with the way I was dressed", he thought anxiously "Maybe I seemed too eager."

"Ping!"

The ring of the elevator brought Allen's mind back to the present moment. As he got on, he noticed several people who were dressed in expensive business clothes, looking very sure of themselves as they stared at the row of numbers above the elevator exit or at their watches or at the floor. Allen felt very small and insignificant. When the elevator opened to the lobby, Allen rushed out past the tinted exit doors into the late morning sun. He walked until he saw one of the green benches that the city provides for its denizens to rest. Before Allen sat down, he took off his jacket to cool down. When he did, he noticed the enormous rings of sweat under the arms of his shirt.

THREE

It was 85 degrees outside, so that meant that it had to be about 105 degrees on the platform of the Bowling Green Station. Jim had just come back from lunch and was waiting to relieve the driver of the northbound 4 train. The morning had been frustrating, especially when he was driving uptown in the Bronx. There were several delays, one involving a sick passenger at Kingsbridge, and the other a 5 train that had gotten stalled on 149th street as he was on his way back to Bowling Green. But such disruptions were fairly common in the underground caverns of the city.

He was a little early for this shift, so he checked in at the dispatch office next to the platform to pick up his belt, radio, goggles and headset and wait for his friend Brian, who would be the CR, or the conductor, on his train for the rest of the day. To his surprise, Brian was already there along with Greg the dispatcher. Greg was about forty or so and, at least to Jim's knowledge, had been there the longest. Brian was African-American just like Jim and was one of his closest associates on the job. In fact, he was the one who had helped him to get a job in transit in the first place. Jim had known him from his days at St. John's University. Brian had the same hard time that Jim had trying to get a job out of college. Fortunately, Brian had an uncle who was a transit worker. It was this uncle who helped Brian get a job as a CR. Later after running into Jim and hearing just how down he was on his luck, Brian was able to help Jim get a job as a motorman. When Jim came in, Greg was already talking to Brian about the rest of the day's schedule. Jim knew there was always some type of interruption, especially with the 4 line. Occasionally, there were signal problems, trains breaking down in the tunnels, or track work going on, in which case trains had to be re-routed, and then once that happened, he had no idea where he would be going. But best to find out before the run than during the run, which happened more often than not.

"Hey, everybody. What's up?"

"Hey, Jim. Great timing, I was just telling Brian about the change."

"Are we going to have to re-route?"

"No, nothing like that yet. Your going to do two runs from Green to Woodlawn and then on the third, you're going to go from Woodlawn all the way to Crown Heights and Utica for the evening rush."

"Brooklyn? But it will only be 3:00. I thought the rush starts at 4:30 for summer."

"This is just temporary, at least until they finish renovating the station at the Bridge", explained Greg.

"Look at it this way, Brooklyn isn't as bad as Manhattan. Once we get over Bowling- Green it's no sweat from then out", said Brian.

"I guess", said Jim, still not completely comfortable with the situation.

"Hey, Jim. I'm going to get a snack from the newsstand before the train comes. You want anything?" asked Brian.

"Yeah, I'll roll with you. Just let me grab my bag."

Jim grabbed his bag from the corner of the office where he had left it and followed his friend out the door onto the steamy platform.

"See you guys later", called Greg.

"See-ya", they both called back.

Brian and Jim headed toward the newsstand, where they both bought candy bars and soda to serve as fuel for the long ride ahead. There was still some time before the train came in so they decided to hang back from the crowd that was starting to gather and engage in some friendly banter.

"So how you been, man?" asked Brian.

"I'm good", replied Jim.

COMMENCEMENT

"Did you hear from any schools yet?"

"Not yet", said Jim with some hesitation, and making sure to avoid Brian's eyes as he spoke.

Both Brian and Jim wanted to be lawyers, and they had both made plans to get started, but only Brian had followed through. They started out taking an LSAT prep course, but unbeknownst to Brian, Jim's determination had exhausted itself after the actual LSAT exam. Jim's scores were actually pretty good, even better than Brian's. They were both supposed to have applied to several law schools together, including Columbia, John Jay, Fordham, and his alma mater, St. John's. But for some reason, Jim choked at the application process. The problem was, he was finding it hard to keep up his momentum. The longer he had been away from school, the harder it had been for him to stay connected to the dynamic that energized him. For some reason, he could not psyche himself up to the tedious process of writing essays, interviewing, and begging for recommendations. Jim felt as if he didn't have the energy and his work for the MTA took up a lot of the precious little time and energy he did have. When he got home at night, he often felt as if he had been run over by one of the trains. If only he had started his legal career straight out of college, it would have been easier. If only he had been able to find a legal job. That's what it had to be. Brian on the other hand had applied to several schools and had recently gotten the green light from St. John's. Ever since, he'd been asking Jim about how he fared, with the hope that they could go to school together. Jim admired Brian's energy and drive, and wished he'd had the same fortitude. Jim didn't have the nerve to tell Brian the truth. Jim had gotten himself into a very sticky situation and he couldn't help but feel a little ashamed.

"You'll make it, man. Maybe I got my letter quicker, since I live in Queens", said Brian, sensing his friend's uneasiness.

"Yeah, but even if I decided to go, how am I going to do law school and transit at the same time? Law school is tough. I can't be puttin' in 12 and 14 hour days here and fulfill my obligations to school. I'd never get any sleep."

"You could get another job that's less demanding, like those jobs at the University. That's what I plan on doing."

"If it's less demanding, it's probably because there's less money, and you know a brother got bills, and law school is going to be a big one. I can't pay my rent and everything with no campus library job."

"I hear you, and transit is good money, but if we're gonna go for it we'll just have to make some sacrifices."

"It's rough out there, man. If it weren't for you hooking me up, I wouldn't have this job. I don't know if I can give it up just like that. I can't go back to livin' with my moms even if I wanted to."

"I feel that. But the long-term rewards make up for the short-term suffering. C'mon, I know you're not going to cut out on me now, are you?"

"No, no. I still want to go", lied Jim. "It's just…I need to think this through. You know, weigh the pros as well as the cons."

"What's to think through? This is your dream right?"

"Yeah, man", said Jim trying to sound confident.

"Then you have to go for it all the way, forget about the things that could hold you back. You deal with them. If it's your dream, you just got to keep going."

"Now you sound like my friend Allen."

"You mean the Harvard dude. How's he makin' out?"

"He's good. Got a lot of interviews. Went on one today. Should be over by now, though. I'll have to ask him how it went", Jim said glad that his friend was changing the subject.

"Interviews are one thing, man. Anybody with a European sounding name can get some interviews, but will he get hired?"

"I tried to break that down to him, but you know how some of these brothers are."

"Yeah, they got they rose colored glasses on, so to speak. They believe in the rainbow. But come on, in New York City more than 50% of black males are unemployed. More than 50%. That's not just some coincidence. That's some systematic scheming. That's why we got to get to law school. We got to get into this system and stop some of this stuff."

That's why Jim liked Brian. It was nice to have someone around who could hear where he was coming from, someone who understood. Jim thought about Allen and the exchange they got into a while ago. He hoped for the best for Allen, but his common sense told him otherwise. He didn't think Allen would get the job, and he felt bad that he could not drum up any more enthusiasm for his friend. But then he thought, "What if Allen did get the job? What would that mean?" Jim's thoughts were interrupted by his friend's sudden outburst.

"What's up with this train, man? This guy was supposed to be here by now!"

"Could be a disruption. There's always a disruption on this line."

"I wouldn't be surprised if the gig we supposed to be drivin' broke down. Greg already told me it's one of those old fashioned jobs."

"Yeah, and the AC isn't working so great on it either. When I left, it was like a sauna in there."

"See. Now this is another reason why we gotta get to law school. There's way too much to put up with in transit. There has to be more to life than drivin' these raggedy trains in circles, going nowhere."

Jim was totally stunned with the intensity of Brian's dissatisfaction with the job. If this had been two years ago, Jim might have agreed with him. At present, Jim didn't see anything so terrible about being a train operator. True there were lots of problems, but for Jim, there were problems everywhere. The salary was solid, and there were opportunities for advancement. He had even begun to think it was a worthy cause, especially when he thought about how important a job it was to get people to and from their jobs on time everyday. It surprised him to think about how much he had changed or even matured.

After a few more minutes of nervous anticipation, the train finally arrived; however, it was not the old clunker they'd expected. Both men were surprised by the fact that they were going to ride in one of the newer models. After the train stopped, he could see Jake, the original motorman coming towards them.

"What happened to 1134?" asked Jim.

"Probably back at the yard by now. Mechanical Problems. The AC finally went dead, and the brakes were acting up. Luckily, I was at the grand central junction when it happened", Jake replied.

"I know the passengers are going to be happy", said Brian sarcastically.

"Tell me about it. The looks I got on the way over."

"You'd think that after that last fare hike, they'd retire some of these old trains and put more new ones on", said Jim.

"Man, please! They just retired the redbirds a couple of years ago, only after a million years of service", Brian complained.

"We better head on out, before the crowd turns on us."

Jim exchanged some final courtesies with the two men, before they each headed in separate directions, he to the motorman's car, Brian to the conductor's car, and Jake to the office, wading through the crowd that had gathered on the platform. Jim and Brian were not surprised by number of people that had aggregated in such a short amount of time. As usual, they were anxious to get where they were going, and upon seeing Jim and Brian in their MTA uniforms, the realization that this was a layover stop for an already delayed train, made them even more apprehensive. Jim could hear the heavy sighs and angry expletives of the passengers as they made their way toward the train. But as he stepped into the motorman's car and put on his goggles and headset, he was able to tune all of those things out. The AC in the car was a welcome change from the stifling platform. After performing his standing break tests, he radioed Brian to see if he had all of the signs changed. Then he punched the timer in the station and checked the signal. Both were green. Just as he was about to start the train up, he heard a call on the radio. It was Greg.

"You're going express in the Bronx on the first run. Just 161st, Burnside, Fordham, Bedford and Woodlawn."

"Got it."

COMMENCEMENT

Jim radioed Brian to let him know. Then Brian made the announcement on the PA system. Immediately following there was a rush of angry passengers who left the train, voicing obscenities to the MTA. Then he led the train out into the darkness of the tunnel. Jim thought about the first time he actually drove a subway train. It was a hot and noisy old-fashioned train. It was creaky, but that wasn't much of a problem for Jim, as he was used to riding in them as a passenger. The one thing he couldn't get over was the darkness within. His trainer had told him that it would be the same as driving around at night, but it didn't seem that way for Jim. There weren't as many lights or signs to guide him. Entering the tunnel for the first time was like driving nearly blind. Jim was terrified. In front of him there was nothing but a narrow tunnel with a few lights strung up here and there. You were never really sure of where you are until you're right up close and by then sometimes, it's too late to change direction. Jim was never totally sure of where he was going most of the time, but he got to the right places somehow. Now he was no longer afraid, and he was pretty sure of himself no matter what route he drove. Jim couldn't see himself leaving his good transit job. Not for law school. That would be like facing the dark tunnel all over again.

FOUR

Today was a new day. Allen had analyzed his failure of two weeks ago. He realized that he had not given the impression that he was willing to learn. Ravitch and Harris probably thought that he was some jerk who thought he could coast on his Harvard degree and connections. He realized that maybe some of his answers did seem to smack of arrogance. Allen decided to change his strategy. He even recruited Tim to prep him with mock interviews. As a result, Allen had passed the first round interview with Concord Group Consulting's human resources department. He now had to interview with the head of the financial consulting department. As he sat in the waiting area of Concord Group Consulting, he was buoyed by his newly restored confidence. Allen noticed that there were other interviewees that had arrived who were also waiting. They were most likely being interviewed for positions in other departments. There was a young Asian woman in a crisp Navy gabardine suit and black pumps, accessorized with a pearl necklace. She was reading one of the complimentary magazines, Harpers Weekly, to be specific. Allen also noticed a white guy with close-cropped brown hair who wore a black and grey pinstriped suit, reading the Financial Times. Allen had been studying his own copy of the Financial Times, scanning for any stray news that would catch his interest. He was a little edgy from the huge cup of coffee he had this morning. Remembering the coffee, Allen suddenly reached inside his briefcase and took out a tin of breath mints. He quickly opened it, popped a mint in his mouth and replaced the tin to its former hiding place. Of all things, Allen did not want his breath to be a strike against him.

By the time Allen's mint had dissolved, a woman walked into the room holding a sheet of paper in front of her. She seemed to be in her mid to late forties. She was tall and thin with short blond hair styled in a bob. Her tall, lanky figure was enveloped by the black wide-legged pantsuit she was wearing. She pushed up her black tortoise shell glasses and looked at the paper and surveyed all of the faces in front of her before walking up to the young white man.

"Allen Sharpe?" she asked him.

"I'm Allen Sharpe", a voice responded.

Puzzled that the response did not come from the young man in front of her, she looked over her shoulder to see Allen rising and extending his hand to greet her.

"Oh! Oh, I'm sorry!" said the woman, her face now red as her perfectly manicured fingernails. "I'm Madeline Aldridge. I'm head of financial consulting."

"It's a pleasure to meet you, Ms. Aldrige", said Allen.

"Same here", she said as she smiled stiffly. "I'm sorry about the mix up, I guess I didn't see you over there", she chuckled nervously.

"It's quite alright", Allen said to relieve her obvious anxiety over the mistake.

"If you please…" Aldrige said directing Allen to follow her to her office. As they walked down the corridor away from the reception area, Allen tried to fill the time with small talk about the watercolor paintings he had observed on the walls. Aldrige responded courteously if not curtly. Finally, they reached a large room with an oak paneled door with a placard that read Madeline Aldrige: President of Financial Consulting Services. As she opened the door, Allen could see that this was what was meant by the term "corner office". The room was as large as a conference room. There was a huge marble desk surrounded by three Corinthian leather chairs, one positioned in back of the desk and two in front, and a huge leather couch behind them, flush against the back wall. Behind the desk there was a huge window, which afforded a view of the Hudson River. The oak bookcases that had a cherry finish, did not escape his notice either. Accenting the beauty of the office were all sorts of curiosities, like the suit of armor in one corner, a huge globe in another. Allen was so taken with the furnishings; he almost did not hear Aldrige ask him to sit down to begin the interview.

"So, Mr. Sharpe, your resume says you went to Harvard. What a coincidence. That's my brother's Alma Mater. How did you like it there?" Aldrige inquired, with just a faint hint of suspicion entering her voice.

"It was challenging, but the professors and the students were very supportive", Allen lied.

"There was one professor there that taught a Macroeconomics course, who was famous for singing during his lectures." Aldrige suddenly stopped looking pensively at Allen. "I can't think of his name right now...."

"You're probably thinking of professor Hunt", Allen suggested.

"Yes!" Aldrige brightened, "That was his name. Were you in one of his classes?"

"Yes. I took Intro to Econ 1. I learned a lot. He's a very brilliant man."

"So I've heard", replied Aldrige. "But I think, we've digressed enough, haven't we. I'm sure you're probably more interested in talking about the position, than reminiscing about your college days", she laughed.

"I am very interested in the position."

"Of course. So, Allen, Why be our financial analyst?"

"From what I understand, your firm specializes in reaching out to non-traditional investors, or small investors: those who have smaller incomes and may not be as knowledgeable about investing. Is that correct?"

"Yes. That's right."

"I have always liked the idea of working with this neglected section of the investment community. I believe that it is important to the economic health of the nation as a whole to try to help all people understand the importance of investing and financial planning. In the past

COMMENCEMENT

I have worked with individuals, families, and small businesses to help them create investment portfolios that would suit their particular needs."

Aldrige was silent. While Allen was speaking, she had taken off her glasses and was chewing on the frame. Allen thought he had answered the question fully, and didn't know if Aldrige was waiting for him to continue or if she was lost in thought.

"Is there anything else?" asked Allen.

"Oh, I'm sorry. I sort of spaced out for a second", she laughed again, more color rising to her cheeks. "I see that you have some experience working with small investors. Could you tell me more about that?"

"For the most part, as I said before, I have worked with families and individuals, primarily with moderate to low incomes, who were looking to either supplement their income or plan for retirement. I have also worked with businesses to help them not only to optimize their investment assets, but to develop strategies to accumulate capital in order to expand their product base. All of the portfolio recommendations would be based on what we knew about the client, their financial goals, how much money they were willing to invest, and the trends we were observing in the market, and what we heard from the indexes. I would lead them to investment opportunities that matched their goals. If they wanted quick returns, I would encourage them invest in funds of small companies who were experiencing rapid growth or get them into low cost real estate. If they were looking for longer-term investments, we would talk about hedge funds, mutual funds, IRA's, or currencies. If the person were a first time investor with very little experience and undue wariness of the market, we would discuss low-risk securities like money market accounts, and bonds. Later on once the client had developed some confidence in investing, we would begin to talk to him about riskier investments like stocks."

"Interesting. Very interesting. You're so articulate."

"Thank you", said Allen as he graciously accepted her compliment. However, then she started to stare again. "Is there anything else that you would like to know?"

"Oh, yes, yes. Uh, well Allen, I was just thinking. You have a lot of sound experience here. In fact, it sounds to me as if the position that we have here may not be challenging enough for someone like you. You seem to be ready for the next level."

"Thank You, Ms. Aldrige. I really appreciate your professional opinion. Do you feel that I could be a considered as a candidate for a more senior position, here?" asked Allen, hoping for a better offer.

"Why yes, of course. However, at this time, we don't have any senior positions open."

"I see."

"But thank you for coming in. It was nice meeting you."

"It was a pleasure to meet you as well, Ms. Aldridge", said Allen rising to leave.

"Yes it's nice to see people like you who are actually doing something with themselves."

Allen was at a loss for words. He merely smiled, and stammered "Have a nice day." before he turned toward the door. As he walked down the hallway back to the reception room, he couldn't help but hear the echo of the words "people like you…"

FIVE

"Should I use the plain blue border or the 'kids playing' border?" Tamiko asked herself. She was standing on a chair in front of the children's coat closet in the classroom. Her classroom. Today was Tamiko's first day at work as a first grade teacher at the Great Expectations School, a Pre-K to 6 school located in one of Manhattan's poorest districts. Technically, she didn't have to report today, but Tamiko was nervous and wanted to get a head start on arranging her classroom.

First, she had to find out where everything was. When Tamiko arrived, the closets were a hodge-podge of assorted odds and ends. Construction paper was in one closet, but writing paper in another. The arts and crafts and math manipulatives were hidden in the same cubby hole of the teacher's desk which was in the center of the room. There seemed to be no particular system applied to warehousing the teaching materials she had at her disposal. It seemed as if the last teacher who had the classroom put things away in a haphazard manner before running off for summer vacation. Tamiko would have to re-arrange her closet spaces to make more sense later.

Earlier, Tamiko had been working to create her teaching space/morning meeting area, a wide space at the head of the classroom near the window, where her mini-lesson rug and morning meeting board would be. Then she went to work on the children's workspaces, arranging the tables in the room. Each table would have a designated color. There would be a red table, a blue table and a yellow table. The tables were actually manila, so she would have to make up signs for each table in the appropriate colors. She also used some short bookcases for her literacy centers, which, by regulation of the Department Of Education, had to be in different parts of the room. Each table was to have its own corresponding literacy center where the children could find paper, pencils, and other things they needed to write stories. Now she was putting up the paper and borders for the bulletin boards. Tamiko decided on doing this sooner than later because she thought it would be a simple task that could be done quickly. However, with all the measuring and cutting of paper and the stapling and choosing colors, it seemed to take an inordinate amount of time. Finally, Tamiko decided on the "kids playing" border, and began to staple it hastily to the bulletin boards. As Tamiko was stapling, she went over in her head all of the other things that she had to do before the opening day of school. There was the behavior chart, the five crates of books in the children's coat closet that would need to be sorted into some sort of library, decisions on where to put the big books, and the word walls. The children's home/school mail boxes needed to be labeled and math centers would have to made, not to mention lesson plans. Then there were the million other things she couldn't think of right now, but would turn up in the course of her work. All of this made her appreciate the relative quiet of the nearly empty school. She would only have two more days before more teachers came, and three more days before the students arrived for their first day of school.

So far, only seven out of the 40 teachers employed by the school were present and working on their classrooms. It was just the six lead teachers for each grade and her. So far, Tamiko had only met them in passing and they all seemed to be nice enough. She had met Charity Fontaine, the tall, effervescent kindergarten lead teacher from Ohio; Grace Weaver, the third grade lead teacher, who seemed very analytical. Then there were the others, all quite reserved, who she couldn't remember, however, there was one teacher who seemed a little aloof. Tamiko would never forget walking into *her* classroom. She had all of the lights off, and Tamiko would have backed away, but then she saw her sitting in a corner of the room where the library was, meticulously cutting out labels. She was an older, heavy-set, white woman with dark hair pinned up in a bun. When Tamiko introduced herself, the woman didn't even bother looking up from what she was doing. Instead, she just said a brief "Hello, nice to meet you" and barely cracked a smile the whole time.

COMMENCEMENT

Tamiko understood that all of the teachers that were in the building were busy, but she could have been a little friendlier. Tamiko would find out from one of the other teachers that her name was Rosalyn Steele, and that she was an "odd ball", who had been working at the school for ten years, four of which she had been a first grade lead teacher. The idea that such a personality would be observing her and taking charge of her professional development, made Tamiko feel a little uneasy. "Maybe, we just need time to get to know each other and break the ice", Tamiko thought optimistically to herself while giving this woman the benefit of the doubt.

Right now everyone was preoccupied with her classroom. This preoccupation or rather obsession is particular for teachers for several reasons. First, the set up of the room determines how one's year will go. If materials and supplies are in short order, or are in difficult to reach areas, and if there is no sense of preparation, the natural result will be disorder and chaos. Children tend to naturally follow adults as their leaders, however, if the adult and the surroundings are disorganized, it naturally causes the children to question and subsequently undermine the authority of the adult. Tamiko also knew the children she would be dealing with had enough problems of their own at home, and some may have behavior problems. A disordered and unorganized classroom was just asking for those behavior problems to manifest themselves. In addition, the classroom is an organic instrument to the teacher, and serves as one of the teacher's primary teaching tools. Bulletin boards teach pride in one's work and self-esteem, behavior charts teach self-control and delayed gratification. And there would be copious amounts of information displayed everywhere in the room to make children's learning easier. Finally, the Principal and other administrators always judged what was going on in the classroom by the look of the room itself. Miss Steele's room was absolutely immaculate, she remembered. Tamiko wished she had taken better mental note of the room, but she was so blown away by Steele's attitude that she didn't get the chance. There was no way Tamiko was going back there again. She'd wait until after the professional development on Thursday, when she would have a better sense of what she was like.

An unexpected knock at the door, almost caused Tamiko to fall off her chair.

"Come in!" Tamiko called out.

It was the Mrs. Nettlenerves, the assistant-principal. Mrs. Nettlenerves was a petite, red-haired woman who talked and walked as if she drank coffee like water. Even when Tamiko was interviewing for the position, she had to ask her to repeat some of the questions because she spoke so fast.

"Hi, Tamiko!"

"Hello, Mrs. Nettlenerves."

"I'm just doing a little informal walk through to see how things are going. I must say you've gotten a lot of work done. It looks great. I love that color for the boards and the border is just to die for."

"Oh, Thank…"

"Tomorrow, some of our school aides are coming in and they will begin handing out starter supplies. You know: crayons, paper, pencils, construction paper, chart paper, glue sticks, color pencils, all those types of things, so don't think you'll have to buy everything yourself. If you've already bought some that's okay, because most teachers run out by the December break, and you may need them because the wait time for Mary to re-order can be a bit long, especially if there's not enough down in the basement. Now, there's a checklist that you're going to get along with your supplies, so don't put any of them away until you've completed your checklist. You'll get your checklist at the professional development meeting on Thursday. And I know you're probably wondering about your class set up, well there's a checklist for our new teachers that you're going to get regarding that as well. It's basically a checklist of all the things that we are looking for in our teacher's classrooms. You look concerned."

"I…"

"There's really nothing to be worried about. It's not that we want the classrooms to look the same, like they came out of a cookie cutter or anything. Believe me we don't want to hamper your creativity or originality, but we have high standards and based on those standards the teachers at this school have agreed that there are certain elements that should be a part of every classroom. You probably have most of them already and they are standard to teaching. Like I don't know any classroom that doesn't have a word wall, or literacy centers, or a math word wall. It's things like that, that a smart girl like you probably already knows about, so there's not going to be any big surprises. That must make you feel better, right?"

"Sure, uh...."

"Well, so far, the room looks fabulous. Keep up the good work. Oh, and before I forget, on Thursday, we are going to have a breakfast in the staff lounge in the morning. It's like our little tradition to get everyone off to a good start. There will be bagels, juice, coffee, pastries, and all sorts of goodies like that. I know you'll be here early, so don't get so busy that you miss it. It's a great opportunity to mix with the other teachers and get to know them and pick their brains for ideas. If you have any questions or anything hold them 'till Thursday, and I promise you everything will be answered then. O.K? See you then!" she said as she hastened out of the door and down the hall.

"See, ya", Tamiko said to the empty space where the assistant-principal had been.

Tamiko was surprised that she was able to get all of that out in such few breaths. She seemed kind and friendly enough, but there was something about her manner that made Tamiko a bit wary. Like the way she tried to give everything a frivolous and light air. And often she spoke so fast, it almost seemed as if she didn't want you to get the full import of what she was saying. Kind of like a used car salesman, who is trying to sell you a really big lemon.

Despite Mrs. Nettlenerves light-hearted banter, Tamiko was concerned about these checklists. It just seemed like a sign of distrust. And why would there be distrust if the teachers were professionals and did their jobs? Tamiko decided to shake off all of her misgivings. "After all, I just got here", Tamiko thought. "I have to give things time to play out before I judge things." That's what she had learned from the scripture she had read last night. After all didn't the Apostle Paul say that we should judge nothing before the time.[1] The words seemed poignant to her, since Tamiko often jumped to conclusions on a regular basis. It was something she was working on in her walk with God. Tamiko had always been a religious person, but only recently had she become a real Christian. This came about after an experience she had during the early years of her college career, in which she felt that God was calling her to teach.

Tamiko would never forget that day during registration, when she had to finally declare her major. She had been praying for what seemed like months about it, wavering between education and sociology. She had always felt particularly passionate about education, especially as a member of the African-American community. The education system here in America was failing so many students of African descent, especially, the young men. Tamiko felt that she just had to do something, and thought about a career in social work. Then while she was waiting to be seen by her advisor, it was like she could hear His voice speaking directly to her. She chose education, and things had been smooth sailing ever since. Tamiko got extra motivation out of nowhere, and breezed through her classes. Her supervising teacher glowed about her student teaching skills and she got an A in the practicum. Right out of college, she landed a job with this school that every new teacher wanted to get into, and she got accepted to the prestigious Bank Street College of Education to earn her masters degree. It seemed like God was blessing her all around, so she had to be on the right track. Best of all, Tamiko loved teaching, and she knew that in this profession she would be able to have a direct impact on the educational outcomes of the children she wanted to reach. Although it is the most tired cliché in the profession, Tamiko really did want to make a difference in children's lives the way her teachers had done for her. After all, she would not have been a college graduate or a graduate school student if she had not had teachers that cared. Tamiko knew she could be a catalyst of change in her students' lives. This was her calling. God meant for it to be. She saw herself eventually rising through the ranks from teacher, to lead teacher, to coach, to assistant principal, then principal, then an upper level administrator capable of making great changes in the ways children, particularly inner city children, were being educated.

In the course of her musings about her career, she thought about Allen. He did not get the job with Hartland Consultants, or the job with the Concord Group. In fact, it had been nearly three months and he hadn't gotten any of the jobs he had applied for so far. It all made her feel a little guilty about her own success at the moment. But perhaps Allen was not in his true calling as she was. If he was, then he wouldn't be having such a hard time right now, would he? Everything would have worked itself out like the way things worked out for her. She knew what she would do. She would pray to God for Allen; that He would help Allen find his true calling. Tamiko wanted to suggest to Allen that he pray about it, but she knew he was still more of a "religious" person rather than a Christian. He believed in God, just not in the power of God. Tamiko didn't want to put pressure on him. Sometimes when she talked about her faith, Allen and the others would stare at her as if she needed to be in a straight jacket. Allen would say that she was being childish, Jim would talk about how Christianity was a white man's religion used to subdue slaves, Tim would start waxing philosophical, Callie would start talking about how all gods lead to the same path, and Richard wouldn't say anything. Overall, she decided she needed to be patient with her friends. Tamiko realized that a lot of young people have a hard time making the spiritual connection to God, because they tend to be too wrapped up in the magnificence of their own person, and their quest for independence. She knew because she had been there herself. No, she would simply wait. Her life would speak on behalf of God. She would be like Abraham. One day she would be so successful, her friends would ask her how it all happened. Then she would tell them, and then they would believe and be converted.

SIX

This was it. It had been four months and twenty-five interviews since his encounter with Aldrige. Allen had been close to a nervous breakdown after so many terrible interview experiences. To make matters worse, the industry in which he had been seeking work had more than collapsed. The subprime mortgage mess was turning into a full-scale disaster of gargantuan proportions. Lehman Brothers, Bear Stearns, Washington Mutual, Fannie Mae and Freddie Mac were the first casualties. Then there were rumors of little banks beginning to fail like Sun Trust out in California. There were bank runs almost reminiscent of the early days of the Great Depression. The financial losses seemed astronomical. Then the DOW fell hundreds of points, on not one, not two, but three days in a row. Despite this, the lame duck president assured the public that there was no real problem with the economy. The recent fall in the DOW Jones industrials was merely a correction. People should take the opportunity to buys stocks at the new lows before the prices went up again. According to certain economists, it was still a bull market. And indeed it was all *bull*. Layoffs of thousands were imminent. There were a few businesses that were still hiring, but for those few jobs the competition was fierce. Allen knew that in this environment, his lack of experience might now be a good thing as those firms that were hiring might be looking to save money with younger less experienced workers. But this alone would not give him much of an advantage. The whole economic crisis made Allen's situation more desperate. He had to make the most of his interviews and land a job while he still could.

COMMENCEMENT

Allen racked his brain to figure out what he was doing wrong. He went to interview workshops, and even paid money for a coach. A couple of days ago, he went on an interview for the position of associate analyst at Towne and Farber with the hope that all the time and money he had spent to sharpen his interview skills would pay off. The interview began like all the others he'd had previously. When he walked into the conference room for the interview, he noticed an uneasiness wash over the people who were interviewing him. Allen managed to sail through the interview, but the whole time he felt as if he were being interrogated. There were some on the hiring panel that were even openly hostile. Allen thought the interview would be a bust like all the others. Then he got a call from one of the panel's members, Mr. Wong, about coming in to discuss an offer. It was as if someone had thrown him a life preserver in the midst of perilous waters.

Allen was now sitting in the same conference room in which he had his initial interview. As Allen waited for Mr. Wong, he contemplated all of the things he had gone through up to this point. He couldn't believe how close he had come to entertaining the idea that maybe he would never find a suitable job. How silly he had been. After all, there was no way someone with his education and skills could be out of work for very long, even with everything that was going on with the economy. In the midst of Allen's meditation, Mr. Wong appeared with some documents in his hands.

"Good Afternoon, Allen. Sorry to keep you waiting."

"Good Afternoon, Mr. Wong. It's no problem, really."

"I know you're probably anxious to get this settled, so I'll get right to it", Wong explained. "As you know, we would like to offer you a position with our firm."

Those were the words that Allen had been waiting to hear for months. He was so happy, he almost felt as if he would cry, and he struggled to maintain his self-possession. Allen knew that in the business world he had to keep his "game face" on.

"Thank You", Allen managed to say. "It's an honor to be an analyst of such a wonderful firm...."

"Actually-, I don't know how to put this, but-I know you were interviewed for the analyst position, but after reviewing your qualifications, we thought we might be able to use your talents in another capacity. The pay is a little less, but we feel that given your incredible management skills it may be a better fit for you. Are you still interested?"

"What is the position?" Allen inquired, trying to keep the suspicion out of his voice.

"You see our firm owns several commercial properties including this one, and we have in-house facility maintenance. You would be working out in our building management office as our Facility Maintenance Director for this property. You would be the leader of a team, and would be managing several of our building maintenance workers, and trouble shooting various problems that occur. You would even manage a lot of the activities in the building. It's a very challenging position, but we think you would be great. You'd be making roughly 40,000.00 a year."

"So basically, I'd be the head custodian of the building."

"Some people would refer to it as that, but at this firm, you would have a lot more responsibility than what such a title implies."

Allen swallowed hard. It seemed as if Mr. Wong just hit him in the face with a brick. Allen had been desperate for work, but not this desperate.

"I'm sorry, Mr. Wong, but I don't think I can accept the position."

SEVEN

"Wow, nice ride, is this new?" asked the second-shift parking attendant at Herns and Marshall's onsite parking facility as he admired Tim's car.

"Yep. So you got to be careful with her", smiled Tim as he handed him the keys.

"No doubt, man. What happened? You got a raise or somethin'?"

"Nah. Just thought I'd treat myself."

"I wish I had it like that."

"Maybe one day, dude", said Tim walking away towards the elevator.

Tim loved the way his new car was able to make people's jaw's drop. He had just brought the Mercedes home from the lot yesterday, and it seemed to bring him a lot of attention and respect. Tim liked seeing the admiration and envy on the young parking attendant's face. It made everything he went through at Herns and Marshall worth it.

And he went through a lot at Herns and Marshall as their President of Business Services. As Tim got in the empty elevator and pushed the button to the 30th floor, he reflected on his tenure with the firm. When he was first hired, he thought the position was as impressive as it sounded. "President of the Business Services Department" seemed to be at title of high renown and significance. Tim thought it meant meeting with major businesses and overseeing their investment portfolios, however, it turned out his duties would not be so challenging.

Most of the time, he was filling in supply request for various departments, and making sure that the company stayed within budget for those request. Not much different from an office manager. Tim was one of the lowest ranked people in his whole division. The only people he was superior to were the admin, the receptionist, and the other business managers in the other departments, who incidentally were also people of color. The day-to-day realities of the job were enough to knock the wind out of Tim's sails for a time. He was often ignored and/or left out of meetings and socials or served as a scapegoat for some crisis or controversy at the moment. Sometimes he went for weeks without important memos and notices, which sometimes left him underprepared for staff meetings and monthly reports. None of his superiors seemed to warm to him, or take him under their wing like the other associates on his floor, and he didn't have a lot of close allies. But even in the face of this, he decided to stay. After all, his salary was excellent, and the possibility of moving up through the ranks to a more responsible position may make itself apparent, eventually. Not to mention, he got a kick out of being able to tell people where he worked. The name Herns and Marshall lent him a certain prestige that opened many doors for him when he went to restaurants and parties. And at least he had his own office, so when all of the craziness was just too much, he could just shut himself inside and everything else out. This made all the missed memos, slights, and aggravation worthwhile. And sometimes there were small victories like the one he had just celebrated.

Tim had just had lunch with the executive director of sales for a major supplier, Brill Corporation, and had miraculously wrangled a deal that would allow the firm to get 30% off of all paper products. This would allow the company to reduce overhead cost by as much as 7%. This was a really big victory for Tim, especially since they just had a meeting about the ways they could cut the firms expenditures. He couldn't wait to get the e-mail from the vendor and finalize everything. Tim hoped the Brill deal would prove to his bosses that he was truly a valuable player with a brain in his head. When he came to his floor, he noticed that Frank and Jason, who worked in the brokerage trading department on the other side of the floor, were loitering about, talking in hushed tones, but the conversation ceased as Tim moved closer to them.

COMMENCEMENT

This piqued his curiosity, so he decided to try to glean the import of their gesture by engaging them in some friendly small talk.

"Hey, Frank. Hey, Jay", greeted Tim.

"Hey, Tim. How was lunch?" replied Jay forcing a smile.

"It was okay. I tried the sushi place everybody's been raving about. The tempura is amazing."

"I know. They're awesome, right. And it's great if you're on a budget."

"Anything happen while I was out?" asked Tim innocently, hoping one of them would bite. Tim always felt that he was the last to know about things in the company. Sometimes he would try to tap his other co-workers for information in order to keep up with things.

"Not much, really", answered Jay.

"I've heard that before", Tim thought to himself.

"Yeah. Kinda dead here today. We're not getting a lot of calls from upstairs, and no e-mails", replied Frank.

"I guess no news is good news. I'd better get back to my desk, check my messages. I'll see you guys around."

This exchange did nothing to alleviate Tim's feelings of apprehension. He knew there was something going on. As Tim walked down the corridor to his office, he thought he heard a familiar voice coming from its direction. As he came closer, Tim noticed the president of his division, Jacob Standoff. Standoff was also the CFO, and one of the four "big cheeses" that could make or break Tim's career. Standoff, noticing Tim, called him over.

"Oh, Tim. There you are. Just in time. I know this is sudden, but I'm having a meeting with your department in conference room C. There's some business we must discuss that requires immediate attention", said Mr. Standoff with an air of gravity to his voice.

Tim could feel the perspiration running down his back and leaking under his arms. Good thing he had kept his jacket on. "This couldn't be good", he thought to himself.

"Is there anything you want me to bring? Like our monthly flow sheets?" asked Tim hoping to elicit more information from Standoff.

"No, just bring yourself. It shouldn't take long. Don't worry about Vera and Clara, they're already there waiting for us", answered Standoff as he vanished away.

Tim felt a bit relieved. It couldn't be that serious if he didn't have to bring anything. Yet he was still a little unsettled at the fact that he was, yet again, the last one to know. Once again his co-workers, who obviously were in the know on this, gave him no warning. "Thanks a lot Frank, Jay", Tim thought bitterly to himself. It made him wonder why people treated him this way. He did everything he could to be a team player. He greeted people often, engaged in polite small talk, but for some reason he didn't seem to fit in. He knew Jim would say it was because he was black. Half black anyway. But sometimes Tim felt the same way around some African-Americans, albeit to a lesser degree. Tim then walked out of his office and down the narrow hall to the elevator. As Tim waited, he wondered what this meeting could be about. In any case, maybe he could use this opportunity to talk about the big deal he just scored for the company.

Upon his arrival to conference room C, Tim saw the familiar faces of his subordinates, the Admin, Clara Mendez, the only Latina in the company, and the receptionist, Vera Watts, a middle-aged African-American woman. The other three business services officers of the other departments were missing. Mr. Standoff and one of the sycophant cronies from the human resources department, Brian Manx, were talking with another gentleman who he did not recognize. He was a deep mahogany-colored African-American man, who seemed to be about average sized. He was clean-shaven and he wore expensive looking round wire-framed glasses. His clothes weren't shabby either. Tim immediately recognized the fine tailoring of his Sea Island cotton twill suit and jeweled cuff links. One thing in particular that caught his attention was the annoying way the guy bobbed his head up and down and smiled at everything Standoff said. It gave the man an air of utter obsequiousness, a quality that Tim despised, despite the fact that he himself possessed a similar disposition on occasion.

COMMENCEMENT

"Afternoon, everyone", said Tim quickly taking his seat.

"Good afternoon", replied the ladies.

"Oh, good. Now we can get started", added Standoff hastily.

"What about the other business services officers?" asked Tim a bit hesitantly.

"That's what we're here to talk about. I know this is a bit abrupt, and you all have a lot of work to do so I'll make it brief. In the next few months we are going to be doing a bit of downsizing..."

"Oh my gosh! So that's what happened!" thought Tim, trying to cover his shock.

"You know that we have four business services heads here for each of our four divisions, but we've decided to merge all of the management positions into one so that interfacing with accounting and human resources will run much more smoothly. Tim will remain with us as our business services man and we will have an additional assistant with him or a vice president that will help him manage and organize tasks."

Tim breathed out a sigh of relief. "Maybe they do respect my work after all, if I'm the last man standing" he mulled cheerfully to himself.

"Everyone I want you to meet Preston Scott", continued Standoff "He's going to be your new vice president so to speak. He's got a lot of experience and drive. We managed to steal him from Wells Farber." At this Standoff laughed to himself a bit. Everyone else smiled or chuckled kindly, patronizing his attempt at humor.

"But enough of me, I'll let him do some talking, too. Preston why don't you tell them a little about yourself."

"Thank you, Mr. Standoff. Well, as Mr. Standoff said, my name is Preston Scott. I graduated from Yale, and in a few years I plan to enroll in the Columbia University business school, to work on my MBA. For the past two years, I was with Wells Farber as the head of customer service, which gave me a lot of experience in business services. Now, I look forward to working with you all to improve business services here at H & M."

"Using acronyms already and he hasn't even started working here yet. Obviously arrogant. And the nerve of him to think his trifling experience as a customer service rep is going to prepare him for the duties he'll have here. This guy is way out of his league", Tim scoffed inside himself. Tim just knew Preston would be a groveling butt kisser. Not to mention competition. And how could Standoff just make this guy his assistant and not even consult him during the hiring process? Allen's experience was way more credible than this guy's. If Tim had known, he could have gotten Allen an interview and they could have worked together, just like they did at Harvard. But then, on second thought, he knew that Allen looked up to him. Allen admired Tim for the fact that he had "made it". If Allen worked at Hearns & Marshall, he would see just how marginal his job was, and well….well he didn't have to worry about that now. Still, he felt insulted, and it made Tim boil on the inside, but he dare not show it.

"Thank You, Preston. Now if you all would briefly introduce yourselves, so he can get to know the other members of the team. Tim, we'll begin with you", said Standoff.

"Okay, I'm Tim Russell. I have a BA from Harvard and an MBA from Columbia and I've been with Herns and Marshall for two years as the president of business services for the Investment Securities division. I look forward to working with our new team player and sharing my expertise."

That's right, brief and to the point. As the others introduced themselves, Tim was thinking about how to position himself against this new enemy. Then part of him chastised himself for feeling this way. After all, wasn't Preston a "brother"? At that moment, he thought about his friend Allen. Allen always talked about how African-Americans should always try to help each other out in the workplace and have each other's backs. Deep down, he knew Allen was right and he began to feel guilty about his negative feelings toward this brother. The guy seemed just as optimistic and as naïve as he had been when he had first started. But then, looking at this Preston again across the boardroom table, his self-confident attitude, his smugness, Tim could not help but to see him as some cut-throat Uncle Tom. After much deliberation, Tim decided that he should protect himself rather than good old Preston. Only the voice of Standoff taking the lead again in the meeting would bring Tim's mind back from his silent musings.

"Preston will be starting next week. I'm assigning him to your office Tim, so you may have to move things around a bit in order to accommodate the new furniture I had Vera, order."

"There's no way in Hades, he's getting into my office. I'll just talk to Standoff later about getting Preston a cubicle adjacent to Clara's", Tim thought.

"In the first few days, I expect you all will help Preston get acquainted with the responsibilities of the department. And then Tim can let him get his hands dirty with orders and tracking. Oh and Tim, I expect to see your time table and preliminary plan for the reorganization on my desk by the end of the month."

"Of course, sir. In fact, just today I met with one of the managers of the Brill Corporation…"

"Just put it in the report, Tim. And if there's no questions, I'm off to another meeting, and this one stands adjourned."

"If I may sir, I wouldn't mind showing our new associate around right now, if he's got some time", offered Tim disingenuously with an ulterior motive.

"That won't be necessary. Mr. Standoff and I have already familiarized him with the physical grounds, and he has an appointment this afternoon to fill out his paperwork. At that time we will acquaint him with our bylaws and policies", one of the human resources guys interrupted, taking on an imperial tone. The human resource guys were the worst. For the most part, they thought they were gods because they were so involved with the hiring, firing, and salary decisions.

"Then, I'll see you in a week, Mr. Scott."

"Yes, see you then", replied the ladies.

"I'm looking forward to it", said Preston confidently.

They all rose and left the conference room, with Standoff, Scott and the sycophant ahead, the rest of them hanging at the back. As the others were heading back to their office, Tim bent forward a little, taken off guard suddenly by a sudden wave of nausea.

"Tim, are you okay?" asked Clara in concern.

"I just need some air that's all."

Or maybe it was his gut warning him about Preston Scott.

EIGHT

"Allen, wake up. Allen. Allen!!"

It took a few seconds before Allen could get a clear picture of the face before him. It was his mother, Lena. This would have comforted him, had the expression on her face been a little friendlier.

"Allen, have you been up here all day?" asked Lena sounding like a mother who was about to give her son a scolding. Allen just rubbed at the pieces of crud that had accumulated in his eyes while he was sleeping. He wished he could have stayed asleep. In his dreams he was the Man in the Corner Office. Now he had to wake up to the real nightmare.

"What time is it?" he asked groggily.

"It's dinner time already, and you're still in your pajamas! Now this is just a crying shame. Get up from that bed and stop feelin' sorry for yourself! And while you're at it, you can come downstairs and get your dinner."

Allen didn't move. He just lay there rubbing his hand over his eyes, hoping his mother would just walk away, but she didn't. Not satisfied with Allen's response, Lena then grabbed Allen's arm and tried pulling him up, which caught him off guard.

"Alright, I'm getting up!" groaned Allen as he began to rouse himself.

"And make sure you wash your face before you come to the table. Don't nobody want to eat, lookin' at you with all that crust all over your

57

face", Lena fussed. And with that, Lena turned on her heel and marched out of the door and down the stairs.

Allen sat on the side of his bed for a few moments, thinking about whether or not he should change his clothes. "It wouldn't do any good now. In a few hours, it would be time to go back to bed anyway", he told himself. He tried to concentrate on the moment, and not the other things that were filling his head right now. Like about how the recent dialogue between him and his mother made him feel like a little boy. Here he was, a Harvard Graduate, and instead of being out and about on a new job, conquering new territory, and learning new skills, he was in the same spot that he had been in before he left for college. The worst part was, Allen didn't quite understand why.

He got up, grabbed some things from a dresser and started towards the bathroom, where he washed his face and put on a clean t-shirt. Then he reluctantly headed down to the dining room of his parents two-story brownstone. When Allen got to the entrance, he could see his father, Vernon, already sitting at the head of the table with his paper. Upon hearing Allen's footsteps, Vernon looked up momentarily and cleared his throat, before returning his attention to his newspaper. Then Lena came out with three plates of food and set them on the table. Allen hoped the silence would continue long enough for him to finish his meal, but not long after they said the grace, his father started in on him again.

"So, you come in here and can't say good evening to nobody?" Vernon grunted.

"Good evening, mom. Good evening, Dad", said Allen straining to be polite "There. Are we straight now?" he added with a bit of attitude.

"I know you're not tryin' to cop an attitude with me!" retorted Vernon ready to rumble.

"Vernon, please. Leave the chile alone! Can't you see he's upset?" pleaded Lena.

"*He's* upset! If he is, it's his own fault. He don't have no right to take it out on us", Vernon grumbled.

COMMENCEMENT

"See! I knew you would bring it up again. That's why I didn't want to say anything", sighed Allen, rubbing his hand over his face in exasperation.

"Don't give me that. You want to come in here and give me and your momma an attitude, but we weren't the ones that turned down that $40,000.00 a year job. That was you! Now you want to mope and moan about the house like a spoiled brat, cause you can't get the job that you want!"

"Let's all calm down..." Lena tried to interject.

"They wanted me to be their head maintenance man! I didn't interview for that position and I certainly didn't go to school for that. Can't you see they were insulting me!" snapped Allen slamming his fork down on his plate.

"Oh, I see. You too good to do that kind of work right? Big Harvard man ain't supposed to do that kind of work right? Well, I been doin' that kind of work all my life to keep a roof over your head, food in your mouth, and clothes on your back. When I started workin' for the city, I couldn't think about what type of job I wanted. I knew I had to work to take care of my wife and my child. I did what I had to do."

"Why are you taking this so personally?! I'm not saying..."

"Vernon, Allen, enough!" Lena scolded. "Vernon, Allen is a grown man. He made a decision, and we have to respect the reason behind it. I'm sure he wasn't trying to insult you. And even you have to admit, that we did not pay as much money as we have for that degree, just so Allen could babysit buildings."

"I know that, Lena," said Vernon taking a much calmer tone, "but it takes time to get where he wants to go. They're not going to take some wet behind the ears know-it-all kid and make him president of the company. He gotta start somewhere. And a job's a job. I mean look at what's going on out there! Bigger and badder corporate fellas being laid off. This ain't no time for pickin' and choosin'!"

"He knows that, Vernon" said Lena turning to her son, "Right, Allen?"

"I have the know how to do the jobs I'm applying for. I have the experience. I did a lot of solid work on those internships."

"Allen, I think you have to be more flexible, too", suggested Lena.

Allen let go of a big sigh.

"Now just listen. I'm not saying to leave the financial field, but you can open up your options a little more. Maybe the job that you want is not what God wants for you. There might be other jobs in the financial sector that may be even better for you. Do you have to work at one of these big firms? Why not a small one? What about working at a bank? There's lots of different things you can do, baby."

"I understand what you're saying, mom, but I've known what I've wanted to do ever since high school."

"I know, but sometimes God makes two paths that lead you to the same destination."

"But what if I take another path and I wind up some place where I don't want to be?"

"That's a possibility. And there's also the possibility that God could lead you to a place that' s better than you could ever have imagined for yourself. But you have to keep praying and keep trying. Sitting at home lying in bed all day isn't going to help."

"I know, but it seems like every time I go for an interview people act like...I don't know how to explain it, but I feel like I'm offending people and I don't know what I'm doing that's causing it."

"Don't so much worry about people. God has ways of using people in spite of themselves. It's like your grandmother used to say: you just do your best and let God do the rest."

"I guess", said Allen sadly.

"Who knows, this may be a blessing in disguise. You may even want to take some of this free time you have and start working on your MBA. You never know."

"Lena, we ain't even finished payin' for the first degree, which hasn't helped so far as I can see, and you want him to go back and get another.

Hmph, if he goes back to school, he's going to be paying out of his own pocket."

"Vernon, God is letting this happen for a reason. Allen, you need to pray about it, and ask God to reveal what your next step should be."

Allen tried to focus on eating his dinner to no avail. He merely ended up pushing his food about his plate. Later that night when he went to bed, he was still thinking about those interviews. While Allen appreciated his mom's advice, he didn't really think prayer was going to get the job done. He just couldn't understand what he was doing wrong. If he could just put his finger on it and fix it. Sure he was high strung, but as he matured, he had been able to tone some of this down. He'd been working with Tim for weeks to polish his interviewing skills, and even went to an interview workshop, where he was given some extremely positive feedback. And then he thought about the Towne and Farber debacle. How could they offer him a facilities management job? Sure he was a relative rookie to the financial consulting field, but so were a lot of other new graduates who had gotten jobs. Tim had told him about one of their white classmates, Troy Lackman, who had gotten a job at Fisher-Pinkerton Advisors without having any experience at all. Not to mention he was the class alcoholic during his whole tenure at Harvard. If anyone should have been offered a facilities management position, it should have been him! Then Allen thought about his connections. Maybe his references were really dogging him out behind his back. Then he thought back to what Jim said the night of his graduation celebration. But it couldn't be that. This was 2008. This new generation of white people had grown up seeing African-Americans operating competently in different fields. Or had they? They had gone to school with and lived near African-Americans for most of their lives. Or had they? They understood the dangers of allowing racism to divide society. Or did they? No. This was the era of the rainbow, the advent of the post-racial society. After all, weren't there white people who liked rap music, and dressed hip-hop? Or was it that simple?

NINE

It was Saturday night. Allen was going to spend it alone sitting in front of the T.V. He had a big bag of Nacho cheese tortilla chips and a liter of soda that he sat on each side of him like two close friends. He was getting ready to fire up the DVD player and watch 'Training Day' for the 5th time when he heard a knock at the door.

"Who is it?" he blared in a semi-threatening voice.

"Who you think it is, son?" replied an all too familiar voice.

Allen walked over to the door and looked out the peephole to see 4 very distorted, but familiar faces. It was Tim, Jim, Richard and Callie and they looked like they were dressed for a night out. Allen opened the door and before he could offer a greeting, they barreled past him like cars on a freight train.

"Alright, grandpa, get out of that ol' funky robe and put on your best gear cause you goin' out", Richard ordered.

"Sorry guys, you're gonna have to give me a rain check. I'm not exactly in the best mood for going out."

"Brrrrt. Wrong answer", insisted Richard.

"C'mon," pleaded Callie "your mom told us all about what's been going on. Al, you can't just sit about the house and mope. Come with us, relax, and take your mind off it for a while. Or if you want, maybe we can bounce around some ideas to help you out."

"Yeah, maybe we could work on some job search strategies", suggested Tim.

COMMENCEMENT

"Thanks for trying to help, but at this point I'm beyond help. It's just so frustrating. I just want to know what I'm doing wrong", sighed Allen pounding a pillow on the couch with his fist.

"Maybe you're not doing anything wrong", suggested Jim somberly.

"So why doesn't someone hire me then?!" Allen found himself half shouting.

"Allen, look there are many different variables that are involved in the hiring process. You have a lot of strengths like your education, and background knowledge, but you have some very real weaknesses like your lack of experience, and dearth of connections. And then there are other variables that have nothing to do with you, like the economy and the demand for...."

"Well, I just graduated from college. How am I supposed to get this experience if they don't give me a chance?!" moaned Allen cutting Tim off.

"C'mon, Tim. Don't even go there", said Jim trying to control his anger. "This doesn't have anything to do with Allen or the economy. Can we please stop dancing around the 5000 pound elephant in the room?! Allen's not getting the jobs because he's black. Period. I know. I've been there."

"So we've heard for the millionth time", sighed Tim, rolling his eyes.

"Don't be facetious, Tim. Even you have to admit what's going on here. Think about the things that have been happening to him on those interviews. Like when that lady at the Concord Group looked at your resume and then walked up to that white guy. Why do you think she made that mistake? In their world the only degree a black man can have is on a thermometer. And if you had a name like Rasheem or Malik, they wouldn't have even looked at your resume", explained Jim.

"Yeah, and that other company, that tried to scam you with that n**ger job", Richard spat out.

"Richard, do you have to use that word?!" chided Callie.

"What would you call it if you went for a good job and they told you all you was good for was managing the trash guys?"

"Guys, I don't think playing the race card is going to help my situation."

"And what about those companies? They're playing it and at your expense", continued Jim.

"Oh, come on, that's enough. Allen and I know plenty of guys who are black with the same creds that have very good jobs. In fact, I'm one of them!" shot Tim.

"No offense, Tim, but with all due respect, your situation is a little different, and you know what I'm talkin' about", Jim shot back. Tim colored a little at his remark.

"O.K., so maybe I'm a little better connected than he is due to circumstances beyond anyone's control. So let's talk about another situation", Tim said defiantly. "In fact, we just hired someone to be my assistant, who happens to be a black guy, who recently graduated from Yale."

"Wait a minute! You mean they was hirin' where you at, and you ain't even put in a word for this brother, knowing his situation?!" retorted Richard, angrily.

"I didn't know they were hiring, it was a surprise to me!"

"Ain't you supposed to be a president or somethin'? How you not gonna know somethin' like that?!" asked Richard incredulously.

"It was an upper management decision!"

"So? Ain't *you* supposed to be 'top brass'? Can't you get them to change they minds? The way you be sashaying and displayin' I would'a thought you had some real juice. Don't tell me you just they pet Negro?"

"You know I'm starting to lose my patience…"

"No, you just lost face, my brother."

"Can we stay focused, please? We came here to help Allen get some perspective, not to fight with each other" Callie reminded them as she placed herself between Richard and Tim who looked as if they were ready to have it out.

64

COMMENCEMENT

"Everyone, please. I've never made excuses for myself. I don't intend to now."

"No one's trying to make excuses for you Allen. But racism is real, and yes, it still exists. When the Civil Rights Acts of 1964 and 1965 were signed, all of the racists in this country did not just spontaneously drop dead. When you were at Harvard, you didn't have a lot of white people banging down your door to be your friend. C'mon Callie, back me up, do any of the white nurses ever invite you to lunch? I didn't think so. Tim never gets invited to after work socials, and I just recently got a ticket for waiting for Miko outside of her building. Do you think these things happen for no reason?" explained Jim.

"You don't have to explain it to me, Jim. I'm very well aware that racism still exists. However, when I interviewed no one called me the N-word, and, for the most part, no one said anything to indicate that they were prejudiced..." Allen stopped as Aldridge's comment popped into his head. '...people like you.'

"They didn't have to. It's not just words. It's actions. Actions, Allen!"

"I could understand if I came in there like some type of walking stereotype. I'm not some thug with his pants hanging down to his knees going "whas-sup!"

"Exactly! Allen's different!" remarked Callie.

"Yeah, he's what they call a 'good n**ger'. However in this world even a 'good n**ger' is still a 'n**ger'. They're not going to let anyone who is black have any type of job with real responsibility or power, especially if they think you're going to use it to our advantage", scowled Jim.

"Even if what you guys are saying is true, what am I supposed to do? Call Al Sharpton? Call for a boycott? Bleach myself?" asked Allen despondently.

"Look, why don't you just let me hook you up with something in transit, so you can get a little cheddar to tide you over in the mean time?

Look at me, I'm just doin' transit till I save enough money to pay for law school."

"Thanks, Jim, but I really need a job that's at least somewhat relevant to my field, or I'll get stuck there", reasoned Allen. Jim appeared crestfallen after this comment. "Not that it would happen to you", Allen added quickly.

"Or you could look into some black owned or operated firms. See if they're hiring", suggested Callie.

"Oh, please. I've already done my research on that. As it stands there are only three black owned consulting firms. One is under investigation by the SEC for fraud, the second has recently filed for bankruptcy, and the last one is listed as Richard's."

"Which leads to my next suggestion. You could start your own joint, which is what you shoulda done in the first place. If you want, I could be your partner 'til you learn the ropes. I could get you the money to get started and everything."

"Oh, really? And just what type of business could you possibly help him to establish? Selling African-American urban lit on a table in front of the mall?" asked Tim skeptically.

"Who you getting uppity with?! I stay paid! You need to keep quiet 'cause you obviously ain't got no juice! You couldn't even hook him up with that assistant job, 'Mr. President'", sneered Richard.

"It's not that simple in corporate America! It's not like I work at some local chicken shack and I can go to my bosses and say 'Yo, hook this brother up!'"

"From the way you always be prancin' around here talkin' all that game and stuff, somebody might think that you were Bloomberg himself!"

"Now wait a minute…"

"Why is it that whenever we get together you two have to start arguing? It's getting to be annoying", said Allen holding his hands to his head in exasperation.

COMMENCEMENT

"My thoughts exactly. In fact, you know what? Could you two agree to not speak to each other for the rest of the evening, please, for all our sakes."

At Callie's rebuke both men went to opposite corners of the room and sat down, mumbling under their breaths like two children who had been put on 'time out'.

"Now, Allen, What about your connections? If they can give you a reference, why not a job?"

"I tried that already. They're not hiring at the moment."

"You mean their quota for blacks is full at the moment", Jim added.

"It's just not fair. All my life I've done the right thing. I went to school. I went to church every Sunday. Never done drugs or been anywhere near a gang. I did the college thing. I treat people with respect and try to give back to my community. What do I have to show for all of it?"

"Al, you're right. You've been working the tried and true path all of your life. Everything by the book. But that book wasn't necessarily written with black folks in mind. Now you have to figure out a new way to get things done. And as for what you have to show for it all, you've got 5 friends who are willing to stick by you in all this", said Callie attempting to reassure her friend.

"Yeah, now it's still not too late, to go out and get dinner, so go upstairs, get dressed and let's roll", said Jim.

"And where are we going?"

"To that new fish joint down on 137th street. I heard the scrimps is bangin'", Richard gushed.

"That's shrimps", said Tim correcting him.

"Look here, Harvard, you don't need to be correctin' my English all the time. You need to chill wit' dat. Actin' like you a dictionary or somethin'"

"I thought I told you two not to speak to one another. Don't let me have to tell you again", Callie reprimanded sounding a lot like a momma. So much so that the two men gave heed to her words almost immediately.

"See now, I was gonna go, but I'm afraid that if I leave these two down here too long, they will have killed each other by the time I get dressed."

"Just go on. Don't worry about these two. I got them", charmed Callie as she nudged Allen toward the staircase to encourage his new mood that was just coming on.

TEN

Manna's Soul Seafood was packed almost to capacity when they arrived. The din of the crowd and the provincial atmosphere took Allen off guard a little bit after being virtually sequestered from the real world for weeks. There were people who were standing near the entrance waiting for a table. Richard led them past the crowd that glared jealously as they headed toward the booth where Tamiko was guarding their seats.

"Hey, it's about time you guys got here. That uptight bougie maitre d was about to have me tossed out of here. What took so long?"

"We had to convince our man here to come", explained Richard.

"Still depressed?" asked Tamiko, her voice full of concern.

"And how would you feel if your future was crumbling before your very eyes?"

"Don't say that, Allen. This is just a temporary set back", offered Callie.

"Yeah, you just need to re-evaluate your options, set some timetables and goals and you should be good to go in no time. Tell ya what. We'll be like your war council for tonight. We'll hit some ideas around and see what comes up", suggested Tim.

"After all, five heads are better than one", said Callie.

"Amen to that", added Tamiko.

"But first things first. Let's get our grub on. I don't know about anybody else here, but I can't get my mind to workin' unless I've had me somethin' to eat", said Jim.

Richard got the attention of the waitress, who took their orders. Allen, Tim, and Tamiko tried the shrimp cocktail, while Jim, Richard and Callie had the fried seafood platter. They also ordered a pitcher of iced tea to wash everything down. As they ate, they began to help Allen get a better picture of his options.

"So let's look at the facts" Tim began as if he were advising a client for financial services. "You have been looking for a job for only three or four months and you have not been offered a position in the field of your choice. Your options from here are to (a) continue to look for work in that field, (b) look for work in another field... anyone else with any suggestions?" he said opening up the conversation to the others.

"He could (c) go back to school, like his mom suggested", added Callie.

"Or (d) he could be his own man and go into business for himself", Richard put in defiantly.

"So by process of elimination, which seems best to you?"

"Well, (d) is out of the question because I don't have the capital to invest in my own business, or at least the type of business that I see myself entering, not to mention this isn't the greatest economic climate for opening a business."

"But it's mad easy, yo", pleaded Richard, "You don't even have to use your own money when you start out..."

"Yeah, but look at what's happening out there, Rich. Guys are losing their shirts. And I don't think many banks will be very magnanimous with their loans now. Timing is everything when it comes to starting your own business."

"But look at that dude that made all that money during the Great Depression from a board game. Even that place Tavern on the Green opened during the Depression. It don't matter what time it is, as long as you got something people want, and you know how to hustle it, that's what counts", reasoned Richard.

"Let's respect his decision for the time being", continued Tim "Now what else were you going to say, Al."

"Going back to school is out for the same reason. Too much money. And you know how it is with grad school. I'd have to go to a school with a reputation that is either equal to or better than Harvard for the degree to mean something. If I stay local that means Columbia or at the least NYU Business school, both very pricey. And there's the matter that I haven't even begun to pay off the loans for undergrad."

"I don't know, Al. Going back to school could make you more marketable with employers. They may be more willing to hire you with another credential. It helped me", offered Tim.

"And you know in the job market of today, employers are looking for people with more education, not less. As a teacher, if I don't get my master's degree in a certain amount of time I'll lose my job", said Tamiko.

"And with any luck, by the time you graduate, we'll have a new president and maybe the country's economic situation will be turning around. And you won't have any embarrassing gaps of time on your resume", offered Tim.

"But you both have jobs to help you pay for school. Al doesn't. I can relate to what he's saying. Sometimes the cost of school is so high, you end up taking out a whole lot of loans. Then the job you get doesn't even make up for what you spent to get it in the first place. And what if the economic situation doesn't turn around? He'll be in a bigger mess than when he started", countered Jim.

"Exactly, and I don't intend to have my parents spending their retirement money on my education, either. Besides, I want to make it on my own."

"If money is the problem, and you don't want to take out a loan, why can't you just apply for some scholarships or some grants? I thought you got those in undergrad", suggested Callie.

"Grants and scholarships paid for about a fraction of my tuition, but my parents made too much money to get any of the need based aid. Anyway, once you leave undergrad, most of the funding for school dries up. Trust me I've researched it."

"While we're talking about it, when are *you* going back to school Jim?" asked Callie turning the question to Jim.

"What?" asked Jim who was thrown off-guard by Callie's question.

"Don't act like you don't know what I'm talking about. You've always say that you only took that transit job to help pay for law school, and I know you took the LSAT last year. When are you going back?"

"My situation is very complicated. I don't live with my parents, and my job is not a short-sweet 8 to 3 like Miko's. I would need to have enough money to live off and go to school at the same time. There are still a few things that have to be worked out."

"But Brian's going back, isn't he? Weren't you two supposed to be going back together?"

Jim forgot that Callie knew Brian through his sister who worked at the hospital. Sometimes it just seemed that even New York City could be so small.

"Yeah, Jim. Why not you? After all, it's what you've always wanted, isn't it?" inquired Allen.

"Look, let's not get off track. We're not talking about me. We're talking about you. That's what tonight is all about. So you eliminated (d), and (c), so all that's left is (a) and (b)."

"Out of those two, my only option would be (a) to keep looking for a job in the financial field. I have always wanted to be a financial consultant. There's no point in looking at any other options."

"So now, if you are going to continue to look for jobs in that field, you're going to have to re-think how you've been looking for work. In the face of all the layoffs, it's really getting competitive. You've really got to start thinking about the people you know who can give some inside information. In the meantime, you may want to try some head-hunters or some employment agencies…." Tim added.

COMMENCEMENT

"If I might interrupt," said Tamiko "Allen, you said that you want to be a financial consultant. Maybe you should think about if that is what you were really meant to be."

"What are you talking about? It's what I went to school for. It's what I've been training for all of my life."

"Yes, but look at what's going on now. Maybe it's a sign."

"Yeah, a sign, that I need to think of a new way of going about things."

"Or maybe it's a sign that… that God doesn't want you in that field."

Laughter and groans abounded at the table after Tamiko's comment.

"What else can we expect from the preacher's daughter?" asked Jim sarcastically.

"I don't know, I could think of some things more typical of preacher's daughters", Tim suggested slyly.

"I don't see what's so funny! And Tim, you better watch that mouth of yours. This is God's chile, you're messin' with", scolded Tamiko.

"Guess I'd better watch out for lightning bolts, huh. Whatever."

"Yeah, whatever. Besides I wasn't talking to you, I was talking to Allen."

"Miko, look, I believe in God just like you do. But why would God not want me to be a financial consultant? It's what would make me happy. God wants his children to be happy, so why would he not want me to be a financial consultant?"

"Maybe you think that's what would make you happy. Sometimes when we go in a direction that's not good for us God will block our path to keep us from harm. Remember what happened to Balaak, when he was on the way to see Balaam to curse the children of Israel?"[1]

"C'mon, Miko. It's not like I want to sell drugs or pimp for a living. What harm could come to me as a financial consultant?"

73

"Maybe she thinks you'll be like the guy that crashed Barron's bank", joked Tim.

"Allen, I don't know why God wouldn't want you be a financial consultant. You'd have to ask Him that. Have you prayed about your situation? Asked Him for guidance?"

"Miko, my mother told me, when I was very little, that God knows what we need before we even ask him. Do you believe that?"

"Well, of course I do…"

"So why should I ask Him? If He's going to do it He'll do it. If He's not, He's not"

"Word, right? I hear that", agreed Richard.

"Because God wants us to. When we pray, it's like acknowledging His power and His control over our lives. And you never know. God can change His mind. Just think about how God spared King Hezekiah when he prayed."[2]

"Miko, those are stories; allegories", sighed Allen. "They're not meant to be taken literally…"

"The Bible is the Truth! These things happened! It's the Word of God!"

"I know you're not talking about a book that was written by white people for white people."

"Say what you want, but I'm not going to doubt the Word of God simply because you all don't believe. I have experienced his power, his mercy, and his goodness. I understand how God has been working in my life. If it wasn't for Him, I wouldn't have any of the things I have now."

"Uh-oh, I feel a testimony comin' on!" sang Richard.

"That's simply it, Tamiko. It's your experience, your personal decisions and beliefs. Everyone worships God in his or her own way. Some go to synagogue, some go to mosque, some call him Allah, some Buddah…" Callie decided to weigh in.

"That has nothing to do with what I'm talking about. Those are false gods…"

"To you! And I'm sorry, but I thought we all came here tonight to help Allen get some ideas about how he could deal with his job situation, not to be his spiritual advisors. You have no right to try to force your beliefs on him or anyone else here!"

"Hold on, Cal. She was only trying to help me. You don't have to jump down her throat like that."

"I wasn't jumping down her throat. I was setting her straight. Someone needed to."

"Excuse you?!" exclaimed Tamiko.

"No, excuse *you*! You may not be aware of it, but some of the things you were saying were quite offensive, not to mention ignorant. It's people like you that give Christians a bad name", snapped Callie.

"I for one can't believe that a college educated young woman like yourself, could so easily adhere to a religion that lead to the enslavement and degradation of your own people. Talk about stupid", said Jim scornfully.

"If believing in God makes me stupid, then I'm glad to be so. As the apostle Paul said: I am not ashamed of the Gospel of Jesus Christ", said Tamiko defiantly.[3]

"Alright, now stop it. No matter what she believes, neither of you have the right to insult her and hurt her feelings", said Tim out of nowhere.

"I didn't insult her! I just made a comment about what she said, and all anyone cares about is poor little Tamiko! What about all of the people she's insulting with those same beliefs?!" asked Callie angrily.

"She's still our friend!" insisted Tim.

"Speak for yourself!" Callie shot back.

"Now this is going too far. Let's just agree to end this conversation", said Allen.

"I've had enough! I'm going home", said Tamiko rising from the table. She was gathering her things and trying to wipe away tears at the same time.

"Miko, c'mon. Sit back down, let's all just cool down…"

"Actually, I think it's best that we all put some space between ourselves so we can cool down. Miko, I'll take you home. Is that O.K.?" offered Tim.

"Are you sure you want to be seen with someone like me?" asked Tamiko defensively.

"Let's just go, okay."

"Goodnight, everyone. See you tomorrow, Allen."

Everyone said a quick "good night" except Callie.

"God Bless you, Callie", said Tamiko before she left with Tim.

"Whoo-ee! This prayer thing done set if off in here! I ain't sayin' nothin'!" Richard called out suddenly.

"A wise man once said: If you want friends then you should never discuss politics, or religion", Allen mumbled to himself.

"Tell that to Tamiko the next time she tries to proselytize us", said Jim.

"Guys, let's just try to enjoy the rest of the evening?"

"So now you want to sit here and act like nothing happened?! Of all people, I thought you would've had my back!" Callie snapped again.

"Uh-oh, I guess it ain't over. Let me go back to silent mode", said Richard.

"How are you making this my fault? Tamiko was talking to me. If you hadn't said anything there wouldn't have been an argument", reasoned Allen.

"So I was supposed to let her go on like that?! You've gotta be kidding me! I'm outta here!" blasted Callie as she bolted away and out the door.

COMMENCEMENT

"Callie!" Allen called after her.

"Don't worry about it Al, I got her. I'll talk to her. See you guys later", said Jim.

"You know what Al? The next time we roll, we gotta leave the chicks out. They just too much drama", advised Richard.

"Not much of a dinner now, is it?"

"How 'bout we jet over to Horizon over on 9th and check out the hotties."

"I'm not quite in the mood, Rich."

"Aiight. If you change your mind, hit me on the cell. 'Cause this is dead."

"See ya 'round."

"I'll holla at you."

So much for a night out with friends.

ELEVEN

"Pass me not, oh, gen-tle Sa-a-a-vior. Hear my hum-ble cry-y-y-y...". Allen sat and listened passively as the choir sang out praises to God. Though the music was loud, Allen felt as if it were somehow lulling him to sleep. He had to struggle to keep his eyes open. "No more late Saturday nights with the guys," he reminded himself. Allen did feel a bit guilty about dozing off in church after his night at Manna's, especially after what happened with Miko and everything. Allen shifted in his seat and repositioned the Bible on his lap, hoping the movement would help to rouse him from his drowsy state. Next to him on his right, his mother sat singing loudly, banging her tambourine on her knee, keeping time with the rhythm of the music. On the other side was Miko. She was also singing and clapping her hands energetically. Allen was in total awe of her given the fact that there wasn't a trace of anger or anything after last night. Sitting on the other side of his mother was his father, who sat looking stoically, as if he was lost in his own thoughts. He was also singing softly under his breath, tapping his feet to the music and swaying to the beat. Everyone seemed to be moved, or inspired in some way by the music, each connecting to God in his or her own way. It all made Allen feel like the odd man out.

Once the song ended, the junior pastor stepped to the podium. "It is now time for our prayer, which will be led by Bishop Jerome Winston, and after that you will be fed the word by our own, pastor, Bishop Julius Bynum." At that moment, Bishop Winston stood up from his seat on the dais and approached the podium as the congregation applauded. He was a tall medium built man, with salt and pepper hair. To look at him, Allen was reminded of Moses. "Praise the Lord, everybody!" was Bishop Winston's greeting and at his word, the whole congregation stood up with one accord and saluted in turn, "Praise the Lord!" Everyone then bowed their head and closed their eyes as the prayer began.

"Heavenly Father, as we come before you this day to worship and praise your wonderful name, we ask that you...." This was all that Allen had heard before his mind started to wander off onto other things. Ironically, he was thinking about last night's argument that had started precisely because Tamiko had suggested he pray. Allen was skeptical of prayer as an effective solution to anything, mainly because he didn't quite know how the whole thing worked. When he was little, he used to pray for things and sometimes he got what he prayed for and sometimes he didn't. When Allen would ask his mom about it, she'd start reciting scripture and then he was even more confused. Then there was just something unsettling about depending on prayer. It was just too passive for him. Allen couldn't see himself talking into the air and then waiting for something to miraculously happen. He liked to be actively doing something. Allen was a strong believer in the principle that "faith without works is dead".[1] He had worked very hard for a very long time. He had had always kept the commandments as well as the "Golden Rule" (do unto other as you would have them do unto you).[2] Allen felt he shouldn't have to ask for what he believed he deserved from God. Anyway prayer seemed like just another Christian ritual that had nothing to do with God. Allen was hoping that their powwow session that night would've given him more ideas about how he could go about getting the job he wanted. One thing he knew was that he would have to change the way he was doing things. All of his original leads, or rather, his best leads, to jobs had dried up. The money he had saved was running low, and he didn't want to become a burden to his parents. He may have to try employment agencies or temping and see if he could find a suitable job that way. It was not until he heard the collective "Amen" rise from the congregation, that Allen realized that the prayer was finished and so hastily added his own "Amen" as well. Then the congregation sat down, as pastor Bynum approached the podium to speak.

"If you all would turn to the book of Genesis, chapter 26 starting at verse 1 and all the way through verse 6."

At once there was the crinkling sound of onion-skin pages turning as everyone who had a Bible was trying to find the day's reading. After several minutes of bumbling about, Allen finally found the scripture, but by that time, everyone had finished reading along. So he just left it open on his lap.

"My subject", pastor Bynum resumed "Are you listening to God?"

Already there were shouts of "Amen" and "Hallelujah" coming from various pews where people were eager to hear more from the man of God. Lena touched Allen's arm and gave him a knowing look, which was basically her way of saying "Pay attention, now." Allen just smiled before returning his attention to the podium. Pastor Bynum started his sermon speaking slowly, his deep baritone voice pausing at times for emphasis. At times, he re-read portions of the scripture passage, pausing at moments, waiting for the faithful to finish his sentences. Then pastor Bynum's voice began to rise in a crescendo as he got to the meat of his message.

"All that Isaac had, he had because he listened to God and was obedient. Now many of us today, we sit around and wonder why things are turning out so bad for us. We don't take the time to listen to God. We listen to our friends, we listen to our parents (not that you shouldn't listen to your parents now...help me somebody), we listen to our mp3 players, we listen to the boss, we listen to our girlfriends or boyfriends, our husbands or wives. We listen to the news and the media. But the one person who we need to listen to, the only one who has all of the answers, we don't make time for. Y'all don't hear me..."

"Hallelujah, praise you Jesus!" Lena yelled out, raising her hand in the air and waving it. A startled Allen looked around nervously as he felt embarrassed at his mother's outburst. He should have been used to it by now, but for some reason, he wasn't. He just didn't understand why she had to act this way. Allen moved closer to Tamiko, and hoped that his mother wouldn't get too wild today. Why couldn't she just clap her hands like Tamiko was doing?

COMMENCEMENT

Soon (though it wasn't soon enough for Allen), pastor Bynum's sermon reached its climax, and the praise music started.

"dr-drrmp, dr-drrmp, dr-dmp, dmp, dmp, dmp da-da-da-dmp"

The parishioners began to get up from the pews and started to dance. Lena darted up from her seat and ran to the aisle to dance, shaking her tambourine vehemently and giving glory to God without restraint.

"Dance, sister! Dance!" pastor Bynum exclaimed. This seemed to encourage more people to get in the aisles and get their shout on. A man in one of the pews up front was led straight up out of his chair and started running up and down the church. Mother Rose, Tamiko's mother had grabbed the hand of a young Latina woman who was sitting beside her and led her to the aisle on the other side where both of them did a victory dance. Every time the Fire got through the church, Allen would get a little overwhelmed. He looked over at Tamiko, hoping to find some camaraderie with another sane, sensible person like himself, however, she too, was in the throws of what seemed to be emotional mysticism. She had one trembling hand raised in the air, and her body swayed back and forth. She was sobbing uncontrollably and her eyes were closed. As a bewildered Allen looked closer, he could even see tears escaping from underneath her tightly closed lids. All Allen could think of at that moment was that one of his best friends had just lost her mind.

Once the music began to slow down, and some of the people began to be seated (Lena was still shouting), Pastor Bynum was ready for the conclusion of his sermon.

"How many of you are ready to listen to God? How many of you need some help to listen and hear his word? Come on down and let us pray for you right now."

All at once people began to get up and the ushers and brothers assisted them in an orderly procession toward the altar. By this time, Vernon had helped Lena back to her seat. Allen had slumped back in the pew and was absentmindedly thumbing through the pages in his Bible when he felt a nudge.

"Allen,....you need to go up there" gasped his mother as she wiped sweat from her face with her handkerchief.

"I don't think…"

"Allen Edward Sharpe, nobody's asking you what you think, it's what you need to do", said Lena sternly.

Allen was a little surprised by the seriousness of her tone. He had looked over at Tamiko hoping she would help rescue him from the situation, but she was already on her way up to the altar. When he looked back at his mother's fixed stare, he knew he had no other choice but to go up. Allen rose hesitantly from his seat and headed toward the altar. In all his time at church, he had never been to an altar call. The line was long and Allen's feet felt like they were lead blocks as he dragged himself forward. He saw some of the deacons and pastors praying for people and holding them so close that it looked a little weird. Some people were falling out on the floor and had to be helped back to their seats, while others started babbling, or so it seemed to Allen. Then he saw his friend Tamiko go up. She was on the line at the other side of the aisle where the assistant pastor was anointing people. Tamiko was still in tears and shaking, her gold colored short sleeved silk dress making her look like a sunflower blowing in the wind. The assistant pastor mumbled something to her, and somehow she managed to respond through all the sobbing. Then he began to pray over her and within a few minutes she too was on the floor. Allen shook his head incredulously at the spectacle. His inner cynic judged the whole affair as a young woman overcome by emotions. "I believe in God, like everybody else," he thought to himself, "but this is just taking it too far."

So wrapped up was he in what happened to Tamiko, he didn't even realize that it was his turn to be prayed for. In front of him was the powerful figure of pastor Bynum himself. Pastor Bynum pulled him gently forward and spread his hand over his forehead almost into his face and asked him "What do you need son?" Allen wanted to say, "How about the job I have worked hard for and deserve?" but instead he just said "prayer". So Pastor Bynum prayed for Allen. Allen couldn't exactly hear much of what Pastor Bynum was saying as his voice seemed to blend in with the voices of the other deacons and pastors who were praying, the shouts and effusions of those being prayed for, and the choir which was now into the fourth verse of "I Know It Was the Blood" which provided the background music for it all. The whole time Allen bowed his head and closed his eyes as tightly as he could, hoping the whole thing would be over as soon as possible. Once he heard the "Amen", Allen quickly thanked the Pastor, shook his hand, before darting back toward his seat.

When he got back his mother was on her knees praying and his father had his head bowed as well, but in the case of the latter, he seemed to be sleeping. Tamiko was leaning on her mother's shoulder, still crying. Allen sat down in his seat and pondered the scene in front of him. He realized that it wasn't just one or two people like his mom who were "over-reacting". As he looked around, he could see that the majority of people seemed to be responding to what they believed was a real and powerful connection with God. "Could there be something genuine going on here?" he asked himself. Allen even began to wonder if he was actually missing something.

TWELVE

Even on a Sunday, trying to get from the west side to the east side and back again was a challenge. Tamiko and Allen were heading home after driving over to Leona's Afro-Carribean bakery to pick up a bread pudding to be served as a dessert for the Sunday dinner that his parents were hosting for Pastor Bynum and his family. As they drove home, Allen couldn't help but think about Tamiko's behavior at church. Looking at her in that yellow silk dress and matching car coat, pillbox hat and pearls, she looked every bit the pastor's daughter. Tamiko had always been "Little Miss Perfect" when they were kids, but even she had some of the playful imp in her. He could remember when they were younger and they used to make fun of the "shouting sisters" in the church. Allen, Jim and Tamiko would be down at the park and Allen would pretend to be the preacher and Jim and Tamiko would pretend to be the congregation. Allen would start to preach and make the silly noises some preachers made when they preached. "And the Lord said….ah-hah- let there be light….ah-hah" and then Jim and Tamiko would pretend to shout and dance like the holy roller shoutin' sisters. They would crack themselves up for hours doing this. One time Tamiko's mom saw them and scolded them for "playing with God", but then Tamiko would be back with them the next day or week to play the same game. Sitting next to her now, he couldn't help but wonder at how she had changed. The same things she used to make fun of, she now seemed to take very seriously. Allen didn't know how to feel about it, whether her actions were pitiable or contemptible. In any case it totally explained her actions last night at Manna's.

84

COMMENCEMENT

"What? Why are you looking at me like that?" asked Tamiko.

"Just wondering about something, that's all" Allen smirked.

"About what?"

"About when you became such a Holy Roller?"

"What do you mean Holy Roller?!" replied Tamiko defensively.

"It's just that I've never seen you get so emotional in church before. It took me by surprise that's all."

"Why's that? If you have a connection to God, you can't helped but be moved by him."

"C'mon, Miko, I believe in God just like any other Christian, but to be so emotional about it. I could expect something like this from our parents, they're from another era, but I didn't think you would succumb to such...such...superstition."

Tamiko's eyes widened with disbelief.

"Here we go again. Are you saying that there isn't any possibility that people can experience the power and presence of God? And what's all this about 'superstition' and how I should know better?"

"I'm not saying that people can't experience the presence of God. I know that everyone experiences God in their own way, but I don't think it has to be accompanied by all the crying out, shouting, babbling and falling out that I see every Sunday. They're just going by feelings and emotions. Reacting to the music and the atmosphere. It's all in their heads."

"And I thought you just said that everyone has their own way of worshiping and experiencing God. So why are you judging this particular way as being crazy or stupid?"

"I know it sounds harsh, Miko, but even you have to admit it's all like a game of musical chairs. When the music stops, they stop."

"That's just some people, not everybody. Not me. Not your mom."

"Don't remind me."

"Are you saying that you're too smart to be touched by the power of God?"

"I never said that I couldn't be touched by God, I just don't think that's how He operates."

"And just how does He operate?"

"Like…like…by arranging circumstances, maybe. I don't know."

"So He would never make anyone fall down and just cry out to Him. He could never have someone speak in tongues, nothing like that. Right?"

"How does anyone know how He operates? He's up there and we're down here."

"If you read the Bible more often you would know. It's not just a bunch of allegories. It's a true historical account. He often speaks to us through his Word."

"If you say so."

"Well, if you don't believe in his Word, then why believe in God at all?"

"I have been wondering that lately."

"Because things in your life haven't turned out the way you planned and you didn't get that dream job?"

"It's not that simple, Tamiko."

"Explain it to me, then."

"Look, I've worked hard all of my life. I'm a good person and I live by the golden rule. I go to church every Sunday and give my tithes and everything. Now, shouldn't there be some type of reward for all that? If not, then what's the point?"

"Allen, we don't just serve God so that we can get the things we want. When you serve God it's not all about you. It's about Him. And there's more to serving God than just going to church, paying tithes, and being a good person. It's about having a relationship with Him."

COMMENCEMENT

"Now you're getting all deep on me. I'm starting to worry about you."

"I don't know, Allen. If, after everything God has done in your life, you can't understand why people like me and your mom praise Him like we do, I think the person you need to worry about is yourself."

"You certainly have changed is all I'll say. And I'll leave it at that."

"And I'll leave it at this. When I was a child I spoke as a child, but when I grew up I put away childish things.[1] We're adults Allen. People need to grow up spiritually too. It's time to stop playing saved and get saved."

The car stopped. They had been conversing for so long, Allen didn't even realize when they had pulled into the driveway of the brownstone. Without another word, Tamiko opened the door to her side of the car, got out and slammed the door. She didn't mean to, for Tamiko wasn't really angry at Allen, but disappointed in him. She always thought Allen was a good, moral, person and had just assumed that this was somehow connected to his upbringing in the church and his relationship with God. The possibility of Allen becoming an apostate to the faith was chilling. However, she hoped the words she had spoken would sink into his heart. Allen was still inside unfastening his seatbelt, and indeed felt very guilty about "offending" Tamiko. He was about to leave the car when he caught a glimpse of something in the rear-view mirror. It was the bread pudding. Given what he believed was Tamiko's attitude, Allen thought the dessert would be the only thing he could look forward to enjoying during dinner.

THIRTEEN

That night the dinner table was alive with the convivial conversation of the elder folks. Tamiko's mom, Mother Rose, and Lena talked about some of the upcoming events in the church, the Pastor interjecting at times when the conversation strayed to gossip. There was not much said between the two older men except noticings about the weather, sports, and current events. Yet there was a silence among the young people that created a tension in the atmosphere and was noticed by all, particularly Lena. She knew Allen could be taciturn when in the company of elders, but such silence from Tamiko was unusual. Tamiko was always bright, upbeat and voluble and tonight she seemed unusually sullen. Lena also noticed that Allen was avoiding eye contact with Tamiko, which led her to assume the two had some kind of disagreement. She hated the idea of two of her favorite children upset with each other, especially since she harbored a secret hope that someday the two would marry. After all, who could be better for her son than her pastor's daughter! In fact, Tamiko had spent so much time in her home as a little girl that she had practically felt like a daughter to her anyway. Lena's maternal instinct would not allow her to simply let things stand.

"So, Allen. How was Leona's? I guess it wasn't very crowded since you and Tamiko got back so soon."

"It was fine. They don't do a lot of business on Sundays", responded Allen, not once lifting his eyes from his meal.

"If that was the case, I'm surprised you didn't come back with a whole bunch of those caramel cookies you love so much. Or maybe he did and just ate them in the car?", Lena suggested as she hunched Tamiko with her elbow in an attempt to get her to talk.

"No, we just got the bread pudding and came back", said Tamiko languidly.

Before Lena could attempt to glean any more information, Pastor Bynum interrupted with a query of his own.

"Allen, my son, how has the job search been going for you? Not as easy as you thought it would be?"

Allen knew that his mom and Tamiko had probably told him everything. However, he would go along with the Pastor to see where this was going.

"Let's just say that there are a lot of obstacles I didn't count on, like the unexpected turn in the financial sector. But it's okay, I've got some other things planned", answered Allen.

"Just don't forget God's plan. You just go to Him. He's bigger than any downturn", returned Pastor Bynum.

"That's what I've been telling him Pastor. Pray and ask God what he wants him to do next", added Lena.

"So have you done that?" asked the Pastor.

"I just figured that I'd go ahead and use the good sense and the Harvard Education that God gave me to think about my possibilities. I don't have time to sit around and wait for a vision or something like that if that's what you're talking about."

"Boy, you better watch your mouth! Talkin' to the Pastor like that!" Vernon warned. "Seems like that Harvard education done turned you into an educated fool!"

"I wasn't trying to be disrespectful..."

"It's okay, Vernon", the pastor said trying to placate the growing tension. "I understand that you must be frustrated by now, but praying is not just sitting around and waiting. It just means that while you are out there doing what you are doing everyday, you take some time to pray and be open to His suggestion. God speaks in many ways, but we have to have our ears open to listen or we'll go the wrong way", cautioned the Pastor.

"Believe me, I'm open. As soon as I see an opportunity, I intend to take advantage of it", said Allen growing weary of the conversation.

"He had an opportunity a couple of months ago, but Mr. Harvard over here threw that away 'cause it wasn't good enough."

Allen bit his lip hard, covered his face with his hands and took a deep breath. He didn't want to lose control, especially in front of the Pastor.

"Vernon, please! Stop bringing that up!" exclaimed Lena who was also tired of hearing her husband's nagging refrain.

"Anyway, I'm not talking about opportunities. I'm talking about having a relationship with God in which he directs and guides you. Tell me, do you read your Bible? Do you pray?" asked Pastor Bynum.

"With all due respect Pastor Bynum, I think I know where you're going with this. In fact, I've already been there with mom and Tamiko. So let me just say this once and for all. Just because I'm a Christian doesn't mean that I'm going to anesthetize myself with religion and try to pray myself away from my problems. God helps those who help themselves."

"But sometimes He wants us to come to Him for help…"

"So, if He wants to help so much, why doesn't He?! Tell me, why doesn't He get one of those big shot executives to give me the job that I've worked my butt off practically all my life for?!" Allen found himself yelling. Then he threw his napkin down on his plate and stormed out of the dining room.

"I'm sorry, pastor. It's just like you said. He's very frustrated right now."

"I can see. I'll keep him in my prayers for you, Lena."

"Yeah, he's gonna need it. Actin' like his Harvard education gives him the right to start disrespectin' grown folk. He keep on, he's gonna end up in the street."

FOURTEEN

For Allen, looking for work had become work. He had renewed his determination to find a position and was sitting on his bed looking through the employment agency documents he got from a Harvard Colleague in an e-mail. Some of them promised to have jobs in banking and finance. He would get his resumes ready tonight and head out early tomorrow to check out some of these places. Then a soft knock on the door interrupted his mental board meeting.

"Yeah"

"Allen, you still up? Are you busy?" his mother asked diffidently as she cracked the door open and peeked in.

"I was just getting ready to get back onto the job search tomorrow. Is it going to take long? I still have some things I need to do."

"I just wanted to check and see if you're okay. You just seemed so upset when you left the table."

"I know. I didn't mean to be rude to the Pastor or anyone else. I just wish everyone would let me handle things in my own way."

"But that's the thing baby. Sometimes we can't...."

"You're not going into the "let go and let God" lecture again, are you?"

"Will you tell me just what is so wrong with taking just a little bit of time to ask God for help? He's the only one who can help!"

"Really?! Because lately I haven't been so sure of that."

"What are you saying?"

"I'm saying, I'm not sure there even is a God, anymore."

"Allen Edward Sharpe! How can you say that after all he's brought you through?! Brought us all through!"

"Well then, where is He now?"

"Allen, you've had a blessed life. Most of these young black boys nowadays don't even live to see their 21st birthdays and yet here you are with your health, strength and an Ivy League education to boot. And you want to say there is no God?"

"Mom…"

"No, Allen. I remember when the doctor told me when I was just thirteen years old, that I would never have any children. Then when I found out about you, they told me I would be able to carry you no more than a couple of weeks, but you were blessed with seven months in my belly. And I remember when you were born, the doctors said you'd never make it, and that if you did, there was a good chance you'd be disabled. But I prayed Allen. I fell on my face and prayed and your daddy prayed, and your grandmother and your grandfather and Pastor Bynum and Mother Rose and Momma Merta, we all prayed Allen. And now you want to forget those things: all the miracles and wonders God has worked for you. You want to forget God because, like a spoiled child, you can't get what you want right now!"

"If I'm so special to Him then why has He abandoned me?!"

"Maybe you've abandoned Him! Ever since you got into college, all you've ever talked about was having that corner office job so you could make a lot of money to spend on worldly pleasures."

"It's not just about money, I want to help the community, too. You know that."

"But what do you intend to give to God? What about that?"

"You know I'll always give to the church, whatever they need…"

"I'm not talkin' about giving tithes. God doesn't need your money. He's got all the money in the world. I'm talking about giving God your soul!"

Allen stood silent not knowing what to say. He had never thought about it in that way before.

"It's getting late, so I'm going to leave you with this. The Bible says that Christ is the corner stone. He who falleth on Him shall be broken, but him on whom He falleth shall be ground into powder.[1] Allen you better watch yourself before you end up nothin' but powder."

FIFTEEN

Jim was on one of the newer trains, so he didn't have to make many announcements. The automated voice took that job. He could just focus on his driving, and punching the stops. Heading south on the number 4 line, Jim had just left Brooklyn Bridge and was heading to Wall Street Station. There wasn't much of a way to go before he got to Bowling Green where he would take a break for lunch. Today he would be alone since his friend Brian was no longer working for the MTA. He had resigned a while ago to attend St. John's school of law, and to work in the law library part time. Jim was actually happy about this for several reasons. First and foremost, he was happy for his friend, who was actually able to go after his dream. Secondly, it put an end to the awkwardness that was beginning to form between them, especially after Jim had to finally confess that he had no intention of leaving transit for law school. That was a moment that stuck with Jim, particularly because of how hard Brian took it. When Jim told him, he could see the hurt and disappointment on Brian's face. Jim knew right then and there that he lost face with Brian. Even as Brian tried to continue their friendship, Jim felt the distance between them. Suddenly, there wasn't much for them to talk about anymore. Brian was busy preparing for all of the new experiences awaiting him, while Jim was still trudging along underground in transit. They were now on two different paths. They saw less and less of each other, until one day, Jim heard from Greg that Brian wasn't coming back. Brian didn't even say goodbye. Maybe that was best. A clean break. Jim couldn't blame him.

As he mourned the loss of this acquaintance with Brian, a feeling of loneliness swept over Jim and covered him like a fog. Lately, even his close friends seemed to be drifting away from him and even each other.

94

COMMENCEMENT

Allen had become totally consumed with his job search and didn't seem to have time for Jim anymore. Even when Allen did have time, he was so cranky and irritable that he wasn't much fun to be with. Richard was laying low somewhere for reasons he had yet to reveal. Tamiko seemed to be drowning in lesson planning and grad school, and Callie was working double shifts at the hospital. In his desperation, Jim was even willing to hang out with Tim, but he was busy with the reorganization of his department after all of the layoffs at Herns and Marshall. The last time they had all been together at once, was when they went to Manna's that Saturday night. Since then, they would meet in groups of two or three, here or there, for a few minutes or whatever. Few words were exchanged if any, each person preoccupied with whatever personal crisis they were dealing with at the moment. Most recently, they had all been reduced to texting each other. Friendships reduced to buzzes from a smart phone. Most days, and now weekends, Jim spent alone in his apartment heating up frozen dinners and watching the latest movie on the On Demand channel.

At least his friends were busy doing something. All he did was drive trains around in perfect circles, at least when there were no delays, track work, or signal problems, which still occurred more often than not. At times Jim would wonder if he shouldn't have just taken the chance and gone to law school. Sometimes he would even stop by a school and pick up an updated application, but soon after, his resolve would wan.

Finally, Jim could see the entrance of the platform as he led the train into the Bowling Green station. When he judged that he was about 60 feet away Jim pulled on the break and slowed the train down almost to a crawl so that he would end up as close to the punch as possible before the train stopped. As close as he was, he still had to use a little stick to reach the punch to signal his arrival into the station. Then he opened the doors and grabbed his bag. Before he left, he made sure the door to the conductor's car was locked and then stepped out of the train car onto the platform with the passengers and waited for his relief. It wasn't long before he spotted Jake. Jim greeted him briefly before handing off the keys and heading up the stairs into the chill October air.

Jim zipped his MTA jacket in response to the change in atmosphere. For a few minutes he wandered about aimlessly, thinking about where he was going to eat. Jim knew that there was a McDonald's not far over by Whitehall, and a fish place, which was a little further over on Court Street. The fish place was always crowded at this time of day, so he decided to go into the McDonald's and grab a couple of dollar menu chicken sandwiches and some fries. By the time he had made this decision, he had reached the restaurant. Jim got on the shortest line he saw and checked out the menu on the wall as he waited his turn. By the time he reached the check out, he had changed his mind and decided to splurge on a number 7: a Big Mac, large fries and large coke and he decided to get an apple pie for dessert. Once his order was ready, he took his tray and looked for a place to sit. There wasn't much space available as the lunch crowd was starting to pour in. He wanted a quiet corner away from everyone where he could just zone out in his own thoughts. As he was scanning the scene, he felt a tap on his shoulder.

"Hey stranger."

It was Callie.

"Hey yourself, what are you doing here?" asked Jim in surprise. He noticed that she was not wearing her nurse scrubs, but rather a fitted yellow oxford button down shirt, dark-rinsed jeans and chocolate Puma tennis shoes. Typical ladies shopping attire.

"After putting in so much overtime, I decided to call in sick and have a day for myself. Come sit with me over here", she said ushering him to a table in a corner near the front window.

"You always pick the best tables."

"Thanks. Did you just get off for lunch?"

"Yeah, I've got plenty of time."

"Good. I haven't seen any of you guys in so long. Lately, it seems as if I've been living at the hospital. You have to catch me up on what's been going on."

"Actually, not much has been going on. I haven't seen much of anyone, either."

"Soon we'll have to start making appointments to see each other. So how you been doin'?"

"You know how it is. Same old, same old. I see you've been shopping. Is that how you spending your overtime money?" asked Jim pointing to her bags.

"Oh, please. This is just a lot of household stuff."

"Since when does Century 21 sell household stuff?"

"They sell bedding and house furnishings there. They had sheets and pillows on sale. I don't want to be one of those sisters who looks all fly and then when you look in her house, all she's got is a sad little mattress and a pot for a toilet."

"Um, hmmm."

"Have you heard from Allen lately?"

"Last time I spoke to him was a week ago. He's still searching for the dream job. He's using agencies this time."

"I hope he has better luck with them than I did when I was looking for a job. Is he still angry with me about the what happened at Manna's?"

"He's not mad at you. He was never mad at you. You were the one that was trippin'!"

"Then why hasn't he returned any of my phone calls or my texts?"

"He's busy Callie. He hasn't really been returning anyone's texts."

"He returned yours."

"Not really. I just drop by every once in a while. I'm just down the block, remember?"

"I bet he's got time for Miss Perfect."

"I guess *you're* still upset about what happened at Manna's. Don't you think that's old by now?"

"It's just that...Never mind. Next topic."

"C'mon, what is it?"

"Nothing! Just forget it."

"Why are you so jealous of Miko?"

"Please! I'm not jealous of her!"

"Then what is it? You're not angry with Allen anymore, but you're not cutting her any slack."

"Oh, I don't know, maybe it's because she's a self-righteous, patronizing, selfish, crybaby who can dish it, but can't take it. And she's always trying to tell Allen what to do."

"Ah, so that's what it is!"

"What are you talking about?"

"You know what I'm talking about?"

Callie shrugged her shoulders to express her lack of clarity with regard to what Jim was referring to.

"Someone's crushing on Allen", Jim sang tauntingly.

"Oh please, stop. If you remember correctly, I was the one who suggested that we should be friends after the prom!"

"And now you've changed your mind?"

"No, I haven't."

"Are you sure?"

Callie rolled her eyes.

"You really don't need to be jealous of Tamiko. She and Allen are really more like brother and sister. He'd never consider anything with her. And neither would I for that matter. It'd be like incest or something."

"It makes no difference to me, cause I'm not interested in him that way. I just wish she'd keep her holy-roller ways to herself, that's all."

"I hear that. All that slave religion stuff can try your nerves after a while."

"It's not believing in God that I can't handle, it's just that she acts as if her way is the only way. Ya know?"

98

"I feel you. Me… I don't know. I used to go to church and stuff, but now, I'm not so keen on religion."

"I mean there's so many religions out there, how can she be so sure about which one is the right one. Who knows, maybe they're all right in some way. It's all very confusing. That's why I don't like thinking about stuff like that."

"Hey, I just believe that if you're a good person, everything will work out in the end."

"But then what does it mean to be a 'good' person. 'Good' means different things to different people."

"Callie, do you know why you're confused about stuff? It's because you over-complicate things. You think too much."

"Me? What about you? Like when are you going to stop thinking about law school and actually go?"

"Now that is a much more complicated matter."

"What's so complicated about it, if it's what you really want to do? I heard from Brian the other day. He's having the time of his life right now. You should have gone with him."

"And how am I going to support myself? Huh? Who is going to foot the bill for law school? You heard Allen the other night. They don't give you money for graduate school!"

"Those sound like excuses to me. Brian is going through the same thing you're going through. He got another job and a roommate to help pay for expenses. He took out some loans and applied for a fellowship."

"Well, that worked for him. It may not work for me."

"How will you know if you don't try?"

Jim began to tune Callie out as he started to pick at the left over ice in his cup with his straw.

"So does this mean that you're never going back to school? You're going to make a life-long career out of the MTA?"

"And what if I did? Would that be so bad? Why does everyone think that every black person has the responsibility to be some barrier breaking 'phenom'. You want to be a head nurse, Allen wants to be a Wall Street consulting big wig, Tim wants to own a multimillion dollar corporation before he's 30, and even Richard wants to be hustler of the year. What happened to being a normal average guy?"

"Jim, are you serious?"

"Look, I've been doing some serious thinking these past two years…"

"Sounds more like you've been doing crack."

"Callie, everybody is not meant to be at the top…"

"So you're giving up? Y'know, you're always talking about how were still in the struggle and how the white man is always trying to keep us down. I guess in your case he doesn't have to try. You're already laying down."

"Wait a minute, are you trying to say I'm a punk?"

"All I'm saying is that I'm disappointed in you, Jim."

"You're disappointed? I'm the one who should be disappointed. I didn't know my friends were so shallow and materialistic. I guess I have to be a "professional" if I'm gonna hang with the set right?"

"Don't even go there! That's not what this is about! This has to do with you accepting less of yourself!" Callie was starting to raise her voice, but caught herself. She didn't want it to seem as if she was angry with him, however she wanted to show her concern.

"Jim, I'm your friend and I care about you. I see that you are an intelligent, hardworking guy with a lot of potential, who, for some reason lately, wants to throw everything away. This isn't you, Jim. What's going on?" she asked in a softer tone.

"It's getting late. I have to get back to the station."

"I'm sorry if I upset you, Jim. It's just that I want you to be happy…"

COMMENCEMENT

"I know. No hard feelings."

"Just think about what I said. Okay?"

"I'll do that."

"If you want to talk, hit me on the cell."

"Sure", he said collecting his tray before heading toward the garbage and finally the exit, leaving Callie alone at the table.

As Jim stepped out onto the sidewalk he was stung by a sudden gust of cold October air. But it wasn't as bad as the sting of Callie's words that still reverberated in his head. They haunted him all the way back to the station. It didn't stop until he was back in the motorman's car of the northbound 4 train heading into the Bronx. Midway through the route, he got a transmission from central dispatch that there was a track fire and that he had to re-route on the 7th avenue line all the way through the Bronx. That meant extra traffic with the 2 and 3 trains. Jim didn't mind. He could handle it because he knew the routes so well. Jim had come to know a lot about how to navigate trains through the complex system of underground tunnels. He knew of other drivers who even got lost down in the system to the chagrin of their passengers and the boss at central. Jim was good at managing the routes. It was the one tangible thing he could hold onto in his life, and there weren't many things he could hold onto.

Jim turned off of the express track at the 149th Street station and headed out onto the tracks at the lower level where the 2 and 3 stop. When he got to the crossing, he had to stop for a red signal. Dispatch radioed that there were two trains ahead of him and to wait for clearance. "Figures." Jim thought to himself. With the 2, 3, and now, 4 and 5 trains using the same tracks it was inevitable. "Attention Ladies and Gentleman, we have red signals ahead of us. When they clear, we should be moving. Thank you for your patience", he announced.

While Jim waited for the signal to change, he thought about how easy this job was in comparison to how he was faring in his life. Most of the time he was by himself, and didn't have to really talk to anyone, except when he was receiving a transmission from his radio. His headset blocked out most of the noise coming from the tunnels. Once Jim got over his fear of driving in the dark, he came to like it even. And he was really good at keeping control over the trains. He knew how to slow down when he came to a shorter platform and he almost always was in the perfect position to punch the clock at the station.

Jim could always keep the trains on the track, but he could never do the same with his life. He lost his dad, his mom, Brian, and now there stood the possibility of losing his long time friends and sometimes he even felt like he was losing himself. Something was happening to him, but he couldn't explain it outright. Sometimes he thought it was a good change. After talking to Callie today, all he could feel was just shame. If only there was a way that he could pursue law school and keep his current job. He could do it, but he just needed something to fall back on. It was really dark out there in the world. Much darker than even the most distant recesses of a closed subway tunnel.

Jim thought about going out into it, but he needed a hand to hold.

SIXTEEN

A few weeks ago, Allen made his first visit to an employment agency. They couldn't find anything for him that day, and told him to call back every couple of days to see if anything came in. Every time he called to check on his application, the receptionist gave the same reply, "We haven't found anything yet". So Allen decided to try to improve his chances by applying to several other employment firms. Today he was on his way to the Black Tie staffing agency. It was located in an impressive 70-story office building just off Madison Avenue near 51st Street. Based on what he had heard from one of his Harvard colleagues, they specialized in matching Ivy League Graduates with top-notch firms. He had already e-mailed his information in advance and had made an arrangement to speak with an employment specialist. Upon arriving at their premises, Allen was even more impressed with the business like atmosphere and clientele. As he looked around the waiting room, he noticed many of the people looked like serious businessmen and businesswomen in their crisp, dark suits, and polished footwear.

"Good morning. I'm here to see Barbara West", said Allen as he walked up to the receptionist.

"Fill this out and have a seat."

"I already filled out my form on-line."

"Then just have a seat, and she'll be with you in a few minutes."

As he waited to meet one of the recruiters, Allen managed to strike up a conversation with a few of the other job seekers who were also waiting. One was a man from Minnesota, who was seeking employment in marketing. Another was a young Indian woman who had already registered with the agency and was on a call back for an interview with a well-known bank for a position as head of client services. One other gentleman was leaving the investment-banking field to find something in human resources. They all had a lot of experience in their respective fields, not to mention several advanced degrees and certifications. Allen would have felt a little intimidated, if he had not been told about how this firm preferred Harvard Graduates over others, since the proprietor of the business had been a Harvard graduate himself. Surely they would be able to find a suitable position for him.

At this point, based on the exigency of his situation, Allen was willing to settle for smaller positions like bank manager or accounts manager. He even thought about the possibility of starting out in accounting or as an office manager. Allen was willing to do almost anything that would help him to earn some money and stay on the path he had chosen for himself. Eventually, he would be able to go back to school and get his MBA. Then he would definitely be on his way to achieving his goals.

"Allen Sharpe", a voice called sharply, almost like a reprimand.

Allen looked up to see an older woman with graying hair and a neat silver shark-skinned skirt suit. She didn't smile or show any trace of emotion. Seeing her reminded Allen of a mean elementary school librarian from his past.

"Yes", Allen responded.

"Barbara West", the woman blared extending her hand for a brief shake.

"Nice to meet you."

"Let's go back to my office so we can talk."

Allen followed her through a door next to the receptionist desk, into a beehive of activity. There were cubicles everywhere, and Mrs. West led the way through the maze of felt boards until they reached one in a small corner in the back. Her set up was impressive for a cubicle. The cubicle itself was fashioned of dark, berber felt. There was a neat little mahogany desk with a state-of-the-art Mac computer, two leather chairs, hers being a recliner of course, and a mahogany file cabinet with silver plated hardware.

"Please, sit", she said gesturing to the smaller leather chair opposite her desk.

"Thank you", said Allen politely as usual.

"So, Allen", West began as she perused his file on her computer. "What kind of position are you looking for?"

"I've heard that you specialize in placing people in the finance industry. I am currently looking for a position as a financial analyst or consulting associate, but I am open to lower level managerial positions like…"

"Finance?! You've got to be joking", she laughed.

The bluntness of her words and manner shocked Allen like a glass of cold water thrown suddenly on him. After a few seconds, however, he was able to recover his wits. Allen was determined to stand his ground and was ready to defend his position.

"I am aware of the fact that there has been a lot of downsizing and layoffs recently, however…"

"They're hemorrhaging jobs out there in the financial sector. There's no way a kid like you has a chance out there. The young people like you are the first ones they cut. Even some of the big pros are having their hats handed to them."

"I understand that, however, I'm sure there must be some entry level positions out there that are open, especially for someone with my credentials and experience. I was under the impression that this firm specialized in placing talent with high caliber positions."

"And that's what we try do, but let's face it, we're not miracle workers. Look, I'll be honest with you. We haven't been getting a lot of great jobs here. Most of our accounts are drying up. We used to have the inside track on jobs with the big advertising agencies, financial firms, public relations giants; you name it. Now a lot of them have been pulling back. The one's who are still with us want people with a proven track record, with portfolios and the like. By the looks of things, you don't have that."

"You don't understand…all of my life…what else am I going to do?" stammered Allen.

"Well, you would need a career counselor to determine that, and we don't provide those services here. What I can do is hold onto your application and see what comes up. Lately, we've been getting a lot of Human Resources stuff, Education, and Health. I'll see if they have anything on the business side that you could do."

West reached over to the caddy on her desk, picked up a card and handed it to Allen.

"Give us a call in about a week or so."

"Thank you for your time", whispered Allen as he took the card, placing it in his jacket pocket as he rose to leave.

"Good luck, kid."

So far there was none to be found.

SEVENTEEN

Tamiko stood outside the doorway of room 415, nervously rocking back and forth as she shifted her weight from one foot to the other, clutching her assessment binder. The assessment meeting was supposed to be during the second part of her third period prep, but it seemed that the school leadership team was still conferring with Joan, better known to the children as Miss Fields. Joan was another new teacher that Tamiko had developed a friendship with. "It probably won't be that bad", Tamiko said to comfort herself. "After all, I've only been teaching on my own for two months. They've got to cut me some slack. I'm still learning."

And it had been the most exasperating two months. During those eight weeks, all of Tamiko's expectations about the profession had been dashed to the ground by the professional expectations of the organization for which she worked. She thought her experience as a teacher would be vaguely similar to that of the teachers who had taught her. Tamiko thought she would have the chance to create and innovate in ways that would inspire her students to learn. She thought she would be a part of an open dialogue with education professionals, who would respect her ideas and observations, and who would help her to improve her practice, however, in reality she found herself in a totally different world.

There were curricula and calendars that were written in stone, to be administered in a specific sequence. The Writing Unit on Narratives had to be exactly three weeks. The Core Math Addition/Subtraction unit ran exactly 4 weeks. It didn't matter if there were children who were not getting the concept. If they didn't get it in the time allotted, it must be due to poor teaching. Lessons were scripted, with the Literacy coach and lead teachers not suggesting, but demanding that she use certain words and phrases when she spoke with the children. She had to begin each lesson with the phrase "Yesterday, we… and today, we are going to…" Tamiko had to end every lesson with "So, today and every day, you can…." Every classroom had to use the same color chart for discipline. Every lesson had to be done using the workshop model, even if it were an exploratory lesson. You must have the connection, teach, active engagement, link, and share. Even if the lesson was a read-aloud and didn't really conform to this structure, you had to make it conform. Read-alouds had to be done using the Expressions curriculum. That meant Tamiko could only read stories like Chrysanthemum by Kevin Henkes, or A Chair for My Mother by Vera B. Williams. She couldn't introduce her students to books written by other authors. Authors that looked like them, that experienced life from a similar perspective. And you couldn't close your door and shut out administrative interference. The coaches and the lead teachers were constantly there, observing, providing feedback, so much feedback, you barely had enough time to digest it all. It all made Tamiko feel as if she was a factory worker. There was nothing of her at all in her classroom or in her teaching. She just did what the curriculum writers, the literacy coach, the math coach, and the older teachers told her to do. And then there was the nightmare of assessments.

There were four assessments that had to be administered individually to each student on a monthly basis. With 24 students in the class, the assessments would take at least two weeks to administer. By the time she finished an assessment, analyzed it, and incorporated information into her lessons plans, it was time for the next round of assessments. Sometimes Tamiko felt she spent most of her time assessing rather than teaching. But at least the people were friendly, and they seemed to care about her development as a teacher. Suddenly, the door opened and she heard the sound of laughter and congratulations, before Joan came bouncing out cheerfully.

"So how did it go?" Tamiko half-whispered eagerly.

"It went great, but I'll tell you more about it later. I gotta go set up my room for math before I have to pick up my kids from art", replied Joan before she hurried away downstairs.

COMMENCEMENT

Her friend's appraisal of the situation made Tamiko optimistic about her own imminent date with the school leadership team.

Tamiko went into the room and was stupefied by all of the people present. There was the principal, Mrs. Stone, the assistant principal, Mrs. Nettlenerves, the lower school literacy coach, Charlotte Booker, the lower school math coach, Milton Resnick, and the lead teachers all assembled together to discuss the progress of her students with her. The presence of so many to discuss what seemed so intimate a topic was more than a little intimidating for Tamiko. She felt as if she was taking the stand at a trial and she was the defendant in question. After greeting the team with a timid "Good afternoon", Tamiko took a seat at the long conference table that placed her furthest from all of the other participants. The inscrutable expressions on their faces set Tamiko even more on edge than she already was.

"Miss Bynum, lets take a look at the data on your students, shall we?" began the ominous Mrs. Steele the first grade lead teacher.

"We'll start with your students progress in literacy. You have 24 students, and last month, you began with 4 students below level in reading, 15 on level and 5 students above level for this time of year. Now you have 5 students below level, 13 students on level and 6 who are above level. On average, the children in your class have moved 1 level, however the average movement for the teachers on your grade level has been 2 levels. Are you noticing anything so far?"

Before Tamiko could answer, the assistant principal chimed in with an observation of her own.

"I'm noticing, that children aren't really moving in this class, and it concerns me a lot. Especially the fact that your bottom 4 students haven't shown much progress at all."

Tamiko was stunned. The assistant principal who often came around with her happy-go-lucky demeanor now seemed so stern and even accusatory with her words. Tamiko, however, would defend herself.

"Actually, they have shown some progress. When these bottom 4 students came into my class, they didn't even know their letters or sounds. Now they have made some progress in that area, even if they have not

109

moved up into reading text yet. And they've only been in school for 2 months."

"That's all well and good," added Booker, the literacy coach, "but a child does not need to know all of his letters and sounds to begin reading text. If you've read Clay, it's very evident.[1] There are other teachers who are in the same situation, and have managed to get children with similar backgrounds up to level 2 by now. We all know about the children and where they started. What we'd like to know is what *you've* been doing to help these children?"

Tamiko was stunned by Charlotte's condescending and critical tone. In her role as literacy coach, Charlotte had observed her on more than several occasions since the beginning of the school year. In follow up evaluation meetings, Charlotte would always tell Tamiko about how great her lessons were. Charlotte was always positive and reassuring. She thought that they were friends even! Looking across the conference table from her now, it seemed as if she had morphed into another person. How could Charlotte question Tamiko about what she was doing to help her students? Most of the things Tamiko had been doing were what Charlotte had recommended. Tamiko definitely felt like she had to speak up for herself, but she would exercise tact.

"As *you've* suggested, I've been pulling the neediest children in small groups for strategy lessons that are tailored to their unique needs. I even work with them during some of my preps. I have been giving them homework that is different from that given to the other children so that they can build the skills that will allow them to catch up to their peers. I have called their parents and discussed how they can work with them at home…"

"But that's just it. You say that you are working with them in small groups and you have tailored lessons to their unique needs, but we're not seeing any change. It makes me wonder just how you've been using the data you've been getting from your class. The whole point is not just to execute lessons, but to plan *effective* lessons", Principal Stone interrupted.

"I must agree. And it's not just the children at the bottom levels that worry me. Every child should be making progress based on his or her individual capabilities. I know that you have some very bright children who are above benchmark who could be pushed higher. For example, you have Jasmine Evans. When she left my kindergarten, class last year, she was a high level 16 and so far she's only moved one level. I'm concerned that you may not be differentiating instruction for these higher-level students", put in Charity Fontaine, the kindergarten lead teacher.

Tamiko was floored by what seemed to be the open hostility of the panel. It sounded to her as if they were trying to tell her that she wasn't a good teacher. If she wasn't, what accounted for those A's in student teaching? Even if she wasn't the greatest teacher, that didn't justify the outright animosity in the tone of these so called professionals. It wasn't like she was giving the children worksheets all day. She stayed up until after 10:00pm most nights planning lessons and preparing materials. Tamiko was doing her best. In fact, Charity was insinuating that Tamiko was ruining the good work she had done with Jasmine last year. Taking advantage of the situation to toot her own horn at Tamiko's expense. "Don't jump to conclusions", Tamiko warned herself. The point of the meeting is to help me find ways to improve, not to judge. But it certainly felt as if they were judging.

"What I think we need to do is to plan some 'next steps' that are going to help you lift the level of your teaching so that your children can move to the next level", suggested Mrs. Steele casually.

"But most of my children are already meeting the current benchmarks for first grade."

"Just because they've met current benchmarks doesn't mean you can just leave them to teach themselves while you take a break…" Mrs. Stone spat out.

"What we mean is," Miss Steele intervened coolly, cutting off the principal, "every child should make at least a year's worth of progress. That means, for many of our students, simply meeting current grade level benchmarks or even meeting end of year benchmarks isn't enough. It's our duty as educators to take them as far as they can go. We don't know what kind of education they'll get once they leave this school."

Tamiko couldn't argue with what the woman was saying, even if she didn't like her very much.

"Not to mention it's the Chancellor's Regulation", Mrs. Nettlenerves added. "This school is being judged by the amount of progress students make in a given year. At this school, we have the reputation for helping children to make a year and a half's worth of progress in a school year. We've been fortunate enough to receive the "Well Developed" Rating two years in a row. This year we're aiming for the "Outstanding" rating and we have to have every teacher on their "A" game if we're going to get it."

"If you'd like, I can come into your class and observe you for a while, and when necessary, provide demonstration lessons in areas of literacy that you may be a little weak in", offered Steele.

This was just what Tamiko needed. More observations, more judgments. She reminded herself that she needed to keep an open mind.

"That sounds fine…"

"I think it's an excellent idea, and Charlotte can help you and Rosalyn work on scheduling the observations. I'm also going to schedule you for several informal observations, before the big formal in April. That way, you can get the feedback you need to develop your teaching skills", said Nettlenerves.

"I will come to you during your first period prep tomorrow, and we'll work on the details", said Steele.

"Thank you for coming in Tamiko. And remember, that the purpose of these meetings is to learn and to improve the practice of teaching. That's what's best for the school and the kids", Nettlenerves said to end the meeting.

Tamiko merely nodded and left the room deeply despondent and dispirited.

****

"Hey, you! All set for lunch?" chirped Joan as she poked her head into Tamiko's classroom. Tamiko tried to force a smile.

"I guess", Tamiko responded weakly.

"You look bummed. What's up?"

112

"My assessment meeting didn't go so well." Tamiko's voice began to tremble as she fought back tears.

"Really? Why? I thought they liked you?"

"But they don't like my teaching apparently."

"Your kids moved up on the Running Records, right?"

"Not as much as everyone else's students."

"Yeah, but you've got a tough class. Considering some of the antics these kids pull, I think it's a miracle, any of them moved at all."

"I know a lot of them have issues, but they're so young. It's not their fault. Besides, it's my job to teach them in spite of their issues."

"So what'd they say? I mean did it sound like they were gonna give you the dreaded "U" rating?"

"Not yet anyway. They're gonna have Charlotte and Steele coach me, and Nettlenerves is going to do a couple of informal observations."

"For the love of Pete! Don't they come in your classroom enough already! What more do they want! And I don't believe that junk about it being "all about the kids". All they care about are their careers. I think they all see themselves as the next Regional Superintendent. Especially Booker and Nettlenerves."

"You can say that again. I couldn't believe how Charlotte turned on me today."

"What'd she do?"

"You know how she's always like, 'That was great, you're in the right direction.' Well, today she just turned on me like a pit bull. You should have heard her, 'I don't see what you're doing to help the kids move'" Tamiko mimicked. "Ironically enough, I've been doing exactly what she's been telling me to do."

"I know. She is such a twit. She's only where she is because her mom is the principal's best friend. How else could someone become a literacy coach after just one year's worth of experience teaching? It's just sick."

"And Steele really takes the cake. I know it's not right, but I just can't stand her. Ever since we met, she's sort of had like this blasé attitude. You know me, I try to give everybody the benefit of the doubt, but I think she's just mean. She was the first one to come out and suggest more observations. What a pill."

"She's a weirdo anyway. No one likes her. Don't say anything, but I heard she's prejudiced."

"Really?! That certainly explains a lot", breathed Tamiko remembering her first encounter with Steele at the beginning of the school year. Most keenly she remembered her dismissive attitude when she introduced herself. Tamiko guessed that maybe she had no time to be bothered with African-Americans.

"Yeah, they say she had some type of incident with one of the parents last year who complained about something she said to one of the students. And she's always trying to get the teachers of color fired."

"Are you serious?! What am I supposed to do with someone like that for my mentor?"

"Rumor has it, she is supposed to be leaving after this year. I heard from Mrs. Lawler that she doesn't like the neighborhood anymore so she's leaving."

"I hope she does leave. In the meantime, I have to suffer that woman in my classroom for goodness knows how long. And given what you just said, she's probably just going to try to sabotage me. I wish there was someone else that I could turn to."

Then after a moment, Tamiko's eyes lit up. "Hey Joan, what about you? Do you think you could help me?"

"I don't know, Tamiko. I'm a first year teacher just like you. What could I help you with?"

"C'mon, your assessment meeting turned out better than mine. Maybe you could share some of what you've been doing."

"Oh please, I've just got a lot of smart kids who are good at teaching themselves. They'd have to with this stupid curriculum."

"Still, if there's anything that you know that could help, I'd appreciate it."

"There is one thing", she said leaning close to Tamiko. "But I don't know … If you're still having trouble after next month's meeting, just let me know."

"What do you mean?"

"Aw man, it's getting late. We'd better go while we can. If we don't pick up the kids from lunch on time, the school aides will blab to the principal. That's another thing about this place. You can barely trust anyone to have your back. There's always someone whose willing to make you look bad to make themselves look good."

"You're right. Let me just grab my purse."

EIGHTEEN

After weeks of visiting agencies with no luck, Allen decided that he could no longer hold onto his dream of being employed in the financial industry. The country's economic crisis had grown steadily worse. The Dow continued to drop hundred of points. This time, AIG and Merril Lynch were the newest casualties of the financial turmoil. As they sunk into the quagmire of corruption and bankruptcy, so did thousands of jobs. Rapidly, the losses in the financial sector began to ripple throughout other industries. Restaurants and retail establishments that once profited enormously from Wall Street bonuses saw their profits dwindle as their customers lost their jobs. Realties couldn't sell houses. In fact, many of the newly unemployed were losing the overpriced homes they already had. The automakers couldn't sell their exorbitantly priced and inefficient cars. Next to succumb to the financial crisis were the big auto giants: Ford, Chrysler and GM. Philanthropy decreased leaving many non-profits who depended upon corporate donations in jeopardy. Then the city itself was hit as the public sector enacted hiring freezes. The nation's unemployment rate suddenly sky rocketed from 4 to 6.5 percent and in the city it was now 5.7 percent. Companies, particularly in the financial industry, were still hemorrhaging jobs. Finding a job was definitely going to be tight, and for an African-American male, almost next to impossible.

There were many bills that needed to be covered, most notably the student loans that Allen and his parents had taken out to finance his education. Allen's chief objective now was to land a job. Any job. He couldn't sit around and watch his parents forego their retirement while he waited for his "dream job". The exigency of his situation demanded that he find a way to help with the monthly bills. It was the only way to preserve what little dignity he had left. So Allen stood on a line outside of the Jacob Javits center, a line that went all the way down to end of Twelfth Avenue to get into the New York Job Fair. After nearly two hours of waiting, he was now on the corner of Eleventh Avenue, just fifty feet from the entrance of the building.

It was cold, rainy, and windy. Allen had a hard time trying to control his umbrella, which at times was flipped inside out by the wind. At times Allen looked down the queue for signs of movement. There were policemen and center security to control the growing crowd. Allen couldn't believe how many people were there; ready to compete for what might be 100 jobs at best. That's the way it worked at job fairs. Sometimes the companies that were represented weren't even hiring, but would send representatives anyway to collect resumes, and to see what the market looked like in terms of skilled workers. Everyone who was there, including Allen, knew the odds, but went anyway in a sort of hopeful desperation.

Allen listened to the conversations of the people around him. Most of the people were recent college graduates like himself. There were some older people who had been phased out of top positions, a few lawyers, bankers, and even some people who his mom referred to as "street". Guys from round the way, looking to see if they could catch a gig to make a few bucks. One guy Allen recognized was a "man on the corner". Even they weren't doing so well these days. Allen remembered how when he was in high school, the guys on the corner would have fresh sneakers every other week, shiny new jeeps and girls hanging all over them. Now there were so many brothers out there flooding "the trade", that wages even in this area were so depressed, the dealers had to get a second job just to keep everything together. But in some way, Allen had expected to see them. They looked like him. There were always a large number of African-Americans and Latinos at these job fairs. What Allen did not expect to see were the large numbers of whites, Indians and Asians who were present (although their numbers were by no means equal to those of African-Americans). It seemed as if the current financial doldrums affected everyone.

The line dragged steadily on until Allen could see the entrance of the building. Security was checking for registration tickets. Ten more minutes and the line began to move faster. Allen could see that they were letting people into the building in groups of about 30 more or less. Allen shifted his umbrella from one hand to another, holding it away from the crowd before he closed it. Then he reached into his raincoat to get his registration form from his inside pocket. Ten more minutes and he would be pasting on his visitor sticker badge and heading forward with the next group of 30 who were making their way into the center and up the escalators to see what job opportunities awaited.

As he stepped off the escalator onto the second floor, he could barely see the little stalls that were being thronged by the other job seekers, and couldn't tell which businesses were there at first. Some of the representatives had the good sense to place their banners high over the table with a collapsible steel framed awning. For example, looking down the aisles of people, he was quick to notice the McDonald's golden arches logo cascading from an awning over their booth, and the famous red, white and blue Duane Reade trademark from their booth over in the corner. Allen decided that he would have a walk around to see just what businesses were there before introducing himself and handing out resumes.

He could barely walk along the busy corridor for the hustle and bustle of the other job seekers. At one stall, Allen noticed a tall red-haired, middle-aged white man who was almost giving a lecture to the people who stood mesmerized in front of him. This piqued Allen's interest so he moved closer to the group to find out what was going on.

"Here is our web address and instructions for filing an application if you're interested", said the man handing out sheets of green paper to the people in front of him. The man fumbled for a bit before handing the papers over to an assistant who handed them into the crowd. Allen took one of the papers, and read what amounted to instructions about how to go online and fill out an application to work at a new M&M super-store in mid-town. Most of the available positions were for sales reps. Even as desperate as he was, Allen just couldn't see himself wearing those brown and yellow aprons trying to talk up the red, yellow and green teddies made after those characters on the commercials.

As he walked further down, Allen made a decision to avoid the tables with too many people crowded around. Such tables often represented companies that offered unskilled jobs. The unskilled jobs were the ones that went the fastest, and Allen knew from experience that they were not looking for someone as educated as he was anyway. He'd have to leave a lot off of his resume if he wanted to work at such places. The bosses were always afraid that too many educated people working for Burger King or the Limited and the next thing you know a foodservice workers union or a retail workers union may spring up. In spite of his desperation, he also had just too much pride to take one of these jobs.

In a lonely corner sat a heavy set bearded man at the Cigna Health Insurance table. Allen decided to walk over and see just what the bearded man had to offer.

"Good afternoon. My name's Allen Sharpe", Allen greeted the man extending his hand for the customary handshake.

"Hi, How are you, I'm Bill Taylor, Human Resources specialist. Are you interested in working in health insurance?"

"Yes, very much", Allen lied. " What kind of positions do you have available?"

"Right now we have a few sales associates positions open? Do you have any previous sales experience?"

"No, but I was a finance major in college. I'm open to new experiences, and I learn quickly. Would you like my resume?"

"Sure I'll take a look at it", said the rosy-faced man cordially, but uninterestedly. Allen thought that at once he would notice the Harvard Degree and then he would have a chance to discuss a possibility for employment. However, Taylor merely glanced over it in a perfunctory way before placing it on a pile of several others. Then he reached over to a little stack of cards and handed one to Allen.

"Here's my business card. I'll bring your resume back to central headquarters to see if they're interested. If they are, they should give you a call."

Allen had heard that before.

"Thank you. I really appreciate it", said Allen as he realized that this was Taylor's way of ending the interview and getting rid of him. He then walked away to scavenge for other opportunities.

After walking around for about 20 minutes, Allen began to believe there weren't that many companies here at all. The crowds began to thin out as people who realized paucity of viable positions began to leave, and Allen could see the wide spaces between the tables. Now he could see more clearly the companies that were represented. There was a representative for the Marriot Hotel Chains. Allen heard that they were planning to build a new hotel on the other side of Harlem. There were a few people at the table already who were engaged in tête-à-tête's with some of the representatives. They did not especially look like the type of people that would be negotiating a skilled position, especially the man with the purple suit and lavender Stacy Adams shoes, or the woman with the burgundy weave and tight fitting burgundy, yellow, and black skirt suit. In any case, it wouldn't hurt to see what they were offering.

On his way there, the woman in the brightly colored suit was walking away and bumped into Allen.

"I'm sorry."

"It's okay."

"Are you sure? You don't look so good", said Allen noticing the despondent look on her face.

"You wouldn't look so good either if you'd been out of work for two years."

Allen couldn't believe what he'd just heard. Two years! How could someone be searching for work for two years! The nearly six months that he had been looking seemed like eternity. Allen couldn't fathom being out of work for two years. Then Allen looked at the suit again. Maybe that was part of her problem. She didn't really know how to dress when looking for work and it seems that no one had ever given her the hint.

"I hope you have some luck here today."

"Thanks, but it doesn't look like it", she said, her voice trailing off as she walked away. At least she was still trying.

Allen made his way over to the stall and spoke with a young African-American woman who was standing behind the table setting up a display of brochures.

"Good afternoon", said Allen offering his usual salutation.

"Good afternoon. I'm Holly, and you are…"

"Forgive me. I'm Allen Sharpe", said Allen extending his hand to the woman.

"So, Allen, what is it that has interested you in working for the Marriot?"

"I've always wanted to work in the hospitality industry. I have some experience in finance and management and was thinking that maybe I could put those skills to work for you. Would you like to see my resume?"

"Sure, absolutely."

Unlike the previous encounter, Holly seemed particularly interested and took the time to inspect the resume.

"Harvard! Wow! You're parents must be proud", she commented before returning her attention to the resume.

"Thank you. They are."

"This is a great resume. You have so much valuable experience, I don't know if you'd even want the jobs we have to offer. I mean, the only positions we have available are for custodians, maids, concierge, and the like. I'm not sure if that's something that someone with your background wants to do. I don't want to waste your time."

"Oh", said Allen he didn't quite know how to feel. On one hand he was encouraged by the fact that the woman was basically expressing he was too good for such jobs, with which Allen agreed. However, he was looking for something to do, and was a little disappointed that she was not able to offer him a better position. Allen wanted to maintain his self-respect in front of this woman.

"O.K., I understand."

"You know what. I'll keep your resume on file and if by chance a position comes up that is more appropriate for you, I can put in the application for you."

"Thank you very much", said Allen brightening. It was almost as if she could read his mind. "I'd really appreciate that."

"Your welcome. And here's my card. My cell phone number is on the back. Feel free to call me anytime", and she gave Allen a knowing wink.

"Thanks, again. I'll be in touch", Allen said coyly. Allen was tempted by the young woman's offer. She was fine, but at the same time he was too busy. He couldn't think about playing the field when he was still trying to make it in the world.

Allen spent the next two hours scoping out businesses, introducing himself to representatives, handing out resumes, and collecting business cards, brochures, and applications. At one point, he discovered there were more employers on the floor above him and continued his search there. The better quality firms and positions were all upstairs. Allen put in applications for Prudential, ING, MetLife, Data Net, a information services company, Lifeline, a healthcare service provider for the elderly, and other businesses. When Allen had exhausted his supply of resumes and business cards, he decided to call it quits.

After nearly three hours, Allen had applied for at least fifty positions. Now all he could do was wait. That was the worst part. Most times Allen wouldn't hear anything from the companies he applied to, and if by chance he decided to call, he would get the obligatory apology followed by rejection. But at this point there was nothing else that he could do, and this frustrated him more than anything. Allen was used to getting things done, achieving, accomplishing things, and most importantly witnessing the tangible results from his hard work. Looking for work was the one challenge that left Allen feeling empty inside. He was putting in all of this work, but he wasn't getting anything out of it. And now that he had exhausted all of his options, he was not even able to think of what he could do anymore. So Allen looked back on the spectacle of people wandering about from booth to booth and decided to leave.

There was a separate exit for the Job Fair to keep things manageable. Allen looked around for the exit signs, which he quickly spotted and headed to the descending escalator at the back of the floor. As he was going down, one escalator and then the next, he could feel his strength, and hope evaporating from him. Today's excursion just seemed like an exercise in futility. He was leaving the same way he came in. Allen knew that it would be that way going in, but in the back of his mind he thought that maybe, just maybe….

As he left the Javits Center, Allen checked his watch. It was now 4:30 pm. It had stopped raining, but the sky was still gray and cloudy. Allen knew his mother had to be home by now, cooking dinner, and waiting for dad and himself. He knew she would want to know how his day went, and he wasn't in the mood to talk about it. His father would unrealistically expect Allen to have found employment. Then, when Allen had to explain that he hadn't, good old dad would start fussing about being picky. Allen walked down to the bus stop in front of the center over by the end of the block. Then he sat down, reached into his coat pocket, grabbed his cell phone, and dialed.

"Herns and Marshall, Business Services. Tim Russell, speaking."

"What's up man?"

"Allen! Long time, no speak. Did your thumbs give out on you?"

"Yeah, you could say that? Are you going to be busy for a while?"

"Kind of, but I should be done here in a hour or so? What's going on?"

"Not much. I just thought that since it's been a while since we've all seen each other, we might be able to just get together for dinner and kick it for a while."

"Okay, sure. What did you have in mind?"

"I was thinkin' Emily Ann's over by the park on 117th."

"Sounds good. What time?"

"How about 6:30?"

"Perfect. I'll call the girls, you call the rest of the guys."

"And maybe we can stop and see that new Denzel Washington film afterward."

"Great. Keep your line open and I'll let you know what the girls have to say."

"Okay, man."

When he heard Tim hang up, Allen quickly called his mother.

"Hello?" his mother answered after the second ring.

"Hey, ma. Have you got dinner on already?"

"I was just about to put together a lasagna. How was the job fair?"

"It was what it was."

"No luck?"

"I'll tell you about it later. Look ma, I wanted to tell you that I'm not going to be having dinner with you and dad tonight. Me and the guys are going to Emily Ann's"

"Oh, okay. So I won't make a big lasagna then. When do you think you'll be coming in?"

"I mean, I'll be by to change, but after that, I'm not sure. We might see a movie after dinner, so I may not be in until late."

"Allen, I know you have a lot going on right now, but I'd like to talk to you about something: tomorrow morning to be exact. You hear me, boy?"

"Yes, ma'am" Allen didn't like the sound of that. Yet another religious lecture, no doubt.

"O.K, now. Talk to you later."

As Allen ended his conversation, the bus pulled up to the stop. Allen reached into the inside pocket of his suit coat for his metro card. He boarded the bus, paid his fare and took a seat in one of the single-seaters on the left side. He would take the bus to Eighth Avenue and then walk down to the subway. As the bus took off, Allen took out his cell and sent texts to Richard and Jim.

"Hey. Everyone's meeting for dinner tonight. Emily Ann's, @6:30pm is the plan"

After scribing his text, he closed his phone and tucked it back into his pocket. It might be a while before he heard from either one of them, since Jim was still driving around in the underground and may not get the message until 6:00 anyway. And heaven only knew where Richard might be. "Maybe, I should have told Tim 7:00 instead of 6:30" Allen thought to himself. He didn't want Jim to have to rush over still in uniform or be late. Richard would be late, because Richard was always late.

It wasn't long before the bus pulled up to the stop on Eighth Avenue. Allen got off the bus and then walked down towards the train station. He didn't have far to go, but the crowd of pedestrians almost rendered the narrow streets impassable. As he walked toward the subway entrance, he could feel the vibrations from his phone in his pocket. Allen stopped and walked over toward a little deserted nook in front of a sneaker store before he checked the phone. Richard had responded.

"u no I'm dwn! See u 18r"

Allen was surprised to hear back from Richard so soon. It had been nearly two months since he had heard from him. He couldn't wait until this evening to find out just what the brother had been up to in all that time. Allen turned off the phone and then headed down the stairs toward the platform. When he got there, the station was crowded and hot. It didn't seem to matter that it was the beginning of November. In the tunnels, summer didn't end until December. Allen placed his briefcase on the platform between his legs and took off his black raincoat and folded it across arm, and pinned his umbrella against it. He shifted his weight from foot to foot as he waited impatiently. Allen wanted to have enough time so he could get to Emily Ann's a little early so he could get a booth, before the place got too crowded.

After a few minutes, Allen could hear the far away shriek of the train as it was nearing the station. He picked up his briefcase from where it had been resting and moved closer to the edge of the platform. When the train pulled in, there was a brief pause, before the doors opened and passengers poured out onto the platform. Allen waited until everyone had exited before he boarded the train. He was one of the first people on and was fortunate to find a window seat. He placed his briefcase and umbrella under his seat, folded his raincoat on his lap, leaned his head against a window, and zoned out trying to let go of all his frustration and anxiety about his future. He just wanted to concentrate on tonight, and the idea of enjoying the company of his friends. Allen hoped that they would all be able to attend and make it through the night without arguments or drama. He needed some fun and a break, especially since tomorrow morning the madness would start again. His mom wanted to "talk", and then his Dad would probably have something to say. Allen pushed these last thoughts out of his mind as he settled in for the long ride home. He didn't want to think about tomorrow. All he wanted to think about was tonight.

NINETEEN

Tim had sent a text to Callie and phoned Tamiko about dinner at Emily Ann's tonight. Both of them had agreed to come. This was the first Friday in a long time that Tim saw the prospect of getting off early, and the fact that he was going to get together with his friends made it just that much better. For the past two months, Tim had been working like a slave. Before the layoffs, Tim had just had to handle supply requests and processing for just one department, but now he had to oversee the supply requests for all of the departments. First, he had to come up with a plan to make sure that the transition went smoothly. Next, had to notify all of the departments of any and all changes ahead of time, make sure they were implemented, troubleshoot any rough spots, and it all had to be done within a week. Clara and Vera were practically lifesavers when it came to the memos, helping to create a new handbook for procedures, the Power Point presentation, and helping to train the staff. Then he had to train Preston, while figuring out a way to handle the increase in the volume of his work, without causing delays for the departments he was serving. Finally, there was interacting with the vendors and the big deal with the Brill Corporation that had to be finalized. At the start of this period of transition, Tim had virtually no social life. It was just get up go to work, then go home (usually bringing more work with him), watch the news, then go to bed and back to work the next morning.

Within the last two weeks, things began to improve. Tim was beginning to find his groove. He had developed a pacing plan to help him with the increased volume of work and was beginning to get used to the new momentum of the office. He was even beginning to come out ahead in certain areas. For example, he had just finished the department expenditure and cost projections for the reorganization plan that he thought would take him into another late night. Now the reorganization was finished, and everything was ready for the final presentation at the big meeting on Tuesday. Tim had just e-mailed it to the departments just before Allen called. Now there was nothing in his way to keep him from enjoying a night out with his friends.

Tim was looking forward to seeing everyone. It had been so long since they all had a real conversation. He wondered how Allen was faring with his job search, whether or not Tamiko and Callie had mended fences, and how Tamiko was making out with teaching. He hoped Richard would just stay in whatever hole he was hiding in. "He's probably in jail, where most hustlers wind up", Tim thought smugly to himself. Most of all, he was looking forward to relaxing and feeling human. All the time he was spending at work made him feel like a robot. Tim had just sent a quick text to Allen to confirm their plans when Preston Scott swaggered into the office about a half-hour late from lunch. He was carrying some mail and files that he had just received from either Clara or Vera, and was wearing a very self-satisfied expression. Preston had been with the firm for only a few months, but he was getting a lot of attention from co-workers and superiors. There was always someone who was inviting him out to lunch, and if it was a higher up, then he was sure to be late.

"Are those projections for the presentation ready yet?" asked Preston not even bothering to look at Tim directly.

"He has some nerve!" Tim thought to himself. "As if he's the boss!" It seemed as if all of the attention had gone to his head.

"I already e-mailed the entire plan to Standoff and had Clara send up a hard copy to the main office", Tim answered, trying to staunch the anger that was welling up inside him. He couldn't believe this guy. Preston was supposed to have helped to put the paper together, but between all of the impromptu social meetings with upper management executives and late lunches, the actual work Preston did was next to nothing. In fact, Tim had to have lunch in the office just to get the projections finished on time, not to mention all of the overtime he had already put in. Recent layoffs left much more work, which his new vice president provided very little help with.

COMMENCEMENT

"Without my approval?" responded Preston, irritation and annoyance in his voice.

"What else was I supposed to do? We have a deadline remember?"

"Which is Monday at 5:00, remember?"

"And you don't have to sign off personally on everything. I'm the head of the department. I'm the one who's going to be held accountable."

"I'm still supposed to know on what's going on, Tim. I don't like being out of the loop."

Tim swiveled his chair around to the computer console on the other side of his new smaller desk. Standoff had ordered all of Tim's furniture taken out and replaced with the new age, feng shui furniture, which he hated, just so Preston could have more space. For Tim, who was six feet one and a half and 160 pounds, it was like working in a Tiny Tikes play office. He then made a copy of the proposal and e-mailed it to Preston.

"There. I just e-mailed it to you", he said when he was done. "Now you have your very own copy to look at whenever you want."

"I wanted to be able to check to make sure that all of our bases were covered. I was just at lunch with the VP of human resources and I got some more ideas about how we could streamline operations here."

"If you'd like, you can always make an addendum and bring it to the meeting on Tuesday. Maybe they'll want us to factor it in next quarter's report. I just went ahead because we already had our guidelines to work with after we got feedback on the preliminary plan. Anything else will just get torpedoed at the meeting. It always does."

"I think Standoff will be pleased with what I have in mind."

"And that is?"

"You'll find out on Tuesday, after I've written the addendum."

'Touché" thought Tim as he noticed how Preston was trying to bite back. Tim knew he'd have the last laugh anyway. They never listened to the lower level officers at those meetings. Even if they liked his idea, if he couldn't spin it in a way to make them think it was their idea all along, they'd hang him and take credit anyway. After all, that's what they had done to Tim about a million times. Tim should have taken him under his wing and told him all of this. He wanted to, but in his heart he knew better. At best, a guy like Preston would think that he was being negative, and at worst, he would go back and tell the higher ups what he said and then he'd really be in for it. "No", Tim thought, "I'll just let Preston find out all these things for himself". They were treating him like their little wonder boy now just to feel him out and get a sense of what he was like. Once they'd gotten used to him and learned enough about him to put him in his place, he'd end up just like Tim. Then maybe he would help Preston out. Maybe.

"I see you've taken care of our e-mails for new orders. Is there anything that you might be able to swing my way?"

"No, I'm taking care of them", Tim said casually. He knew better than to let Preston handle any of the new requests anymore. When he was hired, Tim specifically trained him on how to handle the new intakes, and oversaw him as he handled his first few. Tim thought Preston was capable of doing a good job. He was great on the phone and seemed to handle the orders promptly, and knew to check and cross-check with the budget and existing intakes. Having gained confidence in his protégé, Tim was willing to allow Preston to handle all the new intakes while he handled more complex tasks like finding new vendors that provided great quality and service for less, as well as the tracking and billing to various departments. However, once left to himself, Preston tended to drop the ball. A lot. And Tim was always held accountable. Twice Preston had not responded to departments with regard to statuses of their orders. Preston even delayed the processing of a request for some important software that was needed for a presentation up in accounting and the boss over there was so upset, he complained to Standoff. Luckily, Tim got off with just a humiliating public berating. Then Tim tried to train Preston to be more of a liaison between the department and the vendors and utilize Preston's customer service skills. While Preston was able to talk a good game and make people feel comfortable, he didn't get much work done. Whenever Tim asked him for a status on something, it was always "I'm still working on it." And if Preston wasn't "working on" something, he was passing off work to Clara the admin, which wasn't fair to her. So Tim had to pretty much handle most of the work himself.

COMMENCEMENT

"You always say that. Then you end up working through lunch, and staying late when you don't have to. I'm the Vice-President, your co-leader. Let me help you. I can't do that unless you give me something I can cut my teeth on."

Tim wanted to tell Preston that he had his chance, but he blew it. But he knew he had to take a more diplomatic approach. So instead, Tim took off his glasses, rubbed his eyes and began to address the man in front of him.

"Preston, my friend, you have only been working here for about two months. It's going to take some time before I put you on a major project. For the time being, I think you just need to work on observing and familiarizing yourself with the procedures and routines. I know a lot of the tasks I'm giving you right now may seem fairly mundane, but some of this stuff has got to become second nature before you get into the larger projects", Tim lectured, hoping that he wasn't sounding as condescending as he really wanted to be.

"Tim, would you mind closing the door? I'd like to speak with you privately for a moment."

This couldn't be good. Tim wondered what Preston wanted to talk about. With Preston's disappointing performance over the last few weeks, Tim felt he should have been the one uttering those words. Tim decided to humor him to find out what this was all about. He walked over to close the door, then came back and pulled a chair up to Preston's desk. He tried to appear concerned and conceal his usual sarcastic smirk.

"Tim, I don't want you to get offended, and I'm going to try to say this with as much tact as possible. I know that you're used to being your own man, and very much used to being one of the few African-Americans with any kind of rank in the company."

"And your point is?" Tim sighed heavily.

"The point is, that I don't want you to think that I'm some kind of threat to you."

Tim had to look away from him at this point, so Preston wouldn't notice the smirk that always crossed his face before he was about to let someone have it with some of his trademark sarcasm.

"Really? And just what makes you think I feel 'threatened'?" he said using air quotes. Tim leaned back in his chair, crossed his arms and couldn't help but give Preston an incredulous look. Truth be told, Tim was intimidated by Preston at first, but once he realized that Preston probably couldn't chew gum and walk at the same time, such feelings evaporated. The only thing Tim felt now was a righteous indignation at the fact that Preston had gained the favor of so many people with so little justification for it.

"Well, for instance, the way you've been keeping me from handling major tasks, and leaving me out of major decisions. If I didn't know any better, I might think that you're purposefully trying to make me look bad."

"Preston, really, I'm not trying to make you look bad. As a matter of fact, what would make you think that you 'look bad'?" he said using his air quotes again. "Has someone complained about your performance here?"

"I feel like my talents are being wasted."

Tim could not help the palm-to-face gesture, upon hearing this. Was he stupid or just audacious? Either way, Preston desperately needed a review of the "facts".

"Preston, a few weeks ago, I had you handle some new intakes. Do you remember what happened with those intakes?" Tim asked pointedly.

"Those orders were processed."

"Then how come several very important people sent me some very angry emails? Hmm?"

"Everyone got what they wanted in the end. There were just a few lapses in communication, that's all. I don't think it means I should never handle another transaction again…"

"And what about when I asked you to help me wrap up the deal with the Brill Corporation? All you had to do was get them the contract to sign and send back. We needed that contract on Standoff's desk ASAP."

COMMENCEMENT

"I was just trying to get background information."

"You didn't need background information! It was a done deal. And I didn't know that it was Clara's job to handle the spreadsheets for the reorganization we were working on."

"I delegated the job to Clara, that's what Vice Presidents do. Besides in every case no harm was done…"

"Because, I picked up the ball, not to mention the heat from everyone upstairs."

"Or because you are the President of this division, and that's your job."

"My job is to oversee the smooth operation of this department, not to clean up after you, or hold your hand while you work. If you want more responsibility, you're going to have to show me that you're ready for it", Tim found himself saying sternly.

When he realized how intense the situation was becoming, Tim decided to back off. He didn't want this to turn into an angry confrontation. The next thing you know, good ol' Preston would run off crying to co-workers and starting gossip mill rumors that Tim was out to get him. He may even go blubbering to one of the higher-ups he had been getting cozy with.

"Look, I'll be fair. You're going to be working on this addendum, right? How about we make that your first big project. You can put all of your wonderful ideas in it."

"With all due respect Tim, my ideas should have been included from the get-go. They would have, if you hadn't been in such a rush to make yourself look like the eleventh hour savior", pouted Preston, unsatisfied with Tim's token concession.

"Or, if you hadn't have taken a two hour lunch."

"That wasn't just some frivolous lunch. It was a business meeting. I'm not a slacker Tim."

"I never said you were. But I'm giving you based on what you're giving me. If I get little, then I give little. When I get more from you, I'll give you more."

"That's like a catch 22 isn't it? How can I give you more, when I have so little to work with? In fact, if I didn't know any better, I would think you were purposely trying to sabotage my career."

Tim wanted to say that he didn't have to sabotage Preston. Preston was doing a very good job of that himself. But Tim knew those were fighting words. He didn't want to fight. Tim always chose his battles carefully, and this was not worth fighting over. After all, he knew he had the upper hand if Preston wanted to go complaining. Tim had been collecting a mountain of evidence against Preston, as a safety measure. So to keep the conflict from escalating…

"You're wrong. Just work on the Addendum."

Tim got up and took his seat back to his own desk. He couldn't believe how Preston just seemed so obstinately convinced about the slighting of his self-perceived genius.

At this point, Tim would have loved nothing more than to just grab his coat and leave, but he still had a few more hours to go before he could leave for the day. The tension in the office air was so thick, Tim felt like he was suffocating. He could feel the heat from Preston as he sat stewing in his animosity and disappointment. Preston thought he was holding him back, and in the business world, if you felt someone was holding you back then you had to deal with that person. Tim knew Preston would do something to get back at him, but he would have to wait until that shoe dropped to know exactly what it was. All of a sudden, Tim felt another wave of nausea wash over him. It made him a little disoriented and he thought he would vomit at any moment, but then the feeling passed. "I probably just need some air", Tim thought to himself. He had been having a lot of nausea lately, mostly in the mornings, and headaches but Tim just attributed this to the fact that he'd been under a lot of stress with the reorganization of his department. Not to mention that Preston himself was a headache. The fact that he hadn't been eating well didn't help matters, either. Since Tim had been working so hard, he hadn't really been paying attention to what he ate. Most times it was a cup of coffee here, a sandwich there, and maybe a donut or two in between. Tim hadn't had a decent balanced meal since as Allen's graduation party. He decided to go to the canteen to get some seltzer water. That always helped. Tim was definitely not going to let any physical problems interfere with his plans for tonight.

"I'll be back in five if anyone needs me", Tim said talking into the air. His comment was met by a chilly silence. Apparently Preston was either deep into what he was doing or he was still sulking. "Yeah, let him bring it. Tim thought. I'll be ready."

TWENTY

Emily Ann's was packed when Allen arrived. There were lots of students and professors from the local college having dinner as well as a lot of swanky upper Harlemites. He looked around for a booth, but didn't see one that was big enough for him and his friends. Suddenly and miraculously, a large party of college kids left one of the booths and Allen swooped down on it before one of the waitresses had a chance to clean up.

"I hope I'm not inconveniencing you", Allen said to the large brown skinned waitress in her green and white uniform. Allen could see the beads of perspiration forming along the perimeter of her forehead. She was obviously working hard tonight.

"It's no problem, I understand. It is really crowded. If it wasn't you there'd be someone else", the waitress smiled pleasantly as she continued to work.

Just as they had finished the exchange, Callie walked in. She had her black wool toggle coat over one arm and looked absolutely striking in a purple velour suit jacket with a contrasting lavender v-neck cashmere sweater, and lavender wool A-line skirt. She also had a purple shoulder bag and matching knee-high boots. Callie wore her hair down and parted to one side. Her outfit was a perfect fit as always, showing off her perfect hour-glass figure. Then there was her bright white smile that completed everything. Sometimes when Allen looked at her he thought, "Truly this is a Black Venus", and he had to remind himself that they were "just friends". At first, she didn't see where he was, so he waved his hand to get her attention.

"Callie, over here!" he called, trying not to shout.

COMMENCEMENT

"Hey, you! How you doin'?" Callie greeted him warmly with a hug. She then kissed him on the cheek and settled herself down right next to him in the booth.

"Not as good as you, I see. Lookin' like somethin' off the cover of Essence."

"Thank you," Callie blushed, hoping Allen wouldn't notice. "I still can't believe we're doin' this. When I got the text from Tim, I had to read it twice because I just couldn't believe it. Was this his idea?"

"No, it was mine this time."

"So, is there some special reason for this?" asked Callie, coyly. She was wondering if maybe Allen had gotten lucky and finally found a good job. She didn't want to ask outright because if he didn't, she didn't want to bring up something that would be troubling to him. He seemed in such good spirits and she didn't want to ruin his mood. It had been a long time since she'd seen him so happy.

"Not really. I just thought since we hadn't seen each other in so long, it would be great to get together, catch up, and have some fun. Just like in the old days." Allen sensed what Callie was getting at, but veered away from the topic. Callie immediately understood and went no further. Then before anything else could be said, Allen heard...

"Hey, man! What's Up?"

It was Jim. He had spotted Allen and Callie while they were chatting and decided to walk up and surprise them. "He must have gotten off early", Allen surmised to himself. Jim was wearing a brown field coat, with leather detailing. He took it off to reveal a black mock neck, and dark blue rinsed jeans. Allen got up and pulled him in for the "man-hug". Then Jim hugged Callie who had also stood up. Then they all sat down again. And Jim sat on the other side of Callie.

"I hadn't heard from you in so long, I thought I had missed the funeral" Jim quipped. They all had to chuckle at Jim's joke.

"You did. I just came back from the dead", Allen joked back.

"Welcome back to the land of the living, man."

As Allen and Jim were talking, Callie noticed Tim walking in.

"Hey, there's Tim. Tim, over here!" Callie called as she waved her slender arms. Tim had changed out of the business suit he wore at the office and was looking way more casual than usual. He had on a black wool crepe sport jacket and a fitted black shirt that wasn't tucked in, close fitting low-rise dark blue jeans, and black and white Chuck Taylor sneakers. He wasn't even wearing his glasses, and his hair looked like it had been washed, but it wasn't gelled, so in place of his usual golden waves, his hair was curly and noticeably uncombed. Tim was a little paler and thinner than usual, not to mention he looked a little worn out.

"Whoa", said Jim as Tim approached.

"That's a new look." chuckled Callie.

"What in the world happened to you?" asked Allen, unable to cover the shock from his friend's haggard appearance.

"Don't tell me that new guy whupped your behind already?" joked Jim.

"Nice to see you all, too", said Tim derisively as he slumped down next to Jim and took off his sport coat and rolled up the sleeves of his shirt.

"Looks like he beat about 10 pounds off him", Jim continued.

"No, really man. What's going on with you? You don't look so good", said Allen with some concern.

"You wouldn't look good either if you'd gotten a total of about 3 hours of sleep in the past two months. I've literally been doing the work of 4 people since the downsizing."

"Wasn't your V.P. supposed to have been helping you?" asked Callie.

"My new V.P. is a jackass. The less said the better. Is this everyone? I thought Miko said she was coming", Tim said looking around.

"Oh, look, there she is!" Allen said, spotting her before the rest of the party. Tamiko was wearing a heather grey overcoat and matching beret. She took off her coat as she approached, revealing a close fitting heather gray turtleneck, and long flared black wool skirt that stopped just below her knees and matching black knee high boots. Tim moved over so she could squeeze in next to him.

"Hey, everyone", said Tamiko, her voice lacking it's usual enthusiasm. "Sorry if I'm late. I made the mistake of taking the bus. Seems like that's all I do is make mistakes lately."

"Uh-oh, not another one", said Jim.

"What?" asked Miko petulantly.

"Did you have a bad day at the office, too?" asked Allen.

"'Bad' would be an understatement...." Tamiko paused as she suddenly she noticed Tim's new look. She had to do a double take to make sure it was indeed him.

"Tim?"

"Yes?"

"Are you okay?"

"I am now. But I want to hear more about what's got you so down", he said taking her hand to her surprise. Jim noticed too, and hunched Callie who rolled her eyes.

"Uh...," she said, carefully withdrawing her hand. "Today I had my first assessment meeting with the principal and the rest of the school leadership team, and they basically told me that I'm a screw up."

"What?! But you got straight A's as a student teacher!" said Allen.

"But in the real world, it looks like I get an F."

"Aw, don't worry, Miko", said Tim this time putting his arm around her. "They probably say that to all the first year teachers during the first meeting."

"No! You don't understand!" she said pushing his arm away "They had this spreadsheet, and based on the 'data', I was the worst of all of the new teachers! To top it off, the person who is supposed to help me improve is a racist who hates African-Americans."

Tamiko covered her face with her hands and began sobbing. Everyone at the table was silent.

"Are you sure?" asked Allen.

"That's the word going around the school", cried Tamiko.

"Look, Miko, I'm really sorry."

"Hmm. So I guess I'm not crazy", said Jim.

"Jim, not tonight", warned Allen.

"Miko," Tim said softly rubbing her back, then embracing her "How about we all agree to forget about work and just have some fun tonight? I mean, that's why we all came here. Right?"

Tamiko nodded her head against Tim's chest. He grabbed some napkins from the dispenser on the table and gave them to Tamiko to wipe her eyes. She then straightened herself up next to Tim, but he kept a supportive arm around her. Callie rolled her eyes and sighed heavily. Allen put his hand on Callie's and cut her a look that said, "Now don't start". Jim smirked and shook his head at Tim, who kept his attention focused on Tamiko.

"I'm so sorry about this. I'm ruining dinner for everyone", Tamiko gasped between sobs.

"It's okay Miko. I…we totally understand. The workplace is really brutal out there now. Everyone's going through something nowadays", said Tim.

"Yeah, don't worry about it", Allen reassured her. "Everyone needs space to vent."

"Now that everyone is here, let's order. I know a hot meal might make every one feel better", said Tim.

"Hold on," Allen interjected, "Richard hasn't gotten here yet."

"And he may not get here until Christmas, but I would like to eat before then", Tim sniped.

"He's got a point, Al. You know Richard is always late", seconded Jim.

COMMENCEMENT

Allen assented to his friends' suggestion and he signaled to the waitress that they wanted to order. Allen, and Jim ordered the barbeque spareribs, Callie ordered the hoppin' johns with oxtail and collard greens, Tamiko and Tim ordered baked chicken with wild rice and salad. They all chipped in for a pitcher of Cola to wash everything down, and Jim insisted on getting himself a bottle of Corona. Of the whole crowd, Jim and Tim were the only ones who really drank alcohol of any kind. At times, Jim would drink beer, and Tim would drink some fancy wine or champagne, depending on the occasion. The rest of them rarely ever drank because they simply never got into it. The mood was still flat, but soon Tim brought up a lighter topic while they were waiting for their food.

"Oh, Allen, I got the tickets for the movie. We're in the 9:05 show", Tim said fishing in his pockets for the tickets. Then he gave them out. He handed Richard's to Allen.

"What movie?" asked Callie.

"You know, the one with Denzel and Kerry Washington", answered Allen.

"I've been dying to see that movie!" said Tamiko, her spirits beginning to rise.

"Anything with Kerry Washington in it is good for me. She is fione!" enthused Jim.

"I hope Richard gets here before we head off to the movie at least. I wanted to hear what he'd been up to all this time", said Allen.

"He's probably been in jail, or hiding from the cops", said Tim matter of factly.

"I don't think so. Rich is too smooth for that. He knows how to take care of himself", replied Jim.

"So did Capone, but they got him too", Tim insisted.

"C'mon, Tim. That's not fair. Richard is nothing like Capone or even these brothers on the corner, and you know it. He's just a brother trying to make a livin' the best way he knows how", Callie said in Richard's defense.

"Yeah, and he is makin' it, you gotta give him props for that. And as far as I'm concerned, as long as no one is getting hurt or killed, I don't have a problem", added Jim.

"But people *are* getting hurt. What do you think happens to artists when their works are pirated, and designers who get their profits cut into by people selling counterfeits? The regular people like us suffer, too, especially when the prices for these things go up", reasoned Tim.

"So? Those corporate fat cats are always thinking of ways to steal money from the little man. So what if the little man finds a way to get a cut for himself?" Jim shot back.

"I don't know, Jim. I'd have to agree with Tim on this. Two wrongs don't make a right. And I don't know about anyone else, but I would also have to think about what God has to say about what I'm doing. Piracy is stealing and stealing is wrong, not matter what kind of spin you put on it", said Tamiko, supporting Tim.

"I couldn't have said it better myself. Thank you, Miko", Tim smiled at Tamiko and she smiled back nervously.

"And there you have it. The gospel according to Ned and Maude Flanders", Jim joked.

"Ha-Ha. Very funny", said Tim.

"I'm not convinced the brother is doing anything illegal", Allen insisted. "Richard sells stuff, but I've never seen any evidence that any of the stuff he's selling is stolen or counterfeit. I bought a DVD of that movie *The Great Debaters* from him and there was nothing bootleg about it. I mean I got all the special features and everything."

"Allen, don't be so naïve. You're his best friend and you know where he lives. Of course he's not going to try to put one over on you!" Tim argued.

"You know what? How about we ask Richard himself when he gets here, rather than making baseless speculations behind his back? And Tim, I'm warning you. If and when Richard does show up, you better behave. Everyone wants to have a good time tonight, and no one wants to listen to you and Richard fighting", warned Callie, her eyes narrowing and finger wagging in Tim's direction.

"Yes, mother. But what if he starts it?" mocked Tim.

"Then you end it, or I will", Callie admonished.

"How so? Will you give me a spanking when I get home?" suggested Tim with a sly smile.

Allen and Jim, who both found Tim's insinuation amusing couldn't help chuckling to themselves. Meanwhile the looks on Callie and Tamiko's faces showed they were not.

"You might want to keep your inappropriate innuendos to yourself. Remember, you are in the company of ladies", said Tamiko sharply.

"Sorry."

Tim, stung by Tamiko's reproof, refrained from further comment. After a moment, the doors of Emily Ann's burst open and Richard appeared with a young, slender, almond colored young woman on his arm. Richard was dressed in a Roca Wear denim suit and sporting brand new Jordans. His date wore a car coat over a camel-colored skirt suit with matching high heels.

"Whassup, Dogs!"

"Hey man, we almost thought you weren't going to make it. And who might this beautiful young lady be?" asked Allen.

"Allen, Everybody, this is my boo Leandra Wilson. Leandra these are my peeps Allen, Callie, Jim, Miko, and I want to say that's Tim, but right now, I don't know. It looks more like Buckwheat fell into some bleach and got a texturizer."

Jim and Allen laughed. Callie and Tim exchanged angry looks, right before everyone greeted Leandra.

"Hey, nice to meet you all", said Leandra.

"Y'all don't mind her kickin' it wit' us, right?"

"Of course we don't mind, but I don't know if we're going to have enough space. We're going to need some more chairs."

Allen got up and signaled to the waitress to bring an extra chair to the booth so Leandra could sit down. While the waitress was there, she also took Jim and Leandra's order. Two fried chicken platters with biscuits and gravy.

"So where have you been man? You have definitely been MIA; you don't return calls or texts or nothing. What's up with that?" asked Jim.

"Yo, man, I been handlin' some deep stuff. I been on the trail wit the democrats and all dem tryin to get a black man in the White House, youknowwhatimsayin. That's how I met Leandra here."

"You mean you've been campaigning for Barak Obama!" said Tamiko excitedly.

"Word, yo!"

"Man, that's awesome!" Allen exclaimed, "How did you get involved in that?"

"O.K, now, what had happened was, I was walkin' down 125th street and 5th right, and Leandra was out there recruitin' brothers and sisters to get into the game. You know she was really breakin' it down about how the brothers and sisters need to come together and support each other, you know. And I was like you know what? It's time for a brother to start puttin' all that solidarity talk into action. Next thing you know, I'm sendin' out e-mails, makin' phone calls, interviewing people, scheduling rallies, travelin' all that."

"So you even went out of state?!" asked Tamiko.

"Yeah, I was in Virginia, The Carolinas, Florida, all up and down the southeast, burinin' up the road."

"I wish I had time to go on the road like that." Tim thought bitterly to himself, but he remembered what Callie said and merely asked, "So, Leandra, how did you get involved with the campaign?"

"I work in the democratic party office here in New York. So this is my job year round. If it's not Obama, then there's someone else we're campaigning for."

"I see. Have either of you had a chance to meet Obama in person?" Tim questioned further.

"I got to shake hands with him in Virginia, but Leandra here got to sit down and parlay with the brother?"

"Wow! This is so exciting!" gushed Tamiko, "I can't believe I'm sitting here with people who have actually met Barak Obama. C'mon now, dish! What is the man like?"

"Or more importantly what is his policy like? What is he going to do for us?" asked Jim.

Before either Jim or Leandra could answer, two waitresses appeared with their meals. Everyone was served except for Richard and Leandra who had just had their orders taken. While everyone ate, Leandra began to answer their questions.

"To be honest, Obama has never addressed me personally. I've just heard him speak in person. Maybe just shaken hands with him once or twice. He seems really nice and genuine in his concern about the problems our country is facing right now. From what I've heard, I think he has what it takes to put this country back on its feet. But I'm curious to know what you all think."

"You don't need to use the sales pitch on me. He's got my vote already", said Allen.

"Word, boo. I don't think there's anybody here who ain't down with Obama. Except maybe Annie over there" Richard said gesturing toward Tim. Tim clenched his jaw and glared at Richard, who noticed the angry expression. "C'mon man, you know I had to rif on those girlie curls at some point."

"Riiicharddd...chill" sang Callie with warning in her voice.

"Look, Leandra, I'll agree that Obama is a better choice than McCain right now, but that doesn't mean that I necessarily agree with his whole agenda. Personally, I thought Hillary Clinton would have made a better candidate", stated Tim.

"You can't mean the same Clinton who thinks that LBJ did more for Black people than Martin Luther King, Jr.!" exclaimed Jim in disbelief.[1]

"Everyone keeps bringing up that remark and taking it way out of context", Tim continued.

"I think they pretty much got it right on point. Especially with the way she thought she had the primary in her pocket because she was white", Leandra commented.

"I still disagree. I think a lot of people are just going with Obama solely because he's black. I think that's a dangerous slope to go down. Just think about how a lot of people came out to support Clarence Thomas after he accused the senate of "lynching" him. What's important are the issues, not the skin color", explained Tim.

"You can't compare Obama with Clarence Thomas. Clarence Thomas had a clear conservative history, and Obama doesn't", argued Leandra.

"That's right, preach boo!"

"You're right! Obama doesn't have a history, period. He hasn't been in politics long enough. We don't really know how he's going to handle our issues, or if he'll handle them at all! That's why I think it's ridiculous that there are all these African-Americans acting as if he's the Moses of the Millennium", countered Tim.

"Yeah, Tim, I have to say, I feel you on that. There have been too many so called African-American leaders who use us to get to positions of power and then they give us nothin' in return. I'm willing to give the brother a chance with my vote, but I'm not going to get my hopes up", added Jim.

"But maybe if we got a brother in the White House, he'll do some lookin' out for brothers like Allen over here. Which reminds me, Allen, you still ain't got no gig yet?" Richard asked.

Leave it to Richard to ask the question no one else would dare to. Everyone looked down and stirred in their plates with their forks and avoided eye contact. Leandra looked at all of them in bewilderment. There was a brief pause before Allen finally spoke.

COMMENCEMENT

"I went to a job fair earlier today, and put out some resumes. Maybe I'll get a call, but at this point I've learned I shouldn't hold my breath", Allen admitted.

"See, now that don't make no sense!" Richard fumed. "You got brothers like Allen who got the education, degrees, all that, and they go and give the jobs to white guys who don't even have half that! This is why we need a brother in the White House!"

"Even if there is a brother in the White House, there's still going to be racism. There's still going to be prejudice and discrimination", Tamiko insisted.

"But maybe he can influnce some bills, get some reforms in our favor", reasoned Leandra.

"I understand what you're saying Leandra, but man has been making laws for a long time. First we had the 13th, 14th, and 15th Amendments, then the Civil Rights Act of 1866, then the Civil Rights Act of 1964 and the Voting Rights Act of 1965, then Affirmative Action legislation on top of that. How many laws have been passed and yet the racists find a way around them? I believe that all the problems that have been plaguing our country are not problems with laws, but problems with the human heart. You can change laws until the end of the world, but you can't change people's hearts. Only God can do that."

"What do you mean?" asked Leandra.

"I mean that we can't look to Obama, and we can't look to laws alone for our help as a people. We have to look to God."

"Not again", whispered Callie under her breath. Allen slumped back in his seat and covered his face with his hands. The last thing he wanted to hear was yet another sermon.

"Tamiko, let's not...."

"Here's a fact for you who don't believe. Our first political association was the church. During slavery it was the only institution that we were allowed to participate in. The civil rights movement started in our churches. It was rooted in our belief that God made us, and that we deserved equal rights based on the rights He gave us. We were at our

147

strongest then. Once Martin Luther King, Jr., a man of God, died, and the movement was taken out of the church, everything collapsed and we've made no real progress since. I don't think that was just a coincidence."

"So, what are you saying? That we should all just stop being politically active and just pray our problems away?" asked Leandra.

"I'm not saying that we shouldn't be politically active. Of course we need to vote, and support our institutions, and politicians. But I also think that we need to be spiritually active, too."

"I guess that means we should go out and vote, and then pray that our candidate wins", laughed Tim.

"I know you all think I'm crazy and you don't want to hear this, but I'm gonna say it anyway. I think that we need to let the Word lead us in our politics, rather than the other way around. Look at our communities. They are suffering because of problems with drugs, crime, and poverty. And think about the staggering numbers of African-Americans that go to church, mega churches even. Most of us go to church to hear the Word on Sunday, but never put that Word into action for the rest of the week. I believe that if more people did what Christ said to do, we wouldn't have a lot of the problems we have now."

"That could be said about all of America Miko, not just black America", remarked Tim.

"And what about those people who are not Christians?" asked Callie.

"True. For you to try to make Christian ethics the standard in this country would assume that you and all the people who believe like you are right, and everyone else is wrong", said Leandra.

"So?" said Tamiko defiantly.

"So, you've never heard of a thing called 'ethical relativism'?" asked Tim.

"I know what you're talking about, Tim. I've studied it in philosophy classes at Spelman, but I don't buy all that. I do believe there is such a thing as absolute 'right' and 'wrong'. If there isn't then what keeps people from eventually saying something like murder is okay, just so long as everyone agrees it is? What would keep people from executing a holocaust

148

against African-Americans, or any other people, if there were some tacit agreement among the majority? Just think about what happened in Nazi Germany during World War II. There has to be some authority higher than man that we subscribe to or we're all in trouble."

"Correct me if I'm wrong, but you're saying that the only person who can help us is God, right?" Jim asked with an agenda.

"Yes", she answered confidently.

"If God wants to help us, why doesn't he? You're right. There are a lot of problems in our community and in the world in general. So how come He doesn't come down and do something about these things? There's lot's of prayin' people out there, believing their hearts out, dedicating their lives to Him, and most of them are suffering maybe even more so than the people who don't give a crap. Now how do you explain that?"

"I....I guess I can't" said Tamiko. It made her think about her own situation at work. She didn't really understand why things were going so badly for her either, despite the fact that she recently devoted her whole life to God, and despite the fact that God had told her teaching was her calling.

"Bingo!" said Jim.

"But that doesn't mean...."

"Oh, just can it, Tamiko, will ya! If you were right about anything it's that nobody wants to hear it. Honestly if you're going to keep doing this every time we get together, maybe next time we'll leave you out" said Allen almost glaring at her.

Tamiko's eyes caught his and her face noticeably reddened and became crestfallen. Callie let out a loud unexpected cackle, and Jim snickered.

"Oh snap, that was cold!" jeered Richard.

"Not to mention rude", scowled Tim. "Really, Allen. Was that necessary?"

Allen, realizing the effect of his words as he looked at Tamiko's saddened visage, felt remorseful.

"Tamiko, I'm sorry…"

"No, I'm sorry. Sorry I came", said Tamiko, her voice quivering as she hastily grabbed her coat. She took out her wallet and threw a twenty and a ten into the center of the table to pay for her meal.

"Tamiko, c'mon…it's just that with everything that's been going down…"

"Save it, Allen!" she said cutting him off and putting on her coat. Then Allen noticed Tim was getting ready to leave as well.

"And where are you going?"

"Someone's got to make sure she get's home."

"But this was supposed to be our crew's night out?"

"Tim, it's okay. You stay if you want. I'll be alright. It's not that late."

"It's no problem. Besides, I wouldn't feel right with you being out there all alone."

"Fine. Goodnight, everyone."

Tamiko was about to walk off, but turned around suddenly.

"Oh, it was nice meeting you, Leandra."

"I guess I'll see you guys later. Leandra, take care of yourself", said Tim before he stalked off behind Tamiko. Finally, the waitress returned with two more plates for Richard and Leandra.

"Is everyone leaving?" asked the waitress.

"No, just the cry baby drama queen and the jerk, thankfully. Maybe now we can have some peace", said Callie.

"Man, every time we get together lately its just drama."

"Sorry, Rich. It was my fault. I shouldn't have said what I said", said Allen with regret.

"Oh, you're such a 'Mr. Nice Guy'. C'mon, Allen, she was asking for it", said Callie.

"No, I was angry about my situation and I was taking it out on her. Tim was right. It was uncalled for."

"You did apologize. Don't beat yourself up about it."

"Yeah, man. Don't sweat it. She'll get over it. She always does. And don't worry about Tim. He's just trying to 'get the draws'. If you know what I mean", smirked Jim as he hunched Allen.

"What?!" asked Allen in surprise and shock.

"What you mean 'what?!'? Don't tell me you didn't notice the way that brother was straight beastin' over her since she sat down?" Jim turned to Callie, taking her hand in an effort to mimick Tim. "I wouldn't feel right with you out there all alone." Callie giggled at Jim's impression. "I'm telling you man, the brother is sprung."

"Nah, man, I don't know. Guys like him don't never get with no sisters. They go after the white chicks. Ain't that right, Allen?"

"Tim's actually an equal-opportunity player, but the majority of the women he dates tend to be sisters", said Allen thoughtfully almost to himself.

"I think they'd make the perfect couple, sort of like cheap booze and a hangover", said Callie.

"Tim's all wrong for her", said Allen seriously.

"Why would you say that?" asked Callie trying not to show concern.

"Trust me. He's way too complicated for Tamiko."

"I know she doesn't always act like it, but Tamiko is a big girl. And I think you give Tim way too much credit. He's about as complicated as first grade math", said Callie dismissively.

"You can say that again. Ain't no way she gon' want some corny brother like Tim", said Richard. "And from the looks of him tonight, I think he might be on that stuff. Ain't no way Tamiko tryin' to get with no brothers on that stuff."

"He is not on any 'stuff', man. Stop playin'", smiled Allen.

"C'mon, you know them corporate types like the blow, and he gettin' all skinny like that, what else could it be?"

"Trust me. I've seen him like this before, and it has nothing to do with drugs. He just lets himself get way overstressed sometimes."

"Anyway, man, you know Miko. There's no way he's going to get them draws without a ring. He'd have better luck trying to get into Fort Knox", Jim put in.

"Hey it's getting late. We better hurry or we'll miss our show. Are you guys ready?"

"Yeah, I'm done. What about you Lee?"

"Oh, sure."

"Wait a minute", said Callie "What about Leandra? She doesn't have a ticket."

"That's okay, we'll just grab one for her at the theatre. The line shouldn't be that long anyway at this time of night."

Allen went to settle the tab, while the others got their things together to get ready to go to the theatre. He was so disappointed with how the night was turning out. It seemed no matter how hard he tried the same issues kept confronting him. His unemployment, his relationship with God, and now he had to worry about Tamiko and Tim. There was no way he was going to be able to enjoy the movie now. While he didn't think he had any romantic feelings for Tamiko, he certainly harbored the over-protectiveness that would inevitably develop in their sibling-like relationship. Tim was a good friend, but there was no way he was going to allow Tamiko to become one of his "women". He seriously hoped Jim was wrong. He would have to talk to Tim tomorrow and get things straight.

TWENTY-ONE

Allen awoke the next morning to the smell of frying bacon, crisp hash browns and freshly brewed coffee. He knew this was a trick to get him up and downstairs for a little "talk". His mom knew what his favorite foods were and she always used them to manipulate him into doing something he didn't want to do. He remembered the time when his mom wanted him to join the boy scouts. She brought home a pizza with all of his favorite toppings to convince him the boy scouts were worth a shot. Being only 8 he fell for it. Allen was now way too old to be taken in by a good meal. He just knew the "talk" would end up nothing but an argument replete with recriminations and result in alienated feelings at best. So he decided he would simply feign sleep until breakfast was over and his parents went out on errands. Then he would slip outside for a walk to clear his head.

Allen turned over and pulled the covers over his head. He tried in vain to fall asleep again, but once his brain was on it was no use. All he could think of was the fact that it was another day and he still didn't have a job or a prospect for one. It was now going on six months since his first interview, and to his 22-year-old mind, it seemed like forever. He had exhausted every conceivable resource, every avenue of hope. He had attempted to make networks with important people, went to agencies, and scouted job fairs (well the jury was still out on this prospect). Even though there were jobs that he probably could get if he downplayed his resume, his pride still wouldn't allow him to go there. There was just no way he was going to work at McDonald's or Baskin Robbins, nor was he going to stand on the corner. Tim and Tamiko had the nerve to complain about their jobs. If they were in his situation, they'd actually have something to complain about.

"Maybe you should just give up", he heard a voice inside his head say. Allen surely felt like he wanted to. But then he'd really be a loser. He'd be just like all the other brothers out there who didn't even try. Actually, he'd be worse because he had tried and failed. Then, as time went by, his friends would move onward and upward in their careers. Sure they complained now, but what they were experiencing were just temporary setbacks. Jim would become Attorney General, Tamiko would be schools Chancellor, Tim would have his own company, Callie would be on the board of directors at the hospital, and Richard would be the owner of a fortune 500 company. As they moved forward, Allen would be stuck. They would soon wonder why they were hanging out with such a loser and then they would make excuses. "Sorry, Allen, I have a meeting", "I just can't make it, I have to work late", "I have a very important project that's due tomorrow", they'd say. It had already started happening anyway. Sooner or later, he wouldn't get any calls or get any of his calls returned and he would find himself alone. He wouldn't even be able to blame them.

The worse things went for Allen, the worse he felt. He even noticed his personality had changed. The formerly 'happy-go-lucky' Allen, now snapped at everyone, and what happened with Miko at Emily-Ann's happened at home as well. His father multiplied threats to "put him out", and even his mom, who was more understanding than humanly possible, was beginning to lose her patience.

"Maybe it's you" he heard the voice say again. Maybe it was Allen. Maybe there *was* something really terrible about him that he couldn't see. The employers saw it, and now the people around him were beginning to see it. What if there was something wrong with him that he couldn't fix. What if it was being African-American? What if there was something really wrong with us genetically. He remembered Tamiko's words at dinner. All these years and all the different laws passed, and still we hadn't really gotten anywhere as a people. What if there really was something wrong with us? Or worse. What if God really hates us? He had remembered his mother saying something about the curse of Ham? Was that what this was really about? Or did God just hate Allen?

The longer Allen lingered, the more morose his thoughts became and with each passing moment, he became more and more depressed. The thoughts began to crowd his mind like thousands of little voices. He closed his eyes and all of the negative experiences flashed in front of him: the uncomfortable interviews, the arguments with his friends. Then he became so overwhelmed he had to get up. He had to go somewhere, do something, anything to get away from what he was feeling. Then it came to him. Allen went to his briefcase and searched through the business cards he had gathered at the job fair, and found the one with Holly's number. He would call her and see if she wanted to do something tonight or this afternoon even. He glanced over at the clock to see what time it was. 11:30am. He then went to his coat pocket, grabbed his cell phone, and dialed her up.

"Hello?" a gentle female voice answered after several rings.

"Holly?"

"Yes?"

"Hi, it's Allen. We met yesterday at the job fair?"

"Oh, yes. I remember you" Holly said, sounding pleasantly surprised "How are you?"

"I'm good. And you?"

"Good. Even better, now that you've called."

"Do you have any plans for tonight?"

"Not really."

"How about we do a movie and dinner tonight?"

"Sounds great."

"Do you know the Black Poet's Café?"

"Yeah, I've been there before. I love that place."

"Let's meet there at 7:00pm."

"O.K. What are we going to see afterwards?"

"Why don't you choose? You can surprise me."

"Great. So I'll see you then."

"Can't wait."

Just as Allen ended the call there was a knock at the door. He knew it would be his mother, and he dreaded what was next.

"Come in", he said. He just wanted to get it over with.

"Did you forget that I wanted to talk with you?" She had a breakfast tray with all of Allen's favorite foods: bacon, eggs, hash browns and fresh coffee. It was just as Allen had suspected.

"No. I just got in late last night and overslept, that's all."

"Uh-huh. Who was that on the phone?" she asked suspiciously, as she sat the tray next to him on the bed. Allen knew she had probably been listening at the door for some time before she knocked.

"I just called someone I met yesterday for a date tonight" Allen said putting the phone away. "What's all this for?"

"For you."

"Why?" Allen asked suspiciously.

"Because it's almost noon and you haven't had breakfast yet."

Allen gave Lena a look that said, 'now tell me the real reason.' "Are you sure it doesn't have something to do with the 'talk' we're about to have?"

"Now that you've mentioned it…I was praying to God about your situation, and he put it on my heart to speak with my friend Ms. Bea yesterday, you know the lady from our church whose husband works for that hotel over on 7th."

"Yes."

"Well, she said her husband could get you a job in facilities."

"A janitor? Are you kidding me?"

COMMENCEMENT

"It's a job Allen! And besides, I thought you were ready to take anything to help out around here."

"I am but...what if I hear from one of the employers at the job fair?"

"We'll cross that bridge when we get to it. Right now you got a job, no strings attached."

Allen shook his head and stared down at the food on the plate.

"The hours will be flexible, so you can still go on interviews if you want, or go to school or anything else. At least you will have some money in your pocket until you get something better. And it's a sure thing", continued Lena trying to convince him.

Allen let go of an exasperated sigh.

"All you have to do is go down there on Monday, and ask for Mrs. Bea's husband, Mr. Hardy. He's the head of maintenance."

Lena pulled Allen by the chin until his eyes met hers. "Allen, promise me that you'll go. Don't let me have gone through this all for nothing. Please?"

There was little else he could do once his mother put things in perspective for him.

"Okay, I'll go. I won't like it, but I'll go."

"Thank you", she said reaching out to him for an embrace.

"I guess I should be thanking you."

"And let's look on the bright side. Maybe God is putting you here for a reason. Maybe there is something he wants to teach you before he puts you up higher. Like what happened to Joseph. Before he became the Head of Egypt, he started out as a slave."[1]

"I know, I know."

"I know you learned about Joseph in Sunday school when you were a boy. What I'm not sure of is whether or not you learned the significance of what happened in his life as it pertains to you as a Christian."

"I'm not sure I know what you're talking about mom."

"If you don't, then I don't think I did a very good job as a mother."

"C'mon, you're a great mom by any standard."

"Maybe I was good at providing for you physically and materially, but I don't think I did enough for you spiritually. I thought that leading by example was enough. I should have taken the time to teach you more."

"Like what?"

"Like how to develop a relationship with God for yourself."

"You and Tamiko keep talking about this personal relationship with God. How in the world can anyone have such a thing? How can you have a relationship with someone you can't see, or touch, or hear?"

"You're thinking about the physical. Spiritually, we can hear Him, and see Him and feel Him. But you have to seek Him. By reading the Bible, taking time to meditate on his word, praying and fasting."

"I've read the Bible. I've probably read it twice over. And when I pray, it just seems like I'm talking to the wind."

"That's because when you were doing those things when you were younger, they were just empty rituals for you. You just repeated what your daddy and I told you. You read what they told you to in Sunday school. But believe me, when you are ready to seek God for yourself, when you are ready to have a relationship with Him, and you want Him with your whole heart, He will open those scriptures to you and you will see new things and gain a whole new understanding that will change the way you view and live your life. When you pray, you will not just be uttering words, but praying with your spirit and you will feel his presence. Trust me Allen, I know."

"I don't know."

"Just try Allen. You've tried everything else, what would it hurt to try God? You've got nothing to lose and everything to gain."

"And how do I do that?"

COMMENCEMENT

"Just read your Bible. You don't have to read a whole book. Read as the Lord leads you. Then when you finish, just meditate on it. Think on it. Then I want you to pray. Just do those two things every day for a week, and then you let me know what happens. Can you do that Allen?"

"Yeah, I guess."

"And another thing. Instead of thinking about what you don't have, I want you to think about all the good things God has already done for you. I know I can count 50 ways right off the top of my head without even trying."

"Alright. I'll try."

"And one last thing."

"There's always one last thing. And what might that be?"

"Don't stay out late on that date tonight. Remember, you got church tomorrow at 11:00am sharp! As long as you live under this roof, you will go to church! Is that clear!"

"Yes, ma'am."

"So no funny business on that 'date'! You understand me? I expect you back in this house at a reasonable hour."

"Yes, ma'am."

His mother left and slammed the door behind her. It was almost as if she could read his mind. There went his hot date. He'd still go, but he knew his mother's words would haunt him and there was no way he was going to achieve what he intended. He finished his breakfast and looked at the clock. It was only 12:45pm. He had the rest of the afternoon to himself, and didn't really have much of anything to do. So he decided to do what his mother suggested. He didn't know if it would help, but like his mother said, it couldn't hurt.

Allen moved the tray to the floor on the other side of his bed. Then he went to his desk and looked through his drawers. Then he looked in his closet. He always had to go on a scouting mission for his bible every week before church. This time he found it in one of the bookcases next to his nightstand. Allen flipped through a few of the pages until he got to the

book of Samuel. Seemed as good a place as any to start with. Then he lay
back down on his bed and randomly started from the 13th chapter and
read on. As Allen was reading, he noticed that he and Saul were quite
alike. They were both men of action. When Samuel tarried and didn't get
there in time for the sacrifice, Saul offered his own. Allen thought that
was something like what he would have done. But then Samuel was not
pleased. God was not pleased. But how could Saul have done anything
else? The people were scattered from him and the Philistines were ready
to destroy all of Israel. In the business world, Saul would have been
commended for his forward thinking and ingenuity. How could God get
mad at him?[2]

Allen read the chapter again, but he still didn't understand. Then it
became clearer to him as he went over the verse where it read "I forced
myself".[3] He thought about what his mother had said. Maybe God wasn't
pleased with the sacrifice because it was just an empty ritual. Saul was just
doing it so that he could prevail over the Philistines. God obviously
wanted Saul to wait, but he was too busy looking at his circumstances. But
why did God want Saul to wait? Wouldn't the Philistines have killed
everybody?

He still didn't understand it all very well. So Allen took the time to
say a quick prayer to God. "Lord, God if you love me, help me to
understand Your Word. You said that if we draw nigh unto You, that You
would draw near to us.[4] As I come to You, help me to understand your
Word. Speak to my heart and help me to understand what my mom and
Tamiko are talking about. Let me understand what it means to have a
relationship with you."

As Allen finished his prayer, he waited for a moment. It was as if he
was waiting to hear some voice from the great beyond speak to him,
however, he didn't hear anything. So he got up and put his bible on the
nightstand by his bed. "So much for that", he thought to himself. Then he
reminded himself that he had only started on his journey in seeking God.
Allen would try what his mother said. He would read his bible and pray
every day for a week. But if nothing happened, he'd let it go.

Allen decided to shower and prepare for his date. He grabbed some
of his toiletries from his dresser, and his robe and headed down the hall

toward the bathroom. He stopped briefly at the linen closet to pick up a clean towel before entering the bathroom. When he was inside, he turned on the shower and let the water run. Then he looked at himself in the mirror. "Maybe I should see if I can get a touch up at the barber" he considered to himself. Then he quickly brushed his teeth. His mother would kill him for the waste of water, but he had to let the water in the shower run for a few minutes so it would be hot enough. The plumbing in the brownstone needed some serious tending to.

After brushing his teeth, Allen hopped into the shower and let the spray run all over him. As he stood there he began to think about the real blessings of his life. He had two parents who were still together after 25 years when most of his friends' parents were single or divorced. Allen had pretty much an idyllic childhood, full of supportive adults that were always there for him. He thought about his friend Jim, who had lost both of his parents. First, his father, a New York City Police Officer, was killed in the line of duty trying to stop a robbery. Then, two years ago, he lost his mother to cancer. Allen's parents had filled in the void at times, like during Christmas and Thanksgiving. Other than that, Jim had no family for support. Allen didn't know if he could cope with that type of loss, and was amazed at his friend's strength. Then he thought about Tim whose situation was just bizarre. It was like what he had read about in history books about slavery. Rich white man with a wife and family in the big house, meanwhile he secretly has a mistress and a son in the slave quarters. Although in Tim's case, they were very luxurious slave quarters. Tim rarely talked about how he felt about the situation. He was just grateful that he had a dad who was involved in his life, even if it was just marginally. At the very least, Tim's dad provided for Tim and his sister financially and made sure they were comfortable. But there were times when Allen could see the strain of family issues take their toll on Tim. Like the time when Tim talked about how his dad was coming to visit him on the campus. Allen was actually more excited about seeing him than Tim. Then when they day came, Tim's dad bailed. Tim said that some business issue came up. Tim tried to pretend like he didn't care, but Allen could see that his friend was hurt. It made Allen wonder just how many promises Tim's dad had broken over the course of his son's life. Callie and Richard had strong mothers, but neither of them even knew who their dads were. And they were both at odds with their moms who seemed to choose the different boyfriends in their lives over them. When he thought about his friends, Allen felt very blessed. If he hadn't had the parents God blessed him with, the road to Harvard would have been a lot harder. Maybe God did like him.

Allen also thought about what his mom told him about himself when he was a baby. Everyone in his family talked about how he was the "miracle baby". When he was born, he only weighed about 2 ½ pounds because he was nearly 8 weeks premature. He remember how his mom had told him that all the doctors said that such children tended to develop learning disabilities when they reached school age. His mother had seen such children and had even taught them. The fact that Allen was slow to develop certain motor skills early on seemed to foreshadow the inevitability that when he was five, he would be taking the short bus to school. But no matter what anyone said, his mother had faith that Allen would be okay. He remembered her recounting the story to Mother Rose once. He remembered her saying that she always knew her son was destined for great things. She had faith that if God had allowed him to be conceived and to be born, then he would be okay, and one day God would use him for His purpose. She had faith in God. She believed God.

Allen finished his shower and turned off the water. He dried himself with his towel and put on his robe. That's when he heard it. "Do you believe? Do you have faith?" That was a good question. What did he believe? He knew there was a God. He knew about Jesus, or at least what he learned in Sunday school as a child. But what did he truly believe about them? He never truly understood the relationship between God and Jesus. Did he truly have faith? What was faith? Was it the belief that God exists, or was there more to it than that?

Allen deliberated on these questions as he walked back down the hall to his room. He had to sit on his bed and pause for a moment. His mother believed that he would not be disabled. She believed in spite of what the doctors said, in spite of what she experienced with other children, even in spite of the fact that her child wasn't talking and walking on time. Even when things were at their worst, she still believed. She believed in the power of God. Then it came to him. Maybe that's what Saul was missing. He didn't have faith. He didn't believe that God would come through, so when he made his sacrifice, it was empty and meaningless or "forced". Maybe Saul thought that the power was in his own actions and/or the sacrifice rather than God (activated by his faith). "Are You trying to say I'm like Saul?" That couldn't be. Allen never doubted that he could get a great job in the finance industry. When he graduated from school he knew he was smart enough, and skilled enough to land a job. He had confidence in his abilities.

"That's just it. You had confidence in *your* abilities, what *you* could do. Now you need to trust Me."

"But what do I do next?"

"Just trust Me."

"How do I do that?"

Allen waited, but he didn't hear anything after that. It was as if someone was speaking to his spirit. And then all of a sudden, just as quickly as it had begun, it had ended. "Wait a minute", he thought to himself. "Was God just speaking with me? Maybe. Maybe not."

TWENTY-TWO

Tamiko was sitting on the couch in her parent's home working on making some manipulatives for the lessons she had planned for next week. She had already graded and analyzed yet another math unit assessment, and had finished report cards that were due to be handed in to the principal on Monday. Now she was working on making cards for a word study game she was going to have the kids play in their reading centers. It was basically an onset and rime game where there would be different chunks which students would have to match with an onset to make a word. This was the only part of her work that she actually liked. It was the only part that allowed her to be creative. In addition, the process of cutting and pasting didn't require as much thinking as the other aspects of her work. She could zone out and think about other things.

Tamiko was still kind of upset over the exchange between Allen and herself at Emily Ann's last night. At the time she couldn't believe how mean Allen was, but now in hindsight, she realized that maybe he was right and she should have kept her mouth shut. Hadn't she brought up the same topic a few months ago when they were all having dinner at Manna's and gotten a similar rebuff? Tamiko realized that her friends were not ready for a discussion about God on a deeper level. And maybe she wasn't ready, either. After all, she hadn't succeeded in convincing Jim or any of the others to believe, and when it was over, she found herself questioning her own faith. Especially given what she was going through at work.

Tamiko had always thought that it was God's plan for her to be a teacher. But now it seemed as if that plan was falling apart. She was no good at teaching. That's what they told her, anyway. Tamiko felt horrible. Not just for herself, but for the children she was trying to help. It was her dream to be a positive influence on the lives of the children she encountered, but now she felt like part of the problem that was holding them back. She was just another bad teacher ruining the lives of children. "Did I get the message wrong?" Tamiko wondered to herself. "Did God really mean for me to be a teacher? If He did, then why do I stink at it?" Then she remembered something Tim said last night about a learning curve, and that she would get better as she had more time and experience on the job. Still, she couldn't forget the fact that there were other first year teachers just like herself that were doing a great job already. Tamiko thought she would be a great teacher because when she was student teaching her mentor teacher absolutely loved her ideas. Even Tamiko herself saw how the children responded to her teaching. But then again, the children she taught as a student teacher were from middle and upper-middle class families and were better prepared for school. Tamiko was now teaching in the inner city and many of these children came to school far less prepared, if at all. They were the test to see if she really had what it takes to be a teacher. Presently, it seemed that she didn't. But if she didn't teach, what would she do? She had invested so much time, energy and money in her present career path. As Tamiko was thinking and cutting, her father walked into the room.

"That looks like fun", said Pastor Bynum.

"I guess", Tamiko sighed.

"Would you like some help? I'm pretty good at cutting."

"No thanks, daddy. I'll be fine."

"What's wrong, baby girl? Are you still upset about that meeting?"

"Kind of. I don't know, daddy."

Tamiko put down her scissors and faced her father. "It's just that, I thought that God wanted me to be a teacher, but now I'm not so sure."

"Why? Because a few people said some negative things?"

"They weren't random people off the street, daddy. It was the principal, the assistant principal, the literacy coach, everybody. At least everyone who's important anyway."

"The only opinion that really matters is God's."

"But what if this is a sign from Him that teaching isn't for me?"

"Miko, sweetheart, I told you before, just because God has something for you to do doesn't mean it's always going to be easy or come natural for you."

"But it's not just that I stink. If God wanted me to be a teacher why would he allow a racist to be my mentor? How am I supposed to get over that? I always thought that when God has something for you, He blesses everything you do. Even in the Bible, look at Jacob, and Joseph, and David."

"Whoa, now. Hold on there. What Bible have you been reading? Jacob and David were on the run from people who were trying to kill them before they received their promise.[1] And Joseph was lied on and sent to jail.[2] These were tests and trials that God put them through to test their faith in Him: to see if they would hold onto the promise. This may be a test that you are going through."

"But my situation is different."

"How so?"

"The whole time David had God on his side to help him fight his enemies. I've been praying to God and asking Him to show me how to help these children, and what to do about that Steele woman, but so far there's been nothing. It's probably because He warned me not to go into this profession somehow, and I missed it and now He's just letting me suffer for being disobedient."

"That's a possibility, but you won't know unless you hold out and see this thing through to the end. You've just started teaching. Even if their criticism is warranted, there is still time to learn and grow. And even if teaching is not what God has for you, that doesn't mean he can't take your mistake and make it work out for your good. You won't know any of that unless you hold on. And don't give up on praying. God loves you Miko there's no way he won't answer you."

"Alright. I'll give it to the end of the year. But if things don't change, I'm gonna quit."

"Miko, you remind me of Elijah."

"How so?"

"God has done so much for you, but somebody says something negative to you and you're ready to go hide in a cave."[3]

"I'm not going to hide, daddy! I'm just going to get another job."

The Pastor laughed. Tamiko couldn't help but chuckle herself. Then they both heard the phone ring in the distance.

"I'll get it!" cried Mother Rose from the kitchen.

"Oh, I meant to ask you, how was dinner last night?"

"The less said the better. I got my head bitten off again. By Allen this time."

"Be patient with him, Miko. He's just going through a hard time right now. Still hasn't found a job yet, I assume?"

"No. And I don't blame him for getting mad at me. I shouldn't have opened my big mouth."

"What did you say to him?"

"It wasn't really to him directly. We were talking about Obama and the election, and I was just saying that we can't look to the president to solve our problems, that we had to look to God."

"There's nothing wrong with that."

"Tell that to Allen. He's not really seeing where God has done much for him right now. It's understandable, I guess."

"Yes, I know what you mean. I know you were trying to help him out, but when you are trying to give someone the Word, sometimes you have to wait until they are ready, otherwise they are so wrapped up in their problems, they can't hear the truth you're telling them."

"You can say that again."

"Just wait and let God lead you as to when you should speak. Then let Him speak through you to change their hearts."

"Miko, there you are dear. You have a phone call. It's a Tim somebody", said Mother Rose walking in with the cordless phone from the kitchen. She handed it to Tamiko before sprinting back through the door.

"Tim? Who's Tim?"

"C'mon, daddy, you remember! The guy from Harvard. You met him at the big graduation party and last night when he dropped me off" she said covering the receiver end so Tim couldn't hear her father.

"Oh, you mean that high-yaller fella."

"Daddy! He's not 'yaller'! No one says that any more. He's bi-racial, or bi-cultural. I wonder what he wants."

"Me, too."

"Oh Daddy, not every guy is out for one thing. Tim's nice. About 80% of the time anyway", she said before speaking into the phone. "Hey Tim, what's up?"

"I tried calling your cell, but it was off."

"Sorry about that. Sometimes I shut it off to save the battery."

"Are you busy right now?"

"Kind of. Why?"

"I need some help. It's an emergency. You see my mom's birthday is next week and I wanted to get her a birthday present, and I could use a woman's input."

"You should have asked Callie. She's the one who's up on all the trends."

"True, but you're taste is more traditional, like my mom's."

"I don't know Tim, I still have a few things left to do."

"I promise it won't take all afternoon."

COMMENCEMENT

"Alright."

"Great. I'll pick you up in about twenty minutes. Is that okay?"

"Sure. See ya."

"Well?" said the Pastor expectantly.

"He wants me to help him pick out a present for his mom's birthday."

"Um-hmp. He probably spent all morning thinking of that lame excuse to see you."

"He's a friend, daddy. Just like Allen and Jim. You don't get suspicious when they call or want to go out."

"I've known them since they were children. This Tim fellow is a different matter. I don't know if you should be joyriding around with him alone."

"Daddy! It's not like we've just met. I've known him for years, and he's given me rides millions of times and he's never laid a hand on me. He brought me home last night."

"You mean Allen wasn't with you all?!"

"No. I left the restaurant after he insulted me, and I went to watch the movie with Tim. Afterward we talked, and then he took me home. End of story. You were there when we came in. Remember?"

"I want to talk to him before you leave."

"If you like, but it's not necessary. I better go upstairs and change."

Yes, Tim was just a friend. But even Tamiko had to admit to herself that they had been pretty chummy lately. Or it was more like he was getting chummy with her. It started after Tim had taken her home that night after that big blow-up at Manna's. He listened to her try to explain herself with regard to her beliefs about God. At least he listened. He admitted that he didn't quite understand what she believed, but admitted that her passion "intrigued" him. Whatever that meant. Then last night he was so different. He kept touching her. Taking her hand. Putting his arm around her chair in the movie. Maybe he was.... "Don't start misinterpreting things!" she said to herself. It wasn't like he asked her out, or tried to kiss her. After the movie, all they did was talk about the problems both of them were facing at work. He was supportive and gave her advice, just like Allen or Jim or any of their other friends, with the exception of Callie, who resented her ever since they met. No, Tim was just a friend.

In fact, Tamiko had never ever really thought of him in that way. She remembered when they had first met. It was spring break of Allen's first year at Harvard and he had decided to stay on campus to catch up on some work. Tamiko had felt sorry for Allen, so she decided to pay him a visit. Allen picked her up at the train early and they had breakfast together at a local diner near the campus that was famous with the undergraduates. Then Allen showed Tamiko around the campus and gave her a tour of the dorm he lived in. It was a two-bedroom suite that he shared with three other guys. It was gorgeously furnished with modern appliances. They had their own kitchen, living room, and bathroom. When Tamiko stepped inside she immediately noticed that one half of the room looked very different from the other. On one side there were clothes everywhere, clutter on the desk, a hat hanging on a lamp, and books all over. That was obviously Allen's side. The other half had to have been inhabited by a serial killer. It was so neat and orderly it was scary.

"What in the world? Who sleeps here? Hannibal Lecter?"

"No, that's this guy John's side."

"Is that the guy you're always talking about? The brother that hooks you up."

"No, that's Tim. He's a junior. He lives in one of the dorms over in Cabot House."

Then as they were talking, there was a knock at the door. Allen excused himself and went to answer it. In walked what seemed to be a tall white guy with short brown wavy hair that was combed back and gelled. He was very stylishly dressed in a blue oxford shirt with a navy v-neck sweater, khakis, and burgundy boat shoes. He had an athletic build that showed through the clothes he was wearing. And Tamiko would never forget those piercing hazel eyes.

COMMENCEMENT

"Hey, Allen…Oh, I'm sorry. I didn't mean to interrupt anything…" he said upon noticing Tamiko.

"No way, come in. I actually wanted you two to meet anyway."

Allen turned to Tamiko, who looked rather shocked. "Tamiko, this is Tim Russell. Tim, this is Tamiko Bynum."

"Nice to meet you, Tamiko", said Tim extending his hand for a shake.

"Same here", said Tamiko who was absorbed in examining Tim's countenance. Maybe she had misunderstood Allen when he had spoken of Tim earlier. "There's no way this guy could be a 'brother'. Right?" she puzzled to herself.

"I believe Allen's spoken of you before. Are you the one that's going to nursing school?"

"No, that's our friend Callie", said Allen correcting him.

"Oh…wait a minute, you must be the 'PK'" Tim said a smirk crossing his face.

"What's a 'PK'?" Tamiko asked naively.

"You know, a "preacher's kid", he said slyly.

"Yeah, but her dad's the real deal. He's a real man of God. And Tamiko is just like him."

"I bet. And you go to…."

"Spelman."

"Really? I thought Allen said you were really smart."

"Excuse you?!"

"She is…." said Allen trying to save the conversation.

"So why would you want to go to Spelman? Didn't you get accepted into any of the Ivies?"

"As a matter of fact, I got accepted into Harvard, Columbia, and Cornell, Mr. Russell. I turned them down."

"To go to Spelman?" Tim laughed. "O.K. That's rational."

"Spelman happens to be one of the best colleges in the country!"

"If you say so", he said skeptically.

"C'mon Tim, didn't you say your mom went to Spelman?"

"Yeah, but that was a long time ago. Before our people were given access to better options."

"*Your* mom went to Spelman?" asked Tamiko in disbelief.

"Yes. Why are you looking at me like that?"

"It's just that…I didn't think…never mind."

"Oh, I see. I'll just answer the question I know you're wondering. Yes! I am a product of the infamous "swirl". My mother is black and my father is white. Do you feel better now that you know?"

"It makes no difference to me."

"Yeah, sure", Tim said rolling his eyes at her dismissively before turning away. "Anyway, Al, I just wanted to let you know that this is your last chance to get away. We're leaving in an hour. Just enough time for you to pack a few things in a bag and change the greeting on your voice mail."

"Nah, man. I told you. I've got too much work to do here. You go ahead. Just fill me in on all the details when you get back."

"Are you sure? This is Florida we're talking about. Warm weather. Beautiful women."

"No, really, it's okay man."

"Okay, but don't say you weren't invited."

"Stay safe, man."

"I will. See you around, dude." Then he turned to Tamiko "Good luck at Spellman, Tamika."

"That's Tamiko."

"Whatever."

COMMENCEMENT

Their first encounter left Tamiko with an unfavorable impression at best. Tim seemed arrogant, condescending, and a bit of an Uncle Tom. Tamiko couldn't understand how someone as nice and easy going as Allen could be a friend to someone like Tim. Over time things mellowed out between her and Tim as she got to know him better, but she never really thought of him in a romantic way. That was not to say that she didn't find him somewhat attractive. Tamiko usually favored guys with darker complexions, but Tim was handsome and he did have a very nice build, although recently it seemed he had lost some weight. Even so, he was toned and muscular, but not too muscular. She never did like those guys who looked like they could be on steroids. Yes, he was quite tempting. Especially when he wore his hair curly rather than gelled back into waves. "Keep your head on Tamiko!" she told herself. When it came to romance, Tamiko always tried to put reason before emotions and feelings. She had seen too many young women whose hearts had led them to trouble. Although Allen tended to keep quiet, Tamiko had observed enough of Tim's womanizing ways over the years to make her wary of ever pursuing a relationship with him. Besides as a young Christian woman, she was not going to let romance come before God or the life that He had planned for her. God was going to be her first love; His will for her life would be her main prerogative, and if a potential suitor couldn't accept that then he'd have to step aside. And Tamiko had made many step aside.

Tamiko changed into an outfit that she thought would convey the platonic nature of the excursion. She wore her baggy purple and navy striped rugby with a dark-rinsed denim skirt and sneakers. If Tim was interested, she was going to send him a clear message that she wasn't.

*****

Tim and Tamiko had been to about 15 different stores in Midtown, when Tim finally settled on buying his mom a Hermes handbag and matching belt that Tamiko had picked out. He even offered to buy Tamiko something for her help, but she wouldn't let him. She wasn't going to give him any mixed signals. Then Tim suggested they stop and have something to eat before they headed back. He allowed her to pick

173

the spot and she decided on Manny's pizza shop on 57th and Lexington Ave. Tamiko ordered a plain cheese slice with a sprite, and Tim just ordered a can of ginger ale. They were sitting at one of the small tables in the back of the shop.

"Thanks for coming out with me today on such short notice. I really appreciate it. It's just that next week, I wouldn't have been able to find the time."

"It's no problem. Is that all you're going to have after all that walking around?"

"I'm not really hungry."

"I noticed you didn't eat much at Emily Ann's last night, either. And that ginger ale just says, 'I have stomach trouble' all over it. Are you feeling okay?"

"It's not a big deal. It's part bad diet, part stress related."

"Does the stress part have anything to do with that new vice president you were telling me about last night?"

"Maybe."

"Tim, I don't think it's fair that you should have to work yourself sick like this. Why don't you just tell your boss that things aren't working out? Maybe he can move this guy somewhere else and you can get another VP."

"Because I work in corporate America, Tamiko. As a manager in the corporate world, I have to know how to work with each person in the department to get them to produce. If I complain to the bosses they may think *I'm* the one who's not effective. On top of that, they'll think I'm a whiner. Besides, most of the higher ups are in love with Preston, and they don't really care for me and in the business world, favor can take you where talent can't."

Tamiko wanted to tell him that God's favor was more important than man's favor, but she remembered what happened at Emily Ann's.

"They've got to like something about you. I mean you're still there after the downsizing."

"I don't know. Sometimes I think they just want me to train Preston and then once he's got the hang of everything, they'll hand me my walking papers, too."

"That's crazy! One man can't do all of that work by himself."

"I'm doing it already."

"So, shouldn't that make you more valuable to them?"

"Valuable, but not irreplaceable."

"Well, I think you're irreplaceable", Tamiko found herself blurting out.

"Really? What makes you say that?" asked Tim looking at Tamiko rather intensely. For a split second Tamiko saw a very different Tim. Not the cocky, arrogant, pretentious know it all persona he projected most of the time, but someone much more vulnerable and human. For the first time since she had known him, he actually seemed to be seeking validation rather than granting it. It softened her toward him, but at the same time made her feel a little ill at ease.

"You're one of the smartest guys I know."

Tim seemed to take that as if she were patronizing him with a trite cliché, and sat back stiffly in his chair.

"Now you sound like my mom. C'mon, Miko, there are tons of smart guys out there."

"But you're also loyal, tenacious, resourceful…."

"You mean like a German Shepherd?" he griped, rolling his eyes.

"Sorry. I was only trying to be a friend."

"I know…" he whispered regretfully. "It's just that…never mind. I'm sorry."

"Apology accepted. So when is your mom's birthday?"

"Wednesday. She's going to be the big 50. But don't tell her I told you. Most people think she's 35 and she's not the type to correct them."

"I totally get it. My mom is the same way. So does she always have such expensive tastes, or are you giving her a special treat?"

"My mom is a total diva, so with her it has to be the best. The hard part is finding something she doesn't already have. Since she's a systems analyst with her own firm she can afford to buy most of the things she wants for herself."

"So your mom has her own money?"

"Yes. She's not the 'white man's whore' that Richard makes her out to be. She comes from money. Not Bloomberg money mind you, but good money. We're from what you would call the 'black elite'."

"You mean like that book "Our Kind of People"?"

"Exactly like that."

"So how did she meet your dad?"

"She met my dad when the company she used to work for got a contract from the company that my dad owned. She was the leading analyst on a project to upgrade the accounting software system that was being used in his company. They ended up working closely together and having an affair, which resulted in yours truly."

"Were they in love?" Tamiko asked, but then upon further thought realized the impertinence of her question. "Sorry. You don't have to answer that. I'm just too nosy for my own good at times."

"It's fine. I don't really mind talking about it…with you, anyway. But even I don't know the answer to that question. Sometimes I think they were, and then other times… I'm not sure. He was engaged around the time of the affair, and my mom knew it, but she didn't care. Then she got pregnant and she wanted him to dump his fiancée and marry her, but he said that dumping his fiancée would've amounted to career suicide. He'd lose face with a lot of people he couldn't afford to, and subsequently lose his means of making money. So he told my mom if she kept everything on the 'down low', he'd make sure we were well taken care of. If she didn't, everyone involved would be ruined."

"Your mom told you all this?"

176

COMMENCEMENT

"Of course not. My parent's have never actually tried to explain any of it to me. It's basically what I was able to piece together by eavesdropping on all the hushed conversations behind closed doors over the years."

"So, I guess your parents don't get along very well."

"Actually, they get along quite well. If they didn't I wouldn't have a younger sister."

"You mean you two have the same dad?"

"Uh, duh. I thought you knew that."

"You mean your mom had another child for him? Even after he insulted her like that?"

"He wasn't trying to insult her. He was just telling her how it was and she accepted it. We don't live in a perfect world, Miko. Sometimes you have to be willing to make a compromise if you're going to get by."

"And you're fine with all this?"

"Why shouldn't I be? Getting upset over it isn't going to change anything. Besides, it's not like I don't know who my father is, or he's never spent time with me. He's done quite a lot for me actually."

"I'm sure he has" Tamiko said doubtfully.

"If you're going to pass judgment on my family…"

"I wasn't trying to pass judgment…"

"Yes you were. You probably think that my dad should have just thrown caution to the wind and just up and married my mom and that would have solved everything. In the real world everything isn't so cut and dried. He tried to do what was best for everyone given the circumstances. At least he provided for my sister and I. A lot of other men would have done nothing at all."

"Tim, I'm sorry. I didn't mean to…you're right. I don't know enough about your family or your situation. Besides, no family is perfect. Not even mine. My mom and dad had their own issues, too. They almost ended up getting a divorce at one point."

177

"Really? Who wanted out? Your mom or your dad?"

"My mom. She couldn't handle the fact that the Pastor had to be on call 24/7 for members in the church. She especially hated it when he had to attend to the female members, and believe me, I think she was justified in that. Some of them were total church groupies."

"I guess it's the whole man with power thing."

"You could say that. Anyway, my mom was constantly accusing him of cheating with other women and my dad accused her of trying to sabotage his work for the Lord. At one point things got so bad that my mom took me all the way to Atlanta to start a new life for herself. I was only 9 years old. I didn't know if I would ever see my dad again. It was one of the scariest times of my life."

"How long were you away?"

"About a year."

"That is a long time. How did your parents work things out?"

"I have no idea. When I was a little girl I would just pray to God that He would put my family back together. I just kept praying that prayer every single day. Then one day my dad showed up to talk to my mom. My grandmother took me out for ice-cream while they talked and when I came back, my mother said we were all going to be living together again."

"And you lived happily ever after."

"Not necessarily. My parents still have disagreements sometimes, but they work them out."

"And your dad should be the expert at that."

"I don't know if he would agree with that."

"Speaking of your dad, what was with the third degree he was giving me when I walked in?"

"He's just a little over-protective when it comes to his baby girl, that's all."

"I'll say. And it's not like we haven't met before."

"But he doesn't know you like he does Allen or Jim. You don't come around as often."

"Maybe we should change that", smiled Tim.

"How so?" Tamiko asked warily.

"Lately, I've been thinking that I don't know you as well as I would like."

"Really?" she said, her eyes narrowing with suspicion.

"Yes. We've been friends by association because we both know Allen. But, I'd like for us to be good friends, too."

"I thought I always annoyed you."

"Not all the time. To tell you the truth, I think you are one of the most intriguing persons I've ever met."

"You've said that before. I still wonder what you mean by it."

"I don't quite know how to explain it. I think it might have something to do with what gets you so fired up about your God."

"You mean 'fired at' considering what happened last night at Emily Ann's."

"And yet you still put yourself out there. It makes me wonder what could be so great about your God that you're so willing to be raked over the coals."

"You really want to know?"

"Yeah."

"Are you busy tomorrow?"

"Not at all. You have something in mind?"

"I was thinking that you could come down to the church for the morning service and then you could have dinner with me and my parents. How does that sound?"

"I don't know. I've never really done the church thing."

"C'mon, Tim. It's not a cult or anything. We don't brainwash people or make them drink poisoned kool-aid. Just come once and if you don't like it, you don't have to come back."

"Alright. What could happen? Right?"

"Service starts at 11:00. Don't be late."

TWENTY-THREE

Sunday morning, Allen stood outside the front door of the Greater Apostolic Temple peering through the crowds of people for Tamiko. His date last night with Holly was pleasantly surprising. Now that he had gotten to know her a little better, he was ashamed of his original intentions for asking Holly out. It turned out she was not as forward as their first meeting suggested, and they shared a lot of interests. He ended up asking her to the Election Night party that Jim and Leandra were hosting, and she accepted. But by the end of the night the budding of the new romance only reminded him of what Jim said about Tim. Allen had tried calling Tim during the weekend, but he wasn't answering his phone. He then sent Tim several texts with the message "we need to talk" but Tim never responded. That worried Allen. Tim always responded to texts during the weekend unless he was…busy to say the least. Allen's thought was interrupted by the sudden appearance of a familiar face, although not the one he was looking for.

"Hey, Allen! How's it going?"

"Tim, what are you doing here?" Allen asked suspiciously.

"Miko invited me."

"She's invited you countless times before, and you've always turned her down. What's with the sudden change of heart?"

"Let's just say her passion about God has piqued my curiosity. So, I decided to come down and see what all the fuss was about."

Before Allen could say another word, Tamiko appeared in a lovely white dolman sleeved top, long black skirt, and matching prayer cloth with a double-breasted black wool coat to top it off, and black platform pumps. She completed the look with a black patent leather shoulder bag.

"Hey Allen! See who I brought?!" she squealed with excitement.

"He came with you?!" exclaimed Allen in disbelief.

"He came with me", interrupted Pastor Bynum as he walked up behind them.

"Yeah, Tim gave daddy a ride in his car, and I rode with mom in the family car."

"Pastor, I didn't know you and Tim were so close", remarked Allen.

"Any friend of yours and Tamiko's is a friend of mine. I'm just glad to be able to bring a new sheep into the fold. I hope you enjoy your time with us, Tim. Now if you all will excuse me, I have to go get ready for the service", said Pastor Bynum excusing himself.

"Tamiko, dear, we should be going inside, too. I'm going to help get the congregation into praise, and you are filling in on the choir", Mother Rose reminded Tamiko.

"That's right, I almost forgot."

"Nice seeing you, Allen. Make sure you come with us for dinner afterward", Mother Rose beamed.

"Wouldn't miss it for the world, Mother Rose", replied Allen.

"Yeah, and Tim's coming, too", added Tamiko.

"Oh, he is?" asked Mother Rose who was a bit surprised.

"Yes. Tamiko invited me yesterday", Tim responded.

"But if you have something to do Tim, we'll understand", Mother Rose added rather hastily.

"It's no problem", said Tim.

"Yes, well. I'll see you all inside", Mother Rose said eyeing Tim strangely before leaving.

"See you guys", said Tamiko following behind.

Allen waited until they were both far enough away before he addressed what was on his mind with Tim.

"She's off limits, Tim."

"What?! Who's off limits? What are you talking about?"

"You know very well what I'm talking about! Now you can play your game on any other sister you want, but not Miko. She's not that kind of girl."

"First of all, I'm not trying to play anything on her; and secondly, who died and made you her protector. I thought she already had a dad."

"So what's with the sudden interest in her?"

"I like talking to her."

"Since when?"

"Since for a while now."

"Oh, really?" said Allen raising his eyebrows in disbelief.

"I just want to get to know her better on a platonic level, that's all. We've been friends for the past four years and I don't really know her that well."

"You don't know Callie that well either, but I don't see you wandering around down at the emergency room at St. Luke's."

"I don't see what you're getting so worked up about. Unless there's something going on between you two that you're not telling me."

"Man, please. You know Miko is like a sister to me. And I don't want to see her get hurt."

"And that's not my intention."

"It never is, but it happens a lot anyway. Don't act like I don't know you, playa."

"Look, Allen, I care about her just as much as you do. I don't plan on doing anything to jeopardize our relationship as friends."

"I know that. 'Cause I'ma be watchin' you", said Allen slipping into ebonics. He often did this when he was trying to make a point to another brother.

"Oh, I'm so worried. How about we head in before the service starts? After you."

"And Jim will be watching you, too."

"And God will be watching us all", said Tim jocosely.

Tim followed Allen to the third pew from the front in the aisle where Lena and Vernon were sitting. After introductions and greetings, Allen took his seat next to his mother and Tim took his seat on the other side of Allen. Not long after they sat down, the service began, as the clergy on the podium stood up and Brother Anderson asked the congregation to stand for the procession of the choir. As the music to "Gather In Your Name" began to play, the men walked down one aisle and the women down the other, slowly making their way to the stage and taking their places. Many of the congregants sang along with them as they walked, swaying from side to side. Tim and Allen spotted Tamiko who was in the middle of the procession and she waved to them as she passed by. Allen noticed that Tim's eyes followed her all the way up to the stage. Once the choir had finished their song, it was time for the prayer. Everyone remained standing as the choir belted out "Pass Me Not", the prayer hymn. When they had done, Brother Anderson began.

"Heavenly Father, we come before You this day to thank You and to give You honor and glory for all that You have done in our lives. For waking us up to see another day, blessing us with our health and strength, and protecting us from dangers far and near. We come before You, O Lord, to bless Your holy name, not just for what You do for us, but for who You are. We thank You for blessing us with the knowledge of who You are. Lord, as we stand before You today, we could ask for a lot of things. We could ask for money, and cars, healing, and homes, but we want to ask for something worth more than all that. Lord we ask You to open our hearts and minds to the Word we will hear today. We ask that you bless us with the understanding and the strength to apply Your Word, so that when we leave here today we will be faithful servants that stand out as lights in the darkness of the world. For we know that it is not the hearers of the Word, but the doers of Your Word that are justified. Let Your Word touch our hearts and minds in ways that will enable us to bear forth fruit and become the living embodiment of Your Word. Change us, shape us, transform us, and mold us to Your will. We ask this in the name of Your son Jesus. Amen."

As Brother Anderson closed his prayer, some of the people in the audience were already crying, and shouts of praise were beginning to resound throughout the temple. Even Allen himself, who usually did not pay much attention while they were praying, was moved by the beauty of the words spoken. There was something in the prayer that really touched him. It was not a prayer for the blessings of material things, but something that was harder to fathom: to be changed and transformed by the Word, to become a living embodiment of the Word. Allen pondered what that meant. Is this what it meant to have a personal relationship with God? Did this transformation happen to someone all at once or little by little? Would he…could he be transformed? He thought about his experience just the day before. It would happen, but Allen was beginning to realize that he would have to get out of the way and let God do the work. But for someone like Allen who was used to being in control all the time that would be difficult.

Then the choir director signaled to the choir and they broke into a reprise of "Pass Me Not". When they had finished, Brother Anderson signaled for the congregation to sit. Then there were several songs by the choir including "Living Sanctuary", and "Center of My Joy". After these songs the collection for the offering was taken, followed by meditation time. During the meditation, Tamiko performed the meditation solo "Because of Who You Are".

"I didn't know Tamiko could sing!" whispered Tim, who seemed to be deeply enthralled by her performance.

"And she can play the violin, too", Allen whispered back. Allen was sometimes amazed by how he knew so much about all of his friends, yet they knew so little about each other. When Tamiko finished her solo, everyone clapped and then it was time to collect the tithes. The Choir sang "What Shall I Render?", as the ushers passed the collection plate from row to row. Tim looked at Allen and rolled his eyes as he passed the plate to him without putting a thing into it. When the service was over Allen would have to take Tim to school on how things worked in Greater Apostolic Temple. He didn't want Tim to think Pastor Bynum was just about cash. The offering was just whatever one could afford. Most people gave donations ranging from twenty-five cents to five dollars. The offering was used for the upkeep of the church and services. The tithes, or the tenth of one's salary that most members gave, was used to pay for programs the church sponsored to help the poor and underprivileged in the community. The last collection would be the speaker's offering. The speaker's offering was the only money that was given to the pastor. Each collection had to be taken separately for accounting purposes. Pastor Bynum always made sure the money was used in the way it was intended, unlike some of the other pastors Allen knew.

Once the tithes collection was taken up, the church greeting was made by Mother Rose. During the greeting, Mother Rose welcomed all of the first time church visitors. Mother Rose also made the announcements regarding church activities for the week. When she was done, the collection plate was passed around for the speaker's offering and the choir got into one of the fast songs, which usually got everyone in the place shouting. This time it was "We Worship You". Pretty soon, there were people in the aisles getting their shout on, and Lena Sharpe was leading the way. To his surprise, Allen even found himself clapping and singing along with the choir. Tim pulled at his collar and shifted in his seat uncomfortably, ever so often checking his watch. Soon the song faded into the straight shout music, and it seemed as if the whole church was alight with the Spirit of God. Allen still didn't quite understand what all of the people were feeling, but he knew that for some of them, despite the frantic behavior, they seemed truly happy and at peace. For the first time in his life he was beginning to feel that this might be something that he wanted.

Then Pastor Bynum appeared.

"Go 'head and praise the Lord if you want to."

As he spoke, his deep, powerful baritone sent the people into more of a frenzy. The band went on playing:

COMMENCEMENT

Drmmp-drmmp. Drmmp-Drmmp. drmmp-drmmp, drrmp drrmp drmmp drmmp da-da-da-drmp.

Then Pastor Bynum signaled for the band to stop. For several minutes, there were still people who were praising and shouting to the Lord, but eventually everyone began to calm down and take their seats.

"Praise the Lord, everybody."

"Praise the Lord." the congregation responded.

"Y'all don't mind if I preach for a minute", Pastor Bynum's voice bellowed through the mike.

"Take out your Bibles and turn with me to the book of John, chapter 14, verse 6 and we're going to read through verse 21. When you find it, say Amen."

Allen shared his Bible with Tim, and the two of them struggled to find the passage. The Pastor and his congregation read together until they had finished the reading.

"My subject: What do you believe?" began the Pastor.

"Now I know all of you believe in God, but what do you believe about God? The apostle James tells us "even demons believe and tremble".[1] So believing there is a God is only half of it. It's what we believe that makes the difference between a child of God and everyone else. There are three very important things that we must believe if we are truly the sons and daughters of the Kingdom. First, we must believe that Jesus is the Son of God, whom he raised from the dead and imbued with power from on High to cleanse us from all sin. As you just read, no man can come to the Father except through Him. You must believe in Jesus, there is no other way to eternal life. If you don't believe in Him, He will not abide in you. And if He doesn't abide in you, you can't call yourself a child of God", Pastor Bynum explained.

Allen had to think about this for a minute. He remembered what he was taught in Sunday school as a child. When he was younger it was hard to understand where Jesus fit into salvation. Allen didn't seem to understand how someone could be the Son of God and God in the flesh at the same time. Then he reflected on everything he was taught in college. At Harvard, many of the professors and students would talk about Jesus in his freshman philosophy class. To them, he was just a man who led a religious movement. They said that the Bible was part allegory, and part historical fiction. From the way they talked, it all seemed to make sense. Now the pastor was saying that he had to believe something that didn't seem to make sense to him at all.

"Some of you folks are thinkin' 'Pastor Bynum I don't know if I can buy that.' Some of you don't know how Jesus can be the Son of God. 'Wasn't he just a man?' you ask"

It was as if Pastor Bynum was reading Allen's mind.

"That brings me to the next thing we have to believe if we are truly children of God. Many people want to believe in God for help and healing. 'O Lord, please help me with my children. O Lord, please bless me with a new home. Lord, please heal me of this disease.' How can you believe that God can to help you with anything, if you can't first believe that he wrapped himself in flesh, came down to us, died on the cross taking on all our sins, and then rose again on the third day?"

The audience burst into thunderous applause at his point of logic. When there was a break he continued.

"I know some of you want to say, 'Well, Pastor, I don't believe everything in the Bible is true'. I say if you can't believe everything, how can you believe anything? This book is a Testament of the Power of God. It is in itself Power. The apostle Paul tells us in the book of Romans that 'the Word of God is Power unto salvation to every one that believeth.'[2] As children of God, we must believe in the power of God. Since he's God, can there be anything that he can't do?" You know the answer to that. If you say you believe in God, why would you believe if you think He can't do anything?" Pastor Bynum expounded. His comment was followed by more applause. Again, when the applause began to die down, the Pastor went on.

"Some of you still want to argue. You want to say 'But pastor, what you're talking about isn't logical.' I remember a boy came to me fresh from the university one year. He wants to tell me how I'm a creationist and he doesn't believe in "creationism". He says he's an "evolutionist" because it makes more sense. Said it with his chest stuck out. I told him when you're God, you don't have to make sense. Did it make sense for a man who was 99 years old with a wife who was ninety to have a baby?[3] Did it make sense that a few thousand folk just walked around a wall three times and it fell down?[4] Did it make sense for three men to be thrown into a fiery furnace and walk out unsinged?[5] Did it make sense for a man to be dead three days and just get up when Jesus called him?"[6]

More shouts of agreement came from the audience as well as thunderous applause as the Pastor continued with his message.

"And some of you, I know you out there, got some things in your life today that don't make any sense. Some of you, the doctor said you didn't have but three months to live. Does it make sense that it's a year later and you're still here? I see a woman out there. Her little boy fell from a window four stories and landed on the pavement. Does it make sense that he's sitting next to her alive right now? Some of you had people say to you, you ain't no good, you ain't gonna be nothing. Your parents said it, your teachers said it, and your boss said it, and yet you are sitting here today with the blessings of God upon you. They look at you and say to themselves 'That don't make sense!' but when the power of God comes in it doesn't have to make sense! It doesn't have to be logical! Didn't the Apostle Paul say 'For the preaching of the cross is to them that perish foolishness; but unto us which are saved it is the power of God.'[7] Didn't he say 'God hath chosen the foolish things of the world to confound the wise.'"[8]

"That's why when Jesus was walking on the earth there were some people who he couldn't help. He couldn't help them because they couldn't believe on Him and His Power. The Pharisees, the Scribes, the Elders, and such couldn't benefit from His teaching because they didn't believe in His power. What did it say 'He could do no miracle because of their unbelief.'[9] Do you know why they didn't believe? The devil had them fooled. They were wise in their own eyes and couldn't understand the Power of God. Just like some of these people out here today. You see these wise people out here with their degrees and certificates, and other accolades, think God has to prove something to them. God made us, not the other way around. If we don't understand the fault is with us, not with

God. That's where I'm gonna get to my last point, and I'ma let you go. If you're a child of God, you better believe that the devil is real and he's out there."

"You know you right!" a woman shouted.

"Hallelujah!" a man cried.

"Praise you, Jesus!" another woman called out.

"God loves us and wants the best for us. He wants to bless us, and keep us until it is our time to leave this world and be with Him. That's why He came down in the form of flesh and was tempted, and suffered. He saw us on the road to hell and He came down to make a way for us to be with Him with the gift of grace through his death on the cross in the person of Jesus Christ. But guess who doesn't want you to have it. If you don't believe that there's a devil, believe me that old thing is glad about it. Because then he can come to you and tell you anything to mess you up and you won't know that it's him. If you're a child of God and Satan comes to you with some old mess, you'll know it and rebuke him. If you know who he is and how he operates, you can resist him. It says in James '…resist the devil and he shall flee from you.'[10] But when you don't believe that he exists, you just think that it's just another random thought, and you entertain satan. Before you know it, he's got you. The devil is the one that told you Jesus doesn't mean anything, he's just a man. He told you that because he doesn't want you to believe in the power of God. He doesn't want you to be saved, or healed, or blessed, or anything. Satan just wants you to join him in hell. So he has you look at earthly things like money. C'mon y'all. He'll have you look at things like connections and people. He'll have you focusing on things like degrees, property, status, drugs, alcohol, sex, and just about anything else that he can use. He tells you these things have power, but I'm here to tell you there is no power except the Power that comes from on High."

At this point people were standing on their feet giving glory to God. Lena, Vernon, Tamiko, and Mother Rose were all on their feet clapping and praising God. Allen couldn't help but stand to join them. Tim stood out of respect and courtesy, following the crowd.

COMMENCEMENT

"God wants you to have the best here on earth and also in heaven. He has given us the gift of grace through the cross and resurrection, but we have to accept that gift, and not let the devil take it from us. How many of you want to take that first step and accept that gift? How many of you believe that Jesus Christ is your Savior? How many of you truly believe in the Power of God? Come on up here and give your life to him right now."

As the altar call began, Brother Anderson and other church officers proceeded to the front of the church and people began to make their way down to the altar. Allen had never had the case put so eloquently to him before. Somehow the Pastor's message really ministered to his spirit. He had been thinking about what happened Saturday, particularly, about that something that spoke to his heart telling him to trust Him. But after the sermon it seemed that trusting in God would require him to take the biggest leap of faith he had ever known. He didn't know if he could do it. What could he base it on? Then Allen thought about his life. He was born two months premature, and yet he did not suffer any cognitive or physical handicaps. But weren't there other premature children like him. He certainly was no "miracle" in that context, but it was something to be grateful for. And then he thought about the recent events in his life, especially those pertaining to his search for work. It seemed, as the pastor had said, the wisdom of this world hadn't profited him much after all. Everything that seemed to be common sense had failed him. "Why not believe in Christ?" Allen thought to himself. Then he headed toward the altar.

"Where are you going?" asked Tim.

"I'm going up to the altar call."

"You've got to be kidding! You bought all that?"

"It's like my mother said: 'What have I got to lose?'"

Tim sat back down and shook his head in resignation, while Allen continued to head toward the altar. Lena smiled with approval as she watched Allen move toward the front. Allen stood in the line that was headed by pastor Bynum. As the line moved forward and he got closer to the Pastor, Allen thought more about the decision he was making. It

191

would have to be all or nothing. There would be no doing salvation halfway. If he was going to believe, he would have to believe whether he understood or not. Once he put his hands to the plough he was not going to turn around. Allen had to admit to himself that he wasn't totally comfortable with what he was doing. He had been used to operating by sight, touch, and tangible evidence. Allen was not used to thinking in terms of the spiritual or intangible, but something inside him told him the choice he had just made was the right one.

No sooner than he had finalized his decision, he found himself face to face with Pastor Bynum.

"Are you ready to accept Jesus Christ as your Savior and the gift of eternal life?"

"Yes."

As the pastor laid his hands on his head and began to pray, Allen began to feel something stirring deep within himself. It was like a burden was being lifted from his soul. For the first time he seemed to be awakening to something larger than himself. It was relieving and at the same time, a little frightening. Allen knew within his heart that this was the beginning of something new in his life. Something that would change his life forever.

COMMENCEMENT

TWENTY-FOUR

As everyone sat down to dinner, Tim was astonished at the amount of food on the table. Not that he wasn't used to sumptuous meals and lavish dinners, however he had never seen so many of the entrees placed on the table at one time. Tim was more used to having service workers and waiters bring out dishes for service at different times during the meal, which was more in keeping with his aristocratic upbringing. He was also a little hesitant to partake of the cuisine as well, for he had never eaten much "soul food" in his life. The meal consisted of collard greens cooked with smoked turkey wings, ham cooked with string beans, macaroni and cheese, fried chicken, potato salad, biscuits and pan gravy. It seemed like everything the stereotype called for and the only thing that was missing was the watermelon. It made Tim feel a little uneasy, but mitigating this was the warmth he felt coming from the two families themselves. He had never met any people as warm and as accepting as Allen's mom and dad. The Pastor was a bit uptight, but he was amiable enough. The coldest of them all was Tamiko's mom, Mother Rose, who didn't seem to like Tim and only managed to convey a cool civility at best.

"Mother Rose, you really outdid yourself today! These greens are something else!" exclaimed Vernon.

"And you know I'm going to keep bugging you to give me the recipe for these biscuits, Rose. They're better than the ones from Emily Ann's!" said Lena.

"And you know this ham is tight! Is that how you kid's say it now-a-days? 'Tight'?" gushed the Pastor. Everyone chuckled.

"You all are too kind, really", blushed Mother Rose. Then she looked over toward Tim who was merely picking at his meager plate of macaroni, ham, and string beans. "But I see that there's someone who's not too fond of my cooking."

"Oh, no, really. It's delicious. It's just that sometimes I have stomach issues. It's just the stress from work and not being able to eat properly all the time", explained Tim.

"If it's been bothering you a lot you should see a doctor", Lena suggested.

"I don't think it's that serious. I just need some rest, that's all. I'm scheduled to take a short vacation in December. Hopefully, once I get some rest, I should be okay."

"Are you sure?" asked Lena.

"Yes. I used to get this way in college all the time around exams. Remember, Allen?"

"How could I not? I even got puked on once."

"Was that necessary?"

"You brought it up."

"What's going on at work that's got you so worked up, young man?" asked the Pastor.

"You know how it is out there now. They downsized some positions and now I have more responsibility. It's been a challenge, but I think I'm finding my way. At first it was just crazy, but now things are beginning to slow down a bit and the admins have been helping me to keep things organized", explained Tim.

"I don't see how you do it, Tim. You're doing the work of four people, and with no help from that lazy vice president, uh, uh…what's his face? Winston?" asked Tamiko.

"You mean, Preston", Tim sighed.

"Yeah, Preston. Honestly, I don't know how you put up with it all. And I thought my situation was bad!"

COMMENCEMENT

"I don't know, Tim. If my job was causing me to be physically ill, I'd think of finding another one pretty soon", advised Lena.

"I'd love to Mrs. Sharpe, but in our current economic environment, I don't think I'd have much luck."

"No job is worth risking your health, chile. And anyways you never know how the Lord will work. He blessed Allen finally!" said Lena, spilling Allen's secret.

"He did!" exclaimed Tamiko with delight.

"Allen, how come you didn't tell us?! This is great news!" cried Tim.

"I'm going to be a janitor at the Sheraton. Not exactly Wall Street", said Allen dryly.

"At least it's something. Work is work in my book. Ain't nothin' to be ashamed of", said Vernon.

"And who knows what the Lord will do for you there? What does the word say? All things work together for the good of those who love God.[1] It may not seem like it, but this is in His plan for you. Allen, you keep reading the Word and praying. Let the Lord lead you. He didn't bring you here just for nothin'", added Lena.

"Speaking of the Word, Pastor, I know that God was working through you today! I could feel the Anointing breaking yokes! Praise God!" sang Mother Rose.

"I was going to preach one thing, but I believe God put something else in my spirit to preach. I felt like Jeremiah. It was like 'fire shut up in my bones'.[2] I like to think that God was speaking through me to someone who needed to hear that", said Pastor Bynum.

"It sure spoke to me", said Allen.

"And you don't know how glad I am about that, Allen. You know if you have any questions, or if you need someone to pray with you, I'm always available."

"Thank you, pastor. I'll let you know if I need anything."

"And what about you, son?" Pastor Bynum asked Tim.

"Who? Me?" said Tim taken off guard a little.

"Yes, Tim. Do you think you'd like to come back and join us again?"

"Uh…okay, sure", he said a little diffidently.

"I'm curious, Tim, what did you think of the pastor's sermon?" asked Mother Rose.

"Look, I'll have to be honest…I'm not really into religion. I'm an agnostic", admitted Tim.

"Oh, really?" said mother Rose, her eyes narrowing into little slits.

"While the Reverend, I mean, Pastor, made some salient points, I'm not sure if there is a God", Tim said explaining himself.

"I'm curious Tim. What is it that makes you think there is no God?" asked Pastor Bynum.

"I mean there is the existence of injustice, the suffering of the innocent, war, natural disasters, and famine. If there was a God, why would he allow all of these things?"

"Just because He allows these things doesn't mean He's happy about them."

"So, if He doesn't like it, why doesn't He make them all go away? After all, if He is as all powerful as you claim He is, can't He just stop it and have us all live in peace and fellowship with one another?" asked Tim.

"God doesn't make anyone do anything. He leads us to Him and we either accept or reject His will. The reason why there is so much suffering is because so many people would rather reject God than accept Him. But for those of us who choose Him, one day Christ is going to come back and set up His kingdom down here on the earth, and we will all live in peace and fellowship with one another just like you said."[3]

"But according to Christianity, there has to be this great apocalypse where everyone dies and then after death we're all sorted into different groups, with some people going to 'heaven' and some going to 'hell'. And why would a good God want anyone to be in hell?"

COMMENCEMENT

"First of all, when we go to be with Christ, we will be very much alive. Life consists not in the flesh, but in the spirit of a person. Our spirits will be very much alive and God will put us into a glorified body like that of Christ.[4] Secondly, with regard to your question about hell, do you think a loving and just God would allow someone like Hitler or Bin Laden to just do whatever evil they were big enough to do and think they could go to heaven? That would make every Christian's faith and work in vain and God's law would be a meaningless lie. God loves us, but he hates sin and there are consequences for sin, just like there are consequences for breaking the law. And if you die in sin without repentance and acceptance of grace, you are forever lost."

"Still it's a lot of 'pie in the sky'. What about this life? Isn't that what really matters? It's not like there's definitive proof that heaven or hell even really exist."

"My son that 'pie' in the sky that you speak of is still pie. The next life is going to be just a real as this one, but it's going to last a lot longer. Our time in this world is only preparation for the one that is to come. It will determine where and how we live in the next life. The only thing we should be concerned about right now, is if how we are living is preparing us for eternal life or for eternal suffering. And I don't have to see a heaven to know that there is one. His Word says it and I believe it. You have to have faith and you have to believe. What does he say? 'Faith is the substance of things hoped for, the evidence of things not seen.'"[5]

"Preach pastor!" exclaimed Mother Rose.

"But that's just it. A lot of what is required in Christianity, and most all other religions really, is a blind faith in the unknown. Just like you spoke of today. I don't think I can believe in anything like that. It's like asking me to believe in Santa Claus."

"So you want God to prove to you that He is God?" asked the Pastor.

"When you put it that way it sounds a little scary", replied Tim with some reservation.

"He can, you know. And if He does, I don't think you're going to like it. In the mean time, I'll just keep praying for you Tim."

197

"Don't worry yourself too much, Pastor. You know what the Bible says, 'a sinful generation seeketh a sign and none shall be given unto it, but the sign of the prophet Jonah.'[6] I'm just glad to see Allen making the right choice. Who knows? Maybe we'll see him up in the pulpit someday."

"I wouldn't make any bets on it, Mother Rose." said Vernon doubtfully.

"Oh, I don't know anyone better suited to take over when Pastor retires. That Ruth Joyner thinks her little Daniel is going to be next in line for Greater Apostolic just because the pastor let him preach at the youth service a couple of weeks ago."

"What's wrong with Daniel. He feels he has a calling, he's dedicated to the word, and most importantly, he's effective. He really has gotten a lot of our younger people to become involved in the church. As a matter of fact, I was thinking of making him a Junior Pastor."

"Pastor Bynum, please. Don't encourage him. That would send his mother off the deep end."

"Just let me worry about Daniel, and let God take care of his mother."

"I'm sorry Pastor, but I'm not as impressed with him as you are. He seems very worldly if you ask me. He's into all that Gospel rap and hip-hop non-sense. You can't have one foot in the church and the other in the world."

"And I've heard that Ruth is thinking of trying to set something up between Tamiko and Daniel", added Lena.

"Over my dead body!" exclaimed Mother Rose.

"Well, Miko, what do you have to say about it? It's your life", said the Pastor.

"Everyone can just calm down. I have absolutely no interest in Daniel", Tamiko said flatly.

"Why not?" asked the Pastor who was a little disappointed with Tamiko's lack of enthusiasm. "He's a nice boy. A nice *Christian* boy."

COMMENCEMENT

"He's nice, but he's not my type. He's looking for a woman who just wants to sit around and make babies. I want something more for myself than just being a mom. Not that there's anything wrong with being a mom if that's what someone wants. It's just that's not what I want for myself right now, and I don't think that's what God wants for me, either."

"Amen to that. I don't want my baby wasting her life being somebody's baby machine. Or anything else that some no good man might have in mind for her", said Mother Rose cutting her eyes at Tim. Fortunately or unfortunately, he was too preoccupied with Tamiko to notice.

"And there are plenty of other men in our church to choose from", added Lena.

"Most of the men in our church are married, Momma Lena."

"What are you talking about? There are lots of young men in our church that aren't married. Allen's not married", sang Mother Rose smiling at Allen.

"Mom!"

"I was just using him as an example! I just want you to see that there are lots of young, available, Christian men in our church, so you don't need to be running around with any of these young pagans out here. You know what the Bible says: be not unequally yoked with unbelievers."[7] said Mother Rose, as she cast another unfriendly glance Tim's way.

"If Tamiko wants Allen, she better not wait too long", warned Vernon.

"What do you mean?" inquired Mother Rose.

"Allen's steppin' out with some girl named Halle he met at the job fair."

"Who in the world is Halle?!" exclaimed Tamiko cutting her eyes at Allen.

"Her name is Holly, and it was our first date. I wouldn't say it's serious just yet."

"What do you mean 'just yet'? You're going out with her again?" Lena questioned anxiously.

"Just to the Election Night party at Leandra's."

"What Election Night party?" asked Tamiko.

"You guys wouldn't know because you left early. I was going to mention it to you, but I forgot until now. After you left, when we were going to the theatre, Richard and Leandra invited us to an 'Election Night party' on Election Day. You and Tim are invited, too."

"Allen, you know I don't do 'parties'. Family celebrations, dinners, and praise celebrations, sure. Parties, no", said Tamiko scornfully.

"I'd love to go, but I just don't know if I can fit it in", said Tim.

"I want to know more about this Halle person", blurted Tamiko.

"Does she at least attend a good Bible believing church?" asked Lena.

"If it makes everyone feel better, she does go to church. She goes to Mt. Ebenezer over on third in the Bronx."

"I don't know, Allen. I think the pastor there is a charlatan. Who knows what type of heresies that young woman may be learning. Lena, she may be a corrupting influence", said Mother Rose warily.

"Let's not jump to conclusions, Rose. You think every other preacher that's not me is a charlatan. At least this young lady is in the church", Pastor Bynum replied.

"Let's not get too happy about that. There's a lot of wolves in sheep's clothing running around in the church", cautioned Lena.

"Amen", replied Mother Rose as she eyed Tim.

TWENTY-FIVE

As Allen looked at himself in the locker room mirror, all he could feel was shame and humiliation. How could he feel otherwise? He had spent a good portion of his life working hard to avoid the situation he was in now. The bluish-gray pants felt and looked too big. The light blue shirt felt too tight. Allen unbuttoned the collar and rolled up the sleeves to make the outfit look a little less menial, but to no avail. As he turned away and sat on the long bench in front of the lockers, he kept trying to figure out what kind of plan God had in store for him. "What could God want me to do here?" he thought.

Before Allen could get lost in thought, Mr. Hardy, the facilities manager appeared with one of the other workers to get him acquainted with the responsibilities of his job.

"Don't you look sharp. No pun intended there" beamed Mr. Hardy. Mr. Hardy was a man just like Allen's dad, and he even looked like him, too, but was shorter and rounder. He had worked at the Sheraton for over 30 years. He had started out scrubbing and buffing and had worked his way up to his present position. The same kind of position Allen had been offered months ago. Mr. Hardy was proud of himself and his work, and was yet humble and self-effacing. Many men in Mr. Hardy's position would have loved having someone like Allen working under them. A meaner man would have savored the opportunity to put a young Harvard hot shot down on his luck in his place. Mr. Hardy, however, was friendly and kind and was genuinely interested in showing Allen how the operation worked.

Allen managed a weak smile.

"Thanks", said Allen rising from his seat.

"Allen, this is Davis. He's the repairman that you are going to be working with."

"Nice to meet you" said Allen extending his hand for a shake.

"S'all good" Davis replied curtly, his manner a little distant.

Davis appeared to be a fair skinned Puerto Rican guy with long dark hair plaited in cornrows that extended past his shoulders. He was as tall as Allen, but with a more chiseled physique that was adorned with a number of tattoos. He was probably no older than Tim or Jim, but his worn and hardened expression made him seem a little older. He was what Allen would have called a "ghetto type", and he seemed to be as suspicious toward Allen as Allen was toward him. Allen had had his fair share of bad experiences with "ghetto types" in high school. They were the guys who sold on the corner, had rap sheets that were longer than a Dickens novel, carried firearms like health freaks carried water, and never lived past 25. If they did, it was most likely because they had spent a number of years incarcerated. To Allen, these were the guys who often stole his sneakers, his jewelry, and other things he had worked hard for. They were the guys who always wanted to fight him, who taunted him with names like 'white boy' because he did well in school, and plagued him with all sorts of indignities. Allen was not looking forward to working with or for this Davis.

"You are going to work with Davis on floors 5 through 10 in the south wing of the building. Davis will do most of the repairs and he's going to train you on how to fix small problems, but the bulk of the work you will be doing is maintenance of the floor. You know, mopping, buffing, upkeep of the hallways, small scale paint jobs, changing the lightbulbs, maintaining the fixtures, emptying the trash bins and compactors, stuff like that."

"Okay" said Allen, however he was not okay with a lot of those things he mentioned. Allen barely did any of these things in his own home, except when his mother or father had threatened him. He wanted to go home.

COMMENCEMENT

"Now there are things that are going to be in your routine everyday, like the floors and maintenance of the hallways, but then you are going to have other things that come up. You'll have a radio and you'll be paged if there's anything else that needs to be done. Davis will take you to the equipment area and get you one. Then he'll give you a tour through the floors and show you around. I have a meeting I have to go to in a few minutes. Do you have any questions or anything before you and Davis set off?"

"No, not really."

"Alright then. Davis, he's all yours."

Allen did not like the sound of that.

"Aiight, I'ma take you to the equipment room first and show you how to sign out the radios."

Davis led Allen out of the locker room and down through a dark and narrow winding corridor. Davis remained silent during their trek. He didn't even bother to look back once to see if Allen was even following him. Then finally, they reached the brightly lit office in the far recesses of the basement. There was an open space and plexi-glass counter, and a little gray door that was over off to the side of the counter. Sitting behind the plexi-glass counter was a young copper skinned Mexican woman.

"Yo, Yelitza. Let me get a radio, babe."

The young woman simply lighted off the low backed stool and went to the back of the room, and within minutes came back with a radio that looked like a cell-phone and a clipboard. Davis took the radio and the clipboard from her and handed it to Allen.

"So you just put your name, your I.D. number, and the code number of the radio, but leave the last part blank. You sign that part when you bring it back."

It all seemed self-evident to Allen, but he didn't mention that to Davis. He didn't want to come off as a "know it all."

"How does it work?" Allen asked. He had never seen a radio like this one, and a lot of people he knew used the Motorola ones that have cell phones in them. Allen asked the question as a way to break the ice with

Davis, to get him into conversation and feel out just what type of character he was dealing with.

"If you wanna talk to somebody, you just turn to their frequency and then push the button. Like if you wanna talk to me, you just put in 316 and then push the talk button. When you wanna listen, you just let it go."

Allen tried it out, just to get a feel for it.

"If somebody calls you, they frequency gonna come up, so then you don't have to type it, you just push the talk button. See?" said Davis as he demonstrated to Allen. "Now, I'ma show you where to pick up your cart and supplies, then we gonna get started."

Davis quickly turned on his heel and strode back down the narrow corridor to an elevator in the lobby with Allen following behind him. As they waited for it, Allen tried to fill the dead space with small talk.

"There's so many long hallways, and tunnels, a guy could get lost down here."

"You'll learn" was Davis's terse reply. Davis didn't even bother turning to face Allen.

"I guess, after a while you get used to it. How long have you been here?"

"Four years. Give or take."

"How is it?"

"It's work, man. Keeps them bills paid. And as long as the check clear, I'm not complainin.'" Davis replied rather lethargically.

"I feel you", mumbled Allen, even though he really didn't. If Davis were darker, he would have thought he was Vernon's long lost son.

Suddenly, the elevator chimed and the doors opened. They'd gone up from the basement to the lower mezzanine level. This was where the guests' luggage was gathered from the parking lot and taken to their respective rooms. The area was a hive of activity. There were uniformed security officers scanning luggage, and handing it over to bellhops who were loading the luggage onto huge trolleys so it could be delivered to various rooms. There were also managers and other members of staff hurrying to and fro in the administration of their duties. Davis led Allen to a secluded corner past the security station, through a huge metal door, and then two swinging doors into some kind of equipment room. There were rows of receptacles for the maintenance carts. Some of the rows were empty from which Allen surmised that some other maintenance workers had taken them for use. There were other types of equipment as well, such as buffers, vacuums, leaf blowers and other grounds keeping equipment. In addition to the carts and equipment, there was another plexiglass counter at the far end of the room, this time with an African-American woman manning the station. Through the glass, Allen could see that she kept the cleaning supplies, like the huge bottles of all-purpose cleaners, paint, light bulbs, and other things that the workers used in the daily administration of their jobs. As they moved closer toward the counter, Davis spoke without looking at Allen.

"Usually you not s'posed to come down here for a cart. You s'posed to keep it in one of the closets on the floor you workin' on. You only s'posed to bring it down here if it's broke or somethin' like that. But I know for a fact the last dude that was using it, he brung it down here. So we gotta get it and bring it upstairs" he said before he addressed the young woman at the counter.

"Hey, Kizzy, What's up love?" smiled Davis. It was the first time Allen had seen any trace of friendliness in Davis. It made him a little more human to Allen.

"I'm good. Who's your new friend?"

"This is Allen. He's new."

"Hello, Allen. Nice to meet you", sang Kizzy as she gave Allen a sly smile.

"Same here" Allen blushed, although he should have been used to the way women acted around him by now.

"When you done flirting, could you tell me where Tyron put the cart for the 5th floor?" Davis asked playfully.

"Oh, stop! I'm just being civilized" Kizzy joked.

"Yeah, whatever", teased Davis.

"Ya cart is in station 9, jealous", she teased back.

"That was your goal, right?"

"Please."

"Girl, stop frontin'. You know you want this."

"Take care, loser."

"Aiight. Thanks, babe. I'll see you around."

The smile remained playing about his lips for a few moments after the exchange before the young man's visage hardened into its former glowering mask. "He obviously has some kind of connection to the young woman." Allen thought to himself. Or maybe he was just putting up a front to try to "get the draws" as Richard would put it. Either way, Allen was going to make sure to steer clear of Kizzy. Allen thought about remarking about how nice she seemed, however, he didn't want this guy to think he was trying to take his girl. Especially if he was the type of guy he thought he was.

Davis quickly grabbed the cart and gave it a cursory inspection before taking it and Allen back through the swinging doors, the large metal door and all the way to the other side of the Mezzanine to another elevator marked 'Personnel Only'. It looked like one of those old fashioned elevators. It didn't have numbers that lit up, but a dial hand that moved back and forth as the elevator moved up and down.

"This is the service elevator. That's another thing. Maintenance always use the service elevator. The guests is not s'posed to see you doin' work. That's the rule of the hotel. You gotta be incon...inconsp..." said Davis struggling to pronounce the word he was thinking of.

"Inconspicuous?" suggested Allen.

"Right...right."

They stood in silence until the elevator doors opened. Then they went in and rode the elevator to the 5th floor. When the doors opened again all Allen could see was a dimly lit corridor with two doors almost opposite each other. One was a large metal door.

COMMENCEMENT

"This right here is the water closet", said Davis opening the door with a key on one of the largest key rings Allen had ever seen. The heavy door opened to reveal a long white porcelain sink, which spread across the whole room. The sink had three faucets, and attached to one of the faucets was a rubber hose. Also in the room were two mops, a bucket, and a wet vac. On one side above the sink was a large cabinet full of cleaning supplies and tools.

"The office is on this side", said Davis pointing to a smaller wooden door opposite the water closet. "It's not that big, but you can sit down for a minnit when you on break, and you can listen to the radio, stuff like that. I'ma get you a set of keys from Mr. Hardy a little later, and then you could open up everything yourself when you need to."

Allen peered in briefly. It was definitely not much. There was only space for a small lunch table and two chairs. And it seemed that Davis had a radio, and a small T.V. set up in the place, taking up much of the space on the table. There was also a radiator against the wall next to the table.

"Cool", was all Allen could think of saying at that moment.

"Okay, now we gotta get down to business, and I'ma tell you how it's gonna roll from here on out", said Davis taking as authoritative a tone as he could. Allen's pride immediately brought up feelings of resentment.

"Every single day, you gotta vacuum the hallway carpets, buff linoleum on the uncarpeted areas, check the stairwells for garbage, check the lights in the hallways, make sure the heaters in the hallways is workin, empty the garbage bins in the rooms, and help the other maintenance workers get things ready for the garbage collection. If you see that somethin's not workin' like the heater, or say like one of the guests see you and they tell you somethin's not workin' in they room, then you could hit me on the radio and I'll come down and fix it as soon as I can. Now usually, if somethin's broke, they suppost to fill out a work order and give it to Mr. Hardy at the maintenance desk downstairs, but then you get a lot of these people, they think everythin' is an emergency, youknowwhatimean. I have to do what's on the official work orders first, then I do the other stuff, unless it's a real emergency like there's like a flood or smoke or somethin' like that. You feel?"

"Oh, yes. Totally", answered Allen. He noticed that the longer Davis talked, the more flustered he seemed, despite his attempt at imperiousness. His voice began to quiver a bit, and he never really looked Allen in the eyes, often looking down or around. In addition, he seemed to engage in a lot of nervous gesticulating as he spoke. It seemed so funny to Allen how someone could seem so intimidating one minute, and yet so vulnerable the next. The whole thing made his character very difficult to read and to size up. Only time would tell Allen if this guy would ever be a friend or foe. As for right now, he could settle for a co-worker who just minded his own business and just let him be.

"Oh, yeah, and don't never go in the rooms if somebody's there. If the chambermaid is there, then that's okay, but if anybody else is there don't go there. And most generally, don't go in the rooms unless you really have to 'cuz the last thing you want is for somebody to start complainin' or cusin' you of crazy stuff."

"Sounds like good advice to me" Allen replied after taking a deep breath "So, I guess, I better get started shouldn't I. What's usually done first?"

"Since it's 10:00 already, you could start by pickin' up the lil' random trash in the hall and then vacuuming the floors. Mosta' the guests is up already so the noise won't bother nobody. You could plug in the vaccum to this outlet over here and use the extension cord so you could get all the way to the end. When you finish that, then you can buff the parts wit' the tile. I'll send a guy down from one of the other floors to show you how to use the buffer. That should take you 'till lunch. Then I'll come and check on you, see how you doin'."

"Thanks. I'll see you then."

"If you need help or you not sure about somethin', hit me on the radio. 'kay."

"Sounds good."

Davis strode over to the service elevator and left Allen to begin his humble position as a hotel porter. Allen grabbed the oversized, clumsy looking industrial vacuum from were it lay in the corner next to the sink and began to unwrap the long cord from its dock. He found the extension cord from the cart and hooked it up to the vacuum's cord and then plugged the extension cord into the wall. Allen then dragged the big, awkward device into the hallway and turned it on. It let out a cacophony of whirs and other noises as he began to maneuver the long dust dragon up and down the corridor.

As he vacuumed, Allen tried to buoy himself from despondency by thinking about some of the things he had been reading in his Bible. Last night before he went to sleep, he had been reading about Joseph, and how his brothers sold him into slavery and how then he was betrayed by Potiphar's wife and sent to jail. Joseph had to suffer many indignities before he became the head of Egypt. Maybe he had to suffer the same way. Maybe there was something that God was trying to teach him in all of this. His mother had always said "All thing work together for the good of those that love God." Whatever it was, Allen was hoping that he would be as quick a learner in life as he was in the classroom so he could get out of this mess as soon as possible.

So far it didn't seem so bad. He had to clean, but it seemed to be light cleaning. If he were lucky, he probably wouldn't have that much to do throughout the day. "The class of people that patronized an establishment like this couldn't possibly create much dirt" Allen assumed. Through the din of the vacuum cleaner, Allen thought he could hear a faint chiming sound. He looked over at the radio in his waist belt and noticed that it was lit up. He remembered Davis instructions and took it out and squeezed the little button on the top.

"Yes?" he said, a little self-conscious of how he might sound on the other end.

"Yo' Allen, I need you on level 7. Got a code V."

"Code V? What's that?"

"Some kid lost his breakfast up here in the hall near the front. Bring yo' gloves, the sweeper, a pan and the sawdust, and make it quick aiight."

It seemed like Allen's first day was already taking a turn for the worst.

TWENTY-SIX

The evening wind howled its tocsin song warning the people of the impending winter. As Jim trudged down the street towards his apartment building, he stuffed one hand into his pocket and tried to work his sleeve over the hand that carried his Chinese take out order. Jim lived in one of the large co-op buildings off of St Nicholas on 123rd and a few blocks down from Allen's place. His building wasn't the best place to live, and it wasn't the worst place to live. The super kept the front of the building clean and the stairs were usually free of debris with the exception of a chicken bone here or there. Most of the inhabitants of the building were city workers or workers period. Yet that did not mean that there wasn't a lot of drama in the building. In the past 24 years that he had lived in this building, Jim had seen just as much sordid activity as the denizens of the projects had. The people may have had more money than those who dwelt in the projects, however a good number of them were using it for the same purposes: some weed, hard liquor, and/or parties that ended in shooting fatalities. When his mother died several years ago, she willed the property to Jim. He had wanted to sell his shares and move away and leave the past behind, but Mr. Sharpe had advised him to keep the apartment since it was his mother's last wish that he have it.

As he approached the front gate, Jim dug down into his jacket pocket to retrieve his key. As he stuck the key into the lock, it set off a ringing alarm and the door opened, allowing him to pass into the inner courtyard. From there, he walked toward the entrance of the east wing of the building. As he opened the door, he was greeted by waves of warmth emanating from the radiator in the vestibule, which thawed the frost on his ears, nose, and the left hand that carried his food. He gave a quick nod to the security guard in the corner before he walked over to the mailboxes to get his mail. After that, he headed over to the elevator and pressed the 'up' button with crossed fingers. One of the very big drawbacks of living in this building was that the elevator was always out of service for some reason. As much as the tenants paid for maintenance, Jim would often ponder why they didn't just remodel the elevator. Fortunately, it was working as the signal sounded, heralding the opening of the doors. By the time Jim got out on his floor, he could smell the aroma of the food in his bag and it whetted his appetite.

He looked around before opening the door to his two-bedroom apartment. Since his mother died, he had changed the décor of the apartment completely. In the living room, where there was once a three piece blue and beige floral-print sofa set with mahogany end tables, now there was a leather sectional, and a glass coffee table with pewter accents. In the kitchen, the old oak finished cabinets and counters were replaced by black marble and cheap lacquer finishes. A lovely and homely chestnut dining room set, sideboard and cabinet once graced the corner called the dining area, and in its place was a simple metal and synthetic table set from IKEA. Jim thought that changing the décor would help him to deal with the loneliness and emptiness he felt every time he opened the door and his mother did not appear to ask him how his day was, or with his favorite dish to cheer him up. Jim thought that if he emptied the apartment of the memory of her, he would be able to have peace and be able to get over her death. Instead, he only managed to take away all of the things that would have eased his grief.

Jim threw his keys and the mail on his coffee table and placed his food next to them in front of the 30 inch flat-screen plasma TV. He peeled off his coat and put it on the rack in the hall next to the door before proceeding to the kitchen to wash his hands before he ate. It was one of the things his mother taught him that stuck with him. "Always wash your hands before you eat", she would say. When he was done he plopped himself down on the couch, grabbed the remote from the coffee table and turned on the TV. He turned to a random channel and found an old episode of *The Fresh Prince of Bel Air*. He had always loved this show as a kid. He remembered trying to get all of his homework done before it came on so his mother would allow him to watch it. His mother had never liked the show, but she allowed Jim to watch it. Momma was a very devout Christian, and she didn't like rap music or rappers like the Fresh

Prince. But Jim argued that since he didn't really rap in the show it would be okay. Momma uneasily relented. That was Momma. Everything that went on in the house had to pass the 'what would Jesus want?' test. If she didn't think Jesus would like it, it wasn't happening. Momma lived her whole life for Jesus.

Momma Merta, as most people knew her, didn't just talk the talk of Christianity, but walked the walk. Jim could remember all the times she had taken him down to Pastor Bynum's church on Thanksgiving to help cook and serve food to those who were less fortunate, and the Christmases when she would buy gifts for children she didn't even know. Not to mention the numerous occasions in which she had turned her own home into a sanctuary for young teen mothers who needed help. Everything she did, she didn't ask for anything in return. Momma Merta did everything for the love of Jesus, and yet when she needed Him the most, Jesus let her down. At least that was how Jim saw it.

Jim opened his take out of ribs and shrimp fried rice. It wasn't the best in Chinese cuisine, but it would kill his hunger. As he took a bite out of a rib, which was left rubber like from his trek in the cold, Jim tried to watch the show in front of him to take his mind off of that fateful day. Still his mind went back there. Jim had just visited his mother in the hospital. She was so thin and weak, and had lost most of her hair due to the chemo. Still she managed to smile. Jim could remember what his mother had told him. She said that God was with her and that she wasn't worried anymore. She was in His hands and He knew what was best. It seemed to Jim as if Momma was sure that God would bring her through. Jim thought He would, too. Jim had been praying all week, fasting, going to church two to three times in the week. He thought God would bring her through, if not for all the prayers, at least for the sake of his mother. Momma was the most God-fearing person Jim had known besides Allen's parents and the Pastor. But that night Jim lost her and his faith followed not far behind.

After his mother's death, Jim stopped going to church. It didn't seem fair that someone who loved God so much couldn't even get Him to spare her life for just a few more years. It made Jim think that maybe there was no God. Then he met some real brothers at St. John's who helped to spell it all out for him. He had been worshipping a white man's god, if a god even existed. What he believed in wasn't real, that's why he had been let down. They told Jim that the god represented in organized religion was a political scarecrow that was use to mollify African-Americans, so they would obey their oppressors. Black preachers promised "pie in the sky" for tomorrow, while the white man was having his on earth right now. So he let his belief in God die. It was something that Jim didn't mind doing. There were too many rules to it anyway. In the past, there were so many things that he couldn't do. No women, no secular music, no r-rated movies and just no fun. Jim's decision to abandon Christianity seemed to free him from an arbitrary and senseless orthodoxy. It was all up to him now, and he wasn't beholden to anyone. A notion very liberating, but at the same time very overwhelming as well.

There were times when it seemed like the weight of the world was on Jim's shoulders and he had no one to turn to. Of course, he had his friends, and the Bynums and the Sharpes but there were times when even they didn't understand. It made him think about his conversation with Callie about a month ago. All of his friends thought he should be in law school by now, on his way to becoming some slick lawyer. His friends didn't understand just how big a risk he would have to take in order to make that step. They didn't understand just how hurt he was when his dream of being a law clerk was crushed by the reality of institutional racism. What if he went to law school and for some reason had to drop out? What if he found out that he didn't have what it takes to survive, let alone, succeed in, law school? How could he deal with all those racists out there who were just waiting to give him a hard time? Jim didn't have a guilty white dad who could hook him up with a job like Tim did. He didn't have loving and patient parents like Tamiko and Allen who would support him unconditionally, at least not any more. Nor did he have Callie and Richard's financial acumen and resources. Besides, there was nothing really wrong with working at the MTA. He could make a future for himself there. If not there, somewhere else. But where?

Thinking this way always made Jim feel tense, so he got up from the couch and went to the kitchen and grabbed a beer from the fridge. Jim used to drink only on nights out, then extended his drinking to the weekends so he could wind down from a hard week at work. Now it was only Monday and he had to have a drink. But why not? He'd had a difficult day. He ended up driving one of the worst lines in the city, the C line into Manhattan. It had been a long time since he last drove a train on this line, so he had to take it kind of slow so he wouldn't miss any of the key turns and passes in the tunnels. Then there were signal problems and he ended up idling in tunnels for up to an hour at a time. Now he had to contend with painful memories from his past, and the uncertainty of the future. He needed something to help him relax, and the last time he checked, drinking was not a crime, so long as he didn't get into a car afterward.

Jim alternated between his beer and the Chinese food, which was growing cold and stale. Soon he left off from the take out tray and finished the beer. He tried to concentrate on the program, but had missed most of the funny parts of this particular episode already. So he decided to go back to the fridge and grab another beer. Momma would disapprove. She believed that alcohol was a tool for the devil. That was just a bunch of nonsense. Jim was all too glad that he didn't have to live his life based on such foolish superstitions anymore. And yet what did he live his life based on? Where was he going? What was his life about? As often as he tried not to think about it, these questions just kept confronting him again and again. Fortunately for him, a buzz from the intercom relieved him from having to ponder such questions longer than he wanted to.

Jim walked over and pressed the talk button on the intercom.

"Who is it?!" Jim demanded in an almost threatening voice.

"Who you think it is?" responded the pleasantly familiar voice.

"This ain't no Jehovah's Witness, is it?" Jim laughed.

"Man, open the door! It's cold out here!" the voice yelled back.

Jim buzzed in his visitor and then went to his door and unlocked it. Next, he went to the living room and disposed of his half-eaten take out and empty beer bottle, leaving the one he was still drinking on the table. He cleared off some dirty clothes from the couch and his recliner and threw them in his bedroom. In a few moments there was a knock at the door.

COMMENCEMENT

"It's open", Jim yelled.

"Hey man, what's up?" Allen greeted him from the door.

"Not much man, just layin' back. Have a seat. You had dinner yet? I don't have much in the fridge to offer. I just had some take out myself."

"Nah, man I'm good. I just had a bagel on the train before I got here. I can wait until I get home."

Allen hung up his coat on the rack in the hall and then threw himself into Jim's recliner.

"What is that about?" asked Jim in surprise as he surveyed Allen's uniform.

"What?"

"That get up you got on man."

"You don't know? I thought Tamiko or Tim would have sent you a text by now?"

"Sent me a text about what? You got a job at a parking garage?"

"No. That has a little more dignity to it. Anyway, last night during Sunday dinner, my mom let everyone know that her Harvard graduate son is now working at the Sheraton as... hold on to your hat now... a porter!" exclaimed Allen in mock excitement.

Allen seemed to be taking a page from Tim's book of sarcasm. It sounded to Jim like Allen was on the verge of another 'whine festival', however, Jim was not in the mood to entertain him tonight. It was starting to become a little more than irritating how Allen was always disparaging blue-collar jobs as being beneath him. It sounded like he had been spending too much time with Tim. Being a blue-collar worker, Jim couldn't help but be a little offended at Allen's attitude. But still Allen was his friend, and he knew where the attitude came from. He himself had felt that way just a couple of years ago. He knew what it was like to be the only child of an overprotective mother, who thought everything you did was miraculous. However, the last two years had helped him become more grounded and he hoped to lend some perspective to Allen.

"Look man, you don't have to save face with me. I feel where you're coming from. It's not what you expected. But, hey, it's a job right?"

"Loosely speaking."

"So I take it you got a call back from someone at the job fair?"

"No. This is my mom's idea of a 'hook up'. She had to go begging to one of the church sisters for help."

"Just be glad you got people looking out for you. Besides I could think of worse things to be than being a porter."

"But Jim, I haven't even told you about all the wonderful things I got to do on my very first day. I got to clean up vomit off a carpet, I got to gather garbage from a compactor and put it into these great big ten ton bags and then carry them out to the curb, and I was nearly electrocuted by faulty wiring in a carpet shampooer."

"Still, its honest work and you get paid. They are paying you, right?"

"Fifteen dollars an hour but no benefits until after a 6 month probationary period."

"That's not bad."

"And it's not good either, considering what I have to put up with. The worst part of it is the guy that I work under looks like something straight out of the state penitentiary."

"Oh, poor Allen has to get his hands dirty touching garbage. And he has to associate himself with the lower classes. Oh, the tragedy of it all!" mocked Jim.

"Very funny."

"Welcome to the real world man. Here have a beer. It'll take the edge off."

"No, thanks. You know I don't drink. And since when did you start drinking during a work week?"

"Since I felt like it, Dad."

COMMENCEMENT

"Suit yourself", said Allen resignedly. "I know it sounds a lot like I'm whining…"

"Sounds like?"

"O.K., I'm whining, but not without good reason. And you know where I'm coming from. When you had to take that transit gig, you weren't terribly happy about it either. I just don't like the idea of settling for less. It's like I'm not living up to what I was meant to be."

"So if you feel that way, why don't you just quit? It's not like you have any responsibilities like I did back then. I had to think about how I was going to survive. When I got out of school, and my mom died, I had to think about how I was going to keep a roof over my head and feed myself. I needed a job. Period. Other than your student loans, you don't have any real debts. Your parents aren't exactly in the poor house. You could coast with them until you get something that you consider to be more appropriate."

"I wish it were that simple. I may live with my parents now, but I'm not trying to make this situation permanent. And besides, my conscience won't allow me to just live off of them. They've been working hard for a very long time. They deserve to retire and have fun, and not worry about taking care of me for the rest of their lives. Then I have other, more personal, reasons for why I have to stay."

"What personal reasons? Some hottie there you tryin' to get close to?"

"No, nothing like that. I'm not sure you'd understand. You might think I've gone off the deep end."

"Let's hear it."

"I just think…you know…maybe this may lead to something bigger for me. Maybe I'm supposed to learn something here: you know like in that movie, "The Karate Kid".

"You mean like 'wax-on, wax-off'?"

"Yeah, like maybe this job is preparing me for something."

"Like, what?"

"I don't know. I'm just hoping that God will reveal it to me in time."

"Now you *do* sound like Tamiko."

"I know, but I've been thinking lately. I don't think she's so far off the mark anymore. It's just that for a long time I thought I could do everything on my own. That all of the answers to everything were in me to find, but now I'm starting to realize that I don't know everything."

"Nobody knows everything Allen."

"And that's my point. There has to be somebody who does. Maybe I really do need to start talking to God. I mean, who else can I turn to? Who else can tell me what to do? Maybe I really do need to try to go on a spiritual journey or something, ya know?"

"And do you really think you're going to get an answer?"

"Look, Jim, I know you're skeptical, and after everything you've been through, who wouldn't be, but somehow it just seems right to me."

"Allen, you know I always try to be straight with you, so I'm going to give you my honest opinion and you can take it or leave it. It seems to me like you're trying to find your purpose, but you're not going to find it buffing floors and you're certainly not going to find it in a false religion made up by white people to keep us down. The reason why you got shut out was not due to some supernatural force. It was because we live in a world where people deliberately conspire to hold the black man down. It's called institutionalized racism. I know because I'm in the same place."

"Let's say for argument's sake that you're right. What's the solution then?"

"To resist."

"And how do I do that?"

"By not letting the man brainwash you with his religion."

"Is that all?"

"And by going out and forging your own path. I mean you and the rest of the guys are so bent on showing 'the man' that you're just as good as he is. You all have to have high paying jobs with fancy titles in order to be somebody. You let this White Eurocentric society set the bar for you and you run to jump over it without even thinking."

"And just how does one 'forge one's own path'?"

"By getting out of the rat race and thinking for yourself. You know, the past two years, I started growing up. Life isn't about all the accomplishments and accolades you can accrue. It's about just having peace of mind, and being happy. You know, live today for tomorrow we die."

"You make it seem like life is so simple. I like to think we're all down here for a specific purpose. I used to think I knew what that was, but now... I don't know."

"If everybody is gonna die at some point or another, what does it matter? Everything that happens here is just random."

"I can't believe you really think that. You make life seem like it has no meaning."

"Maybe it doesn't."

"I can't accept that."

"And I can't accept that a just and loving God could allow my father, a good church going man who loved God, to be killed by some crackhead ripping off a bodega. I also can't accept that an all-powerful God let my God-fearing mother die suffering from cancer. And I also can't accept the idea of a God who allows one group of people to commit all types of injustice on another and get away with it."

"Look, Jim. I understand why you don't want to hear anything about God. I didn't mean to...let's just forget I mentioned it."

"Fine with me man. It's your life."

"I told Miko and Tim about the Election Night party yesterday. I don't think they're going to come."

"Figures. You know the Flanders. They would never come to a party in the middle of the week. You're still coming aren't you?"

"I don't know. You?"

"Most definitely. Anyway, I thought you were all on board. What's with the sudden change?"

"I'd feel odd. This is going to be a big party with lots of city bigwigs there."

"And?"

"And what if someone asks me what I do for a living? What if I meet up with people from the old Alma Mater? I'll end up looking like a punk in front of everybody."

"Allen did you ever stop to think that maybe you are not the only Harvard graduate who is having problems finding a posh job?"

"If there are, I haven't heard from them."

"That doesn't mean that they don't exist. And did you ever stop to think that the porters, McDonald's workers, mailmen, bus drivers, and train drivers of this world are human beings worthy of respect just like the CEO's and stock brokers, and other high titled people out there?"

"Now don't get me wrong, I never said people in occupations like mine aren't worthy of respect and human dignity. But you can't deny that there is a reason why people are in those occupations."

"And what do you think the reason is? They couldn't cut it in the so-called 'Big Leagues' where you want to be? They're not 'special'?"

"You're making me sound like some bougie snob."

"You said it. I always thought there are people in those positions because our society needs them, not necessarily because some people are inherently better than others. The way you talk, it makes me afraid of what may have happened if you had gotten some fancy Wall Street position. You'd probably feel you're too good to hang around some mere transit worker like me."

"No way, man. Never. We're blood, you know that!"

"Do I? What if I told you that I didn't want to go to law school anymore, that I had decided to stake my future in transit? Do you think you would still want to be my friend, now that I'm off the white collar track?"

"Of course I'd still be your friend. But I'd be wondering why you didn't want to be a lawyer anymore since it was your dream since we were kids. I would want to know why you gave up."

"Why couldn't you just accept my decision and leave it at that?"

"Is that really your decision?"

"Maybe it is."

"Fine. Then I'd accept it. That doesn't mean that I wouldn't be worried, but I'd accept it."

"Good. So, are you still on the fence about coming to the Election Night party or what?"

"I guess I'll go. Anyway it's getting late. I better head on home. I know my mom is waiting to hear all about my first day."

"I'm telling you, Allen, things could be worse. There are a lot of brothers out there that don't have half the support that you have. If worse comes to worst, you can always fall back on Mommy and Daddy. You could be in a position where you got a lot of bills and all you got in the world is your job as a porter to pay them."

"Jim, just because I have my parents doesn't mean that I have it smooth sailing. Sometimes you need more than that. Way more than that."

"Like what? Money? I hear that."

"I hear you, too, but I wasn't talking about that."

"So what are you talking about?"

"I don't even know enough about it myself. But when I find out I'll let you know. See ya around man."

"See ya."

TWENTY-SEVEN

Tim headed toward the conference room brimming with pride and confidence in his accomplishments of the past three months. It was hard work, made even harder due to battles with Preston's incompetence and his own physical ailments. Even this morning as he worked with Vera and Clara, Tim could feel another headache coming on, but he would struggle through it. He wasn't going to allow anything to ruin this important meeting.

Everything was ready. Clara and Vera had already set up the projector and placed copies of the report, bound neatly in heavy-duty portfolios, on the table. Tim even went to the extra expense of buying some breakfast platters for the executives to snack on. There were platters of fresh fruit, bagels sliced into quarters, mini-muffins, and croissants with the accompanying condiments of margarine, strawberry jelly, and cream cheese. There were also large crystal carafes of orange juice and a silver thermos of coffee, as well as servings of cream, sugar, and half-and-half elegantly displayed in company silver ware. The executives from the upper ranks were used to 'the best' and Tim did everything he could to make this presentation first class all the way. He knew that most of the upper brass either didn't know or care who he was, or didn't like him. With this in mind, Tim knew his presentation had to be flawless if he was going to make a favorable impression on them. He wanted the work he had done to speak for itself. No matter how they felt about Tim personally, they wouldn't be able to say that he didn't get the job done. He'd always delivered when they needed him to and today would be no different.

COMMENCEMENT

Tim had taken great care to fine-tune the reorganization of his department following the layoffs. He was given a directive from Standoff that he had to create a reorganization plan that would fit within the constraints of the new budget and regulatory parameters he had been given. Tim was able to devise a plan that was considerably cheaper than what was projected. In fact, he was going to be able to save the company a considerable amount of money given the new contract with the Brill Company, and his great eye for cheaper products and services that had the same or better quality than the ones they were using. He had already had a dry run with the interface between vendors and departments and was able to trouble shoot problems in advance so the changes happened with little or no fanfare. Tim even had results from a survey that he conducted within the company, which proved that all of the departments were pleased with how smoothly things were running. Some even said that the services were even better than before. The surveys, Tim found, were essential to the fine-tuning process as without the feedback, he wouldn't have had any idea of what to change and how. He couldn't wait to share this bit of information with everyone at the meeting. Tim had been given a lot more responsibility and he wanted Standoff and the others to know that he was worthy of it and capable of much more. Maybe then they might trust him enough to move him up to one of the investment houses into an actual consultant position. Maybe.

The only thing that could possibly derail Tim's hopes was Preston. Preston wasn't very bright, but he was very articulate and charismatic, which made him a very good bull artist. Any other person would probably have been fired after some of the antics he had pulled recently, but Preston was very good at making small things he did seem like miracles, and making all his mistakes look like the work of someone else. Every time something happened it was always "I was told by Tim, blah, blah, blah," or "Tim didn't tell me, blah, blah, blah" But his biggest accomplishment was ego stroking. He knew how to make the big guys feel comfortable around him and that was something Tim could never do, even with his best efforts. He knew Preston was working on an addendum, but Tim didn't particularly feel threatened by it. He knew it would be about 20 pages of the same lame idea worded a million different ways. What made Preston dangerous was his growing influence with some pretty powerful people. The only thing that mitigated Tim's fear of Preston was the understanding that money was the bottom line with the big executives. If you couldn't make money for them, you were done, no matter how nice a person they thought you were. The only thing Preston seemed to be able to make for the firm was trouble.

When Tim entered the conference room, he was a little taken aback by the presence of all the company executives. There were eight of them. One was talking to Clara, and several were taking china plates of food and cups of coffee to their seats, but there was a small crowd around Preston near the refreshment tables. It seemed that he was talking very animatedly with Standoff who was smiling from ear to ear with another heavy weight, Richard Casinoff, who was one of the division heads. Tim couldn't hear what they were saying, and as they saw him approach the table, their faces changed suddenly and the conversation stopped.

"Good morning gentlemen," Tim greeted them cordially, trying to cover his apprehensions. "I hope you are finding everything to your liking."

"Yes, very much. In fact we were just remarking on Clara's talent for refreshments if nothing else."

This was followed by chuckles from Preston, Casinoff, and the others. Tim, who felt uncomfortable with what they were implying simply forced a smile out of politeness.

"Tim, if you're ready, I guess we might as well get started. I do have another meeting to attend at our office in Jersey."

"Yes, of course."

All of the businessmen followed Standoff in a line to the table and everyone sat down with the exception of Clara who was bringing the computer and projector out of sleep mode, Vera who was refreshing the coffee cups of the participants of the meeting, and Tim who was now taking the lead.

First, Tim went over the changes that had been made to streamline the process for ordering supplies. Then he went over how despite the merging of departments, fulfillment of orders and requests would be the same or even better based on the current restructuring. Next, Tim went over the spreadsheets and projections regarding the costs of the new changes to the department. He made sure to emphasize that because of the Brill deal and other changes, the cost to the department would be ten percent less than last year resulting in a huge savings of $4,000,000.00 a year. Tim was confident and he could tell by the looks of the people in front of him that they were pleased with the amount of money saved. Everyone except Standoff, who just sat staring at the projections with a stern, but studious expression, and Casinoff who seemed not to be paying any attention at all, but was whispering to Preston. He was mid-sentence when he noticed, Preston whisper something to Standoff, who nodded his assent to whatever Preston was saying. Tim became a little distracted by their sidebar conversation, but quickly refocused his attention and continued with his presentation. Tim knew that his work had merit, and he had seen how much good it had done for the company. He made sure to mention his work with the surveys and how the method was effective for troubleshooting problems and making things more palatable for the staff. Tim was sure his originality in this area would demonstrate to those present that he was not just some charity case foisted upon them, but someone who took his work for the company seriously and had their best interests at heart.

Soon, Tim was done with the presentation and he opened the floor for questions. Clara stopped the projector and turned the lights on.

"This Brill Corporation is rather new. Do you think they will be as reliable as our other vendors?" asked Casinoff.

"Based on the responses to the quality control surveys, we haven't had many complaints", answered Tim.

"But complaints none the less", remarked Standoff.

"Nothing that was due to inherent nature of services or product. Some people just need time to adjust to change", asserted Tim confidently.

"If you are done, Tim, I hear Preston has an addendum to the re-organization that he would like to present. I'm sure we will all find it to be as interesting as what you have presented to us", Standoff said eerily, almost as if he already knew what it was all about.

"Yes, I'm sure", replied Tim almost glaring at Preston as he took a seat at the conference table near Vera, and Preston strode up to the head of the room.

Preston took a USB drive out of his pocket, put it into the computer and opened up his power point presentation. Tim couldn't believe his eyes as he read the title: An Alternative Plan for the Reorganization of Business Management. This was hardly an addendum at all. Then good old Preston took out a bundle of copies of his handsomely bound proposal and gave it to Vera to distribute to the members present. Clara and Tim looked at each other in disbelief. Tim couldn't believe what Preston was doing. He was trying to usurp Tim's position. Tim's blood was boiling, but he didn't want to make a scene in front of his bosses. It took every ounce of self-control Tim had to keep him from getting up and cramming this 'proposal' down Preston's throat. Now it was clear to Tim that Preston had went behind his back to Standoff. Probably on the evening of their little disagreement. This smelled like a set up, however, Tim was powerless to do anything but to watch events to unfold.

Preston started his presentation by saying that although Tim's plan was a good one, it was too conservative. Preston decided that more aggressive action needed to be taken in face of the economic recession and pressures from the shareholders to reduce costs in the company. He decided that a more radical reorganization was necessary, one that eliminated wasteful spending.

Preston proposed that it was time to automate the supply order process. Instead of having a department for intakes and having people to check budgets, approve the orders, and track shipments and delivery, he wanted to provide every employee with direct contact with the vendors through a personal interface program on the Internet. Vendors and company employees would interface through the company's own supply website. This way people could just submit purchase orders with the click of a mouse and get instant feedback on whether the order was approved and could check statuses over the Internet. Vera and Clara's jobs would be unnecessary and/or redundant and their positions would be eliminated.

COMMENCEMENT

He said that by leaving the responsibility for ordering to individuals in their respective departments, the overhead for supply management would be reduced considerably. The company would only need one person to focus on working with existing vendors, or finding new ones, and maintaining the site. Overall, with the cuts in staff, the firm would save over 15 million dollars a year. That was 11 million more than what Tim's plan managed to save.

The plan was as brash as its originator, and did not mention who would oversee departmental inventory, who or what would interface with the accounting department, or what people would do if things needed to be returned or fixed. Nor were there any specifics about what the site would entail or how it would get started or by whom. When Preston was done with his presentation, he shut off the projector and turned on the lights which didn't shock Tim half as much as what was presented. Preston basically pitched a proposal that suggested that he lose his own job. Even he wasn't that stupid.

"Are there any questions?" asked Preston smiling at Tim almost as if to mock him.

"I don't see how there could be" gloated Casinoff, "I love it. It's totally out of the box. We've really picked a winner this time, Standoff."

"Yes", another executive chimed in "It's right in line with the 21st century. I can't believe no one thought of it before. An Internet site to handle everything would be the most productive and convenient solution. Smart thinking Preston."

Tim couldn't believe what he was hearing. He had to say something.

"Excuse me, Gentlemen, while I agree with you that his ideas are certainly original, I'm just wondering if they are feasible. For example, our department doesn't approve requests ad hoc. I have to check with accounting. Just how would our accounting department be able to use this site? What kind of software would be used? Who would design the website? How much would this cost? And if everyone is ordering their own supplies how do we stop overstock or even theft of services?"

"Tim, let's not be petty", said Standoff cutting Tim off. "I think we all should be professional enough to acknowledge a great idea when it's presented. I think it's gold."

"But his questions do have some merit Mr. Standoff. The last thing our department needs is to have a lot of spending that goes unaccounted for or wasteful spending", replied Middleman, the big cheese of accounting.

"Relax, Middleman, I'm pretty sure that you will all be able to use the website as well," said Standoff nonchalantly.

"Please, Mr. Standoff, hear me out. I don't disagree that we should take advantage of technology, but there are some things in our business which require face to face, personal contact", Tim argued.

"Tim, your point would be valid if this was about doing business with our clients, but it's not. It's just a matter of servicing our employees. And all they're doing is ordering supplies for themselves instead of waiting for someone else to do it for them. I'm pretty sure they won't care one way or the other so long as I sign their checks", replied Standoff.

"It could impact our clients, if our employees find themselves without the needed supplies to service clients, or if time is taken away from our clients to spend on other less important matters…" Tim continued.

"I don't think there's anything you can say that will change how I feel. While I respect the people and the work of the department, we all understand that we have to do what is best for the company. We will continue to work with your reorganization for now as an interim measure but as Preston suggested, the department can be phased out", asserted Standoff decisively.

There was an uncomfortable silence in the conference room that lasted for about a few seconds as the import of what was happening settled into the minds of everyone in the room. Tim knew that they were thinking of choosing Preston to be the site coordinator. He could tell by the way the men were avoiding eye contact with him. It was ironic how safe he thought he was after the first round of downsizing occurred, only to have his whole world crumbling around him now. Then Clara let out a sigh of obvious distress, giving voice to what Tim was feeling.

"I understand that this will not be an easy transition for some of us here, which is why I am also going to offer our excessed workers a very generous severance package, that is, if they are willing to stay on with the firm until the website is fully operational: six months salary and health benefits for six months after excessing. I think that's a fair offer, don't you Casinoff?" recommended Standoff.

"More than fair. Don't you think so Tim?" asked Casinoff pointedly.

"Of course" Tim muttered distractedly. So not only was he going to be fired, but he had to suffer working with, if not for, Preston for the next six months. It was all just too much to bear.

"I just have one question", added Mr. Jacobs one of the bosses from business consulting. "What's the timetable for this restructuring?"

"It shouldn't take more than five or six months", beamed Preston.

"Are you sure? You're talking about hiring a firm to design a web site and software to do all of our supply intakes and then training the staff on the procedures. There are going to have to be dry runs and trouble shooting. Sounds like it could take more than five or six months. Not to mention the new tech staff we'll need to get it done. All that with salaries of the current staff, it just might cost 15 million just to get this thing off the ground", Jacobs cautioned.

"Yes, but we've got to think long-term. Once this new system is running it will be much less of a headache for everyone, and as the years go on the savings will be more evident", rebutted Standoff.

The voices became an indistinct mix of sounds as Tim became distracted by the emotional turmoil within himself. There were so many emotions swirling up inside Tim, he didn't know what he was feeling. There was anger and bitterness toward Preston and Standoff, a despondent sadness about losing his job, and shame for his own shortcomings and failures which may have led to his situation. Tim looked around at the faces in the room. Clara's face was very red, but she kept her eyes down on the table, and fiddled with the pages of Preston's report. Vera was busy clearing the china from the conference table. She looked as if she wanted to cry. So now added to the title wave of emotions that was sweeping him under was guilt. He felt that this whole thing was somehow his fault. It seemed that Preston's quest for vengeance against Tim had affected other people who had nothing to do with what was going on in the office politics. More than anything Tim wanted the meeting to be over. He wanted his life to be over.

Finally, Standoff made the motion to adjourn the meeting and set up a date at which Preston would elaborate on the details of his plan and give them an update about how things were going. Memos were to be sent out to all the departments advising them of the new plan. Tim didn't get much from the end of the meeting. Once the meeting was over, Preston was once again covered in a cloud of executives who were extending praise and congratulations. The sight made Tim sick. Literally. The headache from this morning had morphed into a full-blown migraine. Tim became dizzy and nauseous. There was a sudden rush of acrid bile rising up into his throat. Tim excused himself from the meeting and headed down the corridor to the men's lavatory, as discreetly and as quickly as he could.

As soon as he entered into one of the stalls all of the contents from his stomach spilled into the toilet in front of him. After several painful intestinal convulsions, his stomach was empty. As the episode of nausea ended, he flushed the toilet, exited the stall and staggered over to one of the basins to rinse his mouth and splash water on his face. Then he collapsed on one of the couches in the lavatory. Tim felt drained and exhausted. The emotional strain that he felt was taking on its usual physical manifestation. He'd had more than a couple of episodes of nausea in the past few weeks, but after vomiting his headaches would subside and he would feel better. Tim hoped that if he lay down for a few more minutes the pain would go away. Then there was a knock on the lavatory door.

"Tim? It's me, Clara. Are you okay in there?"

"I will be in a few minutes", Tim said weakly.

"Do you need anything? I can wait for you out here if you want."

COMMENCEMENT

"It's okay Clara. You don't have to do that. I'll be okay."

"You don't sound okay."

Tim was touched by Clara's concern. It took all of Tim's strength to get up from the couch. As he stood up, he began to feel a little light headed and had to hold onto a basin to steady himself. Then he slowly made his way to the door. He tried to gather his composure before he opened it.

"Thanks for looking out for me Clara, but really, I'm okay", Tim said trying to reassure her.

"You don't look it."

"Looks can be deceiving."

"You should really go home, Tim. It's not worth it to stay. Especially after what they pulled today."

Tim didn't want to be a punk. He didn't' want to give Preston the satisfaction of having rattled him, or at least knowing that he had rattled him. If he did that, then Preston really would have won.

"That's what they'd like."

Clara looked at Tim a little puzzled.

"Look, Clara, you go on back downstairs, I'll be there in a few. I'm just going out to get some air, if anyone asks."

"Don't you think you should see a doctor?"

"I don't know Clara. I think an upset stomach is the least of my problems right now.

TWENTY-EIGHT

Allen didn't really want to go to the Election Night party for a number of reasons. First, he didn't really think Obama would win and could wait until the morning for the disappointment to set in. Second, he had to get up early the next day for work and didn't want to be up late at a party. Third, despite his talk with Jim the day before, he was still a little self-conscious about being among the social climbing scene that Leandra was a part of. The only reason Allen was even headed toward Leandra's was because he had kind of promised Jim he would go. In addition, Allen had already invited Holly who was expecting to be introduced to some of Allen's friends. He and Holly had already had dinner before the party at Emily Ann's and Allen was having a pretty good time so far. Allen and Holly had really been hitting it off. They talked for so long that before they realized it, it was time for the party to start. By the time they arrived at Leandra's house it was almost 11:00.

Leandra lived in the posh Lenox Terrace over on 132nd Street and Lenox Avenue. The building had all the amenities of a luxury high rise including landscaped front walks, and a doorman. It sort of depressed Allen because it reminded him of all the things he'd hoped for, but so far, had eluded him. But he didn't want to be burdened down with all of that right now, especially since he was actually having fun for a change. So Allen swept aside all his fears and misgivings and just thought of hanging out with his friends. He just hoped that there would be no arguments or drama, which was becoming the usual, whenever there were more than two of them together at one time.

COMMENCEMENT

"So, is Leandra a friend of yours?" asked Holly as they entered the elevator.

"She's my friend Richard's new girlfriend. He met her while he was campaigning for Obama."

"Wow! Your friend was on the road with Obama? Is he into politics?"

"You could say Richard is into a lot of things."

"You seem to hang with a lot of interesting people."

"You could say that. You'll meet most of them tonight."

"Can't wait."

They got off the elevator and headed down to Leandra's apartment, which was the third door down, where all the music was coming from. He knocked on the door, hoping that the sound would be heard over he music. After a moment, the door opened and Richard appeared, flashing his trademark million dollar smile.

"Hey, big Al! Whas'sup man?" blared Richard greeting him with the pound.

"I'm ready to get my party on, know what I mean?"

"I feel that, yo! And who dis? You got you a shorty, now?"

"I guess you could say that", blushed Allen. "Richard, this is my date Holly. Holly, this is Richard."

"S'all good."

"Nice to meet you, too", said Holly, looking at Allen. She was a little puzzled and shocked by the difference between the Richard she saw before her and the one she had imagined.

"Do you think Leandra will mind that I brought Holly?"

"No problem, man. C'mon in yall, get your groove on. Everybody's here", said Richard taking their coats.

Allen felt a little self-conscious as he entered the room. Leandra's apartment was amazing. It was tastefully furnished in art deco style with

233

an African theme. It was definitely a high-class party with Leandra circulating around with a tray of fancy hor'devores. There was even an open bar. Lots of nicely dressed people were standing around drinking champagne, or sitting on the couch in front of the large screen plasma TV watching the results come in. Allen wondered if he was dressed appropriately enough. Leandra said the affair was going to be kind of dress casual but Allen wondered if he should have worn a tie with his Navy suit jacket, grey poplin shirt, khakis and grey oxford buc shoes. His date, Holly, looked absolutely gorgeous in her little black long sleeved jersey dress and high heels. There weren't as many people as Allen had expected, but there were quite a few none-the-less, and the small apartment was a bit crowded. Allen looked around to see if he could find any familiar faces when he heard a familiar voice.

"Hey, Allen!" said Callie grabbing him for a hug. "It's about time you got here! For a minute I didn't think you were going to come."

Callie paused for a second when she noticed the young woman standing next to Allen who was giving her a very unwelcoming look to say the least. Then she looked inquiringly at Allen.

"Callie, I want you to meet someone. This is Holly. We met at the job fair the other day."

"Really!" said Callie, a little surprised and embarrassed. "Well, how do you do?" she asked extending her hand.

"I'm good, thank you. Nice to meet you."

"Callie is an old friend of mine from high school."

"Yes, we go way back", responded Callie as she narrowed her eyes at Holly.

Allen noticed a little tension starting to brew and tried to engage them in banter to defuse it.

"We would have been here earlier, but we decided to stop and have dinner first. I didn't think it would matter since the polls don't' close until nine and the results usually don't start to come in until later."

"Some of the precincts are already starting to report and Obama has some states in the northeast, but so far they're just the ones we've expected, like New York. So far it's too close to call in North Carolina and Virginia, but were hoping they turn out to be true blue."

"Let's keep our fingers crossed", said Holly.

"Where's Jim?" asked Allen.

"Under the circumstances, I don't think you want to know", answered Callie.

"Why? What's going on?"

Just before Callie had a chance to explain…

"Hey, Allen! Where you been man?!" blared Jim louder than usual. He staggered up to Allen unexpectedly and nearly knocked him over. He was arm and arm with another unexpected guest who was even more inebriated.

"Oh…my…gosh", was all Allen could muster.

"Yo, Al! You came at the right time. Obama is winnin' yo'! You know what this means? It's time for brothers to get paid! Yo, you know me and Tim here, we – we – we – gonna go down there and we gonna try to get a few spots in the cabinet. You down?"

"Secretary of the inferior's already taken, tha's mine. And I call dibs on edmucation secretary for Miko, cause she's not here and I got her back", slurred Tim.

"Allen are you sure you want to introduce Holly to them right now. They're not even making sense anymore. And this one can barely stand up", said Callie pointing to Tim.

"What you talkin' bout 'I'm not makin' sense'. I makin' a lot of sense. It's so much sense, it's too hot to handle baby. Too hot to handle", Jim insisted. "And who's Holly?"

"This is Holly. Holly I'm afraid to say these are my two best buds Jim Reid and Tim Russell."

"Nice to meet you, Jim. And you, too, Tim", Holly said nervously.

"Sleased to meet you, Happy", slurred Tim.

"Same here, sweet thang" laughed Jim. "Yo Allen, I didn't know you had a woman. You met her on yo' job or somethin'."

Allen shot Jim a look that said "Shut up!"

"So you were able to find a job?" said Holly enthusiastically.

"What job?" asked Callie.

"You know, the wack one he don't really want cause he think it's dirty."

Callie was taken off guard and threw a look of astonishment Allen's way. This was the last thing Allen needed. He didn't want to go into the details about his job at a very public event.

"Yes, I did get a position, but it's not worth talking about because it's only temporary."

"It was worth talking about to Jim and Tim", snapped Callie.

"Don't get mad, Callie, don't get mad. He don't want nobody to know cause it's a secret job. He a secret agent. Yeah, he work for the gov'ment, like CIA", chuckled Jim.

Allen put the palm of his hand to his face. The night just couldn't get worse.

"Aw c'mon, Al. It's not like he told her you're a janitor", blurted Tim.

"Well he won't have to be no janitor no more cause he's goin with us to the cabinet", continued Jim.

"I think you two have had enough from the cabinet for one night. Why don't we go in the kitchen and I'll get you two some coffee."

"If it ain't Corona coffee, I ain't interested", Jim grumbled.

"Corona makes coffee now?! Awesome!" exclaimed Tim.

"Yeah, sure. I'll make you a Corona coffee", said Callie rolling her eyes.

"Thanks, Callie", breathed Allen.

"Don't thank me just yet", she glared back.

COMMENCEMENT

As Callie led Tim and Jim into the kitchen, Allen didn't know whether to feel relieved or not. While Jim and Tim couldn't embarrass him any further, they had still spilled the beans about his job to Holly. He was hoping Holly would think they were too drunk to take seriously so he wouldn't have to explain anything to her.

"They're not always like that. And Jim usually doesn't even drink during the week."

"You don't have to explain to me, it's a party. Some people get like that at parties."

"I can't believe my manners. Do you want anything to eat or drink?"

"No, I'm still full from dinner", said Holly who seemed to be losing interest in everything. "So you got a part-time job as a janitor?"

"Full time. But it's only temporary, until something better comes up. I just needed the cash, is all", explained Allen.

"I guess the job market really must be pretty tight if a Harvard guy can't get a job."

"Maybe. It's just..."

"And we have California, Oregon, and Washington!" Allen heard a voice bellow from nearby. "Ladies and Gentlemen, I think we have a winner! Whoo Hoo!" One of the men in front of the television was jumping up and down in excitement.

Allen was thankful for this interruption so that he could find an escape from the awkward conversation he was having with Holly.

In all of the commotion, Callie, Tim and Jim raced back out to the living room.

"Oh my gosh! He won?! He won?!" Callie couldn't help screaming, as she clutched the pearls about her neck. Jim and Tim were stunned silent.

"Hold on, everybody. We don't know for sure", cautioned Leandra nervously. "Richard, turn it up."

Everyone gathered around the television. Richard turned off the music and turned up the volume on the TV so everyone could hear what channel 4's Brian Williams had to say.

"With 358 electoral votes, they are projecting Mr. Obama to be the president elect of the United States."

A unanimous roar of exultation rose from the audience. No one present could miss the significance of this moment. There was hugging, group hugging, dancing, jumping, screaming, praising, and crying. Some of the guests were reassuring each other that the unthinkable had indeed happened. Richard and Tim were even shouting out the windows. As Allen went to join them, he could see that they were not the only ones. There were others who were hanging out of their windows to join the chorus of jubilee. Others stopped their cars in the middle of the street, honking their horns, and some got out for a moment to give a fist pump or a victory dance. Within moments a wave of euphoria swept the neighborhood into a frenzy of celebration. In a nation where a black man's life seemed to be worth less than nothing, a black man had indeed become the President. It was not just one man's victory, but a victory for a whole nation of people who had struggled and toiled for years under oppression. For many it meant the dawn of a new era, a new hope. For others, it was something even more significant.

Soon everyone calmed down as word began to spread that the president elect would soon be making his speech. Everyone stayed close to the television waiting for him to appear on the screen. Allen, Holly, and the others grabbed a place on the sofa vacated by others and waited.

"Oh my gosh! We are all a part of living history now!" breathed Callie.

"I definitely want to remember everything about this moment for as long as I live", said Leandra, who was choked up with emotion.

"Too bad he won't", joked Richard pointing to Tim who had just passed out on the couch.

"I just hope the new Prez got a good body guard", snarked Jim.

"Jim, don't even go there!" warned Callie sternly.

COMMENCEMENT

"I never thought I would live to see this day. If this isn't the hand of God, I don't know what is."

Holly's words echoed through Allen's head even when Obama was making his speech. Logically speaking, Obama shouldn't have made it. He had everything stacked against him. A man with a humble background, very little political experience or exposure, and he belonged to the most disparaged ethnic group in America. According to the way the world works, he should not have had a chance at all. It should have been impossible. Some would attribute Obama's success to the smart way he ran his campaign. Others would give the credit to the disillusioned masses that were desperate for change. But there was something inside Allen that told him it was none of these things. Then Allen heard something or someone.

"With man it is impossible, but with God all things are possible", a quiet voice spoke to Allen's heart.[1]

So it was God that brought this man to the white house. Allen didn't know the reason, but this was somehow in God's plan. If God had an eye on Obama, Allen knew that God had to be looking out for him, too. Allen knew that he would have to learn to trust God. All at once, he finally began to feel a peace about his life that he hadn't felt before. Even though it had just been a few days since Allen had given his life to the Lord, he could tell that something was happening to him. There was a new awareness that was beginning to take hold of him. Allen knew he had no control over it and he was willing to let it take him where it may. It was the beginning of a new life for Allen, and with God in control, endless possibilities.

TWENTY-NINE

Allen was asleep at the desk in the tiny break room across from the water closet. He had stayed up until the wee hours of the morning, first, listening to the New President's acceptance speech and then serving as a livery driver for Tim and Jim who were wasted. To make matters worse, one of his friends relieved himself in his mom's car and he had to explain to her why it smelled like urine. He didn't get home until almost 3:30 in the morning and he had to get up at 5:30 in order to make it to his new job on time. Then, when he came in he had to get right to work. There were railings that needed to be polished, light bulbs that needed to be changed, carpets that needed to be vacuumed, and floors that needed to be buffed. It was raining outside, so the heavy black rubber mats needed to be put down in the common areas to keep guests from slipping on, or ruining the newly buffed surfaces in the high traffic areas. There was a spill and a flood that had to be cleaned up. By lunchtime Allen was totally exhausted, and as unprofessional as he knew it was, he felt he had no choice but to use his lunch break to take a nap.

As he lay slumped over on his desk, a loud beep came from the radio he had laid next to him on the table.

"Yo, Allen! You there?!"

The beep and the voice that followed had startled Allen a bit, and woke him from his sleep, but he was still a little groggy so it took some time for him to realize where he was. The voice from the radio called several times, as Allen shook off his sleep, and sounded more agitated with each call.

COMMENCEMENT

"Yo, Allen! What's the deal man? Where you at?" Davis' voice blared from the radio.

Allen suddenly realizing that he was at work grabbed the radio to respond.

"Copy", Allen mumbled, still a little groggy.

"I need you up in room 811 stat."

"I'm on my way."

Allen slowly stood up from his desk, stretched and let out a loud yawn. He wanted to stop by the bathroom and throw some cold water on his face, but he knew Davis expected him to be there yesterday, so he took the service elevator to the 8th floor and walked down to room 811. The door was open, so Allen just walked in. When he saw the state of the room, his jaw dropped in bewilderment.

The tables and furniture in the front room of the suite had been broken to pieces. Stuffing was protruding from deep gashes in the chairs. There was broken glass all over the floor and red wine stains in the carpet and on the couch. The curtains had been torn down from the windows, and some of the windows themselves had been shattered. The room had the makings of a crime scene all over it. Not long after he had arrived, Davis appeared from the bedroom of the suite. He had a clipboard in his hand and a pen behind his ear.

"What in the world happened in here?!" asked Allen.

"Some lady came up in here and found her man with another chick and went berserk. Only took 'er 10 minutes to do all this. Mr. Hardy had to call the cops. Then we had to take pictures of everythin' for when they go to court."

"So this happened today?!"

"Yeah, man, like half an hour ago."

Allen recalled that he had been sound asleep half an hour ago. Even though it was his lunch break, he still felt guilty.

"Wish I knew who she was. I wouldn't want to mess with her."

"I feel that. But now we got to clean up everythin' and get all the broken furniture outta here, youknowwhatimean. We gonna have to redo the whole place. Right now, I'm just checking out what's broken."

"I guess I'll start with getting up the broken glass."

Allen went back and got his large dustpan and broom and brought them to the room. Then he started to remove the remaining glass shards from the couch and other surfaces before he began to take care of the floor.

"Be careful with that glass, yo. You don't wanna get cut or nothin'."

"Don't worry. I got it."

Allen continued to clean while Davis continued to survey the suite for damages. Allen would have liked to lighten the mood with a little small talk, but given Davis' very business like manner, he didn't know if it would be welcomed. And he didn't really know if he even wanted to get to know Davis better. He was wary of guys like him. And then he thought about the thought that he had just had. What was a "guy like him" anyway? Wasn't that similar to the phrase Mrs. Aldridge used when she spoke about Allen. She didn't try to get to know Allen for who he was. She immediately put him in a box based on some stereotype. Then Allen thought about his conversation with Jim just two days ago. Maybe he was unfairly judging Davis. Sure, he had all of the accoutrements of a "thug" with the tatoos and the cornrows and all, but that was just the outer man. But then Allen thought, that whatever is on the inside of a man often manifests itself on the outside, and this idea made him wary again. But then, after struggling with himself for a bit, Allen decided to put away his misgiving and give Davis a chance.

"That lady must have really loved that guy, if he led her to do all this", remarked Allen.

"Or maybe she's just crazy, period. Some of these chicks ain't wrapped too tight."

"True that. At least for the paranoid, possessive kind."

Davis made no response after this last comment and was continuing to survey the apartment and record the damages on his chart. Allen decided to try to connect with him again on a more personal level.

"I was in a relationship with a girl who could get a bit out of hand. Whenever she got mad, she made objects fly. Usually toward my head."

"Where you come from, I didn't think chicks acted like that."

"What do you mean?"

"You know, like those college chicks. Ain't they suppost to be like high class and all that?"

"Some are and some aren't. I'd say it's 50/50."

"Word? For real?"

"College girls are just like any other girls, man. Women are women."

"You know, I kinda figured that, but you hear stuff. Ya know?"

"Like what?" asked Allen curiously.

"Like people be trippin' bout college and what not. Like it's like Oz or somethin'. You go there and your life will all of a sudden get better than what it is."

"Well, yeah, a lot of people do make it seem that way. It's definitely no Oz, but that doesn't mean that it's all washed up either."

"I guess it's what you make of it, right?"

"I'm not sure if I'm the right person to ask about that."

"I feel you."

There was another awkward silence and the conversation stopped as suddenly as it had started. It didn't seem like Davis was a bad person after all. There were moments when someone like Davis could have just roasted Allen. Davis didn't even sound bitter when he was talking to him about college life. And he was polite enough to not point out the idiosyncrasy between Allen's college experience and his present occupation. In fact, he seemed to have dropped the conversation in such a way as to shield Allen's pride.

Soon Allen became preoccupied with the cleaning of the room. He had gotten up all of the large shards of glass that he could see and put them into the special gray garbage bin that had been brought up to the room earlier. Davis advised him that he didn't have to do a great job, since the carpet would have to be replaced anyway because all of the glass that had broken on top of it made it a hazard. Then they began the perilous task of removing the damaged furniture from the suite and trying to get it onto the freight elevator in the back without causing too much of a stir amongst the guests. Allen was definitely not up to the physical demands of the task. The furniture he was moving was not just regular apartment furniture, but that which was made for commercial use. Naturally, it was heavier than regular furniture, much heavier. As Allen helped Davis carry the sofa down the hall, he could feel that Davis was doing more of the lifting than he was. The only thing that kept Allen from feeling like a punk was the fact that he could blame his weakness on the fact that he only had about 2 hours sleep to go on. Maneuvering the sofa onto the elevator was another herculean feat. Allen clumsily attempted to help Davis with it, but in the end, he had to step aside as Davis brought the whole thing onto the elevator himself. Major loss of face.

And it didn't' end there. This had to be repeated with several chests of drawers, coffee tables, an oblong chaise, and a futon. And that was just one room of the suite! He and Davis had to keep going until they had carried out three rooms worth of furniture. When everything was all done. Allen felt as if he would need someone to carry him out. Meanwhile Davis didn't even look like he was breaking a sweat.

"I think that's it for now. I'll come back tomorrow and start fixin stuff. There ain't nothin' done to the hardware in here so serious that it can't wait."

"I guess I'll go around and pick up the garbage."

"What you mean man? It's quittin' time, yo. We out."

Allen glanced at his watch. It was actually five past the hour. Allen had spent so much time focusing on the jobs at hand, he didn't even feel the time going by.

"Whoa, time flies, doesn't it."

COMMENCEMENT

"When you workin' hard, chief."

"Guess I'll head on out then."

"Don't forget to punch out your time card. You lucky I saw it yestidday. I did it for you."

"Thanks a lot, man. I owe you."

"No big deal. See ya round, man."

"See ya."

It was not lost on Allen that this was the first time that Davis had ever spoken more than one syllable at a time to him. It was still mostly work related, but he seemed to be easing up even if just the slightest bit. It was also not lost on him that so far it seemed that Davis was actually a nice guy. Allen began to feel bad about the way he had originally judged Davis. Yet there was something inside Allen that would still have him wary. After all, why all the tatoos? Had he actually been in jail? Allen had never been friends with anyone even remotely connected to the penitentiary experience despite having lived in the ghetto most of his life. "If Davis had been in jail", Allen wondered, "what could he have done? Was he in a gang? Could he actually be working with someone who killed someone?" Then Allen gave it all a second thought. All of this speculation and fear was just silly. He had some of the same apprehensions when he met some of his other best friends. He thought Jim would be another bully to take his lunch money. He thought Tamiko was a do-good snob. He thought Callie was some brain dead cheerleader. He thought Tim was just some bougie Uncle Tom snob who was just using him for his econ notes (actually, this was true for a while). He thought Richard was a drug-dealing hustler trying to sell him some pot. In every case he would later find out just how dead wrong he was. Hopefully, his initial judgment of Davis would be wrong, too.

THIRTY

Tamiko glanced over her lesson one more time. She had spent extra time making sure that she had all of her materials in an accessible place for the next lesson. She had even rehearsed the exact words that she would say to the students during the ten-minute mini-lesson. There were notes from the last observation referred to in the lesson plan. Tamiko made sure the lesson was differentiated and there were different activities for children at different skill levels. In short, Tamiko had done just about all she could do to make sure that today's Shared Reading and Literacy Centers period went smoothly. However it did nothing to abate the nervous tension inside her. She had to have been observed over ten times by now, and yet every time seemed like the first time, especially since her fiasco of an assessment meeting last week. Today would be her second observation since that day. To make matters worse, now her debriefing sessions were like being put in front of the firing squad.

Tamiko knew that, as with any other observation, there would be a period afterward where the literacy coach, the assistant principal, and the hated Steele woman, and herself would get together to help her see what worked or what didn't. The last time there was very little talk about what worked and a lot of talk about what needed improving. Tamiko was open to learning more and had tried to revise her thinking about the centers as well as the lessons. She just hoped that today, everyone would see just how much work she was putting into the lessons and the children's learning environment.

Then as she looked over at the clock above her morning meeting board, she realized that second period was drawing to a close. Tamiko grabbed her tambourine and shook it in the air. As she shook it, all of the students stopped what they were doing and raised their hands in the air. Everyone stopped except James, an especially mischievous student who always gave Tamiko trouble.

"James, everyone knows what the tambourine means and by now you should, too! Go move your clip down to orange!" scolded Tamiko.

"But I ain't even do nothin'!" the boy pleaded.

"I don't want to hear it! Everyday it's the same thing. You stop when it's time to stop, not when you want to", she reprimanded.

The little boy stomped over to the color chart and moved his name clip from "good-day green" down to "okay orange", which was not a bad color, but not a good color either. Tamiko had to send a clear message to him that she was not going to tolerate any silliness from him today. Then she began to address the rest of the class.

"When I give you the signal, everyone except Jinelle and Eric will put away their writing and their writing folders and come to the rug. Today I am going to sing our good morning song. Remember you have to be at the rug by the time I finish my song", Tamiko warned.

As Tamiko began to sing the song, 24 six and not a few seven year olds raced to different areas of the room to put away their writing folders and their writing tools. Tamiko had to stop her song at one point to remind the children to move quickly, but not to run. Sometimes by ones, or by twos, or by threes they came to the rug and took their places sitting "criss-cross-applesauce" on their rug spot with their hands folded in their laps. It wasn't long before some of the children started to talk, and get silly.

"Our friends Eric and Jinelle want to share what they worked on in their writing today, but they can't because there are too many people who are talking and this makes me very sad", said Tamiko hoping that this would be enough to get their attention, but it wasn't.

"I don't know, but if I keep hearing so much talking, I'm going to have certain students pull their name clips down, and then they won't get to have snack today during reading workshop this afternoon", Tamiko admonished the class.

Silence.

"Remember this morning when we were working on adding details to our writing, well Eric and Jinelle want to share with you how they added details in their writing. First, Eric was just going to write that he went to the park, but then we had a conference and we talked about all the things he did at the park and so he was able to add many more details to his writing. Read what you wrote Eric", she continued wrapping up the lesson.

Eric held his paper in front of his face and quickly mumbled, "I went to the park first I got on the swing my sister pushed me and I went high then I put my legs out so I could go higher and my legs went over the gate."

"Wow, Eric! That was fabulous!" Tamiko praised. "All those details gave me a really good picture of what happened to you and it makes your story so exciting. Good work! C'mon everybody, let's give Eric a roller coaster cheer!"

All at once the children made the motion of a roller coaster going up the slope and going down with a "Woo!Woo!" at the end for a cheer.

Then Jinelle shared her piece about her mom taking her to the dentist. Jinelle, who was not as shy as Eric, made sure all the children saw the accompanying pictures of her story that she drew as well. When she was done she also received the roller coaster cheer. Then both students put their writing away and joined the rest of the class on the rug.

"So today and everyday, when you are writing, you need to make sure that you add lots of details to your writing so that your story will be more exciting to your audience. In fact, let's put that on our "What Good Writers Do" chart. Tamiko was gritting her teeth as she recited the scripted language verbatim. She hated using someone else's words to talk to her students. But they had all this "data" that suggested such scripts made the lessons clearer for student to learn. So Tamiko didn't argue. She just memorized her script.

COMMENCEMENT

Tamiko flipped over a chart on the teaching easel and hastily, but neatly added, "Do I have details" onto a short list.

"Now let's go over some of the things we are going to look for in our writing the next time we write…" said Tamiko concluding the lesson.

And the whole class chimed in to "Are my sight words spelled right? Are my copy-right words spelled right? Do I have a lot of details?"

As the lesson ended, Tamiko looked up to see Booker, Nettlenerves, and Steele all skulking in to see her Shared Reading/Literacy Centers lesson. It was time for act II. Tamiko put her timer on for the lesson. She had 15 minutes for the mini-lesson. Only 15 minutes.

"Alright everyone, today we are going to be reading our Big Book "The Little Yellow Chicken". Today as we are reading, we are going to practice something that good readers do. Good readers get their mouth ready when they get to a tricky word by making the sound of the first letter of the word. Then at the same time, they think about what's going on in the picture to help them figure out what the word is. But before we get to our strategy let's look at some of the pictures and get a sense of what this story is going to be about."

Tamiko went through the book with the children and talked about what was going on in each page, taking suggestions from the children at times. After they all went through the book, Tamiko took extra pains to remind the students of the strategy they were using and then they all began to read the book together. There were post-its on certain words on different pages with just the first letter revealed so that students would get a chance to try the strategy. First, Tamiko modeled the strategy herself with a "think aloud". In a think aloud, a teacher verbalizes her ideas out loud as a way to demonstrate to children how they need to be thinking in order to solve problems they may encounter in a given book. Then for the next few pages, Tamiko had the students join in to help her solve the tricky word. It seemed that the lesson was going well, until Tamiko glanced over at the clock and noticed that she only had 1 minute left to her lesson but several pages of book left. So she basically allowed the students to help her solve two more words, then read the rest of the book with the children while removing the post-its. When they were all finished reading the book, she talked about the lesson of the story with the

249

students briefly before the beep of the timer interrupted them. Tamiko quickly stopped the distracting timer, and told the children that they were going to the reading centers and reminded them to use the strategy during their reading activities. Meanwhile, the women in the back were furiously scribbling onto their pads. Tamiko tried to shut them out as she directed the children to the centers.

"Remember to check the chart to see where you belong. Table monitors bring out the centers to the tables. Tigers you are coming to me first at the banana table."

After the signal, a flurry of activity ensued and the children got busy at their centers. The Tigers (her lowest group) met her at the big crescent shaped yellow table and Tamiko got right into her guided reading lesson with them. They were all level A's, which meant that technically they were not able to read. All five of them were English language learners of various backgrounds including Puerto Rican, Dominican, African, and Indian. Tamiko had to feed them most of the language of the text in order for them to manage it. One little girl had trouble pointing under each word as she read. The others had trouble with some of the concepts in the book. For example, one boy had trouble identifying the objects he saw in the pictures. Instead of reading, "I can see the truck" on one page, he read "I can see the car." Tamiko just pointed out that it was a truck and not a car. The scribbling of the women continued. Finally, she had gotten around to all of them and then it was time for the children to switch centers. Tamiko's group practiced their books while she ran over to get her tambourine. She shook it in the air. This time James was the first one to stop.

"All right, everyone! It's time to clean up and switch to your next center. Remember to check the chart." Remembering James's wonderful turn-around she also hastily added. "Oh, and James, nice work stopping when I gave the signal. You can move your clip back to green."

Tamiko stood in the middle of the room for a while to watch the children during the transition period. She found out the hard way that the transition periods were the times when any trouble that could start, usually did. And since she was watching, she could see that Jerome was being too bossy during clean up and didn't want anyone to help him causing a lot of trouble with his group. Tamiko was able to avert the crisis by saying a few words to the students. She also saw how Nicole was about to start a tickle war with her friend Anastasia. Tamiko warned both girls that they were in danger of having their clips pulled down and found her way out of another potential nightmare. As she returned to the banana table to begin the next round of guided reading, Tamiko noticed Nettlenerves looking at her lesson plan and Booker interrogating some of the children. Tamiko took a deep breath and began to attend to the four children in her second group. They were her second lowest group they were level 3 (or a low level C according to Guided Reading gods Fountas and Pinell) and their book was a little book called "The Lazy Pig". Before she knew it the women were circling her yet again and scribbling in their pads. After the mini-lesson, Tamiko began to listen to the children read one by one. In the process, she found that one of her students, a little girl named Arnetia, was actually trying the strategy and having some success with it. Tamiko praised Arnetia for using the strategy. "I hope someone's scribbling that down." Tamiko thought to herself.

Finally, the bell heralding the end of third period sounded and Tamiko summoned her tambourine once again. Then the women hastily scribbled their final entries onto their pads and left with as much stealth as they came. Tamiko had the children clean up and get themselves ready for the art teacher who was coming the following period. By the time the art teacher came, the children were waiting patiently for her on the rug and Tamiko grabbed her lesson book and her notebook and went upstairs for a meeting with her implacable superiors.

****

"So how do you think the lesson went?" asked Nettlenerves.

They always asked you how you think it went, first. Tamiko decided that she was just going to focus on her weak points. No one really thought her lessons were good, anyway.

"My strategy lesson for the lowest group may have needed some work. Looking back, I don't think it was focused. I also think maybe the book was a bit too hard in terms of concepts. There were still some management issues with some of the transitions…"

"First things first. Let's start with the Shared Reading, since that was the first part of the lesson", Nettlenerves interrupted.

"Yes, of course", stammered Tamiko "I know I didn't get to all of the targeted words…"

"It was a bit too ambitious", said Booker pouncing on Tamiko's words.

"Yes. I was concerned with that, as well", added Nettlenerves, "We have to make sure the lessons are done in ways that the children are getting what we teach them. I'm not sure if you're getting that."

More negativity. More criticism. Tamiko just nodded her head and looked down at her plan. She bit her lip trying to suppress her tears.

"Yes, the amount of work in the book was a little ambitious. Remember, you don't have to have so many teaching points in the book to get your point across, and you have to consider time", advised Steele.

"Yes, timing is key. I noticed that you rushed through the ending of the book", was Booker's critique.

"True, however, that move was warranted and she did get back to the meaning of the story by talking about the theme at the end. It was beautifully done. You took them right back to the meaning of the text." Steele remarked casually "I will also add that the lesson was clear and focused and the children picked it up", Steele asserted.

"Thank you", was all Tamiko could manage, more dumbfounded by where the compliment came from, than the compliment itself.

"The strategy lessons during the guided reading groups were a little unfocused like you said. I noticed that when you conferred with some of your students, you did not engage in teaching that was related to what the focus was", interjected Nettlenerves.

"I know. It's just that it's hard to know how they will respond to the books. Sometimes the things I think they will have problems with they don't, and sometimes there are other things that come up on top of the challenges that I expected them to have", Tamiko explained.

"I think it goes back to really knowing your students. If you know your students, you will choose the books so that they do engage in the problem solving that will get them to the next level", added Steele once again.

"Yes, but part of knowing your students is what you are observing during the lesson. If your observations are off then your teaching is going to be off", Booker commented.

The conversation went on for the next ten minutes or so about Tamiko's conference notes and what she had written and whether or not it was a true portrait of each child's ability as ascertained by the women who had been in the room. There was lots of back and forth discussion about them and it made Tamiko feel uncomfortable to say the least.

"How about we work on conference notes for a while. Tomorrow morning before school, we'll have a professional development session on conference notes, then you'll come and watch me in my classroom, and then you'll do it on your own for a week and we'll check back in and see how things are going", suggested Steele.

"I think that would be good. And I'm going to schedule an informal observation in December to see how much progress is being made. Then we can work on choosing a focus for lessons as well as appropriate books", said Nettlenerves.

Conference notes and book choice were the most basic things to teaching. They were like learning how to float to a swimmer. "If I'm not even good at this stuff, then maybe all hope is lost. Maybe I shouldn't even be a teacher", Tamiko thought dejectedly to herself. The compliment that had been paid earlier had been completely erased from her mind.

Arrangements were made for Tamiko to visit Mrs. Steele, and the meeting was over. At least, no one would be in her classroom for a week or so. And this time she got to be the observer instead of being the observed and that took a lot of the pressure off of her, but then Steele would soon be prying over her conferencing notes, lesson plans, and materials. It was enough to make her want to scream. Once she saw the other women starting to converse amongst themselves, Tamiko slipped away from the conference room and back downstairs to her own classroom.

****

Tamiko had left her professional development notebook in the conference room and had to wait until lunch before she could go upstairs and pick it up. As she neared the room, she could hear several familiar voices in conversation.

"It was okay, but overall, I wasn't exactly bowled over. There's definitely room for improvement. After all, Tamiko is only a first year teacher."

When Tamiko heard her name it piqued her interest. The voice was that of Steele. It seemed that she and Nettlenerves and Booker were talking about her. Tamiko knew she shouldn't have been eavesdropping, and she was afraid of what she might hear. She knew the three of them did not think very highly of her as teacher. Then her curiosity got the better of her.

"There were a few positive aspects of her lesson. At least the management was okay, but teaching is more than just management", opined Nettlenerves.

"True, but I think, she needs to learn that teaching isn't just what you want to do to or for the children, it's about working with them so that they can be independent", said Steele.

Tamiko could expect nothing less from her. She knew she would try to sabotage her at some point.

"And do you really think she's going to be able to learn these things from PD? I think that this is something you should know, regardless", added Booker.

"I see what you mean. Some people just aren't cut out to be teachers", answered Nettlenerves.

"I'm not sure if I believe that. I like to think good teachers are made through good training", asserted Steele.

COMMENCEMENT

"I think we need to be realistic, Rosalyn. We know where this is going. Mrs. Stone was thinking about just making her formal observation early and just giving her a U rating."

"But then you know what happens when they get a rating like that early in the year. They give up and then it just gets worse. And you don't want a loose cannon around when it's time for the quality review", said Steele trying to steer Nettlenerves away from such a drastic measure.

"You're right. How about we just wait until the end of the year, and then let her go. I mean we could do it earlier, but I don't think we'll get anyone better this far into the school year on such short notice. I mean even though we have a couple of subs on hand, they're not very good either", suggested Nettlenerves.

"What about the union?" asked Booker.

"She's a first year. She doesn't have tenure, so we can just get rid of her", remarked Nettlenerves rather flippantly.

"Are we still going to continue with the professional development in the meantime?" inquired Steele.

"Oh, Of course. We've got to cover all the bases. But you know as well as I do, Rosalyn, that all the PD in the world isn't going to help someone who just doesn't have the ability", concluded Nettlenerves.

Tamiko was devastated upon hearing their exchange. It seemed that all of this professional development was just a smokescreen. They didn't think it would help her anyway. She was going to be fired at the end of the year. There was no way she could go in there to get her notebook now. She could feel the tears welling up in her eyes. Tamiko rushed down the hall to the staff toilet. By the time she got inside, rivulets of tears were streaming down her cheeks. Tamiko hated the fact that she always cried when she was upset. When she was younger, everyone called her the crybaby. That was how she felt right now: like a crybaby. Tamiko was going to be fired and she couldn't do anything about it except cry like a baby.

Despite how she felt, she was not a baby. She was a grown woman and a teacher with students who depended on her. Tamiko realized that she had to stop crying and pull herself together. She went to the sink and splashed some water on her face, and then dried it off with the rough brown paper towels from the dispenser. Then she headed downstairs to her classroom where her friend Joan was waiting for her.

"Did you find your notebook?" chirped Joan upon Tamiko's entrance.

"No. They were meeting in there, so I just came back down", Tamiko replied absentmindedly, her mind still in the conference room.

"Are you okay?" inquired Joan who had observed Tamiko's preoccupation.

"No. It's nothing. I was just thinking about something."

"Like what?"

"Nothing important."

Tamiko was too embarrassed to share what she had heard with Joan. Especially with Joan being so favored by all of the other teachers, and the higher ups like Nettlenerves, Booker, and Principal Stone. Although she didn't want to admit it, and despite the fact that such feelings ran counter to her Christian upbringing, she was feeling a little jealous right now. The whole thing reminded her of Tim's situation at work. He too was the black sheep at his place of work.

"O.K. You ready for lunch?"

"I've changed my mind. You go ahead, I have to get ready for math centers."

"I can come back and help you, if you want."

"No, it's okay. I'll be alright."

Tamiko knew she shouldn't have been letting her feelings get to her, but she just couldn't help it. After all, she wasn't in the best mood and she didn't want to risk taking out what she was feeling out on her friend. Joan didn't deserve that. Besides she wanted to be alone to really think about things.

"O.K. I'll see ya later."

COMMENCEMENT

"Later."

Tamiko went over to her desk and took out her lunch bag. She brought it over to one of the student tables, and took out a sandwich. As she took a bite, she began to ruminate over the events of the day and the conversation that she had just heard.

"That's what I get for eavesdropping", Tamiko thought to herself. But then she thought that maybe God wanted her to hear that particular conversation. Maybe He was giving her a heads up so she could make a plan of action. As it stood, the school's administration thought she was a horrible teacher who was beyond all hope. On top of that, there was that Steele woman who was openly trying to sabotage her, and the professional development they were going to provide was merely a sham. It was this realization that made Tamiko really angry. Nettlenerves, Booker, Steele and the rest couldn't even be honest with her. They talked about her as if she was nothing and plotted to fire her behind her back. It was as if Tamiko were a lamb they were planning to slaughter.

"I'm not going out like that", Tamiko thought angrily. "I'll quit before I let them fire me." Tamiko decided that she would stay through the end of next week. She would have left at the end of the day today, but she was helping the children to put on a performance for the school concert and didn't want to bail on them before the big day, which was going to be next Friday. Yes, she would leave. In a way, her decision liberated her and made her feel better. Soon she would not have to deal with Nettlenerves, Booker, Steele or any of the other people at this school the devil was using to try to destroy her.

THIRTY-ONE

When Tim opened his eyes and saw nothing but darkness before him, he thought he was dead and had entered oblivion. But as he became more aware of his surroundings he realized that he was in a room where there was no light. He sat up and tried to think, but his head was throbbing, everything was foggy and the sudden rush of blood to his head made him dizzy, so he lay back down. Then it came to him as he rubbed his hands over his face. He had taken Clara's advice after all, blew off the rest of the day at his job and went to Leandra's Election Night Party. Was he still there in some back room? Was he in jail? He sat up again, a lot slower this time and peered around the room for signs of where he was. He was obviously on a couch of some kind and there was a table in front of him with something on it. So he checked it out and played with it and the TV came on illuminating the scene and yet blinding him at the same time. After recovering from his initial shock, he finally realized he was in his own apartment at the New Towers.

Then he decided to try to stand up, which took a bit of effort since he was still a bit disoriented, and walk over to the window to open the blinds. Then he decided to turn off the TV because it was making too much noise and his head couldn't take it. Now that Tim was fully aware he began to take assessment. It was another full minute before he realized someone had taped a post-it on his shirt. Tim peeled it off and read it.

"I called in sick for you. Your stuff is in the bag next to the couch. Your car is in the garage over on 5th by Leandra's. And you may want to change those pants and take a shower!"

COMMENCEMENT

It was times like this that Tim was glad for a friend like Allen. He always knew how to have a brother's back. Tim looked down at his pants, but didn't notice anything other than they were a little wrinkled. However, on second notice, they were a little damp in the front. A little damp in the front! And down the legs! Tim decided to take a page from Allen's book and swore off all drinking from that moment forward. He only hoped that this embarrassing moment did not happen in public, and that Allen would be a good friend and be discreet. Then, all of a sudden, he felt that wave of nausea that would always sweep over him when he woke up. Within seconds he rushed to the bathroom to vomit. It was mostly just saliva and stomach acid, since he emptied out all of the alcohol on Callie's dress when they were leaving the Election Night party. When he was done he flushed the toilet and leaned his head against the bathtub.

He had been reduced to this: a smelly, drunk loser. Correction: a smelly, drunk loser with no job six months from today, and who in the meantime had to serve as his worst enemy's slave. Tim eased himself up, kicked off his shoes, and took off his pants and threw them in the garbage. He could hear Allen's voice in his head say, "Are you crazy? Those are $500 designer jeans!" There was no way Tim was going to try to explain what happened with them to the dry cleaning guy or the laundry guy, and he certainly had no intention of laundering them himself. He walked back out to the living room and over to the couch to inspect the bag with his things. There was his smart phone, his car keys, his house keys, his glasses, and his wallet. Tim could always trust Allen to look out for him. He put on his glasses and checked his phone for the date and time. Wednesday, 4:30pm. Wednesday! 4:30pm! Today was his mom's birthday, and Tim had to meet her for dinner in two hours! Tim decided to call her and try to get out of it. He didn't want his mother to see him in his present state, and he didn't want to have to talk to her about his job situation, though eventually he knew he would. He tried her number at work, but she wasn't in the office so he tried her cell phone.

"Eleanor Russell", she answered sweetly after several rings.

"Happy Birthday, mom."

"Oh, Tim", she said with some dissatisfaction in her voice. "I was wondering when you were going to call. Allyson called this morning."

"Sorry, mom. Things have been pretty hectic on my end."

"Are you alright, dear? You don't sound like yourself."

"Now that you've mentioned it, I been going through a lot of stress at work lately and you know how my stomach gets sometimes."

"Well it's a good thing for you that we're going to Lydia's tonight. They have an excellent chicken consume that would do you well."

"I'm not sure about that. I really don't feel well at all." For the first time Tim was actually honest about his physical state. He had hoped his mother would be selfless enough to excuse him from his filial obligation.

"You're well enough to work. You are at work, aren't you?"

"Of course", Tim lied. He knew that if he told his mother he wasn't at work it would bring on a fusillade of questions and he was afraid that he might let it slip out that he had been axed. Though six months from now. Tim couldn't risk it.

"If you can suffer through a few cramps at work, surely you can suffer a few more for your mother tonight, right?"

"I don't see why not."

There was no way he could win.

"So Ally and I will see you tonight at 6:30 promptly. I hope you're not pouting, Tim. You would think that as old as I am now, you would cherish spending time with me. Especially after everything I have sacrificed for your well being."

"First of all, I'm not pouting, and you know I don't mind spending time with you."

"I don't know, Tim. When a child waits until almost the last possible minute to wish his mother 'happy birthday', and then in the next breath begins to make excuses as to why he can't even spare a few hours for dinner, it's enough to make one feel very unappreciated."

"I wasn't making excuses, mom. I was just telling you how I was."

"Yes, you were telling me with the hope that I would excuse you so you could go off...tell me, Tim, what could you have to do that is more important than spending time with your own mother? Is it one of those whores you run around throwing money at?"

"No, it's nothing like that! Why do you always have to read into everything I say?!"

"Tim, I'm your mother, I don't have to read into anything. I know. And I suggest you watch your tone when you are addressing me."

"I said I'll be there, alright!"

"I'm not going to go through this with you, Tim. If you really don't want to come then don't come. Heaven forbid that I should be a burden" she retorted angrily before hanging up.

Tim had the better sense to understand that this meant that he had indeed better come.

"I love you too, mom", Tim mumbled into the dead air.

He chucked his cell phone on the sofa and wasted no time getting ready for his mother's birthday dinner. This was a formidable task considering his physical state. His head was still throbbing, and he felt nauseous and dizzy. Tim managed to stagger his way back to the bathroom and turned on the light. In the next moment he was once again kneeling in front of the toilet heaving what little intestinal liquid that was left in his stomach. When the fit was over he stood up, and stared at himself in the mirror. His curly hair was going every which way, and his face looked gaunt and haggard. Not to mention the serious five o'clock shadow. And he only had about an hour to change into a semblance of something a bit more human.

****

It was 6:25 when the cab Tim was riding in pulled up in front of Lydia's restaurant. Tim struggled with his mother's present, the flowers he picked up at the last minute and his enormous hangover, as he exited the taxi. If anyone had seen Tim two hours ago, they would have been pleasantly surprised by his transformation into his slicked back usual self. He knew his mother was very exacting about dress and decorum for occasions and it would have been an egregious transgression to arrive dressed in anything less than formal attire. So he wore his best black

Armani over coat over his custom made dark-grey wool birds-eye suit, with his straight collared pink shirt (his mother's favorite color) and a red silk tie, and black wingtips. It was raining out, but it wasn't heavy rain, so Tim hustled under the awning of the restaurant for shelter before entering.

Lydia's was a small but very expensive Italian restaurant. The décor was old world Italian and very cosy. The place was semi-crowded, but still, Tim was able to spot his mother and sister with relative ease. They were talking animatedly as he approached. The candles on the table highlighted his mother's deep-amber colored complexion. She was absolutely radiant and it was easy to see how any man could have been enticed by her beauty. Eleanor Russell didn't look anything near the 50 years she was celebrating tonight. With her slender frame, that looked like it was poured into her one-shoulder deep-pink evening dress and her long black weave parted down the middle, she looked as if she could be the sister to the young woman sitting next to her. Allyson Russell was just as beautiful with her curly sandy blond hair and complexion that was even fairer than Tim's. Tim knew he was not in his mom's good graces right now, and his sister, if she was aware of it, was probably trying to add fuel to his mother's burning resentment. It all made Tim more than a little apprehensive as he approached. He was definitely hoping the night would pass quickly and bring as little conflict as possible.

"Good evening, mom! Happy Birthday!" He said straining to be cheerful while bending over to kiss her on the cheek.

"Hello, Tim." Eleanor said cordially, if a bit stiffly. However her face began to brighten as she spotted the presents. Presents always had this affect on her. "Are those for me?" she inquired.

"Of course." he said handing her the flowers and the beautifully wrapped box.

"How lovely. Thank you", she said as she placed the presents on a cart next to their table "I look forward to opening them after dinner."

"Hello, Tim", he heard Allyson snarl at him.

"Hello, Allyson. How are you?" Tim asked without the least trace of emotion.

COMMENCEMENT

"Fine, thank you. And you? You look a little thinner than we're used to", observed Allyson.

"Yes, Ally. In fact, I'm noticing that now myself. You know he told me earlier that he was sick and I thought he was making an excuse to get out of dinner, but now that I see you I am concerned. I went ahead and ordered the consume for you as I promised."

"It's just things have been a little stressful for me lately, that's all", explained Tim trying to keep away from the topic of work "But enough about me. How are you, mom?"

"Oh, everything is going so well. And that's no small thing given everything that's been going on in the business world these days. I'm not saying that I haven't had to engage in layoffs to save money, but overall my customer base is stable because the services my firm offers are even more necessary now. And despite the fall of the Dow, Sherman was able to rescue the majority of our financial holdings. I tell you Tim, that man is a more than a genius."

"I guess that means I still have my trust fund", joked Allyson.

"At least the modest one that I have for you. The one that your father has been keeping is another story altogether. Thank Goodness Tim was able to get hold of his already."

"Have you heard from him lately?" asked Tim eagerly.

"Yes. But we'll talk more about that later. Right now, I want to talk about my trip to Belize", continued Eleanor bubbling over with child-like excitement.

"Belize?!" questioned Allyson in surprise.

"Yes. Since my firm is doing so well, I thought I would take some time to go on a short vacation. Of all the places I've never been, I've been hearing from my AKA sisters that it's the new place to be, especially during the winter. I'm planning to hop down there for the holiday season with Terrence. It will be a wonderful break from the usual cold and dreary New York winter.

"And what about us?" asked Tim.

"What do you mean?" was Eleanor's reply.

"Did you ever think that maybe you should spend Christmas with your family? After all it is a special day."

"Well, of course we will be spending Christmas Day together as we always do, just not the days afterward."

"Fine. Best wishes to you in Belize with your boyfriend", Tim said in resignation. He realized that it would have been better off this way. Too much time with his family would put him over the edge anyway.

"Mom is allowed to have her own life, Tim", said Allyson peevishly. Tim knew she didn't care about their mom one way, or the other. She just didn't want her own vacation plans interrupted.

"Thank You, Allyson. I've spent the past 24 years putting my all into my children. Is it too much, to want to do something for myself now?" said Eleanor almost whining.

"Is dad aware of your plans?" asked Tim. He knew his mother would occasionally have other boyfriends, unbeknownst to his dad. However, she had never been so very public about her dalliances with any of them until now, which made Tim curious.

"That man is no longer a necessary consideration in my life", Eleanor snapped. "I have tolerated him long enough for your sakes, and now that you are both adults, he has outlived his usefulness. I just hope they have a Four Seasons in Belize."

"If it's a civilized place, they should", commented Allyson.

The waiter appeared with their food. Eleanor had the gnocchi with spinach salad, while Allyson had the spinach lasagna and artichokes. Tim was served his consume as promised. The aroma from the food exacerbated his nausea. It took all his will and then some to keep from heaving at the table. He was also a little unsettled by his mother's sudden independent spirit concerning his father. It wasn't long ago that his mother was trying to impress upon him the importance of doing things to please his dad. Most times it seemed that everything he did was to gain the favor of someone who could have cared less. However now she seemed as if she didn't care one way or the other. The whole thing made him curious as to what had happened to precipitate his mother's sudden change in attitude.

"You are getting pale, Tim. Eat your soup. It will make you feel better", Eleanor urged in an attempt to be maternal.

"No, I'd rather have some seltzer water."

Eleanor waved the waiter over to their table and had him bring Tim some seltzer water.

"You know mom, I'm reporting for the Columbia Spectrum now", Allyson remarked.

"How nice for you dear. And I was wondering how things were going with rush week. Have you been tapped to pledge AKA?"

"I don't know if I want to be an AKA."

"How could you not want to be an AKA! It is an honor that can open many doors!" exclaimed Eleanor in concern.

"Mom, in certain circles… I've been hearing that the AKA's have become very lower class. Nowadays they let in any black girl who has a few dollars and some humanitarian dream. You should have seen them at pledge week. All these burnt ashy looking girls who are likely from the projects. I'm sorry to inform you mother dear, but I think the AKA's are becoming the laughing stock of our people", moaned Allyson petulantly.

"I find that extremely hard to believe!" exclaimed Eleanor who felt affronted by her daughter's claim. "It just may be that particular chapter at your school. I warned you about Columbia. Too many radicals, too many liberals, and nothing but the riffraff of our race there. It's the absolute ghetto of all the Ivies."

"I thought U Penn was supposed to be the ghetto of all the Ivies", said Tim.

"It is. And Columbia is none other than it's profligate sister."

"Why can't I join one of the other sororities?" Allyson continued to whine.

"You can't possibly mean Delta? Why on earth would you want to join *that* sorority?"

"I wasn't talking about Delta."

"Well, what other sorority could you be talking about? There are only two African-American sororities at Columbia."

"What about Kappa Alpha Theta?" appealed Allyson sheepishly.

"Allyson Eleanor Russell, have you lost your mind!" exploded Eleanor suddenly.

"They've already contacted me and…"

"So tell them you're not interested!"

Allyson's lovely cream-colored complexion turned bright crimson. She bit her lip and looked away from her mother. Then Allyson started picking sesame seeds off the complimentary bread sticks on the table.

"Honestly, I am completely appalled by what I've just heard. I can't believe that you would rather consort with beer-swilling, trailer-trash than with quality people of your own kind! Next thing you know you'll end up like your brother. Hanging out with plebeian types who are good for nothing except trouble", Eleanor ranted.

Allyson remained silent, but Tim couldn't help but be offended.

"Did you ever stop to think that maybe people who don't have a lot of money can still be decent people?" asked Tim defensively.

"Not really as it's highly unlikely", his mother replied scornfully.

There was quiet at the table for a few moments. Soon Eleanor's rage dissipated as quickly as it had materialized and it wasn't long before she was chatting congenially with Allyson once again about less controversial matters. They spent a good deal of time chatting about procuring tickets for fashion week, and social circle gossip. Tim barely entered into the conversation at all except when asked the brief rhetorical question or to weigh in on some shallow observation. Then the waiter cleared their places and brought in his mother's birthday cake. It was a seven-layer raspberry filled white cake with white icing, with a Roman numeral birthday candle. Allyson picked out a fruity, Sauternes wine to go with it.

COMMENCEMENT

Everyone had some cake, except Tim who had his serving wrapped to take home, and then it was time for Eleanor to open her gifts.

"Let's see what my wonderful children have gotten me for my birthday."

"Open mine first, mom" said Allyson practically shoving her gift in her mother's face.

It was a small box covered with silver wrapping paper and tied with a metallic ribbon. Eleanor opened it to find an exquisite gold heart pendant. Allyson carefully studied her mother's countenance.

"Oh, it's lovely Allyson", Eleanor gasped as her daughter beamed and let out a quiet sigh of relief.

"I got it at Tiffany, of course. They say these necklaces are only to be made for a limited run."

"It will go well with most of my dresses. It's beautiful. In fact, help me with it. I'll put it on right now."

Eleanor held up her hair while her daughter fastened the clasp of the necklace. Then she turned her attention to the other gift left on the cart.

"Now let's see what my son bought me. I hope you got a gift receipt, Tim."

"It's in the box, mom."

Eleanor opened the medium sized box wrapped in pink and black wrapping paper and tied with a pink bow. She took out a beaded black silk evening bag with jeweled accents and matching belt.

"Tim, is this from the new Hermes evening collection?" Eleanor asked awestruck.

"Yes. Is there something wrong?" asked Tim.

"For the first time you actually got it right! I love it! It's a far cry from that awful wrap sweater you got me last year. It's as if you and Allyson knew what I would be wearing tonight and you got me the perfect accents to my outfit. It's like a psychic phenomenon. Oh, thank you both!"

She leaned over and gave each one of them a peck on the cheek.

"Oh, it's getting late! I'm sorry, but I'm going to have to cut our dinner short. My Terrence is throwing a surprise party for me over at the grill on 7th. It started at 8:00 and they'll be expecting me around 9:30."

"How do you know about it, if it's a surprise party?" asked Tim skeptically.

"I make it my business to know about everything that involves me", Eleanor chuckled.

"Before you rush off, can you tell us what's going on with dad?" He couldn't let his mother go without finding out what was going on with his father.

"Oh, yes. I hate to be the bearer of bad news, but I must warn you for your own good. Your father is in a lot of trouble. It seems he's been fingered in some type of securities fraud scheme and he's been arrested", Eleanor stated in a matter of fact way.

"What?!" exclaimed Allyson.

"I- I can't believe this!" stammered Tim "How could this happen?"

"I don't know all the details, but it's bound to hit the papers soon. You should be able to read all about it by tomorrow."

"When was he arrested?" asked Allyson.

"Yesterday, I believe. He's out of jail now, but his assets have been frozen. He's trying to raise capital for his defense, or so he says. I think he may be trying to get money to leave the country", explained Eleanor in a more hushed tone.

"So what are we going to do?" asked Tim, still in shock.

"Absolutely nothing, of course. My children I warn you because he may try to contact you to see if he can get some money. If he does, hang up. Do not get involved under any circumstances. He'll suck you under with him. He's a pariah in his own circles now. He's lost all credibility with his associates, his friends, and his family."

COMMENCEMENT

"So you're not going to help him at all?! Even after everything he's done for us?!" exclaimed Tim in disbelief.

"And what has he done for us that we didn't deserve anyway! We don't owe him anything!" retorted his mother who was annoyed almost to anger.

"I'll say. We were never good enough to be in his world before, and finally, the tide has changed", Allyson spat out bitterly.

"Besides, I think I have finally found my soul mate with Terrence. A handsome, rich, African-American man who is more liberal and giving than your father ever was or could be. I only wish I had met him 25 years ago. Then you two would have had the father you deserved. Anyway, I must be going or I'll be late", gushed Eleanor changing moods like a chameleon changes colors.

"Yes, and I better be getting back. I have an art history paper to write", remarked Allyson.

"It was good seeing you both again. We have to do this more often", chirped Eleanor as she rose from the table.

Tim paid the bill for both ladies and escorted them to the front where the valets had their cars waiting for them. He gave each of them the prerequisite kiss on the cheek before wishing them a good evening. Then he walked to the corner to hail a cab. It wasn't raining anymore but it was still cold and damp, and even a little foggy. Luckily for Tim, he didn't have to wait long. Tim almost never had trouble hailing a cab anyway, at least when he was alone. He was so fair skinned that many of the cab drivers either thought he was Puerto Rican or white, so he never got passed over. As Tim settled back for the ride, he couldn't help but think about his dad.

He had always been a very enigmatic figure in Tim's life. Tim's dad was often spoken of around his house in hushed tones, no one every really uttering his name. He was often referred to as either "the father" or "certain persons" or simply a masculine pronoun. When Tim was very young, he had no idea that this person was connected to him in any way at all. Oftentimes it seemed the adults were speaking of some strange, creepy, and dangerous person, like a boogey man or a werewolf.

Whenever 'he' was mentioned, countenances clouded over, and a palpable tension filled the room. He remembered this particularly one time when he heard his grandfather talk to his mother about his dad.

"He's coming to see Tim", Eleanor insisted.

"He's said that before", said her father dismissively.

"He really is coming this time. I have a date and a time."

"I'll believe it when I see it. If you ask me, I think the boy would be better off if that sorry excuse for a man would just stay where ever he is."

Tim remembered being absolutely terrified when he heard the exchange, and he secretly hoped in his heart that the meeting would never happen. It eventually did happen when Tim was about five years old. Until then he had always assumed his grandfather was his dad because everyone he was around always called him 'Poppa'. Tim would never forget that day. His nanny had gotten him all dressed up, while his mother was constantly going back and forth between the nursery and her office phone. His mother had told him that he was going to meet someone very special, and that he needed to be a good boy. But Tim knew from all the conversations he had listened to when he was supposed to be asleep, that it was none other than "him". Tim was actually terrified that "he" would come and take him away to a bad place. He was hoping Brenda, his nanny, would not allow "him" anywhere near the nursery. However unbeknownst to himself, his mother had sent Brenda out on an all day errand while he was playing with his toys.

Then the doorbell rang, and Tim could hear his mother's high, shrill tone mixing with a more masculine one. Tim stopped his play for a moment and peered around the door of the nursery. It was not long before, he saw his mother walking toward him down the corridor of their condo. She smiled at him, and bent down to face him.

"Tim, my love, guess who is here to see you?"

Through a mass of long, curly, blond bangs, Tim cast an apprehensive glance toward his mother, his forefinger planted firmly in his mouth.

COMMENCEMENT

"Take your finger out of your mouth dear", his mother reprimanded softly. "I've told you that's a nasty habit. It will make you sick and it's going to ruin the shape of your mouth."

Tim silently obeyed his mother's request, but he didn't move from the spot where he was standing.

"Come on, sweetheart. It's that special guest that mommy's been telling you about."

Tim eyes welled up with tears and he stepped back from his mother into the nursery.

"I don't want to", he said feebly.

"Now, Tim. Remember, you promised you'd be a nice boy today." said his mother already growing impatient with him.

"Come now, he's even brought you a present", his mother continued holding out her thin golden-brown hand.

It was not without much trepidation that Tim took her hand and went down the hallway to the living room where 'he' was sitting.

'He' was a tall blond white man whose imposing build made it seem as if he was taking up all the space and air in the room. He was impeccably dressed in the dark suit and flashy tie typical of the business people that Tim's mother was acquainted with. When Tim came in, 'he' flashed a weird looking grin, and at once it reminded Tim of those weird clowns he often saw at birthday parties that scared him.

"Hey, little fella!" he said to Tim.

Tim grabbed his mother's leg and buried his face her dress.

"Say hello to your father, Tim." Eleanor demanded.

There was something that seemed very wrong with what his mother said. This man clearly wasn't Poppa.

"That's not Poppa!" exclaimed Tim to his mother before thrusting his head back into the skirt of her dress.

"He's talking about his grandfather", explained Eleanor to the man on the couch. "No this is not Poppa. Poppa is my father and this is your father. I've told you about your father", she said to Tim.

Tim was not satisfied with the explanation and in fact it made him very angry and very hurt. When she spoke of his father, Tim had always thought she had been talking about Poppa. He didn't know she really meant 'him'. How could his mother be telling him that 'he' was his father. Tim did not want the boogey man to be his father. It couldn't be true. His mother was just being mean. Or maybe 'he' had taken hold of her mind and made her believe it.

"No!" he whimpered, his voice muffled within the fabric of his mother's dress where he had buried his face.

"I'm so sorry about this", pleaded Eleanor.

"I wouldn't have expected anything less", the stranger said warmly. "He's a child Eleanor, and I'm a stranger to him."

"Look, sweetheart! He has something for you!"

Tim peeked over and saw the blue and yellow gift-wrapped box sitting on the coffee table. It piqued his interest, to the point that he could now face the man. Like most children his age, he never could turn down a present, even if he was not really sure of the person giving it. He looked up at his mother and then again at the stranger sitting in front of him.

"Here you go, little guy", he said taking the gift off the coffee table and holding it out to Tim. Slowly, Tim took the package and moved back over to his mother. Eleanor then guided her son over to the love seat opposite the couch to sit down.

"Go ahead and open it", he suggested to him.

Tim began to open it, with some assistance from his mother. It was none other than the five, ten-inch ranger soldiers he had wanted. His mother had promised to get him one for Christmas, but claimed she couldn't find any. Now he had a full set.

"Cool!" was all Tim said. The strange man smiled.

"What do you say, now?" Eleanor reminded him.

COMMENCEMENT

"Thank you, Mr...." Tim was thinking even the Boogey man would have better sense than to go around telling people who he was. He knew he had to have some alias that he used when he was running around in the daylight pretending to be normal. So he looked to his mother to supply the "name" of this being.

"Mr. Hurst, dear."

"Thank you, Mr. Hurst."

"Your welcome, kid."

Then Tim played with his new toys while his parents talked in front of him.

"He's certainly a beautiful child, Eleanor."

"I know. He's very bright, too. He's gifted you know."

"Is he?"

"He's only started school and he can read almost anything. He's practically a prodigy in math, especially when it comes to money. I guess like father, like son."

"Oh, really? Let's see", Mr. Hurst said sounding a little skeptical.

The man took a few bills out of his wallet, and some change from his pocket.

"Hey, Tommy..."

"His name is Timothy, but we all call him Tim."

"Sure", said the man a little embarrassed before returning his attention to Tim. "Hey, Timmy. Come here for a minute."

Tim stopped playing with his new toys and looked at his mother before casting a wary eye on Mr. Hurst.

"Go ahead, Tim", his mother urged him, smiling.

Tim slowly walked over to this Mr. Hurst and stopped within two feet of the man.

"Look, kid, I'll make a deal with you. If you can count this, you can keep it", he said handing the money to Tim.

273

Tim took the money clumsily in his tiny hands and sat down on the floor. He spread the bills out by denomination, from the largest to the smallest. Then he did the same with the change. After he had finished going over it, he stood up and faced the man.

"So how much have you got there?" asked the man, who seemed to smirk at him.

"Seventy-Seven dollars and eighty three cents", Tim declared confidently.

Hurst startled at the child's accuracy. Eleanor smiled proudly at her son's accomplishment.

"Hell, you are smart", Hurst breathed. Then to Eleanor he said, "Where does he go to school?"

"Trevor day school."

"Put him in Bankstreet."

"So I can take it, right?" asked Tim.

"What?" said Mr. Hurst absentmindedly.

"The money. You said I could have it if I could count it. We had a deal remember?" Tim reminded him.

"Oh, sure, kid. It's all yours", smiled Hurst.

"I'm going to put it in my cash register. I'll be right back", said Tim tottering off to the nursery with his fortune.

"I tried to get him into Bankstreet, but they said they didn't have any space at the moment."

"Don't worry about it. I know people."

"And who's going to pay for it. I'm not exactly at the poverty line, but Bankstreet is still out of my league."

"I told you. Any thing he needs, he'll have it. You said he could read anything."

"Almost anything. He's still only five you know."

COMMENCEMENT

"Hey, Timmy. Come over here and read this for me." Hurst said to Tim who had just come back into the room. Tim was starting to become more comfortable with this stranger. So far he had given him a gift and a whole lot of money and called him smart. As such, little Tim's apprehensions began to fade. Hurst held out a newspaper to him and Tim read the front matter easily.

"You're a really bright kid, you know that?"

"Are you going to take me away?" asked Tim with some concern.

"No, no. I think you're better off here with your mother. But I promise you I will do my best to make sure you have everything you need." As precocious as he was, Tim had only a very indistinct idea of what this meant.

Then Mr. Hurst looked at his watch.

"I have to go now. But I'm going to talk to one of my associates at Bankstreet later this afternoon. I'll let you know when you can take him down and I'll stop by in a couple of weeks when I can to see how he's getting on", Hurst stated as he rose to leave.

"Thank you. I just want to let you know that I really appreciate everything you're doing for us", smiled Eleanor.

"It's no problem. You're doing a really good job with him Eleanor. He's going to have a good future. I'll make sure of it."

"Thank you."

When Hurst left, Eleanor ran over and hugged and kissed her son.

"Oh Tim, I am so lucky to have a little boy like you", she gushed over him.

"I was good, wasn't I mommy. I won almost 78 dollars", smiled Tim.

"Yes, you were very good. I was so proud of you when you showed your father how smart you were. And he was proud of you, too."

"Is he going to come back tomorrow?"

"Maybe not tomorrow, but he will definitely be back."

When he left, Tim had not learned much about the man other than his name. What he did learn was that if he was a good boy and did things the man liked, his mother was happy and there was a better chance that he would come back. Some how it seemed very important that the man keep coming back. Maybe if Tim were really good, the man would think about staying and being a family with them. Then he wouldn't be a boogey man and he would be a real daddy, just like in a Disney movie. So he suffered through violin and guitar lessons, dance classes, academic competitions, soccer, swimming, and lacrosse competitions. He always had to be the best, earn the prize or the trophy. By the time he was 18 years old Tim (and by then, his sister as well) had a trail of accomplishments longer than an epic tome, but the stranger never came to stay. It was never enough.

But still Mr. Hurst had done a lot for Tim throughout the years. It was Hurst's money that paid for all the fancy day schools, boarding school, and Harvard. It was Hurst that paid for all the trips and vacations cross-country as well as across the world. It was his influence that kept Tim out of trouble at times in his wayward adolescence, and it was Hurst who helped Tim get a job at Herns and Marshall. And now all that was gone. In fact, now his dad needed help, and given the things that had just transpired in his life, Tim was in no position to provide assistance even if he wanted to. What if his father did reach out to him? The one moment when Tim should have been able to be a good son and step in to help his dad out, he couldn't. It made him feel worthless.

As Tim's despondent reverie came to a conclusion, the cab pulled up to the front door of his building. Tim paid the driver and got out. As he stepped out onto the curb, a full day of not eating, the shock of bad news, and the remnants of his hangover began to take their toll and he began to feel light-headed. He decided to sit down on one of the stone benches outside until he felt better. The last thing he wanted to do was go back into the empty apartment. There was so much inside him and he felt like he wanted to talk to someone about it. He looked at his watch. It was 9:45pm. There was a chance that Tamiko was still up. After all it wasn't that late. She would understand. Tamiko always seemed to understand him somehow. And she always had this grace about her that captivated him. He always wanted to know the source of it. Secretly he hoped it some of it would rub off on himself.

COMMENCEMENT

"Hello."

"Hey"

"Tim?"

"None other."

"Do you know what time it is?"

"It's not ten yet."

"But it's almost."

"O.K. it's a little late, but I just needed someone to talk to right now."

"What's going on?"

"I don't even know where to start."

"Try the beginning."

"You know what, Tamiko? It's really complicated. How about I meet you tomorrow after school? Just promise me you'll see me tomorrow."

Tim reconsidered the timing of his call. He knew Tamiko would probably stay up the whole night and into the morning talking to him, but he knew that she had to get up early to go to work tomorrow and would have felt guilty about tiring her out.

"Of course. You can pick me up at school. I get out at 6:30 because of parent teacher conferences. It's the Great Expectations school P.S. 34."

"Okay. I'll see you then."

Now Tim felt like he could go into the empty apartment, knowing that there was someone out there that would listen.

THIRTY-TWO

Allen headed up to the 7th floor to suite 709 with the cumbersome wet vac. There had been a leak that turned into a mini-flood and Davis paged him to come up and clean up the water in the living room. So once again, Allen gathered the necessary tools and headed up to do his job. Allen was quickly getting used to the demands of the job and the routines of the hotel. He was even beginning to see a bright side to everything he was going through. One positive thing about this job was that it would help to keep him fit and lean, since he was constantly moving around. The other great part about it was that he got three breaks in the day: a 10 minute break in the morning, a hour break near noon and another 10 minute break near the end of the day. Allen had used his first 10 minute break to read his Bible. He had remembered the promise he had made to his mother to read the Bible for a week. So far it had been about 5 days, and Allen had hoped that something very powerful would jump out at him that would shed light on how he could get out of his current situation. Since he was working on developing a relationship with God, he thought he'd turn to Exodus and read about Moses who had a really good relationship with God. In fact, Moses was the friend of God. He read a couple of chapters about how Moses spoke to God for the people, and helped bring the children of Israel out of Egypt, but he didn't get anything about what made Moses so special that he was God's friend.[1] What did Moses do that was so special that God chose him to be his friend? This was what Allen was pondering as he rode in the service elevator to the 7th floor. This was another good thing about this job. The work wasn't so intense, and he often found moments in the day when he could just think about things, and meditate.

COMMENCEMENT

When Allen got off the elevator his mind quickly returned to the work in front of him. He would have to continue to meditate on Moses later. He walked down to the suite where the door was already open and came in. There was water leading from the heating unit in front of the window and coalescing into a little lake on the front area rug. Davis had the cover off of the unit and had a section of pipe taken out of it, and was getting ready to install a new section. Allen quickly got to work getting up the water in the living room with the wet vac, and followed behind this with the mop on the hard surfaces. Then he began to move the furniture around, so he could roll the rug up and take it downstairs to be dried. Once he had the rug all rolled up, he took it and placed it outside in the hall. Finally, he decided to stop and ask Davis if there was anything else he needed before he left.

Allen took a moment to study what Davis was doing. Davis deftly replaced the pipe and turned valves, and was beginning to do some sort of check on it. The whole thing looked so complex to Allen. "I could barely put together the bookcase my mom got from IKEA", mused Allen. As Allen watched, he was amazed at how adroitly Davis executed his job. It was funny to Allen. Here he was the Harvard graduate and he didn't have half the skills of the man working before him. Davis was the true professional.

"I got up all the water and I'm getting ready to take the rug down. Is there anything else that needs to be done here?" asked Allen. It seemed like a rhetorical question, given his lack of skills at fixing things.

"Not really, I'm just about finished wit' this", answered Davis as he hefted the large metal cover and put it back on the heating unit. Allen headed to the hall where he had left the rug, when he heard Davis call after him.

"I'll help you wit' that. You don't wanna drag it cause it'll mess up the carpet in the hall."

"Sure, thanks."

Allen took one end and Davis took the other and they took the rug down the hall towards the service elevator and loaded it in the car. Then they took it to the basement through the winding maze of doors and into the service area Davis showed Allen on his first day on the job. Kizzy was sitting behind the glass looking at a magazine when they entered.

"Yo Kizz, tag this for 709. It's gotta be cleaned."

"Sure, Dave, no problem. Just leave it. I'll have Ahmed come and get it", she smiled. "Hey, Allen, how you doin'?" she said winking at him.

Allen tried to keep it brief. He didn't want Davis to think he was trying to flirt with his girl (if this was even his girl).

"I'm good", he said trying to sound friendly but not too friendly. Then he turned to Davis.

"If this is it, I'll just get back to the rounds."

"Chill, man. It's almost lunchtime anyway."

"Really?!" Allen was always surprised at how fast time went on this job.

"Word. No need to be beastin' over the work. It's gonna be here. You goin' out to eat?"

"Yeah, I guess."

"You wanna to roll wit' me an' Kizzy. We goin' to that Chinese store over on 5th."

For the first time, Davis was actually making an overture of friendship to Allen. He was definitely not going to turn it away.

"Sounds good."

"I'll finish up down here. You go up and lock up 709 and put yo' stuff back in the janitor closit. Kizzy and I'll meet you there.

****

Allen, Davis and Kizzy squeezed themselves into the cramped janitors office after getting their Chinese take out. There was barely enough space for all of their Styrofoam containers on the table. Allen sat sandwiched between Davis and Kizzy. Allen had not meant to sit there and he hoped his position next to Kizzy did not offend Davis. So far things were turning out well. Davis and Kizzy had done most of the talking on the way back to he hotel. They basically talked about random stuff, and different people they knew at the hotel. Allen had no idea what they were talking about or how to come in on the conversation, so he just listened. He was content with listening to them while they ate when Kizzy turned to him.

"So Allen, you single?"

"Dag, Kizzy, you don' waste no time! He ain't even got two spoonfuls of rice down and you startin'!" laughed Davis.

"Hey, I'm not tryin' to front. I'ma go for mine. So what you say Allen?"

"Actually, I am seeing someone."

"A boy or a girl?"

"A girl."

"Y'all serious?"

"We just started dating, but I am interested in her."

"What if I told you that I could offer you the opportunity of a life time?"

"Girl, you are too bold!" laughed Davis.

Davis seemed very amused about the whole situation. Obviously, Kizzy was not his girl, nor did he have any intentions for her. Unfortunately for Kizzy, neither did Allen. Her boldness and her directness made Allen very uncomfortable. He couldn't believe she was propositioning him in the presence of other people.

"I'd regret to say I'd have to decline."

"So you a good boy, Allen?"

"I like to think I am."

"It's okay to be bad sometimes."

Allen couldn't think of anything to say to that. So he just said nothing.

"Don't say you never had your chance. It's a little tight in here. I think I'm going back down to the window where there's more space."

Kizzy picked up the remains of her meal and headed out the door without another word.

"Sorry, Allen", smiled Davis, once she was out of earshot.

"Did you set me up?" asked Allen.

"She begged me to introduce her. But I knew you wasn't gonna be feelin' her though."

"She's very direct."

"No, just desperate. Don't get me wrong, I love her and evythin', but she can be a chicken head sometimes. You know?"

"I thought she might have been your girl."

"Nah, we just co-workers. We don't even hang out or anything. I don't have nobody right now. I'm tryin' to get my life together and I don't need the drama. You feel."

"I get that. Don't tell Kizzy, but to be truthful, I don't even know if it's gonna work out with the girl I'm seeing right now."

"Word? Why not?"

"A couple of days ago, she found out that I worked here and when I called to ask her out again, she was a little evasive. She sort of gave me the brush if you know what I mean."

"I hear that. She lookin' for cheddah. That's bad. You know, some chicks they so messed up they see you wit' two twenty dollah bills an' dey throwin' theyself at you. And if it's not one thing it's another."

"Dating is hard when you're a work in progress."

"That's why I don't. I got too much goin' on tryin' to straighten my life out. I wasted a lot of my life on the street, hangin' out on the corner. After a while you get tired. You always gotta have one eye over your shoulda, always gotta be at the drop spot, no matter what, rain, sleet, or snow. It's all good when you a kid and you don't know no better, but then you get older. You want somethin' more out of life. You want to live, period. You see the money you makin' ain't worth the trouble you get behind it." Davis said rather gravely.

"I couldn't agree with you more. So what's your plan?" asked Allen.

"First, I wanna work on getting' my contractin' license."

"With the way you work, I thought you would've had one already!"

"Nah. I got a lot of training certificates, but not the real deal youknowwhatimean. I been going to night school to get my real diploma as like a first step, you know, but it's hard. I never had much luck wit' the books. I can deal with math, but I'm not so good with readin'an' writin papers, stuff like that. That English regents ain't no joke, son."

"What is it that you seem to be having trouble with?"

"Everythin' man. A lot of times I don't even get what they talkin' about in those old-time novels."

"What 'old time novels'?"

"You know the ones by those ol' dead white guys from England and what not. Shakespear an' them. It's like they speakin' English, but not no English I never heard before. You feel?"

"I get you. The language is pretty hard to take, because it really is a different kind of English. Most of those books are written using a lot of expressions and phrases that people of today don't use any more. Do you read the books with a guide, like "Cliff Notes"?"

"I been usin' that, the dictionary, whatever. Sometimes its like I get even more confused 'cause just when you get into what's goin' on, you run into somethin' that confuses you and when you look it up there's like five different meanings it could be or the meanings theyself is confusin'. Then I gotta write these papers. A lotta times, I'm not sure if I'm gettin' what I'm suppost to outta the readin'. You know like the main idea and whatnot."

"Do they offer help at your school?"

"They have tutors, but I have a hard time meetin wit' them 'cause they not available when I'm off. They have daytime office hours durin' the week. I'm only free on the weekends."

"Maybe I could help you. Better yet, I have a friend who is a teacher who may be able to help us, too. We could all get together on Saturday and get our gears turning."

"I don't know, man. I don't want to put you or your friend out."

"It's no problem, I don't mind and I know she won't. How about we meet at the library in the Museum of Natural History over on 81st. It's better than the 40th Street one because there's not a lot of traffic and there's private space where we'll be able to talk."

"Aiight. Is 11:00 a good time?"

"As good as any. I'll let you know what my friend says."

"Cool."

"And how would you feel about meeting on Sunday afternoons if necessary?"

"I guess I could. Just as long as it's after 2:00 'cause I'ma start goin' to church. That's another thing I been workin on: tryin' to live a saved life. A couple of month's ago I met this dude named Daniel at like a church festival or somethin', and he's really been breakin' things down for me. He told me about this church over on 153rd street called Greater somethin' somethin'..."

Allen couldn't help but interrupt at this point.

"Is the guy you met, Daniel Joyner?"

"Yeah. You know him?"

"I went to school with him as a kid. He's our Youth Outreach coordinator at Greater Apostolic."

"Yeah, that's the church! You go there?!"

"Every Sunday."

"For real? Cold Snap! This is crazy, yo! What's the chance of somethin' like this happening?"

"It's almost as if God must've wanted us to meet", said Allen thoughtfully.

THIRTY-THREE

Tamiko had just finished her last conference. Most of the other teachers had finished their meetings and were working in their classrooms. It was only 6:25, and no teachers were allowed to leave until 6:30 on the dot. The extra five minutes seemed like an eternity since Tamiko hated every minute she spent in the building. Each day was like serving hard time. In order to get through, she had to focus on something that awaited her at the end of the day. Something not associated with her work at all. Like today, for instance, she was looking forward to meeting with Tim. She remembered him calling her the other night. He sounded so strange, and so sad. It jarred her so much that she had to get out of bed and say a special prayer for him. Whatever he wanted to talk about, she hoped she would be able to help him. As she waited for the time to elapse, she heard a lot of talking outside her classroom, along with giggles and girlish squeals. When she opened the door and looked out, she noticed several teachers gathering near the window on the far end of the hall. Tamiko might have been curious, but she already suspected what was going on as her friend Joan came running towards her.

"Tamiko, you have to see this! This crazy hot guy just pulled up in front of our school and his ride is to die for!"

"Let me guess. He's tall, fair, with wavy brown hair, glasses..." Tamiko said matter of factly.

"You know him?!" Joan gushed with surprise.

"He's the friend that's picking me up today."

"Which one of your friends is he? I know he's definitely not the janitor."

"He's the one that works at Herns and Marshall."

"Is he single?"

"Yes. Let me guess; you want me to introduce you."

"Would you?"

"Maybe some other time. I'm not sure if he's going to be in the mood for it today."

"Well, you better hurry him out of here. The single ladies here are just salivating over him like starving tigers over fresh meat."

Then the bell finally rang signaling the end of the day, and Tamiko gathered her things from her classroom and headed toward the office. Tamiko could barely escape the gaggle of women who suddenly made a mad dash for the school office. Tamiko quickly signed out and gave a final farewell to Joan before dashing out of the door to meet Tim. She was barely able to get to him due to the throng of young women. All of the single women were ogling Tim and not a few of the married ones, as well.

"Hey, you", chirped Tamiko sweetly as she gave Tim a peck on the cheek, which he returned.

"Hey, Miko", said Tim as he reached for her school bag. "I'll take that. It looks heavy. You carry this thing around all day?" he asked opening his back door and putting it in the back seat.

"No way, just to school. Once I get here I just dump it under my desk."

"Bye, Tamiko! See you tomorrow!" Tamiko heard someone call out. She turned around only to see Charlotte Booker behind her with her fake smile plastered on. Lately, Charlotte wouldn't say anything to Tamiko when she left, which made Tamiko realize the true bent of her intentions.

"Bye, Charlotte", said Tamiko dryly.

"Is this your boyfriend?"

COMMENCEMENT

"No, he's just a friend of mine. Tim Russell. Tim, this is Charlottte Booker, our school's literacy coach", Tamiko said to Tim, giving him a knowing look.

"Nice to meet you Tim. Feel free to stop by the school anytime. We're all family here."

"Thanks", said Tim awkwardly. The fact that Booker didn't know when to leave just increased the awkwardness of the situation.

"We really have to be going. I'll see you around", said Tim as he opened the passenger side door for Tamiko, leaving Charlotte to take the hint that she could in fact leave for her own home now.

"That Charlotte's a real subtle gal", Tim breathed sarcastically as he fastened his seat belt.

"Like garlic."

"And you would think that a woman who looks like big foot's mom would be a little less forward."

"Tim!"

"Oh, come on. It's not like there's any love lost between you two."

"Even so. We shouldn't be mean."

"We weren't being mean. I was being mean."

"So where are we going?"

"You tell me. Have you had dinner yet?"

"If you call a pita melt from the local doughnut shop dinner. How about we go Manna's? It's close to my house and it's on your way home so you won't have to go so far out to drop me off."

"Manna's it is."

****

It was 7:00 by the time they reached Manna's, and since it was during the middle of the week, the place was not as crowded as it usually was. They took seats at a booth near the window, and soon a waitress took

287

their order. As Tim moved forward in his seat, he looked as if he was more than just tired. He looked defeated.

"So how was work?" asked Tamiko taking his hand in hers. She knew that what ever was bothering him more than likely had something to do with Preston.

"Excruciating."

"I guess the presentation didn't go as you expected?"

"Let's just say I now know how Napoleon felt at Waterloo."

Tim breathed a heavy sigh and took both of Tamiko's hands in his. His face wore a very sad expression, that Tamiko had never seen before and it frightened her.

"What I'm about to tell you can't go any farther than where we are right now."

"Of course."

Tim took a deep breath and let it out.

"The firm has decided to phase out my department in favor of an new automated process, suggested by none other than you-know-who."

"What?! That doesn't ... how can they do this after everything you've done for them?"

"It's business, Tamiko. It's all about saving money."

"I'm so sorry, Tim. If there's anything you need right now, just let me know."

"I'm not worried about money, Tamiko. It's just the way everything played out. I feel like I was set up. They're even saying that if I want to collect severance pay, I'll have to stay on for the next six months and help Preston with his reorganization plan. It's like they're making me dig my own grave."

"They have some nerve! Maybe you should just leave. Forget about the money."

COMMENCEMENT

"I thought about doing that, but I'd stand to lose way more than they would. Besides, I need some time to think about what I'm going to do next."

"Who knows? This could turn out to be a good thing. Now you have the chance to get a better job, where you'll be able to work for a company that will appreciate what you have to offer."

"I don't know about that. With the job market being the way it is, I just might end up trying to get Allen to hook me up at the Sheraton."

"Don't talk like that. You've got a MBA and a lot more experience than Allen has."

"Experience doing what? Ordering supplies? A monkey could have done my job, which is why they're going automated. My resume's going to be a joke."

"How can you say that, Tim?"

"Because it's true. In fact, I probably would be at the Sheraton this very minute if it hadn't been for my dad. Truth be told, I had some of the same problems Allen had getting a job even though I had my MBA. I didn't get hired at Herns and Marshall because they thought I was the most qualified candidate. My dad pulled some very long strings to get me set up there."

"So what, if you're dad helped you get the job? You wouldn't have lasted two minutes there if you didn't have some talent."

"Two years isn't that long a stretch either."

"Don't be so pessimistic. I'm sure you'll be able to find another job. And even if things get tough, don't be ashamed to reach out to your Dad again. Maybe he's the person that God will use to help you."

"Not this time. According to my mom, he's been arrested for securities fraud."

"Oh my gosh, Tim! I'm sorry. I know how much you care about him. Have you heard from him at all?"

"No. Not that I could do anything for him anyway."

There was a silence between them for a moment. Tim looked as if he wanted to cry, but was trying to be brave. Tamiko kept trying to think of something to say to help bring him out of his doldrums.

"Do you think your mom could help you out?"

"No. Absolutely not. She'd want me to work for her and then she'd just use the job as a way of controlling my life. I'd rather live in a dumpster."

"Don't you think that's kind of extreme. Your family can't be that bad. After all, they're family: the people you can turn to when things go south."

"If only this were a perfect world with perfect people. But it's not. It's never been for me, and losing my job is yet another reminder. I don't know Tamiko, sometimes I just feel like why do I even bother to get out of bed in the mornings, you know? I spend my whole life trying to make it, but it seems like the harder I try, the worse I fare."

"You're not alone, Tim. Lately, I've been feeling the same way. I didn't want to say anything about this because I didn't want to burden you any more than you already are, but I found out a couple of days ago that my principal is planning to let me go at the end of the year."

"You've got to be kidding! You've only started a couple of months ago."

"Unfortunately, the principal thinks I don't quite cut it as a teacher. Maybe she's right."

"Or maybe it's your racist supervisor! Don't you guys have a union that can stand up for you in matters like this?"

"We do, but I'm a first year teacher. I don't have tenure or anything, so it's pretty much up to the principal. And it's not like I can prove that Steele is a racist. She's never said or done anything overtly racist."

"They never do, do they? I'm really sorry, Tamiko. And here I was thinking I had problems."

"But you don't have to worry about me. I've got this all under control. I'm not going to let them do this to me. I'm just going to wait until the end of next week and then I'll just quit."

"I wonder what your dad had to say about that?"

"I haven't told my dad. Yet. Anyway, it's not his life, it's mine."

"But do you really think that's a good decision?"

"But it has to be the right thing. Why else would God allow me to hear what was going on? Besides, I'd still be losing out if I stay. This way, I'll at least have my dignity."

"You probably know more about what you're facing than I do. But if you can, stay for the extra pay. That way you could get *something* out of the whole thing."

"I wouldn't stay for all the money in Fort Knox. There are just some things that aren't worth it."

"I won't argue with you there. What do you plan to do after you leave?"

"I don't know. I always thought God wanted me to be a teacher, but now I think maybe I was following the wrong path. I guess I'll just be fasting and praying for Him to reveal to me His direction for my life again, while I look for another job. It's just that teaching meant so much to me. It's the only skill I have, or at least, I thought I had. I don't really know what else I'm going to do."

"It's weird, you don't seem too perturbed to say that you're practically ready to give up your entire career."

"I'm not giving up, just changing direction. And that's not to say the decision was easy. I still love teaching, in spite of everything that's happened. But I want to live my life in the way God has ordained for me, and if that means giving up my aspirations to be a teacher, then so be it."

"So you're still devoted to your God. Even after all this."

"If it weren't for Him, I don't know if I could go through all of this. He's helps me to keep everything together."

"And how does that work?"

"Because I know that He loves me and is looking out for me, and He can do what I can't. Like the apostle Paul says, '...my strength is made perfect in weakness.'"[1]

"Sounds very reassuring, but how do you know that your God is truly working for you?"

"Because his Word tells me so and I can see him working in my life. He's the one who allowed me to hear what that principal was planning. If that isn't enough, I know he's with me, giving me the strength to carry on no matter what the situation."

"I'm still not sure if I get it Tamiko."

"Maybe one day, you will."

There was a moment of silence when the waitress brought them their dinners, and they began to eat. Tamiko noticed that Tim didn't really eat much of his dinner and spent a lot of time just pushing the food around on his plate.

"Is your stomach still bothering you?"

"With everything that's been going on in my life recently, I'd be surprised if it wasn't."

"Have you seen a doctor, yet?"

"I don't need to see a doctor. I need a vacation. I still have my time coming next month."

"Still, you're getting kind of thin. If you're not getting enough nutrition, then you'll not only have stomach problems, you'll start to become susceptible to all kinds of diseases. Stuff that could make your stomach problems worse."

"Did you get that from Callie?"

"My mom used to be a nurse, too, before she married my dad."

"And she gave it up to become a preacher's wife."

COMMENCEMENT

"Don't try to change the subject. You need to go to the doctor. Maybe they can give you something."

"That's what I'm afraid of. They'll turn me into an invalid junkie."

"So you're afraid of doctors?"

"I'm not afraid of doctors. I just don't like or trust them."

"I find that to be very strange for someone who doesn't believe in God."

"I never said I didn't believe. I just said I wasn't sure that He exists. Those are two different things. And for your information, I don't think medical science has all the answers either."

"C'mon, Tim. I'm worried about you."

"Really?"

"Yes. If you don't want to go to the doctor for yourself, at least do it for me."

"Since you put it like that, I'll think about it."

"I'll come with you if you want."

"And will the doctor give me a lollipop? Honestly Tamiko, I'm 24 not 4."

"I just meant for support. I know you don't need me there, but I thought you wouldn't mind having a friend to lean on."

"Fine. I'll let you know if and when I decide to go."

"What time is it?"

"8:30."

"I've got to go. I still have some things I have to do for school tomorrow."

"Yeah and unfortunately, I have to go to work early. I wish we had more time to spend together. I really like talking with you. It makes me feel …real… you know."

"It's not so bad spending time with you either. As a friend of course."

"Are you free Saturday?"

"Allen sent me a text earlier about meeting him at the Museum Library on Saturday. He's supposed to fill me in on the details later, but maybe you can come to church with me again on Sunday if you want."

"O.K. It beats sitting at home watching cable. But is every service three hours long?"

"For some people it's long, but when you think of it in terms of the 168 hours there are in a week, it doesn't."

"You are truly amazing", smiled Tim for the first time tonight.

"I don't know if that's completely true, but I'm glad you think so. You're pretty special yourself."

"I wish. Maybe if some of you rubbed off on me."

"If you keep coming to church with me, it just might happen."

THIRTY-FOUR

Allen was setting the table for his mother for Friday night dinner. He had just put out the cloth basket weave tablemats and was now setting out the silverware. Elsewhere in the kitchen, Lena Sharpe was fixing the service trays and platters to be placed on the table. The menu consisted of roasted pork shoulder and string beans with hoppin' johns and rice. Vernon was working on putting the finishing touches on the dessert. Normally, Vernon Sharpe considered himself too manly to cook, but when he did cook, he often stuck to desserts. Tonight, he had made a red velvet cake with vanilla frosting and coconut sprinkled on top. Allen had spoken to Jim earlier in the day and invited him over to have dinner with the family to which Jim accepted. Jim hadn't had dinner very often with the Sharpes since he dropped out of the church about two years ago.

In happier times, the Sharpes, the Bynums, and the Reids, were like one communal unit. They went to church together, they prayed together, and spent a lot of summers and recreational time together. All of the adults looked after each other's children as if they belonged to all of them. Tamiko, Jim, and Allen spent as much time in each other's houses as they did in their own respective homes. With the death of Momma Merta, Jim slowly began to move out of the communal unit and not without some concern on the part of the Bynums and Sharpes. So when Allen told his parents about Jim coming to dinner, they were more than excited about having him over. Allen had finished setting the table when he heard the doorbell ring. He ran to the door and peeked through the peephole, before opening the door for his friend.

"Right on time", said Allen shepherding his friend in. "Hey everybody! Jim's here!" Allen shouted to his parents in the kitchen.

"What's happenin' man?!" Jim said a little more cheerfully than usual. The smell of his breath immediately made Allen a little uneasy. Mingled with the strong mint smell of the gum he was chewing was also alcohol. This was the third time this week that he noticed Jim had been drinking. Although he didn't seem to be totally inebriated like he was at the Election Night party, Allen was still concerned that his friend, who used to drink only on occasions, was now beginning to drink on what seemed to be almost a daily basis. The fact that he had recently revealed to him that he had given up on his life's dream was even more worrying. However, he didn't know whether or not now was the right time to talk to his friend. But Allen felt like he had to say something.

"You know me, man. I'm hanging in there, but what about you? Are you okay?"

"I'm fine, man", replied Jim "I'll be even better after I've had some of your mom's home cookin'. Been a long time since I had dinner here, but if my memory serves me correctly, I think that's roast pork and string beans I smell."

"You got it."

Then Allen's parents came out of the kitchen to greet Jim. After exchanging pleasantries, all of the men sat down, while Lena brought out the food and set it on the table. Then when everything was ready, they all bowed their heads and said grace, in which Jim reluctantly participated, but did not join in by saying the final "amen" on the end. This did not escape the notice of the older adults in the room who merely eyed each other. Lena, Vernon, as well as the Pastor Bynum and his wife were well aware that Jim had been an apostate to the faith for some time now. They all had done everything in their power to avert Jim's tergiversation of his religious convictions and had spent a lot of time praying and waiting patiently for God to change Jim's heart.

"So, how's everything with you Jim? We haven't seen you in so long."

"I'm good. Just glad to be working so I can pay those bills."

COMMENCEMENT

"I hear that", replied Vernon. "Transit is a good place to be. I always wanted to work in transit driving the buses, but I had too many points on my license."

"You think maybe when the recession is over, you'll go back and get your law degree like you planned?" asked Lena.

"I'm not so sure anymore."

"Why not? When you were younger it was all you ever talked about."

"That was when I was younger. I've changed a lot since then. Now, I don't think that's what I want anymore."

"Yeah, mom. It's no big deal. People change careers all the time", said Allen attempting to be nonchalant. He was trying to keep his mother from going where he knew she would eventually go.

"Well, what will you do?" Lena persisted.

"I'm thinking that I'll just stay with transit until I figure it out", answered Jim.

"I was hoping you could've gotten Allen a job in transit. It's more stable than the one he's got", Vernon remarked.

"I don't know dad. Transit's just not my thing. Anyway, I probably have a few points too many on my license", said Allen.

"Yes, Allen. We all know you were meant for bigger and better things", remarked Jim with just the faintest bit of bitterness in his voice. Allen knew what he was alluding to, but decided not to respond to it to avoid trouble.

"Mom these string beans are hittin' it out of the park", said Allen "I think I'm going to have to go back for a second helping."

"Allen, I know how you like my string beans. Just make sure you leave some for anyone else who would like a second helping."

"I think I could use a second helping myself", said Jim.

"Yep. You all had your favorites. Allen loved my string beans. Tamiko always loved Mother Rose's Ham."

"Everybody loves mother Rose's Ham", said Vernon.

"Speaking of Tamiko, what's been going on with her lately. I barely see her anymore. Is she still having problems at work?" asked Jim.

"Unfortunately. Pastor Bynum said she thinks she may not want to teach anymore after this year. I've tried to help her. She called me once to ask me to help her with lesson plans, but I'm not a classroom teacher anymore. I'm only teaching in the resource room now. Besides, everything in the schools has changed so much since I was a classroom teacher. A couple of years ago they started this new "Balanced Literacy" and "New Math" craze and it's taken over all the schools. Everyone says it's good teaching and it's supposed to be "research based", but most of the children wind up coming to me because they don't understand what they're doing. I mean they get these coaches in there to watch the teachers and tell them what to do, and yet no one ever gets it right. It isn't a wonder she's so confused."

"She'll work it out, as long as she keeps the faith. Pastor says she's been praying about it", responded Vernon.

"I know. And it's a shame because it's her calling. I remember when she came to me and told me that God had revealed it to her. She seemed so sure."

"It seems that the only thing you can be sure of in this life is that nothing is ever sure", stated Jim.

"I'm just worried about all you children out there. First, Allen couldn't find a job, Tamiko has one, but doesn't know if she wants to stay, and now Jim doesn't know what he wants to do. It just seems like everybody's drifting."

"I don't think you need to worry yourself so much Lena. That's what young people do. I remember when I was younger. I had a whole bunch of jobs before I got one that was steady."

"But those were different times, Vernon. We didn't have many options back then. Affirmative action was just beginning to open the doors and only for those of us who had the qualifications to go through. These young people today have so much more at their disposal, and yet decisions seem so hard for them to make. I think it's because they don't know who they are", Lena opined with concern.

"But I think that's what we're all trying to find mom. We want to know what our purpose is in this world and to fulfill it", said Allen.

"Allen, as Christians, our main purpose in life is to serve the Lord. The only thing you need to find out is how he wants you to serve Him."

"Do you mean like how we can contribute to making the world a better place?"

"No, Allen. There's more to it than that. It's not about making the world better. The Bible tells us this world is not going to get better. That's why Christ is coming back to the earth to set up his kingdom. In the end there's going to be a New Heaven and a New Earth. So none of these works we do for the world are going to last. It's about living a life that brings glory to our Creator, so that people will see and know who he is, and hopefully want to be saved and join Him in the New Kingdom."

"So everything is about Him. Is that it? What about us? What about the people who serve him? I guess we're nothing to Him, but playthings for His amusement", Jim spat out.

"Jim. I know how you feel, but this is a Christian household and when you are here, you will need to show respect for the God we serve", Vernon said sternly.

"Then I'm sorry Mr. &Mrs. Sharpe, but I can't stay. And I don't think I'll be able to come back."

"Jim, you need to let go of your anger toward God. He loves you and wants the best for you, your mother, and your father. Everybody has to leave this world. Some people die tragic deaths, even Christians. Stephen was stoned to death by a mob, and Jesus Christ himself suffered crucifixion. Life doesn't end with physical death…"

"So they're better off in Heaven, now? Right? Well what about me? Huh? What about me?"

"Jim, please!"

"Let him go, Lena. You've talked to him. Everyone's talked to him. Now we just have to let God talk to Jim Himself."

"I can't let him leave like this", said Allen rising from the table. Then he bolted to the front hall, quickly grabbed his coat from the closet and followed Jim out the door. Allen remembered Jim's breath and was afraid of where he was headed.

Allen looked around to see which way Jim went, and spotted him going in the direction opposite his home. Jim was all the way at the end of the block waiting for the traffic signal to change. This gave Allen some time to run to catch up with him.

"Hey, Jim, wait up!" Allen called out. Jim didn't respond.

"I'm sorry about what happened back there. Don't get mad at them. They were only trying to help", panted Allen who was out of breath.

"I know, but it's not what I'm trying to hear right now."

"How about we go and hang out for a while. Just blow off some steam, you know?"

"Nah, man. You go on home. I just need to be alone for a while."

"Are you sure?"

"Yes, I'm sure", said Jim testily. "I'm not really in the mood for company right now."

"If you change your mind, call me. Please."

As Allen walked away, Jim couldn't help but feel relieved, and this bothered him. Jim and Allen had always been very close friends. Allen was the one person in his life that he felt he could count on, that would understand him, and now it seemed as if they were on divergent paths. The Sharpe's had been his surrogate parents for years and within a few minutes and with a few harsh words, he felt he had become alienated from them forever. Jim was conscious of the fact that he was beginning to lose everything. Momma Lena was right. Jim was drifting, and he had the worst feeling that it was to a very dark place where he didn't want to be. He thought by staying in transit, he had ended all of the dark tunnels in his life. However, the void was opening again and Jim felt himself being pulled toward the deep murky vortex. He wanted to stop what was going on, but felt powerless about what to do about it. Everything he did seemed to bring him closer to it. Jim realized that he needed help, but he didn't know where exactly it would come from. Who could he talk to, now? Who could he lean on? He wanted to talk to someone, but who would understand? Since Allen embarked on this spiritual journey, there was no way that he would. He felt all the others were way too shallow to even begin to talk to.

Jim didn't like the way he was feeling. All the same questions started popping up in his head again. The same questions for which he had no real answers. He had to silence them. Jim crossed the street and headed down toward the Blue Note Bar and Grill on 135th.

It was still early in the evening when Jim arrived and the place was already crowded. Even in a recession, people still found the time and money to get their drink on. Jim maneuvered his way towards the bar and sat down. He thought about ordering a beer, but he had been drinking beer all week, not to mention the fact that he had just had one before he got to the Sharpe's for dinner. No, he needed something a little stronger than a beer right now.

"What'll it be, son?" asked the bartender.

"I'll have a shot of Jack Daniel's, straight", Jim ordered trying to act cool. Jim had never had whiskey before. In the past, he had heard from his friends at St. John's about how strong it was, but then people were known to exaggerate about things.

There was a college basketball game on the flat screen T.V. above the bar and Jim attempted to concentrate on the game while he waited for his drink, but other thoughts kept intruding. Momma Lena said that God loved Jim. "He sure has a funny way of showing it." Jim thought to himself. If there were a God that loved him, He wouldn't have taken his parents away from him. If there were a God that loved him, He wouldn't have allowed racists to hinder him from getting a job as a law clerk. If there were a God that loved him, He wouldn't be turning his friends against him. No, all those things he had been told as a child were lies. His parent's believed in lies. Now he knew the truth. He didn't need a God in his life. Then out of nowhere it flashed before his eyes. He could see his mother's coffin being lowered into the grave; the dirt being piled on. The vivid memory of the sight made Jim feel as if he was in there too, and with each shovel full of dirt, he felt as if he was being covered and suffocated.

The bartender served Jim his drink. Jim gulped it down quickly. After a few seconds he was stunned by a sudden, intense burning in his throat and started to cough violently. The bartender looked over and turned back to his work laughing to himself at the young man's naiveté. Jim played off his coughing fit, trying to stifle it. The drink was strong and it went straight to his head, which Jim liked. It made him feel powerful.

"Yo, bartender. Let me get another hit of that."

"I would've thought you'd had enough the first time, son."

"Please, man. This is like water for me."

"If you say so", smiled the bartender.

The bartender filled his glass again. This time Jim braced himself before pouring the liquid down his throat. It still stung hard enough to make Jim wince, but not as bad as the first time. Now the voices in his head were beginning to quiet.

"What are you going to do now?" he heard one say.

"Who cares? It's like Momma Lena said. We all gonna die anyway."

"Where do you think you're going to go after you die?"

"What does it matter? If I go to heaven I'm better off, and if I go to hell, I've had enough preparation for that right here on earth."

Jim ordered another shot. Then another. Each shot being easier to take than the last. The more shots he drank the less he could feel. The weight and the burden of the responsibility for his life seemed to be lifting from him.

"You know your mother was the only one who didn't want you to be a lawyer. She wanted you to be a preacher."

"She's dead."

COMMENCEMENT

Jim ordered more shots. Soon Jim could feel nothing at all. Everything around him was just dull colors and muffled noises. He was still drifting, but now he was at ease. It was as if he was on a boat in the middle of a placid stream and the warm sun was beating down on him. Jim was peacefully drifting on the stream, blissfully unaware of the falls up ahead.

THIRTY-FIVE

Allen squirmed around in his seat. He was beginning to get a little anxious. It was 10:25 and he was starting to worry. Tamiko was always on time for her appointments. Allen checked his smart phone again to see if he had gotten any messages from her. Then he saw it.

I'm in the library. But where are you?

In the back, all the way back, Allen tapped into his phone feeling a bit of relief.

Allen got up from where he was sitting and went to the corner where he knew she would be able to see him. It took a few moments before they spotted each other. Even on the weekends when she was supposed to be laid back, Tamiko still looked prissy. She was wearing a beige button down shirt under a light orange v-neck sweater, coffee colored corduroy skirt and high heeled coffee colored boots. She looked like something out of a Brooks Brothers ad. Looking at her, Allen felt like a slob in his wrinkled gray sweatshirt, jeans, and vintage Jordans.

"Sorry I'm late, but I had trouble finding parking and the tourists are pouring in right about now."

"You took your car? Why didn't you just take the train?"

"Because I'm going by B.J.'s later to get some things for the ice-cream social the children's church is having. Anyway, what's this all about?"

"Someone I know desperately needs a tutor, and I thought you may be able to help me since you're a teacher and all."

COMMENCEMENT

"Honestly, Allen, with the way things have been going with my teaching career, I'm probably the last person you should be asking for help."

"C'mon, Miko. Even if you don't know a lot, you do know something. That's more than I know right now."

"Fine. Who is it? Does your new girlfriend have a kid or something?"

"This has nothing to do with Holly. Besides we're pretty much over."

"Really, Why?"

"Jim and Tim blabbed about where I worked at the Election Night party, and that was the end of that."

"If she's that shallow, you didn't need her anyway. Now back to business. How old is this kid? What grade is he or she in?"

"He's about 24, and he's trying to get his high school diploma."

"Allen, are you serious?! I'm an elementary school teacher! I have a certificate in elementary education, as in grades 1 through 6. I have no idea how to help someone that old!"

"C'mon, Miko. You have some experience in that area. Remember when we used to be school tutors in high school? That wasn't that long ago", Allen reminded her in an attempt to calm her down.

"So why don't you just tutor him yourself if that's the case? And who is this guy anyway?"

"He's a guy I know from work. His name is Davis Martinez."

"This isn't the guy that you said looks like he's straight out of 'Con Air'?!"

"That was before I got to know him. He's a really good guy. He's had a rough life, but now he's trying to turn things around."

"What do you mean, 'you got to know him'. You've barely known this guy a week! Who knows what he's really like. What if he's mentally unstable? What if he has no intention of studying, but wants us to write his papers for him, and then if we don't cooperate, threatens to shoot us or something?"

"Miko, are you listening to yourself?"

"No, have you been listening to yourself?"

"I just have a good feeling about this guy. Anyway, he needs our help and we are in a position to help him. What do you think God would have us to do?"

Tamiko paused for a moment. Allen had made a valid point.

"O.K, when you put it that way... but you still haven't told me what I'm supposed to do? After all he's your pupil, isn't he?"

Silence from Allen.

"Isn't he?"

"You see, Miko. It's really complicated because I work with him everyday. I don't want to make things uncomfortable between us. It's a guy thing, you know? But if you were to step in at some point, being a girl and all, I think our friend would be more amenable to….."

"Allen!"

"I'm going to be here with you two. Sometimes."

"Sometimes!" said Tamiko, her eyes widening in shock. I'm going home!"

"C'mon, Miko. You'll both be in a public place. I mean it's the library! What could happen here? And besides I'll pick you up and take you home if you need me to."

"I won't need you to, because I'm not staying!"

"Miko, please. C'mon. At least stay for today. He's going to be here in a minute."

Not long after Allen had uttered those words, did Davis appear before them. He was wearing a black wool jacket with a black hoodie underneath, baggy jeans and sneakers. He was also carrying a black canvass school bag on his back.

COMMENCEMENT

"Wassup, Al?" then, after noticing Tamiko's expression, he added "I'm not late, am I? You said 11:00 right?"

"Of course not. You're just in time, man. But first, let me introduce you to my friend I was telling you about. Davis, this is Tamiko Bynum. She's a public school teacher. Tamiko, this is Davis, my colleague from work."

Tamiko couldn't help her open-mouthed stare. However, she managed to shake herself out of it to stammer a few words.

"Nicet to meet you, Davis", she said weakly as she offered a slightly trembling hand.

"Same here", replied Davis giving her a firm, but quick shake.

"Now that we've gotten over the formalities, how about we sit down and get down to business?" said Allen trying to break the ice. They all sat down at one of the rectangular tables. Allen sat opposite Davis and Tamiko sat next to Allen.

"So, Davis, you told me you were having trouble with your English classes, but now we need to find out what your specific problem is. Do you have any of your papers or class work that we could have a look at?"

"Uh, yeah, like I got this paper I did for class last week. I didn't get a very good grade on it, but the teacher said if I could fix it up, he'd score the second one and do like an average of the two grades, but to tell you the truth, like a lot of the comments, I don't get what he's talkin' about. I don't know where to start."

Davis opened his backpack and took out a very smart looking blue vinyl folder, opened it and took out a paper at the front of the pile within, and handed it to Allen. Allen received it from him, and Tamiko peered over Allen's shoulder. They both tried not to seem too startled at the grade (a D-), and then the sea of red ink that covered the paper. In any case, Davis could read their faces despite their attempts to cover their reaction.

"I told you it wasn't good", Davis said looking at his hands.

"What was this paper supposed to be about?" asked Tamiko hesitantly.

"It's suppost' to be about different kin's of heroes and how this guy Achilles is one kin' of hero and how he compares to somebody like this guy named Tom in this other book."

"Tom, who?" asked Allen.

"The guy in this book about these poor people who move to Cali, lookin' for work."

"Do you mean the "Grapes of Wrath"?" asked Allen as he handed the paper over to Tamiko, who was hogging it. It seemed that her teacher's instinct was kicking in, and overriding all of the other feelings she was having at the moment.

"Yeah, that's the one. So whaddoyathink?"

"From what I have read so far, your ideas aren't really that bad. It's just that they need to be organized or arranged a bit better. And they could stand to be a little more developed. But these aren't the biggest issues. It's your grammar that's going to be the real challenge", suggested Tamiko.

"What's grammar?"

"Like the way you put a sentence together."

Davis gave Tamiko a very blank look. Allen and Tamiko looked at each other with grave expressions. Tamiko then tried to explain.

"It's just that you write the way you speak."

"What's wrong wit' that. Ain't you suppost to? That's what my teachers in school taught me when I was little."

"Actually, you're not. I mean it's okay for little kids because they're just learning how to get their ideas down on paper, but once you get older, there has to be a shift in your approach. The way most people talk is very ungrammatical. The only reason it makes sense is because the context of conversation has so many other variables that communicate what our words don't. When you write, you have to be more precise or specific with your meaning, otherwise people won't understand you." explained Tamiko, hoping she didn't sound too much like a nerd.

COMMENCEMENT

"You make it sound like I gotta to learn another language", breathed Davis, a little discouraged.

"Kind of. But it's not that hard. I mean we can start by working on fixing this paper."

"But you think there's hope for me?"

"Of course! Like I said before, your ideas are very good."

"She's right, and you just need to use more precise references from the book to support your ideas", said Allen.

"O.K. so, you just show me what I gotta do and I'll do it."

"Great. Let's get started."

The three of them spent the next three hours helping Davis develop an outline for his new paper, and helping him with deciding on different quotes from the text that would better illustrate his points. All throughout, Davis took notes that he would use to help him to re-write the paper. Then they discussed how when Davis had finished re-writing the paper, he could drop it off with Allen who would deliver it to Tamiko at school, who would then help Davis edit it for spelling and grammar. Then Davis would re-write this draft and hand in the final version to his teacher. All throughout their session, Davis demonstrated a great work ethic. He seemed genuinely interested in learning more about writing than in trying to get either Tamiko or Allen to do his work for him. Allen was impressed by his organization, and his willingness to learn, not to mention his intellect. Reading Davis' paper, Allen realized that Davis was not as ignorant as his speech seemed to indicate. In fact, Allen began to wonder why Davis felt like he didn't understand his reading. The ideas in his paper seemed to be spot on, and Allen was a little jealous about all the different tenets Davis was able to tease out in two really challenging texts. Davis had just as much intellect as he had. He may not have had the opportunities to exercise that intellect as Allen had, but he had just as much potential as Allen did. Tamiko, seemed equally impressed with Davis' intellect, as well as his other more superficial qualities. In fact, she spent a lot of the time wondering about the impression she was making on him.

"Thanks for helpin' me. I really 'preciate it", said Davis when they were done.

"It's no problem man, anytime", replied Allen.

"So how much I owe you?" asked Davis.

"Oh, no! You don't have to pay us anything! Really!" exclaimed Tamiko.

"But I don't like takin' advantage. I know I gotta pay my own way. You feel?"

"But we're all friends here, right?" asked Allen, hoping Davis would accept his offer.

"Yeah, man", smiled Davis "At least lemme get you something to eat. I know you must be hungry by now."

"Sure. How about we get some pizza?" suggested Allen.

"O.K."

"Is that good for you, Miko?"

"I would love to hang with you guys, really. But I have to run some errands for my dad. It was nice meeting you, Davis. I hope you'll hang out with us sometime. Maybe you could go with us to the movies one Saturday when you're free."

"Maybe, but I don't know. I kinda have my hands full right now wit' school and all."

"I understand", said Tamiko trying to hide her disappointment.

"But we'll see."

"O.K. Bye", waved Tamiko, bumping into a table behind her on her way out.

Allen and Davis waved back. When Tamiko was out of sight…

"Your friend is really pretty. How old is she?"

"She'll be 22 in December. All the guys think she's pretty."

"She got a boyfriend?"

COMMENCEMENT

Allen hesitated for a moment. At first, he didn't really know what to say about that given recent developments among their set.

"No."

"For real? Why? Somethin' wrong wit her? She crazy or sumthin'?"

"No. She just has a lot of standards."

"Does that mean she likes the chedda, too?"

"No way. She's not like that at all. She just has a lot of moral standards that most guys have a hard time getting with."

"Like what? She don't sleep around?"

"Yeah, but that's just the start of it", laughed Allen. "You're not interested in her, are you?"

"Nah, man. It's like I tol' you before, I got too much goin' on right now to get involved with any females. I was just curious that's all. She's not like any of the girls I know from round the way. She seems real classy."

"Yes, Tamiko is truly one of a kind. But if you hang around us long enough, you'll find out all about her for yourself."

"Doesn't sound like a bad idea, man."

THIRTY-SIX

It was another Sunday morning at Greater Apostolic. The Elder sisters of the church - Mother Rose, and Lena, and the other older women were up front leading the congregation in praise songs, and calling people up to testify of God's greatness in their lives. Allen was sitting in a pew sandwiched between his dad and Tamiko. He was actively taking part in the praise and worship, and as he did, he could not help thinking about his life. His mother had challenged him to read his Bible for a week, and to pray, which he had done. However, he did not see or feel any miraculous change in his life. Allen was not overcome by some feeling, or calling, and he wasn't totally sure if he had heard the voice of God. Allen was still a Harvard graduate who was working as a porter until he could find a more suitable position. But he did feel that *something* was different. It was almost as if his eyes and his heart were starting to open to something new. He was beginning to acknowledge God's authority over his life. Allen's anxiety over his situation had lessened considerably, since he began to recognize that it was God's prerogatives that took precedence and not his own. He didn't know how long he would have to be a porter, or when another really good opportunity would open up, and he was trying to make peace with himself about these facts in his life. Allen was willing to follow this path where God would lead him. Allen also began to develop a different perspective about his work as a porter. It was like Jim and his dad had said. It was honest work, and he would do his best at it, for as long as this was his position. After reading his Bible for a week, Allen understood that God loves a good and faithful steward. He thought about Joseph, and David, who started out in very humble positions. These men were faithful, and God rewarded them for their work. Allen hoped

312

that he would be rewarded for his work, and that God would show him what to do. Allen now understood that he couldn't do it all himself, and he didn't have to. However, he couldn't help but wonder what was next. He just wished that God would explain what He was doing and make His plan clear to see.

Allen was also beginning to develop a deeper respect for God, and a sense of real humility. Allen fully realized who he was with respect to God. His mother was right. God did not owe him anything. He was God, after all. "It was he who made us and not we ourselves."[1] Since God was the maker, it was Allen who owed God. It was Allen who owed God praise, adoration, and above all else his whole life.

This new awakening had several secondary affects in Allen's life. First, since he was no longer as anxious, he began to get along better with everyone around him. His relationship with his parents and his friends had improved (with the exception of Jim, but that is another story). It also opened him up to making a new friend. Allen thought about Davis and the circumstances surrounding their meeting. Here was someone who had had a hard life and who was trying to turn his life around and give it to God. At the same time, here was Allen who was seeking a relationship with God. Maybe God had allowed them to meet so that they could help each other on a spiritual level. Allen recalled that Davis had said that he was going to join this church a few days ago, but hadn't mentioned it since. Yesterday, when they were having pizza together, the subject didn't come up. All morning, Allen had been looking around to see if Davis would appear, but the later it got, the less likely it seemed. Maybe Davis felt weird about going to the same church as Allen. Allen felt like maybe he shouldn't have mentioned that he went to Greater Apostolic. Maybe that's what scared Davis off.

Allen's train of though was interrupted as someone approached his pew.

"Is there space here for one more?" he heard a familiar voice ask.

"Of course", he heard Tamiko say while moving down a space so Tim could squeeze in between them.

"So you're back?!" squealed Tamiko who was pleasantly surprised.

"Sure, why not? It's not like I have anything better to do."

"Here we go", Allen said under his breath.

"Allen, don't be so rude", whispered Tamiko "I for one am glad that you've decided to come, Tim. And you've got to come with us to the luncheonette after church. We're just gonna have coffee and hang out before dinner."

"Sounds good to me."

"I bet it does", Allen scoffed. Allen felt guilty about having such feelings toward his friend, but he didn't like the idea that Tim was only coming to church to get close to Tamiko, especially when Tim's motives for getting close to her were not very clear. In fact, Tim was never clear about anything when it came to women. He always started out saying he just wanted to be "friends", then slowly escalated things, to the point of no return. Then, just when a poor girl thought she had something with him, he'd draw back quickly and dump her. Tim had left a trail of tears and broken hearts at Harvard this way, and he did not want Tamiko to be another casualty.

Soon the church band started to play the processional hymn and the choir began to make their way to the stage, marking the beginning of the service. As usual, everyone stood and sang along as the choir marched, swaying to the music. Once the hymn finished, the choir was seated and Daniel Joyner came to the podium to lead the church in prayer.

"Heavenly Father, we come before you once again to thank you for blessing us to be able to come together on another Sunday to praise your Holy name. We thank you for your love, grace, and mercy, without which we would have nothing. Thank you for loving us despite our fallen nature and sending your Son to die on the cross for our sins. Thank you for being patient with us as we walk this long road to salvation; picking us up when we fall and giving us those second chances when we fail. Thank you for chastening us and helping us to see our failings; for living through us and abiding with us and helping us live lives that bring honor and glory to your name. Thank you for being with us through life's trials and tribulations letting us know you are there, that you have not left us nor forsaken us. And thank you for those miracles that you are going to accomplish in our lives…."

As Daniel prayed, Allen prayed along with him, and he was touched as Daniel spoke of God being with us through life's trials. This was exactly what Allen wanted. He wanted to feel that God was indeed with him; directing him and guiding his life. Sometimes Allen could feel His presence as he read the scriptures, and he knew God was there when he prayed and meditated. Allen was much more aware of the presence of God in his life as he spent more time with God. However Allen wanted more. He wanted a special relationship with God, where he spoke to him directly.

Once the prayer ended, everyone sat down and the choir rose from its seats and led the church in praise once again. They sang, "Lord I Just Want to Thank You." It was an upbeat song and many of the people in the church started to sing along. Allen found himself singing and clapping his hands to the music. He actually empathized with the sentiments of the song. Instead of being down about his situation, he actually felt grateful to God. After all, he did have a job in one of the worst economic downturns in American history. He had lots of supportive friends and family, and he was semi-independent. Allen was able now to contribute to his household and his parents were not the type to try to dictate what he could and couldn't do beyond reasonable limits. His life wasn't as bad as he thought and he had God to thank for it. He was even hoping that maybe Tim might share some of this joy that he was feeling. He looked over at him, but he seemed to be too busy studying Tamiko who couldn't even stay seated. She was standing and clapping enthusiastically, while swaying to the music. She almost looked as if she was going to go "Lena Sharpe" and get into a full out shout. Soon the song ended, however, but for a few moments after it ended, Tamiko was still standing, and applauding; praising God with loud, effusive Hallelujahs.

The service went on through its usual course with moments of praise occurring between moments of prayer and meditation. Then there were the customary announcements, and then Mother Rose did the welcome address. Mother Rose loved doing the welcome addresses and she always stood out with her flamboyant attire. Her broad hats, and sparkly outfits were typical "church Diva" attire. This Sunday she had on a wide brimmed lavender hat with real ostrich feathers and a silk band, which was a perfect complement to her lavender, organza dress with sequins at the top. The whole thing looked more appropriate for Saturday evening than Sunday morning.

"Praise the Lord, Everyone!" Mother Rose greeted the congregation.

"Prasie the Lord!" the congregation responded.

"At this time we would like to welcome all of our new members to the Greater Apostolic Temple. Here at Greater Apostolic, we are honored to be able to spread the message of the Gospel, and it is with open arms that we welcome new sheep to God's growing pasture. As your name is called, please bless us by standing, so we can welcome you with a hearty praise. Sister Dimas Jones from Brooklyn, NY, Brother Kevin Sanford from Bronx, NY, Sister Grace Anunke, from South Africa, Brother Davis Martinez, from Bronx, N.Y...."

"He's here!" Allen thought excitedly to himself. He looked around to see where he was. Allen managed to spot him just as he was about to sit back down. He was all the way over near the back of the church in the pews over on the right side. Allen almost didn't recognize Davis because he had cut his hair into a curly fade, and was wearing a dark suit. Allen couldn't wait until the address was over so he could get up and welcome Davis himself. As he was waiting for his moment, he felt a paper slap him in the back of the head.

"You invited Davis to our church!" Tamiko tried not to whisper-yell, but was unsuccessful. She had switched places with Tim who was looking on curiously from the other side.

"No. Daniel did," said Allen still rubbing the back of his head where Tamiko hit him with the paper bulletin. He hoped she hadn't given him a paper cut in his scalp.

"What do you mean 'Daniel did'?"

"He met Daniel at the Youth Outreach Festival. When he told me about it, he didn't know that I was a member. Then when I did tell him, he never mentioned it again. I just thought that maybe he was uncomfortable with the fact that I was member and wouldn't show up."

"And you didn't mention this to me because…"

"I just told, you. I didn't think he'd show up."

"Well, now he has."

"Could someone explain to me who this 'Davis' is? And why Miko is so upset about him being here?" asked Tim getting into their whisper conversation.

"I'm not upset. I'm just surprised", Tamiko said suddenly patting her hair and smoothing her dress. This did not go unnoticed by Allen.

"You've got a funny way of showing it", said Allen dryly.

"Are you sure he's not stalking us?"

"Tamiko, get a grip", said Allen rolling his eyes. He noticed the address was over as the audience sent up applause for the new members. Allen decided to head out to where Davis was sitting.

"I'll be right back. Don't let anyone take my seat."

"Where are you going?" asked Tamiko nervously.

"Excuse me, I'm still in the dark, here!" said Tim still waiting for an explanation.

"Tamiko can explain it all", Allen told him.

"You still didn't answer my question!" Tamiko shot at Allen.

"Because you may not like the answer."

Allen walked to the far end of the pew away from the center aisle and used the aisle at the far end of the church to walk toward the back and then to the other side where he saw Davis sitting. Thankfully, the pew was almost empty with the exception of Davis and an elderly woman who was sound asleep at the end. Allen excused himself to the somnolent elderly woman as he made his way to Davis.

"Hey, man. I hope I'm not disturbing you." said Allen taking a seat next to Davis.

"Allen! Hey! Nah, man you not disturbin' nothin'. I was looking for you when I came in. I saw you was up front, but it looked a little crowded so I decided to sit back here. So, What's up?"

"Just wanted to give you a personal welcome. It's good to see you here man. You clean up pretty good."

"Yeah. I didn't want to come in disrespecting God by lookin' like whatever, ya know?"

"Don't sweat it man. It's the heart He's lookin' at anyway."

"True that."

"I'm going to leave you to get your praise on, but before I go, let me ask you something. How would you like to meet with me and some of my friends after the service? We're going to the luncheonette over on 6th to have some coffee before dinner."

"I don't know man...I got studying to do and everything..."

"C'mon man. It's not a lot of people. Just me, Tamiko, who you already know, and our friend Tim. He's cool."

"Aiight. But just for a few."

"Cool. Meet us in front over by the gate."

"You got it, man."

By the time Allen walked back to where he was sitting, the welcome address was over and the meditation was about to begin. As Allen sat down, Daniel had just signaled the start of meditation. Upon sitting down, Allen bowed his head and closed his eyes to participate in the meditation. He tried to meditate, but he couldn't help but feel Tamiko's eyes burning a hole into his face. He knew she wanted to know where he went, and if it had anything to do with Davis, and he was glad for the forced silence imposed upon the church, so a possible whisper argument could be avoided.

Once the meditation was over, it seemed that Tamiko must have forgotten the subject of her interest because she did not look Allen's way at all. In fact, for the rest of the service, she spent a lot of time whispering back and forth to Tim who was now seated on the other side of her.

COMMENCEMENT

When Pastor Bynum came out to deliver his message, she even shared her Bible with him. Allen tried hard to put away his apprehensions about what was going on and focus on the sermon.

Today the Pastor's subject was holding on through the storm. The reading was from Matthew chapter 14 vs. 22-33, Allen had remembered reading this passage previously one evening before going to sleep. It referred to when Jesus was on a boat with his disciples, and the storm was so fierce that the boat seemed like it would capsize. During the storm, Jesus was asleep on the boat and the apostles woke him up because they were afraid that they were going to drown. So Jesus rebuked the wind and the waves, calming the storm. That being done, Jesus then rebuked his apostles for their lack of faith. They should have had faith that Jesus loved them so much that he would never let anything happen to them that contradicted what he had already promised them. After all, hadn't he already told them that they would be fishers of men? Hadn't he already chosen them as his apostles? Pastor Bynum preached that their faith should have told them that Jesus would protect them in their commission. The whole sermon succored his spirits and helped to reinforce his own faith. Allen was just beginning to trust God. Sometimes, it took everything within him to hold onto his faith. There were times when doubt lingered and played around at the back of his mind. Like the Apostles on the boat, the circumstances around Allen often distracted him, and they would almost take him under. He realized he had to stop thinking about what "the world" said about his situation and try to think about it from a biblical standpoint. So Allen listened attentively, and at one point found himself jotting down notes from Pastor Bynum's sermon on his program. The more Allen learned about the Lord, the more he wanted to learn. Many times he was left with more questions than answers, but Allen did not find this in the least discouraging.

Soon the service was coming to its conclusion. Pastor Bynum wrapped up his sermon and then there was the altar call. This Sunday, Allen did not go up. He had already dedicated or rather re-dedicated his life to the Lord. But he did notice a familiar face headed in the direction of the altar. Allen leaned over to tell Tamiko about Davis, when she started up from the pew with Tim.

"Wait a minute. Where are you two going?"

"To the altar."

"You mean you convinced Tim to get saved?!"

"Not so much. I just told him that maybe it wouldn't hurt if daddy said a prayer for him."

"*You* want to be prayed for?!"

"It's like Tamiko said; it couldn't hurt."

"O.K., but I don't know if the Pastor will have enough time for a case like you. They might need to take you to the Upper Room."

"Very funny, Allen", said Tamiko rolling her eyes.

"Wait a minute. What's this 'Upper Room'?" asked Tim nervously.

"It's just a place upstairs where people tarry in prayer. They pray for hours at a time."

"Your dad's not going to take me in there, is he?"

"Don't be silly. Let's go", said Tamiko, dragging Tim by the arm.

Allen shook his head and laughed. Then after a moment he bowed his head for a quick prayer.

"Heavenly Father, my friend Tim is one of my best friends in the world. He has one reason for being here today, but as he goes up to your altar, give him another reason for coming. Open his eyes and circumcise the foreskin of his heart to bring him into the knowledge of who you are. I know he's a challenge, but Father God, I know there's nothing that is too challenging for you."

Once the altar call was over and the Pastor had given his final benediction, the people began to empty out of the church. Lena gave Allen a quick kiss on the cheek, before she headed off with Vernon to the parking lot. Pastor Bynum, headed into the inner sanctuary with his wife to perform a baptism, which left the three young people to themselves and their afternoon plans. They walked out of the church and toward the gate where Allen stopped them.

COMMENCEMENT

"Hold on, guys. I told Davis, we'd meet him here after the service. I invited him to have coffee with us."

"You what?!" exclaimed Tamiko.

"So you're saying you don't want him to have coffee with us?"

"No. I'm just saying that you could have given me some warning", she said, anxiously smoothing her clothing.

"I just did. Anyways, why are you trying to make this drama?" asked Allen, although after knowing Tamiko as long as he had, he was pretty sure he already knew the answer.

"I don't know, maybe it has to do with the fact that none of us really knows him all that well", offered Tim "And given what Miko has told me about what little she knows, don't you think this will be a bit awkward for him."

"Oh, really? And just what has Miko told you?" asked Allen.

But before Tim could answer Allen's question, the person who was the subject of their discussion approached. Here was Davis, and to Tamiko's astonishment, with a very new look. Davis was wearing a black suit jacket with a grey oxford cloth shirt, and matching black tie. He also wore dark grey twill pants and black, square-toed leather shoes. It was a stark contrast to the look he had the other day at the Museum library.

"Hi, Davis", Tamiko swallowed hard. "Love your new look."

"Thanks. You look real nice, too", Davis said shyly "And I don't think I met you before", he said referring to Tim.

"Davis, this is Tim Russell. He's an old friend of mine from college", said Allen introducing them.

"Whassup, man", said Davis putting his fist out for the pound.

"Nice to meet you, Davis", said Tim extending his hand for a shake.

After an awkward moment, Davis took Tim's hand and gave him a firm shake.

"So let's hit the café. I could use a cup of Joe right about now", said Allen.

The Luncheonette wasn't very busy at all until Allen and his friends arrived. The tiny little establishment was just a few tables and a long counter that ran across the back where the orders were placed. Allen and the others took seats at a table across from an old woman who was nursing a plate of chicken and waffles. Allen sat next to Davis and opposite them were Tamiko and Tim. The one waitress on duty took their order and them left them to themselves.

"So how do you like Greater Apostolic, Davis? Do you think you'll stay with us?" asked Allen.

"Oh, mos def. I like the pastor. He seems mad real, yo. He really knows how to break it down, so you understand. Now I know where Daniel get's it from", answered Davis.

"Tamiko, I know you must be glad to hear that", Allen said giving her a knowing look.

Tamiko simply smiled shyly.

"Pastor Bynum is Tamiko's dad", said Allen.

"Word?!" Davis replied a little unnerved by the revelation.

"Yes. She is the preacher's daughter. She grew up in that church."

"So did you", Tamiko reminded Allen.

"Yeah, Tamiko and I have been friends since kindergarten. Our parents practically raised us together so we've both been a part of the church for years."

"Whoa, so you like church royalty or somethin'?" asked Davis a little awestruck.

"I don't think our church has a 'royalty'. Although my mom would probably like to think so", laughed Tamiko.

"Yeah, man. Her dad doesn't allow people to head-trip over titles. Everyone is treated with respect, whether you clean the kitchen or on the Deacon board."

COMMENCEMENT

"Oh. And how long you been there, chief?" Davis asked turning his attention to Tim.

"I'm not really a member. I go with Tamiko sometimes as a friend, but I'm agnostic."

"What's that? Is that like the Presbyterians or somethin'?"

"No," chuckled Tim "It just means that I'm not sure there is a God."

"Yeah, I used to be like you, but after everythin' that's happened in my life in the past six or seven years, I know there's a God. True that."

"What happened?" asked Allen.

"I don't know if you ready for my story. I mean you guys bein' raised in the church and what not…my life has been kinda…rough, if you knowwhatimean. I don't know if it's what you're used to."

Then the waitress came to the table with their coffee. There was silence between them as the waitress placed the cups and condiments on the table. They all thanked her before she left. Then Allen picked up the thread of their conversation again.

"Look man, just because I've grown up in the church, doesn't mean I've always been on the straight and narrow. I've made a lot of mistakes in my own life and taken a lot of foolish turns that I've… I mean, God, had to work out. All of us have. Nobody here is in a position to judge you."

Davis paused briefly before he reticently began to relate an episode from his past.

"I'll make it short. My life was so rough that I used to think there couldn't be a God with everythin' that was goin' on. There were times when I didn't care whether I lived or died. To this day I don't know who my dad is, and my mom had a string of boyfriends that was mad abusive. So I spent a lot of time on the streets tryin' to get away from it all. Needless to say, I was runnin' wit' a bad crowd and eventually it caught up wit' me. One day a dude took a 45 magnum and blew a hole in my chest. I went down on the pavement. I couldn't move. I couldn't say nothin'. Then I started to feel this cold. It started at my feet and was inching it's way up my body. I knew I was gone. It started getting dark. I couldn't see anything, but I could feel somebody's hand on me, and I

323

could hear someone say to me, 'This is not your end. This is your beginning.' Next thing I know, I woke up in the hospital and they was tellin' me that if I wasn't dead yet, I would be soon. I had a collapsed lung, and I lost like more than a pint of blood. They had the hospital preacher there and my moms and my sister. He asked me if I wanted to give my life to God. I said yeah. I figure if He's keepin' me alive, He's doin' it for a reason: for me to give Him my life."

"Look at how good God is!" gasped Tamiko.

"And that's not the end of it. When word got back to the street that I was alive, the dude that put me in the hospital was lookin' to finish the job. But I thank God that by the time I was ready to go home, I heard that my would-be executioner was in jail, and the others who set him on me was dead. They all got shot up by some dudes that had beef wit' them. It was like in the Bible when God took care of the Assyrians when they was threatenin' to get the Israelites. They didn't have to do nothin'. They just woke up and all they enemies was just dead in the camp."[2] Davis continued.

"That is some testimony Davis. God has really been good to you", said Allen.

"These people who were after you…were they like, gang members? " asked Tim.

"Tim!" exclaimed Tamiko at Tim's brazenness. "It's okay Davis, you don't have to answer. It's not any of our business."

"It's aiight. I ain't tryin' to front or nothin'. They were, and drug dealers, too. So was I. But I don't roll wit' that no more. I been outta the thug life for a long time now."

"Really? It's seems your conversion experience was quite some time ago. You're just now beginning to attend church," Tim continued with his examination.

"Tim, you don't just go from being saved to a church going saint overnight. Sometimes people want to take the time and find the right church. Right, Davis?" said Allen in Davis's defense.

COMMENCEMENT

"Yeah, man. I had been to a few churches before. But in some churches, it's like you go in and nobody talks to you. Or you go in and you find out that there's different sections for different kinds of people: saints up front, sinners in the back. There's even a VIP section."

"I hear that!" laughed Allen.

"I got tired of all the drama. I was just gonna try to study my bible on my own, but then one day I was comin' down near the park 'long 135th and I saw this block party. And it wasn't no ordinary block party neither. They was singing gospel songs, and there was a lot of kids havin' fun getting' they faces decorated, young adults playing games. I was just standin' around wishin' I could be a part of it, when this dude comes up to me an' just invites me in. Then when I went in, the atmosphere was really different. Everybody was nice. There was people that would walk up and talk to me like I had known them for years. The old folks wasn't all suspicious an clannish. Then when Daniel started preachin' I knew that this was the kind of church that I wanted to be part of."

"Well, I think I can speak for everyone, when I say that we are glad to have you, Davis." said Allen.

"Yes, we certainly are. Next week, when you come, you meet us out front and then you can come in and sit with us", offered Tamiko.

"Aiight, thanks. I'll do that."

"Our folks have Sunday dinners together, too. If you want, and if you have some spare time after studying, maybe you could come to dinner with us", she continued.

"You mean like have dinner with the pastor? I don't know if I'm ready for all that."

"He may be the pastor of the church, but he's still a regular guy." said Allen.

"Maybe later on. Tonight I have get that paper ready you guys was helpin' me wit'. I wanna finish revising it, so I can give it to you tomorrow. Guess that means I'm gonna have to jet", said Davis rising from his seat. He took out some money to pay for the coffee, when Allen stopped him.

"No way, man. I let you get the pizza yesterday. Coffee's on me."

"You sure?"

"Of course."

"Thanks. See you guys around."

They all gave their good byes to Davis who left the Luncheonette.

"So what was that about, Tamiko?" asked Tim.

"What was what about?"

"First, you're all shocked when Allen asks him to have coffee with us, then you turn around and ask him to Sunday dinner?"

"He's a friend of ours, now. Right, Allen?"

"I don't see why he can't be."

"Are you kidding me? He's a gangbanger and drug dealer! What if there are other people that are out to get this guy? Do you really want to risk being a picked off in a "drive –by"? Risk getting arrested just by being with him?"

"He's an Ex-gangbanger and an ex-drug dealer. He said he's been out of that life for years", said Allen in Davis's defense.

"And you really believe that?" asked Tim incredulously.

"Davis has been working at the Sheraton for four years, and Mr. Hardy likes him. Besides, the whole time that I've been working with him, I haven't noticed anything that would indicate he's leading a double life as a drug dealer. He's got too much going on for that. He's going to night school for crying out loud", Allen insisted.

"You've known Davis seven days, not seven years, Allen!"

"I don't know about anyone else, but I trust him. When he talks he's very …genuine", Tamiko remarked with a dreamy look.

"You don't say", Tim responded sarcastically.

"Look, let's not waste time arguing about Davis. He's our friend now Tim, get used to it. Now let's go or we'll be late for dinner."

COMMENCEMENT

"Fine. I just hope I don't end up having to say 'I told you so'", warned Tim.

THIRTY-SEVEN

"What was going on between all of you children during the welcome address?" asked Lena after the Pastor had finished saying grace over the meal.

"Allen just noticed that his friend from work was one of our new members. We had coffee with him this afternoon", answered Tamiko.

"Just look at that! Allen is working to bring people to Lord. Maybe the ministry is your calling Allen", beamed Mother Rose.

"Actually, I really can't take credit. That belongs to Daniel."

"And what does he have to do with this?" asked Mother Rose peevishly.

"Our friend Davis, went to the youth festival that Daniel organized and he was the one that invited Davis to our church. It's just a coincidence that we happen to work together", Allen explained.

"May not be much of a coincidence, after all. God has ways to bringing people to himself. Maybe Daniel brought him in, but you may be the person that will help him to stay", suggested Lena.

"Maybe."

"But he is planning to stay at our church already. He's going to sit with us next Sunday, and we all may get a chance to know him a little better, once I convince him to come to one of our Sunday dinners", sang Tamiko.

COMMENCEMENT

"You seem to be very happy about this new friend", observed Pastor Bynum.

"I'm always excited to see people come to the Lord!" exclaimed Tamiko.

"Really?" said Mother Rose with a hint of suspicion.

"This is a sudden change from last week. You were so down in the dumps because of what was going on at work. Things getting better?" asked the Pastor.

"Actually, they're not", Tamiko sighed. "It just so happens that I'm actually planning to quit after the end of next week."

"What?!" gasped Tamiko's mother "What could possibly make you want to do that?"

"God blessed me to overhear a conversation that the assistant principal was having with the lead teacher and the literacy coach. The principal doesn't think I can be helped, and she's planning to fire me at the end of the year. I figure I'd just beat them to it."

"I can't believe they would do something like this! And after all the work I've seen you put in!" Mother Rose huffed.

"Are you sure this is what you want to do?" asked Pastor Bynum.

"I think it's what's best, daddy. I can't see myself trying to explain to a prospective employer why I got fired. Besides, I think God allowed me to find out what they were planning so that I could quit, without being disgraced."

"Or maybe He let you find out so that you would be able to see and experience the Glory of God. I don't think you should quit Tamiko."

"But daddy, the principal thinks I'm a loser, and that racist lead teacher is probably doing everything she can to keep the principal from changing her mind."

"I know what it looks like. Were you listening to my sermon today?"

"Yes, I understand all that about how we can't look at our circumstances, but…"

"But what? God didn't bless us with a record of what happened to his apostles just so that we could feel good at the end of the day. He did it to provide an example to us for how we should put our faith into practice. Tamiko, you need to learn to stand still and keep your eyes on the Lord. Stop thinking about what this one says about you or about what someone else is going to do. Don't let those waves toss you. God told you, you were supposed to teach. He put you in this school. If he has let you know that you will be gone at the end of the year, you don't leave until the end of the year. I'm not saying you can't look for another position, but until you find another, you need to remain a good and faithful servant and do your best no matter what. Keep in mind the One you're really working for."

"But how can I do my best under these circumstances? I constantly feel so isolated and depressed when I'm there. I just think that if I quit, things can only get better."

"You may feel better for a while, but the situation may not get better, in fact it could get worse. And what would really make you feel better would be to change your focus. Don't go to that school everyday thinking about people. You go to school thinking about God and how he can use you to help those children. That's the only thing that counts. You do like Nehemiah: stay on the wall."[1]

"With all due respect sir, if her boss is out to get her, what else can she do?" asked Tim.

"Though you may not think so, I know there is no boss on this earth bigger than God."

"For Tamiko's sake, I hope so", said Tim doubtfully.

"I believe the Lord is putting a Word in my spirit for you young man. I don't know if you are still having problems down at your job or not, but I feel God telling me that you need to learn to love your enemies. That no matter what they have done to you down there, you need to keep on working and doing good for them. You may be tempted to just give up and not do your best just to get back at them, but I want you to know that God is looking down and having mercy. Continue to do good, despite what they do to you. Now, I don't know if that makes any sense to you, but that was what I believe the Lord wanted me to tell you."

Tim thought for a moment about what the pastor said. He had to admit that when the pastor said it, he was kind of shocked because in some way it did resonate with him. He was going to just sit back and let Preston run everything and try to get away with doing as little as he could until he was let go. After all, with what they did to him, they deserved it. He knew Tamiko hadn't told her father about what had happened, and Tim hadn't told her about what he had planned to do. It was eerie: almost as if the pastor was able to read his mind. But how could he "love" Preston or any of the others at Herns and Marshall. It was stressful enough just being civil with them. Tim couldn't picture himself working merrily with them like elves in Santa's workshop. That just seemed ridiculous.

"I'll take it into consideration", Tim responded politely.

"So, Pastor do you have a word for me?" inquired Allen hoping that the pastor would give him some insight into what was in store for him.

"I don't have a particular word for you Allen. Anyway, I think you are doing just fine where you are."

"I don't think I'm doing fine. It's hard being in the dark. I know God is with me. I just wish he would reveal more of his plan to me. Tell me what's next, or what to expect, or what it is that I'm supposed to be learning from him at the Sheraton."

"Allen, I couldn't tell you those things. You may not learn them until you are on the other side of this trial. You're just going to have to wait."

"It seems like the hardest part of having faith is the waiting."

"That's because when you're young, you want everything to happen right away. But trust me, God will never leave you hanging too long. What's that saying 'He may not come when you want Him, but He's right on time.' That's the way he's worked in my life. Just keep holding on Allen. Everything will fall into place."

Allen simply smiled half-heartedly at what the pastor said. All anyone could do is hold on. In real life it was much easier said than done.

THIRTY-EIGHT

November came in with gusty winds and left as quietly as falling autumn leaves. Then on came December with it's dry cold, that gave no indication of the weather that waited. Some had even harbored a secret hope for an unseasonably mild winter. On this December morning, the forecasters had predicted a light rain that would clear out toward the end of the day. However, some time toward mid-morning, the rain began to change over to snow, creating slush on the streets below. Caught unaware, many commuters trudged through the slush with their canvas sneakers and ballerina flats, the cold freezing their feet and toes. Then the temperature dropped suddenly to 30 degrees, freezing the slush and creating icy conditions on the roads and resulting in traffic nightmares that unfolded all over the urban landscape. Storeowners and proprietors hustled to have sidewalks shoveled and salted, and people in offices worried about what their commute would be like when they started home.

It was upon such a scene that Allen found himself shoveling the sidewalks in front of the Sheraton. He and two other porters had started on the front walk, but it seemed their efforts were made futile by incessant snowfall. They had just spent the last twenty minutes or so cracking up the ice that was forming under the snow and shoveling it. When they had finally finished the long block that ran in front of the hotel, there was a new coat of snow waiting to be shoveled. So the second time around, Allen and another porter shoveled as the two others spread salt behind them. When they were done, Allen understood why people often died of cardiac arrest while shoveling their driveways. It was 30 degrees outside, yet Allen had worked up a sweat that had drenched his thermal underclothes. He knew he should head inside before the dampness of his clothes caused him to catch a cold, but he desperately needed time to catch his breath.

Allen leaned on his shovel and surveyed the city scene in front of him. Watching the people struggle with the unexpected turn in the weather, made him think about the past six weeks that he had been struggling at the Sheraton. The work was hard, and it seemed the winter months made it harder. The physical labor required to do his job was beyond back breaking. Since Thanksgiving weekend it seemed as if every room in the building was occupied with tourists who were in town for the Christmas season. With more guests there was always more to be done and it had to be done quickly. The only thing that made up for it was the fact that he had developed a physique that rivaled Tim's during his heyday as a member of the Harvard lacrosse team. But the best development of all was Allen's burgeoning friendship with Davis. For the past six weeks they had been working together and helping each other in various ways. Allen and Tamiko's tutoring had helped Davis to improve in his English literature, history, and writing classes in night school. In return, Davis was helping Allen to learn more about buildings and how to make small repairs. Allen had learned all about how to detect mold, how to lay down tile and linoleum, and how to fix small plumbing problems. They also spent more time together off the job and were fast becoming good friends.

In addition to church, Davis had been hanging with Allen and his friends when they went out to dinner or to some event or show. As with the integration of new friends into an old set, there is always some conflict that arises. Tim, didn't like him, but then he was the type of guy who jealously guarded any friends he had, mostly because he had very few real friends he could trust. Tamiko and Richard, however, were nuts about Davis. Allen thought Davis and Jim would hit it off, because of Davis's blue-collar background, but strangely enough, Jim seemed very cool towards Davis. Not that Jim had spent much time with their set anyway. For the past week or so, it seemed as if Jim were avoiding them all, and Allen had a sinking suspicion as to why. The few times Jim did hang with them he seemed very sullen, moody, and worst of all, inebriated. It was ironic and almost prescient that Davis should enter Allen's life just as Jim seemed to be leaving it. It made Allen suspect that maybe God knew that Davis was the kind of friend he needed right now in this particular time in his life. The only one Davis hadn't met was Callie who seemed to be MIA since the night of Richard's Election Night Party. Jim mentioned speaking to her a few times, but she never returned any of Allen's e-mails or texts, and whenever he called her, he always got her voice mail. When it first started happening, he thought maybe she was just busy, but now it seemed that maybe she, too, was avoiding him. However Allen could not fathom why. He knew he would actually have to go to her house to visit her to find out, and he didn't know if he was really looking forward to that.

Allen already knew, he had spent too much time outside and headed inside with his shovel. First he stopped off at the supply area to return the shovel, and had to wait for Kizzy to finish flirting with another porter who had joined the staff shortly before Allen. When he was done, he got on the service elevator and was going up to finish his rounds on the ninth floor when he heard Davis paging him on the radio.

"Copy" Allen murmured into his radio.

"We got a situation in 621 wit' a toilet. Bring the bucket, a mop, and the wet vac."

"Got it."

"And make sure you got yo' gloves man."

"Hear ya. Over."

Allen used his key to override the elevator and stop at the fifth floor to get the bucket, mop, and wet vac from the water closet. He also took some of the industrial cleaning rags as well. He almost forgot his gloves, but remembered when he was near the doorway. Allen ran back and grabbed them from the shelf above the sink where he left them and shoved them in his pocket. Then he headed back toward the elevator. In the past few weeks, Davis and Allen had been like the Batman and Robin of the Sheraton, extinguishing the small troubles in their wing of the building. They worked together so well that sometimes he could anticipate what Davis wanted before he even asked. And Allen was always in awe of the different things that Davis could do. He was not just some guy with a sketchy knowledge of repairs. Davis really could fix anything because he had a deep understanding of the science and engineering involved in his job. When he talked about fixing things, his persona would change. Davis would become more confident. His vocabulary seemed to expand as he spoke the jargon of plumbing repair. So it was no shock to Allen when he found out that Davis had excellent grades in math and science in Night School. Straight A's to be exact. No wonder he didn't want to settle for a G.E.D. It would have totally undersold the brilliant mind that he had.

When Allen came to room 621 the door was ajar so he opened it and came in. Then he headed toward the bathroom where he found Davis who looked as if he had been working for some time. He had his toolbox with him and there were other sundry plumbing items lying around the bathroom.

"Whatever is clogging it must really be stuck. Are we going to have to take it up?" asked Allen.

"Maybe. I mean I plunged it, used the toilet augur on it...everything. Now we gotta get down and dirty. You got everything?"

"Yes, sir. What do we do first?"

"Bring the wet vac over here. We'll try that first."

Davis put the nozzle of the wet vac into the toilet drain and then turned it on. It sucked all of the water out of the toilet, and He hoped the obstruction would come out with it. When all the water was gone, Davis turned off the machine and took the hose out.

"Okay. Cross yo' fingers."

Davis flushed the toilet and he and Allen looked over in the bowl with anticipation. The water came in and eddied before rising to the top of the bowl without flowing back out.

"Dag. I was hopin' but...looks like we're gonna have to take it up. You ready?"

"Just let me put my gloves on."

Allen quickly put on his gloves as Davis turned off the water supply to the toilet. Then Allen used the wet vac to get the remaining water out of the bowl. After this Davis deftly disconnected the water supply from the toilet.

"Here," said Davis handing his putty knife to Allen, "you could use this to get the caps off the base."

Allen took the knife and got to work. After taking the caps off, he then worked on unscrewing the bolts. He went through it easily as he had assisted Davis with installing a new toilet in one of the suites just a few days ago.

"Okay it's done", said Allen when he was finished.

"Good, now stand back a little cuz, I don't want nothin' left up in here to come down on you."

"I hear you", replied Allen as he stood up and moved back.

Davis lifted the porcelain stool and moved it to one side. A small trickle of water flowed out from the bottom onto the newspaper that Davis had spread around earlier. After that, there was nothing left except the forbidding looking hole in the bathroom floor.

"Are you going to have to put your hand in there?"

"You really shouldn't ever, especially if you don't have gloves. But I don't think that's where the problem is. You gotta rag or somethin'?"

Allen handed Davis one of the cleaning rags he brought up and Davis used it to cover the drain to keep the sewer gases from escaping.

Allen looked over and saw that Davis had leaned the toilet back against the tank, so that the base was facing them. Then Davis took the pocket flashlight from his belt to look up into the bottom of the toilet. Davis would have to put his hand into the base to pull whatever it was out. Thankfully he had on his work gloves as well. Allen merely gawked as Davis put his hand in. He would have not wanted to trade places with Davis at this moment for anything in the world.

"I really hope this isn't what I think this is", grunted Davis as he started to pull out the obstruction. Allen grimaced with disgust.

COMMENCEMENT

"Okay, I think I got it."

Davis slowly pulled his hand from the toilet, but Allen's view was obscured by the position of the toilet.

"Here, catch this", said Davis unexpectedly making a pitching motion toward Allen.

"No way, man!" exclaimed Allen scrambling to get out of the way and falling into the bathtub.

Davis was laughing hysterically as Allen struggled back to his feet. Allen began to realize that Davis had not actually thrown anything at him.

"I'm sorry, man, but the look on yo' face…I just had to."

"Very funny. What was in there anyway?" said Allen half-laughing at himself.

"Just this", said Davis still laughing. He opened his hand to reveal what looked like a building block from a child's duplo set. "Not what you was expectin', right."

"Now how in the world…?"

"I don't know man. Probly a kid not big enough to reach the sink decided to play in the toilet."

"I'm just glad it wasn't something…well, you know."

"I hear ya. Now we gotta clean up. I'll let you take the lead here if you think you could handle it."

"Sure man."

There was a lot of work involved in re-installing a toilet. All the old ceramic sealant had to be scraped away, and the wax ring would need to be replaced. Fortunately, Davis had foreseen all this and had brought all the necessary materials needed. Allen got right down to business. Allen liked the added responsibility that Davis allowed him. It showed that Davis trusted him and his newly acquired skills and that meant a lot to Allen. It was a relatively simple job, but it was one Allen knew he couldn't do a few months ago. As Allen prepared for the toilet to be remounted the two young men engaged in the chatter that usually surrounded their work.

"So how's your new paper coming? Have you chosen your topic yet?"

"Yeah, I decided to go wit the one on *Of Mice and Men* since it's somethin' I'ma little more familiar wit, and they say that stuff like that is going to be on the test."

"When is the exam anyway?"

"February."

"That's coming up soon."

"I know. I got a handle on the multiple-choice questions. That's no sweat. It's just the essays that I'm worried about. There's three of them."

"I think your writing has really grown a lot over the past couple of weeks."

"Yeah, but that's because you and Miko is there to spot me. These essays are gonna be cold. No drafts. No re-writes. You feel?" said Davis with some concern.

"I get it. But don't be so hard on yourself. Your grammar has improved a lot, as well as the clarity of your writing."

"I just hope it's enough to get a 75."

"I thought you only needed a 55 to pass."

"Yeah, but the program that I'm tryin' to get into to get my license is requirin' at least 75."

"Oh." Allen remembered Davis briefly mentioning the program before. "I believe you'll make it man."

"I hope so. I'm like sweatin' it wit' a sponge- no joke."

"So, what's next once you get your license?"

"I'm hopin' that I can do some independent jobs and eventually start my own business. Then hopefully, I can help my mom get out of the mess she's in."

COMMENCEMENT

"What mess?"

"She got caught up in one of those bad loans they been talkin' about. She got a house in Queens. The one I grew up in before I moved to the Bronx. See, my brother got locked up and she needed money to get him outta jail, and hire a lawyer and all that, so she went to the bank for a loan. The people at the bank told her to do somethin' called a 'refinance' on the house and then the monthly payments wouldn't be that much. Everything was good for the first year or so. Then one day she got a bill for like $6,000.00."

"Sounds like the hidden balloon payment."

"I don't know what it was. All I know is my moms didn't have no $6,000.00. I mean me and my sister are helping her out now, but once I get into this program, I don't know if I'm going to be able to help out no more. I got my own bills to pay and soon I'm gonna have tuition to deal wit' on top of that. There's no way they gonna let her keep the house if she don't pay. I'm just prayin' to God about it."

"I'm really sorry about what's going down, man."

"Then she might have to move in wit' my sister, and they don't really get along, at least when they in the same house. I want my mom to stay wit' me, but I don't have enough room. The worst part is that her credit is gonna be all messed up for good. At her age she don't need that. How's she gonna retire?"

"I wish there was something I could do to help you and your mom."

"Don't sweat it, man. You done more than enough for me already. You been better to me than people I knew way back in the day. Beside I'm looking to God to make a way. He's brought us all this far. I'm sure he's gonna work somethin' out. If He doesn't, it's all good because He's got His reasons, ya know? They can take the house but that's all they can take. And who knows? One day maybe I'll be able to buy my mom an even better house."

"That's one way of looking at it", replied Allen, still mulling over something in his mind. At times it seemed that Davis had more faith than he did, despite Allen's church upbringing.

"What you gonna do, son? I know you ain't fixin' to be no porter forever", asked Davis. The question caught Allen off guard.

"I don't know. Everyone's been telling me that I need to develop a relationship with God and allow him to show me. So far, I haven't heard anything."

"You will, eventually."

"Has God spoken to you in your life? Like did you hear God telling you to go for the program you're trying to get into?"

"I don't know if you could use my experience. I always thought God works for different people in different ways."

"You're probably right, but just for curiosity's sake."

"It was like, one night a couple of years ago, I was just layin' in my bed thinkin' about what I was gonna do wit' my life. Then I started thinkin' that I really should get my license 'cause then I could get more jobs and maybe even start my own business. Only thing was I didn't have any idea how to get started. I was thinkin' and thinkin' myself in circles. So then a couple of days later, Mr. Hardy told me about a program I could get into that they was offerin' at the City College. So I went out and I got an application and everything, but you had to have a high school diploma, and I had dropped out a few years before. And you couldn't get into the program wit' a GED. I didn't think they would ever let me back into school given my past and how old I was, so I just threw the application in a bunch of old papers and forgot about it. Then some more months passed and I was prayin' about my situation when somethin' spoke to me and told me to go get the paper. At first, I was like 'why should I do that?' I knew I didn't qualify for it because I wasn't a student. But then, I just went and got it. As soon as I got the paper in my hand it was like God started to show me how I could do it. He led me to a school that had a night school program where you could get a real diploma. So I got registered and God worked it out from there."

"Really?" said Allen a little awestruck. "So he just spoke to you out of the blue?"

COMMENCEMENT

"Yeah, like he was speaking to my heart. But then I had been praying about it for a while. It wasn't like I prayed and then ten minutes later I got the answer I needed."

"One time I thought I heard God speaking to my heart, but that was over a month ago. I haven't heard anything since. Sometimes I think maybe he's angry me. After all, here I am having grown up in the church, but all my life I've just sort of taken Him for granted. I've even been ungrateful to God for all the great things He's already done for me. I was like the children of Israel when they were wandering in the wilderness. Maybe God is punishing me now for being such a jerk."

"Don't get so down on yourself. The Bible says that 'God is slow to anger and plenteous of mercy. He will not always chide neither will he keep his anger forever,' and then, 'If we turn to him with our whole heart, he will forgive our sins.'[1] God loves you Allen. He sees that you're sorry about everything and that you really want to have a relationship with Him. He's not gonna leave you hangin'. You just gotta keep seeking Him."

"Now you sound like Pastor Bynum."

"I don't know if I got it like that."

"I think you do."

"All I do is just read the Word, pray, and trust God believing."

"I guess it's easy for you since He's done so much in your life and He's always speaking to you."

"It's not like he speaks to me everyday. Even in the silences you have to trust that when there's a need he will speak. I'm not sayin' it won't be hard, but we have to keep on goin' inspite of what everything seems like. That's what keeps me goin' atleast."

"I think you're right. In fact, I know you're right. You don't know how good it is to have someone to talk to about these kinds of things."

"But what about the Pastor and your friends. You don't talk to them about stuff like this?"

"Not really. The Pastor's a great guy, but sometimes I feel like he's on a whole other level. It's been a long time since he's been where I've been. And as for my other friends, the only one who's really workin' on a relationship with God is Tamiko. She's sweet, but sometimes you just need another guy to talk to."

"I feel you. You know what. I was actually going to sign up for the Brotherhood Bible study group Daniel's hostin'. I read about it in the church bulletin. Why don't you join wit' me?"

"Bible Study??!"

"Why not? You said you wanted a deeper relationship wit' God. What better way than to study his Word? Like the Bible says 'study to show thyself approved unto God.'"[2]

"But I already know about the Bible. I read it everyday."

"But do you know what it means for yo' life? Like how you suppost to live. I'll admit that there are some things I need to learn."

"Okay, I'll think about it."

"It's at 2:00pm right after service on Sundays. But you probly already know that."

Allen didn't but wasn't about to reveal this to Davis.

"Look at the time. We gotta finish up here so we can get through the rest of our rounds before quittin' time.

Allen and Davis finished the preparations for remounting the toilet. Then Allen helped Davis to fit the toilet onto its base and they re-bolted it and replaced the caps.

"Nice work on the fixtures, Al. Now it's time for the moment of truth."

After reconnecting the water supply and turning on the water, Davis flushed the toilet. It flushed normally. The seat was on securely and there was no water leaking from the foot of the toilet.

"Guess we make a pretty good team, don't we?" suggested Allen.

"Yeah, we do", replied Davis.

THIRTY-NINE

Tim wanted to put his head down to rest if not for just a minute however, this would be impossible in the tiny cubicle where he had recently been banished. He had just finished checking over intake orders and sent a bunch of receipts to accounting. Now he had to update Preston's calendar. It was 1:30, and he still hadn't had a lunch break, not that he was in any condition to eat anyway. He woke up this morning with an excruciating headache that only went away after throwing up what little breakfast he had eaten. Now his headache felt like it was coming back, and the nausea along with it. Tim desperately needed a break, some respite from the constant flow of work that came at him from the time he walked in the door. Tim thought that with Mr. Big Shot taking over the department, his workload would have been reduced. After all, Tim wasn't in charge anymore, so why should all the responsibility fall on his shoulders? However, in the aftermath of the most devastating professional coup he had experienced so far, there seemed to be an endless stream of work for Tim, and working at Herns and Marshall had become like working at a forced labor camp.

As could be predicted, Preston's triumph at that tell tale meeting changed him into a Stalinesque despot. In a short period of time he became well versed in how to employ bullying, intimidation, and threats to get what he wanted, no matter how big or how small. Preston fumed when files were lost, but raged when no one bothered to check to see if the chicken wings in his lunch order were fried hard enough. He was annoyed when he didn't receive important messages, but was livid if you used staples instead of coated paper clips on his documents. Two weeks of his swaggering was enough to make Clara turn in her resignation and forego her severance pay. Since then, they would hire an administrative assistant only to lose them soon after an encounter with Preston's vituperative ego. The longest they'd had an admin since Clara's departure was two weeks. Vera hung around for as long as she could, but soon the stress of the environment caught up with her. Nearly a month into Preston's reign of terror, Vera collapsed suddenly while photocopying documents for him. It was luck that Tim found her not long after she collapsed. She had to be taken out in an ambulance. Word got back to the office that she had developed hypertension and was on an indefinite medical leave. This meant that Tim was now the secretary, admin, and office manager for Preston. So now on top of his daily duties of keeping his department running under the interim organization he'd developed, Tim also had to answer phones and take messages, make copies, organize files, manage Preston's appointment calendar as well as his own, and anything else that Preston dictated. There were times when Tim didn't know if he would end up taking a ride in an ambulance or a hearse.

Tim's health problems gradually worsened. He was at the point to where he was living off of a diet of seltzer water, soda crackers, soup, and Ensure, since he couldn't keep down much else. However, he was determined to stick it out. After all, he had his vacation coming in two weeks and then he could finally work on getting some rest. This fact was the only thing that kept him going, and the fact that Preston's behavior and work (or lack thereof) were slowly coming back to haunt him.

It had been more than a month since Preston presented his Big Idea of the All Powerful Website. There was supposed to be a presentation that was to have taken place several weeks ago in which Preston was to have expounded in detail just how his idea would take shape and manifest itself within the company. The problem was the Big Idea was easy, but trying to pinpoint and organize the details was much more complicated than Preston had anticipated. He just couldn't put everything together. First, there was the problem of choosing and settling on a firm that would design the website. There were several that Preston had been in negotiations with, but he had not signed a deal with any one of them yet. Then there was the whole glitch with how the accounting department would interface with the website, the design of the website itself, possible changes in department policies and procedures, procedures for troubleshooting, all which had yet to be done. It was a big task, and after the departure of Clara and Vera, Preston pleaded for and got additional time to work on the project. However, that time was now running out. His final deadline was just before the two-day Christmas break, and he was no closer to finishing his final plan than he had been weeks earlier. At this point in time, even Standoff was becoming impatient. Sometimes it was even fun to watch Preston, squirm as he made excuses for why he had not met any of the timetabled goals for the project. He would try to blame Tim, but Standoff would always remind him that this website was his idea, and he was ultimately the one responsible for its taking shape. Yes, the Fall of Preston Scott was imminent. Tim was just hoping that he would be sitting in the front row when Preston came down.

Tim was halfway through the updates, when the Despot walked in a half-hour late from lunch for the umpteenth day in a row.

"Where's Sarah?" Preston asked looking around the office in bewilderment. Sarah was an admin from the accounting department who had graciously lent her support after Tim practically begged her for help.

"She left. She said she could only stay for a couple of hours. She had to get back to accounting to work on a bigger project there."

Preston ran his hand over his scalp in frustration.

"Get on the phone with that temp agency again: see if they can get someone over here for the afternoon. In the meantime, did you hear anything from HR about interviews for the admin position?"

"No." Tim replied as he dialed the agency. "I called them this morning and they said they haven't found anyone who wants a interim position."

"And you let them get away with that?" Preston cried "Tim, you see how short-staffed we are! You should have lit a fire under their pants and told them to stop lollygagging and send some candidates for interviews! Hello! It is what you're being paid for!"

Tim decided to try to be reasonable rather than let Preston goad him into an argument.

"With all due respect Preston, I can't just go around making threats. It's not like I'm their boss."

"And at this rate you never will be. Just call the agency and get Joe on the line. I hope you can at least do that!" growled Preston before he stormed back into what used to be their office.

Tim was trying to call the temp agency for the second time when he heard the dictator's blustering bellow.

"Tim!"

"Yes." Tim replied in exasperation.

"Where the hell are those bids from the tech firms?!"

"On your desk, I suppose. I gave them to you before you left for lunch."

"Oh, is that so? And do you think I would be standing here talking to your sorry butt if they were?"

Tim got up and went past Preston into the office.

"What the hell do you think you're doing?! That's my office!"

Ignoring Preston, Tim grabbed a bunch of files from Preston's disaster of an 'in-box' and sifted through them.

"Do you want me to call security?"

"Do you want your precious bids?"

It didn't take Tim much time at all. After flipping through some of the folders in the in box, he found what he was looking for.

"Your bids, sir", said Tim slapping the papers against Preston's chest as he walked past him back to his cubicle.

"Cute, very cute. You probably moved them from where I had them in the first place. I'll have to remind myself to lock my office door when I go out for lunch."

"You're welcome", sneered Tim.

COMMENCEMENT

"So what did the agency say?"

"With all of the interruptions, I haven't had the chance to put the call through."

"Get it done yesterday already!"

The dictator withdrew to his office and Tim dialed quickly hoping to finish his business before some new complaint brought Preston stamping out again like a terrible ogre in a fairy tale. Tim felt bad having to call Black Tie Staffing for what seemed like the thousandth time. As he sat listening to the phone ringing on the other end, Tim felt even worse for the poor victim who would be sent out for the position. When the receptionist answered the phone she recognized his voice immediately and Tim could sense her irritation.

"Hey, Maggie. It's Tim From Herns and Marshall. We need another person who can fill an administrative position."

"If this is for the Business Services Department, we don't have anyone."

"You can't be serious! Let me speak to Joe!"

"Fine. I'll transfer you."

"Joe Tarantillo."

"Hey, Joe, it's Tim. What's this I hear about you not sending any temps to our department at H&M? What's going on?" said Tim trying to be diplomatic.

"I'm sorry, Tim, but the last kid I sent there went to the BBB to have me reported. I've got a reputation to uphold and a business to run. Standoff and I had a conversation and we decided in order to keep things good between us, I don't have to send anymore temps to your department until further notice."

"Standoff knows about it?"

"Yeah. It was his idea. I thought he would've let you guys know by now."

"No, not yet. But I understand", Tim said resignedly.

"You're gonna have to try to borrow someone from another department. Sorry about this, Tim."

"Not as sorry as I am."

Now Tim would have to be the bearer of bad news. He went over to Preston's office door, which was now locked, and knocked. I wasn't long before he could hear Preston stomping toward the door.

"Yes?" he asked peevishly as he cracked the door open.

"I just got off the phone with the agency…."

"And? Don't tell me they can't get someone here until tomorrow."

"No temps are going to be coming at all. They're not sending temps to our department."

"Why the hell not? What did you say to them? Don't tell me you've managed to alienate us from one of our closest business associates?"

"Of course not! All I did was ask them to send another admin. It seems the admins who have been sent here have been complaining about the work conditions…"

"Get Joe on the line!"

"It won't do any good. He's spoken with Standoff. They've made an agreement."

Preston was crestfallen.

"That can't be…why would he…I mean he knows I have a deadline. How could he expect me to…I'm going to call Joe myself. There has to be some mistake. You probably got the message wrong anyway", stammered Preston before slamming the door in Tim's face.

At that moment the phone began to ring at the front desk. As Tim went to answer it, he could hear the echoes of Preston's conversation with Joe through the office door.

"Herns and Marshall, Business Services. Tim Russell, speaking", Tim answered.

"Standoff here, Tim. Put me through to Scott. It's urgent."

COMMENCEMENT

"Of course, sir."

Tim tried passing the call through to Preston's office, but the line was still busy. So he got up and knocked on the door.

"I'm on the phone!" Preston screamed from behind the oak door.

"Standoff's on the line! He says it's urgent!"

There was a moment of silence.

"Pass him through."

Tim went back to his cubicle and passed the call through successfully. As he tried to put his mind back on his own work, he couldn't help but pause to wonder why Standoff had called. Tim knew it probably wasn't to congratulate Preston for a job well done. Tim wished he could hear the conversation Preston and Standoff were having right now.

It wasn't long before Preston appeared from his office. He had a very wild expression on his face that seemed to hint of fear.

"Standoff's on his way for a status report. He'll be here in an hour. I want all the preliminary files together. Don't mess up. I've got a lot riding on this."

"You have everything in your office."

"I know that, genius", Preston sneered. "I'm giving it to you to straighten out and create the status report."

Tim felt he shouldn't have been surprised by the outrageous nature of the request. Preston wanted him to complete a status report of their work in less than an hour. Under any other circumstances the task would have been impossible if not for the fact that Preston hadn't done a thing since the last status report meeting with Standoff. Tim knew he would merely take the last report, add a few meaningless bullet points and reprint it. The bigger surprise would be Standoff's reaction to the report.

****

"Afternoon, Tim", greeted Standoff who had just arrived for the meeting with Preston.

"Good afternoon, Mr. Standoff. I'll let Preston know you're here."

Before Tim could go over to Preston's office, the man of the hour came out flashing his trademark grin.

"Mr. Standoff, sir. It's so good to see you", he gushed as he shook Standoff 's hand.

"Yes, but enough of the formalities. I'm anxious to see the status report."

"Of course, sir. Right this way."

"What about Tim? He is a part of this department."

"I thought this would be a private meeting, since this is my project, sir."

"No, it's a department meeting. And since Tim's a part of this department, he should be at the meeting."

"Right. Tim, would you mind? You can put the answering service on until the meeting is over."

"Sure."

Tim was curious as to what Standoff was getting at. After all, Tim had not been invited to any of their previous meetings. They all entered into Preston's office and sat down.

"What's new, gentlemen? How is the website coming along?"

"Well, sir, we've gone through all of the bids, and so far we've settled on a short list of three companies that we're in negotiations with…"

"You're still looking through the bids!" exclaimed Standoff in shock.

"No, sir!" exclaimed Preston, who was surprised by Standoff's choleric reaction. He wasn't used to incurring the displeasure of his superiors. "As I've said, we've selected three…"

"According to the timetables we set at our last meeting, you should've settled on one already! I came expecting to see plans for the site at the very least", Standoff fumed. "Now you have the gall to tell me your still at phase one. I have to say, this is way past disappointing."

COMMENCEMENT

"Mr. Standoff, although it's not readily apparent, much progress has been made. I felt that taking our time to find the right firm for this project would save us a substantial amount of money in the long run."

"More than this waste of time is already costing us?"

"Sir, if I may explain…"

"Preston, you do realize that you have only two weeks left to bring this project to life. Do you really believe you will be able to do this if you haven't even chosen the firm for the website!!!" Standoff said, his voice rising in a crescendo of fury. Tim and Preston were both taken aback by Standoff's raw rebuke. Tim originally thought he would have been enjoying this moment, but for some reason, it made him feel very uncomfortable.

"More would have been done, sir, but you do realize that my department is greatly understaffed. Mrs. Williams is on medical leave, Mrs. Quinones has resigned, and now that we don't have access to any temps…"

"And whose fault is that! I heard from Joe that your unprofessional behavior has caused some trouble for him and potentially this firm."

"But Mr. Standoff…"

"But Mr. Standoff…" mocked Standoff "Is this going to be another excuse? Since the day after you took on this project it's been one excuse after another and frankly I'm sick of it all. I've been practically holding your hand for the past several months and you still have yet to deliver. And what's more is, I'm not sure if you can."

"Mr. Standoff…please…I…" Preston stammered weakly.

"Mr. Standoff," Tim cut in "we still have two weeks. Just give it two more weeks. I'm sure we can turn things around." Although Tim had no idea why he seemed to be sticking up for Preston.

"Fine. Preston you have two weeks, at the end of which I will expect the finished product or your resignation. As there is nothing further to discuss, our meeting stands adjourned. Gentlemen."

Standoff strode out of the room while Preston and Tim sat in silence for a moment.

"I'm going back to man the phones if you need me", said Tim trying to provide himself with an escape from the tension in the room.

"Are you happy now, Tim?" asked Preston in resignation.

Tim returned to his cubicle without answering.

****

As Tim worked through the rest of the afternoon, he couldn't help but be haunted by the images from the status report meeting with Standoff. Most vivid was the impression of Preston's voice as he asked Tim if he was happy now. Tim felt that he should have been happy. After all, Preston got exactly what he deserved and Tim got a chance to see it. It was providential retribution, but Tim was more unsettled by it than anything else. It reminded him of what happened to him barely two months before, but not in the way that he had expected.

Tim now knew why Standoff wanted him there. He wanted to humiliate Preston in front of his subordinate as a way of punishing him for his failure. Hadn't Standoff done something similar to him almost two months ago? Tim was angry with Standoff for manipulating them against one another. It made Tim lose respect for him. At the same time it made him feel bad for Preston. The pained look on Preston's face said it all. It reminded him of his own pain and humiliation. No longer could he see Preston as simply "The Jerk". He was just another brother with the same struggles and problems that he had. Maybe that's why he spoke up for Preston at the meeting the way he did.

Just then, Tim was hit by a sudden wave of nausea, not as bad as the one he had this morning, but it unsettled him nonetheless. He needed some air and perhaps a drink of water. Tim went over to Preston's office to let him know that he would be stepping out for a few minutes. He knocked but he heard no response. Then he tried the door, which was open. Tim stuck his head in. Preston was sitting at his desk with his head in his hands looks as dejected as ever.

"I'm going to take five, if that's okay with you."

COMMENCEMENT

"Yeah, that's okay with me, Tim. You take five. In fact, I was thinking you take as much time as you want. I'm done" said Preston somberly.

"I'm not sure what you're talking about."

"I'm talking about all this. The corner office and all that", replied Preston whose manner became more peculiar with every word.

"Look man, maybe you should just take the rest of the day off. Get some rest. I'll handle things while you're gone."

"Yeah, I think it's best that you handle everything from now on. You win brotha! You win! It's all yours!" exclaimed Preston.

Without warning Preston darted toward the window.

"What the hell are you doing? Are you crazy?" yelled Tim trying to keep Preston from jumping more than 18 stories to his death. If this had been about six months earlier, Tim would have been able to take him without breaking a sweat, but in his current condition, it was taking everything he had.

"Get off me or you're going with me!"

"Preston, don't do this", said Tim as he backed off.

"Now you want to be the hero, too! Not if I can help it."

"Preston, this isn't about me. It's about you. Think about what you're about to do to yourself. Once you go off that ledge there's no turning back."

"Don't try to use psychology on me! You're no saint! You don't give a damn about me!"

"Preston, you may not be my favorite person in the world, but I do care about you. If I didn't then I'd just walk out of here and let the police or whoever pick up your broken pieces, and try to take your place, but that's not what I want to happen. I'm pretty sure your family and friends don't want that to happen either."

"My family doesn't care about me. All they care about is money. And I don't have any friends."

"What about all your friends here at Herns and Marshall?"

"Since Standoff's started to give me the business, all of my former associates have been acting as if I caught the plague. And you heard him today. In two weeks, he's gonna put the word about me in the street. Then what am I going to do? What's left for a black man once his reputation is marred."

"Preston, H&M is not the center of the universe. This may be a powerful company but not powerful enough to determine the rest of your life. I have a friend, and she believes that there is more to this life than our jobs, or money, or anything else we can see. There are infinite possibilities, things that defy our sense of logic or what we can reason. You talk about the next two weeks as if you know you're going to fail, but you don't know that for sure. You won't know until you go through it and come out on the other side."

"There's no way I'm going to get everything together in two weeks. It's not humanly possible."

"Still, we could try. I'll help you. We'll work it one task at a time until we're done."

"And what if it doesn't get done?"

"Then there are other options. Preston, you're not the only person on Standoff's hit list. I'm on borrowed time here, too. Remember? So if you're gone, that doesn't mean they'll automatically have me take your place. They'll just hire someone else for your position and I'll still be out in the cold."

"Yeah, but a guy like you must have a lot of fancy connections. Don't act like you don't have someplace else you can run to."

"To tell you the truth, Preston, I don't. I'm in the same situation that you're in. I can't depend on my family, and my friends couldn't help me find another job even if they wanted to. Truth be told, I might end up with my best friend as a janitor in the hotel downtown for all I know."

"So what keeps you going?"

"I don't know. Maybe it's the hope that there's someone or something out there that's bigger than me who can handle what I can't.

Someone or something that can work things out in ways I could never expect."

"What? You mean like God?"

"I don't know. Maybe. All I'm saying is this project isn't worth throwing your life away. This is just one moment in time and you don't know what the future holds."

"You mean like more misery."

"Look, Preston, everyone has good and bad times, but if we don't hold on through the tough times, we'll never be able to reap the benefits when the good times come. C'mon, Preston. Come down from there and let me call someone who can help you."

"I don't want those doctors to come and take me to the loony bin."

"You can check into a hospital yourself for a few days. Then you can see someone as an outpatient. No one's going to lock you up, and no one here has to know. You could just say you had a medical emergency."

"Why should I trust anything that you say?"

"O.K., Preston, I'll be the first one to admit that I've been a jerk in the past, but one thing we both know is that I've never lied to you. I always say what I mean and mean what I say."

It took some time before Tim's words were actually received by Preston. He had a pensive look on his face, as he thought about what Tim said.

"I'm still the boss though", Preston remarked apprehensively.

"Fine, just come down."

Preston began to come down from where he was at the window, looking almost as if he were coming out of a daze.

"I think I had too much to drink during lunch. I don't feel so well."

"If you want to go home, I'm sure everyone will understand."

"Standoff wouldn't. Just give me some space for a minute. I'll be okay. I just had a little too much to drink at lunch."

"Are you sure? I promise, I'm not going to do anything behind your back. If you need to go home or if you need to see a doctor…"

"I'm not crazy, Tim! I told you…I had too much to drink at lunch. I need some rest. Who knows, maybe this is some kind of hormone imbalance. Maybe I will see a doctor."

"That's a good idea. Is there anything that I can do for you in the meantime?"

"I need you to help me put together the final presentation. It's all there. Somewhere. You're a big boy. You can figure it all out."

"Alright….just go and take some time for yourself."

Preston grabbed his suit jacket, coat, and brief case and left leaving Tim still feeling a little weakened and shaken by the ordeal. The adrenaline rush was wearing off now, and Tim was dizzy from being emotionally spent. He just needed some time to process everything that had just happened. But before he could gather his composure, there was a knock on the outer office door. Tim didn't want to answer it, but he knew there were probably some people in the other departments who heard all of the yelling (although they should have been used to it by now). Tim had to do damage control. He got up from his chair went out and closed the back office door to hide the mess that was inside. Then he went to the front office administrative area and opened the door.

"Hey, Tim. Is everything okay in here? Sounded like Preston was having another meltdown."

"That shouldn't be unusual."

"True", laughed Frank "That guy's something else, isn't he?"

"He's just under a lot of pressure, trying to get his big presentation together before the deadline."

"So it seems from the looks of the way he just stormed out of here. He taking yet another lunch break?"

"I don't know. We really don't talk much except for business."

"I don't blame you. Word has it, he'll probably be gone after the end of the month."

COMMENCEMENT

"Really?" sighed Tim who was tired and showed almost no interest. He really wished that Frank would just go away. Tim just wasn't in the mood for the gossip right now.

"Yeah, everybody knows he's not even close to finishing the presentation. Standoff's already got his eye on his replacement. Everyone's saying it's going to be his niece who just got out of Yale."

"Interesting. Well, I'd love to chat, but I've got a lot to do right now."

"If it's something for Preston, don't sweat it too much. But take care of yourself. I don't think that guy's playing with a full deck if you ask me."

"I'll do that. Thanks for looking out."

"See ya 'round Tim."

Tim closed the door and headed back to the back office. The wind coming through from the open window had blown papers everywhere. Tim went over and closed the widow, stooped down to the floor and tried to put everything together including his own sanity in the process.

Everything had happened so fast. Tim needed time to go over it all. If he was correct, Preston had been on the verge of a nervous breakdown of suicidal proportions, and he had just reached out to keep his worst enemy from a catastrophic end. How did this happen? How did he even know what to say? Where did it all come from?

Tim couldn't help but see a lot of himself in Preston. There was a time in his life when he was Mr. Popular: confident and self-assured with lots of friends, or so it seemed. Yet on the inside he was nothing but an insecure mess always in need of constant reassurance and validation by others. So Tim was driven to perform; to be the best; to be 'successful'. To be honest, he was still like this. Like himself, it seemed that Preston was always chasing the carrot of success. The problem was that with each accomplishment, more would be expected. You always had to keep working, keep striving. And what happened when you couldn't keep up anymore? For Preston it seemed that life wasn't worth living. Tim himself understood that feeling and had contemplated suicide himself on more than one occasion in the distant past. But he was thankful for friends like

Tamiko and Allen who were some of the few people in his life who didn't have expectations for him, or hoops for him to jump through. They taught him that there was more to life than accomplishments. Tim knew they would stick by him even if he were the biggest loser on the planet. Tim was now beginning to understand that who he was as a person was more important than any accomplishment. Most of all, he was beginning to see that there was indeed more to this life than just work, being successful, and accumulating wealth. After all, what if you didn't have these things? Or what if one had all these things and then suddenly lost them all? What was this life all about then? Thinking back on all of those philosophy classes he took at Harvard, not one provided him with an answer to that question. That's partly why he became an agnostic. For years, Tim had been satisfied to just believe that there was no reason for life and no need for God. However, now this theory bothered him. A lot.

There had to be some meaning to it all. There had to be some definite answer, otherwise, why not jump 18 stories to one's death. If life is meaningless, then why hold it to be so sacred?

Perhaps there was something to the religion that Allen, Tamiko, and the Pastor believed in. Maybe that God was in work in him right now. How else could he explain it?

Looking through the folders, there was not much to be had. There was still so much that had to be done. It was already almost 3:30, and Tim didn't even know where to begin. He had promised Preston that he would help him and he meant it. The present moment conjured memories of Pastor Bynum's prophetic word for Tim a month earlier. He had said that Tim needed to love his enemies and to do good for them. If anyone had told Tim back then he would be in the situation he was in now, he would have laughed. He had just practically saved Preston's life, and now he was going to save his job. The presentation was due in two weeks. It would take nothing short of a miracle to get even a half-baked presentation finished by then. Tim was just one man, and he couldn't count on Preston to fill in the gaps especially given what happened just moments ago. Then Tim remembered what Tamiko said that night that he took her to Manna's after work. She believed that God was there to do the things that she couldn't "for my strength is made perfect in weakness."[1] This mess was way bigger than Tim. "If there is a God, I sure need him right now", Tim thought to himself.

FORTY

"Lord, help me to get through this day. Show me how to help these children learn what they need to know. Open our hearts and minds to your will and your wisdom. Help me to love my enemies. Keep my footsteps in a straight path and let not iniquity have dominion over me."

Tamiko prayed quickly before the start of the morning bell. Just as she finished she heard a knock at her classroom door. When she looked up, she could see Rosalyn Steele peeking her head in.

"I hope I'm not interrupting you."

"No, not at all. Is there something you needed?" Tamiko asked straining to be civil. She knew it wasn't right as a Christian, but she absolutely despised Rosalyn Steele.

"No. There are some schedule changes you need to know about. I'm coming in to your class to see the literacy block during periods 2 and 3 and Miranda is going to cover you 4th period so we can debrief."

"Okay. I just wish I had been told about this in advance. I thought I had a prep second period. I was hoping to use that time for assessments." Tamiko tried not to sound as annoyed as she felt.

"I know it's short notice, I didn't even know until I got in this morning and read the daily bulletin."

"But I read the daily bulletin when I got in. I didn't see that on there."

"They made changes on it. That's why I came up to tell you before you went to pick the kids up."

"Just what I need." Tamiko thought to herself trying not to get angry. In the past few weeks it seemed that she and Steele had been working together so much it seemed like they were team teaching. For Tamiko, that wasn't a good thing.

"I guess I'll just have to make it work. Thanks for letting me know."

"If it's any consolation, I had things that I had planned for my own class that I have to scrap now."

"I understand. If you don't mind, I have to go and pick up my class, so we can be ready for you when you come", said Tamiko trying to end the conversation.

"Of course."

Tamiko and Steele walked out of the class together but took opposite stairwells to the lunchroom where the children lined up for school everyday. As Tamiko walked down, she wished she had not taken her father's advice to stay. Every day for the past couple of weeks there was always some new issue. First, they had her spend a lot of time shadowing Steele, which meant that Tamiko didn't have a lot of time to spend with her own class. Then she got a notice from Nettlenerves about how her bulletin boards were not updated. Tamiko would've had time to update them with new work, had she had time with her own students! Then one morning when Tamiko came into school, she found that Booker, Steele, and Fontaine had come into her classroom and totally changed the room around! Apparently they had issues with the learning environment and felt that the way Tamiko had things set up was not conducive to the children's learning. To add insult to injury, they made her room into what was practically a carbon copy of Steele's. It was just sick. Now there were these random "drive by" observations, probably done just so that they could catch her off guard and find something to complain about and/or write her up about. There were days when Tamiko thought she would lose her sanity. Today seemed like it was going to be one of those days. All she could do was think about Jesus and how what he suffered on the cross was way worse than having your class constantly audited. Tamiko stopped off at the office to look at the daily bulletin again, to see if she would get an extra prep to conduct assessments. Of course not. Her only prep was 4th period and she had to spend that debriefing with Steele and planning next steps.

When Tamiko reached the table where her class was, she did her best to put the upcoming observation out of her mind and greet her students with her beautiful smile.

"Miss Bynum, I make dis for you!" chimed little Syreeta as she handed her a beautifully colored picture of Snow White."

"Oh, Thank You! It's beautiful! And look at how neat it is! I know you probably worked very hard on this."

"I make her brown! Now she look pretty like you!"

This did not escape Tamiko's attention. The things that the children said would sometimes touch her heart. They were the only bright spot in her day here.

"I'm going to hang this up on my desk where everyone can see it. I love it!"

After a few minutes the school aides began to call the classes upstairs.

"1-purple, Staircase A, 2-blue Staircase B!" Miss Jackson called out.

"1-pink, Staircase A!"

Tamiko signaled to her students to stand and line up, which they did in an orderly fashion. Tamiko led them out of the cafeteria and to the staircase where they waited for another class to clear the stairway. Then she led them the rest of the way to their classroom. Once they were outside the classroom door…

"Good morning, 1-Pink!"

"Good morning, Miss Bynum!" they greeted in chorus.

"When you go in, you're going to unpack and put your homework in the bins. Take out your take classroom library books, and those of you who have jobs are going to do them. When everyone is done, we'll meet on the carpet for morning meeting. Today's greeting is high fives."

The children entered the classroom, girls first, each one giving Tamiko a high five before they went inside. When Tamiko had finished greeting the girls, the boys went in, each one giving Tamiko a high five.

COMMENCEMENT

Tamiko quickly changed the centers board and got all the guided reading materials ready. She took out the book she was going to be using for her Word Study lesson and put it on the easel. This time they were going to be reading 'The Drippy Dinner Drippers' by Joy Cowley, and the students had already read the story together twice before. As she was trying to get everything together, she was interrupted by some conflict amongst her students about jobs.

"Miss Bynum! Jinelle keeps trying to do my job!" exclaimed Anthony.

"Cause you takin' too long!" Jinelle complained.

"Anthony does have a point, Jinelle. After all, he is the pencil sharpener", reasoned Tamiko.

"But I'm the helper, and I'm supposed to help", pleaded Jinelle.

"Sweetheart, you're the teacher's helper, not the student's helper. Let Anthony do his job. O.K."

"But he's just playing around, and he's trying to make all the pencils little with the sharpener. Look!" said Jinelle showing Tamiko a pencil that was about an inch and a half long.

"Oh, is that right?"

Anthony just shrugged his shoulders.

"Anthony, if you're not going to be responsible, I won't have any choice but to fire you and give your job to someone else. Understand? No more whittling the pencils to stubs."

"What's 'whittling' mean?"

"It means to wear down by cutting or shaving. That's what the pencil sharpener does to the pencils", explained Tamiko.

"Oh."

After settling the conflict, Tamiko used her tambourine to signal that morning meeting was about to start and took her place on the chair between the easel and the morning meeting board. All the children scurried to their places on the rug. The morning meeting was just a set of routines in which children reviewed basic mathematics and literacy concepts as they went through the calendar, named the days of the week, updated a weather graph, counted the number of children present, counted the days of school in various ways, and finally, solved a morning message math equation. When the meeting was over, the bell rang signaling the end of period 1 and the beginning of period 2. Steele came prowling in and took a seat at one of the student tables just as Tamiko was leading the children in a transition activity so they wouldn't have to sit on the rug for such a long stretch of time, making them restless. They were doing the alphabet dance to a song that used melody and dance to help children remember basic letter/sound relationships. When the movement activity was over, Tamiko went right into the word study lesson using the shared reading book. Tamiko explained to the students that sometimes words will have a Y at the end that could sound like an e and gave an example with the word "happy". Then she asked the students to read the book again with her and check and see if they could find any words with the same kind of y ending. She read the story with the students and on a separate piece of chart paper she neatly wrote down the words the found. When they were done, she challenged them to find words with the y-ending in their reading, and sent the students off to read books that were in their book baggies, but not before she gave each of them two sticky notes to write down any special words they found.

When the students went off to read, Tamiko set the timer for 20 minutes so there would be enough time to have a "share" or a period of time in which students would talk about what y words they found in their books. While the class was reading, she went around to confer with various students taking notes as she read with each one. Steele followed her around taking her own notes, but it didn't faze Tamiko anymore. She knew Steele wouldn't approve of anything anyway. Soon the timer's alarm sounded. Tamiko called the students back to the rug and the students shared what they found and attached the sticky notes to the board. There were a few cases in which students found a word that ended with y that had a different sound like the words fly and try, and she explained that while these words ended with y, they didn't have the e sound they were looking for, and that she would keep sticky notes for another lesson when they looked for words that had these kinds of y-endings.

COMMENCEMENT

After the Reading Worskshop session, Tamiko began the guided reading/literacy centers activities with a strategy lesson on taking words apart when reading. For this she used a short poem that she had written on chart paper about a chicken that didn't want to come out of an egg. Although Tamiko hadn't planned on it, one of the tricky words was a word with a y-ending. When she asked the students to help her take it apart, one of them yelled out,

"It has a y at the end that sounds like an e."

It made Tamiko feel good that someone had gotten the idea from the lesson. Once the strategy lesson was over she sent the children to their respective literacy centers. In the first rotation, she would meet with her lowest group for guided reading, while the high achieving children engaged in a making words activity in which the students who could use the letter tiles at the center to make the most words got a prize. At another table her second lowest group played sight word bingo, and at another table the intermediates worked on making words using word families. On the second rotation, Tamiko met with her second lowest group for guided reading, while her lowest group visited the classroom library, the highest group practiced with their old guided reading books, and the intermediates browsed through the extra large sized Shared Reading books on the rug. Then the final bell sounded signaling the end of the third period, and yet another ordeal had been passed. After Tamiko had the children clean up their centers, she gathered them on the rug for another movement activity while she waited for Miranda the social studies teacher to arrive. In the midst of the transition, Steele stalked away unnoticed. After the activity was over, Miranda still hadn't showed up, so Tamiko played the "Quiet Game" with the students. In the quiet game, the students tried to stay as quiet as they could for as long as they could. Anyone who talked or laughed, or who deliberately tried to make other students laugh, was out. This game could never last more than a minute or two, which was all Tamiko needed before Miranda finally arrived. Then Tamiko headed upstairs to the dreaded meeting room.

When she got there, Steele was sitting at the conference table reviewing her notes. She didn't even notice when Tamiko came into the room.

"Sorry I'm a little late", Tamiko said to get her attention. "Miranda had some trouble with her supply cart in the elevator."

"It's okay. I guess it's just you and me today, the rest of the team is at a network meeting."

"I guess it's a busy day."

"I won't keep you long. I really think you're teaching is developing. That was a great lesson with the y endings for word study. I liked the way you had them search for it in the Shared Reading, which modeled and was connected to what they were doing during their independent reading."

"Thanks", said Tamiko flatly. She couldn't be very enthusiastic, especially since she knew that the bad part was coming up.

"I also think that your conference notes are much more detailed and give a better picture of what the children are doing. I like the checklist that you're using."

"At your suggestion, of course."

"Of course. And I also think your centers were more differentiated than previously, but…"

"But there's still something wrong", said Tamiko, her voice quivering a little.

"Tamiko, I hope that you don't think that these observations, or at least my observations are about picking on you."

"To be honest, it does feel that way", Tamiko found herself blurting out.

"Tamiko, I'm going to give it to you straight, no chaser. I know that a lot of you young girls today get your heads juiced up in the Ed schools, and a lot of these principals get caught up with gimmicks that look like good teaching, but are really nothing but fluff. No one is born a good teacher. Good teachers are made through patience, reflective practice, and perseverance. You are getting better and you will get better still, but it takes time and thoughtful reflection. Your motivation needs to be what's best for these children and not being a hotshot teacher. It's not about you."

COMMENCEMENT

"Still, I wonder why I am the only teacher that's being singled out for this intensive professional development."

"Tamiko, I know that there's a lot of politics that go along with this job. But you can't allow that to suck you under. I won't lie to you. Some people have singled you out for failure, but not me. I think this can be an opportunity for you to turn it around. You are turning it around. I only want to help you."

Tamiko couldn't believe what she was hearing. How could this woman who was a racist, be trying to help her? Tamiko couldn't help but be suspicious of her offer.

"I don't know. I just wonder if you'll say this to me now, and then say something else to someone else behind closed doors."

"I totally understand where that is coming from. I know there's a rumor mill here. I'll just tell you this, you can only believe half of what you see and none of what you hear. I've had my character dragged through the mud in all sorts of ways. I've been called a racist, and on the other hand I've been called a bleeding heart liberal, I've been called cold, calculating, evil, and have been blamed for every bad thing that's happened to this school, but none of that fazes me. I know who I am. All I care about is if the children are learning and growing."

Tamiko couldn't believe the woman's candor. It forced her to re-evaluate everything she had been through the past few weeks.

"So what is it that you think I need to work on now?"

"You still need to work on differentiating instruction for your students. Now this is something even the best of us have a hard time doing. I'm going to a workshop on Saturday afternoon that covers a lot of issues on this topic. They had it last year, but it wasn't an open workshop. This year it is because there's been such a great demand for it. I think you should sign up for it. They have a lot of good ideas and they give you free copies, lesson plans and other stuff you can use in the classroom."

"It does sound interesting."

"Good. I'll e-mail you the information."

"Thanks."

"I'm not going to keep you any longer Tamiko. You've got 25 minutes left to the period. If you want you can go back upstairs and work on testing your kids. I've got a writing celebration to prepare for myself."

"Thanks. I'll do that. And good luck with your writing celebration."

"And Good luck with your assessments."

Tamiko was almost floored by the exchange that just took place. It seemed that things weren't as they appeared to be. The 'racist' Rosalyn Steele seemed to be trying to help Tamiko, an African-American woman. It just seemed too weird to be true. Tamiko couldn't believe that she had so misjudged this woman and as a result misinterpreted all of her past actions. "This must be the hand of God", Tamiko thought to herself as she made her way back to her classroom. Tamiko didn't know what God had in store for her in this new relationship with Rosalyn Steele, but she was very curious to find out.

FORTY-ONE

Tim was sitting in his pajamas amongst a mass of paperwork on his couch, when there was a buzz on the intercom. It buzzed a number of times before he was able to free himself from the morass of papers to walk over to answer it.

"Go ahead."

"Mr. Sharpe to see you, sir."

"Send him up, Brad."

It was nine thirty, and usually Allen would be at home during this part of the evening on a Thursday, no less. Tim went over to wait by the door. He couldn't help but wonder what could be on Allen's mind at this time of night. When he heard Allen's familiar tread he opened the door.

"Do you know what time it is?"

"Don't act like you were asleep. I've never known you to go to bed before midnight."

"There's a first time for everything, you know. And don't forget to wipe your feet."

"Oh, yeah. What in the world is all that?" asked Allen after noticing the sea of papers covering room.

"My kamikaze mission", said Tim taking Allen's coat.

"I guess I came at the wrong time."

"No, no, no. Have a seat, if you can find one. It's really not as bad as it looks."

"For your sake I hope so. Man, maybe you should ask if you could have two VP's."

"No thanks, one's trouble enough. So what can I do you for, Al?"

"I'll make this quick. Let's say someone got caught up in a mortgage or a refinance that they can't afford. What do you think would be the quickest and cleanest way out, without destroying their credit?"

"You came all the way over here to ask me that?"

"What you mean 'all the way over here'? It's not like you live in Brooklyn. Besides, I wanted to have a face to face conversation. This is important."

"Oooooo-k. So, you want to know how someone can get out of a really big loan that they can't pay without any damage to their credit?"

"Yeah."

"Let me think…a magic wand. Root worker, maybe."

"Can we be serious for a minute?"

"C'mon Al, there's no way out of that kind of mess. Some people get forbearances, or they get a refinance on the loan, but that only delays the inevitable which is usually declaring bankruptcy, hence, ruining their credit for a long while."

"That's kind of what I thought."

"Why so interested in loan defaults all of a sudden? Someone you know in trouble?"

"Yeah. I just thought that maybe there was something I could do to help them out of it."

"Who is it?"

"Nobody special."

"This 'nobody special' wouldn't happen to be Davis? Would it?"

"What would make you think that?"

"Because it would seem more than coincidental that your interest would suddenly develop so shortly after you two became fast friends."

COMMENCEMENT

It would seem that 'the children of this generation are wiser than the children of light'.[1] Allen didn't know how to respond so he was silent.

"So I'm right! I knew there was something fishy about him! Don't tell me: he's hit you up for some money, hasn't he?"

"No, it's not even like that. Davis isn't the one in trouble. It's his mother. And he didn't ask me for anything. He's trusting that God will deliver."

"I bet. So why don't you let God deliver them and stay out of it. I mean, don't you think you've done enough for this guy? He's already got you and Miko doing his schoolwork for him."

"We're not doing his work! We're tutoring him. Tamiko's been doing most of the tutoring, though. Besides, I think this may be why God brought Davis and I together."

"So you heard this voice from above speak to you in the middle of the night and it told you to save the Martinez family?"

"No, it's just a feeling that I have. I mean I am the guy with the financial background. Who better to help?"

"And you think a little financial background is going to be enough to extricate them from that kind of mess? There are experts who don't have a clue."

"What about the guy that handles your trust fund?"

"Sherman's a financial genius, but something like Davis' situation is like going to the doctor and asking him to cure someone with a severed head. And if you want to talk to him, I'll just warn you, he'll charge you $400.00 for a 20 minute phone consultation."

"There's got to be something that can be done. There are other people who are offering assistance to people who got caught with subprime mortgages even and..."

"And all they're doing is either stealing what little money they have left or buying them a little more time before their inevitable financial ruin."

LAWRENCE CHERRY

"I'm just going to have to do some more research. Maybe there's something specific to their case that can help them. Maybe some loophole that was overlooked. Look, man, don't say anything to Davis about this okay. I don't want him to think I'm putting his business in the street."

"Whatever, man. But just watch yourself with that guy. I know you like helping people Allen, but there are people in the world that are just looking for people like you to use."

"I don't think Davis is looking for anything. He's never asked me to do anything."

"That's the whole point. The users of this world never have to ask. They always seem to know just the right words to say to get someone like you to volunteer. Think about it, Allen."

"Speaking of volunteers, did you just so happen to volunteer for all this: your 'kamikaze mission'?"

"This is a long story that is better left unsaid. I warn you from experience, Allen."

"Would you like some help?"

"No, I'll be okay. I know it doesn't look like it, but I've got a system worked out here, and I've already gotten a surprising amount of work accomplished before you walked in. In fact this whole project has been turning out be easier than I thought it would be."

"Have you been doing this everyday?"

"Of course. You know I'm a one man act down at H&M."

"You're killing yourself man. You look like…like… a crack head."

"My vacation isn't far off."

"That's what you always say. You better hope you make it to vacation."

"I'm optimistic that I will. I'm thinking of spending some time in the Caribbean, if I can get some of you guys to go with me."

372

"You look like you need to spend some time in the hospital. The only thing missing from your outfit is the plastic bracelet with your name on it."

"Would you be less concerned if I told you I feel better than I look."

"No, because I know you'd be lying. You need to ask for some early time off. At least take a three day weekend or something, man.'"

"No can do, my friend. There's a lot of big things that need my attention right now."

"You know what man, I was right. You are a crack head. This job is your crack, and it's killing you. I bet you stand in the hallways like 'you got any files, man.'"

"Don't blame me. Blame Pastor Bynum. This was all his idea. Or God's idea. After all, he's the one that said 'Just keep working hard young man and love everyone at Herns and Marshall'."

"You remembered that?! Tim, are you...converting."

"Oh, please."

"Tamiko is going to be thrilled!"

"If she's not too busy with our new friend Davis."

"I won't argue about that."

"So she's told you she likes him."

"Not in so many words, but let's just say, it's kind of obvious."

"Yeah, I guess you're right. He is so wrong for her."

"I don't know about that."

"Allen, are you kidding me? You were so worried that I might be interested in Tamiko, but now you think Mr. Rico Suave is perfect for her?"

"You're one to cast aspersions! Do I have to remind you about Veronica? And how about Liz? And Tasha? You remember Tasha right, she was the one who stole some of your clothes, put them on a dummy and burned you in effigy on the college walk."

"O.K. Allen…"

"And what about Monique? You had to get a restraining order against her and you had to go into hiding for a week. You even had me into some covert operations nonsense, wearing your clothes, and a Davy Crockett hat to serve as a decoy…"

"Alright already! I'm not saying that I'm a saint. But you don't know much of anything about Davis's past relationships or how he treats women."

"He's a Christian man, and he loves God. So he fulfills all of Tamiko's pre-requisites anyway."

"He seems to be Christian."

"Why do you care so much, anyway? I thought you just wanted to be good buddies with Tamiko."

"I do. I just don't want to see her get hurt. Just like you do."

"Well, you won't have to worry about that for two reasons. First, Davis said he's not really into the dating scene right now because he's too busy trying to put his life together and he doesn't want to complicate things with a romantic relationship."

"That's what he says, now."

"I'm not finished. Secondly, Tamiko is the Pastor's daughter and I think that makes approaching her a little bit intimidating, for him at least."

"So he understands that she's way out of his league."

"I'm only assuming. Does that make you feel better?"

"Kind of. Does Tamiko know all this?"

"This is guy stuff. I'm not going to tell her and neither are you. It's none of her business."

"But what if she pursues him?"

"So Davis will tell her himself. She might get hurt, but it's better that way. Just let it play out.

"You mean let Davis play her out?"

COMMENCEMENT

"Just go to bed, man. I'll see you when I see you."

"All right. Nice talking to you, Al. This was kinda like old times back at Harvard. We gotta do this more often."

"We would be able to if you didn't work so hard."

"Touche. Goodnight, Al."

"Goodnight, Tim."

FORTY-TWO

Jim slowly awakened from his sleep. At first, all he could do was open his eyes. Although he was groggy, he had a good feeling about where he was. The one thing that he could distinctly remember before it all got fuzzy was that he got in a cab and gave his own address. There was a 90% chance that he was somewhere in his own apartment. All of his body seemed numb, except for his head, which was buzzing. He needed some time before he could actually move.

Jim took a deep breath before he eased himself up from where he was. Taking time to survey the room, he realized that he was indeed in his own bedroom. He had gone to bed with his MTA uniform on. It was no longer night because he could see a few rays of sunlight cascading through the open folds of the blinds at his window. He looked over at the alarm clock. It was 8:30am. He was already an hour and 45 minutes late for his shift at work. Again.

"Should I go in late, or call in sick?" Jim asked himself. Either way, he had to make up an excuse and he didn't feel like going through it with Greg. Jim had been using up quite a few of his sick days recently, but he still had a lot left in any case. In the past two months he had been out about 7 times. He had been late more often than that. His supervisor had been threatening to give him a negative performance review if he kept it up.

"Let them do whatever they want. I'm calling in sick", he finally decided.

Jim reached into his pocket to see if he had his cell phone on him. Luckily it was still there. He took it out and turned it on. He had two missed calls. They were both from the depot where he reported for work. This was not going to be an easy phone call.

"Supervision, Bowling Green."

"Hey Greg, it's Jim…."

"How good of you to call, Reid. And so soon. Why it's only been an hour, since the last message I left", Greg scoffed.

"Look, Greg, I'm not going to be able to come in today. I'm not feeling well."

"Next time could you call before your shift starts so we don't have to scramble around like headless chickens looking for someone to cover your irresponsible butt."

"I'm sorry, but I really am sick. I took some medication and I overslept."

"Yeah, right. It's always something with you lately. I'm warning you, you're skating on thin ice. You better report bright and early at 6:30 Monday morning or your gonna be facing suspension. And don't think I won't be writing you up for the stunt you pulled today."

"It's not a stunt. I really don't feel well…"

"I'll believe that when I see a doctor's report. So when you come in, make sure you bring it with you."

"But…"

Jim's supervisor had hung up.

"More problems", Jim thought to himself.

"You've got to stop this, Jim. Everything is spiraling out of control", the voice warned.

"I already have control", Jim shot back.

"Oh, really? Is that why your facing suspension? Is that why you can't stop drinking?"

"Drinking is not the problem. Lots of people drink."

"Lots of people don't get in trouble on their jobs."

"I just have to keep it tight, that's all. After all, there are millions of people who drink a lot and are high functioning people. I just have to make sure I keep my shirt tucked in."

"Why don't you just stop drinking?"

"I don't want to stop."

"Or maybe you can't stop."

"Please, I can stop anytime I want to. I could stop today. Right now even. And I can do it all by myself. I don't help from anybody or anything."

"All by yourself? Are you sure about that?"

"You'll see."

Jim got up and went to the shower hoping to wash away all the worries and thoughts that constantly chased him. He began to regret calling in sick. Had he went to work he would have had something to do; something to focus on so he wouldn't have to listen to all the thoughts and questions of his conscience. He wouldn't have to work so hard not to drink. Now he had a lot of time that he didn't know what to do with. He didn't have any friends to visit. He couldn't go around Allen and the others anymore. It seemed like Tamiko had everybody trippin' on Christianity. Even Tim was going to church. And now Allen had found a new faith buddy on his spiritual journey; some Puerto Rican dude named Davis Martinez, aka, the "new Jim".

Everybody loved Davis. Tamiko acted like a schoolgirl with a crush around Davis. Richard and Davis got along like old friends. Even Tim, who usually hates on everyone at some point, managed to be civil, but what really stung was watching Davis with Allen. Jim had to admit to himself that seeing how well Allen and Davis got along really hurt him a lot. When they went to Emily Ann's about a couple of weeks ago, Jim felt like the third wheel. He felt like he was invisible to Allen whenever Davis was around. This was the same Allen he had grown up with, who was like a little brother to him. People used to say they were like fries and ketchup: you often wouldn't find one without the other. Now, Allen had someone else to look up to. To make matters worse, Allen was always on his back about how much he drank and Jim had gotten tired of his nagging. Things had recently reached a breaking point when Allen openly confronted him about it on one of their nights out. Since then, Jim decided to just let the relationship die. He knew that he and Allen were on two disparate paths.

Jim finished his shower and dried off. Then he wrapped the towel around his waist and headed back to his bedroom. "I need something to do", he thought. "Where could he go? What could he do?" he continued to ponder. Maybe he could go down to the Blue Note. He wouldn't drink anything. He'd just sit there and watch the T.V. Maybe he could go shopping and get some new sneakers or browse around the Apple Store and pick up a new gadget. Anywhere would be good. Anywhere where he would not have to be alone with himself.

After dressing in a hooded sweatshirt, jeans, and hiking boots, Jim grabbed his winter coat and left. He still didn't really know where he was going. When he got to the lobby of his building, he checked his watch. It was now 9:30am. He didn't have an appetite for breakfast. It was way too early to go to the Blue Note (not that he would drink anything if he decided to go there). Christmas shopping was out. Now that he had no friends and family, he had no one to shop for. "Maybe I'll take in a movie." Jim thought to himself. The Magic Johnson Theatre wasn't that far away and they always had really early matinees. Jim walked down to the bodega on the corner to get a newspaper. The sun was out but it was freezing outside. Going to the movies would be a great way to get out of the cold. After making his purchase, Jim went to the diner across the street to get a coffee and have a seat while he combed through his paper.

The diner was almost empty since it was a weekday and most everyone was either at work or on his or her way. Jim took a seat at the counter and almost immediately a waitress took his order: one black coffee, two sugars. Jim opened his paper to the movie timetables and quickly located the listing for the Magic Johnson. There were several movies out; none of which he was really excited about: two romantic comedies, two kids movies, and an action flick. By the time waitress brought his coffee out, Jim had settled on the action flick. It was going to start at 10:15 so he had a little time. Jim decided to browse through the rest of the paper while he drank his coffee. This didn't take long, and soon afterwards he was on his way to the movies. He chose to walk because he didn't want to take his car and have to look for parking, nor did he want to wait in the freezing cold for a bus.

The walk was short and all the energy he expended along with the coffee he had just had, kept him warm as he traversed the frozen concrete. Even though the morning rush hour was over, there were still a lot of people out, most likely because of the holiday season. 125th Street certainly wasn't 5th avenue, but there were a lot of little niche stores and outlets where people could resort for their holiday shopping. When he finally reached the theatre, there wasn't a crowd or line at all, so he was able to purchase his ticket with ease. There was barely anyone around and the theatre workers were just beginning to prepare concession snacks at their counters. There were two people waiting for the popcorn to be made as Jim passed by on his way to the screen room where his movie was being played.

The room was dark and the trailers were running when Jim came in. He would have preferred coming in before the trailers because he hated trying to find a seat in the dark. Luckily, there were only about 5 other people in the theatre so he didn't have to worry about too much noise or talking during the show. Jim finally sat down in a seat in middle of the isle toward the back. As he settled in, the main feature began and he started to relax. Jim planned to sit back and think of nothing but what was in front of him. He just let himself be taken in by the spectacle of the show. The movie wasn't very interesting and the plot was total nonsense. Despite the coffee he'd had earlier, Jim's eyelids began to grow heavy. He tried to keep his eyes open but they just kept closing. All of a sudden, Jim got a jolt, as he realized his surroundings had drastically changed. He was on a boat in the midst of a river. The sky was cloudy and through the sounds of rushing water he could hear a faint and almost indistinct voice calling him. He sat up and tried to focus on the sound of the voice. It sounded vaguely familiar, almost like his mother's voice. But how? She was dead? He stopped and listened again.

"Jim, come back. Jim, come back. Don't leave us."

It was Momma! She wasn't dead. She was here somewhere. He needed to find her.

COMMENCEMENT

"Momma! Momma where are you!" Jim screamed.

He grabbed the oars of the boat and tried to steer the boat toward the direction where the voice was coming from.

"Momma!"

"Jim come back!" the voice was fainter, and the noise of the water grew louder. Jim continued to try to go forward, but it was taking all of his strength. The current was pulling him away from it."

"Momma! I can't! I need you to help me!"

"Jim, please. Come back!" the voice grew weaker still.

Jim looked back to where the noise of the water was coming from. He was about to go over the falls. He tried to steer the boat toward some rocks, hoping to get stuck there, but to no avail. Finally in an act of desperation, he jumped from the boat and tried to swim away, but it was no use. The current was too strong. Then in an instant, he felt himself being swept away into the shower of the falls.

"Nooooooo…."

When Jim woke up, the closing credits were scrolling down the screen and the lights had come on. He was drenched in sweat and was a little more than shaken. As he looked around, Jim noticed that he was the only person in the screen room. He leaned over, rubbing his face with his palms to gather his composure, trying to forget the images that loitered in the back of his mind. Then Jim checked his cell phone for the time. It was now 12:00. Jim had slept off the lingering remains of his previous hangover and he was ravenously hungry. So he decided to stop off at the nearest fast food place that he could find to get something to eat. As he exited the theatre, Jim was drawn to the tantalizing aroma of fried fish that wafted through the air and ended up heading over to Joe's Fish and Chips, which was right across the street.

The shop was primarily a small take out place. There were only two booths where a few people could sit and eat, however, a woman already occupied these with her three kids, as well as a young woman and her boyfriend. The line was a little long, but Jim figured it would give him time to think about what he wanted. Service was quick and by the time it was Jim's turn he had settled on a whiting sandwich with seasoned fries and a cola. When he got his order he double tied the white plastic bag to keep the cold air out. He looked at his watch again. It was only 12:20. The day was going by at an excruciatingly slow pace.

By the time he had gotten home, Jim didn't feel like doing anything but eating. When he opened his bag, his food was barely warm, so he put it in the microwave for a few seconds. When it was ready, he took it out and put it on a plate he had gotten from the cabinet. Then he took the food and the soda to his living room. Next, he put on the television and turned to the food network and watched Emeril cook while he ate his food. The fish sandwich smelled better than it tasted. There was more breading than fish. The fish underneath the breading was hard and greasy. The fries tasted as if they had been fried twice. Fortunately, Jim's hunger excused the poor preparation of meal. It was barely satisfactory but then he was not expecting it to taste like home cooking. "No one could cook fish like momma could", Jim thought mournfully to himself. No one could do anything like his mother could.

Jim needed to stop himself before the lugubrious train of thought that began to ensue consumed him. He got up and turned off the T.V. It just wasn't distracting enough to keep the thoughts out of his head. Next, he went into his bedroom and took the clothes out of the hamper and put them into a laundry bag. Jim then dragged the bag to the kitchen where he got some detergent and fabric softener from a cabinet and put those into the bag too. Next, he doubled back to bedroom to get the change jar off the dresser, and his mp3 player and stuck those in the bag as well. When he was done, he left his apartment and went down to the laundry room in the basement of his building.

The laundry room was a small, brightly lit room that had four large washers on one side, four large dryers on the other and a long narrow white table down the middle. The place was swept and neat, but the furniture and appliances looked well worn. There was no one else in the room when Jim arrived and for the first time he had the place to himself. Jim put on his mp3 player and then quickly got to work sorting the clothes, putting them into the machines, and finally putting in his coins and soap powder. Together, the work and the music were keeping his mind occupied and therefore safe from intrusive thoughts. It wasn't long before the machines had stopped and he was busy again taking them from the washer to the dryer. Then the next thing he knew he was fluffing and folding. By the time he was done, he was sure that it might have been late in the day, but when he checked his cell phone it was only 2:30pm. So Jim brought his clothes upstairs, all the while trying to think of another way to keep himself occupied during this dreadfully long day.

When Jim got back he went to his room unpacked the clothes from the laundry bag and started to put them away. He was just about finished and was thinking of cleaning the whole apartment when his cell phone began to ring. Jim looked and was shocked to see Callie's number come up.

"Hey, Callie. What's up?"

"Hey!" said Callie sounding surprised "I thought I was going to get your voicemail. Did you take a day off or something? Are you sick?"

"No, no. Just playing hooky. So what's going on?"

"Nothing. Literally nothing. Look, I really need to talk to you…I can't think of anyone else who would care."

"Callie, are you okay?"

"Honestly? No."

"When do you get off?"

"At 3:00."

"How about we meet for an early dinner. Anywhere you want."

"I'm going to need a drink. How about the Blue Note, that's close to you. Do you know where it is?"

"Uh, yeah."

"I have the car today. It shouldn't take me more than half an hour to get there. Meet me at around 3:30."

"Sure. See you there."

"Later."

Jim changed out of his sweatshirt and jeans into something a little classier. He put on a light blue button down shirt with a navy v-neck sweater and khaki colored cords. As he dressed, he wondered what was bothering Callie. She had been MIA for a long while, but sometimes that would happen. Oftentimes one person from their set would be missing for a while, mostly because of work or some personal crisis. The last time he had spoken to her was a couple of weeks ago. She had told Jim at that time that she wasn't speaking to the others. Jim had no idea why Callie was mad at them, as she didn't go into details. In any case, Jim was glad that there was still one person in their set that he could count on. How could he have forgotten about Callie? She was the only one who wasn't trippin' on Christianity. She was probably the only person who would understand where he was coming from.

"So you're going to the Blue Note after all?" Jim heard the nagging voice ask.

"I'm only going there with a friend. I'm not going to have anything to drink."

"Sure about that?"

"Of course. I've made up my mind."

"We'll see."

****

When Jim arrived at the Blue Note, the crowd was a bit thin since not many people had gotten off of work yet. Instead of sitting at the bar where he usually sat, he got a table near the door so that he could spot Callie when she walked in. It was not yet 3:30 and he wasn't expecting Callie to be on time, so he took the liberty of ordering a drink. Jim stuck to his resolve and only ordered a ginger ale with ice. From where he was sitting he could see the T.V. at the bar. There was a Lakers game on and Jim watched while he waited and nursed his drink.

"Hey stranger", he heard someone say after a while.

Jim looked over to see Callie. She was wearing a long black goose down bubble coat, a knit scully and those ugly black suede snow boots that were popular at this time. She looked as beautiful as ever with her hair down, and cascading around her narrow face. Beautiful, but sad.

"Take a load off", Jim offered.

"Thanks."

She took off her coat to reveal a mint green cashmere v-neck and black skinny jeans.

"What? No scrubs?"

"I don't wear my scrubs in the street. It's unsanitary. What have you got there?"

"Ginger ale."

"Ginger ale?" scoffed Callie "I don't think so, I'm going to need something a lot stronger", she said. "Waiter!"

"I didn't know you drank?"

"I do now."

"Hold on. I'd like to hear what's wrong before you get incoherent on me."

"You want to know what's wrong? I'll tell you what's wrong. I just realized that the people who I thought were my friends really don't give a damn about me."

"Hey, Hey! Where's all this coming from?"

"Oh, please. Like you don't know."

"No, I don't."

"I'm always the last person in our group to find out anything. Like at the Election Night party. You have no idea how stupid I felt when everyone knew about Allen's new job except me."

"He didn't really want anyone to know."

"Just don't", she said waving her hand. "And you know I was so angry at them, especially Allen. I just decided to give everyone the cold shoulder, just to see if anyone would notice. Do you think anyone came by to ask me what was wrong? Was anyone concerned?"

"Maybe they think you're still angry about Tim throwing up on you at the party."

"Really? After more than a month? Do you really think I'm that petty? I could have been abducted or something for all anyone knew."

"Richard's been missing in stretches longer than that. And everyone knows you know how to take care of yourself. It's not like you're Miko or something."

Callie glowered at the mention of that name.

"Sorry. Poor choice of words."

"It's probably all her fault anyway. She's probably been badmouthing me to everyone there."

"No, you know Miko's not like that. I just think everybody's preoccupied with finding out God's purpose for their lives. Tamiko's got everyone drinkin' her Christian kool-aid. Even Tim's been going to church."

"The agnostic is going to church?!"

"I think we both know why he's there."

"Because he can't get enough of Thumbelina? I hope he gets her pregnant. And what about Richard? Has he gone mad, too?"

"No, he's too into his new girlfriend. Besides he's always been in and out."

"So is that the new hang out now? Greater Apostolic?"

"I guess. Allen's even got a new spiritual partner. Some guy from his job. Seems that he's a new member of the Church, too."

"And yet another thing I'm the last to know about! Where's that waiter already?"

The waiter came and Callie ordered a bottle of Alize.

"Don't feel so bad about being out of the loop. You're not the only one. I haven't hung out with them in I don't know how long."

"And yet you still know a lot more than I do."

COMMENCEMENT

"Sometimes I wish I didn't."

"What do you mean by that?"

"It's just that Allen and I go way back. We were like brothers. But now...ever since he's been on this spiritual journey, it seems like we've been growing further and further apart. One day I wake up and it's like we have nothing in common anymore. Allen was the one person who I thought I could always rely on and now I don't even know if we're still friends. And then to see him with this Davis dude and they're hitting it off like they've been friends for years..."

"I understand that you and Allen were really close, and I'm sorry that your bromance with him has ended, but did you stop for one minute to think that maybe you have other friends, you could talk to. Like say...me, for instance?"

"I can't argue with you, Callie. I'm sorry. You're right."

At that moment, the waiter arrived with a bottle of Alize and two glasses.

"Alright! It's party time!" buzzed Callie as she poured herself a large drink.

"I can't believe you're about to get your drink on. I've never seen this side of you Callie."

"You're about to see a lot of different sides of me. I'm tired of being good old reliable Callie. Taken for granted Callie. I'm done with that."

"I don't know if I should."

"Oh, come on. One drink won't hurt."

"You don't want to be rude," a new voice reasoned "and Callie needs you to show her your here for her right now."

"Why not."

"Here's to Saints and Sinners. Allen, his skanky girlfriend, Tamiko, Tim, and what's his face are the Saints and you and me can be the sinners."

"Here, here. And Allen's not seeing that girl anymore. She dumped him after she found out he was a porter. So it was over before it even started."

"Serves him right. Especially after the way he's treated me lately. And he calls himself a Christian. Is this how Christians treat their friends? If so, then good riddance."

"Christianity is full of contradictions as the Christians are apt to be."

"I'm not trying to trash their religion or anything, but I just don't understand why Allen wouldn't want to share what he's going through with me or at least try to explain. I mean Tamiko was putting it down for Tim."

"That's because Tamiko is more sure than Allen. Allen doesn't really understand it himself. He's hardly in a position to explain it to you or anyone else."

"Yeah, but he could have talked about how he felt. Instead he just shut me out. And after everything we've been through together, I just can't believe…" Callie's voice trailed off as she began to choke up.

"Hey. It's gonna be okay", said Jim gently stroking her hand.

"It's just that…it's like I don't mean anything to him at all."

"I don't think that's true."

"Then why hasn't he come to see me?"

"Maybe he thinks you're too busy. Or maybe he thinks you don't want to see him. After all, you are giving him the cold shoulder."

"I didn't think about it that way."

"Why don't you call him and tell him how you feel?"

"That's just it. I'm always calling Allen, always cheering him up when he's down, encouraging him, worrying about him when he's not around. Now it's time for him to worry."

"I do think he tends to take you for granted."

"Who knows? Maybe it's better this way. If he can't come around to see about me then the relationship...I mean, our friendship is over."

"I don't think you mean that, Callie."

"Oh yes I do. As a matter of fact, let's make a new clique. You and me can start a new clique and we can make more friends who aren't too caught up in their religion to show their friends that they care. What do you say friend?"

"Sure why not?"

Jim and Callie spent the rest of the afternoon and into the evening talking and commiserating together, finishing two bottles of Alize in the process. The alcohol had lightened their moods and they moved on to less weighty topics such as their old high school days, and the prom. Gone were their troubles, anxieties and fears. They stayed in their spots all through out the night oblivious to everything and everyone around them.

"Oh my gosh, what time is it?" asked Callie "It's real dark out there."

"Let me see", replied Jim pulling out his phone. The screen was nothing more than a bright blur.

"I can't tell. I think someone changed the language on my phone", he laughed.

"It was nice talking to you, Jim, but I need to get home."

Callie stood up and then wobbled a little before falling back into the chair.

"I guess that didn't work", she laughed.

"Maybe you should take a cab."

"Are you crazy? Ain't no cab stopping for no black woman this time of night."

"You right. You right. You know what. You can crash at my pad. I have an extra bedroom and in the morning you can drive yourself home. How's that?"

"Alright. I don't feel like driving anyway. It's too much work."

Callie attempted to get up again and this time, Jim put his arm around her waist to steady her. Then he helped her with her coat and her purse before they exited the Blue Note and headed toward his apartment.

When they arrived, Callie was not in the best shape to say the least. He could tell that she had never drank as much as she had tonight and was truly out of sorts. But at least she could hold her liquor. She hadn't thrown up once since they left the bar. Jim himself was a bit disoriented. By the time they reached the entrance of the building, she was not able to remain vertical without Jim's assistance. This was a struggle for Jim who was not only dealing with trying to coordinate Callie's movements but his own as well. Yet she was very voluble, at times breaking into choruses of the song "That's What Friends Are For". By the time they reached Jim's apartment door, he was practically carrying her. Jim set her down for a moment to open the door, while she picked up her song once more.

"Shhhh, girl. You gonna wake up everybody in the building!" Jim whispered as he fumbled clumsily with his keys.

"So. They need to wake up."

After several tries, Jim was able to locate the lock with his key and opened the door. Then he went over to where he deposited Callie on the floor, picked her up and carried her across the threshold, and kicked the door closed behind him.

"Oh, Jim, you're my hero."

"I don't know about that", he groaned depositing her on the couch, and then slumping beside her.

Callie leaned her head against Jim's chest and put her arms around him.

"You're a good friend Jim."

"You're a good friend, too, Callie."

"Promise me you'll always be my friend."

"I Promise."

"And you'll always call me, and come over, and invite me to cool parties."

"Promise."

"And you won't leave me alone."

"I won't leave you if you won't leave me. Deal."

"Deal."

"Goodnight, Callie" said Jim attempting to extricate himself from her embrace.

"Don't, please. Don't leave me."

Even in the darkness of the apartment Jim could see the plaintive, pleading expression in her eyes. It spoke to the longing and loneliness within his heart. For a long time he had been drifting on his raft, alone on the quiet water, the noise of the falls growing louder and louder. Now there was someone else struggling in the water. Jim pulled her closer to himself. He was going over the falls, but he was glad he was not alone.

FORTY-THREE

Tamiko checked herself in her small compact mirror for what had to have been the 60th time. When she last glanced at her watch it read 10:49. Davis would be here in about 10 minutes, and she wanted to make sure she looked okay. "Just relax." she told herself. This was a difficult task given the fact that she was tutoring the hottest guy on the planet! Hot and a Christian! No. Hot and a Christian and crazy smart! Tamiko thought she would have gotten over these feelings as she and Davis spent more time with each other. After all, wasn't familiarity supposed to breed contempt? And yet the opposite happened. The more she got to know Davis, the more she became infatuated with him, and the more infatuated she became the more she thought about him. It had gotten to the point to where Tamiko even thought about him during random moments of the day. Sometimes she'd find herself wondering what he was doing, what he was wearing, whether or not he was thinking about her. Did Davis just like her as a friend, or was he interested in her at all as a girlfriend? Did he even already have a girlfriend? Sometimes the kind courtesies he paid her, or that warm smile he often bestowed on her encouraged her to think that maybe Davis did like her. But he had never asked her out, never 'made a move' that would overtly suggest it. But Davis wasn't a guy who was as transparent with his feelings like Allen, or Tim. Davis was a bit enigmatic, and this made him all the more alluring to Tamiko.

So Tamiko sat in the library waiting for Davis wearing an outfit she picked out especially to impress him. Her navy blue three-quarter sleeved boat-necked cashmere sweater with the bow on the shoulder, a gray form fitting pencil skirt and long high-heeled boots. Tamiko wore her hair parted to one side and down over her shoulders without any curl at the ends so she would look more mature. She knew Allen would not be here again because he was supposed to be doing research for a special project he was working on. While Tamiko was glad to be able to spend some time alone with Davis, she was still nervous and self-conscious in his presence.

Just as Tamiko was starting to daydream, in walked the main character of her fantasies. Today he was wearing his goose down parka with a wool Pendleton shirt and jeans, and hiking boots. He beamed his trademark smile her way as their eyes met across the room.

"Hey. I see Al's cut out again."

"Yeah, he said he's busy doing research for some project he's working on."

"Oh."

"Are you disappointed?"

"Nah, no way. You're just as good as he is. Maybe better in some ways. But don't tell him I told you that", he winked.

"I won't. And thanks for the compliment."

"You're welcome."

"So, let's get started." blushed Tamiko "Where's your latest assignment?"

"Righ' here. It's the draft though."

Tamiko took the paper and began to read it over.

"It's pretty good for a draft."

"Yeah, I've been studyin' that book you gave me. That Bedford book...and the Style book too."

"It shows."

When Allen told her about Davis, Tamiko would have to admit that she thought he might be a slow guy with a learning disability, but the more she worked with him the more she understood just how much the opposite was true. Tamiko only had to explain a concept or idea once and

Davis would take hold of it and be able to apply it to his writing. At times he would go beyond what she would teach him. He asked intelligent questions, inquired about resources that he could use and took his work very seriously. Each time Davis brought her a paper there would be less and less to correct on it.

"And I did my own outline for the paper this time. Is it flowin' like it's suppost to."

"Yeah, it really does, actually."

"And you're not just sayin' that 'cause we're friends, right?"

"Davis, I think way too much of you to patronize you. Your writing has come such a long way. Really."

"But there's still probably something I could do to make it better right?"

"I would be reaching, but you might want to work on your punctuation. You've got a few comma splices here and there. But I don't know anyone who doesn't have trouble with that. It's tricky even for pro's."

"I've been beatin' myself up about that for the past coupla days, but I just can't seem to get wit' it. It's kinda frustratin'."

"It's okay, Davis. No paper is going to absolutely perfect."

"I know, but writin' and readin' has always been a big deal for me. See, my family came to this country from Puerto Rico when I was five years old. They put me in school and I didn't know any kind of English. So I had a hard time learnin' to read and when I wrote or when I talked stuff didn't come out right. Like I had trouble communicatin' and what not. Kids would laugh at me, call me stupid."

"But you weren't dumb. You just didn't know the language."

"Guess they must've realized that 'cause when I went to second grade, they put me in a bilingual class, but I didn't learn much English. The teacher just spoke Spanish and I did everything in Spanish. My grades got better in the class, but when I took the state tests, which were in English, I would get a low score. So then they had me evaluated and they said I had speech and language learnin' delay. They put me in a special-ed class. And that just really made me discouraged, like you know when they put you in special-ed, it's like they sayin' it's no hope for you. The teachers in those classes didn't do much teaching anyway. So I just gave up on school."

"I'm so sorry, Davis. You shouldn't have had to go through all that. The system is so unfair."

"I just wish I had a teacher like you when I was younger. Somebody nice and patient. I bet you don't even yell at the kids in yo' class."

"Oh, I don't know. I can be pretty stern at times."

"And I bet those times is few and far between."

"You're really too kind."

"Nah, for real. You're a really good teacher. Those kids in your class are lucky."

"Actually, I'm not a good teacher. But I hope one day I will be."

"Why would you say that?"

"Because, looking back I think I've been too preoccupied with myself. I didn't focus on my students like I should have. I closed myself off to learning and growing."

"I still say you're a good teacher, 'cause a bad teacher would not be thinking the way you are now. They wouldn't care less. And if you're still not convinced, let me show you somethin'."

Davis took another paper out of his bag and gave it to Tamiko. It had a B+ on the top of it.

"Davis, this is wonderful! How come you didn't show me earlier!"

"I wanted to surprise you."

"Oh, Davis! I am so proud of you!"

"I couldn't have done it without you and Allen."

"And don't forget to give yourself some credit."

"I think I better not forget to give God the credit. I mean, if it wasn't for Him I never would have met Allen or you. I feel blessed that God has brought some really good people into my life."

"C'mon Davis, we're just regular people."

"Tamiko, I've been around a lot of people. Unfortunately for most of my life, the people I was hangin' wit' only brought me trouble. Then when I gave God my life, I had to cut a lot of people loose and a lot of the others cut me loose, 'cause they couldn't get wit' what I was about. For a long time I didn't have nobody to be wit'. I was gettin' real lonely. Kinda like the prophet Elijah. For a while, I thought I was the only Christian person my age on the face of the earth. Then I met Daniel and Allen and the rest of y'all. Now I know I don't have to be alone no more. I mean 'any more'."

"Never, not so long as I…I mean, we're around." Tamiko was touched by what Davis had said. Tamiko had taken hold of his hand, but upon realizing what she had done, she quickly let go. "Davis, are you sure you don't want to come to Sunday dinner with us. I'm sure my dad would love to get to know you", offered Tamiko, attempting to be more casual.

"I don't know, Miko. I don't want him to get the wrong idea. I mean I'm kinda new to the church community. I don't want to seem like too forward…"

"Oh, no! No one would ever think that. Besides there is no set decorum. It's not like you'll be coming to the house on church business. It's just dinner at a friend's house. There's nothing wrong with that."

"Aiight. And since I don't have to spend a lot of time reworking my paper this time. I guess I'll have some free time to come."

"Excellent! Dinner is at 5:00. If you want you can hang out with me and Allen after the service."

"Actually, I'm joining Daniel's Brotherhood Bible Study Group."

"Really?!"

"Yeah, so I don't know if I'll be able to hang out."

"All right then. That's probably the better choice anyway."

COMMENCEMENT

"I guess we done here, right?"

"I guess. I would stay longer, but I have an afternoon workshop that I'm planning to attend."

"Oh", said Davis looking a little disappointed. "Then I'ma jet back home and edit this and get it ready for school and everythin'."

"See you on Sunday."

"No doubt." he smiled.

FORTY-FOUR

Allen was furiously writing down notes on a legal pad, pausing at times to sift through some documents in front of him. He also had his laptop out checking various websites as well. Finally, he had figured out why God had led him to work as a porter at the Sheraton. Although Allen couldn't explain it, he knew that he was supposed to meet Davis at this point in his life and he also knew there had to be a reason for it. Ever since he had spoken to Davis that day when they were fixing the toilet, the idea of helping Davis and his mom out of their financial conundrum had just stuck in his head. Allen thought about what Tim said the other night, but why would that idea resonate so strongly if God didn't want him to be the one to help? And why not? Hadn't he helped other businesses and clients with their finances in the past? Maybe this was what God was calling his attention to. Working with people like Davis and his mom, helping the poor and less able manage their financial resources rather than the rich and wealthy. Allen couldn't even count all the times in the Bible where God spoke about how the poor are the apple of his eye and how God favors those who help the poor. Now everything was making sense. Maybe Davis was his test case. If Allen could help Davis's family out of their financial mess, then it may lead to something bigger. If Allen succeeded, not only would he be able to help his good friend, but maybe God would lead Allen to start his own non-profit organization dedicated to helping struggling families manage their finances and lift themselves out of poverty. How grand and noble it all sounded when Allen thought of it. "This must be the plan that God has for me", mused Allen. Yet, there was a small problem. Allen had no idea where to begin or what his plan of action was.

COMMENCEMENT

Earlier he had spent most of his day at the library, researching various consumer loans and what options were available to those who were unable to manage them. He found the subject of subprime loans of particular interest. Allen learned that the irony about subprime loans were that they were loans to people who most likely would not be able to pay. The banking executives knew this. Candidates for subprime loans, mortgages, and refinances were mainly those people who had poor credit and payment histories. The only options that were available to them were pretty much what Tim had spoken of earlier. They could work with the bank on restructuring the loan and working out better terms (i.e. smaller payments over a longer period of time), try to get a deferment on payments due to hardship, or they could try to sell the house and use the money to pay off a large part of the balance. Still, there was no real evidence that Davis's mom had been the recipient of a subprime loan or refinance. Her credit could have been stellar, but taking on another mortgage at this point in her life could have just been too overwhelming.

There was so much that Allen didn't know and he knew Davis would probably not tell him. Allen knew he could probably help him work out something with a restructuring, but he would need information that was specific to Davis' particular circumstances. Like what kind of lending institution did they broker the refinance with? How much money was involved? Had they been making payments or were they past due? Had they even spoken with their lender about their options? Everything would be contingent upon their history with the lending institution. There was a lot of legal stuff involved that Allen needed to learn more about as well. Allen couldn't really do anything more until he got more information from Davis.

In the midst of this activity, Lena sharp wandered into the living room, studying Allen for a brief moment and wondering what her son was up to.

"What you doin' baby?" she inquired.

"I'm just working on a project", answered Allen succinctly.

"Is it for work?"

"No, I don't think this type of work would be required at the Hotel."

"You looking for another job?"

"No, I'm just researching something to try to help a friend."

"Oh, well, I'll let you get back to what you were doing."

"Since you're here, there's been something that I wanted to ask you. Do you think God leads people into situations and gives them these sort of missions? Sort of like if you pass the mission, you get to go to the next level?"

"I'm not sure if I know what you're talking about sweetheart."

"It's just that I was reading the Bible the other day, and I was thinking that maybe my time at the hotel is like my mission. Like there's something that I'm supposed to do there and then once my work is done, I'll get to move on."

"Did you hear a Word from the Lord confirming this?"

"No, not like a voice from beyond or anything, but it's just like a feeling. You know?"

"Be careful, Allen. Sometimes your feelings can fool you. What do you think is your mission from God?"

"I think he sent me to the hotel to be a help to someone there, and in the process help a lot of other people."

"How would you do that?"

"I can't really say too much right now, but I think God wants me to use the skills that I have to help someone who is in need. I was even thinking that if this works out, I'd be able to start something that may help other people."

"I don't know, Allen. Only God would be able to tell you if you're on the right track."

"Maybe this feeling that I have is His way of letting me know."

"Pray about it, Allen. The last thing you want to do is rush ahead of God."

"I *have* been praying about it. Sometimes I feel like I've been praying forever."

"I know this isn't easy for you because you're so used to doing and helping, but maybe what God wants you to do is to stop doing. Now God could have a mission for you down there at the hotel or He could simply have put you there to learn. It could be that you're the one who needs the help."

"I've thought about it that way, but how can someone grow spiritually through manual labor."

"I don't know, but God has spoken to and worked through a lot of manual laborers. David was a shepherd, Amos was a gatherer of sycamore fruit, the Apostles were fishermen, Paul was a tent maker, and even Jesus himself was a carpenter. So don't knock it."

"I'm not saying that there aren't jobs that involve manual labor that aren't important or that don't involve real skill or brains. I think Davis is amazing with the way that he can fix just about anything. But my job is so different. All I do is sweep, mop and buff. If it wasn't for Davis showing me how to do small repairs, my job could be done by a ten year old."

"Allen, I can't tell you how God will work, but one thing I do know is that he *will* work. Don't worry so much about finding out what's supposed to happen next. Just keep working on your relationship with God. Remember: Seek ye the kingdom of God and his righteousness, and all other things shall be added unto you."[1]

"But I thought that having a relationship with God meant that I would be walking in His will for me. Is it so wrong to want to know what that will is?"

"No. But if we want to know his will, we first have to learn how to trust God so we can be obedient. That means believing, trusting, reading his word and praying. Remember the relationship is not about us, so much as it is learning to love the Lord with your whole heart and your whole mind."

"And just when I thought I was figuring things out."

"Allen, when you have a relationship with God you don't have to figure out. He shows you.

FORTY-FIVE

The sky was grey and cloudy, but it wasn't as cold as it had been previously. The wind was calm and still. It almost seemed like fall rather than winter as Tim and Tamiko walked through the park on Sunday afternoon. The church service had ended a while ago and Allen and Davis stayed behind to attend Daniel's Brotherhood Bible Study class. This left Tim and Tamiko wondering how to pass the time until Sunday Dinner. They were both much too restless to sit around in the coffee shop so they opted to take a walk through the park and take in the view.

"Ready for the Holiday Season?" Tim asked.

"Not really. I haven't finished my Christmas shopping and I still have things to work out for this year's Christmas Celebration", answered Tamiko. "What about you?"

"Same. Not much done on the personal front. I hate Christmas shopping. I never know what to get. I need a personal shopper. Like you for instance. I don't think I told you, but my mom absolutely loved the handbag you picked out."

"Glad to hear it. Guess she and I do have the same tastes, after all."

"You think maybe you could help me out again?"

"I don't know, maybe. So long as you don't wait until Christmas Eve."

"No, I'm not one of those people who gets a rush from being in the crowds."

"When is that often talked about vacation of yours finally going to get here?"

403

"I've only got one more week before my vacation. Then I'll have three whole weeks to myself, the week before Christmas through the week after. I just need to figure out what I'm going to do with all this time on my hands."

"I know one thing that you should do, if you haven't made time already."

"Yes, I know I need to see a doctor. I am. I already have an appointment if you must know."

"Good. So when are we going?"

"It's the Friday before I go on vacation. I decided to take a half-day the Friday before and see the doctor in the afternoon at 4:00."

"And then you are going to need to go on a long rest. You should get out of the city and go some place nice and quiet and relaxing."

"That's exactly what I was thinking. Just get away from the insanity of Herns and Marshall."

"Things haven't gotten any better I take it."

"It's funny. In a way it's worse and in a way it's better even."

"Okay...."

"It's like...How can I say this...there are things going on that I can't explain...It's almost like there are some supernatural forces at work."

"By supernatural forces, do you mean like God?"

"First, let me explain it and then you tell me. Now this is just between you and me, okay."

"Sure."

"You know Preston is the big cheese now and he was supposed to have this big presentation where he sort of works out the details of the reorganization under his plan."

"Yes."

"Well, he never got it done on time, and the date kept getting pushed back and next thing you know, the final deadline was fast approaching. So you can imagine the office was like a pressure cooker and, of course, Preston practically morphed into Pol Pot. I kid you not."

"I can imagine."

"Then Clara quit because she couldn't take it anymore, Vera got really sick, poor woman, and that just left me and Preston. We got temps, we tried to hire other people, but no one would stay because of course, no one could stand to work with Preston."

"Which would be understandable."

"So as the deadline approaches, rumors were circulating that Preston Scott was going to go down. And Even Standoff himself really let him have it. We had a meeting and Standoff just stopped short of canning Preston right there. Then after Standoff had left, Preston just lost it."

"He got violent?"

"Kind of. But not to me or anyone else. I mean, he was literally going to jump out of the window and kill himself."

"Are you serious?!!"

"Deadly so. It was so surreal. About a month ago, I would have been tempted to push him myself. But at that moment, seeing him like that...something happened inside of me. I just couldn't.... I don't know how to explain it without sounding all '7th Heaven' corny."

"Who cares if it sounds corny. I'm not judging you. Say what you need to say."

"Seeing Preston like that...I just understood, because I had been where he'd been. There were times in my life I felt like doing what Preston was about to do. I knew what the suffering was like and I didn't think anyone should have to feel like that. Not even Preston. I didn't know what to say, but it was like something spoke to him through me to get him to come down."

"Is he okay? Did they take him to a hospital?"

"No. Nothing like that happened. He took a few days sick leave, but no one knows why. He and I were the only ones there when everything went down, and I didn't want to make spectacle of it. I don't think he really wanted to die, he just wanted a way out of his situation. He probably just got so desperate that he freaked out."

"What did you say to him to get him to come down?"

"To tell you the truth, I don't even remember most of it. But I do remember telling him I would help him with the presentation and that I wouldn't say anything about what happened."

"Really? That's convenient. Don't get me wrong, I don't mean to sound cynical or make light of the situation, but are you sure that he wasn't performing to manipulate you?"

"I thought about that afterward. He very well could have been without consciously knowing it, since being manipulative is such an ingrained part of who he is. But that's not important. I'm not helping him because he's such a great guy."

"You mean you two aren't friends now?"

"Hardly. But we have worked out a 'truce' if you can call it that. He's still the same old Preston, but that doesn't matter. It's not like I was expecting anything from him anyway. Loving your enemies isn't about what you're going to get in return."

"So you've actually been listening to my dad's sermons."

"And then some. You remember a while ago at Sunday dinner, your dad gave me a word to "love my enemies" so to speak."

"I think I do."

"Well, when Preston had his melt down, I thought about what your dad said that day, and what you had told me about Christ when he was on the cross praying for his accusers and everything. All of that made me realize why we should 'love our enemies'.[1] We're all on this planet together. As human beings we have a responsibility toward each other that's somehow Divine in nature. It was a really deep thing for me to get."

"I can tell."

"Sometimes I think if I had only loved my enemies from the beginning, I wouldn't have a lot the problems I have now."

"What do you mean?"

"I mean, I have some confessions to make. I know that I've made it sound as if Preston was the bad guy a lot of the time, and there were times when he was, but I didn't help things. I'll admit I was jealous because he was popular with a lot of the higher ups. And maybe my jealousy kept me from being the co-worker I should have been. It may have been part of the reason why Preston decided to go after my job in the first place."

"This is really new. You sound like a different person."

"I know. It's crazy right. But you know what's really crazy? There was so much work to be done I thought that we were doomed from the start. I even found myself trying to pray at one point. But little by little, it was like someone was guiding me. I was working 16-hour days, but I wasn't tired or as exhausted as I usually am. Things just started happening. Just too many coincidences for this to be attributed to dumb luck. And it had nothing to do with me by myself. I know a lot of people in my situation would like to think it was just a little sweat and elbow grease, but this…this…this was way bigger than me. You understand right?"

"Of course, I do. But do you?"

"I guess you mean that God is doing all of these things. I'll admit Tamiko sometimes it does seem like it. But then I think, here I am, a person who has never believed on Him or worshiped Him, and then there's Preston, who probably thinks he's a god all on his own. Why would God do such great things for us, and someone like Allen, who is trying to commit his life to Him, is working as a janitor? And look at what happened to you even!"

"First off, I'm starting to learn that being a Christian doesn't make you exempt from problems. The Bible says 'all that live godly shall suffer persecution'.[2] Sometimes we go through trials that test our faith and make us stronger, other times we suffer persecution from others who don't understand us. But as a Christian, God is with you in the midst of it all. Secondly, God is merciful. He sends his rain on the just as well as the unjust.[3] He hates sin, but he doesn't hate us. Jesus sacrificed himself not because we were just so great, but because He loved us. He saw us suffering in sin and he wanted to save us."

"So you think this is God's way of getting me to understand that He's real. Like he wants to save me?"

"I believe so."

Tamiko couldn't believe her ears. Here was Tim, pondering the possibility that God was real and working in his life. She never thought this day would come so soon and under such circumstances. Tamiko thought that it would take nothing short of bringing Tim practically to his deathbed to get him to believe in God. And yet all it took was an incident at work. It was like when Nathanael believed that Jesus was Messiah simply because Jesus told him He saw him under the fig tree.[4]

"Hmmm…I won't say you're wrong."

Tamiko and Tim talked on until it began to get dark. Before they realized it, it was time for dinner and they had to rush back to the Bynum homestead. When they arrived they could hear the faint voices of those inside through the door. Tamiko was fishing in her purse for her house key when Pastor Bynum opened the door.

"I thought I heard a car pull up. It's about time you two got here. I was about to get worried."

"Oh, I'm sorry, daddy. It's just that Tim and I were talking and talking and we forgot the time."

"I'll say", Pastor Bynum replied casting a suspicious glance over at Tim "Well, come on in, everyone's ready to eat."

"Tamiko, where have you been?!" scolded Mother Rose.

"Tim and I were walking through the park talking…"

"Dinner should have started at least 20 minutes ago. Next time, please be considerate of our guests."

"Yes, momma", Tamiko said reticently. Then as she surveyed the room, her eyes lit up as she noticed the presence of a special guest. "Davis, you came!"

"I couldn't break my promise, right."

"Have you met everyone?"

"It's okay, Miko, I already did all the introductions", chuckled Allen.

"Oh my goodness, I'm so crazy, of course you did. How was the Brotherhood Bible Study?"

"It was good. I felt like I learned a lot", Davis replied bashfully.

"How about you guys continue this conversation over dinner. Cause I'm really hungry", said Allen interrupting them.

"Oh, yes. Right this way", said Tamiko taking hold of Davis arm and leading him to the dining room.

"Are you okay, man?" Allen asked Tim who was noticeably disturbed.

"I'll deal", Tim replied somberly.

****

"Davis, I hear you're Allen's boss. How's that workin' out. He doin' right?" asked Vernon.

"I wouldn't exactly say that I'm his boss, like he don't report to me or nothin' like that. I just let him know some of the things that need to be done, and he helps me sometimes. He's a good worker, good wit' his hands and eveythin'. He even helps me wit the repairs sometimes."

"Are you talking about the same Allen who couldn't even put together a paper church fan?" joked Vernon.

"Aw c'mon Dad, that was when I was 6." laughed Allen.

"Allen, now that you know how to fix things maybe you'll be a little more handy around the house", hinted Lena.

"I don't know if I'm ready for that yet."

"What exactly is your position at the Sheraton?" queried mother Rose impertinently.

"I'm just one of the repairmen that they have on hand. I fix things, install things, stuff like that." answered Davis.

"I see", remarked Mother Rose coldly.

"That's a good skill to have young man. Everybody needs someone to fix things recession or not", stated Vernon in approbation.

"Are you a licensed contractor?" asked Mother Rose.

"No, but I'm working towards that right now. Allen and Miko have been helping me on the weekends."

"So I hear", said the pastor. "How has school been coming along?"

"Good. Better, now. I'm making good grades an' eveythin'."

"That's because he is so smart. Did you know he got an B+ on his last paper", added Tamiko.

"I did have help though."

"Don't be so modest. Most of the work was yours."

"So you're currently working on your BA?" asked mother rose continuing her interrogation.

"No, I'm trying to get my high school diploma so I can get into this program they got that's gonna help me get my contractin' license." explained Davis.

"Aren't you a little old to be working on your high school diploma?" asked Mother Rose, condescension dripping from each word.

Tamiko shot her mother a look, then sent another one to her father that pleaded with him to intervene.

"Now, Rose, there's different paths for different people. Not everybody does everything the same way", reasoned the Pastor.

"It's okay Pastor. I'm not gonna try and front. I've made some bad choices in my life, like droppin out of school when I was 16. But now wit' the help of the Lord, I'm going straight."

COMMENCEMENT

"And that's the most important thing, letting God direct the choices you're making now, like joining our church. How are you liking Greater Apostolic so far, Davis?"

"It's been good. I've been learnin a lot from you and Daniel. I've made a lot of friends as you can see."

"You don't know how glad I am to hear that. I hope in time, you will want to get more involved in our community. We have need of young people like you in service."

"I don't think I'd mind that at all."

"But he's already getting more involved", gushed Tamiko. "How do you like the Brotherhood Bible Study Group that Daniel's got going?"

"I'm really feelin' it you know. It's like he's teachin' things from a male perspective, like how to be a godly man. Like today, he was talkin' about how a man could be a godly leader, and the different characteristics of leadership like humility, submission to God, all that. It was very interestin'."

"And how about you, Allen? You were there, too. What did you think?" asked Lena.

"Like Davis said, it was interesting. And I didn't know how well Daniel could handle the Word. It seems like Pastor's right, God has really anointed him to preach."

"And I'm glad to hear that. I can't think of a better way for you to spend your Sunday afternoons, Allen", said Lena enthusiastically.

"Since we're on the topic of how people spend their afternoons, I'd like to know what you and this young man…Tom, is it?" began Mother Rose.

"It's Tim ma'am", said Tim politely.

"Oh, yes. I'd like to know just what you and Tom were talking about that was so interesting that you forgot all about dinner and kept our guests waiting for nearly 20 minutes?" asked Mother Rose, her voice full of accusation.

"We were just talking about work, that's all", pleaded Tamiko.

"Really? For nearly two and a half hours? Must have been quite a story he was telling."

"We took a walk through the park and we went farther than we should have", Tim tried to explain.

"Interesting choice of words", said Mother Rose bitterly, her eyes narrowing into little slits.

"Are you still having trouble on your job young man?" asked the Pastor, trying to rescue the conversation from where it was going.

"Actually, I was telling Tamiko that I think things are changing for the better."

"That's good to hear. Did the Word that I gave you lend any clarity to your situation?"

"It did actually. In fact, I've found that a lot of things you've said have been making a lot of sense lately."

"I see. I've notice that you've been with us for quite some time now. Have we convinced you to join us yet?"

"I… I'd…You're kind of putting me on the spot here, Pastor."

"I don't see how. The answer is either yes or no", barked Mother Rose.

"Rose, please!" the Pastor said to his wife sternly. "I'm sorry, Tim. I didn't mean to. If you need more time it's no problem."

****

After dinner everyone bid each other farewell and headed out for the night. Mother Rose excused herself to clean up the mess left behind, taking Tamiko with her to help. Allen and Davis went out together and the Pastor followed Tim out to his car.

"Pastor, could I have a word with you for a second."

"Sure, Tim. What's on your mind?"

"I wanted to know if I could talk to you privately at your office about some things."

"Of course."

Meanwhile Allen decided to take advantage of a spare moment with Davis.

"Hey, Davis."

"Whassup, man."

"I've been thinking about what you told me a while ago. About your mom's situation with the house. I think I can help you, but I'm going to need some information from you."

"Look Allen, don't sweat that none. I told you. God will work things out. "

"But I know there is a way out. I could broker the deal for you. I have a degree in finance. I can help you."

"Allen, please, it's okay. We've already been through it wit' the guy at the bank and everythin'. If I'm not worried about it, why should you?"

Allen realized his mission was going to be harder than he thought. Especially if Davis wasn't going to cooperate."

FORTY-SIX

"Heavenly Father, I know you want me to help Davis. Please show me what I need to do to help him and his mother with their financial situation. As you already know, he doesn't want me to help him. How will I get the information I need to do the work that you want me to do? Please let me know what I need to do. In your Son Jesus' name. Amen."

It had been a couple of days since that Sunday Dinner when Allen had spoken to Davis. He had spent a lot of time since then praying, as he had just done, that God would enlighten him about what to do to convince Davis to work with him on the re-finance restructuring. Allen had tried broaching the subject with him several times, but Davis often bristled at his suggestions. Allen just couldn't understand why Davis was rejecting his help. What was the stumbling block that was hindering Allen's work and Davis' blessing? Once again Allen waited for a moment before he got up off his knees, hoping that God would speak into the void. Once again, he heard nothing. Allen was becoming very discouraged.

Everywhere he turned everyone was telling him he had to wait. Be patient and God will answer. Even during the Brotherhood Bible Study when Daniel was instructing them on the virtues of a godly leader, he talked about patience. He spoke of how Abraham had to wait 20 years before God fulfilled the promise that he made to him about Isaac. Joseph spent a good number of years in jail before he came into the promise he saw in his vision as child, and how Moses spent 40 years in the wilderness of Midian before he delivered the people of Israel. Allen couldn't fathom waiting even a year without God speaking to him. And Davis' situation couldn't wait 10 or 20 years if he was going to help him with it. Something had to be done. Now.

Allen got up off his knees and got his things together to finish his remaining rounds. That was his last 10-minute break before the next hour and a half stretch until quitting time. Today he had started on the 9th floor and made his way down to the 5th floor cleaning the hallways and polishing fixtures, removing trash and whatever else needed to be done. Now he was just going through the 5th floor to finish up. Today was a quiet day at the hotel, despite the fact that it was getting ever nearer to Christmas. As much as Allen liked doing repair work, he was glad that he didn't hear the beep of his radio today. Many times the constant interruptions kept Allen from his regular duties, and there had been days when he had to work overtime to finish. Maybe the guest were out doing their last minute Christmas shopping or taking time out to see the Broadway shows. Whatever they were doing, Allen was just glad they weren't in the building ruining all the hard work he was putting in right now.

The slow pace of the day also gave Allen more time to think. If he was going to help Davis, he would have to think about it. Maybe that's what God wanted him to do anyway. Maybe as he was thinking about it, God would let a really good idea pop up into his head. So Allen thought.

If Davis wouldn't provide the information, there would be no way to help him broker a deal with the lender. The only other thing Allen could possibly do in this case would be to speak to his mom herself or find some way to get Davis enough money that would help him with his situation. The first idea was out of the question since Davis' mom didn't speak English very well. The second seemed not only much more feasible, but may even be more palatable to his friend. Maybe he could raise some money amongst his friends and invest it to get a return that would enable Davis to pay off the mortgage. Sure the market was in the midst of crisis, but even now there were stocks that were surging. Besides, with the installation of the new presidential administration, the Dow index began to rise, slowly, but rise nevertheless. The stock market would rebound back and with it, the chance for the Martinez's to keep their family home.

This was it! Allen would have to act quickly. He knew he would need the resources of all his friends. Wait a minute. His friends would not be willing to contribute enough money necessary unless they knew about Davis' situation. That meant putting Davis's business "out in the street". But then again, it's not like Davis' told him to keep everything on the down low. Allen would only tell his immediate friends and family. When everything was said and done, who wouldn't be grateful to a friend that looked out for them in this way. Allen would have to convene a meeting and soon. It would have to be this Saturday. He knew Tim started his vacation this Friday, and he heard from Tamiko they would be going to the doctor on Friday afternoon. This meant that he'd had to have everybody on deck including Callie, Richard, and Jim. He knew he could get Callie and Richard, but Jim was another story.

Jim tended to spend most of his time drunk, and even when he wasn't drunk he was bellicose and hard to deal with. Jim seemed to be going on a downward decline into a dark place. If there were any of Allen's friends who needed help the most it was Jim. But Jim had choices to make; choices that Allen couldn't make for him no matter how much he wanted to. But still, Jim was more than a friend. He was family. Maybe this would provide the opportunity for them to reconnect. Maybe Jim would open up to him about what was bothering him and Allen could help him along toward the path of sobriety.

Allen decided to stop by Callie's after work to mend fences with her as well. He had no idea why she had been ignoring him for nearly two months, and he was afraid to find out. He was hoping it didn't have anything to do with the way Jim and Tim behaved at the Election Night party. Tim ended up throwing up all over her new dress. Or maybe she didn't like his date, Holly. Either way both issues were resolved. Tim had told Allen he sent her a check for the dress, and Allen wasn't seeing Holly anymore so she'd had no reason to sulk. But Callie always could hold a grudge. He knew that when he knocked on her door, he wouldn't be greeted with hugs and kisses.

Time passed quickly as Allen finished his work. The next thing he knew it was quitting time. Allen began to put all of his cleaning tools back in the water closet. Then he went downstairs to punch out before heading to the locker room to change his clothes. Upon entering the locker room he saw Davis, who was collating and signing work orders to be filed away.

"Slow day today", remarked Allen.

"Yeah, it kinda dragged by. I like it when there's more to do. It makes the day go faster. Feel?" responded Davis still rummaging through the orders.

"Yeah, but sometimes you need some time to catch your breath, too."

"I betta hurry up if I'ma make class on time", Davis looked up and noticed that Allen was in a rush. "You seem to be in a hurry today. Where you off to?"

"To see my friend Callie. She's the only one you haven't met yet."

"She real busy?"

"No, I just think she's mad at me, maybe all of us, about something."

"Like what?"

"I have no idea. You know how women are."

"Say no more, man, say no more."

"If we mend fences tonight maybe you'll get the chance to meet her at the Tamiko's Christmas Celebration."

"This must be some party. Tamiko's invited me like a hundred times already. I even hear Daniel's sweatin' it."

"First of all, don't let Tamiko or her mother hear you call it a "party". According to them "parties" are the work of satan for the people of the world. They have "Celebrations". Tamiko throws two big celebrations each year. She has a Christmas celebration on Christmas Eve and then she has a big Praise and Worship Celebration in April right around Easter. She puts a lot of work into both. She says she's just trying to make a way for Christian people to have some fun without getting worldly."

"So what kind of par-, I mean celebration is it?"

"I don't want to spoil it for you. You're going to have to find out when you come. But I'll tell you this. You'll be glad you came."

"Good to know. Oh, Snap! It's getting late. I have to jet."

"Okay, man I'll see you."

"See ya."

****

Allen couldn't help but feel a little nervous as he approached the brownstone where Callie lived. Allen pressed the buzzer to her apartment, and not without much reticence.

"Who is it?" He heard her ask.

"It's Allen", he answered, his voice cracking a bit. There was no buzz back. Yep, she was mad all right. Allen took out his cell phone and dialed her number.

"Hello", she answered with an attitude.

"I'm sorry, Callie. Whatever it is that you're mad about, I'm really sorry. Now could you please buzz me in so we can talk about this like two mature adults?"

"You should have called first. How dare you just drop by unannounced! How do you know if I have company or not? And what kind of apology is that if you don't even know what you're apologizing for?" Callie blared into the phone.

"You've never had a problem with me dropping by before, and how would I know what you're mad about when you're giving me the silent treatment?"

"So it took you nearly two months to figure out I was giving you the silent treatment? It took you two months to even think of coming by to see me? Really makes me feel special."

"Callie, as much as I'd like to work things out between us, I'm not going to do it from the front stoop. You can either let me in or I'm hanging up and going home."

COMMENCEMENT

Callie hung up the phone. A few tense seconds passed before Callie rang the buzzer to let Allen in. It was a two family house and Callie lived on the second floor. Allen took the stairs two at a time until he reached her apartment. He tried the door, but it was still locked so he knocked. Allen could hear her stomping toward the door in fury. All at once the door swung open.

Callie stood with one hand on her hip. She was wearing the cutest little flower print pajama set with a matching terry robe along with a very angry glower on her face. Allen couldn't help but notice that even when she was angry she was beautiful.

"Can I come in?"

"The door's open, isn't it?"

Allen maneuvered carefully past Callie into her tiny apartment. Allen hadn't been here in such a long time that at first he thought she had changed the décor, but then realized that she had only had the walls painted ice pink instead of the white he remembered. It was neat and sparsely furnished with a feminine touch. The rose-colored velvet sofa was still the same, as well as the tapestry covered armchairs, and the mahogany tables.

"I'm sorry about leaving you out of the loop. But you have to admit your part, too. If you want me to know that something's wrong, the last thing you should do is give a brother the silent treatment."

"It's not just leaving me out of the loop, Allen. For a long time now you've been taking me for granted. There have been times when I have done nothing short of walk on live coals for you and then to have you treat me like a mere acquaintance? That hurts, Allen."

"When have I ever treated you as less than a friend?"

"Like at the Election Night party. How come I was the last one to know about your job? Huh? And what about you and Tamiko and Tim having dinner together every Sunday? Every Sunday, and you don't even think of inviting me. And what about your new friend, David? When was I supposed to meet him?"

"First of all, I didn't want anyone to know about my job. My mom blurted it out when we were having dinner. Then I thought word would get back to you anyway. And maybe you would have been invited to dinner and you would have met Davis had you not decided to throw a temper tantrum and cut everybody off."

"Now you're saying I'm childish."

"Don't put words in my mouth, Callie. I didn't say that."

"Well, only children have tantrums."

"I want to make things right between us Callie! What do you want me to do?!"

"Maybe be there for me for once!"

"I'm always here for you, Callie."

"Not since you've been off on your spiritual journey. It's all about you and your God and it seems like you don't have time for anyone who's not a church going Christian."

"So that's what this is really about, isn't it? You can't deal with the fact that I want a real relationship with God."

"Allen, I could care less who or what you worship, but does it have to consume your whole life? Isn't there room for people of different faiths?"

"Callie, I'm a Christian. For a long time, I didn't know what that meant. Now I know that my life is in Christ. He is my life now. I can't and won't compromise that for anybody."

"So are you saying that we can't be friends any more?"

"That's up to you Callie. If you can respect my beliefs…"

"You mean that your way is the only way and if I don't believe in Jesus I'm going to hell? Right?"

"Could you tell me just what is so repulsive to you about believing in God and in Jesus His Son? The Buddhists believe their way is the only way, so do the Hindus, and the Muslims, but no one ever gets upset when someone espouses one of those faiths. But let someone say they're a Christian and you're ready to pillory them for what they believe."

"Maybe because Christians have used their God to sanction the senseless suffering of so many people on this planet…"

"And people of other religions haven't?"

Allen was silent for a moment. He wanted her to understand.

"Callie, why don't you come to church with me. Then maybe you'd understand…"

"Or maybe you could get me to convert? Be what you want me to be?"

"That's not what it would be about!" said Allen trying not to shout. He was losing his patience. It just seemed like he couldn't win with her. "You said you wanted to be included and then when I try to include you, you say no."

"Because again it's all about you! I have to get with your program! Why aren't you interested in what I think or believe? Why can't you be more open to me!"

"I'm open to you, Callie, but not to anything that goes against the Word of God."

"Then I guess there's no more to say then."

"Fine. If that's your choice, so be it. Remember it's your choice, not mine. If you should ever change your mind, you know where to find me."

Allen didn't want to, but as painful as it was for him, he knew he had to walk away. Never in his life had he imagined that it would come down like this between him and Callie. He had always felt that she had a deep understanding of him. There were times when they would be able to finish each other's sentences. Allen thought that things would have gotten a little bit easier after committing his life to God, but now it seemed that the opposite was true. He had just lost one of his best friends. Allen wondered just how much more he would have to lose to establish a relationship with God.

FORTY-SEVEN

Tamiko had been going over her latest round of assessments during her prep period. There had been some improvement in the children's progress, but it still wasn't on par with what other teachers at her grade level had been able to produce. She knew she was going to be roasted at the next assessment meeting, but Tamiko wasn't worried about that anymore. She now realized she had to focus on her students and think about each of them deeply, and what they needed to succeed. Thankfully the workshop Rosalyn had suggested had provided her with a lot of ideas on how to differentiate her instruction for all of her students' needs. They even gave her all kinds of classroom materials that she could use with her students. Tamiko was looking over her assessment spreadsheet when Rosalyn came in.

"Hi, Tamiko. How are assessments going?"

"Everyone has been assessed, and I've done all the write ups and entered the information into the database. I just printed out the spreadsheet. Not a lot of improvement, in spite of everything that I've been doing."

"It's going to take time, Tamiko. Don't get discouraged."

"I know. Oh, and I went to that workshop you suggested."

"Great! I was hoping to see you there, but we must have missed each other. Did you find it to be helpful?"

"Yes. You were right, I got a lot of great materials that I'm going to use with the children."

COMMENCEMENT

"But you have to know your children really well if the materials are going to be effective. Knowing your students is key. Some one can give you a tool, but if you don't know your students you won't know how you can use it."

"I know that now. That's why I've been really pouring over this grid to see how I'm going to plan the next week."

"And don't just limit yourself to the data. Think about their personalities, their likes and dislikes. For example when you're choosing a guided reading book, don't just think about the target words they'll have to decode or the strategy your going to teach. If you choose the kind of book a particular child likes to read, anything you teach will be made just that much clearer to them."

"I see. And I've even been thinking of the kind of learners they are. Like I've noticed that I have quite a few students who are kinesthetic learners like Jinelle, Sandra, and John: they have to move around and use their bodies. So I've been adding more opportunities for children to move during lessons. For starters, I've been using skywriting during word study and math, using dances and acting to explain concepts, choosing Shared Reading books that are more rhythmic and adding movements, and even just using more manipulatives in my lessons. It's even helped my ELL students who are learning English because it helps them to connect the words they are learning to concepts."

"That is wonderful! See! This is what I've been talking about. Your best teaching is going to come from what you learn about your students, not from some pre-packaged program."

"I'm starting to see where you were right before. Rosalyn, I'm sorry about the hard time I gave you at our last meeting."

"It's okay. I understood where you were coming from. This place can be crazy sometimes. If there's anything I can do to help, you let me know."

"Actually, I would love to see how you do your writing lessons. I know you use multisensory techniques, and with all my kinesthetic learners, I figured you could show me something that might help them.

Then maybe you could come and watch me to see if I'm on the right track."

"Of course. I'll talk to Nettlenerves and Booker so they can put it in the schedule."

"And can I ask you a question? I hope it doesn't seem odd. That first day that we were setting up classrooms, I came in to say hi and you were sitting in the dark on the floor…"

"Oh, that. I'm sorry. I have migraines. I know it's no excuse for being rude but I was in the midst of a horrible migraine and I wasn't feeling well at all."

"That's a relief. Wait a minute… that didn't come out right. What I mean is, I thought you were upset with me or that you didn't like me."

"Don't be silly. I try to make my decisions on a person's character after I've had a chance to get to know them. And now that I've known you for a while, I happen to think you are an intelligent and caring young woman."

"Thanks. And I'm finding out that you're definitely nothing like I've heard."

"And I can imagine that you've probably heard some things."

Both women giggled. At that moment Booker entered the room in a frantic hurry with some memos.

"Glad I caught you ladies before the period was over. Mrs. Stone and Mrs. Nettlenerves wanted everyone to be served with these personally", said Booker as she barged into the classroom.

"What's the big deal?" asked Tamiko.

"We've just heard from central. Our quality review is going to be early this year. We always used to be reviewed in late March or early April, but this year it's going to be in February. All the details are in the memo. We're going to have an emergency staff meeting about it during the lunch periods", explained Booker.

COMMENCEMENT

"I wonder why there's such a fuss. We've always done well on the Quality Review. At least for the past two years", wondered Rosalyn out loud.

"But this year they've changed everything: the process of the review, the criteria for the Well Developed rating. It's really a big shock to all the schools", continued Booker.

"This is crazy. Why would they change everything on such short notice?" asked Tamiko.

"There's not a lot in this system that makes much sense", sighed Rosalyn with an air of resignation.

"I've got to be going. I still have seven more classes to hit before lunch. Everything is in the memo. Just make sure you report for the meeting either 11:30 or 12:30 sharp in 415." said Booker backing out of the classroom with her stack of memos.

"Rosalyn, you probably know more about this more than anyone. What happens during a Quality Review?" asked Tamiko full of apprehension as well as curiosity.

"An educator from some consulting firm all the way over in England comes to our schools and judges us based on a set of criteria. They meet with the administration, some of the teachers, do a walk through of the school and visit certain classrooms. It's really intense."

"How do they decide whose classrooms to visit or which teachers to interview?"

"The principal has always chosen the classes. She'll just choose her favorite people as usual."

"That takes a lot of pressure off me. I'm probably the last teacher she wants them to see."

"But even if they're not in your room, you still have to be on your best. The reviewers watch everything. You never know what they'll notice and criticize."

"I just hope I don't turn out to be the 'weak link'."

"Don't worry about it Tamiko. You just keep focusing on your students. Teachers who get in trouble are those who aren't doing their job, and then try to fake it during the review. Those kind of teachers are very obvious because the children always give them away."

"Really?"

"Yeah, I remember this teacher a few years back named Mrs. Bowen. She's not here any more. Her classroom was a train wreck. No order, no discipline, and no learning. All the teaching was lecture based, very little independent work. Then the reviewers come and she tries to put on this act. Big fancy lesson with lots of manipulatives and time for student directed work. It totally blew up in her face. The kids weren't used to using the manipulatives and some of them were playing with them instead of using them in the way they should have been. Then one of the kids tells the reviewer that and I quote 'Today is fun. We always do workbooks, but today we get to play with the toys.'"

"You're kidding! That had to be priceless!"

"The reviewers had a field day on Stone. It was our first quality review and we only got a score of proficient because of that incident. The reviewers citing the fact that administration didn't seem to know what was going on in their own classrooms."

"Mrs. Stone probably wanted a rock to crawl under."

"And you know what made it even more embarrassing? She was one of Stone's top protégés. You see, she knew all of the jargon of the business and could talk a great deal. Stone and Nettlenerves thought she could do nothing less than walk on water. After the review, she ended up transferring to another school."

"If I were in her shoes, I think I'd want to transfer to another country."

"Then there's the other end of the spectrum. There was another teacher who was good at these "hands on" lessons, but she wasn't providing the children with a conceptual framework for their learning. The kids worked well with the tools, but they had no idea why the activities were important. Like the kids could play a rhyming game with onset and rime, but they didn't see how they could use onset and rime to help them decode words. They could play the "Get to 100" game with the hundreds chart, but couldn't explain where the tens place or the ones place was in a number. They couldn't solve addition or subtraction problems without manipulatives. And these were third graders! All the "hands on" stuff made it look like the children were learning, but they really weren't."

"I guess it takes a balance of things."

"And that's what a lot of people in our field don't get Tamiko. Everyone's caught up in how things look, and putting on a show for these educrats who are wedded to some new fad or ideology. And with every change at central there's a new ideology. I remember when readers were the rage and phonics was the key. Then they threw out the readers for the "cloze" method. Now it's balanced literacy and "hands on" learning. Here everyone has fancy charts all over the place, tons of student work on the walls, all these 'manipultives' and 'centers', but at the end of the day if it's not helping them to learn, then what good is it?"

"You're so right. And like you said, we can use a method or technique, but it will only be useful if it is effective with the student you're working with. And I'm beginning to see that there's no one method that's going to work for everybody."

"Exactly. But one thing that can't be denied no matter what, is good teaching. I do what I do regardless. If any administrator or whoever wants to question me about whatever is going on in my classroom, I'm always ready to answer based on what I know about my kids. And my kids prove me right, because in the end they're learning."

"I wish I could be so confident."

"Tamiko, I've seen a lot of teachers over the past two decades of my career. Believe me when I say you have nothing to worry about."

****

It was 11:30 and Tamiko was almost late for the big emergency meeting. When she arrived she had just enough time to scrawl her name on a sign in sheet and find a place at the crowded table and sit down. She was squished between Miss Moss and Miss Fields. Tamiko knew she wouldn't see Rosalyn here since her lunch was next period. Not soon after Tamiko was seated, Booker hurriedly closed the conference room door and Nettlenerves rose to address everyone.

"Has everyone has gotten their memo? If you've read it then you know that we are going to be having our Quality Review early this year. Now that's not such a big deal as we are always providing our students with a quality education. What is a big deal is that there are going to be some changes to the review process and to the criteria for the ratings. Charlie's going to hand out the copies of the new guidelines that I got at a Network meeting."

At Nettlenerves cue, Booker passed out copies of the Quality Review guidelines and procedures to all of the teachers. After briefly perusing the pages, Tamiko felt overwhelmed. There was so much information in such detailed technical jargon, she could hardly make out what it meant.

"We don't have time to go over everything, so I'm just going to go over what the important changes are and how they affect us. The first big change is there is no longer an "Outstanding" Rating. There are only 4 ratings Undeveloped, Undeveloped with Proficient features, Proficient, and Well Developed. Of course we're going for Well Developed. The next big change is the criteria for Well Developed. This year the department wants every child to be able to articulate a set of personal learning goals for every subject and be able to tell reviewers what their goals are. This is for every child in every grade. You will need to post these goals on a classroom goals board, and keep copies in a special goals binder. You will also need to keep track of how the students are progressing toward their personal goals."

"Even Pre-K!" asked Miss Smith, one of the pre-kindergarten teachers.

"Even Pre-K", affirmed Nettlenerves.

"But that's absurd. I could understand if the children were older. But 4, 5 and even some 6 year-olds don't understand what a goal is, much less make a bunch of them and remember them", complained one of the kindergarten teachers.

COMMENCEMENT

"And I could see if it were just one goal, but for one kid to try to remember all these different goals for all the different subjects. They're having enough difficulty learning the academic content we're teaching them and then they want to pile this on top of it", added another teacher.

"This is what's coming out of central and it's not going to change. So we've got to find a way to make it work", Nettlenerves replied.

"Maybe you could make songs out of them, that way it would be easier for the children to memorize them", suggested Booker.

"And what about the paperwork for us? A goals binder and a goals bulletin board?" the kindergarten teacher shot back.

"No one said this was going to be easy. I'm not going to have a picnic in the park either. All teachers will have to make goals as well. I'm going to have to keep these goals in a binder and keep track of your goals", Nettlenerves argued.

A lot of mumbling and disgruntled moans echoed throughout the conference room.

"There is another big change to the Quality Review which is even more important. You know that in years past, Mrs. Stone was able to choose the classrooms for visits, as well as the participants of teacher committee that would speak to the reviewer. Now it's out of our hands. Central will be providing the reviewer with a copy of our organization sheet and they will be picking classrooms at random", Nettlenerves continued.

Tamiko's hear leapt into her mouth.

"They are going to want to see our professionals across a spectrum. They will want to see one first year teacher, one seasoned professional, one cluster teacher, and a resource room specialists. The team that will be interviewed will be composed of these teachers."

"Lord, God, please let them pick Joan. Please let them pick Joan." Tamiko prayed silently to herself.

"I would like to impress upon everyone here that this Quality Review is very important, not just to the school but to the community. It is imperative that we all put our best foot forward in order to keep this building open and to continue to provide the great educational experiences to these children who need it most. Now I know that we all don't always see eye to eye, and some of you are not pleased with the procedures and policies of this organization. However, I ask that you do not use the Quality Review as tool of retaliation or to make your grievances public. Not only is it unprofessional, but there will be consequences."

Tamiko thought it was unprofessional even to bring something like this up. She was sure that no one in his or her right mind would ever use the Quality Review to settle personal grievances.

"We are going to have another meeting on Tuesday afternoon before the break. Hopefully some of you will want to volunteer for our Quality Review Team and help us prepare. In the meantime, I want you to go over the criteria rubric and the new regulations over the weekend and think of the ways in which we meet the other criteria listed, and how we can integrate these goals more seamlessly into the fabric of our school culture."

As the meeting ended Tamiko dashed back to her classroom. She needed time by herself to digest everything that she learned at the meeting. When she got back she realized that she had 15 minutes left to the period to eat her lunch, but she was way too distracted. Tamiko flopped into her teacher's chair at her desk and stared into space. They were going to pick people at random, and they were definitely going to pick a first year teacher. There was a 50 percent chance that she would be picked and that was a very good chance. She wondered when they would know who was picked. There would be nothing worse than finding out a few days before the actual Review. "You're being silly." Tamiko said to herself. "You may not even be picked and all this worry will have been for nothing. And with the way Stone and Nettlenerves feel about you, I wouldn't be surprised if they bribed someone not to pick you." But then what if she was picked? What kind of lesson would she do? What if the kids had an off day? What if she ended up making a really stupid mistake, causing the school to receive some sort of sanction? "Lord help me to leave this in your hands. Let your grace be sufficient enough for me", Tamiko prayed.

COMMENCEMENT

FORTY-EIGHT

Allen had finally worked up the courage to make the call. It had been nearly four weeks since he had heard from or seen Jim. The last time they had been together at Emily Ann's was a total disaster. He was totally wasted, and had been really rude to everyone, especially Davis. Allen had no choice at that time but to take him aside in the men's room and call him out on his drinking. Allen had begged him to talk to him about what was going on, and to get some help, but his pleas fell on deaf ears. Jim stormed out of the restaurant absolutely livid after the confrontation and cut off all contact with Allen and the others. He rarely answered texts, or emails, and when Allen called his phone it went to voice mail. Even when he went to his apartment building, he wouldn't answer the intercom. So Allen decided to give Jim his space. Maybe they needed some time apart. Allen only hoped that Jim had taken time to consider what he had said and get some help. He also hoped this phone call would not turn out the way his visit to Callie had.

Allen had racked his brain thinking of a suitable pretext for calling, but he couldn't think of one. He had thought about using Davis's situation and the upcoming meeting at Uptown Soul restaurant, but knowing how Jim felt about Davis, he didn't think that would be a good idea. So Allen just decided to take a chance with the hope that he could get Jim to open up about what was going on with him. He knew it had something to do with the death of Momma Merta. Jim and his mom were really close, and after her death, Jim began to change. First he left the church, and now he had abandoned his ambitions to become a lawyer, only to take up the bottle. Allen couldn't let his best friend in the world continue down this path without reaching out to help him, but Jim wasn't making it easy. Allen couldn't help but be a little nervous as he dialed Jim's number. "What if he was still angry?" Allen thought. Allen's anxiety was put to ease when he heard the phone ring on the other end.

"Hey, long time, no hear", answered Jim after the sixth ring.

"I know. So what's up, man?"

"Me? I'm good. Got nothin' to complain about. You?"

"Same. I was wondering if you'd be interested in meeting up with me and the guys for dinner, or if you want we could just go down to the court, and shoot hoops like old times."

"I don't know. I've been working a lot of overtime lately. I'm not in the mood for a whole lot of running around."

"C'mon, Jim. This is Allen, your boy. We go all the way back to comic books and cookies, man. I don't like the way things are between us right now. We really need to talk."

"Isn't that what we're doing?"

"Jim, you know what I mean."

"Whatever you have to say, just say it."

"Okay. If you want to do it this way, then fine: what's going on? Why have you been avoiding me lately? You rarely return calls or texts and when I come by, you pretend you're not home. What's up with that?"

Allen could hear Jim taking a deep breath during the brief pause in the conversation, and it worried him.

"I was just trying to make things easier for you, Allen."

"I don't get it, man. How can having my best friend act like a total stranger make things 'easier' for me?"

"Allen, I think you know just as well as I do that we've reached a fork in the road of our friendship. I want to go one way and you want to go another."

"Could you please stop using bad clichés for a second and explain what you're talking about? I always thought that we would be boys no matter what."

"I'm talking about the fact that we've changed. We've outgrown each other. We have different wants and different needs. You're into the church scene and I'm not and because of that, we don't really have much in common anymore."

"I've been going to church for years since you quit. You never had a problem with it before."

"You weren't as committed back then. Back then we could talk about stuff without getting into a major argument."

"It's not religion that has been causing arguments between us lately, Jim. You know that."

"And that's another thing," said Jim, bristling at Allen's implication. "You're not the same dude I grew up with! Now you're just like the church people we used to make fun of. All those sanctimonious, judgmental, know-it-all's who think they know everything about everybody. Maybe I don't want to be friends with someone like that."

"Jim, I have never stepped to you out of condescension. Anything I've said has always been out of the love a man has for his brother. Can't you see that I'm afraid of what's going to happen to you? I don't want you to end up strung out or processed through the system like some of these other brothers out here."

"It's my life Allen! And just because I'm not living it the way you think I should, doesn't mean I'm going to be a screw up!"

"I'm not asking you to live my way. I just want you to deal with what's been bothering you."

"The only thing that's bothering me right now is you! You need to stop trying to be Superman for everyone else and save yourself!"

"Jim, the last thing I want to do is be a bother to you and I didn't call just so we could get into another argument. All I want is to have my best friend back. Tell me, how can we fix this?"

COMMENCEMENT

"There are some things in this life you just can't fix."

FORTY-NINE

Tim sat nervously in the hospital waiting area. He tried to look through magazines to pass the time, but there were only the tabloid rags in which he had no interest. Tim looked back for signs of Tamiko. She said she would be here. He took a glimpse at his watch. It was only 4:07, so it wasn't that late. Tim hoped she wasn't in the wrong wing of the building looking for him. He really needed someone to talk to right now, if not but to keep his thoughts from wandering onto the morbid. Like the idea that the doctor would find something... luckily Tim didn't have time to finish this thought before Tamiko walked in through the door.

"Sorry about being late. But I had a student whose mom forgot that dismissal is at 3:00. Then there were signal problems in the tunnels." She said plopping down next to him out of breath.

"I'm just glad you're here now."

"So, how was work?"

"Now hold on. Are you ready for this?"

"What?"

"The presentation went off. And it went very well. We have a tech firm that is working on the website as we speak. And I was able to figure out the glitch in the communication between accounting and the rest of the departments."

"How?"

"I thought that what accounting could do is give every department a pin number that they would use every time they accessed the website. When the pin would be linked to their budget and if they went over

436

budget they wouldn't even be able to log onto the website. The accounting department would get like a status after every transaction and then it would feedback to the website. Everyone loved it."

"That's wonderful news! I knew everything would work out!"

"And we're still going to have to have one person in each department who oversees all of the intakes and purchases, so unfortunately the VP's of the divisions are going to have extra work. But all of the big bosses agreed that this was inevitable. The new restructuring is more of a headache than my original plan, but since Standoff gave it the go ahead and so much money was invested in it, the company has no choice but to follow through."

"And how much did Preston contribute to the project?"

"He did some work. I just found a way to use Preston's strong points to my advantage. Since he's good with the gift of gab with higher-ups, I used him as my front man. My negotiator and public relations guy."

"That's great! It would be even better if this new system wasn't going to cost you your job."

"True. And now I don't even think they're going to keep Preston either. I'm not certain, but I think they're going to have one of the tech guys from H&M to oversee the website."

"Is all the work done?"

"No. There are still some loose ends, but the important thing is we're still keeping the timetable for the new restructuring, which is the big Christmas miracle. And what about you? How are you hanging in there at the school?"

"There's good news and bad news."

"I'll take the good news first."

"The good news is that Mrs. Steele doesn't seem to be a racist after all. It was nothing but a bunch of unsubstantiated rumors. The whole time she was actually trying to help me."

"Just goes to show that you can't always judge people by appearances. I'm really glad it worked out that way."

"In the past couple of weeks, she's been really helping me with the students. She's got a lot of great ideas. If I hadn't been such an idiot, I probably would have learned a lot sooner."

"Speaking of the kids, how are they doing?"

"Better, but still not as well as everyone else's."

"Every class is different. Just give the kids some time."

"That's what Rosalyn says."

"Besides, if you could help Davis get an B+, you certainly should be able to help these kids."

"Cut Davis some slack. He may not have gone to Harvard, but he's a very bright guy. He's just had some unfortunate experiences. I'm sure if he had wealthy parents he probably would have been one of your classmates."

"I'm sure. So, is that all the good news?"

"Pretty much. The bad news is there's going to be a review of our school a whole two months earlier than expected. They go through the classrooms and watch the teachers. There's even a group interview. It's really intense."

"Sounds stressful. Is it like a whole committee that's coming?"

"No, it's just one person, but they hold the fate of the school in their hands."

"Now that's scary. When is it going to happen?"

"February. Just before the midwinter recess."

"That's not that far away."

"I know. And the worst part is that they want to look at different teachers from across the spectrum of professionals. They definitely want to pick a first year teacher and there are only two: me and Joan."

"There's still a chance you may not be picked."

"But what if I am?"

"Tamiko, as long as I've known you, you've always been top notch at everything you do. I think you'll be fine."

"That's just it. All my life I've been so used to things being easy for me, but teaching, real teaching, is hard."

"It's hard, but not impossible. Especially when there's someone greater than you in control of it all who's looking out for you."

"Where's this coming from?" Tamiko asked in surprise.

"From you."

"What?"

"After all, that's what you'd always say when you were reassuring me or Allen or the others when things weren't going right in our lives. For a while I thought it was because you were naïve, but then I realized that wasn't it. I used to look at you and think, 'Man, she is always so confident about who she is without being arrogant, so positive, and always hopeful.' Now I think I know where that comes from."

"You do?"

"I wish I had what you do."

"Maybe you already have it."

"I'm not so sure. If I did I wouldn't be as nervous as I am now."

"I don't think there's anything to be nervous about. The worst thing they could probably find is a stomach ulcer. If that's the case, the doctor will just prescribe a change in diet and maybe some medicine to heal the ulcer."

"I just hope you're right. They're supposed to do an endoscopy on me today. You know when they put that tube down your throat with the little camera on the end and look around inside your stomach and everywhere."

"That doesn't sound like it's going to be fun."

"Tell me about it. They'll probably give me an anesthesia or a sedative or something. If I seem out of it, could you help me get home.

When we get to my place you can drop me off and take my car home. I'll pick it up in the morning."

"You didn't even have to ask, of course I will. And I don't need the car. I can take a cab back. It shouldn't be that late when we get done here."

"Now I won't hear of that. I don't want to have to worry about you in some strange cab all by yourself."

"I'm a big girl. I can take care of myself."

"You don't look all that big. You can't be more than 5'2, and 100 pounds soaking wet."

"Just because I'm small doesn't mean I'm totally defenseless. I know Karate. I took it for my phys-ed requirement at Spellman."

"Well excuse me, Ms. Dangerous. But I'd still feel better if you took the car."

"Fine."

"Excuse me, Mr. Russell?" asked the nurse interrupting their conversation.

"Yes?"

"You can go on back. The doctor is ready for you."

Tamiko and Tim exchanged glances before Tim headed off with the nurse to see the doctor. When he and the nurse disappeared behind the nurse's station, Tamiko bowed her head and prayed.

"Heavenly Father, be with my friend Tim and help him through the examination. Lord, we know that by your stripes we are healed from all our infirmities. If there be any illness in his body I ask you to heal it. In the name of Jesus, I pray. Amen."

FIFTY

Allen sat in a booth at the Uptown Soul restaurant waiting for the others to arrive. This was a new hangout that Allen had scouted out and he hoped that everyone would be able to find it. He had sent out texts to all of his remaining friends now that Jim and Callie had put him on their "no friend" list. He told everyone to meet him here at 7:00, but he didn't get many responses to his text. Allen had only heard definitive responses from Tamiko, and surprisingly enough Richard. Astonishingly, the first person to show up was the last person he would have expected.

"Hey, Big Al, Whassup!"

"You're here and early at that!"

"Yeah, man. I had to get away from da crib. I love Leandra and all, but she's startin' to wear a brother out."

"What's wrong? I thought she might be the one."

"Yeah, the one to drive me crazy. She's jus' too clingy man. It's like she tryin' to have me on Lojack and what not. She got to know everywhere I go and everything I do. I mean jus' all up in my business. I need some breathin' room, yo."

"Funny, she didn't strike me as that type of girl."

"Me neither man. I thought these educated chicks was suppost to be independent. Not! I'm tellin' ya I feel like I'm gonna have to cut her loose. Soon."

"If it's as you say I can't blame you, man."

"So what's this big meeting about?"

441

"It's about a friend that needs our help. I'll explain it more when the others get here. If they get here."

Tim and Tamiko walked in on cue just as Allen had finished his sentence. They were arm in arm, with Tim wearing the same haggard expression that Allen had gotten used to seeing by now.

"Hey, everybody." Tim said hoarsely.

"Hey, man. Are you okay?" asked a concerned Allen.

"I'm still a little foggy from the medicine they gave me at the doctor yesterday and my throat is kind of scratchy from the procedure, but I'll be okay." Tim managed sounding a bit hoarse.

"So what happened? Did they find out what was wrong?"

"They did some tests, but so far it's all been inconclusive."

"What dey testin' you for, man? It ain't nothin' somebody could catch, is it?" Richard asked moving his chair over.

"No." Tim said flatly, rolling his eyes.

"They were checking to see if it's stomach ulcers. But it isn't." explained Tamiko.

"Yeah, they already ruled that out. They did an endoscopy on me and they didn't see any evidence of ulcers", added Tim.

"If it's not stomach ulcers, what else could it be?" asked Allen.

"I don't know. I guess I'll find out soon enough. Anyway, I'm curious as to why you called us all down here."

"Let's order first before we get down to business."

Allen signaled for a waitress. She took their orders quickly and left the party, which resumed their original conversation.

"Wait a minute. This is all of us? What about Davis, and Jim and Callie?" asked Tim.

"Jim and Callie don't want to hang any more. Especially, not with me", answered Allen sadly.

"Word? What's up wit dat, man?" Richard asked.

"Jim has decided that we need to go separate ways. Callie feels the same way."

"But y'all was boys, man! Like blood!"

"And I always had the feeling that Callie was sort of your female half. What gives?" inquired Tim.

"They're not too thrilled about my choice to have a relationship with God."

"I can't believe they cuttin' you off over somethin' like dat! That's just triflin'!" exclaimed Richard.

"I can believe it, especially after the way Jim's been acting lately. Sometimes things like this happen. Christ said he did not come to bring peace, but a sword..." said Tamiko shaking her head.[1] "And what about Davis? Why isn't he here?"

"Because the meeting's about him. He and his family need our help. That's why I called you all here today", Allen replied.

"What he need?" asked Richard with some concern.

"Uh, Al, this doesn't have anything to do with what we were talking about the other night? Does it?" asked Tim uneasily.

"Yes it does. You see, Davis' mom took out a second mortgage on their house to get some money she desperately needed. Now she can't afford to pay it back and she stands to lose the house."

"How much does she owe on the house?" inquired Tamiko.

"I don't know. Davis never told me."

"So what's your plan, Al? Where do we fit in?" asked Richard with some reservation.

"I was hoping that we could all contribute to a fund that I could manage and invest. When it turns over, we could give it to Davis so his mom can pay off the mortagage. Each of us can contribute say, $2,000.00. I could probably get some money from my parents and Tamiko's parents as well. We could even get the church involved to help too."

"Whoa, wait, hold the phone…what happened with the whole, 'I'm going to help Davis restructure the loan with the bank' plan?" asked Tim.

"I pitched the idea to him, but he won't let me."

"Are you saying he'd rather have the money instead?" Tim questioned further.

"No. He insisted that I stay out of it altogether", answered Allen.

"So how about we go with that plan and stay out of it", suggested Tim.

"We can't. He's our friend. And I think this is what God wants me to do."

"Maybe Allen's right. As Christian people, we should be looking out for each other's needs. Like the Bible says: how can we say that we love God and see a brother in need and turn away?" Tamiko offered.

"But we don't even know how much they owe. It could be hundreds of thousands of dollars! And let's say you get enough money for the initial investment. You don't know when the money is due. The house could be in the process of foreclosure as we speak. And even if it wasn't, do you really think you have enough time to turn over the investment before the bank forecloses on them?" reasoned Tim.

"And I don't know about evybody else, but $2,000.00 is a lot of cheese. Davis is cool and evything, but I don't know", said Richard doubtfully.

"I thought you said you stay paid", sneered Tim.

"I do. That's because I don't be shellin' it out", responded Richard.

"We've got to do something!" Allen pleaded.

"But is this the best thing? I really want to give Davis the benefit of the doubt, but I think we're all being suckered into a ghetto ponzi scheme", argued Tim.

"You think Davis is goading Allen into this? No way!" said Tamiko.

"And give me some credit, too, Tim. Do I really seem that stupid?"

444

"O.K. Fine. I'll bite. I will give you $2,000.00 to invest in Davis', or rather his mom's mortgage troubles. No, just to show how magnanimous I can be I will give you double that. Now, when you have all the money together and flip it to give to Davis, let's see if coincidentally he happens to leave town soon after. Any other takers?" offered Tim.

There was silence as the others pondered over the commitment to making such a large contribution.

"Oh, come on. Am I going to be the only one? After all, Davis is such a great guy", goaded Tim with his trademark sarcasm.

"I'll give. And I'll ask my parents, too", resolved Tamiko.

"Aiight. I'm in", Richard said resignedly. "But how you gon flip it man?"

"I've been watching some stocks and I've been researching the companies, and I think I know what to invest it in. All I need is just one or two quarters to double the investment."

"Sound real risky, Al", cautioned Richard.

"There's no gain without risk."

"Stocks are a big gamble. It's like you'll be taking our money to a casino!" exclaimed Tamiko.

"Now I know this is a ghetto ponzi scheme", sighed Tim.

"Just relax guys. I know what I'm doing."

"Yeah, that's probably what Madoff told his investors, too", Tim added.

"And we've got to keep this thing quiet. I don't want Davis to find out until we have the money together."

"I have an idea! Let's not wait until Allen invests the money. Maybe when we have the initial investment, we can let Davis know. It will be like a Christmas gift. We can present it to him at my Christmas Celebration." Tamiko proposed.

"I don't know. I'd rather wait until we had everything together."

"I second Tamiko's idea. After all, Al, what if your investment scheme doesn't work out? Then everyone's contribution goes down the tubes", said Tim in agreement with Tamiko.

"Don't you have faith in my abilities?" asked Allen.

"As much as I love you, Al, no. And you can't blame me. This is potentially tens of thousand of dollars you're going to be handling, and not just our money, but possibly some of the church's money, too."

"Yeah, Al, I don't always agree wit' red bone here, but he's got a point. It's not like you got a lot of sperience wit' da stocks", Richard put in.

"Now you guys sound like a lot of those people I interviewed with."

"Al, when you were interning, you had the pros to spot you. You're going to be flying solo on this. Do you really think you're ready? I mean you don't even have your broker's license!" continued Tim.

"What if I worked with your man Sherman to invest it. Would that make everyone feel better?"

"Now that would make me feel better. But you do realize Sherman's not into get rich quick schemes, so we can't expect our investment back after just two quarters. And remember, his skills don't come cheap. He's going to want 10% of any of the profits. That has to be factored in."

"Who's Sherman?" asked Tamiko.

"He's my family's financial manager."

"He any good?" asked Richard.

"If he wasn't I don't think I'd be living at the New Towers and driving a brand new Mercedes, now would I?"

"O.K. I'm wit' the flippin' so long a you use Tim's man Sherm."

"But you just heard Tim. Sherman's not going to be able to pull it off in time", whined Allen.

"Which goes back to my original suggestion. Let's just take up the collection and give him whatever we get. It may not pay off the whole mortgage, but it should buy his family some time until they can come up with a long term plan."

"Again, I think that's the best idea I've heard all evening. No offense Al."

"None taken. All right, let's vote. All in favor of just giving Davis the initial collection."

Tim, Tamiko, and Richard raised their hands in favor.

"I guess I'm out numbered 3 to 1."

"Oh, this is going to be wonderful! I'm going to tell Daddy as soon as I get home."

"When's the deadline to pony up da cheese", asked Richard.

"It'll have to be at least a few days before the party. How about next Friday."

"Okay. No prob."

"And remember, keep this under your hats. I don't want Davis to find out before the party."

"Oh, but I'm just bursting with excitement….I think we can handle it, Al", scoffed Tim.

"I can't wait to see Davis's face when he get's his gift."

FIFTY-ONE

"That's it for today everyone. Next week, we'll be looking through the book of first Samuel and continuing our study of what it means to be an obedient servant to God." said Daniel closing today's Brotherhood Bible Study Session. Allen was too preoccupied by his own thoughts to hear anything Daniel said. Allen was still reeling from the disappointment of not being able to invest the money he was collecting for Davis' mortgage payoff. He thought that this was what God wanted him to do: to use his skills and abilities in finance to help Davis. Now he had been relegated to just collecting money. He felt like he was going out of the will of God, and that he was on the brink of failing his 'mission'. Allen didn't want to have to keep working at the Sheraton any longer than he had to and he felt that if he failed his mission, God would leave him there indefinitely. Allen needed some guidance with this situation.

"Hey Al, you ready?" asked Davis nudging him into the present moment.

"What? Oh? Is it over?"

"Yeah, where was you?"

"I guess I was thinking about something?"

"Yeah, Daniel was laying down some real deep stuff. Especially when he was talkin' 'bout how obedience requires submission and puttin' yo'self aside. Like the things you want that you think is good for you because God knows what's better. I know what that's like."

"I hear you."

"You sure? You seem kinda out of it."

"There's just something that's bothering me."

"You still ain't heard nothin' from God yet?"

"That's the problem. I'm not sure."

"The Pastor's still here. Maybe you could talk to him about it."

"You know what, that might not be a bad idea."

"Yeah, I think I saw him go into his office earlier. You could go up and see."

"Are you sure? This might take some time."

"Don't sweat it, man. I'll meet you at Miko's, aiight."

"Okay, see you there."

Allen left Davis and headed upstairs to the offices. He was about to knock on the door when he heard voices and footsteps approaching. Then all at once the door opened.

"Thank you for your time pastor, I really appreciate it", said a familiar voice.

"Any time, Tim. I'm just so glad you've decided…Oh, Allen I didn't see you there."

Allen was stupefied.

"Tim what are you doing here? I thought you left with Tamiko a while ago."

"Oh…well…She went home to help her mother with dinner, and so I just thought I might have a word with the pastor about a personal matter."

"Really?!"

"Yes. And what brings you to my office, Allen?"

"I guess the same as Tim. I also had something rather personal to discuss with you."

"In that case, I'll just excuse myself. Thanks again, Pastor. I'll see you all at dinner."

"Any time, Tim. See you at dinner." said Pastor Bynum bidding Tim farewell. When Tim was out of sight, the Pastor turned his attention to Allen. "Come in, Allen. I guess I have few moments to spare. What's on your mind?"

"To put it simply, I feel like I'm moving out of the will of God."

"And what makes you think that?"

"A couple of weeks ago, I got this feeling that God put me at the Sheraton for a reason and I think that reason was to meet Davis and help him with his need."

"Oh, yes. Tamiko has told me all about it, and the fundraiser you're doing. I'm willing to contribute needless to say."

"Thank you, sir. But did she tell you that I wanted to invest the money so that Davis would be able to pay off the whole mortgage? No one trusts me enough to handle it. I believe that God wants me to use my skills to help Davis. I think he may even want me to use this gift to help other people who are in need financially."

"How do you know for certain that God wants you to do this? What did you hear from him exactly?"

"There was no booming voice from above, but I got this feeling. And then when I started thinking about it, it all made sense."

"Really, and how would you go about investing this money for Davis?"

"You see, I've been following some stock picks for a while now…"

"*You've* been following some stock picks. Did God reveal to you what to invest in?"

"I think He did. I noticed some patterns occurring…"

"Again it's all about *you*, Allen."

"What are you trying to say, Pastor Bynum?"

"I'm trying to say that when we are waiting for God to speak we have to be careful and make sure that we are listening to Him and not our own desires, wishes, or reasoning."

"So you don't think this is the leading of his Spirit?"

"Again, Allen, only you can be certain of that. But let me tell you this. When God wants you to do something, when he speaks to you, he will give you direction. If he wanted you to invest this money for Davis, he would show you what to do with it. You wouldn't have to figure it out on your own."

"But don't we have some agency even in His will?"

"We do. We can believe what He says and act on it. When we try to figure it out for ourselves we just mess up. Look at what happened when Sarai reasoned that the child God had promised her would have to come through Hagar.[1] And again, think about what happened when Moses reasoned the way to deliver the Israel was by the strength of his own arm. He slew the Egyptian and then had to go on the run and spend forty years in Midian.[2] And finally think about what happened when Saul did not destroy all the belongings of the Philistines, but reasoned that he could use the sheep and the goats for a sacrifice."[3]

"I see. But I know that Davis and I were meant to meet each other. I know that I have a lot of good skills in finance that I'm not using. Then comes Davis with this situation. There's just too much here for this to be just circumstance."

"Allen, God put you at the Sheraton, and yes he may have wanted you to meet Davis. But there may be another reason he put you there as well. It may have to do with the work you are doing. Did you ever think of that?"

"I still don't get why God would want me to be a porter? Why allow me to get a Harvard degree in finance if this is what he wants me to do with my life?"

"This is what he is allowing for now, Allen. Eventually you will see where your degree will come in. Concentrate on what God wants you to do right now. That's the first step towards coming into promises for the future."

"That's what I thought I was doing."

"I think you need to spend more time in prayer. You may want to consecrate yourself through fasting even. I could even tarry with you in the Upper Room if you want."

"I'm not sure I want to go there yet."

"Just think about it Allen."

"I'll do that." Allen looked at his watch. "Speaking of tarrying, I think we've tarried a bit too long here already. It's almost time for dinner."

"You're right. Mother Rose will have a fit if we're not there on time. She came down pretty hard on Tamiko a while back. And I know she'll do the same to me."

"I guess we better be going then."

"You said it."

FIFTY-TWO

Jim was lying in a small boat on a placid stream drifting. There was a lulling breeze, and the sun warmed his body. Jim had never felt a peace like this before. Then he began to hear something in the distance. It was the sound of rushing water. Jim sat up in the boat. It was the falls! Jim took the paddles that lay next to him and tried to row away from them, but it was too late. His boat was caught up in the strong current that was pulling him closer to the edge. Then all of a sudden, a pair of hands sprang up on the side of the boat, tearing off pieces of it. Water began to flood in. Jim tried to fight with the hands.

"Stop it!" screamed Jim "Get off! You'll kill us both!"

The water continued to come in. At this rate, Jim would end up drowning before he even got to the edge of the falls. The hands kept clawing, the boat continued to fall apart and Jim sank deeper into the water and went under.

"NOOOOOO!"

Jim opened his eyes in darkness once again. He could barely remember the details of the past few hours. Everything was hazy. He sat up on the edge of a bed and tried to think, through the buzzing in his head. Slowly things started coming back to him. The last thing he remembered was that he was at home when he got a phone call from Callie. This time she was worse than the first time she called him. She was absolutely hysterical...something about Allen walking out. Then he came over. He brought some Alize, which had recently become her favorite drink. They drank and talked...he comforted her through her pain...

Jim flinched and looked around. He wasn't alone in the room. There was someone in the bed beside him. He wanted to find the light and turn it on, but he was afraid of what he might find. Jim went to the window of the room and opened the blinds a bit to let in some light from the moon and the street lamps outside. As he surveyed the room in the darkness, he slowly realized where he was and what had happened. He had to get out of there.

Jim, still a bit inebriated, did his best to gather his clothes and dress in the darkness as quietly as he could. His hands were shaking as he struggled to button his shirt. He found his jeans and jumped into them. Checking the pockets he found his cell phone, wallet, and his keys. That was a big relief. He couldn't find his socks but he did find his boots, however, he didn't put them on. Instead, he crept quietly across the carpeted floor to the bedroom door turned the knob slowly and eased on out. In the living room, he bumped into the coat rack where he found his coat, hat, and scarf. He didn't bother putting them on either, but carried them out in the hallway. Once he was outside the apartment, he finished dressing and dashed down the steps and kept going until he was outside the building.

It was still dark. Jim checked his cell phone for the time. 4:30am. He had to go to work in about two hours.

"Nothing may have happened, after all." Jim tried to persuade himself "I was way too drunk for anything to have happened. Probably just fell asleep, like the last time."

Jim walked on faster and faster until he reached the train station. He hopped onto the first D train that came by and took it to 145th street. Then he went home, quickly showered and changed. Jim ended up leaving for work at his usual time. He was lucky to have awakened when he did because he remembered his boss' warning. Jim was walking a fine line at work. When he came in on that fateful Monday, Jim's boss had given him a formal reprimand. Even though Jim was now a union worker and didn't foresee himself losing his job anytime soon, he could be suspended if he didn't straighten up. He had been present and accounted for on time now for nearly a week, and he didn't want to lose his momentum. He was trying to keep his shirt tucked in. Things were going good until last night.

COMMENCEMENT

On the subway ride to the station, Jim tried to put what happened last evening out of his mind and tried to think about the day ahead of him. He was thinking of how good it would be to be driving his regular route with no interruptions, signal problems or the like. Jim was thinking about where he would go for lunch, when he heard that voice again. That old nagging voice.

"You know you really messed up this time."

"Shut up! Nothing happened! It couldn't have. I was way too drunk."

"So what happened to your clothes, then?"

"I said shut up! I don't have time for this right now."

"You know Allen really liked her."

"If he liked her he wouldn't have treated her the way he did. He wouldn't have taken her for granted, or walked away from her."

"Still, you remember what Allen told you. Just you and no one else."

"That was a long time ago. People change, feelings change. How do you explain that chick he went to the Election Night party with, then?"

"You knew that was over before it started. Now let's tally the damages. You have no friends, no family, you're stuck in an unsatisfying job which you just may lose because can't seem to get your act together, and who knows what will come of certain recent developments. Especially if certain people got word of it. I don't even need to mention all of the bad 'habits' you've picked up lately. It's a good thing your mother isn't here to see what you've become."

"Shut up! Leave me alone!"

"How can I? Look what you're doing to yourself!"

"I'm not doing anything that no one else hasn't done before. I'm human. I can make a few mistakes, can't I? I haven't really messed things up that bad."

"Not yet, anyway."

"What do you mean by that? I've got my life in control. I'm holdin' it down on the job. As long as I got some money comin' in what does all that other stuff doesn't matter?"

"You mean like Callie? Is that all she is to you? Other stuff?"

"She's a big girl, and she's not stupid."

"You made a promise to her though. Don't you think she'd be devastated if you broke that promise? What if she did something desperate because…"

The voice kept talking, but Jim tried not to listen. The voice just made him feel ashamed, guilty, and depressed. It was not that the voice wasn't right, but Jim felt helpless in the face of its accusations. He didn't feel that there was anything that he could do to change things. Just when Jim thought he was doing the right thing, he'd end up doing something that was wrong. No matter how hard he tried to take control of his life, something would happen that he didn't foresee. His actions would cause a chain reaction leading to events that would totally blind side him. Jim needed help, but he didn't know where to turn.

Soon Jim was at his stop. He got off the train and reported to the station office to punch in and get his equipment for work. Then he boarded the train that was idling in the station. Jim put the train in gear and did his standing break tests. He checked his watch. The train would not be leaving for another few minutes. Jim stood staring down into the dark tunnel as he waited. He thought back to when he was a child, and how frightened he used to be of the dark. Momma would always let him sleep with her and even then he needed a night light. Jim used to believe that the devil was the ruler of all darkness and that he would use the cover of darkness to sneak in and steal Jim's soul. Jim no longer believed in the devil. At least he thought he didn't. But he was still afraid of darkness. Jim had been fighting a darkness that had slowly been wrapping itself around him. It seemed the harder he fought, the tighter its grip took hold of him.

Jim was startled by the loud, sharp noise from the radio.

"You're clear", the dispatcher said.

COMMENCEMENT

Jim started up the train and turned on the automated announcer. Then he punched the signal and headed out into the tunnel. Jim felt a lot better now that the train was in motion. He could focus on the task at hand: keeping his train running, monitoring the signals and turns. It was predictable. Even when there were disruptions, they were always dealt with using the same predictable permutation of possibilities. This job was the only thing that Jim had left. His tiny hold on sanity. It seemed to be the only place where he could shut everything out, where nothing could touch him. He was in control here. "I'll call Callie, a little later. I'll leave a message on her cell phone and explain everything." This thought made Jim feel a little better about the situation he had walked away from earlier. Then another voice began to speak.

"Callie's a grown woman. She knows the deal. I don't think she's gonna read nothin' into it."

"Yeah, it's not like she's new to the game. She's been around."

"And who cares about anyone finding out. You don't run with that set anymore, so what does it matter?"

"I can't be bothered with analyzing every move I make. Life is sloppy. Sometime you get good and sometimes there's bad. You just deal."

"That's right."

"No, it's not right." the other voice interrupted.

"No! You can't be here! I won't listen!"

"Look where you're going!"

Jim accelerated the speed of the train as if he could outrun the voices in his head. Then he heard a call from the radio.

"Slow down there's a local train crossing in front of you."

The operator of the crossing local train honked his horn loudly. Jim jerked out of his trance and put on the brakes, which made a loud squeal that resounded throughout the tunnel. He could feel the car shift as the force pushed him forward. Any passengers who were standing in the other cars were most likely thrown to the floor. Jim was shaken, not by the accident that had almost occurred, but that his solitude within the tunnels could be disturbed. As he waited for the oncoming train to pass, Jim bowed his head and tried to collect his composure. Soon the train had passed and supervision had given Jim the all clear. His hands shook as he put the train into gear again. He started off slowly, leading the train into station up ahead. Jim couldn't do his job like this. He needed to calm down. He needed an escape from the voice that seemed to follow him everywhere, and now even into his inner sanctum. But what would he find and where would he find it?

FIFTY-THREE

Allen took his first personal day off to tend to the collection of donations to help his friend Davis. He had just arrived at the bank to open an account and deposit all of the money. Tim had made good on his promise to give double the required amount, and he had also gotten contributions from Richard, Tamiko, his parents, the Bynums, Daniel, and even Mr. Hardy from the hotel. So far he had a grand total of $18,000.00, which wasn't a bad haul. If they were still making payments on the mortgage of $6,000.00 per month as Davis had intimated earlier, then this would hold the bank off for at least another three months. Pastor Bynum was in the process of approaching the church board about setting up a fund that would not only contribute some more money to Davis' fund, but would also help other members of the church who were facing foreclosure on their homes as well. It seemed Allen's idea was being expanded upon, after all. This was definitely the hand of God.

Thanks to automated and online banking, the bank wasn't crowded at all and Allen was able to complete his transaction without any hassle. His task being finished, he decided to call Tim to see what he was doing since he was the only one on vacation. Being a teacher, Tamiko wouldn't get out until nearly the last minute, and Richard was trying to get in a few more hustles before the season was over. After exiting the bank and finding a nearby bench to sit on, Allen made his call. Tim answered after several rings.

"Tim Russell, speaking."

"Hey, Tim. It's Al."

"Hey, Al. How's it doin'?"

"Good. How's the vacation so far?"

"Restful. I've been sleeping a lot if nothing else."

"I didn't wake you? Did I?"

"No, I've been up for a little bit. I don't want to get used to sleeping in too late."

"You feel like hanging out?"

"Hanging out? Aren't you at work?"

"Not today. I took a personal day to deposit the money for 'the Davis Fund'. Now that I'm done, I've got all this free time on my hands and I thought maybe we could hang out."

"Okay. What do you have in mind?"

"I never really gave it much thought. Anyway it's your vacation, what do you want to do?"

"Let me think…It's kind of early…oh, I know! Tamiko promised to go Christmas shopping with me later if I picked up some stuff for her party. You want to go hunting for party supplies?"

"You mean 'celebration' supplies don't you? Sure, why not?"

"Give me some time to get dressed and find the list she gave me and we'll meet up. Where are you right now?"

"At the Carver Bank over on 3rd."

"Come on over to my place. I should be ready by the time you get here."

"Okay. See ya."

Allen hung up the phone and headed over to the New Towers.

****

The New Towers was on the other side of Harlem and Allen wished he could've taken his mom's car instead of public transportation. The only way to get to Tim's from the bank was the cross-town bus, which

460

usually took forever. Allen had to wait 20 minutes for the bus to show up and then the ride itself took 30 minutes because of all of the traffic and congestion. The bus was crowded, of course, so he had to stand all the way. When Allen finally arrived he felt like he had been through a marathon. Allen managed to drag himself through the lobby where Bradley greeted him with his usual cheerful pleasantries.

"Good morning, Mr. Sharpe."

"Good morning, Bradley."

"I'll page Mr. Russell for you."

Bradley dialed Tim's number. "Mr. Russell? Mr. Sharpe has arrived. Very good, sir." The call completed, Bradley hung up the phone.

"He'll be right down."

"Thanks, Bradley."

"My pleasure, sir."

Allen went to have a seat in the waiting area. No matter how many times Allen came here, he was always in awe at how refined Tim's building was. The doorman was always so polite and formal. There were so many amenities like the elegant waiting room he was sitting in complete with sofas, coffee tables, magazines, a vending machine, and a water cooler. There was also a gym, a swimming pool, a restaurant and catering facility on the top floor, a terrace, and a garden. In addition, there was always some local celebrity that could be found visiting or living here. On previous occasions, Allen had seen two very important African-American politicians, and a few actors and actresses he hadn't seen on T.V. in a while. It was also the home to many black elites who were doctors, dentists, lawyers, architects, therapists, and other white-collar professionals. Allen hoped to live here one day, but his present situation caused him to doubt that possibility. Allen was considering whether or not to grab a quick snack from the vending machine when Tim finally made it down. He was very casually dressed with his grey fleece jacket, wrinkled orange and grey plaid shirt, jeans and grey dress sneakers. Not to mention some strange-looking tortoise shell glasses.

"Sorry to keep you waiting. I had trouble finding that list Tamiko gave me."

"What's with those glasses, man? What happened to your old wire-rimmed jobs?"

"I couldn't find them. So it's back to these. I haven't worn them since high school."

"I hope you find your other ones. Soon. Those make you look like Urkel with a chemical peel."

"Hilarious. Let's get rolling, we may have a lot of different stores to hit because I'm not sure we'll be able to get everything at one place."

"I think we could get everything at Party City down on third."

"I don't think they sell dessert boxes at Party City."

"Dessert boxes?! I guess Tamiko's going upscale this year, huh?"

"You know she tries to outdo herself every year."

"I guess it's going to be Pier One or one of those other stores."

"I think I know where to go. Let's head out."

Allen and Tim took the latter's Mercedes and began their scavenger hunt for party goods. They ended up going to about five different places before they were through. Then they stopped to have lunch at one of those fancy grills that Tim liked to frequent.

"I don't know Tim this place is a little pricey for my taste."

"Relax, it's on me."

The waiter came and took their orders. Allen ordered a cheeseburger with sweet potato fries and a cola, while Tim decided on chicken soup and ginger ale.

"Still not feeling well, huh?"

"No. It's really bad in the mornings. That's when I'm puking my guts out. After that there's just a low grade nausea that's sort of off and on throughout the day."

"All that and the doctor didn't find anything wrong with your stomach? Maybe you need a second opinion."

"Maybe. But there have been other things. Like headaches. And now I think my vision is starting to give out on me."

"Seems like you've stressed yourself out so much, your body is falling apart. Hear anything back on those tests yet?"

"The blood test was normal, so was the urine test and all the other basic stuff. They want me to come back in a few weeks for a CT scan and an MRI."

"Isn't that like when they look at your brain."

"Yeah."

"You don't think..."

"I don't know what to think, Allen."

For a few moments there was silence between them. The waiter came and served them their food, but neither one of them had much of an appetite anymore.

"Maybe it's a hormone thing."

"If it was, it would have shown up in the blood test."

"It could also be psychological. Like some kind of stress response."

"Could be. I hope so, anyway."

"It would have to be. You're the healthiest guy I know. You swim, you play tennis, and you eat better than most guys."

"I'm not sure if it's that simple, Al."

"Come on man, don't start with the negative talk. Like my mom says don't start claiming negative stuff. If the doctor hasn't said it's anything serious yet, don't worry about it."

"You're right. I'm not going to worry about that bridge until I cross it. Besides, the holidays are here. It's time to be merry and all that stuff. Right?"

"And have you made any plans to go away?"

"No. I've got no one to go with. You're working. Tamiko certainly wouldn't go unless her parents were chaperoning, and I don't know Davis well enough to invite him, not that I'm that desperate. Callie and Jim have us on the blacklist. And Richard...I wouldn't even go to the corner store with him."

"But what about your family?"

"Are you kidding me? You have noticed that we're not exactly the Winslows."

"You all make it a big deal to spend Christmas together. Why not go away together?"

"Because the more time we spend around each other, the better the chance that there's going to be some kind of conflict, especially since my mother is a control freak and my sister is a drama queen. In fact, the last time we went on an extended vacation together, we ended up in family therapy for months afterward."

"Sorry to hear that, man."

"Not as sorry as I was living through it. Besides, I'd rather stay in the city anyway. You guys are here, I get to have great Sunday dinners with the Pastor, and there's always something to do."

"Speaking of the Pastor. What were you two talking about last Sunday?"

"Now that's a personal matter?"

"Too personal even for me?"

"Even for you."

"I hope it's something good."

"Well, it's nothing bad. Whoa, time flies", said Tim checking his watch. "I gotta pick up Tamiko. Sorry to cut this short Al, but I don't want to be late."

"I'm starting to notice that you two have been spending a lot of time together."

"So? We're friends. We're supposed to spend a lot of time together."

COMMENCEMENT

"Are you sure about that? The way you looked when Tamiko started gushing about Davis during Sunday dinner..."

"I told you. I just worry about her that's all. None of us knows Davis that well."

"He's good peeps, man."

"I'm not entirely sure. Let's just see what happens when he gets his Christmas Eve surprise."

FIFTY-FOUR

Christmas Eve had finally arrived, and not without a lot of fanfare for Tamiko. Since her first day of vacation was literally the day of the celebration, she had to hustle and make a lot of last minute preparations. Tamiko really did thank God for Tim's kindness in picking up all of her celebration supplies. Allen helped her make place cards and gift baskets the night before, too. That left Tamiko with just a few hours to decorate and help her mother prepare all of the food. Tamiko had been up since 5:00am working tirelessly with her mother in the church kitchen making all of the desserts. First there was the gingerbread nativity scene, then the famous chocolate covered star cookies and angel cookies that would go in the dessert boxes the guests would be able to take home. Next, the 4-layer vanilla and strawberry birthday cake with white icing and strawberry filling between the layers, and the banana pudding had to be made. Finally, there was the signature chocolate mousse. After the desserts were finished, they had to work on decorating the church hall. Her father and Daniel had moved all of the furniture to its appropriate spots and Tamiko and her mother put up the fancy curtains and the streamers, set up the tables for the gift boxes and dessert boxes, put tablecloths on all of the tables in the dining area with the attendant center pieces and place cards. The stuff for the sound system was in the corner. Jim would usually stop by early and set it up for her, but this year Allen would have to do it. Tamiko tried not to think about Jim. She did miss him terribly. He was not only a big brother to Allen, but to her as well. She couldn't believe that after all those years growing up together, he was no longer going to be in her life. Well, then again….maybe she could. The last time they were together, Jim was horrible to Davis, and everyone else for no reason. Not to mention he smelled like a brewery. Tamiko suspected what might be going on with Jim, but she knew she couldn't help him with his problem. All she could do is pray that God change his heart and open his eyes to what was happening. And right now she didn't have time to dwell on it too long. There was just too much to do.

Once the hall was decorated, Tamiko moved on to helping her mother with the main course: baked salmon steaks with rosemary and lemon marinade, steamed vegetable medley, and rice pilaf. Next, the hor'deovres had to made. There would only be three kinds: cheese puffs, shrimp cocktails, and fish cakes. After everything was prepared, the china had to be washed and the place settings had to be set at the tables. The food had to be put into steam tables and the hor'deovres had to be set on trays. The punch had to be made and put into one of the large crystal punch bowls they had brought. So did the eggnog. The canned sodas had to be set up in a tub of ice next to the punch bowls. By the time all the celebration preparations were done it was 5:00 and Tamiko had barely enough time to go home, shower and change while the sisters in the church presided over last minute details.

In honor of the special occasion, Tamiko wore her black short-sleeved merino wool keyhole sweater with princess sleeves, and white trim around the edges. She paired this with an ivory colored pencil skirt and black and white spectator pumps. Tamiko took her hair out of the doobee she had it in all day and unwrapped it. She parted it to one side and just let it fall to her shoulders. Then she put two sparkly hair clips in one side to keep her hair from falling into her face. Then she checked herself in the mirror. Tamiko thought she looked good enough. She just hoped Davis would think she looked good, too. She was so excited that he was coming, and had spent a lot of time making things perfect just for that reason. Tamiko was also hoping that he would like the gift that she got for him when she went shopping with Tim yesterday. She had gotten gifts for all of her friends, but she took special care when choosing Davis' gift. She didn't want it to seem romantic, but she did want to show that she cared about him. He wondered if he got her a gift. Even if he gave her a friendly card, she'd be pleased. At least something that showed that he was thinking about her. Realizing the time, Tamiko shook herself out of her train of thought and grabbed her purse and the bag of presents that she had for her friends before heading downstairs to wait for her parents. When she finally came down she found it was they who were waiting for her.

"It's about time, baby girl! I was about to come up there."

"Sorry, but it takes time to look beautiful."

"Tamiko, get your coat" Mother Rose ordered. "We have to get back to greet our guests. I'm hoping Allen is there setting up the sound system."

"Don't worry, mom. He knows. Allen won't let us down."

"That's because he's a responsible young man. The kind of man any woman would be lucky to have."

"So, are we ready?" asked the Pastor.

"Yes, sir!", was Tamiko's enthusiastic reply.

Then they all headed out into the car for the 10-minute drive to the church. When they got back, Allen was there indeed, dressed in a prince of whales plaid wool twill suit, blue shirt and red tie, setting up the sound system as promised. After exchanging greetings with the Pastor and Tamiko, Mother Rose went into her usual bit.

"Hello, Allen. It's so good to see you", charmed Mother Rose.

"Hello, Mother Rose. It's good to see you, too. I'm almost finished setting everything up."

"Thank you so much for your help. Such a sweet young man, and so responsible. I was just telling Tamiko that any woman would be lucky to find a gentleman like you."

"Thank you, Mother Rose. You're too kind", responded Allen politely.

"Your parents are on their way, aren't they?"

"They should be. They were getting ready when I left. Which songs do you want first?"

COMMENCEMENT

"How about O Little Town of Bethlehem, followed by Silent Night, anything else can go in between, but just make sure that we have Joy to the World and Oh Night Divine towards the end of the evening."

"Got it."

"And when you're done, would you be a dear and help Tamiko check on the food."

"Of course, Mother Rose."

Allen finished setting up the auto play for the songs and then went to help Tamiko with the food. He went back to the kitchen where he saw Tamiko struggling with the large platters of hor'deovres.

"How about I take one?" asked Allen taking a platter from Tamiko.

"Thanks."

"Where do they go?"

"Outside on the front table near the entrance."

"I gotta hand it to you and Mother Rose; the place looks fabulous. This looks like one of those swanky affairs Tim's mom puts on."

"Thanks. God only knows how much work this was. I'm exhausted. We're definitely going to need more people on hand to help next year, God willing. Oh, and thanks for all of your help."

"No need. It's the least I could do. Oh, and what's with all that stuff over there?"

"In years past we always have so much stuff left over. I decided that I would just put a lot of the goodies into dessert boxes for people to take home at the end. And then we have the family gifts we give out. It's just our family Christmas card, a psalm calendar, and a daily devotional day planner."

"Sweet."

"Did you bring the big surprise?"

"I gave it to your dad this morning. He has it."

"I can't wait to see Davis' face. He's going to be too thrilled!"

Before Allen got a chance to respond, Mother Rose came rushing into the room in dramatic fashion, with the Pastor not far behind.

"The guests are arriving! I just saw your parents pull up along with the Hardy's and the Joyners. Allen, start the music please. I want our guests to be greeted by the sweet melodies of song. Tamiko you need to be up front. Smiles, everyone!"

Allen turned on the music and not long after, Mother Rose booming voice could be heard welcoming the guests. First were Allen's parents, then the Hardys. Allen greeted Mr. Hardy before the latter joined the Pastor and his dad in their conversation. Then the Joyners came in. Mother Rose curtly greeted Ruth Joyner and her son Daniel. As usual, all the older folks showed up first. Allen and Tamiko struggled to have a conversation with Daniel, but it didn't go beyond formal inquiries into health and the like. Daniel seemed pleased to have some time to speak with Tamiko, but she didn't reciprocate. Tamiko was polite, and kind, but she wanted to send the message to Daniel that she was not as interested in him as he was in her. After a while, more guests showed up this time more of the younger folk from the church. Mr. Hardy's daughter, Dorcas, had shown up. She was around the same age as Tamiko and Allen, but she never really hung out with them. Dorcas was a member of the church in name only. She was wild and street, which probably contributed to the fact that she and Tamiko didn't like each other. Then finally some of the regular crew showed up. First to arrive was Richard who even in his attempt to be modestly attired, still stuck out like a sore thumb in his Roca Wear black and white pinstripe suit, black gators and matching pimp cane.

"Merry Christmas, yo."

"Hey, man. Merry Christmas."

"Merry Christmas, Richard. You didn't want to bring Leandra?" asked Tamiko.

"Man, I quit her like a bad job. Don't even ask me why 'cause that would take all night."

"Sorry, man."

"Don't be. I sure as hell ain't. Scuze my language. Now where do I park these gifts?"

"Right under the Christmas tree over there."

Then Tim showed up in a new slate grey wool skinny suit with white shirt and a black skinny tie.

"Merry Christmas, everyone!"

"Wow! You look the best I've seen you in months, man", said Allen.

"Yeah, you look great! Is that a new suit?" asked Tamiko.

"Yeah. Thanks. All of my others were getting too big, so I decided to get a new one for tonight."

"You really do look wonderful. Oh, and thank you for all of your help with the shopping!"

"It was my pleasure, Miko. I see you really did out do yourself this year!"

"Thank You."

"Put your presents by the tree over there, and then take a load off."

Soon the hall was filled with people as guests continued to stream in. Everyone was talking and enjoying the hor'doevres and the cheerful atmosphere of the celebration. The pastor went around offering drinks (of the non-alchoholic persuasion) and Mother Rose made sure to greet everyone who came. Tamiko and Allen sat with their friends who were also enjoying the appetizers and drinks. Everyone who was invited was there, with the exception of one notable person.

"So where's the man of the hour?" asked Tim.

"He should be here in a while. He called me to ask when the par- I mean, celebration was starting", answered Allen.

"I hope he gets here soon. My mom is about to get everything started. Maybe I should call him. To see if he's stuck in traffic or something", said an anxious Tamiko.

"Chill, girl. No need to be sweatin' a brother", said Richard.

"I'm not sweating him. I just want everything to turn out alright."

"Come on, Miko. Davis is a big boy and he knows his way here", remarked Tim.

Mother Rose interrupted the conversation to start the first part of the celebration, which was the prayer.

"Excuse me everyone, if I may have your attention! Please, everyone take your seats!" she boomed over the mix of voices. "First, I would like to thank you all for coming to our Annual Christmas Celebration. It is an honor and a privilege to be able to share this joyous occasion with all of you in our church family. As you know, we are here to celebrate the birth of our Lord and Savior Jesus Christ, who came into the world to save us from sin. To start our celebration, I feel it would be most appropriate to dedicate some time in prayer to the Heavenly Father to thank Him for his most blessed sacrifice. Now if you will welcome my best friend and our valiant prayer warrior, Sister Lena Sharpe, who will lead us in prayer."

Everyone clapped as Lena approached the mic at the head of the room.

"I ask that every one take the hand of someone at their table and bow your heads."

As everyone complied with Lena's request, Davis slipped in and over to the table between Richard and Tamiko and placed his bag of gifts on the back of his seat. Tamiko smiled shyly as he took her hand. She then bowed her head hoping her hair would hide her blushing cheeks. Allen and Tim who were on the other side of the table from Tamiko exchanged wary glances. Then Lena continued with her prayer.

"Heavenly Father, we thank you for blessing us to live to see another Christmas Eve, and giving us the opportunity to come together once again to worship and praise Your Holy Name. We praise you for who You are and what You have done; for all of Your loving kindnesses and tender mercies. Tonight, Lord, we want to thank You for looking down on Your creation and having mercy on us. We want to thank You for sending Your only begotten Son Jesus down to earth to be a propitiation for our sins. Lord, we know we didn't deserve it, and we thank You for loving us so much, that you looked past what we deserved to provide

COMMENCEMENT

what we needed. Lord God, as we come together tonight to honor the birth of Your son, we thank You with our love for You and we thank You with our lives that we submit to Your will. Help us all to walk in Your Word and Your Love and to live lives that are acceptable in Your sight. Help us to show love to one another the way that You love us. Amen."

Everyone applauded the prayer and Mother Rose stepped back up to the mic.

"Thank you Lena; a beautiful and moving prayer, as always. At this time, we will take time to reflect on that blessed moment as my husband and our Pastor reads from the Word of God. Pastor Bynum."

"Merry Christmas, everyone."

"Merry Christmas", the audience replied in unison.

"If you have brought your Bibles and would like to read along, I'm going to Luke, Chapter 2, vs. 1 to 21."

The Pastor read the scripture to everyone and then followed up with a mini sermon on the importance of celebrating Christ during the Christmas season rather than commercialism, with the giving of gifts symbolizing the gift we were given by God in his Son Jesus. Once the sermon was over. Mother Rose came back to the mic again.

"Now that we have been fed spiritual food, it's time to eat of our earthly bounty." At Mother Rose's cue, the church volunteers came out dressed in white to serve the guests. They had carts, on which they carried plates of food for the guests. Once everyone had a plate, the Pastor led everyone in the grace. Then the guests all ate and chatted in between bites, and Davis, Tamiko, Allen, Tim and Richard got lost in conversation.

"What happened Davis? You gave Tamiko quite a scare. For a moment there, she thought you weren't going to show up", said Tim straining to be polite.

"Sorry I came late. You know how traffic is on Christmas Eve with all the last minute shoppers out", explained Davis.

"Don't sweat it, man, as long as you made it", remarked Allen.

"And I see you brought gifts", noticed Tim.

"Oh, Davis, you didn't have to do that", said Tamiko.

"I wanted to. You're my friends."

"So what do you think of the celebration?" asked Allen.

"Pretty cool. I've never been to a Christmas par- I mean, celebration like this one. Most of the celebrations I've been to, it's just an excuse for people to get sloppy drunk, or some people just come for food, to get they dance on, or to see what they can get. But here we're keeping it real; remembering the real reason for the season, which is Christ. It can't get no betta than that. And that was a beautiful prayer your mom gave, Allen."

"Thanks. I'll tell her you said so."

"Being here wit' you all like this…It just makes me just that more grateful to God for all that he's done to turn my life around. You guys are like his blessing to me."

"And you may not know this, but you are just as much a blessing to us", said Allen.

"C'mon, man…"

"No really. You may not know this, but we've had a few friends who've decided to go their separate ways. We understand that good friends are hard to find, and even harder to keep."

"How about we make another toast: to friendship", motioned Tim.

Everyone gave a "here, here" and tapped glasses. Then they finished their dinner, and soon after, Mother Rose brought out the cake and everyone sang Happy Birthday to Jesus, even though it was a few hours too early. Once everyone had cake, it was time to exchange presents. All of the guests gathered around the Christmas tree and got their gifts and handed out presents to other guests exchanging lots of "Merry Christmas" greetings, "God Bless You's", hugs, and in some cases tears. Gifts were exchanged, but not opened. Then they went back to their seats and joined Mother Rose in singing Christian carols and finally, Pastor Bynum came to the front to address the revelers.

COMMENCEMENT

"If I could have everyone's attention, please. There's one final presentation for the night before we send you home. You all know that we are facing some tough economic times. There are many people who are losing their jobs, struggling to keep their homes, and put food on the table. I just wanted to announce that Greater Apostolic is starting a new initiative. Starting now, we have set up a fund to help those sheep in our pasture who need help keeping their shelter over their head. We will be providing financial assistance and financial counseling for those who are in need."

The Pastor's announcement was met with thunderous applause.

"Tonight I would like to present the first gift to someone in our community who is present here today. He is an upstanding, well-deserving young man. Davis Martinez."

The audience clapped up a storm, especially everyone at the center table. Davis was shocked. All of a sudden his face was bright red. He just stared down at the table. He didn't move despite the fact that Tamiko was nudging him with her elbow. Allen had to pull him up and push him to the front.

"Davis, on behalf of Greater Apostolic Church in Christ, I would like to present you with this check. We hope that you will allow us to be a blessing to you and your mother in your time of need."

More applause.

"Thank You, Pastor Bynum. I know you all probably sacrificed to do this, and I am truly grateful and appreciate everythin'…but I can't accept this gift."

"It's no trouble at all, son. Please, take it. We want you to have it."

"No. I can't. I think it would be best if you put it back in the fund, where it would help someone who truly needs it. Thank you", he stammered handing the check back to the Pastor.

Davis rushed away and went back to the table where he collected his coat without saying a word to the others.

"Davis, what's wrong?" asked Tamiko.

"Yeah, man. What's the deal?" asked Allen.

Davis ignored their pleas and darted out of the hall. Allen rushed out behind him. Davis was almost out of the parking lot when Allen caught up with him.

"Davis! Davis, Come on!"

"No, you come on, man! I thought we was boys! How could you do me like that?!"

"What are you talking about?!"

"I'm talkin' about you putting my business on blast like that! Now you got the whole church thinkin' I'm some type of gutter rat lookin' for a handout!"

"I'm sorry, Davis, but I was only trying to help you!"

"And I told you I didn't need your help! What you think I am? Some kinda charity case?"

"I…we were trying to be a blessing to you! You yourself said you thanked God for…"

"That was before I realized what you and your crew really think of me. Like I'm some kind of broken toy for you to fix. I thought I had your respect, but now I see all I had was your pity."

"That's not true!"

"Yes it is! You think you better than me 'cause I'm from the hood. Cuz I didn't go to college, and all that. You just like all the other church people out there! You don't care nothin' bout people like me."

"I wouldn't have done this if I didn't care!"

"Yeah, right! I bet you was thinkin' you help a loser like me, you'd score some saint points wit' God! Forget you, man!"

"Davis, wait! Please!"

But it was no use. Davis kept on going until he disappeared out of sight into the darkness of the evening. Then Tamiko and the others came outside to see what was going on.

COMMENCEMENT

"I heard a lot of yelling. What happened?" asked Tamiko.

"Let's just say, I think we've lost another friend. And again, it's all my fault.

FIFTY-FIVE

As Allen tied his tie, he looked out of the window to see what the weather was like. Other than a cloudy sky, there was no sign of the nasty storm that the weather service had forecast for today. It was supposed to be the worst storm of the winter, but Allen wasn't worried. The snow was not expected to start until after 8:00 and by then, he would be at home watching T.V. or reading. His mother had been grocery shopping the day before and his father bought a few bags of salt that he planned to spread out over the driveway and on the front sidewalk after they came back from church. If the storm was coming, he was prepared. What Allen had not been prepared for was the storm that had taken hold of his life.

It had been more than a week since the night of the Christmas Celebration and the disaster that ensued with respect to his friendship with Davis. He had tried to call Davis to make amends only to get his voice mail each time. Allen thought he may get the chance to see him at church, but Christmas Service and Watch Night service had passed without any sign of Davis. Even at work, Davis had become a relative phantom. Each day, Allen made his rounds with few or no hits on his radio. Even when his radio did go off, oftentimes it was the voice of one of the other repairmen or Mr. Hardy requesting some task to be done. Davis wouldn't even let Tamiko tutor him anymore. When Allen thought of these things and the things Davis had said to him the night of the celebration, it made him worry. Not for himself, but for Davis.

Hadn't Davis told him that he had been looking for a church, a place of worship where he could find people who lived out the true meaning of what it was to be a Christian, and not some place where he would be judged and stereotyped? Hadn't he said he was glad to have finally found friends who would be able to help him in his walk with Christ? Now with one act, all of that was gone for Davis. Allen hoped that Davis wouldn't think that all Christians were as condescending as Allen himself had been. He hoped that Davis would not lose his faith in God because of what happened. Allen knew he couldn't forgive himself if Davis became an apostate because of what happened at the celebration. Looking back, Allen was ashamed that he had viewed Davis as his "mission". "Who was I to think that Davis needed anything from me?" Allen mused to himself. He was about to put on his shoes when he froze. "He was confiding in me as a friend. All Davis wanted was a friend, but instead, I had to try to be his Savior."

Now Allen could see how God had been warning him all along, but he didn't listen. God had spoken to him through his mother, Pastor Bynum, his friends, even Davis himself. Allen had been so caught up in himself and his 'quest for purpose' that he had been deaf to everything and everyone else, including the voice from God that he was so desperately waiting to hear from. He wished that he could go back in time and undo everything, but he couldn't. Only God could fix it. Allen wanted to pray to God and ask him to fix everything, to restore him and Davis, but he felt guilty. In the face of his disobedience, Allen felt as if God wouldn't hear him even if he did pray, so why bother. The whole episode had thrown him into spiritual turmoil.

Allen was now totally confused about God and how He worked, how He spoke and what, if anything, He wanted from Allen. The last few times Allen went to church, he didn't have any joy. He just felt isolated and lonely. What little connection to God that Allen felt he had, he'd lost. Allen didn't know what to do. In the midst of his self-pity and despair, Allen heard a knock on his door. He knew who it would be.

"It's open."

"Allen, are you ready?" his mother, Lena, asked.

"Actually, I'm not feeling well. I'm not sure if I'll be able to go today."

"What do you mean you don't feel well? What's wrong?"

"I don't know. It's not physical. I just feel off. I just need some time alone to think."

"Are you still upset about what happened Christmas Eve?"

"Mom, if you don't mind, I really don't want to go over all of that again. What's done is done. I messed up. Again."

"Okay, so maybe what you were thinking wasn't right for Davis. But on the bright side, that church fund the Pastor set up is helping a lot of people. If it weren't for you, a lot of people wouldn't be getting the help they needed."

"That's nice and everything, but it still doesn't change what happened with Davis. I mean what if he abandons his faith completely because of what I did?"

"Allen, God is in control. He knows all and he sees all. He's the one that brought Davis to Himself, and He will keep him. God knows that you didn't mean to hurt him. Maybe He will help Davis to see this in time. But you have to give God time."

"But I've been giving Him time. How much more time do I have to give? I've been asking God to direct my path, to talk to me, to show me what to do. Just when I feel he is speaking to me, I find out it's…He's never clear with me!" Allen couldn't help raising his voice out of frustration.

"He is clear. But you've got to focus on Him: on your relationship with Him. It's not about missions or helping people. If that were the case then we wouldn't need Jesus. We could do some good works and that would get us into heaven. We have to focus on becoming the people He wants us to be. Stop looking for your purpose and look for God."

"What if He doesn't want me to find Him?"

"That's silly, Allen. God doesn't want to see anyone perish. He wants all of us to have everlasting life. But we have to accept it. Come to church Allen. Don't stay here at home moping around. This is just the opportunity the devil is waiting for, so he can wreak more havoc in your life."

"But what's the point if my heart isn't there?"

"If your heart isn't there, then put it there. Otherwise the enemy will have it, and trust me you don't want that."

"Alright. Just let me put my shoes on."

"See you downstairs, then."

Allen finished dressing and met his parents downstairs, where the three of them headed off to church. When they got there, Tamiko and Tim were already seated and the service had already started. The Sharpes took their usual seats, and the service went on as it usually did, but Allen couldn't muster up any interest. Allen didn't bother looking for Davis because he knew he wouldn't be there. At times Allen could hear Tamiko and Tim whispering back and forth to each other, but he was too upset to care what they were talking about. His mother had told him to put his heart there, and though he wanted to, he couldn't. He just felt numb. So, Allen went through the motions of attending service. It made the service longer and almost unbearable. By the time the service was over, Allen was ready to go home.

"Allen, aren't you supposed to be going to the Brotherhood Bible study group?"

"I'm not feeling it today, Tamiko."

"We're going for coffee. Do you want to come with us?"

"Nah, you guys go on ahead. I'll see you at dinner."

"Allen,..." Tamiko started to say something, but changed her mind. "Never mind. We'll see you at dinner."

Tim and Tamiko walked out and Allen was about to try to find his parents, when he heard a familiar voice calling him.

"Allen... Allen!"

It was none other than Daniel Joyner. He was the last person he wanted to be talking to right now.

"Hey, Daniel", Allen said flatly.

"Bible study is going to start in a few minutes..."

"Sorry, Dan. I'm not feeling well. I think I'm just going to go home."

481

"Come on, man. Don't tell me you're dropping out, too!"

Allen already knew who the other drop out was.

"I'm not dropping out completely, it's just…"

"It's a new year. What better time to revive your relationship with the Lord."

Allen didn't really want to go, but then he heard it. Like a little voice inside his heart, telling him to go. At first Allen was just going to make up another excuse, but then thought that he may as well.

When Allen and Daniel reached the little conference room, there were only two other people there and they seemed to be new faces. It seemed a lot of people had dropped Daniel's brotherhood bible study.

"Is this it?" asked Allen, a bit surprised by how many people dropped out.

"I told you there were some drop outs. And I thought I would have gotten more brothers to join with the passing of the New Year, given so many brothers out there making resolutions to be saved."

"What's the Word for today?"

"I want to start a new topic. I want to talk about having a right relationship with God. Our relationship with God is the most important relationship we will ever have. It determines the course of our relationships with all the other people in our lives, and it determines how we think of ourselves. When we go back to the Bible, who are some people that you've read about who had special relationships with God?"

"Noah, Abraham, and Moses", answered one man.

"Yes. Anyone else?"

"The prophets had special relationships with him, so did the apostles", answered the other man.

"Right. What about you, Allen? Do you know any other people who had special relationships with God?"

"Some of the kings. Like David and Solomon, and then there was Job."

COMMENCEMENT

"Right. Now what do you think all these people had in common in their walk or relationship with God?"

"They were holy people?" answered the first man with uncertainty.

"And what do you think made them holy?" Daniel asked purposefully.

"They were able to perform miracles", answered the second man.

"And why do you think they were able to perform those miracles?" Daniel asked again.

Silence.

"Let's go to our Bibles so we can understand, shall we."

After taking them through several scriptures involving many of the people previously referred to, Daniel began to make his point.

"So as we can see, the common denominator in all these relationships is they were obedient to God. They did everything that God told them to do. But in order to do all the wonderful things they did, there had to be a first act of obedience on which rested all of the other acts. That first act of obedience was faith", lectured Daniel.

"You mean they believed that there is a God, right? We all believe there is a God, Daniel", said Allen.

"But having faith is more than believing there is a God. 'Faith' is believing in His power, and his love toward us. It is believing that he can and will do. It's knowing what his promises are to us and believing those promises are sure. Let's go back to Hebrews 11 vs 1: "Faith is the substance of things hoped for, the evidence of things not seen.""

"I'm not sure I get what you're talking about. Do you mean like believing something before it happens? For example, that if you want a car and you claim it, you will have it", asked the first man.

"Not exactly. I'm not one to endorse naming and claiming. Let's go to the scriptures for an example. Let's look at Matthew chapter 9 vs 28 – 30. What did Christ say to the blind men before they were healed? First he asked them if they believed that he could do it. They said yes. Then he laid hands on them and said 'According to your faith, so be it unto you.'

483

Jesus also said to the woman with the issue of blood "your faith hath made you whole." And look what it says in Matthew, chapter 13 vs 58. It says that 'he did not many mighty works their because of their unbelief.'" continued Daniel, hoping the others were following his point.

"So it is believing in the Power of God?" answered Allen hesitantly.

"Yes. But now when we think of faith we have be honest with ourselves about whether or not we have faith, true faith, because although some of us profess with our mouth that we believe we tend to 'second guess' God. We have a wait and see attitude. We say we believe, but then we say to ourselves, 'O.K. now let's see what's going to happen', as if you didn't believe in the first place. When you have real faith, there is no 'let's see', because you already know what the outcome is going to be. When you pray you go in faith believing, knowing that when you get up off your knees, God *is* making things happen", Daniel continued to expound.

"But I've heard of the situation of a family where the parents believed that God would deliver their child from an illness, but the child died and the parents were prosecuted because they didn't provide proper medical care. Would you say their child died because they didn't have this kind of faith?" asked the second man.

"I can't judge that situation because I don't know those particular people, and I don't know what they believed or how they believed. I can only tell you what the Bible tells us. And I can tell you about the people in this church who have experienced the power and glory of God. I'll use myself as an example. Everyone knows that I was in a car accident when I was 16 years old. The doctors said there was very little chance that I would walk again. But I didn't believe them. I believed in God and his unlimited Power. The Power of God was there and my faith unlocked it. Now it didn't happen overnight, but by the Grace of God, and by his healing power, I stand before you here today defying the expectations of the doctors."

"But everybody has doubts at some point, don't they? How can anybody have faith like that?" asked Allen skeptically.

"Again let's read our Bible. Let's go to Romans, 10 vs 17 where it says 'faith comes by hearing, and hearing by the Word of God." It is the

Word that establishes and strengthens our faith. This goes back to what I said about knowing what his promises are. We have to stay in the Word and feed ourselves this word everyday because within this Word are his promises to us, and his love for us. As we learn and grow, we learn not only these promises, but we learn to love God. Where there is *love* there is absolute trust and faith, which erases all doubt."

"I think I get it now. That's why the greatest commandment of all is to love the Lord with all your heart, mind, soul, and strength", said Allen thinking out loud.[1]

"Exactly, my brother."

Now Allen realized what he was missing.

FIFTY-SIX

Davis was kneeling down by a table in his living room praying silently. This was the second time today that he felt he needed to unburden himself before the Lord. He really thought he was making progress in his Christian walk when he found the Greater Apostolic Church, and some decent Christian friends. But then came the Christmas Celebration and the deep humiliation that came with it. Since then, Davis didn't know what to do. He didn't want to go back to church, and deal with the drama of "church folk". Davis was becoming disillusioned with organized religion and the so-called "people of God". "Was it always going to be like this?" he thought. "People who judged you and put you down because you happen to be different." After reading his Bible, he found the scripture with the parable about the wheat and the tares.[1] In every church there were people that were truly people of God or 'the wheat', and amongst them would be people who were not committed to God, but to religion or the 'tares'. "How come I can't find any of the wheat?" Davis asked himself. His situation made him feel very lonely. Once he heard a voice telling him that maybe he would be better off if he went back to his old friends in the street, but he knew in his heart he couldn't. Now that he had tasted the goodness of God, there was no way he could go back to the old ways. It was like being caught between heaven and hell. So he prayed.

"God, you see this situation that I'm in now. Lead me in the right direction, and show me the right path to follow. I need you to guide my actions. Help me to forgive my enemies and love them the same way you loved me when I was goin astray. I'm not going to lie. This is very hard for me right now because I'm really feelin' a lot of hurt. I trusted some people and now I feel like I don't want to trust nobody no more. I need you to help me get through this…"

It was hard for Davis to admit, but he did feel hurt. Davis thought Allen respected him as his equal. When he talked to Allen, he though he could trust him and confide in him about his problems. He didn't necessarily want help, just someone who would listen and understand. Davis and his sister were already in the process of working things out with the bank. They got a three-month forbearance and his sister was in negotiations with the bank about lowering the payments. God was working for him. His family didn't need or want anyone's charity. Looking back Davis probably wouldn't have minded some financial assistance, solely for his mother's sake, but he didn't like the way Allen went about it.

Why did he have to make Davis's life a public spectacle? Why did he have to put his family's poverty on display for the whole church? Davis felt as if Allen was using the situation to make himself look like a good Samaritan, seeking the praises of men, rather than God. Or maybe Allen was jealous of his position at work, and concocted this scheme to make Davis feel little. Did Allen think he was better than him? Did they all think that way? Did they make fun of him behind his back? Call him stupid and rude? In his past, a lot of the "upper-class" people like them did. He knew Tim probably did, and he and Allen were good friends. Maybe that was the case. Davis couldn't believe he didn't see this coming. Being that he was from the 'hood' and after everything that he had seen and been through, he should have been able to see through Allen's front. Davis felt he was getting too 'soft', letting his guard down like that.

"…and God please give me a more discerning spirit, to be able to tell the good from the bad; to know the difference between the people who serve you and those who serve themselves. In Jesus name, I pray. Amen."

Davis got up off his knees and was going to work on finishing an assignment for school when there was a knock on his apartment door.

"Who?" asked Davis.

"It's Pastor Bynum, son."

Davis couldn't believe his ears. Why was the Pastor knocking on his door? Without any other thought, he went to the door and opened it. As he faced the Pastor, he was speechless. He had no idea what to say.

"May I come in?" asked Pastor Bynum.

"Yeah- I mean, yes Pastor-sir." stammered Davis, stepping aside so the pastor could enter.

"Nice place you got here."

"Thanks. Pastor Bynum, no disrespect, but what you want to see me for?"

"I was worried about you, son. I haven't seen you in church for a while."

"Pastor, I'ma be real wit' you. I don't think I'ma be comin' back to Greater Apostolic no more."

"Does this have something to do with what happened at the Christmas Celebration?"

Davis didn't answer.

"Davis, I am truly sorry about what happened. Neither my church members nor I meant to offend you. I was told that you needed assistance and was only trying to provide it. That's what we do at our church. We're all a family and we look out for each other. Looking back, I realize that calling you out in such a large group of people probably wasn't the best way to go about it. I guess I got too carried away."

"Thanks for the apology. I accept it and all, but that don't change that fact that I'm not going back."

"I'm sorry to hear that, Davis, but I think I understand. But even if you don't come to our Church, I hope you find some place to be a sanctuary of God for you."

"I don't know. I think I'ma just be wit' God by myself for a while."

"In the meantime, if you should ever feel like you want to come back, you're welcome at any time. And if you need anything, just ask. I want you to know I mean that with all my heart."

COMMENCEMENT

"Pastor, sir, I don't mean to be rude or nothin' but I got a lot of work I gotta do for school, so if that's all you wanted to say…"

"Say no more, I don't want to keep you from your work. And I have to be at dinner. Oh, but before I forget, Tamiko asked me to give you something", said the Pastor pulling an envelope from his coat pocket and handing it to Davis. Davis took it half-heartedly and chucked it on the table, and this did not escape the notice of the Pastor.

"It's just a letter, Davis."

"I know. So she's the one that talked you into coming over here?"

"No. Davis, I'll have you know I'm not the type of man to be manipulated by my daughter for any reason. I came over here on my own volition, and when I told her about it, she asked me to give that to you."

"Oh."

"Goodnight, Davis. God bless you."

"God bless you, too, pastor- sir."

The pastor then left. Davis didn't know how to feel at that moment. He couldn't believe that the Pastor had come all the way to his house to see about him and to apologize for what happened. Had he been wrong about the church, or the pastor at least? Then there was the note from Tamiko. The pastor said she didn't influence him to come over, but Davis didn't know if he should believe that. He had to admit to himself that he was curious about what she had to say, but the part of him that was still hurting didn't want to read it. There was so much he wasn't sure about, and he was wary of opening himself up again to people who had hurt him so badly. Davis knew before the night was out he would be on his knees to God again praying for guidance. He would keep Tamiko's letter and he would ask God if he should read it, as well as if he should go back to Greater Apostolic church. Davis would leave it in His hands.

FIFTY-SEVEN

Allen came home from work exhausted. The snowstorm that the weather service predicted came as promised. During the late evening hours, there was a Nor'easter that dumped more than a foot of snow on the city. There were blizzard-like conditions as the wind whipped up the snow into the air and sprayed it into the faces of those walking about. Commuting to work was a nightmare, as everyone who usually took the bus crammed onto the subways, which began to experience service delays. Thankfully the mayor had decided to close the schools or it would have been worse. When Allen got to work he had to help shovel the sidewalks while fighting the strong gales of the storm. Now that the New Year was well underway, there were not as many occupants of the hotel, however, the few that remained didn't dare venture out into the storm. That meant there was a lot of foot traffic on his newly buffed floors, and the garbage cans needed constant re-emptying. Overall it had been a very trying day and Allen was glad to be home when he got there.

There was dinner with his family as always, and after that, his mother retired to work on lesson plans for school, while his father fiddled with his hobby of making model boats. That left Allen to retire to his room where he could be alone with his thoughts.

Once again the day passed without hearing anything from Davis. This still bothered Allen, but he had resoled to leave the situation in God's hands. After all, he had left voice mails, and sent e-mails containing the most contrite apologies. Allen had done everything he could to reach out to Davis. There was nothing else he could do, so now he would wait for God. And yet there was something else on Allen's mind. He thought about what he learned in the Brotherhood Bible study class the day before. He thought about 'the greatest commandment of all': to love the Lord with all your heart, mind, and strength. Allen had to stop for a minute to really think about what that meant. Many times when he heard people testify in church and talk about how they loved the Lord, it was usually because He had done something for them. They loved what the Lord did, but did they necessarily love God? He had heard his mother and Tamiko talk about how we need to love God for who he is, almost as if he was like a person, like your mom or dad. "How could you do that?" Allen asked himself. With people you could spend time with them and talk with them to get to know them and let love grow out of the relationship. How could you do this with God?

Allen opened his Bible to read. He turned to Matthew chapter 10 vs 37-39 when Christ admonished his disciples that he who loved mother or father more than Jesus was not worthy of him. And that he had to hate even his own life as well. How could this be?

Allen felt like his relationship with God was very one-sided. Allen read his Bible, he prayed, he went to church, he was even into meditating on the Word, but still he rarely heard God speak to him. There were times when Allen felt something speak to his heart like when he came out of the shower that day, and at the Election Night party, and even before he was about to skip the Bible Study, he felt something speak to his heart and tell him to go. These were very small things, though. It was nothing like the instructions that God gave to Abraham, or to Isaiah, or like when he appeared to the Apostle Paul in a vision.[1] That's the kind of thing Allen was expecting. Something big and bold. There were times when Allen felt that God was with him and then there were times when he felt abandoned. How in the world could he get to know God like this? How was he going to learn to love Him in the way that he should?

Allen needed to talk to someone about this, and who better to talk to about this than someone who really loved the Lord: his mother. So he went downstairs and knocked on the door of her room.

"Come in, Allen."

"How'd you know it was me and not Dad?"

"You're the only one that knocks."

"Right", laughed Allen.

"What do you need sweetheart?"

"I wanted to talk to you about God."

"What about?"

"What does it mean to love God? How do people love God?"

"That's a funny question coming from someone who just recently got saved. Don't you love God, Allen?"

"I thought I did, but after the Brotherhood Bible Study class with Daniel, I'm not so sure."

"But how can you decide to devote your life to God if you don't love Him?"

"Because I stand in awe of Him as the Creator, and I fear Him. I serve him because I think I should, but I don't know if it's because I love him. I know how to love people, but with God it can't be the same, can it?

"Well, when you love someone, you want to be with them all the time. You want to give of yourself to them. And if push came to shove, you would lay down your life for them, right?"

"Yeah, I guess."

"We have to love God like that, too; even more than that. When you love God, nobody has to tell you to read your Bible, or pray or go to church because you love him so much you can't help but want to be in his presence all the time. Nobody has to tell you to praise him, because you always have a praise in your spirit that has to come out."

"Still, how do you get that way? And how can I love Him more than anyone else?"

"Allen, You love Him more than anyone else because He's God and He's the one that first loved us. He is love. You learn to love him by taking the time to learn about Him. Now we can't learn everything about

God, because as the Bible says "His ways are unsearchable", but we can learn something. But you have to pray, and fast and read your Bible."

"But I've been doing that."

"Really? And how often do you read your Bible? How many times a day do you pray?"

"I don't know. I guess once a day, each."

"Once a day! Daniel prayed 3 times a day."[2]

"Mom, I work and I get really busy! I can't pray and read the Bible all the time."

"Allen, I work too, and have been working since I was 14 years old, but I make time for the Lord because He's important to me. If He's important to you, then you will do the same thing. And you need to read your Bible and meditate more often, too. The Bible should be the first thing in your hand when you wake up in the morning and the last thing you put down before you go to bed at night."

"But I have to get up so early to go to work."

"So? When you were a baby Allen, I had to get up earlier than I was used to in order to feed and care for you. It wasn't an inconvenience because I loved you. Now if you want to love God the way you say, you can get up a few minutes earlier to give yourself enough time for a morning devotion."

"I never thought of it like that."

"And if you have nothing to do you can start right now."

"Alright. I just hope everything works out in the end."

"Just believe Allen, and it will.

FIFTY-EIGHT

Tim felt anxious as he sat in the waiting room of the neurologist's office at New York Presbyterian Hospital. Just a few days ago, they had taken images of his brain with the MRI and CT scans. Then yesterday the doctor called him to make an appointment to discuss the results. After he received the call, Tim knew it couldn't be anything but bad news. The doctor was curt and brief, hardly providing any information at all, other than he had to see him right away. If the doctor hadn't found anything he would have told Tim over the phone to reassure him, but such was not the case. Tim had an idea of what he would hear when he went into the doctor's office, in fact, he had been thinking about it ever since they told him his nausea had nothing to do with his stomach. Tim tried to brace himself for this meeting, to prepare for what he felt may come, but he couldn't think about it without being gripped with absolute terror.

"Tim Russell!" the nurse called out from behind the administration desk.

"Yes." Tim replied.

"If you'll come this way."

Tim got up and followed the nurse back to an office.

"The doctor's finishing up with another patient, but he'll be in with you in a few minutes. Have a seat."

"Thank you", replied Tim, who was preoccupied by his thoughts.

In the silence of the room, Tim could hear his own heart beating. He took a deep breath and took out his smart phone to check his messages as a way of distracting himself from his worry. There was one message from Preston. He probably wanted a status on the contracts with the vendors. At least now work was becoming a bright spot in Tim's day. The site was on its way to completion, but Tim needed permission from the vendors for the links to the secure portions of their respective sights. The majority of them had already verified their permissions, which were on his desk. They were waiting for the one from the Brill Corporation, and Tim wasn't worried about it because he had already spoken to them. The next big thing that had to be done was to test run the site, and make up an employee regulations manual. Things were going according to schedule. There was also a message from Pastor Bynum about their next meeting. Tim was actually glad to see that he had called given recent events, but the one person he wanted to call didn't.

Ever since Christmas Eve, Tamiko had sort of been in mourning over Davis. Tim felt bad about what happened, especially since he had totally misjudged him, but he couldn't help but feel a little upset by the way Tamiko seemed obsessed with Davis. It seemed He and Tamiko couldn't have a conversation without Davis's name coming up at least twice. Tim had told her about his appointment today, hoping she would come with him, but she couldn't because of some assembly they were having at her school. "She'll call. She's probably just busy with the children and everything. After all it was only 10:00, and she wouldn't have lunch until around 11:30 or so." Tim reasoned with himself. It surprised Tim to realize how close he and Tamiko had become. A few months ago, he probably wouldn't have given her a second thought, whereas now he thought about her more often than not. If he wasn't thinking about her, he was thinking about God. Tim was also surprised by how much Tamiko influenced him with respect to religion. He had thought more about God in the past few months than he did in his whole life. Tim even had to admit that he was beginning to believe in God. Especially after all that he had been through recently. He even found himself praying as he did this morning. Looking back, he realized that he had done the work of about 7 people. Preston attempted to do what he did and literally had a nervous breakdown. "How was I able to do it?" Tim thought to himself. In the past, Tim had really worked through the midnight oil, but even during those times he would become all but bedridden. That didn't happen at all this time. It was as if God was giving him the strength to go through it all. Tamiko said she prayed for him, not to mention he prayed (or tried to), and he knew the good Pastor was praying for him. That had to be it. Tim only hoped this God that had delivered him through the toughest two weeks of his life would deliver him from what he was about to face now.

Tim had just finished going over his messages when his doctor, Dr. Rabinow came in.

"Hello, Tim. How are you today?"

"I don't know. I was hoping you would have the answer to that."

"You're ready to get down to business. I totally understand."

The doctor sat down behind the desk and opened the file in front of him.

"I'm going to start by saying that this is just a preliminary diagnosis. There are still more tests that are going to have to be done, but…"

"You found something."

"Unfortunately, yes. The MRI and the CT scans reveal that there's an unusual growth within the posterior-fossa region of your brain. There's been some intracranial pressure that has resulted in swelling and the hydrocephalus has increased pressure on some of the cranial nerves in that area which has been causing your headache, nausea, and vision problems."

"I see."

"The growth is fairly large, and there are indications that if it gets any larger it may obstruct the flow of cerebral spinal fluid which can cause herniation, which would be fatal."

"This growth… is it cancer?" Tim could hardly get the last word out without choking up.

"We don't know yet. We would have to go in and do a biopsy to see what kind of growth we're dealing with. It could simply be a colloid cyst that can be drained or it could be a tumor. But we would have to go in to find out. I recommend that you get it done as soon as possible, so that we can decide how we're going to proceed with removal."

COMMENCEMENT

"Sure. Of course."

"Let's see… today is Wednesday…I can fit you in the beginning of next week. How about Monday at 4:30? Does that fit with your schedule?"

"I guess it will have to now, won't it."

"Good. It's a simple procedure, but it is invasive surgery. We would drill a hole in your skull and then insert a stereotactic needle to extract tissue from the growth. A computer that uses the MRI or CT scan as a map will guide the needle in order to prevent injury to healthy areas of your brain. There are risks to this procedure as with any. There may be some scarring, which may lead to seizures, and there may be some swelling and fluid around the brain. But we will be monitoring you for these things."

"So I'll be in the hospital for a couple of days."

"Yes. Would you like me to write a notice for your employer."

"If you don't mind."

"And if we're lucky, I may be able to get a diagnosis in the same week. But we'll discuss those options during your recovery."

"This is certainly a lot to take in."

"Like I said Tim, all this is just preliminary. I don't want you to go home overly concerned. Even if this is a tumor, we have to diagnose what kind it is. It could be benign for all we know. For the most part, tumors in this area of the brain usually are."

"Don't worry, doc. I'll be okay. Thanks for everything."

"Do you have any questions or concerns that you'd like me to address?"

"No. It's okay. I'll see you Monday."

As Tim got up and walked out of Dr. Rabinow's office, he felt as if his air supply was being cut off. They had found a growth, just as he had suspected. The doctor said it might not be cancer, but there was still a good chance it could be. When Tim got outside he hailed a cab (because he couldn't trust his vision anymore) and headed back to work. As he sat in the cab, he thought about the significance of what he just learned from the doctor. The first thing that came to mind was death. Tim had always taken for granted that at just 24 years old, he had his whole life in front of him. Never before had he contemplated that it could come to an end so quickly and without warning. Sure he knew that an accident could potentially take him out of the world before he was ready, but he had always taken precautions on those ends, at least those things that he could control. Now, in the face of this illness, he had no choice but to confront his own mortality.

At first he thought about all the time he had taken for granted. Tim had taken for granted that he would have time to build a business and make Allen his partner. He had thought that he could wait until he was 40 to get married and have children, but now he didn't know how much time he had left. Tim thought he would one day get to the bottom of what stood in the way of a loving relationship with his sister, and that he would reconcile things with his dad. Now he didn't know if these things would happen at all. Then finally, he thought about God. If there was a God, (which Tim was beginning to think that there was) was he ready to meet Him? What would Tim say to Him? How could Tim justify all of what he knew deep down inside was wrong in his life to God? And what if there was a Hell where he could be sent to for all eternity? Life on this earth had been hell enough. He didn't want to wind up there. There were so many things that Tim pondered and as he mused, he felt an overwhelming desire to make things right. There were certain things that weren't in his control to fix, but those things that were, he was determined to take steps to rectify while he still had time.

Finally the cab pulled up in front of Herns and Marshall, and Tim paid his fare and got out of the cab. Then he went up to his office, trying to prepare what he was going to say to Preston on the way. He needed to let him know that he would need some time off without getting into specifics. He didn't want anyone at work to know anything unless it was absolutely necessary. By the time he got off the elevator and arrived at his office, he had it down, that is until he came face to face with Preston at the entrance of the office. Tim was about to open the door, when it swung open and he was assaulted by Preston's angry tirade.

"Where the hell have you been? I've been calling you for the past hour now?"

"I was at my doctor's appointment Preston, which is where I told you I was going before I left", said Tim. By now, he had become so inured to Preston's rages, they no longer had any effect on him.

"You should have gotten back to me when you were done! Standoff came up here while you were out looking for those verifications. Thankfully the Brill Company sent theirs a few hours before. So at least I had that to show him."

"Perfect. I'll give you the rest, and we'll copy them and send the copies to Standoff."

"You should have just told me where they were and I could have done it a while ago."

"You're right. Sorry about that. In fact, I'd like to meet with you tomorrow if you're available to sort of give a status report on how things are going and what needs to be done, especially since, in the next couple of days I'm not going to be here for medical reasons."

"You're cutting out on me?"

"Preston, I would hardly call it cutting out. I am going to debrief you on everything and it's not like I'm taking a personal day. It's a necessary medical leave."

"What's wrong with you?" asked Preston, who almost appeared to be concerned.

"I'd rather not go into detail, but if you would like to call my doctor to verify that I'm going to need recovery time, go ahead."

"Fine. We'll meet first thing tomorrow at 9:00."

"I'll be ready."

After their conversation, Preston went back into the office, and Tim retired to his cubicle. He was about to begin to prepare some files for tomorrow's meeting when his cell phone rang. It was the call he'd been waiting for.

"Hey, you. What did the doctor say?"

"Hey, Miko. I'm at the office, and I don't want to really talk about it over the phone. Are you busy tonight?"

"Never, for a friend. Where do you want to go?"

"You pick. Just make it some place where we'll have some kind of privacy."

"How about the gym in your building. See if you can get one of the dance rooms and we'll talk in there."

"That's a great idea. I'll do that. I'll meet you after dinner?"

"Sounds good. I'll call you before I leave."

"Thanks, Tamiko. I don't know what I'd do without you."

"It's going to be okay, Tim. God is going to see you through this."

****

Tim paced up and down one of the dance rooms waiting for Tamiko to arrive. He felt like a rubber band that was going to snap, so taut were his nerves. He started to walk laps around the room to keep himself sane. Tim was on his third lap around when he heard footsteps echoing through the dance room. He turned around and saw her standing a few steps away. As their eyes met, Tamiko was able to read the anguish on his face almost immediately. She ran over to him and threw her arms around him. Tim put his arms around her and lifted her up a little bit, holding her tight. He didn't want to let go.

"I'm so glad you're here."

"So what happens now?" asked Tamiko as she pulled out of the embrace to face him.

"I'm supposed to have a biopsy done on Monday, so they can find out just what it is."

"What time are you going in?"

"At 4:30."

COMMENCEMENT

"Do you need me to do anything for you while you're in the hospital? Like run errands or something?"

"No."

"How soon will you have the results of the biopsy?"

"I don't need the results to know what this is. We both know what it is."

"No we don't. What ever it is, it may not be life threatening. Maybe the doctors can operate and remove it…"

"And what if they mess up? Or What if they can't get it out? What happens then?"

"Don't even go there! God is going to work this out!"

"And what if He doesn't, Tamiko? What if this is one thing He doesn't want to work out? This is a very real possibility that we have to face."

"I can't believe that! I won't believe that, especially after all He's brought you through! I don't want you thinking that either!"

"When I was in the cab going back to work, I was looking back over the past couple of months and I was thinking that maybe it was no coincidence that I should begin to experience God in my life at this time. Maybe you were right. Maybe He wants me to get my life right… because I don't have much time left."

"No! Tim, you're going to just stop this right now! I'm not going to allow you to sit here and wallow in self-pity. Yes, God has brought you to Himself, but I don't think it's because you're going to die. I think it's because he has a plan and purpose for your life. You are going to come through this."

"You don't know how much I want to believe that."

"Then believe it."

"I just…what if…"

"Tim, I know you're used to being let down by a lot of people, but God won't let you down. That much I know. But you have to come to Him and surrender everything."

"I know. I want to, but…I'm not sure if I have what it takes to be the kind of person like you or Allen. I'm not exactly the nicest guy in the world."

"You don't need to be the nicest guy in the world. Tim, all you need is to believe in His Son, Jesus, and have the desire to live right. Do you have that?"

Tim had to think about this. He did believe that there was a God. He did have the desire to live right, but he didn't know about Jesus as God's Son and the only way to God. He had spoken with the Pastor about this on a previous occasion. In some ways it seemed to make sense and in some ways it didn't.

"I don't know. I think…I mean I know there's a God. I know that my life isn't what it should be, but I'm not sure about much else."

"Tim, as long as you've been a part of our church, have you been reading the Bible?"

"Funny you should ask. Haven't really. I've always thought that's what the good Pastor was for."

"The Pastor isn't the only one who's supposed to read the Bible. We are, too."

"But there's so many different versions. How do you know which one is authentic and which isn't?"

"In our church we use the King James Version of the Bible. This version was translated directly from the original Hebrew, Greek and Latin texts. I hope you still have the one I got you for Christmas."

"I have it."

"Read the New Testament. Read about Jesus. Listen to him speak through the Word. If you truly believe in God, it will clear up a lot of your confusion. Will you do this?"

"O.K. Couldn't hurt right?"

"Of course not. In fact, it will help you in ways you can't begin to imagine."

"I guess I'll take your word for it. Tamiko, I don't want this to get out…"

"You know you've got me keeping a lot of secrets."

"I know. I'm sorry. It's just that I don't want a lot of drama. I'm planning to let Allen and the others know, soon. I just want to be able to tell them myself. And I don't want to get my family or the people at my job involved just yet."

"I can understand the people at your job, but your family! Tim, isn't that what your family is there for? Shouldn't you be able to lean on them in times like this?"

"In theory yes, but my mom always manages to take my crises and turn it into her own personal melodrama. And all my sister would do is sulk because she's not the center of attention. I don't need that right now."

"O.K. I'll let you handle this your way. But if you need anything, you know you have me and Allen, and my family you can turn to. And best of all, you always have God."

"Thanks, Tamiko. Why do I always feel better after talking to you?"

"I hope it's because God is using me to help you."

"I think He is."

FIFTY-NINE

The Brotherhood Bible Study group had just finished for the day, and Allen was on his way home for the Sunday Dinner, which would be held at his house this week. He walked downstairs to the vestibule and was about to leave when he heard some familiar voices behind him.

"Thank you again for your time, Pastor Bynum."

"You know you're welcome any time, Tim. I don't mind."

"I thought I heard you two", interrupted Allen. "Pastor, are you grooming Tim to take over Greater Apostolic? " he joked.

"Not just yet, anyway", laughed the pastor. "I'd love to talk, but I have to run home and change before dinner. See you boys later."

Allen and Tim headed out of the church together.

"Hmm...If I didn't know any better."

"I just had some philosophical questions."

"And did you get any answers?"

"Always. Sometimes, it's not what I expect, but I always get an answer."

"Does this mean I can now call you 'brother Tim'?"

"Wait a minute. You guys have orders?"

"No...never mind. It was a joke. You didn't get it. So where's your car?"

"I took a cab. My vision's gotten so screwed up, I can't even drive anymore."

"That reminds me, how did your appointment go? I wanted to wait until we were face to face to talk about that."

"I'm not going to mince words, Al. They found something."

Allen stopped in his tracks. He couldn't believe what he was hearing.

"Are you sure?"

"Unfortunately. The doctor showed me the scan results."

"Is it...?"

"They don't know. I'm going in for the biopsy tomorrow. They'll have the results by Thursday. No matter what it is, I'm going to have to go under the knife."

"Maybe this is for the better, man. Just think. If you hadn't found out and this thing kept growing..."

"Then I could have died happy without having to look over my shoulder every five minutes for the grim reaper."

"You can't be serious, man."

"Allen, I have a brain tumor. Do you have any idea what this means?"

"There are a lot of things that it could mean, but nothing's certain yet. Let's just take it one day at a time. That's the only way you're going to get through this. You start going into 'what if' mode, all you're going to do is worry yourself sick and make this worse."

"You're right."

"So let's start with Monday. What's going to happen with the biopsy?"

"Nothing too serious. They're just going to drill a hole in my head and stick a needle in my brain, not to mention there's the possibility that I could end up seizing into a coma. But other than that it should be a walk in the park."

"You don't have to worry, man. The doctors have probably done this thing thousands of times. And Presbyterian is the best. Don't sweat it. It'll probably only be a few minutes and then you're done."

"Try more like an hour. Then they're going to put me under observation afterward, so it's more than likely I'll be in for a few days."

"What time are you going in? I'll be there."

"You don't have to do that, Al."

"Tim, I want to. You're my friend. I'm not going to let you go through this alone."

"Alright. Thanks, man. It's at 4:30."

"Does Miko know yet?"

"Yeah, she called me after I got back to work, but enough about me. How are you doing? You didn't look so good when I saw you last Sunday. You're not still bummed out are you?"

"A little. I still feel bad about the mistakes I made, but there's only so much I can do. I've put things in God's hands I'm going to let Him handle it."

"I kinda feel bad myself. Seems like Davis wasn't the hustler I thought he was. Got a lot of pride though. He still hasn't said anything to you? Even at work?"

"No. I think he even had Mr. Hardy switch his floor assignments so we wouldn't have to work together anymore."

"So he has a flair for drama. I think that's going a bit far, don't you? It's not like we all didn't apologize a million times."

"In his book, I punked him. That's not something you take lightly when you're from round the way."

"Considering his past, I hope he stays saved for your sake. I'd hate to hear round the 'hood that you got a 'mark' on you."

"That's not funny, Tim."

"Right. Sorry. Anyway, are we actually going to walk all the way to your house? Let's just grab a cab?"

"Do you really think they're going to stop for a couple of black guys in Harlem, on a Sunday no less?"

"What if they didn't know they were stopping for two black guys? What if they only saw one white guy? Or a guy who they thought was a white guy?"

"Tim, no!"

"No, Al. They want to play games, so can we. You know the drill, go stand over there."

"You know, one day this is going to get us arrested."

"The last time I checked, head games weren't illegal."

"What if the driver thinks he's being set up for a stick up and drives us to the police station?"

"Allen, we're dressed in suits, and we don't have firearms."

"What if the police plant some...?"

"Will you just get over there?!"

Allen stood farther along the sidewalk while Tim walked to the curb to hail the cab. He got one almost immediately. Then while he was asking the driver "if he knew the directions" Allen would walked up and when Tim got in, he got in after him. It always worked, which annoyed the daylights out of Allen. They rode in silence during the short drive to Allen's house. When they arrived Allen opened the door to find everyone assembled in the living room in lively conversation.

"Speak of the devil, we were just talking about what might have happened to you two", remarked Vernon.

"How did you get here?" asked Lena.

"We took a cab", replied Tim.

"Cabs are stoppin' for black men now?" asked Vernon skeptically.

"It's a long story. Is that roast chicken with wild rice that's got this place smelling so good?" asked Allen.

"Yes it is. I was trying to make something that would suit everybody. You think your stomach can handle it, Tim."

"I'll be fine Mrs. Sharpe, thank you."

"Speaking of your stomach, son, have you been to the doctor?" inquired Pastor Bynum.

Allen, Tim, and Tamiko exchanged knowing glances among each other. Tamiko looked down, visibly upset. This did not go unnoticed among the older folk who also exchanged puzzled looks in the silence that ensued.

"Well?" asked Mother Rose breaking the silence.

"There's nothing to worry about, really. They're still doing tests to see what the problem is."

"Maybe you need to see another doctor if this one can't find out what's wrong", suggested Lena.

"Sometimes these things take time. I'm not in a hurry. Anyway, I feel fine right now. Good enough to have two helpings of chicken."

"I hear that. Let's go get some dinner", said Mr. Sharpe.

They all went into the dinning room for dinner. There wasn't much talk at the dinner table. The young people were noticeably quiet. The older people were concerned and were thinking of how to steer the conversation so that they could find out what this silence was all about.

"This must be some really good food, Lena. Seems no one can talk for eating."

"Thank You, Pastor. I think you might be right. Not even your Tamiko has anything to say", remarked Lena.

"I'm just tired, Momma Lena. It's been a long week."

Silence.

"How's things going with the Brotherhood Bible study, Allen."

COMMENCEMENT

"Everything's good."

Silence.

"How was your vacation, Tim? Did you get to go away at all?"

"No. Just stayed in town."

Silence.

The conversation went on this way throughout the night, leaving the older folk with perturbed feelings that lingered long after the aroma of seasoned chicken had gone. When dinner was over, the elders tried to extend the evening with dessert, and again attempted to extract any information they could, but it was futile. Finally, Tim excused himself from the company to go home, ending the evening and any chance the elders had to discover what was amiss.

"But it's still early. Do you have to leave so soon?"

"I'm sorry Mrs. Sharpe, it's just that I have a lot of things to prepare for tomorrow."

"Good evening and God bless you, dear."

"Thank you, Mrs. Sharpe. God bless you, and everyone else. Goodnight."

Everyone else bid Tim good night, and he left for home hailing another cab at the corner. Once he had gone, Tamiko grabbed Allen and pulled him toward the front door. She took her coat and gave Allen his. Allen played along as he was beginning to understand what she was doing.

"Daddy, Allen and I are going to the store for a minute. I want to get some sunflower seeds for a math game I'm going to play with the kids tomorrow. Do you want anything while we're out?"

"But we were just about to go, sweetheart. We have to get back to the church for evening service."

"It'll only be a minute. We're only going to the store on the corner. We'll be back before you know it."

Once they were outside, Tamiko waited until they were a few feet away before she brought up what they both had been thinking about throughout dinner.

"So did you and Tim have a chance to talk?"

"You mean about his having to go into the hospital tomorrow for a biopsy?"

"I still can't believe this is happening."

"I know. You know he already thinks it's the end."

"It's not… Right?"

"I'm going to do just what I told him, Tamiko. I have to take this one day at a time. But we have to be prepared for…"

"No! We can't go there! We have to be strong for him and go to God and cover him with our prayers! We need to have faith. God can save him! He will save him. He has to…" Tamiko was now sobbing uncontrollably. Allen took her in his arms to comfort her as he struggled to fight back his own tears. It seemed that ever since he devoted his life to God, things had gone from bad to worse. Not only had he lost direction for his own life, but now he was beginning to lose all the people he cared about. First, Jim, then, Callie, then Davis, and now there was the possibility that Tim was terminally ill and would be gone with no hope for return. Allen knew he needed to have faith in God. He had to trust God despite everything that was going on, but he couldn't help being scared, and a little angry about what God was allowing to happen.

SIXTY

Jim went into the 24-hour bodega on the corner a few blocks down from his house. Jim had been frequenting this particular store for a few weeks now. He always came after work on Fridays. That had been his plan when he started. Only on Fridays. Now it was late Sunday night and Jim found himself headed toward the spot.

That voice was bothering him again. Especially after he had started seeing Callie. He had only meant to drop by to see if they were cool about everything and to bring her a Christmas present. Then he ended up in the same position he had been in before, only this time he couldn't fool himself because he wasn't that drunk. Then came more promises she forced him into. Now he would have to see her more often, which Jim did not relish. Their relationship made him feel ashamed and guilty, and whenever he felt this way, the voice would come back. He should have just kept it at quick phone calls like he had been doing for the past few weeks, but she sounded so desperate that he couldn't help but be concerned. Jim knew the pain she was going through because he was feeling the same way at times and he thought it wouldn't have been a bad idea to have some company to commiserate with. But it just led to the voice getting louder and filling Jim with more anxiety about his future.

When Jim entered, the place was empty. There were dusty bags of chips lining the shelves along with old boxes of cereal and instant mashed potatoes, whose packages had faded to another color. Jim passed all these and went to the plexiglass counter.

"Let me get some wraps", was Jim's coded request to the guy at the counter.

"To the back, man."

Jim went to the back of the store and stood near a little door that looked as if it were part of the wall. The man came through and Jim handed him some money and the man handed him a bag. Jim stuffed the bag in his pocket and quickly walked out of the store into the street. Since it was late, there weren't that many people about. Jim decided to duck onto a side street. He frantically took the bag out of his pocket and pulled out one of the joints inside. He put it to his mouth and lit it. He inhaled deeply and let the smoke fill his lungs. He could feel his burdens begin to lighten themselves as the smoke passed through his nose and mouth.

Just as the beers had lost their effectiveness, so had the hard liquor. Jim reasoned within himself that at least he wasn't drinking as much anymore. The marijuana would help him get rid of his dependence on alcohol. And it's not like he did this all the time. In the past three weeks since he had started, he'd only had three or four joints. He didn't even smoke them all the way through – just enough to get his head straightened out, so he could wind down.

"Do you think you'll be in any condition to drive a train tomorrow morning?"

Jim responded by taking another drag. Then another. He kept on until he couldn't hear that voice any more. Then he put out the joint with his fingers and put the rest of it back in his little plastic bag which he deposited into the inside pocket of his jacket. Then he walked back home to his apartment.

All at once Jim began to feel hopeful. What had he been worried about? His life was headed in the right direction. They couldn't really do anything to him on his job. After all, he was in the TWU. The worst thing his bosses could do to him was to suspend him. And every man needed a woman at hand every once in a while to fulfill those needs. It's not like Callie wasn't down. She knew the risks. And those old phantoms from the past, they were long gone. There was no need to worry about them. Besides, he didn't need a bunch of people hanging around him all the time with their nosy selves interfering in his personal business. He was better off flying solo the way he was. If he wanted to, he could go out and make new friends who were down with the new program he had for himself.

SIXTY-ONE

Davis had been avoiding Allen for the past three weeks. At first it was because he was angry about what Allen had done to him, but now it was for a different reason. After praying and hearing God respond through his word, Davis was beginning to see the situation a bit differently than he had before, and he was embarrassed by his own fleshly response on that particular night in question. It had led him to read Tamiko's note, which further convinced him of how wrong he was about all of them. Now he had to confront his own weakness in order to make reconciliation with Allen and God, and it wasn't going to be easy.

Davis had to acknowledge that he had a lot of pride, and although the world would say that was a good thing, he knew from reading his Bible that "Pride goeth before a fall."[1] It was pride that had led him out into the street life, searching for "respect" and "cred", both of which came with a very high price that almost cost him his life. It was pride that ruled his flesh in his angry response to Allen and the way that he interpreted the events of that Christmas Eve.

He had been praying and when he had finished, something told him to read his Bible. He just happened to be reading in the book of John in the 9th chapter. It was about when Jesus opened the eyes of the blind man and the Pharisees were questioning the blind man about who opened his eyes and how.[2] They just couldn't accept that Jesus opened the man's eyes because of their pride. In fact, they couldn't accept Jesus gift of salvation because of their pride. Their pride blinded them to the truth of who Jesus was. They were too caught up in their status and their position to learn from Jesus. God revealed to Davis through the scripture that he had done the same thing; he had focused too much on his reputation in the church rather than accepting the gift and being thankful to God and the people who he was working through for their generosity.

Looking back he realized that Allen was not "looking down on him". It was Davis' own insecurity about himself in relation to Allen. It was Davis who was looking down on himself, believing that because of his background, he wasn't good enough to hang with people like Allen and Tamiko and the others. He remembered that Allen's other friend, Richard, didn't have a college degree, either and he hadn't seen Allen show him any less respect than anyone else. Coming to this realization, he took out Tamiko's letter and read it.

Dear Davis,

I'm so sorry about what happened at the Christmas Celebration. Our friends and I all realize just how wrong we were to put you on the spot like that in front of so many from our church community. We've all been deeply distraught over seeing how much you were hurt and for that we are truly sorry.

We all miss you here at Greater Apostolic. Daniel misses your insightful questions. My father misses your sobriety and respect, and we all miss your warmth and quiet affection. Most of all, we miss your friendship. You once said that we were a blessing to you. Well, you were just as much a blessing to us. You're a person with character and integrity, something not often found in this world that we live in. Please consider this apology. It is meant with all my heart. If you want to talk, you can call me any time.

Sincerely and Affectionately Yours in Christ,

Tamiko

This wasn't a letter that could have come from a so-called "stuck up bougie snob." Davis had even felt guilty for judging them in the same way that he thought they were judging him. In fact, if they had not respected him as an equal, there would have been no way that any of them would have thought of apologizing (Even Tim left an apology on his cell at one point). If they were the people he had judged them to be, they would have all been indignant and called him ungrateful. They wouldn't have cared less if he came back to their church or not.

Adding to everything else, Davis was lonely and he missed the company of Allen, Tamiko, Richard, and even Tim to an extent. But he felt he had been such a fool. "What if they were re-evaluating things just as he had been?" Davis thought to himself. "What if they were beginning to feel that he had acted like a fool and they didn't need someone like that hanging with them?" It was these kinds of thoughts that kept him from going back to Greater Apostolic or approaching Allen to reconcile.

And in the last day or so, he had tried approaching Allen. Yesterday he saw Allen working on replacing light bulbs on the 5th floor, and thought about walking up to him, but he didn't know what to say that didn't sound stupid. How could he just walk up to him after avoiding him all this time and just strike up conversation like nothing happened. So he backed off. Then after reflecting on the moment, he realized that this was just his pride again. He was just afraid of being hurt. Davis realized he needed to put his pride down and just talk to Allen. That's what he had worked up the courage to do now.

Davis finished up on the cabinet he was working on quickly because he knew that Allen would be having his last 10 minute break within the next few minutes. Davis knew Allen always spent his breaks in the little office on the 5th floor. He would just go down there and ask him if he would talk to him for a second. Davis took the elevator down to the 5th floor and went to the office, but there was no sign of Allen. He thought of calling him on the radio, but that seemed too impersonal. So Davis headed down to the next place where he might find him: the locker room. The longer it took to find Allen, the more nervous he became. As he traveled the complex system of corridors to get to the locker room in the basement, another voice tried to talk him out of what he was doing, but Davis kept to his resolve. Yet, upon arriving at the locker room, Allen wasn't there either. This was strange. He knew Allen had punched in today because he saw his time card this morning. Then he went over to Mr. Hardy's office.

"Hey, Mr. Hardy. Have you seen Allen?"

"Oh, he left early today. He's helping a sick friend who's going into the hospital."

"What?! Who's sick?"

"He didn't say."

"Did he say which hospital he was going to?"

"I'm not sure if I remember. Presbyterian maybe. Do you need him for something?"

"Nah. It's not that important."

As Davis left the office he couldn't help but feel a little shaken. Who could it be? As one familiar face flashed before him, it nearly took the wind out of him. He thought of going over and checking in at Presbyterian to see them, but then he had another thought. "With everything that's going on, I'm probably the last person any of them want to see." But he couldn't help but be concerned for whoever was in the hospital right now, especially if it was the person he thought it was. Davis looked at his watch. He had five minutes of his 10-minute break left; just enough time to go back to the little office and pray for his friends.

COMMENCEMENT

SIXTY-TWO

Tamiko couldn't help but be distracted a bit as she waited in the hallway of room 415. Nervous energy had her shifting her weight from one foot to another swaying back and forth, and fumbling about with the assessment binder she was holding. It wasn't the anticipation of the meeting that made her tense. Today, Tim was supposed to get the results of his biopsy. Tamiko tried to keep her mind on the meeting, but she couldn't help but think about Tim and what he was going through at this moment, sitting in the waiting room of New York Presbyterian waiting for the news.

Tim's appointment was for 1:30. He tried to get a later appointment so Tamiko would be able to be with him, but the doctor's schedule would not allow it. Tamiko wanted to be there to keep Tim positive, because she knew how pessimistic he could be. She wanted to help Tim keep his eyes focused on God and what He could do, and not on the disease.

Suddenly the door opened and Tamiko was brought back to the reality of the present moment. Joan came out smiling, casting an awkward glance toward Tamiko.

"Hi, Tamiko", she offered flippantly before passing by without another word.

"Hi, Joan", replied Tamiko. As Tamiko's unpopularity with the administration grew, she and Joan grew further apart. It seemed that Joan didn't even want to be seen with Tamiko at lunch any more. Tamiko was hurt at first, but then she decided not to let herself get to caught up in her emotions. She was just glad to learn what kind of person Joan was before she put too much trust in her.

Tamiko went into the room and sat in the seat that Joan vacated. She wasn't too worried about the meeting this month because this time a lot of her kids had made significant progress. Tamiko did not forget to take time to thank God for his guidance and mercy in making this happen. In fact, two of her lowest students moved five levels each in reading and seemed on their way to approaching grade level benchmarks for reading and math which was quite an accomplishment for them. Tamiko thought that given this fact, the faces about her would be more cheerful, but they were not. The only one who seemed to be in any kind of a good mood at all was Mrs. Steele.

"Good afternoon, Miss Bynum", Principal Stone said gravely to start the meeting.

"Good afternoon."

"Your students have made a lot of progress since the last meeting", beamed Mrs. Steele. "I was telling the others that I was impressed with the growth of your students."

"Thank You. I don't think the students would have done half as well if God hadn't blessed me to be able to work with you", was Tamiko's reply.

"Yes. It almost seems too good to be true", sneered Nettlenerves.

"I'll say. Five levels is a lot of movement for a child in one month. Some of our best teachers haven't seen that type of movement. It's very unusual to say the least", Booker added with a hint of suspicion.

"I don't think so. Miss Fields, had a student who moved 7 levels in a month, and no one found it unusual", Mrs. Steele said in Tamiko's defense.

"That was isolated to one student. In this case, there are several. Even you have to admit it seems highly irregular", countered Nettlenerves.

"Well, you've seen the running records and the other assessments. They speak for themselves don't they?" asked Tamiko.

COMMENCEMENT

"I'm more interested in what you have to say Miss Bynum. Why don't you explain what you've been doing in the classroom to precipitate this sudden change?" Stone suggested with a hint of sarcasm.

Tamiko explained what she had been doing in elaborate detail beginning with the observations lessons and mentoring she had received from Mrs. Steele and how she used this to change her lesson plans and revise her teaching with regard to word study, centers, and guided reading. She spoke of the various talents and strengths she noticed in particular students and how she used what she had learned to design lessons that would use student's strengths to help them overcome weaknesses, and in the process, develop new skills for learning.

"You seem to know your students really well and it shows", Mrs. Steele lauded.

"Yes, so it seems. I'm sure they've made progress, but we have to be careful when administering assessments. Sometimes our own subjectivity can tarnish the results. Just to be on the safe side, I think we should have Mrs. Bedford the reading specialist go in and re-assess some of the children, especially those who seemed to move more than two levels" said Principal Stone as she glared at Tamiko.

"That's a good idea. I think we can get the math resource room teacher to re-test some of the children with the Math assessment as well", Booker put in.

"Yes, we must always take caution on the side of error", said Stone, focusing a laser like stare toward Tamiko.

Tamiko struggled to hide her shock and disbelief. They were accusing her of fudging her students' records! They had some nerve! They badgered her for months because her students did not do as well as other teachers, and then when they were learning and doing well, they still found fault! "This school is like the twilight zone!" Tamiko thought to herself. Part of her wanted to tell them off, but she remembered what kind of person God wanted her to be and she also remembered what Mrs. Steele had told her. "Lord, God, keep my mouth and my tongue from uttering something that I shouldn't", Tamiko prayed inside herself.

"That's fine with me. I'm sure they will do well", replied Tamiko with confidence.

"Once the assessments have been completed, we will meet again. Thank you for your time Miss. Bynum. You are dismissed", remarked Stone coldly.

"Have a nice day everyone."

Tamiko took her assessment binder and left, at the same time trying to staunch the anger and indignation that had welled up inside of her. "I really shouldn't be surprised by now," Tamiko thought to herself. Ordinarily, the thought of having her children assessed by someone else would have rattled her, but she knew that this was just another test that God was putting her through. It was God that had helped her to understand her students, who opened her eyes to who they were and what their needs were. It was God that enlightened the students understanding so they could learn. If God had brought her this far, then she knew He would continue to be with her, even through this inquisition that they were imposing upon her.

Tamiko went back upstairs to her class to finish the lessons for the day. The guided math cluster teacher was covering Tamiko for the assessment meeting and had started the lesson that Tamiko had planned. When Tamiko got back the children were in the middle of the math centers activities and groups of children rotated through the centers, taking turns practicing different skills until all of the groups had completed all of the activities. Tamiko was actually thankful for the hustle and bustle of her work at this moment. The classroom required all of her attention and didn't allow her mind to wander onto other things. Once math centers was over there was a read aloud, and then she would review tonight's homework with the children, hand out the behavior chart colors and rewards and then have the children line up for dismissal. Then during dismissal, Tamiko had to learn to have eyes in the back of her head to make sure the children stayed in place and that each child was picked up by someone who was responsible for them. She stayed in her 'alert' mode until the last child was picked up. When she finally came up for air, it was 3:15. Tamiko left the gym where the children were dismissed and went back upstairs to her classroom and checked her cell phone. Tim hadn't called her. He should have gotten word from the doctor by now. She then called Tim to see what had happened. All she got was his voicemail. He still couldn't be at the doctor, could he?

Tamiko gathered her belongings and went downstairs. On her way to the office to sign out she ran into Mrs. Steele.

"Tamiko, I'm so sorry about what happened at the meeting today."

"That's okay, Ros. I know it's not your fault."

"I tried to talk them out of re-testing the students, but they just wouldn't listen."

"Don't worry about it. I'm not. It's like you said, the students will prove me right by what they can do. And no one can take back the knowledge God has given them."

"Good for you, Tamiko. That's the way to think. And by the way, I was really proud of the way you handled them in there. They were hoping to break you, but you didn't flinch."

"I had help. God was with me."

"And He sure was working. Well, I have to go. I'll see you tomorrow."

"See you, Rosalyn, and thanks for standing up for me."

"Anytime, my dear."

Tamiko left her and signed out. Then she walked up the block to the train station and headed to her grad school class at Bankstreet College. It was raining lightly now, but since the walk wasn't long Tamiko didn't bother getting the umbrella out of her bag, but simply tucked her hair underneath her hat so it wouldn't get wet. Before she went underground to the platform, she tried Tim's cell one more time. Still, nothing but the voicemail, so Tamiko left a brief message telling him to call her in an hour when she was out of the subway. Now she was worried.

Tamiko went down the stairs to the station entrance where she went to the turnstile, swiped her fare card and then headed down another flight of stairs to the platform. As she descended, she wondered why Tim wasn't answering. Was he still with the doctor? Did he get bad news? He said he'd been having trouble with his vision lately. Did he have an accident? When Tamiko had last seen Tim, she was helping him home from the hospital after the biopsy. She remembered him being really quiet, and kind of sad. She hoped that today's news hadn't led him to do something desperate. Tamiko recalled what he had said when he told her about Preston's melt down. Tim had said that there were times when he felt suicidal. She hoped he didn't feel that way now. Didn't he know that he could talk to her or Allen, or even better, he could talk to God about how he was feeling? Tamiko desperately hoped Tim was all right.

"Heavenly Father, please be with my friend, Tim, right now. He's going through so much with his job and now this disease. Please keep him in his right mind and help him make right decisions. Let him know that You are with him and ease any pain or grief that he might be going through right now. Help him to keep his eyes on You and let him know he can trust in You. In Jesus name. Amen."

After her short prayer, Tamiko still felt burdened in her spirit. She knew she couldn't go to school like she planned. Tamiko went past her usual stop and transferred to a local train so she could stop by Tim's place to see if he was home. When she came out of the station, she discovered the light rainfall had changed over to snow. The stairs of the subway exit had become slippery and her leather high-heeled boots were no match for them under these conditions. When she had finally made it up the stairs and onto the street, she was nearly knocked down by a ferocious gust of wind that pelted her with tiny ice crystals. They stung her face like little shards of glass, and Tamiko had no choice but to bring out her umbrella. She teetered, tottered and wobbled for a few steps in the thickening slush, before taking cover under a bus shelter to gather her bearings. Tamiko took out her cell phone. It was now 4:15. She checked to see if she had any messages. There were none. She put her cell phone back into her coat pocket, slung her school bag over her shoulder, adjusted the umbrella and headed the rest of the way to the New Towers.

Tamiko was out of breath when she arrived, after fighting five long blocks through the worsening snowstorm. She barely had enough breath to greet Bradley the doorman.

"Good afternoon Miss Bynum, what brings you out in this weather?"

"I know it's pretty bad out there", said Tamiko trying to be nonchalant, "Is Tim in? Did you see him come in?"

"I was on break from 12:00 to 1:00, but since I came back, I haven't seen him. But sometimes he slips by me if I'm signing for a package or something. I'll page upstairs for you to be sure."

"Thank you, so much."

Bradley picked up the intercom phone and dialed Tim's apartment. Tamiko followed his every movement. Her heart leapt higher in her throat with every moment of silence.

"Seems he's not there. Sorry. Would you like to leave a message for him?"

"No, that won't be necessary. But thanks for your help, Bradley."

Tamiko walked over to the waiting area and took out her cell phone. She called Allen.

"Hello."

"Allen, it's Miko."

"You're lucky you got me. I thought my phone was off. You do know I'm at work?"

"Allen, this is important. You know Tim was supposed to get his results today, right?"

"He called you?"

"That's the problem. He hasn't called me, and when I call him it just goes to his voicemail. I even came all the way to his apartment, but no one's seen him. I'm really worried", Tamiko's voice began to choke up.

"Tamiko, relax. Do you know when his appointment was for?"

"1:30 and now it's almost 4:30. That's like three hours ago."

"That's not that much time. Calm down. You know how long they can make you wait at the doctor's office."

"But three hours? What if he got bad news and got really depressed and decided to do something crazy."

"Miko, I've lived with him for more than a year, and I think I know what he's capable of. If he got bad news he might get into a funk and go sulk somewhere, but I don't think he'd do anything crazy."

"Allen, it's not like he's been dumped by some girl! This is a life and death issue he's dealing with! Can you really say what he would do in a situation like this?"

"Miko, trust me. Go to school. If he's in a mood, you probably won't want to find him."

"How can you say that! He probably needs us right now."

"Or maybe the brother just needs space."

"What if you're wrong? I just feel this burden in my spirit like something's not right."

"Listen, I get off in about half an hour. If it will make you feel better, I will go out and check a few spots where he might be at, make a few phone calls, and get back to you. But there's one condition. You have to go to school."

"Fine. I'll go, but that doesn't mean I won't worry."

SIXTY-THREE

The snow was now more than ankle deep and still coming down fast when Allen left the hotel. He had just checked his cell phone to see if he had any messages, but there were none. Previously he tried to call Tim's cell phone thinking that maybe he just needed time to digest whatever the doctor had told him. All he got was his voicemail like Tamiko had said. Then he called Bradley at the desk of New Towers. He still hadn't seen him. Next he tried Allyson, but she hadn't heard from him in a week. It seemed like Tim was in one of his 'I want to be alone' moods. There was no way that he could have gotten good news if he was pulling this stunt. And contrary to what Allen told Tamiko, there was no way of guessing where Tim could be. Despite what he told Tamiko, Allen was now beginning to worry. He would try his best to think of where he should go next.

The first place Allen went was Tim's own building. There was the chance that Tim could've sneaked past Bradley and then locked himself in the apartment with the lights off. The fact that Tim hated winter weather also made this possible, as it was highly unlikely that he would want to be out in all of the snow. Allen had Tim's spare key so he was able to actually go in. He looked through every room, but he didn't find him. Where could he be? Allen knew that any place Tim would go would be the last place where someone would look for him. The bar next door was too obvious. Then he thought of his mother. That was indeed the last place where he would expect Tim to turn up, especially given what he was going through. It was worth a shot though. Allen went back out into the winter tempest and took the train over to the Battery Park condo where Tim's mom lived.

Allen remembered the way from when he visited Tim during one Thanksgiving break a long time ago. The building had a doorman just like Tim's where the tenants were paged. It turned out that she wasn't at home, either. As Allen left the building and walked back into the stormy night, he tried desperately to think of where Tim could be. Then all of a sudden it came to him.

****

On Tuesdays and Thursday, Greater Apostolic Church was open throughout the night for those who wanted to come in and pray. The pastor was not there, but the deacons would come and open the church sanctuary and the upper room for those who wanted to sit in silent prayer to God. The sanctuary was basically the pulpit and surrounding areas where the choir, pastor and church laity were seated when church services were held. Upstairs, the upper room was divided into two parts. First there was a big spacious room where people tarried to be filled with the Spirit. Then over on the other side of this room, there were little stalls or booths where people could have more privacy. When Allen entered he saw a few people sitting in the pews and some kneeling at the sanctuary in silent prayer to God. Allen walked past as quietly as he could, so as not to disturb them. Then he went upstairs to the upper room. When he arrived, the front space was empty, so he walked off to the side and checked the stalls. Allen breathed a sigh of relief as he saw a familiar pair of hiking boots sticking out from under one of the booths. Allen went to the booth next to this one and got down and prayed as well.

"Heavenly Father, I come before you this evening for my friend. He is in desperate need of your love, mercy, and grace. Help me to help him through this trying time of his life. Please speak through me and help me to comfort him in the midst of his pain and suffering. Let him know that You love him and are looking out for him. Put Your hand on him and touch him. Let him know that this disease does not have control, but You. Give us both the faith and the strength to overcome this…"

COMMENCEMENT

Allen continued to pray until he heard movement in the next stall. He got up and went over to look, and saw Tim sitting on the floor of the booth. He had his field coat stowed to the side and his head on his knees.

"Tim?" Allen called out softly.

Tim looked up startled. He got up and turned his face away from Allen so he wouldn't see how red, puffy, and tear stained it was.

"Hey. What are you doing here?" Tim voiced wavered as he tried to put on a carefree veneer.

"Same thing as you, man."

"I just came to be alone for a while."

"You don't have to front, Tim. It's me. Remember?"

"I don't know if you could call what I was doing 'praying'. I was just talking to Him about different things…you know?"

"I know. So do you think you're ready to talk to me about what's going on?"

Tim paused for a moment and put his hand over his mouth. Then he looked away from Allen, fighting to hold back the tears that wanted to come down.

"They call it an anaplastic astrocytoma." Tim's voice quivered as he spoke. "They can operate, but they don't know if they'll be able to get it all. It can come back. It can even turn into something more malignant."

"But they can give you treatments to prevent that right?"

"You mean the lethal doses of radiation and chemo I'll have to endure just to extended my life a measly two or three years when I'll be nothing but a vegetable. I'd be better off dying on the operating table."

"It doesn't have to be that way. God can and will give you the strength to go through this. He can heal you, but you've got to believe." Allen couldn't believe what he found himself saying; especially because he wasn't sure he believed it himself. Sure he knew what the Bible said, but he had never experienced it.

"I don't know if I can."

527

"Yes you can. You wouldn't be here if you didn't believe God could help you."

"I'm too scared", said Tim, his voice cracking in spite of his best efforts to hold it together.

"That's because you're looking too far down the road. I told you one day at a time. And stop trying to do this by yourself. You just brought this burden before God. Leave this here with Him. And let me and Miko help you, too. You know she was worried sick when she couldn't get through to you."

"Really?"

"What you mean 'really?' You should know how much she cares about you by now. She is your friend, too."

"I'm sorry. I'll call her right now."

"Let's wait until we get outside. You want to get something to eat? It is kinda late and I know you've probably been here for a while."

"I'll be alright."

"You'd be in a better position to fight this thing if you keep your strength up. And dinner doesn't take that long."

"There's that Chinese take out place down the block from me."

"We better hurry, some places are closing early because of the snowstorm."

"What snowstorm? It was only raining when I came in."

"You must have been here an awful long time. There's about five inches of snow out there, now, bro."

"Aww, man! There's no way we're going to be able to get a cab now!"

"So we'll take the subway."

"I hate having to trudge through the snow."

"Well, at least you won't be alone."

"I know. Thanks, man."

SIXTY-FOUR

It was a cold and blustery Sunday morning after what seemed to be one of the worst snowstorms in New York City's history. Total snowfall accumulations reached 12 inches. In the early hours of the morning the New York City Sanitation crews had been hard at work removing the snow from city streets. There were still mounds of snow in piles at the edges of the curb where storeowners and other property owners had shoveled snow, and lots of slippery spots on the sidewalk where melted snow became ice, making the streets treacherous booby traps. And yet there was still a crowd of people who made it to Greater Apostolic for the morning service. Among them was Tim who arrived early with a purpose in his heart.

Tim was sitting in the half-empty pew reading the exquisitely made hand crafted leather Bible that Tamiko had given him for Christmas. He had taken her advice and had begun to read the New Testament. He started with the book of John and went from there to Matthew. He had to admit that he was fascinated by what he read. In college, he had been told that Jesus was a philosopher, not unlike Plato or Socrates. Tim had read excerpts of the Bible for some of his courses, but never gave the verses much thought, until now. As he had been reading, there was something different about the words that Jesus spoke. His Word was more than a mere philosophy. A philosophy implied a rationed thought or perspective of life that was theoretical, based on supposition. When he read the words that Jesus spoke, he couldn't help but remember that it was said "He spoke as one having authority, and not as the scribes and pharisees."[1]

Then he remembered in John where Jesus said, "these words I speak unto you, they are spirit and they are life."[2] When Jesus spoke he wasn't wondering about what this life was about. He wasn't trying to figure it out. He knew because He was from God.

The more Tim read, the more he was drawn to read. A lot of the things he had spoken to the Pastor Bynum about and that he had preached on before became clear to him. Tim was moved by Jesus' compassion for the people, especially those who lived in sin. Jesus had mercy on a lot of sinful people who repented to believe on Him. Tim remembered the woman caught in adultery, which Jesus forgave.[3] He also thought about the blind men who begged for mercy.[4] Jesus even called Matthew the tax collector to be one of his apostles.[5] Tim felt like one of those people. He had spent his whole life doubting God and living his own way. It was good to know that God was merciful and full of compassion. Tim had experienced that compassion, mercy, and power, and in light of his present situation, he needed them now more than ever. Yes, Tim could now believe that Jesus was the Son of God. He was ready to finally repent and commit himself fully and completely to living the way God wanted him to live in the little time that he may have left.

"Hey there", said Tamiko softly. Tim stood up and greeted her with a hug and then they both sat down in the pew.

"As you can see, I've followed your advice."

"And what do you think?"

"You were right. It put a lot of things in perspective for me", he said quietly.

Just then Allen came in and sat on the opposite side of Tim.

"Hey man, how's it going?"

"I'm taking it one day at a time, just like you said."

"Good. I see you're into the Word."

"Yeah. I had to make sure the Pastor was telling me the truth", Tim joked trying to be more casual.

COMMENCEMENT

"Next thing you know, you'll be joining me for the Brotherhood Bible study."

"To tell you the truth, I don't think that would be a bad idea."

Soon, Brother Anderson was at the podium to announce the entrance of the choir and the beginning of the service. As they sang and prayed, Tim prayed and sang along, actively participating in the service. When he first started coming to the church he was a mere voyeur, observing the goings on, listening to, but not actually hearing the sermons. Tim was skeptical of the people's religious expression, believing as Allen had, that it was all a mere paroxysm brought on by an overabundance of emotion. As time passed, he began to listen and to wonder. Then there were things that were said that began to speak into his life. And he would never forget the prophetic word the pastor had for him that came to life. Now he was beginning to feel a part of the church and to understand what the people were feeling. Even if their outburst were just emotional, he was beginning to understand why the people were so emotional.

Soon it was time for the sermon, and Pastor Bynum took to the podium to speak.

"Praise the Lord, everybody!" he greeted the congregation.

"Praise the Lord!" the congregation responded in unison.

"I'd like to read from the book of John, chapter 3, vs 14 to 18. When you find it say Amen.

There was a loud rustling of onionskin pages as the members of the congregation sifted through their Bibles to find the scripture followed by a collective "amen". Pastor Bynum led them through the scripture reading and then he began his sermon.

"My subject: The Greatest Love of All. What would you call the greatest love of all? Now there are many things that we call 'love'. There is a love between a man and his wife: a kind of romantic love. Some people think that's the greatest love. There's the love between family: like between a mother and child or between siblings. Some people think that's the greatest love. There's a love between friends: a bond of friendship.

Other people think that's the greatest love. But I'm here to tell you that none of that compares to the love with which God first loved us. What does it say in chapter 3: it says that 'God so loved the world'. He loved us. Now I'm not saying he loves what we *do* all the time, but he does love us. In fact, God loved us so much, that he sent his only begotten Son to save us. How many of you understand that sacrifice that He made? How many of you know what it meant? Say Amen."

And the congregation responded with a hearty "Amen".

"I say this because there are some of us that don't understand that sacrifice. If they understood it, they wouldn't want to live any old kind of way. If they understood just how much God loved us and how much He sacrificed for us, they couldn't just be satisfied with just coming to church on Sunday. You couldn't just worry God all the time about what you want. If you knew just how much God has sacrificed for you, you couldn't sit in that seat like a stone, you'd have to get up and praise Him and say 'Thank You, Jesus!'"

At this there were shouts of "Hallelujah!" and "Thank you Jesus!" that resounded throughout the audience.

"So I'm going to try to explain it to some of y'all who don't know, or you want to act like you don't know. Help me somebody. What does the rest of the scripture say? 'He gave His only begotten Son, that whosoever believeth on Him should not perish, but have everlasting life.' Think about that. Did you get that? Everlasting life. Do you know what that means? That means that when the physical life is over, you're not going to die. There's a lot of people that will die, and when they leave this world, they are going to experience a second death: a spiritual death. That's what hell is you know. If you don't have Christ you're dead. Even life here on earth without Christ is hell. Yeah, life is tough. If you have Christ you can make it, but if you don't it's like living in hell. But for those of us who want to accept this gift that God has given to us out of his love for us, we will have life here on earth and after we leave these physical bodies! I don't understand why some of you aren't excited by that! What did Jesus say? 'I came that you might have life and that they might have it more abundantly.' I don't know about you, but I can't help but be grateful, I can't help but say Thank Yaaaaaa! Hallelujah!"

COMMENCEMENT

Many of the parishioners stood up to praise God and give the Pastor a standing ovation. When the audience's enthusiasm subsided, Pastor Bynum continued his message.

"And don't think that it came easy. You know when you get a gift that doesn't mean anything. It's usually something cheap, and it didn't cost the giver anything. For example, if someone who's very wealthy gives his wife a diamond it may not be meaningful to him or to his wife because it didn't really cost him anything. But if a poor man scrimps and saves to buy his wife a diamond, it probably means more because it cost him more. There was a sacrifice involved. You know that abundant life that we got. It cost a lot. That's how we know the love of God is real. God sent his only begotten son, Jesus, who suffered to give us life. He was tempted by the devil. He was lied on and talked about. They called him a demon and a drunk. And it didn't stop there. He was spat on and buffeted. He was slapped and mocked and if that wasn't enough He was hung upon a cross and suffered the pains of death. What does the Bible say 'No greater love hath a man than one that will lay down his life for his friends'.[6] Jesus laid down his life for us! I don't know about you, but there is no greater love than that! What other god has done that? Did Buddha lay down his life? Did Mohammed? Did the Dalai Lama?"

The audience responded with thunderous applause at this point. Tamiko was standing and praising God, along with the Sharpes and even Allen was on his feet. So was Tim, who found himself clapping as well. The more he listened, the more he knew it was true. He had been looking for the kind of love the Pastor was talking about all of his life and now he finally found it.

"And you know how else I know he loves us? He did all that and we didn't even deserve it. What were we doing? Down here serving wood. Bowing down to stones. Some of us still bowing. They don't call it Ashtoreth any more, now we call him 'money'. It's not called Baal any more, now us call him 'technology'. Some of you spend more time on the computer than you do reading your Bible. There are a lot of different names for it now. And none of these things has done anything for us. Some of us are sitting down here destroying ourselves, profaning His holy name, and doing anything we're big enough to do, wallowing in sin. If

God was like us, He would have looked down and destroyed us all. He could have said 'I'm sick of these ungrateful beings, let them perish', but He didn't do that. God looked down and had compassion on us. He loved us. He wouldn't let us go out like that. So He came down and He humbled himself. He sacrificed Himself even though we didn't deserve it. Now you tell me have any of you ever known a person who can love you like that? I don't know anyone else who can love me like that!"

Tim knew what Pastor Bynum was talking about. God had mercy on him and blessed him in so many ways. It was God that took the hatred and envy out of his heart toward Preston and Standoff and enabled him to work with them. It was God's love and mercy that spoke through him to talk Preston out of suicide. It was God's mercy that allowed him to do the work of 7 men. And more than anything else, He had blessed Tim with loving and caring friends that had been better to him than his whole family. Friends that had led him to God. Tim hadn't deserved any of that, and he was thankful for God's grace and mercy. All of Tim's life he had worked hard to gain love and acceptance and never got it, even when he thought he deserved it. And here was a God who loved him in spite of everything. Pastor Bynum was right. There was no greater love than this. There was no doubt about it. He was a mighty God. A God that could do anything even send his Son, Jesus, to die for the sins of the people.

Pastor Bynum concluded his sermon.

"So I know God loves us. He paid a price for us that we can never repay. And I don't know about you, but when I think about that loving sacrifice, I can't help but love Him. I can't help but to serve Him. I can't help but to praise Him. I can't help but to surrender my life to Him because without Him there is no life, and there is no love. He is the Greatest Love of all!"

Now the church was on fire. There were people praising God, some people were shouting in the aisles without music, and some people were crying. Tim himself found himself praising God with a "Hallelujah", which caused Allen to turn a startled look toward his friend. He noticed Tim was trying to wipe away tears that had begun to form in the creases of his eyes. Then Pastor Bynum began to make this week's altar call.

COMMENCEMENT

"How many of you are want to surrender to the Greatest love of all? How many of you want to be baptized and receive the gift that Jesus paid so dearly for? Come on up right now."

Tim headed toward the altar, but not before he felt a hand on his arm, pulling him away.

"Tim, you do know what this means? Are you sure that you're ready?" Allen asked.

"I've never been more sure about any thing in my whole life."

SIXTY-FIVE

"Praise God, Hallelujaaaaah!" shouted Lena. "Glory to God!! Glory!!"

"Thank You, Jesus! Oh, Thank You, Jesus! Hallelujah!" Tamiko praised.

Allen was astonished at the miracle he had just witnessed. Here was a person who had believed more in his own self than in any conception of God, who was now willing to be baptized as a Christian, no less. It reminded him of the voice that spoke to him at the Election Night party: "With man it is impossible, but with God all things are possible."[1] Yes, Allen knew Tim believed in God. He didn't know how deep Tim's belief went, but apparently it went deeper than his own.

"Allen, why don't you go on and be baptized?" Vernon suggested to Allen.

"Why? I thought you had me baptized when I was a baby?"

"You weren't baptized, you were christened."

"Isn't that the same thing?"

"Not that I can see. When you were a baby you didn't have a choice. Now you do."

Allen thought about what his father said for a moment. At first he didn't want to get caught up in what could be a meaningless ritual, but then he reflected on the sermon. A while ago, Allen had wondered how one could love God, but after today's sermon, he was beginning to understand. His father was right. It was his choice now. He had to devote his own life to God for himself. But he was still so unsure about a lot of things. He wavered back and forth in his faith, so much. But then he thought about what his mother had said. He wanted a relationship with God, and if he really wanted that, baptism would be another step in the right direction. However he was a little ashamed that his father had to suggest it.

"You're right."

Allen went to the altar call where the people were lining up to be baptized. The women went to one side of the altar and the men went to the other. Since Allen had taken so long to make his decision, he was one of the last men on the line, and Tim was way ahead of him. There had to be at least 30 people on the line. Brother Anderson was now leading the men to the changing rooms on the mezzanine level above the altar. As Allen proceeded forward with the rest of the men, he thought he saw someone else on the line that looked vaguely familiar. Then he recognized the curly fade haircut. He must have sensed Allen's eyes on him, because he looked back, at which time Allen looked down as the line slowly moved forward. Since Allen had looked away, he didn't notice when Davis got off the line and came to the end.

"Hey, Allen."

"Hey!" said Allen shocked that he was speaking to him. Neither of them knew what to say next and so there was a moment of awkward silence.

"Kinda surprised to see you here. I thought you would've been baptized already", Davis continued.

"You would think, but no. I'm kind of surprised to see you here, too. You haven't been here in a while."

"I know. I wanted to talk to you about that, man to man. Do you think we could meet up after the baptism?"

"Sure. How about we go for coffee after church." Allen knew he would miss the brotherhood bible study, but he felt this was more important and he didn't want Davis to feel like he was blowing him off.

"Cool. I'll meet you out front and we'll walk over."

The Luncheonette where they had coffee was as empty as it always was on Sundays. Allen and Davis ordered their coffee and the waitress came back with it not long after. There was another moment of silence between them as each of them pondered what to say next.

"So when did you decide you wanted to be baptized?" asked Allen who couldn't take the silence any longer.

"In the last week or so. I realized that if I'm accepting God into my life, then I have to submit to Him making me a new person in Christ. There's a lot of stuff I still have to let go of. That's why I wanted to talk to you."

Then Davis paused for a moment.

"I'm listening."

"Look, Al, I just want to apologize for how I acted at the Christmas Celebration. And for cuttin' you off like that. I been praying to God, and he opened my eyes to see that, I got too much pride. I know now that you wasn't tryin' to clown me or nothin'. You were just tryin' to have my back. Feel?"

"I hear you. But you had every right to be angry, Davis. It wasn't just your pride. You were right. I was being a disrespectful jerk. I should have listened to you when you told me that it wasn't my business, but instead I tried to play God with your life. I'm just glad that you've forgiven me."

"Yeah, but still I know you didn't mean anything by it. Sometimes I get too caught up in the whole 'respect' thing, you know. Probably 'cause I don't have enough of it for myself. I keep thinkin' people are looking down on me, but really it's me looking down on myself."

"But Davis, you're a really great guy. Why would you think otherwise?"

" 'Cause I see you and Miko, and Tim, and you guys are like all proper and all that. You know a lot of things about life that I never knew 'cause I didn't have nobody to teach me. Like you know how to relate to people without fightin' all the time, and you know how to kick back without getting' into trouble. And you all went to college and everything.

It's like you guys are from a whole other world and sometimes I'm not sure how I fit in."

"I don't know Davis. Just because we've had a certain kind of upbringing, that doesn't mean that we're perfect. Trust me, we've had our fair share of arguments. We make mistakes and get in trouble, too. That's just life."

"Yeah, but you guys have helped me so much. I feel like I have nothing to give back to you."

"No way, man! Davis, you are highly intelligent, caring, humble, selfless...just about everything I thought I was until I met you. I can't tell you what a privilege it is to be able to call you my friend."

"Really?"

"Really. And I realize now that you have something that is worth more than all of our education, and family background combined. You have something that I've been searching for, for months and still haven't found. You have a real relationship with God. He speaks to you. He guides you. Like you said earlier, he opened the word to you so that you could understand what you needed to let go of."

"But Allen, you're a Christian, just like me. All of us have a relationship with God."

"No. A lot of us go to church and pretend. We go through the motions, but we don't have a real connection to God."

"You don't go through the motions, right? You pray, and I know you believe, right?"

"Yes, but not the way you do. It's like you really love God and you trust him completely. Tamiko has that, and now Tim may even have it, but somehow, I'm not sure if it's happening for me."

"We're all going to have our doubts sometimes. There have been times in my life where I wasn't sure God was going to step in but he did."

"Yeah, but at least you know how you feel about Him. Sometimes I can't help but feel angry and frustrated with Him."

"We all feel that way sometimes, but we can't let ourselves stay there. Jonah was angry with God, and there were times when Moses got really frustrated, but we have to remember that He is God and it's His world. He knows what's best. Maybe it's your anger that's hindering your relationship. The fact that things haven't turned out the way you think they should have. Maybe you need to pray about that and ask Him to help you let it go."

"You know what, maybe you're right about that. You see Davis; this is why you're so important to me, and everyone else. So will you hang with us again? Come to dinner tonight?"

"I don't know. Are you sure the others are going to be as forgiving as you?"

"There's nothing to forgive, Davis. Come on, man. Even Tim misses you."

"Well, if you put it that way…Oh, and there's something else I wanted to talk to you about Al."

"What?"

"I heard you went to the hospital with one of the guys? Is everything ok? Tamiko isn't sick, is she?"

"No, Tamiko is fine. It was someone else."

"Then it must be Tim."

"I'm not sure I can confirm or deny."

"It's okay Al, I get you. I won't say nothin'. Now I think I understand why he went up today. Is it really serious?"

"Yeah…yeah." was all Allen could muster.

"I figured. I'm gonna pray for him. God's going to work this out. No doubt."

"I hope so."

"I know so."

COMMENCEMENT

****

This had been a very full day for Allen, and he was glad that it was now time to turn in for the night, so that he could digest everything that happened today. First there was Tim, who became baptized as a Christian. Allen noticed that after it was done, Tim had seemed happier than he had been in a long time. At dinner, he talked more than Tamiko did. Which led Allen to think about the next occurrence. Allen had totally given up on his relationship with Davis. He let go and submitted to God. Then out of nowhere it seemed that Davis was reaching out to Allen. Maybe God was listening to his prayers. Davis came back and it seemed like things just picked up where they left off. Even Tim wasn't as standoffish as he used to be with regard to Davis.

Then Allen thought about what Davis had said. Allen thought he had let go of his anger at God, but now he wasn't sure. In the past, he was angry and disappointed because God did not allow his life to turn out the way he wanted it. Allen had to admit that even now he was still angry and disappointed. He was disappointed that God did not speak to him when he wanted. He was angry about the loss of his friends, and about Tim's illness. If he was going to trust God, he had to love God with all his heart, mind, and strength. How could Allen love God if he was holding on to anger? Then he thought about the Pastor's sermon today.

Allen thought about God's love for him. If God loved him like that, how could he keep hold of his anger? Maybe God wasn't doing these things to hurt Allen as he had thought. Maybe the things God was allowing in Allen's life were to help him and make him stronger. To keep him on the right path. To keep Allen's eyes on Him. Allen got down on his knees and began to pray:

Father God, thank you for all of the blessings you have bestowed on me, my friends, and family this day. Thank you for saving my friend Tim, and restoring my friend Davis to our lives. Heavenly Father, I ask that you keep us all until the day when we are called from this earth to stand before You in Your glory. Father God, be with my friend Tim and heal him of his illness, and if you should choose not to heal him, then Lord help us to accept Your will for his life. Lord, I also pray that You reach out and touch my life in the way that You have touched my friends' lives. You

541

said if we draw near to You, You would draw near to us. If there is any anger in my heart towards You, please, Lord, help me to deal with it and take it out of me so that I may love You and praise You the way I should. I ask this in Your Son Jesus' name. Amen.

Allen got up off his knees and went to bed still thinking. He began to re-evaluate why God had put him at the Sheraton and why He allowed him to meet Davis when he did. His mother may have been right. Maybe he was not put at the Sheraton to help Davis, but maybe it was Davis who was supposed to help him.

SIXTY-SIX

Although it was 7:00, the winter sky was as dark as if it had been the middle of the night. Thunder rumbled as dark clouds threatened to let loose a torrential rainstorm on the city below. Tamiko hurried along the street hoping to get to the school before the first drops began to fall. Luckily she made it. After signing in at the office, Tamiko took a look at the Daily Bulletin posted on the office bulletin board for any schedule changes. There was only one change listed in big bold print:

THERE WILL BE NO ENRICHMENT PERIOD THIS MORNING FOR THE FOLLOWING TEACHERS: MISS ROBINSON, MRS. WOOD, MR. HULE, MR. ORVIS, MS. RICHARDS, MRS. STEELE, AND MISS BYNUM. INSTEAD THERE WILL BE AN EMERGENCY FACULTY CONFERENCE IN ROOM 415 AT 8:00am. ALL INVOLVED PLEASE BE PROMPT.

"Now what do they want?" Tamiko sighed. She would have thought it was bad news except there were other teachers on the list that the administration liked. Tamiko hurried upstairs and got her classroom set up for the day's lessons. She hoped she could get everything done before the meeting started.

Tamiko was in the middle of changing her math centers chart when she heard a knock at the classroom door.

"Come in."

"Hi, Tamiko. Here are the games you wanted for the math centers."

"Thanks, Rosalyn. You're the best."

"The 100th day of school will soon be upon us. Do you have anything planned yet?"

"I was going to do cereal necklaces for math and a 100 words book during word study…oh, and I bought this book over the weekend on the 100th day of school that I was going to use for a read aloud, but I don't know what else I'm going to do."

"I have an 100 days of school activity book for teachers. If you'd like you can flip through it and see if there's anything that catches your eye."

"Thanks, that'd be great. Ros, before you leave, I wanted to ask you something. Do you have any idea what this emergency faculty conference is about?"

"I haven't heard anything from Stone or Nettlenerves, so I'm not sure."

"Do you think this has anything to do with…"

Before Tamiko could finish her sentence, an announcement came over the PA system.

"Please excuse this interruption. Good morning to all teachers in the building. It is now 7:55. I hope those of you who will be involved in this morning's meeting are making your way to the conference room in 415 for our emergency faculty meeting. We need everyone to be there on time so we may begin promptly. There is a lot of information that needs to be discussed, so it is imperative that everyone be on time. Thank you."

"I guess we better be going. We wouldn't want to be late now, would we?"

"Not after that announcement", laughed Tamiko.

****

All the teachers involved in the meeting arrived at the same time, and they were all equally in the dark about what was going on. After a few minutes, Principal Stone and Nettlenerves arrived, with Booker tagging along behind them. Principal Stone sat at a desk near the front of the room, allowing Nettlenerves to take control of the meeting.

"Good morning, everyone", Nettlenerves greeted her audience.

544

COMMENCEMENT

"Good morning", the faculty responded in unison.

"I know you're all anxious to know what this meeting is about so let's get right to it. On Friday, Principal Stone got an e-mail from Central about the Quality Review. The Quality Review inspector has chosen all of you to be observed. Some of you are familiar with the process, but there are many of you that have never participated before which is why we have convened this meeting today."

Tamiko's heart was gripped with fear as Nettlenerves uttered those last words.

"Not only will you be observed in your classrooms, but you will also serve on a panel in which the reviewer will ask you questions about the school. As you know, the Review is going to be in two weeks, which is not a lot of time to prepare. This is really important because you will all be representing this school and what happens in your classrooms may be a deciding factor in determining our school grade. Our state scores for the upper grades aren't that great, and neither are our parent surveys, so this Quality Review is going to make or break us. I can't impress upon you enough how serious this is, since our grade can affect our school's budget. Miss Booker and myself will be conducting 'walk-throughs' of each of your classrooms and providing you feedback that you will use to prepare classroom environments. You will also need to submit any and all lesson plans that you will be following that day for approval."

Tamiko's head was swirling. She was still struggling with the last task of setting goals for all of her students in various subject areas, then there were the children that were being reassessed, now she had to go through observation boot camp again. It all just seemed like too much to bear. Then she thought about what the apostle Paul had said had said:

"I can do all things through Christ who strengthens me."[1]

Tamiko repeated the verse over to herself and tried to listen to Nettlenerves as she continued her lecture:

"Now because of the importance of this review, we are going to be conducting your formal observations at the same time. So you can consider the Quality Review your final observation for the year."

"My strength is made perfect in weakness…" Tamiko meditated.[2]

"And we expect that no one here will use the interview as the opportunity for critique. It's unprofessional at best. Remember, this is your school. What ever you say about this school is a reflection on you as well. Now are there any questions?"

"When are the walk-throughs going to be conducted?" asked Miss Robinson.

"We'll start today and continue through Wednesday. Mr. Orvis and Miss Bynum will be first."

"If there's something wrong with our classroom environment, how soon will it have to be fixed?" asked Orvis.

"Once we do a walk-through, we'll schedule a meeting with you to debrief. At that meeting we'll let you know the date for turnaround, because it's largely going to depend on how much needs to be worked on."

"How long are the reviewers going to be in the classrooms?" Robinson asked.

"Probably not more than 10 to 15 minutes. But no matter when they come in or how long they stay, you've got to be on your A game."

"When is the panel meeting and how long is it going to last?" queried Hule.

"The panel meeting is during your lunch period and shouldn't take longer than 20 -30 minutes."

"When is the deadline for lesson plans?" Tamiko asked timidly.

"In a couple of days we're going to have another meeting where we will be giving you guidelines for your lesson plans and we'll talk about due dates at that time."

"What types of questions are they going to ask on the interview?" asked Mrs. Woods.

COMMENCEMENT

"They will be asking you about the school and it's mission, about our goals and programs, things like that. We're going to be providing you with fact sheets so everybody is on the same page."

This question and answer session went on for some time until the teachers had exhausted their brains of all questions, and Nettlenerves adjourned the meeting.

"Are you going to be okay?" Mrs. Steele asked Tamiko.

"It is a bit overwhelming, but I think I can handle it."

"Remember, I've been through this before, so if you have any questions we can talk later."

"Oh, thank you, Ros. Maybe I will later. Right now I'm just trying to focus on getting through today."

"Miss Bynum," called Nettlenerves "may I speak to you for a moment?"

Mrs. Steele and Tamiko were about to leave as the rest of the teachers had done, when Nettlenerves interrupted them.

"Of course" Tamiko said civilly.

"I'll see you later, Tamiko", Rosalyn said quietly as she left the room. There was no one left except Tamiko, Nettlenerves, and Stone.

"Miss Bynum, I don't want you to take this the wrong way, but we're very concerned about your teaching…"

"This goes way past concern", interjected Principal Stone, angrily. "I'm putting you on notice. We're watching you. Don't even think about pulling any slick tricks on the Quality Review. If you do I'll make sure you never work again. Don't think I can't make it happen."

Tamiko couldn't believe the temerity of this woman. Then Tamiko had a second thought as she began to recognize what this was. Tamiko had been with God too long not to recognize the devil working through this woman. "The Lord rebuke you in the name of Jesus." Tamiko said inside herself, before responding.

LAWRENCE CHERRY

"Mrs. Stone what have I ever done that would make you think I would do something like that? Haven't I cooperated with everything that you've wanted?"

"I'm not going to play cat and mouse with you, Bynum. You're on notice. If you think you can't be broken, you just cross me. Now I think you better go and pick up your class while you still have one."

"God bless you, Mrs. Stone", Tamiko said before she turned to leave.

"Save it for yourself 'cause I don't need it."

Tamiko left without another word. She knew what she was up against now. The forces of satan were out to try to destroy her, but she would not play into his hands. It was satan who wanted her to give up teaching, and he had planted enemies in her path. But God had been merciful to Tamiko. As she walked down to her classroom, she began to reflect on the last few months. It was God that worked through her father to encourage her and stop her from quitting her job. It was God who worked through Rosalyn to help her learn more about teaching. It was God who had helped the students under her care to grow and blossom. She even heard from the reading teacher that, so far, the children who had been re-tested did as well or even better on the assessments than when Tamiko gave them. God had been with her all this time, and had kept her from falling into the snare of the enemy. Tamiko knew He would continue to keep her now. She didn't know what would happen at the Quality Review or the rest of the year for that matter, but she wasn't worried because she knew God was in control. She even thought about her dear friend Tim and his situation. Tamiko had been praying for him for a long time and finally, he was a baptized believer. If God could change his heart, couldn't he heal his broken body? There were many storms raging in Tamiko's life at this time, but she had learned from her earlier mistake. This time she wasn't going to look around, but keep her eyes focused on Jesus.

SIXTY-SEVEN

It had been three days since Allen had decided to go on a fast. He had gotten the idea after reading in the book of Luke when Jesus had been tempted in the wilderness after fasting. When the devil told him to turn the stones to bread, Jesus responded with the Word: "for man shall not live by bread alone, but every word of God."[1] Allen couldn't help but feel that was what he needed right now. He was also hoping that in the process of fasting and praying, he would be able to confront and deal with his anger towards God. Allen wanted to remove the obstacle that was hindering his relationship with God. Allen decided to fast until the evenings, replacing his meals with prayer to God and the spiritual food of the Word. Then he would eat his dinner and pray and meditate on the word. Allen thought it would be easy, but so far it was proving to be a real struggle.

It seemed as if it wasn't until he made a decision not to eat, that he saw and smelled food everywhere. His job didn't make things easier because there was so much physical work to be done, that often times he would feel weak, but he knew that he had to believe that God would give him strength through the Word. By the time he got home, sometimes he would eat like a pig, and then be so full that he would fall asleep instead of reading his word and praying like he should. But Allen was determined to keep going.

In addition to dealing with his anger, Allen was hoping that God would speak to him. Allen had read in the book of Samuel, where God spoke to Samuel when he was a little boy. He called Samuel by name and gave him a prophetic word.[2] God also spoke that way to a lot of the prophets and to the apostles as well. He gave them great revelations, visions, and dreams. Allen still wondered why God hadn't spoken to him like that. This was what he was pondering on his lunch break while reading his Bible in the little office on the fifth floor when Davis dropped in.

"Hey, Al. How's the fast going?" inquired Davis.

"Okay, I guess", said Allen sadly.

"You don't sound okay."

"It's just that…I don't want to be angry and frustrated, but I feel like I can't shake it. When I think of all the things that are going on right now…"

"So don't think about those things, man. That's what the devil wants you to do. Now that you're fasting I think you should get into the Word and read the scriptures that talk about the goodness of God. Like some of the Psalms. Try to meditate on all the ways God has been good to you. That's going to counter all that other stuff the devil is going to try to put in your way to make you angry. If you want I can e-mail you some scriptures that you could read."

"Thanks, man. I'd appreciate that. I think the real source of my frustration is that I don't hear anything from Him. I've never had a vision, or a dream, or even heard him calling me."

"But Allen, think about it. Have you read about what happened with Elijah?"

"What do you mean?"

"Like when God wanted to speak to him, there was a wind, and an earthquake, and a fire, but God wasn't speaking to Elijah through any of that. It was the small still voice.[3] I mean, I can only speak for myself, but that's how I've experienced it. It's real subtle. Sometimes it wasn't even like a lot of talking. It wasn't a big vision or anything like that, and I'm not saying God can't operate that way, but he's got a lot of ways of doing things. That's why his ways are past finding out."

"Yeah. 'Past finding out' just about describes Him for me." Allen said dejectedly.

COMMENCEMENT

"Don't be so down on yourself, Al. He's gonna come through for you."

"Speaking of Him coming through, how is your study for the English regents coming along?"

"I've been taking practice exams all this month. On one I got a 70 and on the other I got a 76, so I'm not doing too bad. I'm getting better. You and Miko helped me a lot with my grammar and that's made a huge difference."

"That's good to hear."

"Yeah. I can see where I've improved a lot because at the beginning of the year, when I took the pre-test, I only got a 35. It was really bad. But I said, you know what? God, You blessed me to get back into school, and You know the program I want to get into requires a 75. If this is what You want for me, it'll happen. And that's what I'm believing now. If this is what God wants for me I'm going to have it. I'll get the 75. After all, I've done my part. If not, He's got something better."

"So when's the big day?"

"Two weeks."

"If there's anything I can do to help you in the meantime, just let me or Tamiko know."

"Thanks, but I think I'm okay for right now. I'm more worried about our man, Tim."

"Yeah, I hear you man."

"You know he called me the other day. He wanted to make sure we was straight and everything. He told me about the tumor."

"Really? So you know it's pretty bad."

"Yeah. But like I told him, it's never too bad for God. I told him that if he wanted, we could all get together and go to the church one day during the week when it's open and just go before the Lord and pray together. It's like the Bible says "if two of you agree touching anything that they shall ask it shall be done for them by my Father which is in heaven."[4] You could join us."

551

"Of course, man. Just let me know when."

"I'll let you know when Tim gets back to me."

"Do you really believe Tim will be healed? I mean I know there were lot's of people who were healed during the time when Jesus walked the earth, but I haven't heard of a lot of people being healed now."

"Allen, I believe that God is the same, no matter what time it is. If He did it then, He can do it now. Look what He did for me. I told you, I had a hole in my chest the size of handball. I should be dead, but by the grace of God, I'm not."

"And what if He doesn't heal Tim?"

"Then He doesn't. Tim is saved now. If God calls him home, he'll be in a place where he won't have to worry about sickness or pain or anything else. We'll be hurt, and we'll miss Tim, but we'll see him again some day. No matter what happens God is still God."

SIXTY-EIGHT

"You look gorgeous", smiled Tim as Tamiko came down the front steps of the brownstone. Her black cashmere over coat was open revealing a burgundy wrap sweater dress, accented by an onxy and garnet necklace.

"Thank you. But are you sure that you're not just saying that because you bought it."

The dress had been a Christmas gift from Tim. When Tamiko initially saw it, she felt it was too extravagant, but Tim refused to take it back. Since it was a Christmas gift and she didn't want to hurt his feelings, she kept it.

"Not necessarily", said Tim opening the door of the cab for her.

They both got in and Tim gave the driver the directions for Lydia's.

"Thanks for coming with me tonight."

"Don't worry about it, Tim. I don't mind. But at the same time I don't see why it's necessary. I mean what could possibly happen?"

"Spoken like a person who has never been around any of my family for more than 10 minutes at a time. You just wait."

It wasn't long before the cab pulled up in front of Lydia's. Tim and Tamiko went in and the concierge had the waiter direct them to their table.

"Wow, this is really swanky."

"I told you. My mom always has to have 'the best'."

"What did you tell her about why we were having dinner?"

"I basically told her that I had some news that would greatly affect her."

"And your sister?"

"I didn't have to call my sister. Once I tell my mother, she'll force my sister to come. Oh look, here's my mother now."

Eleanor glided in wearing a black, form fitting, sleeveless, wool crepe v-neck, dress with ruffles down the front and along the hem, flashing her radiant smile.

"Tim, my dear, how are you?" asked his mother. Tim stood up to receive her and gave her the customary peck on the cheek.

"Well, that's what we're here to talk about mother."

"Of course. And who might this be?"

"Mother, you remember my friend Tamiko?"

"Not really, dear."

"We met at Tim's grad-school graduation dinner last spring. I'd understand if you don't remember. It was a while ago."

"Yes, you must forgive me, I don't. And Tim has so many friends of the female persuasion, it's hard for one to keep track."

"Please, sit down mother."

"Thank you. Tim, you can't possibly keep me in suspense while we wait for your sister. You must give me a hint. Does this news that you have involve this young woman?" inquired Eleanor with a bit of trepidation.

"No. Tamiko is just here to lend her support as a friend."

"That's encouraging at least. I was worried for a moment", chuckled Eleanor, however, her snide insinuation did not escape Tamiko. Then Allyson arrived, breaking the tension that was beginning to form at the table.

"Hello mother, how are you?" she beamed as she pecked her mother on the cheek.

"Wonderful. Belize was much more than I could have imagined! And yourself dear?"

"I'm more than fine. You are looking at the newest member of Alpha Kappa Alpha!"

"So you finally pledged! How wonderful, dear! I'm so pleased."

"Hello, Allyson", said Tim interrupting them before they began to engage in a full-blown sidebar conversation.

"Hello, Tim", Allyson offered curtly.

She sat down before Tim could receive her, but he leaned across the table to give her a peck on the cheek, which she wiped away with one of the napkins on the table. She virtually ignored Tamiko who had also been waiting to greet her.

"Allyson, you remember Tamiko, don't you?"

"Not that I recall, no."

"Hi, Allyson. We met at your brother's graduation dinner", offered Tamiko.

"I'm sure", Allyson snarled, sending Tamiko a sarcastic little half-smile before opening her menu.

"Let's get our order out of the way so we can talk", suggested Tim.

"Wonderful." said Eleanor.

Eleanor signaled for the waiter who came at once.

"And what will be your pleasure this evening?"

At his request, everyone placed an order, except Tamiko who was still trying to figure out the menu.

"Is something wrong?" asked Eleanor.

"I'm fine. It's just that I'm trying to find something that suits my taste."

"This establishment doesn't serve collard greens or chitterlings if that's what you're looking for", sniped Allyson.

"And you've decided to be rude to my friend because..."

"Is that what you call them, now? Friends?"

"You owe her an apology!" demanded Tim.

"She'll have to put it on my tab."

"Allyson, you have no right to…"

"Children, please! We are in a public place", said Eleanor through gritted teeth, while gesturing toward the waiter.

"It's okay, Tim. I'll just have the lasagna and fresh spinach salad."

The waiter collected the menus and left.

"Now that we're all here, Tim, what is this all about?"

"I've been having a lot of issues with headaches and nausea lately, more so than in the past."

"You've always had a nervous stomach dear. Ever since you were a boy."

"I told you, it's been different lately. I went to the doctor and they conducted some tests. It seems they found that… I have a brain tumor."

Allyson looked away. Eleanor opened her mouth as if to say something several times, before she was able to say anything.

"A tumor? Are you sure?"

"Yes. I had an MRI and a CT scan. They also did a biopsy."

"Well, there are lots of kinds of tumors. As long as it's not malignant there shouldn't be anything to worry about", said Allyson dismissively.

"Yes, you are right Allyson. That's true. They can operate on it and then you'll be fine in no time."

"It's a grade III tumor. They call it an anaplastic astrocytoma. Even with surgery and therapy, not many people make it past the two year mark."

"No. This can't be. Not my son", Eleanor said softly as if she were talking to someone that the others couldn't see. Then her visage hardened in determination.

"Who is your neurologist?" demanded Eleanor.

"Dr. Rabinow, the same one that helped Poppa."

"That quack! No!"

"And have you had a second opinion?" asked Allyson.

"Not yet, but I'm..."

"How could you put us through this grief without having had a second opinion?" huffed Allyson.

"Yes, Tim, you must have a second opinion! I've never trusted Presbyterian, especially after what they did to Poppa."

"I don't mean to pry, but who's Poppa?" asked Tamiko.

"That's my grandfather. He died of cancer about 10 years ago", answered Tim.

"My friend Dr. Jacobs has some connections at Johns Hopkins, and he's been telling me they are the best at everything. In fact, they put Presbyterian to shame. I want you to go there for your second opinion. You must go there even if I must take you myself!"

"Mother, that's all the way in Baltimore!"

"Honestly, Tim. It's Baltimore, not China. It's less than an hour away by plane. You could stay at the Rhine Gardens for a week or two while you confer with the doctors", said Allyson sounding as if she was annoyed by the whole conversation.

"But I have work to do. I just missed nearly a whole week of work recently, on top of my vacation."

"Tim, this is your life we're talking about! You need to take a leave of absence until this matter is resolved. I'm sure the chiefs at Herns and Marshall will understand."

"I have to agree with your mother, Tim. Your health is what's most important. You need to let your boss know just how serious this is and you need to take some time to deal with it."

"I know", sighed Tim, assenting to Tamiko's plea. "I'll talk to them Monday and..."

"And I'm going to call Dr. Jacobs first thing and see if he can have you seen by one of the neurologists as soon as possible. When that's done, we'll have to see what's available at the Rhine Gardens. I just hope they have rooms on their upper floors available. The view is so much nicer there. Then I'll have to check my calendar…"

"Mother, I'm a big boy. I can do this by myself."

"Absolutely not. I will not sit idly by as my son becomes some doctor's lab experiment. Things must and will be done properly. Besides, I don't believe for one moment that the situation is so exigent that surgery will even be necessary. The doctors at Presbyterian have obviously made a mistake."

"And what if they haven't made a mistake? What if we the doctors at Johns Hopkins find the same thing these doctors found?"

"Let's not think about that right now dear."

"No, we need to think about this right now!"

"No! I am not going to lose my son!"

"Tim, stop this! You're upsetting her!" barked Allyson.

"And how do you think I feel? I'm the one that may not have much time left!"

"Don't you think you're overreacting?"

"Overreacting? I didn't think even you could be that heartless."

"I think we all just need a moment to calm down" interjected Tamiko.

"And I think you should mind your own business. This is a family matter", Allyson snapped.

COMMENCEMENT

"You have no right to talk to her like that! She has every right to be here; Tamiko is like family to me."

"How so? Is she pregnant?"

"Allyson! Timothy! Stop this bickering, both of you! This conversation is ending. As far as I am concerned, there is nothing more to say until we hear from the doctors at Johns Hopkins!"

There was complete silence at the table. Tamiko looked at all the faces around her in astonishment. She was surprised by the amount of control Eleanor had over her "grown" children. Tim sat back resignedly in his chair. While Allyson, who was now colored crimson, stared down at her plate and played with her napkin again.

"Now let's talk about something a bit lighter", said Eleanor struggling to regain her composure. "Allyson, when are they having your induction ceremony?"

"Next week. There are going to be a lot of celebrities there, and they say the President's wife may even attend."

"Now that would be splendid wouldn't it?"

"You are coming, aren't you?"

"I'll have to see, what with recent developments and all. Where is our food? I feel we've been waiting an eternity."

"Tim are you okay?" asked Tamiko noticing that Tim seemed to be kind of staring into space for a while.

"Tim, dear. What's wrong?"

Tim didn't answer either of them. Then his head and neck started jerking and he fell out of his chair and began to convulse on the floor.

"Oh my gosh, Tim!"

"Somebody, call 911!"

SIXTY-NINE

Allen's heart was beating out of his chest as he bolted through the doors of NYU medical center. When Tamiko called him she was crying and could barely put together a coherent sentence making it hard to understand her. But he definitely knew that she told him to come to NYU medical center. Something had happened to Tim. From what he could piece together from Tamiko, it probably was a seizure. Tim had told him that this could happen as a side effect from the biopsy or from the increased pressure from the tumor. Allen hoped it was more the former rather than the latter.

Allen headed to the emergency unit waiting room, and there he saw Tamiko sitting with Ms. Russell and Tim's sister, Allyson. Allyson seemed to be consoling her mother while Tamiko was doubled over holding her head in her hands.

"Hey, what's going on?" asked Allen, out of breath.

"Allen, what are you doing here?" queried Allyson incredulously.

"I called him", said Tamiko weakly.

"Do you really think all this is necessary?" hissed Allyson.

"For heaven's sake, he already knows, Allyson!" Tamiko spat back out of frustration.

"Can somebody please tell me, what's going on with Tim?!" Allen asked again.

COMMENCEMENT

"He had a seizure. They were able to stabilize him in the ambulance, but they're checking him out now. They think he's going to be okay", said Tamiko trying to keep herself composed.

"Thank God for that", breathed Allen.

"Excuse me, I'm looking for Ms. Russell, Tim Russell's mother." said the doctor on duty. He was a tall dark-haired white man in scrubs.

"Yes, I'm Ms. Russell", said Eleanor springing up from her chair.

"I'm Dr. Michaels. Your son had a seizure, and we gave him some Klonopin to stabilize him. We're going to keep him for observation overnight, but overall we think he's going to be fine for now. He's awake and you can go in and see him now. I suggest two at a time, family first."

"Thank you, doctor. Come, Allyson."

Eleanor and Allyson followed the doctor through the swinging doors into the emergency unit, while Allen and Tamiko remained in the waiting room. Allen took a seat next to Tamiko.

"Are you okay?"

"I don't know. One minute we were sitting at the table, and the next thing…I didn't know what to do. You don't know how much I thanked God that there was a doctor in the restaurant that helped us… I was so scared…I thought I could be strong for Tim, but now I'm not sure."

"Everything's going to work out", said Allen putting a consoling arm around Tamiko "Tim's going to be all right. He told us this kind of thing could happen. It doesn't mean it's the end."

"After having dinner with his family, I realize just how much he needs God's love and our support."

"I guess they didn't take the news well."

"His mother is in denial, and his sister doesn't seem to care at all."

"Sorry to say, but I kinda expected that."

"I'm going to keep praying. I know God can bring him through this. We just have to help Tim keep faith in Him."

"Excuse me." Dr. Michaels came back. "You can see him, now, but try to keep it short. He needs to rest."

"Where is he?"

"Right this way."

Dr. Michaels took them upstairs to a general observation room. Tim was sitting up, playing with his smart phone when Allen and Tamiko came in. Tamiko swooped down on him for a hug.

"Hey."

"I'm so glad you're okay", she said, her voice muffled by the fabric of the hospital gown he was wearing.

"I hope I didn't give you guys too much of a scare."

"Don't worry about us, man. How are you?" asked Allen.

"I'm okay."

"Really?" asked Tamiko.

"Yeah, I'm fine. It's not like Dr. Rabinow didn't warn me. But I will say that losing control of one's body does take some getting used to."

"We have to keep believing. God is going to see you through this."

"Yeah. But I think this just might be a sign that I better get my second opinion soon."

"Remember, man: one day at a time" said Allen.

"I'm trying. But it's hard when you get these little reminders that your brain is falling apart", said Tim struggling to be brave.

"So when are they letting you go home?" asked Tamiko.

"Tomorrow morning."

"We'll come by and pick you up."

"You guys don't have to do that. I don't want to become 'poor Tim'."

"Tim, we're family. We got you", insisted Allen.

"That's right. Speaking of family, what happened to your mom and your sister?"

"They went home. My mother is determined to haul me off to Baltimore. But at least now she seems to be coming out of denial. My sister...I don't know. She didn't say much of anything. I'm really sorry you had to put up with all her nonsense at dinner."

"Don't worry about that. I'm developing a thick skin for insults. But I think your mom is right. You should go", said Tamiko.

"I don't think I have a choice, now."

"Maybe this will all work out for the best. You never know, man", said Allen.

"I don't know. If the tumor doesn't kill me, two weeks with my mom just might."

"Maybe she won't be so bad."

"I love my mom, but I just wish she wasn't such a control freak. You know, I told her all they have to do is send my records and the biopsy sample to Johns-Hopkins for the new doctor to review, but she wants me to have another MRI, CT scan, and biopsy. I don't want to have to go through all of that again."

"Did you tell your mom that?" asked Allen.

"Talking to her is like talking to the wall, especially if she's determined to get what she wants."

"You're not a minor, Tim. She can't make you go through with something you don't want to", suggested Tamiko.

"You obviously don't know Eleanor Russell very well."

"And I think we'd like to keep it that way", joked Allen.

"Is there anything you need right now?" asked Tamiko.

"No. Not really. But since you guys are coming by tomorrow, could you stop by my apartment and bring me my field coat and some regular clothes. I don't want to be out Saturday morning with a formal suit on. And bring a couple of garment bags for my suit and my dress coat."

"Will do. But right now I think we need to let you rest for the night. Good night man, see you in the morning."

"Goodnight, dude."

"Good night, Tim" said Tamiko pecking him on the forehead.

"Good night, Miko. "

SEVENTY

It was Saturday night, and time for Jim's obligatory visit with Callie. Jim had already had two joints and had brought some Blue Agave and some Jonnie Walker Red for Callie. She loved to drink, not Jim. As he walked up the front steps to her building, Jim was in an extremely good mood. And this was despite everything that happened during the week.

First, he had gotten in trouble at work. He came in one Monday morning with bloodshot red eyes. Jim's appearance was so disheveled that one of his co-workers reported him to supervision. Then they called Jim into the office for a random drug test, which he failed. He was immediately suspended without pay. Next, he had gotten in trouble with the police. Jim went to the Blue Note one night to watch the Lakers game (at least this is what he told himself) in HD. He only incidentally kicked back a few shots. Then he got into an argument with another patron about Kobe Bryant. Jim had to defend Kobe's honor. In the end, he wound up being charged with aggravated assault, and was issued a summons to appear in court. He forgot when he had to appear. It didn't matter, because he didn't feel like going to a hearing anyway. So what if he caught a warrant. This summed up his week. Jim was a little down at the start of it, but now after the two joints things were looking up. And besides, there was Callie.

Jim pressed the buzzer to her apartment. After a few seconds she buzzed back, and he went upstairs. Yeah, she knew what time it was.

When he got to the landing where her apartment was, Jim could see her standing at the door in her bathrobe.

"Hey, Cal. You ready for a night to remember?"

If Jim hadn't been high, he would've recognized the very somber expression on her face.

"Are you high again?" she asked with an attitude.

"Only off of your love." He said as he came face to face with her. He tried to close in for a kiss, but Callie pulled away.

"C'mon, girl. Is that any way to treat your best friend?"

"You haven't answered my question? Are you high?"

"Callie, you know me."

"Do I, really?"

"What's wrong? Why you so serious tonight? It's Saturday! Time to hang back and let all your problems go."

Callie stepped aside and let him into her apartment. Jim put the bottles of liquor on the coffee table. Then he went back to Callie and put his arms around her.

"We have to talk, Jim."

"Later. First, let me turn that frown into a smile."

Jim tried to kiss her, but Callie pulled away.

"No. We have to talk *now!*"

"Fine. What's the problem, now?"

"What do you mean 'what's the problem, now? Am I a burden to you all of a sudden?"

"How would you feel, if you went somewhere to kick it, and every time there's always some kind of drama."

"Oh, so now I'm 'drama'. What about you? You don't think you bring enough drama in my life?"

"I'm not the one always moanin' and gropin' over nonsense."

"But you can come to me high as a kite."

"I just told you I wasn't high."

"I'm not a fool, Jim! You got bloodshot eyes, and you reek of reefer!"

"I also work hard Callie! They got me doing all kinds of shifts on my job lately!"

"Oh, spare me!"

"Look, let's not fight. I been fightin' all week. I'm tired of that. Let's just relax and enjoy the evening."

"There's something you need to know, first."

"What?!" Jim snapped annoyed.

"Never mind. Just leave."

"I'm listening to you, Callie! Why you being like this?"

"Just go!"

"Fine. I'll come back when you're in a better mood. This is ridiculous!"

"I don't want you to come back."

"Callie, why are you trippin' like this? Weren't you the one that made me promise not to leave you! Now you kickin' me to the curb?"

"Yeah I remember when you made that promise, but too bad you couldn't keep it."

"I'm here, Callie!"

"No, you're not! You're everywhere else but here! You know what just do us both a favor and leave!"

"Forget you then, skank! I don't need you or your drama!"

Jim stormed out of the apartment, but not before taking his liquor with him.

"Now look what you've done."

The voice was back. The joints and the liquor had not been enough. What was it going to take to get rid of that voice?

"You need help."

"I got this. I don't need you", Jim responded angrily.

"You've lost so much. How much more are you willing to lose?"

"I didn't lose nothin' but problems. And I'm sick of you bothering me. It's time I got rid of you once and for all."

The whiskey and the marijuana were not enough, but Jim knew something that was strong, real strong. So strong it could take him to another world; far, far away from that voice.

SEVENTY-ONE

It was Tuesday and since the church was open for prayer, Allen decided to drop by after work to sit in the house of God and be alone with Him. Allen had fasted and prayed a whole week. He read the scriptures that Davis had suggested and concentrated on all the loving mercies that God had bestowed on his life. When he thought about it, God had done more than enough for him. There were a lot of things he had taken for granted. Especially when he thought about how God was sustaining him now, even through Tim's illness. Allen faced his anger toward God. Allen had to admit to himself that he was still angry that God had not allowed him to find that dream job. He was angry about losing some of his friends, and he was angry about what was happening to Tim. But now Allen had come to an understanding that had caused him to put away his anger.

Originally, Allen believed that God might have been punishing him. But now he was beginning to see that maybe Tamiko was right all along. Maybe God did not allow him to go into the field he wanted because he was protecting him from something. Most likely it was Allen's own arrogance. Thinking back on everything, Allen could now see that when it came to finance he knew a lot less than he thought he did. Recently he'd been checking the stocks that he had planned to invest on Davis' behalf. He thought they were prime deals that would weather the tumultuous twists and turns of the stock market. He had been wrong. They all had dropped sharply over the past few weeks. Had Allen invested the money as he had originally planned, he would have lost all of it, destroying his friend's trust in him, the reputation of the church, and any chance of helping Davis at all. "What if I had made a big mistake like that working for one of the big consulting firms?" Allen wondered. His career would have been over before it even started; his reputation destroyed. Allen thought he knew too much. He would have relied more on himself and his own knowledge instead of allowing God to lead him, which inevitably would have meant disaster.

As for his friends, Allen could now see that he was removing people from his life that would have just brought him down. Callie and Jim would only hinder him in his relationship with God, planting seeds of doubt. As much as Allen loved both of them, he knew they each had their own issues that only God could help them with. Just as he had done with Davis, he had to let go of them for now and pray that God open their eyes and reveal Himself to them.

Allen also realized that God, in His loving mercy, was protecting Allen, not just from physical or material harm, but also spiritual harm. God led Allen to take his eyes off himself and focus on God. Allen now thought more about God, talked more with God, and read his Bible more than he had done in his entire life, or ever thought he would. Allen's inability to get a job made Allen realize that he needed a relationship with God. The people that were left in his life helped to direct and guide him to God. In this way, God had saved Allen from something much more dangerous. What if the job he desired changed him in such a way as that he lost his faith in God? Allen had to admit that he had felt that he was beginning to lean in that direction. But, fortunately, God worked through Allen's friends and family to bring him back from the edge. Allen was humbled when he thought about these things. He just wished that God would speak to him. Then as he thought on this he realized something else.

Allen began to realize that he had indeed heard from God. God had spoken to Allen's spirit on more than one occasion. Allen remembered the time he was coming from the shower and he heard someone speaking to him, telling him he had to stop thinking about what he could do, and think about what God could do. Then there was the time at the Election Night party. God had also spoken through Allen's friends to keep him from the disastrous "ghetto ponzi scheme", as Tim called it. God spoke to Allen that Sunday afternoon, and told him to go to the Brotherhood Bible study, where he got that awesome realization about how he needed to love God. God had even helped Allen figure out where Tim was hiding after he had gotten that disturbing prognosis from the doctor. The problem was that God spoke to Allen in a way that was different from what he had expected, so he didn't value it. He was like Naaman the Syrian who scoffed when Elisha told him to go bathe in the Jordan seven times to cure himself of leprosy.[1] Naaman, too, was expecting something really grand, and because of this, almost missed out on his blessing to be healed. Allen was indeed in the process of forming a relationship with God. Allen just needed to trust Him.

This is why Allen found himself in the church now. Allen was no longer bitter toward God, however he was still reticent to trust Him. Now Allen knew that God heard his prayers. But Allen couldn't help thinking about the fact that he had been out of school almost a year and he still had no direction for his life. Then he thought about what was happening to Tim. Allen was terrified about what he might witness with his friend's condition over the next few years. It made him think about what happened with Momma Merta. Allen remembered all of the times he, his mother, his father, Jim, Tamiko, the Pastor, Mother Rose, and Mrs. Hardy had all but sequestered themselves in the upper room praying for her. Momma Merta believed that she could be healed, and so did everyone else, but yet they all watched as her condition went from bad to worse. It didn't seem like God was answering their prayers at all. Then one day, three years into her struggle, she was admitted to the hospital and that night she was gone. Everyone seemed to have no choice but to be consoled by the fact that Mother Merta was now in the arms of God, in a place where she wouldn't have to suffer anymore. Pastor Bynum even suggested that maybe her time down here was over and she had done all that the Lord had called her to do. Allen knew that Momma Merta would have to die, but he didn't understand why God hadn't healed her before she did. Jim didn't understand it either, and when Jim abandoned the faith, Allen couldn't think of anything to say in God's defense.

So now, as Allen sat in the church pew, he was afraid that the same thing would happen to Tim. Davis wanted to get as many people as possible to go with them on Thursday to pray for Tim and tarry for him.

The way Davis and Tamiko talked about it, they were sure that Tim would be healed. But Allen wasn't as certain. It wasn't that Allen didn't believe in the power of God. He knew that God could do anything He wanted. Allen wanted to know if God would heal Tim. If this is what He wanted.

"Heavenly father I come before you this evening to ask you what is your will for my friend Tim's life? Help me to understand what you are doing and for what purpose is this disease. Lord, you know I want you to heal Tim, and I know you can heal him, but I also know it's not that simple. You said that if we asked anything according to Your will, it would be granted. Lord, please tell me what is Your will for my friend and help me to accept it, whatever it may be. Is the purpose of this disease to bring glory and honor to Your name? Has Tim's time run it's course and has he accomplished what you wanted for his life on this earth? Have you brought him to Yourself at this time in his life so that he may come and dwell in Your house forever? In Jesus name, please reveal this to me. Amen."

The minute that Allen finished his prayer, the burden that had been on his soul when he came into the church had been lifted, and all of a sudden he felt as if he was at peace. Allen was glad for it, even though it didn't provide any insight into the answers he wanted. Then he thought back to what his friend Davis said the other night: No matter what happens, He's still God.

SEVENTY-TWO

Tim was nervous as he got in the elevator. He had put in his request for a leave of absence on Monday, and didn't think there would be any problems. Then he got a call from human resources telling him that Standoff and the President of Business Consulting wanted to speak with him in reference to his request. Tim was thinking that maybe they were upset that he had taken so much time off in addition to his vacation for medical procedures. Tim had tried to offset his absences by coming in earlier and staying later. And it wasn't like he was faking. Tim always brought in notices from his doctor after every visit. He only hoped he wasn't jeopardizing his severance pay. After all, there were only two more months that he had with the company before he would be let go. It might even be sooner, since things were going ahead of schedule. The web site was now up and they had done a couple of test runs. It wouldn't be long before the memos were sent to the departments letting them know about the change in services. Hopefully, Tim could stay employed until then. He didn't want to have to worry about explaining what had happened with his job on top of dealing with his disease. "One day at a time; one battle at a time", he told himself.

When Tim got off the elevator, he went down the corridor to the two big brown mahogany doors where Standoff's name stood emblazoned upon a bronze placard. Tim opened the door and walked up to the reception desk in the waiting room.

"I have an appointment to see Mr. Standoff and Mr. Silver."

"You must be Tim, right?"

"Yes."

"Have a seat, and I'll let them know you're here."

Tim sat down. Under less strenuous circumstances, he would have taken the time to admire the opulence that Standoff's position afforded. All Tim could do was to wonder just what this meeting was about. He hoped it wasn't an ambush. After all, he knew he wasn't Standoff's favorite person in the world.

"Mr. Russell?" the secretary called, interrupting Tim's thoughts.

"Yes?"

"If you'll come right this way."

As Tim followed the young woman to the office in the back, he tried to steel himself for what may come. When they entered the office, Standoff was chatting pleasantly with Silver who had taken off his jacket and was reclining in one of the leather chairs in front of Standoff's desk.

"Tim, come in and have a seat", called Standoff rather jovially.

"Thank you, sir", said Tim trying to put on a confident pose as he took his seat.

"So, Tim, your department has got the whole company talking."

"Good things, I hope."

"Very good things, indeed. The reorganization is now proceeding ahead of schedule, true?"

"Yes, sir. We've already done several runs of the website, and everything seems okay. We should be able to bring it to the employees by the end of the month."

"That's good news. The sooner it gets up the more money we'll save. But onto other matters. You must know why you're here, don't you?"

"I assumed it was to discuss my application for a leave of absence."

"Yes. You're right. That's part of it. I hear you're going away to get a second opinion for a serious illness. Now, you don't have to disclose this illness whatever it is, but I'd like to know if you feel that eventually you would be able to return to us or whether this leave would be indefinite."

"I would love to be able to give you a definite answer, but I can't. At least not until I've gotten the second opinion. After that I could probably give you a time table of surgery, recovery and when I could return."

"I see. Makes sense. And how soon do you think you'll have the results of the second opinion?"

"I have an appointment for the week after next. If everything goes as scheduled, it should be no later than the middle of the week following."

"Would you be willing to keep in touch with us?"

"Of course. Would you like me to send an e-mail to H.R.?"

"That would be good, but don't send it to the general mail box, send it directly to Mr. Silver here."

"Yes, I will. Does this mean that my request for a leave of absence has been approved?"

"Oh, certainly, that goes without saying. But I wanted to talk to you more about it because there's something else that needs to be discussed. You see one of the associates in Business Consulting has decided that she is leaving in a few months to take another job in Seattle. Silver and I were thinking of who could replace her. We came up with a short list, and after the big turn around in business services, we thought you would be perfect for the job. Are you interested?"

"This is kind of sudden. I never would have expected…"

"Neither did we, but in these last few months, you've demonstrated that you're capable of handling more responsibility. That turnaround in business services was nothing short of miraculous."

"But I did have help. Preston was there, and I like to believe we were the recipients of God's favor."

"Yeah. You would need God's favor to work with that guy. You don't have to be a nice guy, Tim", joked Silver. "I think everybody in the whole company is aware that he was no help."

"Even I'm willing to admit he was one of the biggest mistakes I ever made. He didn't even get the idea for the website on his own, you know. Got if from Casinoff."

"He must be good for something", said Tim in Preston's defense.

"Let's not dwell on Preston. Do you think you'd be interested in working in Business Consulting? Since you seem to have a keen insight for running the systems of your department, we thought that your skills would transfer well to helping us with planning long-term solutions for the company."

"Yes, of course, sir."

"Good. You can take your leave of absence to think about it. The position doesn't open until June or July, but remember to keep in touch with us. We'll expect to hear from you in a few weeks after your second opinion."

"Thank you both for this opportunity. I promise I will get back to you as soon as I can."

"Thank you for your work in this company."

****

When Tim got back to his office he could hardly focus on his work. He couldn't believe what just had happened to him. He went from being virtually unemployed (in two months time) to the possibility of a promotion to Business Consulting. Tim was so overwhelmed that he took the time to thank God in prayer.

"Dear Lord, thank you for revealing yourself to me through this opportunity today. You said "When a man's ways please the Lord, he maketh even his enemies to be at peace with him."[1] Thank you for blessing me to experience the truth of Your word. Please continue to lead and guide me during these difficult times. Help me to stay steadfast both in my faith and in Your word. In Jesus name. Amen."

When Tim was done praying he thought about how weird it was that he was being considered for a promotion, just as he had been diagnosed with this illness. There was the possibility that Tim wouldn't even be able to accept it. If the second opinion were consistent with the first, he would have to arrange for surgery, and then he would have to have treatment. He had been reading over the Internet just how much the radiation and chemotherapy could ravage a body. There would be no way he would be able to perform to their expectations under the strain of this disease. Still it was a blessing of the Lord that he was even being considered for the position. Then Tim thought of another possibility. His next thought was to call Tamiko to talk to her about it. Tim looked at the clock on his desk. It was only 2:30 and Tamiko was still with the children. He would have to call her later after dinner.

Just as he was thinking, a call came in on his cell phone. Checking it, he saw that it was his mother. Again. In the past week, she called him over 30 times about the trip to Baltimore and the appointments with Dr. Burstyn, who would be his neurologist. Tim didn't mind talking to her to arrange stuff that was important, but she was constantly giving him status reports to things he didn't really care about, like the room reservation, the meal package, the time the limo would be at the airport, whether or not to have a personal physician on hand. As Tim answered the phone, he wondered what little trifle she would have to talk about.

"Yes, mother."

"Tim, I just wanted to let you know that we now have a personal physician on hand. His name is Andrew Smythe and he's absolutely the best."

"Mom, don't you think that's going a little overboard?"

"Absolutely not! What if you have another episode like you did the other night? Someone must be there to make sure you pull through. I'm not willing to take any chances."

"Fine. Is he going to be with us the entire time?"

"Of course. I wouldn't have it any other way. He'll be in the room directly across from you, should you need him, and I'm going to have an intercom link set up between your rooms as well."

"Is that all you wanted to tell me, or is there something else?"

"No, that's all, but I was hoping you would be more excited."

"Mom, believe me, I really appreciate everything your doing to make this whole thing go as smoothly as possible."

"That's right! This has been a lot of work. You have no idea."

"I know. Thanks, mom. I love you."

There was a brief moment of silence.

"Mom? Are you still there?"

"Yes…it's just that I haven't heard that from you in a long while. Not since you were a boy."

"I know. And I mean it. Just thought I'd let you know."

"I love you, too, Tim."

SEVENTY-THREE

Time seemed like it was rushing by. Already it was the middle of February and Valentine's day to boot. This would be a very special Valentine's day because it was the last day Tim was going to be in town before going out to Baltimore for his second opinion. Allen and Davis had made arrangements with some of their friends to have a special prayer service for Tim in the Upper Room of the church. Allen was the first one to arrive. As he stood in the main area of the Upper Room with it's red, carpeted floor and little white podium in the middle, Allen was overcome by the solemnity of this gathering. Everyone wanted this day to be a turning point for Tim. Yet, Allen couldn't help but think about what happened with Momma Merta.

Allen and Davis had called as many people as they could, just like what had been done for Momma Merta, but none of the elders were there. It was just going to be the younger people. And there weren't that many of them. Tamiko, and Daniel were coming; even Richard was coming. Given the urgency of the situation, Allen thought about contacting Jim (to at least make him aware of Tim's illness), but given how similar the circumstances were to those that had caused his apostasy, he didn't. It would be too much for him to bear, not that he'd come anyway. He didn't even consider Callie after what she had said the last time they were together. Allen didn't know if he should have called his parents, and the Pastor and his wife. Since they had known the Lord for a lot longer, maybe God would be more apt to listen and have mercy. But like Davis said "If two of you agree touching anything that they shall ask it shall be done of them by my Father which is in heaven." Soon Allen's silent reverie was broken by the sound of footsteps coming up the stairs. It was Davis and Daniel. They exchanged friendly greetings of "Praise the Lord" and then there was a quiet moment between them, when finally Allen broke the silence.

"So what's on the program for tonight? How's this going to work?"

"Daniel is going to lead us in the main prayer. Then we're all going to pray individually. You can stay here in the main sanctuary or if you feel you need privacy you can go to the booths", answered Davis.

"How many other people are going to be here?" asked Daniel.

"There should be six of us; Tim included."

"Are you sure you don't want me to see if the Pastor can come down and join us? He's a man of God, Allen. He can intercede for us, like the way Moses did for the people of Israel", suggested Daniel.

"It's probably too late for that. We'll just have to make due with who we have", said Allen thoughtfully.

"I don't think it will matter. The Bible says: the prayers of a righteous man availeth much.[1] We've got at least 5 men and one woman. As long as everyone here believes in God and His power, there's no reason why he shouldn't hear us. I mean he heard the people of Ninevah when they prayed, didn't he?" said Davis confidently.[2]

As they were speaking, Richard came bounding up the steps.

"Praise the Lord", greeted Davis.

"Oh, is that what you say? Yeah, Praise the Lord, y'all."

"Thanks for coming, man. We really appreciate it."

"Yeah, I know me and Tim - sometimes we cross paths, but when it comes to somethin' like dis, I'ma have his back. Fa real."

"You've prayed before, right Rich?" asked Allen.

"Yeah, man. I be prayin' all the time. How you think I stay large man?"

They all laughed.

COMMENCEMENT

"So where's the man of the hour?" asked Jim.

"He probably stopped by to pick up Tamiko. They should be here any minute", replied Allen.

And no sooner had their names been mentioned than they arrived.

"Praise the Lord Everyone!" greeted Tim as he came up the steps with Tamiko.

"Praise the Lord!" they all responded.

"Wow! This is a bigger crowd than I expected!" he beamed "Hey, Rich. I didn't expect to see you here."

"Hey, I know we don't always eye to eye, but I'ma always have your back."

"See, I told you", said Tamiko.

"Thanks, man", said Tim humbly.

"Since we're all here, I guess we should get started."

"Hold on Al. There's something I'd like to say first. I'd like to take the time to say thank you to all of you for being here with me tonight and for all of the love, support, and guidance you've provided me in my life. I was thinking the other night about the ways that God has blessed my life and I didn't even realize it. But of all the ways that he has blessed me, you guys are the most special blessing of all.

Daniel, I just want to thank you for your time and your prayers. You didn't even know me that well, and yet you've treated me just like a friend. And thanks for spotting me in the baptism pool.

Davis, thank you for having patience with me. I know I gave you a hard time when we first met, with my snide comments and sarcastic innuendos. Now I know you're a real Christian man of character. You would have to be to put up with me, right? I have to say, I am more than proud to call you my friend.

Look Rich, I know I've always given you a hard time. I'm ashamed to say it was because I always envied you because you were so independent. You made your own standard and didn't try to fit into the one society made and you succeeded. That's because you had the one thing I didn't have: courage. Now instead of envying you, I admire you.

Allen, what can I say? I didn't know what friendship was until I met you. I didn't know what family meant until I met you. I'm not sure if I even knew what love was until I met you. In fact, I think I first experienced the love of God through you. There were so many times in the beginning when I was just absolutely rotten to you, but you kept coming back and you treated me with so much compassion. At first I thought you were crazy, or stupid, or naïve, but finally, I realized that you are proof that there are still good people in this world. We've been through our highs and lows together and you've been better to me than I've been to myself. I can say with certainty that you are my brother.

Tamiko, it was your example of unwavering faith that drew me into God's fold. You were always so passionate and so bold. You always held fast to what you knew and you never backed down, even when things got heated. And no matter what you were facing in life or how down you would get, I noticed you have something inside of you that would always pick you up. I would look at you sometimes and wonder what it was that kept you going like that. And because you were so willing to share yourself with me, I know what it is. It's God living on the inside of you. You opened me up to a love that I never thought was possible. You're an angel on earth if there ever was one.

So thank you all. There were times when I was first thinking about giving my life to God that I doubted that He would want me. I didn't think God could love someone like me. Now I know He does love me, because if He didn't, He wouldn't have blessed me with friends like you."

By the time Tim was finished, Tamiko was sobbing and the men struggled to keep their composure. Allen quickly wiped at the tears that had gathered in his eyes. Then everyone started reaching out to Tim for hugs. When they had done sharing the emotionally charged moment. Daniel began to start the prayer service.

"If everyone could just form a circle around the altar, join hands and bow your heads please."

COMMENCEMENT

Everyone did as Daniel directed. Daniel was at the head of the circle leading the prayer.

"Heavenly Father, we have come together in your presence this evening to send up a petition for our friend, Tim. Father God, You know his condition, and the trials he has to face concerning his health. Lord we know that You are all powerful and full of mercy. We know that You are a Healer as your word has revealed the countless times how You have healed the sick. We are faithful to believe that You are the same God then that You are now. We beseech You Lord, God, in the name of Your Son, Jesus, that You have compassion on our friend Tim. Please God, show him the same compassion that You showed to the woman with the issue of blood who was sick in her body. We ask that you show our friend the same compassion that you showed the Ninevites when you were ready to destroy them. They prayed and you had compassion. We ask that You come down and touch his body and rid him of this disease. Lord we pray that You break the bands of the enemy and let this illness be for Your glory. We will give You the glory, the praise, and the honor. Lord, God, we give You the glory right now for what You are about to do. Hear us, Lord, God. You said that where two or three are gathered together in Your name You are in the midst.[3] We ask that You come in the midst of us and deliver. You said in your word that if we believe, there was nothing that would be withheld from us. Lord, we believe in You today and everyday and we know You will do. So we come before You in sackcloth and ashes. We come before You knowing that we don't deserve it, but we beg for mercy. And so we present this petition to You in the spirit of humility acknowledging that there is nothing that we can do but to ask You to speak into this situation. In the name of Your precious Son, Jesus. Amen."

When the prayer was over there were more hugs and tears. Then everyone spread out for silent prayer. Allen, Tim, Daniel and Richard went into the booths, while Tamiko and Davis stayed in the main sanctuary. At first, there was total silence as each person poured out his and her hearts to before the Lord. Then after a while, muffled sobs could be heard rising up throughout the room as they prayed more earnestly and fervently. Allen was soaked with tears and sweat. When he grew tired and weak he felt something take over him and keep him going. It was as if his spirit was praying separately from himself. Everyone else felt it to. They stayed on their knees for hours tarrying and travailing into the night.

****

"So I guess this is it", said Tim as he loaded his bag into the trunk of the limousine his mother had rented to take them to the airport. She was waiting on the inside, while Tim bade farewell to his friends.

"Don't' make it sound so final", pleaded Tamiko.

"It's only going to be for two weeks, Tim. God willing", said Allen.

"I'm still going to miss you guys."

"Same here", said Davis.

"Allen, would you check on my apartment while I'm gone. I already told Bradley you'd be back and forth."

"C'mon man what could happen in two weeks."

"How about fire, break-ins, plumbing problems. Besides you could take this opportunity to try out living on your own for a while or you can use my place to crash when you feel like you need to get away. Just don't throw any wild parties."

"I hear you man."

"Tamiko, I have something for you that I want you to keep safe for me until I come back." Tim reached into his jacket pocket and pulled out an envelope. "But don't open it until I'm gone, deal."

"Deal. What is it?"

"You'll find out later. Just hold onto it and promise me you won't lose it."

"I promise."

"And Davis, my friend I am trusting you with a very valuable gift."

"What's that, man?" asked Davis kind of puzzled.

"Her", Tim said looking into Tamiko's eyes "Watch out for her for me. Don't let anything happen to her while I'm gone."

Tamiko was speechless.

"I won't", replied Davis smiling.

"Tim! We're going to be late!" screeched Eleanor from the limo.

"I'd better go."

"God bless you, man."

"God bless you all, too."

They all exchanged hugs before Tim disappeared inside the black limousine with its tinted windows, which soon sped off down the street into the bustling traffic. Then the three that were left walked away in silence knowing there was nothing more they could do. Tim was in God's hands now.

SEVENTY-FOUR

Davis barely had enough time to catch his breath as he took a seat in the classroom. "Thank You Lord God, for blessing me to get here on time." he prayed silently to himself. The only testing center that was available to him was the old William H. Taft Complex all the way over on 170th Street, so he had to take the bus to the D train. Davis tried to give himself over an hour and a half to get here, with the hope that he could stop off and grab a quick breakfast from McDonald's before the exam. Train delays made this impossible.

"Good morning, everyone. Thank you for being on time. The English Regents exam is about to begin. Please put away all cell phones, mp3 players, and other electronic devices, and make sure they are turned off. If not, they will be confiscated. The only thing that you should have out are pencils, pens, and your ID information." the test proctor admonished the students.

Davis took out a neat little pencil case, which contained everything the proctor asked for. Then he let out a deep yawn, and stretched as he waited for the tests to be handed out. Davis had been up all night studying, and after that praying. Now the moment was upon him, but he had no worry or anxiety. It was God that had showed him how to get back into night school. It was God that had led him to the information about the program. His weak reading and writing skills could have been a stumbling block, but it was God who had led him to Allen and Tamiko who provided him with the help he needed. The same God who did all those things would help him now.

COMMENCEMENT

"We will now be handing out the scantron forms. Please fill them out completely in print. You may use pen only for the top portion or the lined portion of the scantron. Do not use pen for anything you must bubble in."

Several proctors handed out the scantrons. When Davis received his, he filled it out carefully. He took the time to say one final prayer before the test began. After a few moments the lead proctor was back at the podium again.

"Is there anyone who has not received a scantron sheet?"

No one from the audience responded.

"Proctors will now be coming around with the testing booklets. Please do not open your booklet until you are instructed to do so. Otherwise your test will be forfeit."

The proctors handed out the booklets. Davis left his where the proctor put it, not even touching it to move it.

"You will have two hours and thirty minutes to complete this exam from the time you are told to open your booklets. If you need assistance, please raise your hand and a proctor will assist you in any way that is permissible. You are not allowed to talk to anyone other than the proctor and that is with permission. If you finish before the time is up, raise your hand and a proctor will come and collect your booklet and you will be dismissed. Once you are dismissed, you must leave immediately and you will not be allowed back into the testing area, so make sure you take everything with you", said the proctor. "Is there anyone who does not have a testing booklet?"

Silence from the hopeful test takers.

"You may now begin."

Davis let out a deep breath as he opened his test booklet and gave himself over to the power of God.

SEVENTY-FIVE

Tamiko couldn't help but feel a little nervous as she set up her classroom for the lessons that she had planned today. Everything had to be perfect. There would be no room for error. Tamiko made sure that all the materials she needed for the mini-lessons were placed discreetly under her chair. The morning meeting materials were out and accessible. The biggest challenge would be the children themselves. Overall, they weren't bad kids. They had more good days than bad days, but when they did have bad days they were awful. But Tamiko couldn't control that. That's where God stepped in. She had been reciting the 23rd Psalm to herself since she came in this morning. Tamiko had faith that God would be with her on this most important day.

He had been with her through so much by now, she wondered at how she could still be so nervous. In the past two weeks alone, she had been taken through so much by the administration that she felt like David when he was being pursued by Saul.[1] First, they had directed her to change aspects of her classroom setup and bulletin boards despite the fact that they had been re-arranged earlier in the year by the same people who were finding fault now. Then when she submitted her lesson plans for today's Quality Review, they were rejected and had to be re-written, not once, but four times. There were constant surprise observations in which the feedback amounted to little more than nitpicking. Suggestions like "don't use dark colors to back children's work on bulletin boards" and "math word wall words should be in the times roman font" bordered on harassment. If this wasn't enough, she was told to re-organize the way that the children's goals were kept and tracked. The work kept her up well past midnight and then she had to get up at 5:00 in the morning for work, not to mention all of her graduate school obligations and assignments that had to be taken care of as well. Sometimes Tamiko felt as if she didn't have any strength left. At those times she would call upon the Lord, and He would help her make it through. There were even times when she thought she would lose her mind, but she was grateful to God that He didn't let that happen. God would be there with her today, as well, but she only wished she knew exactly what His plan was.

Now that she was done, she stood in the midst of the room, giving everything one final survey. Then she prayed:

"Heavenly Father, You have been with me in the midst of all the trials and tribulations that I have faced up to this point. Please continue to hold me up as I go through this Quality Review. Please guide my hands, my feet, my mouth, and my heart to do Your will this day. I ask that You give me wisdom to make right decisions this day. Heavenly Father You also know that the enemy is out to destroy me here. You said that no weapon formed against Your children will prosper.[2] I ask that you break the bands of the wicked and confuse every evil device. In Jesus name, I pray. Amen."

When Tamiko had finished her prayer, she looked up to see Mrs. Steele in the doorway of the classroom.

"Hey, Ros. I didn't know you were there."

"It's okay. I didn't want to interrupt you. I should have asked that you say a prayer for me, too."

"I do pray for you, actually. I pray for everyone here. Even the people who don't like me that much."

"We're going to need it, too. I just came in to wish you luck. But from the looks of it you probably won't need it. Seems like you've got something much better."

"Thank you. And may God be with you today, too."

"Thank you. You know I'm going to let you know now, that no matter what happens today, I think you're a fine teacher."

"That means a lot to me, coming from you. Thank you, so much."

"And not just a fine teacher, but a fine person. I've seen a lot of people come and go at this school, and I must say that I haven't met anyone like you. I've seen so many people fall away, not just from this school, but from this profession who hadn't gone through half of what you have this year. And so far you've come through with a grace I've never seen before."

"But you've been in this field for a long time. You've probably been through and seen more than I have. That would make you a lot tougher than me."

"Or so it would seem. I don't know what you have, Tamiko, but I sure wish I had it. If I did, I wouldn't be leaving at the end of the year."

"What? I thought that was a rumor?"

"It was a rumor. That is until this morning. I've just grown so discouraged with the system. Some friends and I are in the process of starting a non-profit group that empowers underserved parents to make better educational choices for their children. The way I see it, the main reason why the system won't change is because corrupt local officials deny parents access to the information that the teachers have. Then they use this to divide and conquer us in order to continue the status quo. Someone's got to make sure the parents know just as much about education as the teachers and administrators do."

"I'm sorry to hear that you're leaving, but this new venture sounds wonderful. I hope God blesses it to grow. We surely need something like that."

"Thank you. Oh, look at the time. We'd better be getting downstairs. The reviewer is probably here already."

"You're right. After you", said Tamiko, respectfully giving way to the older woman.

As Tamiko descended the stairs, her anxiety began to lift as she put on her spiritual armor. She was in God's hands. Always had been and always will be. And as long as this was true she had the victory already.

SEVENTY-SIX

When Mr. Hardy had asked Allen if he would go on a special errand for him, he was more than happy to do so. In the past few weeks, Allen's attitude toward his job had changed. He found that he actually liked working at the Sheraton. At first, Allen thought the work would be boring; the same mundane tasks over and over again. However, he was doing a lot more than just cleaning the building. There was Davis who was teaching him all sorts of things about repairs, and even Mr. Hardy had been sharing his insights on building management, which were very interesting. Yes, there were tasks that he had to do everyday, but because of all of the things that could happen in the process of his duties, everyday was different. There was always something that came up that would make his work just that much more remarkable.

On this occasion, Mr. Hardy was trying to find some special parts for the washing machines the laundry women used to clean the sheets. He'd been searching hardware stores on the Internet to find the part when he discovered a little shop over on 115th and Broadway sold the part. Mr. Hardy called the store to place an order and then arranged for Allen to go over to pick it up. Allen took the 1 train and got off at 116th and Columbia University. Upon reaching the surface, Allen took a few moments to admire the stately looking campus and watch the traffic of students coming in and out of the huge wrought iron front gates. Something stirred in his heart, but Allen didn't quite know what it meant. So he just walked the rest of the way down to the hardware store and picked up the package of parts that he was sent for.

Allen's errand did not take much time at all and it was not long before he was headed back toward the train station. Allen slowed his pace as he passed the campus gates of Columbia University again. Allen felt something drawing him in, so he went past the gates to take a tour of the campus.

The buildings seemed a lot like the ones at Harvard, but the campus here was a bit smaller. Allen walked down the college walk to where the fountain was. He looked up to where the Alma Mater sat in front of Low Library. Allen took a walk up the steps and past the grand hall to the other side of the campus dotted by stately cherry trees and surrounded by more imposing looking structures until he came to Uris Hall, home to the Columbia University School of Business. Allen knew Tim had just graduated from here last spring, and had thought of applying here himself at one time, but it was very expensive. He always thought that when he graduated from college he would get a job in finance and then he would either have the money to go or his employers would sponsor him to go. Thinking about it brought up Allen's old dreams for himself and it made him kind of sad. This school was totally out of his league. His current job was barely enough to keep the loan officers off his back as it was. Besides, God had taken him away from that life. It was God that did not allow him to get a job in the financial sector in the first place. "Why in the world did I come here?" Allen pondered. "I really should be getting back to the Sheraton."

Allen was about to turn away when he heard it.

"Keep going."

Allen walked a little further along the campus, and past a small footbridge until he reached East Campus. There he was faced with the imposing Columbia University School of Law.

Law School? Allen had never ever once entertained the idea of becoming a lawyer. That was Jim's thing. When Allen was younger they both had it all figured out. Allen would be the corporate tycoon and Jim would be his counsel. Besides, even if he was interested, there was no way that he could afford graduate school. He didn't want to end up living with his parents in perpetuity and/or having them forsake their retirement.

"No, this couldn't be God speaking. Could it? He put me at the Sheraton", he puzzled. Allen turned away again.

"Go in and get an application."

It didn't make sense. But Allen went inside the huge building. He found the admissions office and picked up an application and the accompanying financial aid forms. He put them in his bag with the package he was carrying and headed back over to the Sheraton Hotel, with a confidence he had never before experienced.

SEVENTY-SEVEN

It was late and Jim was on his way to the special little bodega on the corner. The voice had come back and Jim needed the only thing that would silence it. The bodega was only a few steps away, but it seemed that he couldn't get there fast enough.

When he finally arrived, he bolted to the window and made his request.

"Sugar."

Then he went to the hidden back door to get his package. He checked it briefly, stuck it in his pocket and headed back out. As he was leaving, he noticed pair of men coming in. Jim kept his head down and walked out. He had gone halfway down the block and back to his building where he was confronted by two men. One was African-American and the other was White.

"NYPD" said the African-American man as both men flashed their badges "We want to talk to you for a minute."

All Jim could think about was the package that was in his pocket. It carried with it a mandatory 10-year jail sentence. What if they searched him? Jim did the only thing he could do: he ran.

"Stop!" he heard one of the officers call after him.

COMMENCEMENT

Jim ran as fast as he could. He had no idea where he was going, but he knew he had to get away from the officers. He ran into the traffic even though the signal was against him. He'd rather be dead, than just another brother in jail. Luckily or not, most of the cars just stopped short of running him over. Jim kept running until he saw a large housing project. He thought with so many buildings and alleys he would easily be able to lose them.

Soon, Jim could no longer hear the tread of their footsteps behind him. He was too scared to look back, but he hoped he was losing them. Then Jim ran onto a grassy lawn and through a narrow footpath. He had almost made it to side alley when he felt a huge weight take him down.

"Stay on the ground!" the officer ordered.

The cop had tackled Jim to the ground and was kneeling on Jim's lower torso. Jim could feel the metal tip of the officer's revolver pressing into his back. It was over.

After a moment, the African-American cop had caught up with his partner.

"Did you search him?"

"I'm about to."

The other officer came and cuffed Jim's hand while the one on top of him searched him. It didn't take long for them to find it.

"Well, well, well…what a surprise", the white officer sneered.

The African-American officer started to read Jim the Miranda law. And over the officer's voice, he could hear another.

"It's time to stop running."

SEVENTY-EIGHT

"At least it's starting to get warm. Maybe we'll have an early spring", remarked Allen just before taking a sip of his coffee.

"I hope so. It feels like it's been winter forever. And I'm tired of all these snow storms", said Tamiko responding to Allen.

"I don't know it depends on how you see it. I personally can do without the summer", added Davis.

"Word, yo. If you cold it's easy to get warm, but if you hot it ain't that easy to cool down", said Richard.

Then there was a moment of silence between them. They had all gathered at their usual spot at Emily Ann's. All they could muster was this polite banter. No one had the courage to talk about the one thing that was on all their minds. At least not yet.

"So Al, when are you going to officially submit your application for the law school?" asked Davis.

"It's too late to for me to be considered for the fall term. I may try to see if I can get it in for the next year, but we'll see. I'm still praying to God about it."

"Any idea what you're going to major in when you go?"

"Nothing definite yet." Allen didn't want to give away too much of what the Lord had revealed to him just yet.

"Speaking of school, how did your test go?"

"I got an 80", Davis declared proudly.

COMMENCEMENT

"That's fantastic, man. So now you're ready for that program."

"And not only that, but I passed my other tests, too. In June I'm going to be able to graduate with a real regents high school diploma, God willing."

"Are you kidding?! Of course you will. That's awesome!" smiled Tamiko.

"You could probably get into any of those college joints you want with that Regents diploma", Richard added.

"I'm just trying to see what this program is about. You have no idea how good it feels to even be one step closer to getting my contracting license. Oh, and how's things with you Miko? They still harassing you at school?"

"Actually, things have gotten much better. I'm so glad I listened to my Dad. The Quality Review went way better than I expected. The reviewer said he could hardly believe I was a first year teacher. After he gave me such a great review the Principal had no choice but to give me a satisfactory rating. And believe me she didn't want to."

"So does this mean you get to keep your job?" inquired Allen.

"Yes, but I still don't know if I want to stay there. That principal is still out to get me, and my only friend there is leaving. I'm thinking of transferring to another school for the fall."

"But look at how much God has worked out for you there. He took your enemies and made them your footstool, just as He said He would. If God wants you there, you won't have to worry about them", Davis reminded her.

"You're right, but I haven't made my final decision yet. I'm still praying about it."

"With all of these wonderful things happening, you would think we'd all be jumping out of our seats", said Allen dryly.

"I just wish..." Tamiko stopped in the middle of her sentence unable to finish it.

"Has anybody heard from him?" asked Richard in an unusually staid tone.

"Not since Wednesday, before they were supposed to do the MRI again."

"He probably just got caught up with everything. He's supposed to be back in a couple of days. I think we'll definitely hear from him before then", said Davis as confidently as he could.

"I always meant to ask you Tamiko, what was in that envelope he gave you?" asked Allen.

"A gold watch on a chain. Like those old fashioned ones men used to carry around in the 1900's. Why?"

"Did it have the initials TR on it?" Allen continued to inquire.

"Yes. How did you know? He showed it to you before?" asked Tamiko a bit puzzled.

"Yeah. It's his grandfather's", Allen said quietly.

"Is there something special about it?" asked Davis.

"He never parts with it."

There was another silence.

"I don't know about y'all, but after that prayer meeting we had last week, I felt like…like, peaceful. Like everything is gonna work out", said Richard.

"Funny. I felt that same peace too. In fact, even lately when I've been praying for him, this peace comes over me", said Tamiko.

"Same here", agreed Davis. "But, it's kinda strange…like…like…"

"Like you want to be upset, but you can't. You want to be scared, but you can't. He doesn't tell you specifically what's going to happen, and yet, you know. You already know, and all you can do is wait", remarked Allen in the same sober tone.

"You think…" started Tamiko.

COMMENCEMENT

"I think the will of the Lord will be done. And no matter what happens, He's still God", said Allen. After that no one else had anything more to say. Allen had said it all.

Suddenly, Allen couldn't hold back the flood of tears that began to roll down his cheeks. Something was taking hold of him. It spoke to his spirit. He knew. Just as surely as he knew his own name, he knew. And he knew Tim knew as well. He could feel it in the depths of his soul.

"Hallelujah", he said out loud in spite of himself.

Allen couldn't help himself, all at once he felt the need to praise the Lord. He stood up and raised his hands to God.

"Glory to God. Hallelujah. Thank You, Jesus!"

Allen collapsed back into his seat, but he couldn't stop praising God. He couldn't stop crying. No one else at the table said anything. They could all feel it, too. Tamiko put her arms around Allen, before growing weepy herself. Soon they were all crying and praising God. The other patrons of the restaurant looked over at their table with concern. A waitress stopped by to see if everything was okay. No one was able to respond. Instead, Richard and Davis helped Allen up and they all proceeded to leave.

Allen had always wondered why the people at church shouted, wailed, and danced. Now he knew. It was because no matter what was going on in their lives, God still ruled on the throne. He is a loving God, a just God, a merciful God and a God of judgment. And Allen was glad for that because he knew that as long as that is true, then God's promises are true. And as long as God's promises are true, there is always reason to rejoice. The victory had already been won.

NOTES

One
1. "danced like David": Refers to 2 Samuel 6:14 "And David danced before the Lord with all his might…"

Five
1. Refers to 1 Corinthians 4:5

Ten
1. "remember Balaam": Refers to Numbers 22: 1-35
2. Refers to Isaiah 38: 1- 7
3. Refers to Romans 1: 16 "For I am not ashamed of the gospel of Christ…"

Eleven
1. "faith without works is dead": Refers to James 3: 14-20
2. Refers to Matthew 7:12

Twelve
1. Refers to 1 Corinthians 13: 11

Fourteen
1. Refers to Matthew 21:44, & Luke 20: 17-18

Seventeen
1. Refers to Marie Clay a prominent figure in education, who was a specialist in the area of teaching reading, author of "Literacy Lessons".

Twenty
1. LBJ: Lyndon Baines Johnson; President of the United States from 1963-1968 and signed the famous Civil Rights Act of 1964 and Voting Rights Act of 1965.

Twenty-One
1. Refers to Genesis 37
2. Refers to 1 Samuel 13: 1-14
3. 1 Samuel 13: 12

4. Refers to James 4: 8

Twenty-Two
1. Refers to Genesis 27: vs 41-45 and 1 Samuel 20
2. Refers to Genesis 39
3. See 1 Kings 19: 1-4

Twenty-Three
1. Refers to James 2:19
2. Refers to Romans 1: 16
3. Refers to Genesis 21
4. Refers to Joshua 6: 1- 20
5. Refers to Daniel 3
6. Refers to John 11
7. Refers to 1 Corinthians 1: 18
8. Refers to 1 Corinthians 1: 27
9. Refers to Matthew 13: 54-58
10. Refers to James 4: 7

Twenty-Four
1. Refers to Romans 8: 28
2. Refers to Jeremiah 20: 9
3. Refers to Revelation 21- 22
4. Refers to 1 Corinthians 15: 37-58
5. Refers to Hebrews 11:1
6. Refers to Matthew 16: 4
7. Refers to 2 Corinthians 6: 14

Twenty-Eight
1. Refers to Matthew 19: 26

Thirty-Two
1. Refers to Exodus 33: 7-23

Thirty-Three
1. Refers to 2 Corinthians 12: 9

Thirty-Six
1. Refers to Psalms 100: 3

2. Refers to 2 Chronicles 20

Thirty-Seven
1. Refers to Nehemiah 6

Thirty-Eight
1. Refers to Psalms 103:9 and Ezekiel 18:21
2. Refers to 2 Timothy 2: 15

Thirty-Nine
1. Refers to 2 Corinthians 12: 9

Forty-One
1. Refers to Luke 16: 8

Forty-Four
1. Refers to Matthew 6: 33

Forty-Five
1. Refers to Luke 23: 34
2. Refers to 2 Timothy 3: 12
3. Refers to Matthew 5: 44-45
4. Refers to John 1: 43-51

Fifty
1. Refers to Matthew 10: 34-36

Fifty-One
1. Refers to Genesis 16
2. Refers to Exodus 2: 11-15
3. Refers to 1 Samuel 15

Fifty-Five
1. Refers to Matthew 22: 35-37

Fifty-Six
1. Refers to Matthew 13: 24-30

Fifty-Seven
1. Refers to Acts 9
2. Refers to Daniel 6: 10

Sixty-One
1. Refers to Proverbs 16:18
2. Refers to John 9

Sixty-Four
1. Refers to Matthew 7: 29
2. Refers to John 7: 63
3. Refers to John 8: 1-11
4. Refers to Matthew 9: 27-31
5. Refers to Matthew 9: 9
6. Refers to John 15:13

Sixty-Five
1. Refers to Matthew 19: 26

Sixty-Six
1. Refers to Philippians 4:13
2. Refers to 2 Corinthians 12: 9

Sixty-Seven
1. Refers to Luke 4: 4
2. Refers to 1 Samuel 3
3. Refers to 1 Kings 19: 5-19
4. Refers to Matthew 18:19

Seventy-One
1. Refers to 2 Kings 5

Seventy-Two
1. Refers to Proverbs 16:7

Seventy-Three
1. Refers to James 5:16
2. Refers to Jonah 2: 5-10

3. Refers to Matthew 18: 20

Seventy-Five
1. Refers to 1 Samuel Chapters 19-31
2. Refers to Isaiah 54:17

Also Available From SJS DIRECT

The Temptation of John Haynes
ISBN 978-0-615-42592-4
Suggested Retail Price $15.00

Death kills the Flesh.
Compromise Kills the Soul.

All About Marilyn: A Screenplay
ISBN: 978-0615342580
Suggested Retail Price $14.00

Fame Ends at 34.
Life begins at 35.
A story of Hollywood in Black and White.

The Cassandra Cookbook
ISBN: 978-1602642294
Suggested Retail Price $14.95

A pinch of hard work.
A dash of determination.
A recipe for success.

ISIS
ISBN 1-58939-236-1
Suggested Retail Price $12.95

A lost goddess.
A heritage found.
A greater destiny to be achieved.

www.ingramcontent.com/pod-product-compliance
Lightning Source LLC
Chambersburg PA
CBHW020453020726
47493CB00001B/20